MAN'S BOOK

MADE AND PRINTED IN GREAT BRITAIN
BY ODHAMS (WATFORD) LTD.

S.369.SCP.

THE WORLD IS FULL OF MARRIED MEN

Jackie Collins

★

TO GLORY WE STEER

Alexander Kent

★

A WIND OF DEATH

Gavin Black

ODHAMS BOOKS
LONDON

CONTENTS

THE WORLD IS FULL OF MARRIED MEN

Jackie Collins

'The World is Full of Married Men' is published by W. H. Allen & Co.

The Author

Jackie Collins, born in London, comes from a theatrical family. She has appeared in more than thirty films and in many TV shows, and she also toured Britain playing the lead in *French without Tears*. She gave up acting to get married and has two small daughters. Having lived in both Hollywood and Rome, she really prefers living in London, and her interests include dress designing, photography and driving fast cars. The inmates of California's San Quentin jail once voted her 'the girl we would most like to be in solitary confinement with'.

CHAPTER ONE

'WHEN I WAS FIFTEEN, I was a doll, an absolute doll! Mother was terrified to let me out on my own, she felt I was bound to come home pregnant, or something silly like that.'

The speaker was Claudia Parker. The listener was David Cooper. Claudia was in bed. She was a very beautiful girl, and she knew it, and David knew it, so everyone was happy. She had long shiny ash-blonde hair, which fell thickly around her face, and a deep fringe down to her eyebrows, which accentuated her enormous slanty green eyes. The face was perfect, with a small straight nose and luscious full lips. She wore no make-up and no clothes, and she was covered by a thin silk sheet.

David sat at the end of the bed. He was forty, and looked it. He had black slightly curly hair, and a well-lined rugged face. His nose was rather prominent, and he wore thick square horn-rimmed glasses. He was a masculine-looking man, and enjoyed a great deal of success with the opposite sex.

'Well, eventually I left home,' continued Claudia. 'I mean it was just all too impossible and dreary. So, one night I sneaked out, never to return! Actually, I met this marvellous boy, an actor, and he brought me to London with him.' She sighed and wriggled around under the sheet. 'Got a cigarette, darling?'

David produced a packet of filter-tips from his dressing-gown pocket, and handed one to Claudia. She took a long drag. 'Want to hear more of my lurid background?'

'I want to hear everything about you.'

Claudia smiled. 'You're so sweet. Not at all dull. I thought when I first saw you, you would turn out to be an absolute bore. But how wrong I was. I'm mad about you!' She leaned over to where David was sitting, the sheet was left behind, and she wound her arms around his neck, and started to nibble at his ear. She had quite a fabulous body.

David pushed her back on the bed.

'Want me, baby?' she whispered. 'Want me badly?'

David grunted his assent.

Suddenly, she twisted herself free, jumped off the bed, and ran to the door. 'You're too much,' she said, 'but not now, darling. Maybe you can so soon again but I need a little rest.' She giggled. 'I'm going to have a shower, then maybe we can get some lunch out; and then, baby, then we can come back and make it all night long!'

She vanished through the door, and David heard the water running in the bathroom.

He thought about Claudia, he thought about how they had first met. Was it really only three weeks ago? He had had a particularly hard day at the office, and Linda had been nagging him about all the extra work he seemed to be doing, and how she never saw him any more. It was nearly six, and he was just getting ready to leave, when Phillip Abbottson had come darting into his office. 'Listen, Dave,' he had asked, 'got a spare moment to come down to the studio and make a decision for us? We've got two girls testing for the Beauty Maid soap product, and it's a dead heat; we just can't decide.'

Reluctantly David had gone with Phillip to the ground floor studio in the enormous Cooper-Taylor advertising building. It was owned by his uncle, R. P. Cooper who had two sons, and Sanford Taylor with no sons but a son-in-law. Therefore, David came sixth in the line of importance, which in a business of such a size was quite important, but not important enough as far as David was concerned. He was in charge of the T.V. section and, since Beauty Maid soap was to be featured quite heavily on Channel 9, it was necessary to pick the right girl. However, Phillip Abbottson usually made the decisions about who was to be featured in the commercials, and David had never found fault yet.

They entered the studio, and David immediately spotted her. She was sprawled in a canvas chair, wearing a white terry cloth robe. Her hair was piled high on her head, and she was eating an apple. The other girl came into focus next. She was chocolate-box pretty, prim and virginal looking. However, her figure belied her face. She had a protruding bust, the largeness of which was emphasized by the flesh-coloured swimsuit she was wearing.

'What tits!' muttered Phillip.

'Well, let them do their stuff,' said David.

Phillip called for silence in the small studio, gestured to the Chocolate Box girl, and she made her way on to the small set where a fake bathroom was located. She climbed daintily into the large round marble bath, flesh colour swimsuit and all, and a prop man rushed eagerly over, and started to spray her ample proportions with bubbles. Someone else thrust a large bar of soap into her hand, and then Phillip shouted, 'O.K., let's take it.'

The cameras started to turn, and David watched the scene on a small closed circuit T.V. screen.

The girl flashed a toothy smile at the camera. 'I'm a Beauty Maid,' she cooed. She lathered the soap in her hands and spread it luxuriously up her arm, first one arm, and then the other. 'Beauty Maid was made for me. It's so creamy, so smooth, so datable.' She drew one long leg out of the bubbles and lathered that too. 'Why don't you try Beauty Maid, and then you can be a Beauty Maid too!' She smiled at the camera again, and shifted slightly, so that her ample bosom was well in focus.

'O.K., cut it,' shouted Phillip. 'Miss Parker now please.'

David turned to watch as Claudia changed places with the other girl. She had a panther-like grace all her own. Her voice was low and sexy as she read her lines. When she had finished she casually shrugged her way back into her terry cloth robe, and went and sat down. Chocolate Box was still bouncing around the set.

'The Parker girl,' David said to Phillip. 'She's the one.'

As he left the set, Claudia caught his eye. She smiled, and he felt a hint of promise in her smile. He returned to his office, packed up a few papers, called Linda to say he would be home for dinner, and then left.

Claudia was standing outside the building.

'Hello,' she said, 'small world.'

They talked for a few minutes about the tests, and Beauty Maid soap, and the weather, and then David suggested dinner. Claudia said she thought that would be a divine idea.

They went to a small Italian restaurant in Chelsea, where David knew he was unlikely to be spotted by any of his or Linda's friends. He called Linda on the 'phone and made his excuses. She sounded upset but understanding. Claudia called a boy-friend and cancelled him out. They ate cannelloni and talked and held hands, and there it all began.

Suddenly Claudia returned from the bathroom. 'Darling, what have you been doing?' she questioned. David pulled her down on the bed. 'Thinking about you, and how you picked me up.'

'It's not true!' she protested, 'you're just a dirty old man who fancied me as soon as you saw me in that bath!' She was wearing her white terry cloth robe again. David ran his hands underneath it. She shivered. The 'phone rang. 'Saved by the bell!' she giggled, and rolled over to answer it. It was her agent.

David dressed slowly, watching Claudia all the time. She spoke animatedly to her agent, occasionally pausing to stick out a small pink tongue at him. Finally she hung up. 'Oh baby, you're dressed,' she said accusingly. 'I've got simply marvellous news though. I have an interview with Conrad Lee tomorrow. He's over here looking for a completely new face to star in his latest film; it's all about the Virgin Mary or something. Anyway, I'm to see him tomorrow, six p.m., in his suite at the Plaza Carlton. Isn't it all too exciting?'

David wasn't too pleased. 'Why do you have to see him at night, what's wrong with during the day?'

'Oh baby, don't be silly. My God, if he wants to get laid, he can get it just as well at eight a.m. as any other time.' She marched crossly over to the dressing-table and meticulously started to apply her make-up.

'All right, I'm sorry I spoke. I just don't know why you want this silly career of yours. Why don't you . . .'

'Why don't I what?' interrupted Claudia coldly. 'Give it all up and marry you? And what do you suggest we do with your wife and kids, and all your other various family entanglements?'

David was silent.

'Look baby.' Her voice softened. 'I don't bug you about things, so just forget it. You don't own me, and I don't own you, and that's the way it should be.' She applied her false eye-lashes with a flourish. 'I'm starving, what about lunch?'

They went to their little Italian restaurant, and good humour was restored. 'Sunday's such a dreary day,' said Claudia, 'it sort of sags along.' She drank her red wine with relish, and smiled at the short fat proprietor who grinned happily back. 'Do you know everyone believes they are beautiful, I'm sure of it. They look in the mirror, and they see two eyes, a nose and a mouth, and that's it, they think, what a gas!' Her laughter lit up the restaurant, and David laughed with her. She was such a beautiful, vital girl. He had had affairs outside marriage before, many times, but this was different; this time, for the first time, he wished he was free.

'I met this man once,' said Claudia. 'He promised me a yacht in the South of France, a villa in Cuba! Lots of jewels and all that jazz, and then he just disappeared. I heard later he was a spy, and got shot. Isn't life funny. . . .'

After lunch they drove through the West End looking for a film they would like to see.

'Look at all those nuts,' exclaimed Claudia, watching a large procession heading towards Trafalgar Square. 'Can you imagine spending all your spare time rushing around tying yourself to Embassies, and sitting down all over the place? And all the chaps have beards, I wonder why . . . ?' She snuggled up closer to David. 'Let's forget the movie,' she said, 'let's go back to my place and swing.'

CHAPTER TWO

'BAN THE BOMB,' the banner attached to the stout lady's back announced quite clearly.

'Peace everywhere,' declared a large notice held aloft by a bearded young man.

'End Nuclear Warfare,' stated a large piece of cardboard

clutched gamely by a harassed woman, also clutching two scruffy looking children by the hand.

This group, along with several hundred others, marched slowly into Trafalgar Square. Many had arrived before them, and there was a milling crowd round about Nelson's Column and the fountains. Linda Cooper was already there; she stood squashed between an earnest-looking group of young girls with long, untidy hair, and grubby-looking outfits, and a bespectacled gentleman, who kept up a constant muttering to himself.

An attractive woman in her early thirties, with short auburn hair partly concealed beneath a chiffon scarf, she wore a cream Chanel suit which looked out of place in the company she was with. One would imagine that ten years earlier she had been very pretty indeed, but the prettiness had been replaced with an expression of the acceptance of life. There were little lines, a certain amount of tiredness, and slightly too much make-up; but the overall effect somehow seemed to make her more attractive.

She glanced around her; it seemed so funny to be standing there, part of the crowd, without David. It was so seldom that she did anything or went anywhere without him, but more and more lately there had been long business trips, and late meetings, and he seemed to have become so completely involved in his work, almost to the exclusion of all else. She sighed. It was only by chance really that she was at the meeting today. David was away, and suddenly she felt she must get out of the house and do something different for a change. The children were in the country with her parents for the week-end; she had declined to go, thinking that David would be home, but at the last moment he had had to rush off as usual. She had found herself all alone, and eventually decided she couldn't bear to sit around the house all day, so she had 'phoned Monica and Jack and they had asked her over to lunch. But it was a mistake; they were really David's friends from his bachelor days and she always sensed a certain forced gaiety about them, a sort of 'so David finally married you' attitude, 'well, he could have done worse'. After an hour and a half she excused herself on the pretext that she had to get home, there was so much to be done before the children arrived. What, she could not imagine, but Monica and Jack didn't argue, so she left.

It was while she was driving home that she noticed the marchers and the banners and the crowds, and it was on impulse she parked her Mini in a side street and made her way into Trafalgar Square, which appeared to be the general gathering point. It was a subject she had often thought about, and secretly wished that she could be part of. To protest seemed the very least one could do, if not for oneself for one's children.

The bespectacled man standing beside her suddenly looked at his watch. 'It's three o'clock,' he announced excitedly.

There was a sudden surge forward of the crowd, and a general shouting and yelling, and small groups of people seemed to disintegrate from the mass and rush towards the road where they promptly sat down in front of the traffic. Linda was carried forward with the crush and found herself near the edge of the pavement. There were a lot of policemen pushing and dragging and lifting the squatters from the road and as soon as one person was removed another immediately took his place. The mob was delighted. They chanted various slogans and cheered and booed the police. The large blue police vans gradually began to fill up, but still undaunted new squatters appeared.

Linda felt marvellous. 'Ban the Bomb,' she shouted. *She* was protesting about the bomb. *She* was actually involved in a meeting of world wide interest. *She* was in a minute way helping to protect the future of her children. It was an exciting experience.

'Ban the Bomb,' joined in the people near her.

'Come on, darlin',' a dark-haired young man grabbed her by the arm, and together they rushed on to the road. They sat in the face of an oncoming taxi and the irate taxi-driver growled, 'Bloody barmy, the lot of 'em.' Linda had a feeling of complete exhilaration, and then a pink faced constable was grabbing her under the arms and pulling her to the side of the road. She started to struggle and another policeman joined them and took hold of her legs. There was a moment of immodesty as she felt her skirt hike up above her knees, and then they unceremoniously dumped her back on the pavement.

Helping hands got her to her feet where she discovered she had lost her shoes and somehow or other cut her arm. Her scarf had vanished and her hair fell around her face.

'Well, you look a right mess,' it was the dark-haired young man again, 'want to give it another bash?'

A girl grabbed him by the arm. 'Oh, come on, Paul,' she said, 'let's go. We don't want to get lumbered down to Bow Street again.' She was small, with long lank pale yellow hair, and she was very young.

Paul ignored her. 'Look,' he said to Linda, 'you had better come with us. I've got a mate lives near here and we can maybe get you some shoes.'

'Well . . .' started Linda.

'Oh, come on, Paul,' said the girl crossly.

'Well all right,' decided Linda, and the three of them started to push their way to the edge of the crowd. Paul took hold of Linda's arm and guided her through the mass of people, his lank-haired girl-friend trailed miserably behind.

'My name's Paul Bedford, what's yours?'

Linda glanced at him. He was tall, with slate grey eyes. She guessed he must be about twenty-two. She found him uncomfortably attractive. 'Mrs. Cooper,' she said firmly.

He gave her an odd look, half amused, half puzzled. 'All right, Mrs. Cooper.'

The pavement was cold and hard on Linda's stockinged feet, and suddenly she found herself wishing she was safely home, and not rushing around Trafalgar Square with some strange young man whom she had only met ten minutes before.

'Listen, I have a car parked close by,' she said. 'I think it would be better if I got back to it. I'm sure I have some old shoes in it.'

But Paul was already leading her across the road into Newport Street. 'We're here,' he said, banging on a battered yellow door, 'at least come up and we'll bandage your arm and then I'll take you back to your car.'

The girl-friend looked sulky in the background.

'All right,' said Linda.

A make-up-less, white faced, black-haired girl finally came to the front door. She wore a slightly tattered-looking blue and gold brocade Chinese housecoat and once-white fur slippers. 'Hi baby,' she greeted Paul brightly, 'and how's little Mel,' she nodded at the girl-friend. 'Come on up.'

They followed her up a narrow staircase into an enormous room painted completely black. There was a large bed in one corner, a lot of books and cushions scattered and piled around, and a record player with Miles Davis turned up full volume. This appeared to be the full extent of the furnishings of the room.

'Where's the old man?' asked Paul.

'Oh, he went down to join the crowd,' said the girl.

'We need a drink,' said Paul, 'got hung up in the middle of it. This is Mrs. Cooper, she cut her arm and lost her shoes. Had a right punch up.'

The girl smiled. 'You always manage to get people involved. Sit down and I'll get you a beer, it's all we've got.'

'Come on,' said Paul to Linda, 'we'll fix your arm up.' He took her into the bathroom which was surprisingly white and antiseptic-looking. 'So where's Mr. Cooper?' he asked.

Linda looked at him coolly. 'He's away on business.'

'What's your name?'

She hesitated, then said, 'Linda. Why?'

'I just wanted to know.'

They looked at each other and then Linda glanced nervously at the floor. This is ridiculous, she thought. What am I doing here with this boy whom I find so very attractive. What would David think. I must get out.

They discovered a box of Elastoplast and Paul put one over her cut arm. 'Was this your first meeting?'

'Yes,' she replied. 'Look, I simply must get back to my car now; it's really awfully nice of you to have taken all this trouble, but I have people expecting me at home and they will be worried if I'm late.'

'All right,' said Paul. 'I'll take you. Can't have you wandering about London with no shoes on.'

They went back into the large black room. Lank-haired Melanie was sitting clutching a can of beer. She jumped up when Paul came in and rushed over to him. Linda decided she wasn't very pretty, much too thin, and that awful hair!

'Have some beer,' Melanie offered. She had a slightly whiney voice.

'No, we're splitting now,' said Paul, 'I'll be back soon; you wait here.'

The girl obviously wanted to argue, but didn't quite dare.

Paul kissed the owner of the room. 'Be back.'

Linda said goodbye and they left.

In the street Paul took her arm again but she shook it free. 'I don't like my arm held.'

'What do you like?'

They walked in silence to where Linda had left her car. She felt embarrassed and inelegant in her stockinged feet. Besides that, the pavement was cold and hard and she wished she was safely home. They reached her car and Paul helped her in.

'Where do you live?' he enquired.

'Finchley. We have a house there.'

'Well, we're neighbours then. I live in Hampstead.' He stood on the pavement leaning against the car door. 'You could drop me back there. Do you mind?'

'I thought you had to go back for your girl-friend,' said Linda nervously. She just wanted to drive off now and leave him standing there. She knew how attracted she was to him, and somehow she felt very vulnerable.

'That's all right, Mel will find her own way home. She usually does anyway.' He walked around to the passenger seat and got in.

It's now or never, Linda thought. Either I tell him to get out now or I'm accepting the fact that he's interested and letting him know that I'm interested too. She felt him staring at her. She started the car.

Linda drove expertly through the traffic. Paul sat silently beside her, his silence making her even more aware of his presence. Eventually she spoke. 'You know, your girl-friend isn't going to be too pleased with you, saying you will be back and then just disappearing.'

'It doesn't matter.' They lapsed into silence again. Linda decided that when they reached Hampstead she would stop the car, wait for him to get out, and then wave goodbye and drive quickly away. She would give him no chance to talk about seeing her again, instinctively she knew he would want to.

'I noticed you immediately,' he said.

'What?' she replied, startled.

'I said I noticed you immediately,' he repeated, 'in the crowd. You looked so out of it, so sort of lost. You wanted to be part of it and yet couldn't quite make it. So I grabbed your arm and pulled you into the road and then you were all right, you forgot yourself, y'know?'

'I don't know what you mean,' she said defensively.

'Oh, come off it, you know what I mean, you dig, you're hip. Where's your old man then? Where's your kids? You have got kids, haven't you?'

'Yes, how did you know?'

'It's easy, I could sum you up in a minute. Married maybe ten years, nice little house, mink stole, husband away a lot, kids growing up and leaving you behind. It's true, isn't it?'

Linda's first reaction was one of anger, stop the car and tell this rude little boy to get out, but wait a moment, what he was saying was very near the truth, wait, hear him out, what harm could it do. And then there was curiosity, how did he know? Did she look the part so completely? She forced a smile. 'You're very sure of yourself, aren't you?'

'Yes, I am. I can see it in your face, the way you look, everything about you.'

'We've reached Hampstead,' said Linda quickly. She swerved the little car abruptly into the kerb, 'thanks for the summing up. It was great fun for you, I'm sure. David would have been amused. Goodbye.' She stared straight ahead and waited for him to get out. He didn't move. Eventually he said, 'Can I see you again?' She turned to look at him, his eyes penetrated deep into her own.

'I don't understand you. First you dissect my life, pull me to pieces and then you ask to see me again. No, you can't. I'm in love with my husband. I have two lovely children and I live a very nice life, thank you. I think you are a very rude boy, and do you mind getting out of my car and going away.'

'I would like to see you again. I think you need someone like me.' He opened the car door and got out. 'Anyway, if you change your mind, I'm in the 'phone book.' He turned and walked away.

Linda watched him go. He's a beatnik, she thought angrily. He's very thin, probably never eats. So young, but so knowing. I would like to sleep with him. She halted her train of thought abruptly. I would like to what? she asked herself incredulously. Sex had always been synonymous with David. She had never had an affair, she had gone to her marriage bed a virgin, and now this thought was in her head. Oh, there had been many boys she had dated, necked with, before getting married, but never anything more serious than that. David is a wonderful husband, she thought, a wonderful lover. But when did he ever make love to her these days? Maybe once a fortnight, and then it was a quick ten minute affair, out of which she derived no particular pleasure, and afterwards he would turn over and go straight to sleep and snore, and she would lie awake for a long time thinking how it used to be before the children, when they were first married. She sighed and started the car, it was impossible to turn the clock back.

The house was empty, even the dogs were away with the children and their live-in Spanish maid, Anna, was out for the day. It was depressing. Linda switched the television on in the bedroom. It was nearly six; David had said he would be home around nine, so there were three hours to kill. She had no intention of watching the television, but it was nice to have human voices around her. She decided to 'phone her mother and see how Jane and Stephen were behaving themselves. She dialled the operator who put her through. Her mother's voice, placid and comfortable, came on to the line. 'Hello, Linda, is that you, dear?'

'Hello, mother, how's everything?'

'Oh, fine dear, fine. Jane's having her bath now and Stephen's right here. Wait a minute, hang on, he wants to speak to you.'

There was a pause and then Stephen's thin excitable voice came on the line. He was eight. 'Hello, Mummy. We're having a smashing time. Grandma made lots of gooey cakes for tea and that pig Jane tried to eat them all so I pushed her off her chair and she started to cry and . . .' He carried on at great length about the cakes and then her mother's voice came back on the line.

'Daddy will be driving the children back after lunch tomorrow, so you should expect them about four. How is David? Did you have a nice peaceful week-end together?'

'Yes, Mother, very peaceful,' replied Linda ruefully. 'All right, then, I will speak to you later in the week. Thanks for having the children, kiss Janey for me. 'Bye.'

What now? Feeling slightly hungry she went to the kitchen,

but she hated cooking just for herself, so she finally settled for a cheese sandwich. There seemed nothing else left to do except go to bed and wait for David. Bed, David, the two thoughts connected in her head, and a sudden idea formed. She rushed to her wardrobe and hunted around until she found what she was looking for. A long slinky black négligée she had bought in Paris several years ago and never really got around to wearing. It had always seemed too frivolous. She held it up against her, and then returned to the kitchen to iron it. Well, this is what they say in all the women's magazines, she thought, smiling, shock your husband into realizing how utterly sexy and devastating you really are!

After the négligée was ironed, she ran a long hot bath and borrowed some of Janey's Baby Bubbles to throw in. For good measure she added some Chanel No. 5 cologne and the whole thing looked very luxurious and inviting. Next she creamed her face, set her hair, and then climbed into the bath and relaxed. The 'phone rang. Wrapped in a bath towel, trailing bubbles, she hurried into the bedroom to answer it.

'Hello.'

'Hello, Linda.'

'Yes.'

'This is Paul Bedford.'

A long silence, and then his voice again. 'You mentioned David and Finchley, so it was easy to trace you in the 'phone book. Look, I'm sorry, I wanted to apologize for earlier. I didn't mean to be so rude. Will you forgive me?'

'There is nothing to forgive,' said Linda coolly. 'It certainly didn't bother me one way or the other.' She was tempted to say goodbye and hang up, but she waited to see what he would say next.

'Oh well, that's all right then.' He sounded relieved. 'You know, when I like people, I mean really like them, I always seem to rub them up the wrong way. I don't intend to, but it just happens. Sort of reverse action, I suppose.' He paused, then continued. 'Listen, a friend of mine is having a party tonight, he lives near you, and I thought you might like to come.'

'I'm sorry I can't,' she answered quickly.

'Well, no harm in trying. Maybe some other time.'

'You will have to excuse me, I'm in the middle of taking a bath.' She paused, and then added, 'thanks for the thought anyway. Goodbye, Paul.'

'Goodbye, Linda. Sorry about dragging you out of the bath. The party doesn't start till after ten, so if you should decide you would like to go, my number is Hampstead 09911. 'Bye.' He hung up.

O-double-nine-double-one, so easy to remember. She shivered and made her way quickly back to the bathroom. The bubbles in the bath had gone flat and the water when she got back in was luke-warm. She was secretly pleased that Paul had 'phoned, it made her feel desirable and wanted, a feeling she couldn't remember having had for a long time. Tonight things would be different, she would make David realize that everything could and should be as romantic as it was when they first knew each other. After all, just because two people were married didn't mean that romance had to go by the board. She sang softly to herself. I'm only thirty-three, she thought, that's still very young, well certainly not old. She climbed out of the bath, and studied her naked body in the bathroom mirror. I could do with going on a diet, she mused. Her legs were shapely but a little heavy around the thighs, her waist was quite slim and her breasts, although large and full, were still firm. She slipped into the négligée. It clung flatteringly and she was pleased with the effect. She applied a light make-up and combed out her hair. Then she went down to the lounge and fetched the portable gramophone, taking it to the bedroom. She searched around and found some Nat King Cole albums and put them on, his dreamy voice was much more acceptable than the noise of the television, which she switched off.

The stage was set, the player was ready, it was nearly nine. A little glass of wine would be nice, she thought. There was a bottle of rosé in the fridge, so she went and got it.

An hour passed. The wine was drunk, the records had come to a stop, the black négligée had been replaced with something a little warmer. The television was back on and Linda huddled morosely in front of it, watching an American crime serial.

She was a little loaded. The emptiness of the house seemed to press around her. Where was David? He had said nine o'clock. If he was going to be late, he could at least 'phone. He was usually very prompt, it was one of his better habits. Perhaps he had had a car accident. Perhaps he was lying badly injured or even . . .

The 'phone rang. First, the operator's cool efficient voice, and then David, obviously in a hurry. 'Look, I'm held up with these people here. I had to drive over from Leeds to Manchester, and I'm absolutely bushed. Not going to risk driving back tonight, it's a filthy night. I'll leave early in the morning and be home about eight.'

'But, David, I'm expecting you,' she tried to keep her voice pleasant. 'Why couldn't you have let me know earlier, it's nearly ten, and you promised to be home by nine.'

'Look, I can't talk now, I'll explain tomorrow.'

Her temper suddenly snapped. 'I don't care about tomorrow. What about me? I've had a bloody miserable week-end and tonight I've just sat around waiting for you, and you couldn't even bother to 'phone. At least if I'd known I could have gone to the films or something. You're just selfish, and I can't . . .'

His voice was cold and unemotional, 'I'm with people now. I'll see you tomorrow. Goodbye.'

The line went dead in Linda's hand and she sat very still trying to control a choking feeling of complete frustration. He had hung up on her, he hadn't even bothered to wait for her to say goodbye. At last she replaced the receiver, only to pick it up again and dial. The ringing tone seemed very loud in her ear. I've had too much to drink, she thought vaguely, then a voice was saying hello and she found herself replying with, 'Hello, Paul, this is Linda. About that party . . .'

CHAPTER THREE

IT WAS FOUR O'CLOCK when David and Claudia arrived back at her flat. She lived in a converted house at the back of Knightsbridge. It had been made into six flats and was all very new and modern. She occupied the top flat which had the advantage of having a small roof garden. David had often found himself wondering how she could afford it. All her furniture was new and obviously expensive and she had an enormous wardrobe of clothes.

She was an actress and model and from what David knew of both professions unless you were extremely successful you didn't earn an awful lot of money. Certainly not enough to keep Claudia in the style she was living. He had mulled this problem over in his mind and come to no real satisfactory conclusion. Eventually, he had decided that she must have a rich father, although this didn't really tie in with the bits and pieces he knew of her background.

She had left home at fifteen and come to London, and now she was twenty and had ambitions to be a successful film actress. She was very beautiful and sparkled like champagne. He had known her only three weeks, and in that time seen her as much as twelve times. She had always been free to see him; there didn't appear to be any other man in the picture. She accepted the situation that he was a married man, and didn't nag about it as a lot of women might. She had never mentioned money to him. He had seen that she did the Beauty Maid commercial, but apart from that she didn't appear to have worked at all. David decided that he must find out more about her; maybe she needed money and was embarrassed to mention it. He resolved to bring the subject up.

When they entered, Claudia rushed about making a great show of fixing the bed and generally tidying up. She was most undomesticated and had a daily woman who came in except for week-ends. She made a disgusted 'ugh' when she came to the dirty dishes in the kitchen. David followed her in. 'I'll buy you a dishwashing machine,' he said, slipping his arms around her waist.

She turned laughing. 'You're joking, of course. A dishwashing machine! What a terrible present. I'll have something more romantic than that, thank you!'

'What do you want? We'll go shopping tomorrow.'

'I want, let me see now, I want a Facel Vega, two mink coats, lots of diamonds, a beautiful penthouse in New York, and a villa on the Riviera!' She started to laugh. 'Can you afford me?'

'I'm serious. Will you settle for a mink jacket? Go and order it tomorrow.'

Claudia looked at him. 'Well, you really are serious. Baby, that's fabulous, I would adore that. But if you want me to have it, surprise me, none of this ordering jazz; I like surprises.'

'All right, a surprise it will be.' He wondered if now was the time to bring up her financial situation, and decided against it. Later, when they were in bed.

'What time do you have to turn into Cinderella tonight?' asked Claudia.

'Well, I should leave about eight thirty,' he stroked her hair, 'but I can always stretch a point, depending on what the main attraction is.' She giggled and suddenly pulled off her sweater. 'The second feature is starting now. The main attraction should prove to be very interesting indeed!'

Sometime later, when David looked at his watch, he was surprised to find it was well after nine. Claudia lay asleep beside him, her long hair in disarray around her face, her make-up smudged and faded. She looked very young. Her clothes were scattered around the bedroom, leading in a trail from the kitchen. As if she sensed him looking at her, she opened her eyes, yawned and stretched and made contented noises.

'You're like a cat,' he said, 'sometimes an innocent little kitten and sometimes the wildest dirtiest alley cat around.'

'I like that. I can see myself telling it to someone in the years to come. There was this guy and he said to me, you're just like a cat, sometimes. . . .'

He put his hand over her mouth. 'Don't say that. There will

be no other guys in the years to come, only me. I love you and I want to marry you.' He was surprised himself to hear the words, but there they were, spoken aloud for all to hear.

'You know, it's amazing,' she said, 'how very easy it is for married men to propose. I guess it's an easy thing for them to say, because really they are all safe and secure, and they know they can lay out this tasty bit of bait without a hope in hell of getting trapped themselves. Marry me, my darling, only don't let my wife find out!'

David was furious. So all right, he hadn't really meant it. Correction, he had meant it but, as she had said, was secure in the knowledge that it was not possible. However, the fact that Claudia realized this infuriated him. Why did women always seem to have so much insight into the things men said? 'I could get a divorce,' he said.

'Are you going to?' replied Claudia.

'I don't know,' he pulled her to him, 'it's not just me and Linda; there are the children to consider. But I love you, and I want to look after you, and one day when my kids are a little bit older, well then everything will work itself out. I don't want you to be in that rat race you're in. I can look after you, and you needn't do anything. I don't want you to work.'

She stared up at him with her large slanty green eyes. 'Well I'm glad you have it all figured out.' She caressed his back, and he felt desire rise up in him again. She had only to touch him and he wanted her. 'There is only one problem. I don't want to marry you. Not even if you were free, and we could rush off and do it now.' She wriggled away from him and got off the bed. She stood looking at him, completely naked, and continued, 'I want to do what I want to do whenever I want. No ties, no strings. I don't dig this marriage bit, it means nothing to me, so don't offer it like it's the golden hoop, because I'm just not going to jump. I love you now, today, but tomorrow who knows? That's me, I don't make any pretence to be something I'm not, so why don't you do the same?'

He couldn't control the choking excitement he felt for her as she stood there; her words didn't matter. He dragged her back on the bed, and let loose his fury and frustrations on her. She tried to struggle but he crushed her beneath him, until her struggling stopped and became part of him.

For David it was devastating; with Claudia it always was. She was unlike any other woman he had ever known. And each time it was more, both emotionally and physically.

'You had better get up, it's past the witching hour and wifey will be waiting.'

'Don't be a bitch; anyway, I think I'll stay.'

She kissed him. They 'phoned Linda, and Claudia pretended to be the operator so that the call appeared to be coming long distance. Afterwards, she said, 'No son of a bitch would talk to me that way and get away with it. I feel sorry for your wife.'

'Do you?' he said shortly. It annoyed him when Claudia discussed Linda.

'Yes, I do, although it's her own fault.'

'What do you mean?'

'Well, darling, I mean really, what made me more exciting to you than her? Because I was new and younger and prettier. Am I prettier?'

'Yes, you're prettier.'

'But you shouldn't have to look around. She should be new to you, she should make bloody sure that she's always new to you. Most women seem to get married and then stop trying. Well, we've caught the fish, now put away the bait and only bring it out on special occasions. I'm not saying that you wouldn't screw around once in a while, all men do, even the happiest of married men. But that's all it would be, there would be no affairs like me, you wouldn't need one.'

'Thank you, marriage councillor Parker, but I have a feeling that you are addressing the wrong party.'

'Shall I speak to your wife? What shall I say? Darling, in strict confidence I'm banging your husband. This isn't really necessary, if only you weren't so dullsville he might fancy you again. Liven up a bit, and back he will come.'

They both started to laugh. 'You are a bitch. Is that why I love you?'

'No,' she giggled, 'you know why you love me.'

They got up and Claudia busied herself in the kitchen making sandwiches while David prowled around the flat thinking how he could bring up the subject of her finances. She had annoyed him with her little speech about not wanting to marry him. But really he wasn't too annoyed, because on thinking it over he decided she had only said it as a defence mechanism. She knew they couldn't get married, so to save face she had probably convinced herself that she didn't want marriage anyway. On thinking it over even further, he became almost pleased about it, because it put him in the enviable position of being able to have his cake and eat it too.

He didn't really want to leave Linda; in his own way he loved her, although she had ceased to attract him sexually shortly after they were married. He had compensated for this by different affairs through the years, and to Linda he had been more than generous materially. She was the perfect wife figure. A lovely hostess and mother. No, he certainly didn't want to leave

Linda. He felt no particular guilt about being unfaithful to her, although if the shoe had been on the other foot, so to speak, but no, that was unthinkable: the very idea of Linda being unfaithful to him was ridiculous.

Claudia was licking mayonnaise off her fingers in the kitchen. She was wearing a pink kimono and had tied her hair away from her face.

'You look about fifteen,' he said.

'And you look about fifty. What *is* on your mind? Are you brooding because I turned down your gallant proposal?'

'I want to talk to you seriously. Bring the sandwiches and come and sit down.'

She followed him into the living-room and, munching a sandwich, she sat down on the floor near his feet. 'Now isn't this cosy, so what seems to be bothering you?'

'Look darling, I've been thinking a lot about you.'

She giggled. 'I should hope so.'

'This is serious, Claudia,' he continued. 'I've been worried about you, about how you manage financially. I mean, well this flat isn't cheap and I want to help you out. I mean, well frankly, where do you get your money?'

Claudia sat very still, her eyes glinted dangerously. However, she managed to keep her voice pleasant. 'Well, baby,' she said sweetly, 'what makes you want to know?'

David didn't observe the danger signals. 'Well, of course I want to know. Do you get an allowance from your father or what?'

'Oh, come on, I haven't seen my family for five years and I don't care if I never see them again. My old man wouldn't give me a penny to go to the bathroom with.' She sat silently then, and David realized that she had no intention of answering him.

'Claudia, I want to know.'

She arose. 'I don't like being questioned. I'm not asking you for anything. I don't want anything from you.' She started to shout, 'Leave me alone with your questions. What's on your mind? Where do you think I get money from? Do you think I'm a whore? Well, if I was, wouldn't I be asking you for money?' She was crying and David was shocked that he had provoked such anger. 'It's my business where I get my money from and if you don't like the idea of that then let's just forget it.'

David had caught her mood of fury by this time. 'All right,' he said coldly, 'we'll forget it.' He marched into the bedroom and dressed. Claudia didn't follow him. When he came out she was sitting on the sofa reading a magazine. She didn't look up.

He stood there, undecided about whether to walk out or not. 'Well, are you going to tell me?'

She continued reading and didn't answer him.

'Goodbye,' he said, and left.

In the hall outside her front door he immediately regretted this move. He couldn't go home and he debated making it up with Claudia, but that was impossible. If he gave way to her now he would be admitting defeat and he never admitted defeat to any woman. No, he decided to let her stew a little and she would come running back, they always did.

He went downstairs to his car, having decided to spend the night in a Turkish bath. He was puzzled why Claudia was so secretive about the source of her income; it could only mean that it was something he wouldn't like. Well, in that case, when she told him he would stop it, whatever it was, and then she would be dependent on him, which was exactly the way he wanted it.

He drove to the Turkish baths in Jermyn Street, and, after going through the hot and cold steam baths and having a massage, he was quite happy to settle down in his small white cubicle, where he promptly fell asleep. Tomorrow he would settle everything.

CHAPTER FOUR

PAUL LOOKED YOUNGER than Linda remembered him. He was wearing a black sweater and tight black trousers. She had decided to wear a plain dark blue cocktail dress after discarding several other outfits. They met at a pre-arranged spot and Paul helped her out of her car and said he would drive as he knew the way.

'I'm glad you changed your mind. What did it? My irresistible charm?'

'I don't know.' All the wine she had drunk and the rushing to get ready had finally made her tired. 'Maybe I shouldn't have come. I don't know why I'm here really.'

He looked at her. 'I'm glad you're here. I don't think you will be sorry you came. In fact I promise you that.'

They drove a short way along the Heath and Paul eventually pulled into the drive of an old rambling house. Its windows were ablaze with lights and the belting voice of Solomon Burke screamed out. A couple were arguing in the open doorway and, as they arrived several more people came pushing through the door with much laughter and yelling. Paul parked the car and they went in.

The scene that greeted their eyes was somewhat wild to say the least. The front door led into a small hall with big rooms off either side of it and a large staircase in the centre. The staircase was littered with various people, a lot of men with beards, girls sitting and standing, and everyone steadily drinking. The room on the right was filled with dancing couples, shaking, or just standing and necking. There appeared to be no furniture, only a rather battered old record player balanced precariously on the window sill. The room on the left featured a thin girl with stringy red hair taking off her clothes to the beat of some bongos being hammered on by a West Indian clad only in white slacks. No one was taking much notice of them, mostly people were watching a blond boy at the other end of the room who was standing on a chair reciting an obscene poem.

Paul squeezed Linda's arm. 'Come on,' he said, leading her up the stairs and greeting people as he went. 'Let's get rid of your coat then we can get a drink.'

Upstairs there were more rooms which seemed equally devoid of furniture. Paul steered her into a room with a bed creaking under the weight of many coats. Two girls were staring deep into each other's eyes in a corner, and another girl was either asleep or had passed out at the bottom of the bed. Linda took off her coat and felt too dressed-up in her neat cocktail dress. Paul said that she looked great and took her to find a drink. They went downstairs to the room on the left. The redhead had abandoned her strip and was sitting on the floor, someone's sweater covering her. She grabbed hold of Paul's leg as he went by. 'You look sexy, want to make it?' Her voice was slurred. 'I've got a great body.'

Linda found herself separated from Paul and she headed towards a table where the drinks appeared to be coming from. A fat man pounced up behind her. 'You look very smart,' he said, 'who are you?' His face was beaded with sweat and his breath was a combination of onions and stale beer. 'Do you want a drink?'

'Yes, please,' said Linda, trying to edge away from the full blast of his breath.

He poured her a very large scotch in a cracked glass and she drank it down hastily. 'Let us go and dance,' he said, and put his arm around her waist. She could feel the hotness of his hand penetrate her dress through to her skin.

'Not just now,' she said, trying to disentangle herself from him.

He licked his pudgy lips and then Paul arrived. 'Hello, Bruno, I see you've met Linda.'

The fat man removed his arm. 'Oh, she's yours, is she?' he said hastily. 'I don't know what they see in you.' He wiped his mouth with a plump pink hand and ambled away.

Paul laughed. 'Don't take any notice of him,' he said, and then was suddenly serious. 'You're very lovely.' He took hold of her hand.

'Oh,' said Linda. She had never been able to accept compliments easily. She drained her glass. 'I'd like another drink.'

Paul poured her another scotch and she drank it quickly, feeling its burning effect almost immediately. 'I think I should go home,' she said weakly, 'I'm a little bit drunk, you know.'

'I know.' He pushed her towards the wall and then he leaned forward and kissed her. She closed her eyes and felt the intimacy of his tongue penetrate her lips. His mouth was persistent and demanding. She felt she should push him away but didn't have the strength and anyway she didn't want to. It was a long time since she had been kissed like this. David never kissed her any more and she had forgotten how exciting a kiss could be.

'Oh, so here you are,' the whiney voice was familiar and the note of anger was unmistakable. Paul straightened up. Melanie was standing there, her yellow hair hanging in a straight curtain around her thin flushed face. 'I thought you were coming back for me.' She glared at Linda. 'Or have you been so busy that you couldn't find time.'

'Oh. I'm sorry, Mel, thought I said I'd see you here.'

'Well, you didn't.' Her voice was becoming almost shrill. 'And how's Mrs. Cooper? Recovered I see.'

'Can it, Mel,' said Paul sharply. He steered her away from Linda and into the hall. 'Look, I'm sorry, but that's the way it is.'

'That's the way what is?' Suddenly her eyes filled with tears.

'Look, Mel, it's been great, but we've been heading this way a long time now, and I think that it's best to forget it. I still dig you and all that bit, but, well you know . . .'

'No, I don't know. And anyway, what can you see in that old bag in there.' She started to cry. 'I hate you, Paul.'

'Look, kid, you're seventeen, there will be lots of other guys, you'll soon forget me. We're just not . . .'

'We're not what?' she interrupted angrily. 'I think you're rotten and I hate you.'

He shrugged and walked away. Linda was deep in conversation with the fat man again. 'Do you want to go?' Paul asked her.

'No.' Her eyes were bright, she was very drunk. 'Bruno's going to teach me to shake.'

'Bruno can find a girl-friend of his own. I'll teach you.' He took her into the other room where the dancing was going on, and then he held her very tight. 'I want to sleep with you,' he whispered.

'I want to sleep with you too,' she whispered back. 'I mean I don't want to, but it would be nice, but I . . . Oh, God, I think I had better get some air.'

He kissed her again. This time she kissed him back and their mouths met in mutual enjoyment. They stood still amongst the dancers, lost in their own little world. His tongue explored her mouth and she felt a sudden hot desire for him. He pressed her very close, and then released her.

'You wait here,' he said. 'I'll get your coat.'

She stood patiently waiting, the liquor she had drunk falling over her in waves. She couldn't think clearly at all, her head buzzed and she wanted to be back again in the safety of Paul's arms. There was a lot of noise coming from the hall and she wandered out there. Two men were fighting. It was the fat man, Bruno, and the West Indian who had been playing the bongos earlier. They screamed obscenities at each other, and rolled about on the floor. No one tried to stop them.

'Why are they fighting?' Linda asked a girl standing near her.

'Oh, darling, Bruno always has to fight with someone,' the girl said, 'it wouldn't be Bruno if he didn't.'

The West Indian's nose had started to bleed and there was a lot of blood. Linda suddenly felt very sick. She edged her way to the front door and got out. The cold air had a slightly sobering effect. She went over to her car and sat in it.

Eventually Paul arrived. 'I was worried, I thought you had walked out on me.' He got in the car and put his arm around her. She pulled away. 'What's the matter?' he continued.

'I feel terrible. I think I'm going to be sick.'

'Oh great, let's get back inside and I'll get you upstairs to the bathroom.'

'No, I don't want to go back in there.'

'You'll feel better in a minute.' He put his arm around her again and this time she didn't pull away. He kissed her and his hands started to explore her body. She felt weak and her head spun, and when she shut her eyes everything whirled round and round. She could feel Paul touching her and his mouth on hers, but it all seemed like it was happening to someone else.

Abruptly he let go of her and started the car, and they seemed to be driving for ages, but really it was no time at all. Then he was helping her out of the car and they were climbing a lot of stairs, and then they were in a room, and he was pushing her on to a bed. She didn't struggle when he unzipped her dress and pulled it off because, after all, this wasn't really her that this was happening to. He kissed her slowly and the bed was very soft and she felt very comfortable. His arms were strong and warm, and his hands created a fantastic excitement in her. He rolled her over on her stomach and she felt him undoing the hooks on her strapless bra.

'I'm not here,' she whispered, 'I'm on another planet. I'm very drunk, you shouldn't take disadvantage of me, I'm at an advantage . . ." She started to giggle.

He began to kiss her back, and she was suddenly lost in a raging enveloping holocaust of love, which seemed to go on forever and ever.

'I love you,' one of them said.

'I love you,' the other said.

Linda awoke about five a.m. She opened her eyes in disbelief. She felt parched with an awful thirst. Her eyes felt heavy and her face like sandpaper. She looked around her. She was in a small untidy room, and Paul was sprawled across the end of the bed asleep.

She sat up slowly and looked around for something to cover herself. Her head felt it would split open if she moved too rapidly. She pulled a cover off the bed and, wrapping it round her, she got up. Paul didn't stir. She groped her way to the door and found herself in a tiny hallway piled high with clutter. She made her way through to the bathroom which was a small dusty room with everything rusting and old. She switched on the light; it was a naked bulb, and then she turned on the cold water tap. A large black spider ran disdainfully across the basin and she almost screamed. She found a tooth-mug and quickly drank four mugfuls of water. It tasted faintly of toothpaste but made her feel a little better in spite of that. She stared in the mirror above the basin. Her make-up was smeared and etched into deep lines about her face. Her hair was untidy and matted. I look like I belong here, she thought vaguely.

She padded back into the bedroom and searched for her clothes. When she found them she dressed quickly. She looked at Paul. He slept deeply. She stared at him for a long time and then, finding her coat, she left.

It was cold and silent in the street. Her car coughed and spluttered and she thought that it would never start. At last it did, and she drove home through the deserted streets.

She let herself quietly into the house and went straight to her bedroom. Everything looked clean and new. She took a hot bath and collapsed into bed, where she lay and thought. She couldn't exactly remember what she had done or what had happened between her and Paul. But obviously she had slept with him.

She felt a tremendous feeling of guilt and also a certain horror at herself for having allowed it to happen. Yes, she had been drunk, but was that any real excuse?

At last she fell asleep, knowing that in the morning she would have to face herself and David. For Linda this wasn't a pleasant thought.

She tossed and turned and slept restlessly.

CHAPTER FIVE

DAVID LEFT the Turkish baths at eight in the morning. He felt refreshed and invigorated. He had contemplated 'phoning Claudia, but had then decided to wait the day out and see if she called him. He parked his car, and bought the morning papers, and then made his way along Piccadilly to Lyons where he planned to breakfast before continuing on home.

He ordered bacon and eggs, toast and coffee, and then sat back to scan the papers. His eye was immediately caught by a half page picture on the front page of the *Daily Mirror*. It was captioned More Near-Riots in Trafalgar Square, and the picture was of an angry mob of people surrounding two policemen in the process of carrying a woman away from the road, and obviously about to dump her back on the pavement. The woman's skirt was high above her knees, so high that you could see the tops of her stockings. Her hair was flopping over her face, and one shoe was about to fall from her struggling foot. It was an effective picture.

The waitress arrived with the order. She was plump and Cockney. She peered over his shoulder at the paper. ' 'Ere what does she think she looks like,' she muttered, 'about time all this rubbish was stopped. A load of show-offs, that's all they are. They should lock the lot of 'em up!' She wandered away, cluck-clucking about nothing in particular. David was staring at the photo, horrified. The woman was unmistakably Linda. He shook his head in disbelief. What was she doing? What was she thinking of?

He gulped his coffee, scalded his tongue, swore, found himself unable to eat anything and called for the bill.

The waitress padded slowly back. 'What's the matter, dear? Isn't everything all right?'

He thrust a ten-shilling note at her. 'Everything's fine,' he said, and stormed out.

A parking warden was in attendance beside his car. David brushed impatiently past him. 'I'm afraid you'll have to wait while I finish writing out this ticket, sir,' said the warden. 'I suppose you are aware that this is a restricted zone for parking?'

'Just give me the ticket and get on with it,' said David brusquely.

The warden glared at him, then proceeded to take his time.

David drove away, his face grim. He envisaged what he would say to Linda. He couldn't quite make up his mind what he would say. The whole thing was so utterly ridiculous. His wife, at a protest meeting! It was ludicrous. She didn't know anything about politics or bombs. The kitchen and the children and social activities such as tea with the girls and dinner out twice a week were her province. Ban the Bomb indeed! Who did she think she was? Claudia was forgotten. He put his foot hard down on the accelerator and raced home.

Anna let him in. 'Mrs. Cooper, she slept late,' she announced. 'You like tea?'

'No,' he grunted, already halfway up the stairs to the bedroom. Linda was asleep, curled up and buried beneath the covers. He drew the curtains, throwing glaring daylight into the room. Linda didn't stir. He paced the floor, coughed loudly and, when she still didn't appear to show any signs of waking up, he went over and shook her roughly, thrusting a copy of the *Daily Mirror* in front of her face as she sleepily opened her eyes.

'What's all this about?' he demanded angrily.

A feeling of dread ran through her. He had found out about her and Paul! How? So soon. She sat up quickly. David stood there glowering at her. He continued talking, 'What is this then? Some secret ambition of yours to make yourself look a complete fool?' He brandished the paper at her again, and she took it from him. A feeling of relief passed over her when she realized that this was what he was so furious about.

'What an awful photo!' she exclaimed. 'I didn't know they were taking any photos.'

'Is that all you have to say?' He mimicked her, 'I didn't know they were taking any photos.' He snatched the paper away from her and continued in a loud angry voice, 'What were you doing there anyway? What were you thinking of?'

'I had nothing else to do. I just found myself there. I'm sorry that you're so angry about it.'

'I'm not angry,' he screamed. He always screamed when in a temper. 'I like to see photos of my wife smeared all over the papers, with her skirt around her waist, accompanied by a load of scruffs.'

She got out of bed. 'I'm not going to sit here while you yell at me. Perhaps if you spent a week-end at home for a change this might not have happened.'

Just then the telephone rang. Linda suddenly felt very hot and flushed. Supposing it was Paul? Should she answer it, or would it be best to let David pick it up and then maybe Paul would hang up. She was convinced it was him.

David swooped down on it, and barked into the receiver, 'Hello.'

Linda held her breath, and then David launched into a long conversation with someone from his office.

She took advantage of his preoccupation on the 'phone and dressed. When he had finished talking he seemed a little calmer. 'Do you want some breakfast?' she asked him.

'No. I have to make some calls. There's this party tonight to launch the Beauty Maid soap product; I had forgotten all about it. You had better meet me at the office at seven, and we'll go from there. I hope to Christ nobody has noticed all your publicity.'

She groaned inwardly at the thought of another party, and then mentally planned her day, which included being at home to greet the children and a definite visit to the hairdressers.

David meanwhile had his own thoughts. Claudia would most certainly be at the party; she was being paid to be there. He wondered if it would be possible for him to effect a quiet reconciliation without everyone in the room noticing. He must be sure that Linda didn't become suspicious, she seemed to be getting too concerned about him being away so much. Maybe she was beginning to suspect him, although this seemed unlikely as he had managed to get away with various affairs throughout the years and she had never found him out yet. At least he would be able to see Claudia. He started to make his business calls.

The children burst back into the house at exactly four o'clock. Linda's father was always prompt. She had just returned from the hairdressers and Stephen flung his small wiry body at her, practically knocking her down.

'We've had a smashing time, Mummy,' he exclaimed. 'I'm starving. What have we got for tea? Grandma makes lovely cakes!'

His sister Jane gave Linda a small kiss. She was six and rather shy. 'I'm glad we're home, Mummy. Your hair looks all pretty, are you and Daddy going out?'

Linda greeted her father and then they sat and chatted while Anna served tea and the children rushed around rediscovering their various toys.

Linda was only half listening as her father droned on about Stephen and Jane's activities during the week-end. She thought about Paul. What did he think of her? Why hadn't he telephoned? What would she say if he 'phoned and David was there?

Finally her father left and the children were settled with Anna having their dinner; and then she got herself ready. Just as she was about to leave the house the telephone rang. She so expected it to be Paul that she felt herself break out in a sweat and her hand started to shake as she picked up the receiver. 'Hello.'

'Hello, darling, it's Monica. How about *you*, then! Aren't *you* the dark horse! Fancy leaving us yesterday and not saying a word about where you were going. You are a deep one. What does David think about it all?'

'Oh,' replied Linda, 'he's not too pleased.'

Monica laughed. 'Well, darling, not to worry, Jack and I think it's marvellous. Anyway, sweetie, we're having a few people over after dinner tonight and we should love you and David to come.'

'Well, Monica, we have to go to a sort of a press party launching the new soap product tonight, and I don't know what time we will be able to get away.'

'Never mind, darling, just come along when you've finished. You know us, we're *always* late.' She gave Linda no chance to protest. 'See you later then, 'bye darling.'

Linda replaced the receiver. She really wasn't too fond of Monica and Jack and she certainly didn't feel like seeing them later. However, she would have to tell David as he would probably want to go.

She left the house in a bad mood. She had a headache, and she was half angry and half relieved that Paul hadn't 'phoned her. She desperately wanted him to 'phone, otherwise what had it all been? A quick one-night affair, a meeting of two people with no more in common than a few hours in bed. However, if he did 'phone, she wanted to tell him that she couldn't possibly see him again, that it could lead nowhere, and that it had all been a mistake. She sighed, at least that way she would be regaining a small amount of self-respect, by denying herself something she really wanted.

It was all so unexpected. She had really never thought of herself as the sort of woman who could have an affair. And this boy Paul, he was so much younger than her, and so different from the type of people she knew and mixed with. How had it happened? She searched her mind and finally concluded that it must be a failure on her part to have reached a complete fulfilment in her marriage. She resolved to try and put the episode with Paul out of her mind and to work desperately and make things more satisfactory between herself and David.

It was nine o'clock before Claudia appeared at the Beauty Maid soap party. David had been watching for her all evening, and suddenly there she was. She materialized beside him, looking exceptionally beautiful, and she murmured, 'Good evening, Mr. Cooper.'

David was taken off guard. He was standing talking to a group which included several press boys and their wives, and Linda. He was flustered and Claudia smiled faintly. The group of people were looking expectantly at him, waiting to be introduced. At last he said, 'Oh, this is Claudia Parker, our Beauty Maid girl.'

Claudia smiled round at the group. She was very flushed and her eyes shone. David knew at once that she was a little loaded. She wore an orange dress, dangerously low cut, and the women in the gathering found themselves standing up straighter and throwing out their bosoms, as if in answer to this sudden challenge. The men were all obviously impressed. 'Miss Parker,' Ned Rice, a small beady-eyed reporter, pressed closer towards her. 'What do you really think of Beauty Maid soap?' His eyes darted towards her bosom.

Claudia played up to him; she fluttered her very long eyelashes and gave him one of her deep sexy looks. 'Well,' she said at last, 'actually I'm an actress really, therefore I don't feel I can give you a serious opinion on soap! As a matter of fact, I've just come from seeing Conrad Lee and he's very interested in having me in his new picture.' She shot David a triumphant look.

Ned Rice was most interested. 'Well, that sounds wonderful. Perhaps we could do a piece about you on our film page.'

'Yes, that would be lovely,' Claudia smiled. 'I'll give you my 'phone number.'

David suddenly could stand it no more. He gripped her by the arm, smiled tightly and said, 'I hope you will excuse us, Miss Parker is here for a purpose, she will be demonstrating our product and I think she's due to begin pretty soon, so I had better get her over to Phillip Abbottson.'

'Oh well, Miss Parker,' said Ned Rice, 'I'll see you later and we'll get together on this.'

'Yes, fine,' she gave one last radiant smile around the group and then followed David.

As soon as they were out of earshot he exploded. 'You're drunk,' he accused, 'where have you been? You were supposed to be here by eight.'

She gave him a cool look. 'David baby, you're nothing in my life, so why don't you just leave me alone.'

'You bitch,' he said in a low voice, his grip tightened on her arm.

'I'm going to make a scene if you don't let go of me,' she said quietly, 'I'm tired of you telling me what I should do.

I'm not someone's wife who has to answer questions and account for every second of her life.'

At that moment, Phillip Abbottson rushed up to them.

'What *is* going on?' he asked. 'Claudia you were supposed to be here an hour ago. We're waiting to unveil the display, get changed for Christ's sake, you think we want to be here all night?' He gave David an odd look and then with Claudia in tow rushed off again.

Ned Rice sidled up to David. His plump pasty wife was talking to Linda across the other side of the room. 'Quite a bit, your Miss Parker,' he said with a leer, 'I bet she's a hot little number, a real tiger!'

David endeavoured to remain calm. 'I wouldn't know.'

'Oh well then, in that case I expect it's all right for me to have a bash.' He nudged David. 'These starlets are all the same, y'know. You've just got to tell them you can get their name in print and they pull their drawers down without you even asking!'

David was saved from answering by the arrival of Mrs. Rice and Linda from across the room.

Ned affectionately patted his wife's plump shoulder. 'Enjoying yourself, love?' he asked, then he waggled an accusing finger at Linda. 'And what were you up to making front page news this morning?'

David was beginning to dislike Ned Rice more and more.

Just then, the lights in the room were dimmed and a spotlight was focused on a mock stage, set at one end of the room. Phillip Abbottson was standing poised at a microphone, and as soon as the hubbub of chatter died down he launched into a long speech about Beauty Maid soap. He was a good promoter and made a simple bar of soap sound like a solid block of gold. At the end of his speech there was polite scattered applause and then he stood to one side and said, 'And now I would like to introduce you to Miss Beauty Maid herself!'

The curtains were drawn back, and there sat Claudia, in a marble bath surrounded by bubbles, in fact an exact replica of the set that was used in the television commercial. She was wearing her flesh-coloured swimsuit, but of course no one could see it, so the general assumption was that she had nothing on beneath the bubbles.

David felt a surge of sudden excitement. Claudia smiled at her audience and started to recite her Beauty Maid speech. Ned Rice whispered something obscene in David's ear. Mrs. Rice said to Linda, 'Isn't she a pretty little thing.' Linda stared blankly into space, her thoughts on the night before.

When Claudia finished talking there was hearty applause

from the men and a few jealous titters from the women. Then the curtains were drawn on Claudia and Phillip appeared back at the microphone with more to say.

David excused himself from the Rices and Linda and made his way to behind the stage. The marble bath was now empty and he noticed a small door at the back of the dais. He hesitated, and then went through it. Claudia was standing, patting herself dry with a towel. It was a very small office, and Claudia's clothes were scattered around in her usual untidy style. She was wearing the flesh-coloured swimsuit and it clung to her like a second skin.

She looked at him wearily. 'What now?'

He walked over to her and put his hands on her shoulders. 'I'm sorry,' he said, 'no more questions.'

She threw him her wide-eyed look, 'Promise?'

'I promise.'

She smiled then, and snaked her arms around his neck. 'All right then, you're forgiven.'

He bent down and kissed her warm soft lips. Her body was still wet and he put his hands in the top of her swimsuit and slowly peeled it off. 'Not here, you idiot,' she whispered, 'some-one might come in. Anyway, you'll be missed.'

He let go of her, and went and turned the key in the door.

She was giggling softly. 'Oh, David, you're really nutty!'

He cupped her breasts in his hands and bent to kiss them. She moaned, 'Go on then, you son of a bitch. Do whatever you want, I don't give a damn!'

CHAPTER SIX

THE GATHERING at Monica's and Jack's was in full swing when Linda and David arrived. There were about ten people there, a mixed crowd, for Monica liked 'group variety' as she put it. Monica herself was a largish woman heading rapidly towards forty, and desperately trying to pull back the other way. She had a lot of very bright red hair, which was inclined to be frizzy, and her face, although heavily laden with Elizabeth Arden, was somewhat outdoorsy and even a little horsy. She used a heavy overpowering musky perfume, which enveloped you like her personality. She was given to talking in a shrieky sort of a voice, and her conversation was always well peppered with 'dahling' and 'sweetie' and 'oh my God!'

Jack, in contrast, was rather reserved. He was a little older than David, but they had been close friends for a number of years. He smoked a pipe, and had a twirly grey moustache. He always wore suede jerkins, or some sort of similar sporty attire. One could imagine him with an enormous mansion tucked away in some rural part of England, walking some type of large dog through his spacious grounds. He owned a chain of garages, and in his younger days had fancied himself as a racing driver. Even now he would often take a test spin on the track to keep his hand in.

Monica grabbed hold of Linda when she arrived, and proudly, with her arm around her, she marched her into the living-room, where everyone was, and announced dramatically, 'And this is our famous ban the bomber!'

Linda was terribly embarrassed, Monica made her sound like some new type of aeroplane! She knew most of the people there, and they all made some sign of greeting. There was one couple she hadn't met before, a thickset, very dark man, and a silver-blonde haughty-looking girl. Monica, as soon as she had finished with her dramatic announcement, introduced her.

'I'd like you to meet Jay and Lori Grossman, friends of mine from America. Jay's here to direct the new Conrad Lee picture.'

'Oh really,' said Linda, 'how interesting. I met a girl earlier this evening who's going to be in it.'

Jay raised a quizzical eyebrow. 'That is interesting,' he spoke with a short sharp New York accent, 'we haven't cast at all yet apart from the male star.'

'Oh well,' Linda smiled, 'I expect she's suffering from delusions.'

'What's her name anyway?' Jay asked.

Linda frowned. 'I can't really remember. My husband would know, she just did a commercial for his company.'

Just then Monica arrived with David, and made the introductions again. He had been in a very good mood since leaving the other party, and he put his arm around Linda and started to chat easily to the Grossmans.

'Darling,' Linda interrupted him, 'what was the name of that little girl who was doing the Beauty Maid thing?'

'What?' asked David, feeling at once guilty. 'Why do you want to know?'

Linda looked at him strangely, or anyway he thought she looked at him strangely. 'Do I have to have a reason?' she asked.

David felt slight tension build in the short silence that followed, and then at once he laughed weakly and said, 'Of course not. It's Claudia Parker, why?'

Jay shook his head. 'Never heard of her.'

'What is this?' questioned David.

'Well,' said Linda, 'you remember she said she was going to

be in the new Conrad Lee picture. Well Jay's directing it, I thought he would know about her. Anyway apparently she isn't in it or going to be.'

'She didn't say she was in it at all,' said David coldly, 'she said she had been to see Conrad Lee and he liked her, that's all.'

'Oh,' Jay laughed, 'that accounts for the confusion. Conrad is always seeing these poor little chicks and stringing them along. Actually, confidentially, the girl is already cast. An unknown Italian kid of sixteen. It builds up the publicity for a film though if we put on a big search for the right girl, and Conrad enjoys seeing the chicks so everyone is happy.'

David scowled at him. 'Everyone is happy except the poor little girls whose hopes he builds up.'

Jay shrugged, 'That's show biz, most of them know the score, and the ones that don't soon learn.' He turned to his wife who so far hadn't opened her mouth, 'Isn't that so, honey?'

Lori Grossman nodded. Her face never seemed to register any expression. It was like a beautiful, but quite blank, painted doll.

'That's how Lori and I met,' Jay continued, 'she was an actress, came for a part, and instead got me. She's my third wife, the other two were actresses as well. I probably met them the same way, don't even remember now.'

At last Lori spoke. Her voice was a thick Southern drawl. 'I sure would like another drink, honey.'

'Certainly baby,' Jay stood up. 'How about you, Mrs. Cooper?'

'Please call me Linda. I'd love a gin and tonic.'

Jay went off to fetch the drinks, and Monica arrived back and claimed Linda, dragging her over to some other people to show them the famous newspaper clipping.

Lori crossed long shapely legs.

David said, 'What part of America are you from?'

'I come from Georgia, honey,' she blinked lazily at him, 'but I've lived in Hollywood for the last five years.'

David studied her. She was older than Claudia, about twenty-seven he reckoned. She looked like one of those thin models out of *Vogue* magazine, everything carefully perfect. He found himself attracted to her. The very perfection made him wonder what she was like in bed. He wondered if that beautiful chignon of silver-blonde hair stayed in place, one somehow couldn't imagine her with it out of place. 'How long are you here for?' he asked.

'Several months, I guess,' she drawled. She apparently had no conversation except to answer questions.

There was a silence until David said, 'Well you and your husband must come over to our house for dinner one night.'

'That would be fun.' She smiled at him, displaying two rows of even, white, obviously capped teeth.

Jay returned with the drinks. 'Where's that lovely wife of yours?' he asked David.

'Honey, there's no ice in this drink,' said Lori petulantly.

'Oh, screw the ice,' said Jay, 'this is England, baby, they don't go so big on the ice bit.' He turned to David, 'Listen, we have to meet some friends soon at the Candy Club, how about you and Linda coming along with us?'

'Well, this is our second party tonight, and I don't know how tired Linda is, but it sounds like a good idea. I'll ask her.'

'Hell, you must come,' said Jay. 'Lori does the craziest cha cha cha you've ever seen. I'll go and ask Linda myself.' He went off.

Lori said, 'Gee honey, what do you do without ice!'

David laughed. 'We usually have ice, we're not that un-civilized. I suppose they've run out.'

She screwed up her nose. 'I like ice,' she stated, and then stared blankly off into space.

David looked at his watch, it was past twelve. Claudia would be safely at home in bed. After the incident in the office, she had promised that she was going straight home, 'You've left me fit for nothing else!' she had joked. He wondered if he could tele-phone her, but then decided it was too late; he didn't want to wake her, and anyway there was nowhere really private that he could 'phone from. The Candy Club sounded like a good idea, and Lori Grossman's cha cha even better.

Jay returned with Linda, smiling broadly. 'I never get no for an answer,' he said with a wink, 'we're all set. Shall we move?'

Monica was quite frosty when she found David and Linda departing with the Grossmans. 'Well honestly, darlings,' she said, 'you've only been here two seconds!'

However they left, and piled into David's Jaguar.

Lori was wrapped in a full length black diamond mink coat, and it reminded David that he had promised Claudia a jacket. He would get it the next day, she had been so sweet earlier. Or was sweet the right word?

Linda and Jay hit it off very well. They chatted away about the differences between England and America, and schools, and where it was best to bring up children, it seemed that Jay had three children, all from his previous marriages. Eventually Jay said to David, 'Hey, your wife is a doll! She's beautiful *and* intelligent, quite a combination.'

Linda was beginning to feel much better, her headache had gone, and she had had just enough to drink to take away any tiredness and make her feel quite gay. She had pushed Paul away to the back of her mind, and was enjoying talking to Jay.

They arrived at the night-club. Jay made a grand entrance, as most Americans do, and asked to be taken to Mr. Lee's table.

The great Conrad Lee was a tall, voluble, half French, half White Russian man in his late fifties. He was totally bald, very suntanned, with piercing eyes which seemed to glare right through you, even in the dimness of the night-club.

He was at a table with six other people, and he leaped up and embraced Lori, and when Linda was introduced he kissed her hand. He smelled strongly of garlic.

The waiters busied themselves trying to squeeze more chairs around the already crowded table, and Jay attempted a few introductions, but it was more or less hopeless, as the noise of the band was so loud that you couldn't hear yourself speak anyway.

David stared in amazement and fury at Claudia. She sat beside Conrad, her hair tousled, one strap of her dress falling off her shoulder, much cleavage. She was very drunk. When Conrad sat down his hand caressed her shoulder, pushing the other strap of her dress down. There was another girl on the other side of Conrad, a plump brunette. He had his arm around her too, pinching chunks of her fleshy back between his fingers.

'Got two lovely little girls here,' Conrad said to Jay, and then with a wink, 'maybe we can use them in the picture.'

Jay raised an eyebrow at Linda. 'See what I mean,' he said with a smile.

'That's the girl I was talking about,' Linda whispered.

'Sure,' said Jay, 'she's got as much chance of getting in the picture as fly!'

Claudia noticed David then, she was too drunk to be surprised or shocked. She just waved gaily, and said, 'What a small world!'

David remembered her saying those exact words to him the first time they met. He scowled at her.

Conrad took Lori off to dance, then Jay claimed Linda, and they went off to dance too.

David sat down in the now empty chair beside Claudia. 'You lousy little bitch!' he said in a low voice. 'Going straight home to bed, well I suppose you'll be doing that eventually.'

She looked surprised. 'Baby, what's the matter? I did go home, and then Conrad called and said he would like to see me again, so he could come to some decision about the part. Well, I mean I have to think about my career, don't I?'

'You're drunk,' he said with disgust, 'you're acting like a whore. Do you honestly believe all this shit Conrad is telling you about putting you in his stinking film? I credited you with more brains than that.'

She looked at him coldly. 'Oh shut up, you make me sick. You're just jealous, that's all. The only time you act sweet is when you've got a hard on!'

He wanted to slap her. She sat there, glaring at him, and for one lucid moment he saw not his beautiful Claudia, but a hard calculating face over a well developed, highly exhibited body.

'Your tits are hanging out!' he said.

'So?' she replied. 'Why not? Are you the only one that's supposed to see them?'

The plump brunette the other side of David suddenly tugged his arm. 'Are you a film producer too?' she asked. Her eyes were large and round and somewhat bloodshot.

'No,' he said curtly.

Conrad and Lori returned to the table, and David stood up. Lori was very tall. She stood there remote and cool. David could see that Claudia was watching her jealously. He took hold of Lori's arms quickly. 'What about another dance?' he said. 'I want to see this wild cha cha of yours.'

Claudia shot him a dirty look, and then focused her charm on Conrad again.

'That would be fun, honey,' drawled Lori, and they headed for the dance floor.

She danced beautifully. 'I used to be a showgirl in Vegas,' she confided.

The evening dragged on. Claudia got drunker and drunker, and she and Conrad closer and closer. The plump brunette was obviously forgotten. Linda and Jay chatted on. Lori sat silently. only speaking when someone spoke to her. David lounged morosely watching Claudia and Conrad, and occasionally attempting to flirt with Lori in case Claudia should be watching him.

At two in the morning Linda eventually said to him, with a yawn. 'I think we had better be going, I'm absolutely tired out.'

No one else in the party seemed interested in leaving, so they said goodbye, and David tried to press some money on Jay, as their part of the bill, but Jay refused to accept it. Claudia said goodbye with a drunken smile, and then turned back to concentrate on Conrad, who by this time was as drunk as she was.

Jay insisted on coming with them to the car, and they exchanged 'phone numbers and promised to all get together again soon.

At last they were alone. Linda leaned back in the car and closed her eyes. David said, not really meaning it, but wanting to take his bad temper out on someone, 'You and that phoney director were getting very friendly.'

She opened her eyes. 'No more friendly than you and that tatty soap model.'

He shot her a dark look, 'I didn't even talk to her, I don't know what you mean.'

'Oh, David, really,' she sighed, 'you didn't even talk to anyone you were so annoyed she was with Conrad Lee. Any fool could see that.' She paused, then added curiously, 'Have you ever taken her out?'

He stared furiously at the road ahead. 'What a ridiculous question.'

'Well I just wondered, I mean you seemed so sort of interested in her. Even at the first party you kept on getting in little huddles with her.'

'She works for us, Linda, I was trying to see that the display thing went off smoothly, that's all.'

They lapsed into silence. He switched the car radio on.

'Darling,' Linda said quickly, tentatively, 'what's wrong?'

'What do you mean what's wrong?'

'I mean what's wrong with us? What's happening to us? Why are we so far apart all of a sudden?'

He turned off the radio. 'I didn't know we were so far apart.'

She looked out of the car window, they were driving through the park, and the trees looked dark and ominous as they sped past them. 'It's funny, David, this must have been starting to happen to us for years, and yet neither of us realized it, neither of us tried to stop it. We're almost like strangers now, two strangers, and the only thing we have in common is our children.'

'I think you're overtired, you're talking a lot of nonsense.'

'A lot of nonsense,' she repeated, 'is that what you really think?' Tears started to roll silently down her cheeks. 'When did you last make love to me? When did you last really want to?'

'Oh, so that's what this is about.'

She fought to keep the tears under control. 'No, that's not what this is all about, but I suppose it's a part of it.'

He pulled the car into the side of the road and stopped, and then turned to face her. What could he say? That he didn't find her very exciting any more? That Claudia was a better lay? She was right really, they were far apart.

'Do you remember our honeymoon?' she questioned.

Yes, he remembered their honeymoon. Spain, hot and sticky and long pleasurable nights with Linda; an innocent young Linda, who awoke all sorts of desires and ambitions in him. 'Yes, I remember our honeymoon,' he said quietly.

'Well, why can't things be like they were then?' She looked at him plaintively.

'Linda, we're both ten years older. Things don't stand still, you know.'

'Yes, I know.' She thought—Paul makes me feel ten years younger. He makes me feel attractive and desirable. He makes me feel wanted.

David said, 'We'd better be getting home. I want to get to the office early in the morning.'

'Yes, all right.' She thought—Why don't you take me in your arms? Why don't you throw me down on the back seat and make love to me here?

They drove home in an uneasy silence, both realizing that there was more unsaid than said.

The house seemed cold and dark. Linda went in to look at the children. Jane slept curled up in a ball, her thumb stuck firmly in her mouth. Stephen had kicked all his covers off, and had nearly fallen out of bed. She covered him, and kissed him lightly on the forehead. They were so innocent, her two precious children. So young and pure.

David was taking a shower. Linda undressed and settled into bed. She wondered if because of what she had said, he would want to make love tonight.

He didn't. He returned from the bathroom, got into bed, switched the light off, muttered, 'Goodnight', and appeared to go straight off to sleep.

She lay there angry and frustrated. I tried, she thought, I really tried to talk to him. But he doesn't seem to care what's happening to us, he doesn't seem to *mind*.

The morning dawned bleak and raining.

David was up at seven. He shaved, showered, and dressed without disturbing Linda, and was out of the house by eight.

She awoke shortly after. Jane was standing beside the bed. " Mummy, can I come in for a cuddle, please?' she requested.

'Yes, of course, darling.'

'I hate Stevie,' Jane confided, 'he's a nasty rough boy. I wish boys were girls!'

'Yes, that's a very good idea,' replied Linda, smilingly.

The morning passed in a flurry of domesticity. The children started at school the following day, and there was a lot to be done. School uniforms to be assembled, books to be found, everything clean.

Linda had no time to think, and in the afternoon she had promised to take them to the news theatre to see the cartoons.

There was no message from Paul. She was both hurt and yet relieved.

When they returned from the cinema she 'phoned David. He wasn't in the office; she left a message for him to call her as soon as he returned.

Jay Grossman had 'phoned and left a number, she rang him back. 'We were wondering if you and David would care to join us for dinner tomorrow night?' he said. 'Lori just can't wait to go to the Savoy Grill, she's heard Princess Margaret goes there, and figures we're bound to be at the next table!'

Linda laughed, 'I'll have to check with David, can you possibly call us back later?'

David didn't 'phone until past seven. 'I'll be late,' he said.

'How late?'

'How the hell do I know, probably around twelve.'

'Where do you have to go?'

His voice was angry. 'What is this, a cross examination?'

She replied coldly, 'No, it's not a cross examination, but I think I'm entitled to know why you're going to be late.'

There was a silence, then, 'I'm sorry, of course you're entitled to know. I'm tired, I suppose. Actually I've got a late discussion with Phillip.'

'Well, why don't you bring him back here and I'll give you both some dinner.'

'No, it's all right, we'll get a sandwich next door and get on with things.'

'I'll see you later then.'

'Yes, don't wait up.' He hesitated, then asked, 'How are the children?'

'They're fine. In a state of excitement about school tomorrow.'

'Give them a kiss for me. 'Bye.'

' 'Bye.' She hung up and yawned. It's an early night for me, she thought, then she remembered that Jay would be 'phoning back about dinner the following evening. Quickly she picked up the 'phone, and dialled David's private number at the office. It rang and rang, but there was no reply.

'Oh bother,' she muttered. She hung up and went and looked in the 'phone book for Phillip's number, David was probably in *his* office. She couldn't find Phillip's office number, but his home number was there, so she dialled that. His wife Mary answered.

'I'm sorry to bother you,' said Linda, 'but can you give me Phillip's private number at the office?'

'Yes, of course,' said Mary, sounding slightly surprised, 'but I'm expecting him home any minute, so I shouldn't think there would be any reply.'

Now it was Linda's turn to sound surprised. 'But isn't he working late with David?'

'No, he's definitely on his way home, his mother is here for dinner, he'll be here any minute.'

'Oh,' said Linda quietly, 'I must have made a mistake.'

'Hang on a sec,' said Mary. 'I think I hear him at the door.'

Linda was left hanging numbly on to the receiver. She felt stunned. So David was lying. Why was he lying? How long had he been lying? And why was it only now, when she herself had been unfaithful, that she had to find out? It was obviously another woman. She felt sick.

Phillip's slightly harsh voice boomed down the 'phone. 'Hello Linda. What's your problem?'

She forced her voice to be light. 'Oh, no problem, Phillip, I'm just trying to track David down. I thought he said he was working with you, but I must have got it wrong.'

Phillip sounded embarrassed, 'Well actually I can't help you. David left the office early today.' He added as an after-thought, 'he's probably out with Mr. Smythson or someone from up north, we seem to have a whole group of people down this week.'

'Thank you, Phillip,' said Linda, she wanted to say—you don't have to try and make excuses for him, instead she said, 'I'm sure you're right, goodbye.'

So this was it. This was the answer to all her questions. It all tied in, late nights home, week-ends away on business, no real physical interest in her. This must have been subconsciously why she found herself in bed with Paul. They say there is a certain point in every marriage where a woman is at the crossroads as to whether to go to bed with someone else or not and, depending on the state of her marriage at the time, she makes her decision.

It's true, thought Linda, if things had been all right with David and me, then I would never have looked twice at that boy. She started to cry. It all seemed so wrong, and to add insult to injury Paul hadn't even rung her.

She threw herself down on the sofa, and gave way to her tears. 'I hate men,' she sobbed, 'selfish, lousy, horrible bastards. . . .'

CHAPTER SEVEN

DAVID AWOKE on Tuesday morning early, with one thought uppermost in his mind, and that was to get out of the house, reach a telephone, and 'phone Claudia.

It was seven o'clock and Linda lay sleeping quietly, so quietly in fact that for a moment he contemplated using the 'phone in the house, but realizing the probable folly of this decided against it.

He shaved, showered, dressed hurriedly, and left. He drove as far as Baker Street before stopping to use the 'phone. It rang dully in Claudia's flat, but no one answered it. He re-dialled, but still no reply. He let it ring for a long time but to no avail. At last he reached the obvious conclusion that she was either out, or too deeply asleep to be disturbed.

He jumped back into his car, and with a sudden flash of decision drove to where she lived.

This time it was the doorbell he rang to no avail.

'Little bitch!' he muttered to himself, 'dirty little bitch!'

He hung around outside for a while, but eventually realizing the futility of this, he drove sourly to his office.

Every half hour he rang her number, getting more and more angry each time it wasn't answered. Until at last, at eleven, it was finally picked up by Claudia's daily.

'Is Miss Parker there please?' he asked.

The daily's voice was full of Cockney richness. 'I fink she's asleep. 'Old on a tick, I'll go an' 'ave a look.' She returned after a short pause. 'She ain't in,' she stated. 'Any message?'

He said, 'You don't happen to know what time she went out?'

'Can't say that I do. Don't fink she's bin in since yesterday, 'cos 'er bed ain't bin slept in.'

'Thank you,' said David, 'there's no message.'

He imagined her with Conrad. Her smooth, beautiful body crushed to his, going through the motions of love which she practised so expertly. He could almost hear her small exquisite cries of excitement, her little moans, and the way she muttered crude words in a low throaty voice. He swore.

After that he rang her flat every hour, hanging up when the daily answered. He was furious with himself for being in such a state about her. He had always prided himself on never getting too deeply involved emotionally, always being able to shut other people out of his life when he had had enough of them. But this time it was different. Whatever she did, he couldn't seem to get Claudia out of his mind.

At four o'clock she finally picked up her 'phone. The record player was very loud in the background, and she sounded in good spirits. He listened to her voice saying 'Hello,' then a pause, then—'Hello, is anyone there?' Then another longer pause, and then—'Oh, screw you whoever it is!' And the 'phone was slammed down.

He left the office at once, and drove straight over to where she lived. He didn't want to row with her on the 'phone, he wanted to see her, hear the excuses, watch her lie.

She answered her front door and looked surprised and a little guilty to see him. She was wearing very tight white slacks, and a large black polo-necked sweater. Her face was devoid of any make-up, and although she looked a little tired, her brilliant green eyes shone with an alert, triumphant expression.

'Well, surprise, surprise!' she said. 'Come on in.'

He followed her into the flat. A very loud Sinatra singing 'Come Fly With Me', was turned up full volume. A half bottle of Scotch, and a giant pink fluffy toy poodle stood on the table.

'Want a drink?' asked Claudia.

'It's four o'clock in the afternoon,' he said coldly.

'Square . . .' she muttered, like a naughty child caught doing something wrong.

She poured herself a stiff Scotch, lit a cigarette, and flopped down on the floor. 'Well, David, what is there to say?'

'There's plenty to say,' he paced the room angrily, and added menacingly, 'plenty.'

She giggled, 'Oh stop it with the wronged husband bit. I *told* you I wasn't tied to anyone. I warned you that no man tells me what to do.'

He shook his head at her, 'I don't understand you, you act like some cheap little whore.'

She rolled over on her stomach, taking a long drag of her cigarette and, blowing the smoke towards him, said calmly, 'I'm in a very good mood today, nothing can spoil it, not even you.' She rolled on to her back and stretched, the taut outline of her breasts appearing through her sweater. He felt the familiar hot desire creep up on him.

'Conrad Lee is a very important man, and he's going to do a lot for me.'

'Oh yes, he'll do a lot for you,' said David bitterly, 'he'll do a lot for you in bed.'

'I'm testing this week for his new film, how about that?'

'Balls!'

'Oh, you're just jealous, that's all. You see, he's going to make a star out of me. You wait, you'll see.'

'You're making a fool of yourself, the *director* of the film said that this is Conrad's hobby, stringing along little girls like you.'

'I'm not a little girl. I'm a big girl. I'm not a fool, I do know the score.'

'How was he in the sack?'

Her eyes met his. They were big and green and bright. 'He wasn't anything like you.' She stood up, and wrapped her arms around him. 'No one's like you,' she whispered, 'no one's ever been like you.' The fight was over.

It was slow, and warm, and tender. Afterwards they lay on the floor where he had taken her, locked in each other's arms.

She kissed him softly. 'You must understand,' she whispered, 'it doesn't mean I don't love you. When I sleep with him it's nothing. He's a pig, an old pig. But baby, I want to be in his film, I want to be in it so much. I'm going to be in it, I promise you that.'

He flicked his hands over her soft breasts. 'You're so beautiful, when I'm with you I don't care what you've been doing. All right then, get in his lousy movie if you must. But don't sleep with him or anyone else again, or I'll beat hell out of you!'

She pressed closer to him. 'I wish you would beat me, that would be good.'

It's impossible, he thought, impossible that it could happen again so soon, and be that much better. She's like a tigress. They should cage her naked in the zoo for all to see, for only seeing is believing: and they should pin a notice to her cage—'Do not feed, only eats men'.

Out of the blue Claudia said, 'Your wife's very attractive, isn't she?'

'She used to be. I suppose she still is really.'

'How old is she?' asked Claudia, a typical woman's question.

David wasn't interested in discussing Linda. 'Oh thirty something, I don't know.'

'I wonder what I'll look like when I'm thirty.'

He was saved from answering this by the telephone ringing. Claudia reluctantly lifted the receiver.

'Oh, hello,' she said softly. She glanced quickly over at David. He immediately wondered who it was. 'I'd like that,' she was saying, 'about what time?' She balanced the receiver under her chin, and fumbled for a cigarette from the table. 'All right then, see you tomorrow. Look forward to it.' She hung up. 'I'm starving!' she exclaimed. 'I feel like going out for a fabulous exciting dinner.'

'Who was that?' he asked, trying to keep his voice casual.

'Who was what?' she asked, knowing perfectly well what he meant.

'On the 'phone.'

'Oh, that!' she hesitated for just a second too long before saying, 'It was my agent. He wanted me to have dinner with him and his wife tomorrow night.'

'Friendly of him, just like that he starts asking you to dinner.'

'Yes, just like that,' she said patiently. 'As a matter of fact I called him earlier and told him I wanted to see him about this Conrad thing. I'm going to bathe, can we go out later? Or have you got to rush home?'

He thought she was lying, but what was the point in arguing. 'Do you want me to be free?'

'Silly! Of course I want you to be free, otherwise I wouldn't have asked you.'

'I'll 'phone home, where do you want to go, I'll book a table.'

'Oh, let's go somewhere swinging for a change. We always have to hide out in some old dive. What does it matter if we're seen. After all I am Miss Beauty Maid, so I'm business really! Let's go to Carlos.'

Carlos was a fairly new, very expensive, very fashionable Italian restaurant. It was *the* place to go, *the* place to be seen at. He knew that he was taking a ridiculous risk going there with Claudia. He was sure that he would see people he knew there. However, on the other hand, he wanted to be seen with Claudia, he wanted people to know that this was his. Then also, Claudia wanted to go there, and now she had him by the short hairs, and they both knew it. He had come running back after what she had done, and now it was she who was able to call the tune.

'O.K., you go and make yourself pretty, and I'll book a table for eight o'clock.'

She kissed him lightly. 'Divine, darling.'

He gave her a playful tap on the bottom. 'Go put some clothes on, or we'll never get out!'

Giggling, she retired to the bathroom.

David read the evening papers, booked a table at the restaurant. He felt guilty about 'phoning Linda, but eventually he did, and then snapped at her when she asked what he had to do. He produced some suitable lies, felt badly about the whole thing, enquired after the children in a fit of conscience, and then hung up.

Claudia reappeared after a time, transformed. Her glossy ash-blonde hair was piled on the top of her head in studied confusion, her make-up was smooth and perfect. She wore a plain black dress, and rows and rows of jet beads. She looked stunning.

David told her so, and she smiled and preened and showed off her dress to him, flitting around the room, like some beautiful exotic bird. 'Isn't it *exciting* going out somewhere *decent* together!' she exclaimed. 'I do wish we could do it more often.'

In the car on the way to the restaurant, he had second thoughts. It was a stupid thing to do. Linda was bound to find out, and then what? Especially as she seemed to be so sensitive about their marriage lately. He glanced quickly over at Claudia, she was fiddling with the radio trying to find some music on it.

'Why don't we drive out somewhere nice in the country instead?'

She looked over to him, her big eyes frosty. 'I knew you'd get cold feet, *you* go to the country, drop me at a cab rank, I'm sick of hiding all over the place.'

'All right, we'll go to Carlos.' To hell with it, Linda probably wouldn't find out, they said that wives were always the last to know.

The restaurant was very crowded. The head waiter said their table would be a few minutes, so they sat in the bar. Claudia greeted several people. David was relieved to see no one he knew.

A girl came up to them, dragging a weedy-looking young chap behind her. She was very thin and sun-tanned, and quite pretty.

'Darling!' she said to Claudia, 'you look fabulous! Where *have* you been, haven't seen you for ages!' She dragged the young man alongside her. '*You* remember Jeremy.' Jeremy blushed and stuttered 'Hello'. 'Well darling, we're engaged! Can you imagine!' she giggled and gave Jeremy a playful poke in the ribs. He looked acutely embarrassed.

'Shirley!' exclaimed Claudia. 'How marvellous!' She turned to David, 'Shirl darling, this is David Cooper, a very old friend of mine.' Shirley extended a small suntanned hand, and David shook it briefly.

Claudia continued, 'And David, I'd like you to meet Shirley's fiancé, the Hon. Jeremy Francis.'

Jeremy edged forward. 'Jolly glad to meet you, old boy.' He had sandy-coloured skin, liberally dotted with angry red spots.

'Sit down and have a drink,' said Claudia, 'we must celebrate!'

They found extra chairs and sat down. The girls immediately went into a huddle about the dresses they were wearing. The Hon. Jeremy sat uncomfortably on the edge of his chair. He was extremely tall, and his knees bumped David's under the table.

'We're going to have an *enormous* wedding,' Shirley was now saying, 'it will be simply marvellous. Jeremy's parents know absolutely everyone!' She flashed a large emerald and diamond ring at Claudia. 'Look!' she said dramatically. 'Asprey's!'

Claudia said, 'It's divine, I love it. I'm so happy for you both.'

'And now what about *you*?' questioned Shirley, shooting a coy, meaningful look at David.

Claudia laughed, 'You know how *I* feel about marriage. It's not for me, Shirl baby. I dig the single bit. Anyway *you* met Jeremy first!' Jeremy blushed, and looked suitably flattered.

David stood up. 'I think our table's ready.'

'Oh, did you *book*?' said Shirley wistfully. 'We forgot, and now we've got to wait simply ages for a table, and I'm *starving*.' She hesitated for a second or two, and then continued, 'I say, why don't we all have dinner together. I haven't seen you for *such* ages Claudia, and it would be such fun!'

'We have a table for two,' said David grimly.

'Oh well, we don't mind being a bit cramped, do we, Jeremy?' Jeremy nodded blankly.

'Well, what do you say?' Shirley turned to Claudia.

Claudia looked hopelessly at David. 'Fine, we'd love it.'

They followed the waiter to their table, Shirley waving and smiling to several people on the way. 'I think this is a simply marvellous place,' she said to Claudia as they reached their table. 'I'm sure if one just sat here for a week one would see absolutely everyone one ever knew pass by, sort of like London Airport!' She giggled loudly.

David sat through the dinner in sullen silence, and Jeremy didn't have much to say at any time, so it was Shirley who did all the talking, with Claudia occasionally joining in. Shirley was an avid reader of *Queen* magazine, especially the society pages, and her main topics of conversation were who had been seen with whom, and what good parties were going on. Jeremy, apparently, was asked to most of them, and Shirley went into minute details about the most boring items. For example, Lady Clarissa Colt wearing the same dress to two different parties, and the Hon. Amanda Lawrence having a coming-out party where they ran out of champagne. 'It was too awful,' wailed Shirley, 'one just *never* should run short of champers! Too embarrassing!'

Eventually, when they had reached dessert, Jeremy took her off to the small dance floor, and they clung limply together to a Bossa Nova beat.

'Let's get out of here,' said David, 'I've heard just as much as I can take from that stupid, snotty little cow.'

'I'm sorry, baby,' replied Claudia soothingly, 'she is a bit much.'

'A bit much! That's an understatement if ever I heard one. Who is she anyway?'

A smile played softly around Claudia's mouth. 'When I first came to London I worked in a club, Miss Fancy Pants worked there too.'

'What were you doing in a club?' asked David surprised.

'Well darling, I had to earn some money, it doesn't grow on trees you know, and this actor I arrived with never seemed to work, so I took a job in this club.'

'Doing what?'

'The dance of the seven veils!' Claudia replied laughingly.

'What! You must be joking.'

Claudia's smile faded slightly. 'I'm not joking. Look I had no talent for doing anything else, it was either that, or being a hostess and getting pawed about by a lot of dirty old men, and I would sooner take my clothes off any day. They could look, but they couldn't touch.'

'I don't know anything about you really, do I?'

Claudia's large eyes turned suddenly remote. 'You've never bothered to listen, like all men, your prime concern is to get me in the sack as fast as possible.'

There was a short silence, then Claudia gave a quick brittle laugh. 'I'm sorry, my past is a big drag anyway, why should you want to hear about it.'

David was about to reply when Shirley and Jeremy returned.

'Jeremy's made the most divine suggestion,' said Shirley.

'There is a simply dinky little night-club opened down at Windsor, and he says why don't we all pop down there.'

David looked at her sourly. 'At the Castle, naturally.'

For a moment Shirley's pale blue eyes glinted angrily, then she grimaced and laughed quickly, replying, 'No sweetie, not at the Castle.'

'Well count us out then,' said David.

'I say old chap, are you sure?' stammered Jeremy.

Claudia broke hurriedly into the conversation. 'David's a bit tired, you two run along, and if we change our minds we'll join you later.'

'All right then,' said Shirley, 'but do try and make it.' She grabbed Jeremy by the arm, 'Come along sweetie, we'll leave these two lovebirds on their own.'

She shot a dark glance at David, waved gaily to Claudia, and towing Jeremy along behind her, they made their exit.

Claudia started to laugh.

'I don't happen to think it's so funny,' said David grimly. 'I suppose I'm stuck with the bill as well. Many thanks for a delightful evening.'

Claudia's laughter increased. 'Oh, I'm sorry. But honestly it is funny. If you had known Shirley a few years ago, well I mean, you just wouldn't believe it. She was anybody's and everybody's!'

His tone was cold; 'and you?'

Abruptly Claudia stopped laughing. She stared at him for a few seconds, and then said slowly and deliberately, 'I think we have just about reached the end of our relationship, if you could ever call it that.' Before he had a chance to reply, she got up from the table, and threading her way through the restaurant she vanished out of sight. Quickly he called for his bill.

'It's David Cooper, isn't it?' the voice was loud and American.

David looked startled. There stood Jay Grossman. 'Well, hello,' he said uneasily.

'Where is your lovely wife?' Jay stared pointedly at the obviously recently occupied place across the table.

David wondered if he had seen Claudia leave, then decided he hadn't, otherwise, as he was more or less only a casual acquaintance he would never have made such an obvious remark. 'Oh, she's at home,' said David, then indicating the rest of the table he continued, 'I had a business meeting, they all had to rush-off.'

At that moment the waiter presented the bill, and leaving a wad of notes David got up quickly.

'You must come on over to say "hello" to Lori,' said Jay, 'she would be most upset if I told her I'd seen you and hadn't brought you over for a drink.'

'Well, only for a minute then,' said David reluctantly, 'Linda's expecting me.'

The Grossmans were sitting at a table right across the other side of the room, and he was pleased to note that they couldn't see his table from where they were. Jay had only spotted him by chance on his way back from the men's room. Lori looked as aloof and perfectly groomed as before. Every shining blonde strand of hair arranged carefully in place, her face a mask of smooth clear flawless make-up. She wore a pale brown chiffon dress, which dipped revealingly between her breasts.

'Nice to see you again,' said David unable to keep his eyes from straying down her neckline.

'Likewise,' she replied, in her faintly suggestive, empty American drawl.

'Come on—sit down, you must join us for a drink,' said Jay.

'Well,' he sought wildly for an excuse, couldn't find one, and anyway, what the hell—eyes fixed firmly on Lori's neckline he sat down.

'What will you have?' asked Jay.

'A scotch on the rocks.'

Jay summoned the waiter while Lori produced a small gold compact and proceeded to touch up an already perfect make-up.

'I spoke to Linda earlier,' Jay said, 'she mentioned she was going to talk to you about joining us for dinner tomorrow night.'

'Oh,' said David blankly—his mind was half on the fact that Claudia had walked out on him—what a bitch! and half on the fact that he had a strong fancy for Mrs. Cool, dumb Grossman. What a revelation to get her into bed and penetrate beneath the layers of make-up, eyelashes, and hair pieces. 'That would be a good idea, where do you want to go?'

'Well, Lori wants to see the Savoy Grill.'

'Yeah,' Lori put down her compact for one brief moment, 'I've heard it's a gas. You get to see Princess Margaret and that cute guy she's married to.'

'Well, they don't exactly do a cabaret there,' said David smiling, 'but they have been known to go there.'

Jay said, 'Shall we meet at our hotel?'

They chatted a short while longer, and then David made his excuses and left. He tipped the attendant who brought his car round, and sat morosely in it. Screw little Miss Hot Pants Parker. She was becoming too much. First of all she talked him into going to a restaurant he didn't even want to go to, then she lumbered him with her dreary friends, then she admitted to working in a strip joint, and got insulted when he commented on it, and then had the utter cheek to get up and walk out on him. On top of all this she had been to bed with that fat slob of a producer the previous evening. She was nothing but a little tramp, an easy lay. If he wasn't dead careful he might even catch something from her. She could get lost, he was going home.

He headed his car towards Hampstead. It was ten o'clock.

CHAPTER EIGHT

AFTER A WHILE Linda stopped crying. She went into the bathroom and washed her face, her eyes were red and swollen. She stared at her reflection in the mirror. She didn't know what to do, she knew she couldn't face the prospect of sitting around waiting for David to finally arrive home, fresh from the arms of some tart. She had no one to telephone. Since marrying, she had gradually lost touch with all her girl-friends—they had all drifted apart, got married and gone off to live in different parts of the country. She thought of 'phoning her mother, but to confide in her would be ridiculous. Her mother had never really approved of David, and would be only too pleased. She had warned Linda against marrying him. 'After all, he's a Jew,' she had said, as if that explained everything.

In desperation she 'phoned Monica, she had to talk to someone. Monica was cool. 'Well dahling, absolutely charming the way you stayed five minutes and then dragged off my most important guests. I mean, really dahling—a bit off.'

Their conversation was brief, and when Linda hung up she thought—the hell with it, I'm not a child and she picked up the 'phone again and dialled Paul's number.

He answered the 'phone—'Hallo?'

She got cold feet and froze not saying anything, quickly she hung up the receiver. It rang again almost immediately. She said 'Hello'.

'Linda, this is Paul, I know you just 'phoned me.'

She was taken aback.

'Look—I've been waiting for you to 'phone. Can I see you? Can you come over?'

'When?' she muttered weakly.

'Can you make it now?'

'Well, I don't know . . .'

'Please, I must talk to you.'

'Well, all right then, I'll be there in half-an-hour.'

'Great,' he gave her the address.

She was surprised. Ego had told her that he wouldn't have forgotten her, but she hadn't expected him to be waiting to see her, expecting her to 'phone.

She got ready swiftly, before she changed her mind, and drove the five-minute distance to where he lived. It was an old house converted into flats squashed between a butcher's shop and a vet on the main High Street. She climbed five flights of stairs before reaching his flat—number 8, with a peeling yellow front door.

He answered her knock immediately.

'I don't really know what I'm doing here,' she blurted out. He took her by the hand and led her inside.

'You look lovely, I've been going mad waiting for you to 'phone.'

'Why didn't you 'phone me?'

'Look Linda—I dig your scene. I didn't want to put you in a bad position, it was up to you to make the next move.'

He made her feel very young, although she could give him at least ten years.

'I know nothing about you.'

'You're always saying that,' replied Paul. He was wearing paint-stained faded old blue jeans, and a white polo-neck sweater. He looked very attractive.

They were standing in a small dark room which Linda presumed was the lounge, dining room, study, etc. The walls were painted black and hung with lots of paintings, some framed, some unframed, mostly nudes with exotic thin faces, masses of hair and voluptuous bodies. The furniture in the room was a teak Danish dining-table—piled high with papers, and a battered old scarlet sofa. She sat on the sofa and he said she could have a beer or 90% proof Russian Vodka—brought direct from Moscow by a friend of his. She elected to have the Vodka. It was very strong, he mixed it with water and it tasted vile, but she struggled to get it down. He put a Billie Holliday record on and sat beside her.

'Look, about the other night,' she said nervously, 'it should never have happened—I mean well—I'd had a row with my husband and I had too much to drink. . . .'

He took her hand. 'You don't have to make excuses, it happened and it was great, and if you're embarrassed about it, well you didn't have to see me again. I didn't call you for that reason.'

She took another gulp of Vodka. 'I just wanted to explain!' she hesitated and then rushed on, 'I mean I didn't want to leave you with the wrong impression of me.'

'You left me with a beautiful impression, your perfume was all over my bed and the smell of your body, and the way you cried out when you came.' He reached over for her and she half-heartedly tried to pull away. But their mouths met and she was lost. He was young and trying to please and full of strength, and this time she was almost sober. His whole feeling seemed to be to try to please her, and in return she found herself twice as adept at thrilling him. They made love for two hours—starting on the sofa, the floor, and then the bedroom. Afterwards they lay and talked.

She felt so peaceful and protected by him. He listened quietly while she told him about David and his indifference towards her. She told him everything about herself, about the children, about her life. They smoked cigarettes and drank more Vodka.

She found out about him too. He was an artist, he had left Art School a year before and was now working as assistant to the Art Editor of a glossy woman's magazine. The paintings on the wall and in the other room were all his. She found out they were of a girl-friend he had called Margarethe. It was a sad story, they had met at Art School and fallen madly in love. Margarethe was from Sweden, and had worked as an au pair girl for three years to earn enough money to study art. She was a lovely girl and after living together for six months they decided to get married. Paul's mother was dead and his father, a retired businessman lived in Cheltenham. So to the house in Cheltenham they went to have Margarethe meet father. She met father and three days later she married him. Paul was stunned, he couldn't believe it. He had a terrible row with both of them, and hadn't seen or heard from them since.

'I couldn't accept it,' Paul said, 'I mean, I don't believe she could have loved him, I suppose she wanted his loot, I couldn't offer her any security.'

'How do you feel about her now?' questioned Linda.

'I don't know,' said Paul moodily. 'I think she's a cow. They just went off one afternoon and came back married.'

'Why do you still keep your paintings of her around?'

'I don't know,' he shrugged, 'just to remind me not to be such a berk again, I suppose. I can't make it with girls any more, y'know. Maybe once or twice, then I just don't want to know.'

She remembered whiney voiced, pretty little Melanie.

'I imagine I'm all right because I'm married?' said Linda.

'Yeah, I guess so, but listen darling, I really do dig you. I think you're great.'

They lay in silence for a while, both mulling over their individual problems.

'The thing that really gets me,' said Paul, 'is imagining Margarethe living in Cheltenham with my old man. She was such a swinger, really a cuke. She liked to ball more than anyone I ever knew. I just can't see her fancying him. He's a drag.'

'What was your mother like?' asked Linda.

'It's a long story,' said Paul.

Linda leaned over and kissed him lightly on the forehead. 'Tell me about it,' she said gently.

'You sound like a psychiatrist,' he laughed. 'Actually it's a lousy story, she killed herself when I was fifteen.'

There was silence. Linda was shocked. She wanted to ask why —but Paul had turned over on his side and closed his eyes. 'It's a drag, Linda,' he muttered, 'I'll tell you about it some other time.'

After a while Linda looked at her watch and seeing that it was past eleven, she said, 'Look, I had better be leaving, David's going to be home at twelve.'

'Can't you stay the night?' Paul mumbled, his back still to her.

'Oh, honestly Paul, I would like to but I just can't not be there when he gets home—I mean he would be worried. He knows I never stay out—he'd probably call the police.'

'It's funny, isn't it,' Paul said. 'All these little birds that I bang I just can't get rid of.' He put on a high thin voice, 'Oh darling, let me stay the night—Mummy and Daddy never expect me before morning.' They both laughed.

'I tell you it's horrible, they just will not go. And you must know what it's like to screw someone and then not be able to stand them near you after. Y'know Linda, you're the first female since Margarethe I've asked to stay the night—and you say no.'

She dressed slowly and Paul lay lazily back in bed watching her. 'Y'know, you're very sexy, I'd dig seeing you in long black nylons and a black garter belt.'

'What would you do, take pictures?'

'No—I'd paint you—sort of lying on a sofa. Very sexy indeed. Can I?'

'I'll think about it,' she laughed, slightly embarrassed.

Eventually she was ready to go.

'When am I going to see you?' he asked.

'Well, I don't know.'

'Tomorrow?'

'I don't know Paul, it's very difficult for me to make plans.'

'Well, you can't just leave without telling me when.'

'I'll 'phone you in the morning.'

He gave her his 'phone number at work, kissed her long and hard, and she set off on her journey home. It was eleven thirty.

CHAPTER NINE

CLAUDIA LEFT the restaurant angrily. She hailed a taxi and directed it to Conrad Lee's hotel. She was fed up with David Cooper. Stupid bastard—who did he think he was! At first their affaire had been fun. She dug having affairs with married men, they were a race apart, and always a challenge. Also, she had misguidedly thought he might be able to help her career. Nothing he had done, absolutely nothing. Being Miss Beauty Maid appeared to lead to a dead end. He hadn't even given her a decent present, just a lot of unkept promises. So where was the famous mink jacket she was supposed to get? She didn't want money from him, how dare he offer her money like some cheap whore, but presents were a different matter.

'Cheapskate,' she muttered under her breath. Why he even complained about paying the bill in the restaurant.

The taxi pulled up at the hotel and a doorman leaped forward to escort her in. She strolled coolly over to reception.

'I'd like to speak to Mr. Conrad Lee.'

They put her through on the house 'phone. After a while the operator said there was no reply.

'Would you try the 'phone in the bedroom please,' said Claudia.

The 'phone rang several times, then a voice answered thickly —'Yeah?'

'Conrad, this is Claudia Parker.'

'Who?'

'Claudia Parker,' she repeated patiently. 'Listen darling, you can't have forgotten last night already?'

There was a short pause, then—'Oh yeah, of course, how are you baby? What can I do for you?'

'Well, your secretary called me earlier about seeing you to-morrow night—I was out with this dreary guy, and I suddenly thought the hell with it, what about tonight.'

He laughed, coughed unattractively and said, 'Listen baby, I'm all tied up tonight.'

'Oh,' she sounded disappointed. 'Look, I'm cool,' she continued, 'I never find three a crowd.'

'Do you mean what I think you mean?' he questioned.

'Of course I do,' she purred, 'you were so fantastic last night I don't mind sharing.'

'Hang on a minute,' Conrad said, and the 'phone was muffled. She waited patiently and soon his voice came back full of interest—'Come right up baby, we'll be waiting.'

She hung up smiling and made her way leisurely to the powder room, where for the next twenty minutes she touched up her make-up and re-arranged her hair so that it fell around her shoulders thick and shiny. She looked very gorgeous, young, sexy and pretty. Her figure was shown off to its best advantage in the low cut black dress she was wearing.

A half hour had passed by the time she finally knocked on

the door of his suite and he answered almost immediately—wearing a livid green and orange striped bathrobe. 'Where the hell have you been?' he demanded.

She smiled apologetically, she knew she looked great. She walked into the living-room and sat down, crossing her legs carefully to be sure there was the maximum amount of thigh showing.

'I'm so sorry,' she said, 'I know you're going to think I'm terrible. But what I said on the 'phone about a threesome and everything. Well, I'm sorry but I just can't.'

He stared at her disbelievingly. 'You can't?' he said thickly.

She shook her head slowly fluttering long black eyelashes. 'I guess I wanted to see you again so much, I just said it—but really, it's not my scene.'

'It's not your scene,' he repeated blankly.

'No,' she licked her lips, crossed her legs the other way and waited.

'Look baby,' he said at last. 'You called me while I was balling this chick,' he indicated the bedroom, 'you called me up right in the middle. Nobody asked you to—but there you were on the 'phone—asking, and I mean asking, to join us. So what happens—you get me all hot over the idea of a scene—I stop halfway with this other broad—wait a goddamn half hour and then you mince in here saying you can't make it.' His voice had been rising excitedly and now he was almost screaming!

She stood up—'What can I say?' She walked over to him and put her hand on his arm. 'I was drunk last night, but in spite of that I remembered last night as something special. Now I'm sober and can I help it if I don't want to share you?'

He looked at her admiringly. 'You're a smart little cookie, I suppose you want me to get rid of—' he gestured towards the bedroom.

She kissed him, pressing herself up against him hard, 'That's the general idea.'

He pushed her away. 'All right baby—but don't think you're fooling me, because I'm hip to exactly what you're doing. You happen to be a lot prettier than her, so I'll pay her off. Is that what you want?'

She looked at him wide-eyed. 'I don't know what you're talking about,' she said, 'do whatever you want. I'll still be available tomorrow night, I can always go now.'

His eyes swept over her body—'No, you stay, wait in the bathroom.'

She smiled and walked obediently into the bathroom which was in the hall. He kept her waiting about five minutes and she heard a shrieky female voice and then a door slammed. Eventually he threw open the bathroom door—he had discarded his vibrant bathrobe and stood there with nothing but his sun-tan and a hard on. 'Let's go baby,' he said, 'I just had to give that broad fifty bucks, so you'd better make it worth my while!'

David parked the car in the garage and let himself into the house. It was strangely quiet, and he supposed Linda had gone to bed early. He made his way upstairs and looked in on the children who both slept peacefully. Jane woke up and sleepily requested a glass of water. He got it for her and she threw her arms around his neck and said 'I love you Daddy'. He settled her down and went into the main bedroom. It was empty. He was mildly surprised. Where on earth was Linda? He knew the rest of the house was deserted. She must have gone to a movie or something, but it was most unlike her.

He checked through the window and saw her car was not in the drive, and then he looked around for a note—no note. He went along to Anna's room and knocked. The maid came to the door—she was clutching her transparent nylon nightdress around her and she featured a heavy black moustache.

'Where's Mrs. Cooper?' he questioned.

'She went out maybe eight o'clock,' said Anna. Her English was not too good, and she didn't volunteer any further information.

'Did she say where she was going?'

'No.'

'What time she would be back?'

'No.'

The conversation was finished.

He went back to the bedroom, showered and fell asleep reading the papers on the bed.

That was how Linda found him when she came in. She was surprised, he had said twelve o'clock and he was always later than he said he would be.

Fortunately he was asleep, as her make-up was all off and her hair a mess and she knew if he saw her he would surmise something. She made it into the bathroom quickly and got out of her clothes and into a robe; at least if he woke up now it wouldn't matter. She ran a bath. David awoke. 'Where the hell have you been?' he said.

'I went to a movie, where were you?'

'You know where I was. The movies get out at quarter to eleven—where have you been for the last hour?'

'I suppose you were with Phillip,' said Linda, ignoring his question to her.

'Yes—you know I was with Phillip.'

'Well, I was with Phillip too.'

He stared at her blankly. 'What are you talking about?'

'I was with Phillip as much as you were with Phillip.'

'Have you been drinking?'

'No, David, I haven't been drinking. I called the Abbottson house after speaking to you earlier, and while I was talking to Mary, Phillip came in and he knew nothing about a meeting with you.'

'Oh,' David thought quickly, 'yes, things were a bit of a mess. I thought Phillip was coming back later, but then I realized he had said he couldn't so then I had to take those people from out of town, out to dinner.'

She raised an eyebrow at him—'But you just said you were with Phillip.'

'Yes—well that was because I knew you wouldn't understand.'

'Well, you were right, I don't understand. Now please can I take a bath?'

'Oh, you're so ridiculous, Linda,' his voice was becoming louder—'Look, I've been home for hours. I took these three men to Carlos and I ran into Jay and Lori Grossman. Now do you believe me? They want us to have dinner with them tomorrow, and I said it was all right. Now you can ask them who I was with. O.K.?'

She was surprised, maybe he was telling the truth. 'Oh all right,' she said wearily.

He stalked back into the bedroom. She took her bath. Their thoughts were on separate planes. Neither of them really wanted to get involved in long discussions about who had been where as it was dangerous ground and they could end up getting found out themselves.

She came to bed. He thought how pretty she looked. She was wearing a long pink silk nightdress that clung seductively to her.

He broke the silence. 'Where would you like to eat tomorrow?'

She was non-commital, 'I don't mind.'

'Jay says Lori wants to go to the Savoy Grill—a bit conventional but I suppose as they are visitors here we should oblige.'

'Yes, I suppose so.' She turned out the light on her side of the bed and lay with her back towards him.

'What's new with the children?'

'Oh nothing much.'

He lit a cigarette. 'I'm not tired,' he remarked.

'Well, why don't you read? There's that book back there that you started about three months ago.'

'I don't feel like reading.'

'Well, turn your light off and go to sleep then.'

'That's a pretty nightdress, is that new?'

'No, I've been wearing it for the past two years,' she said patiently.

He leaned over and cupped her left breast with his hand. She shrank away immediately.

Oh, God no, she thought, not tonight—please God not tonight. After all those nights I've lain here and ached for him he couldn't possibly pick tonight.

He lounged across the bed after her. 'What's the matter?'

'Nothing,' she forced herself to turn around and face him.

Fortunately he took her quickly. He had long ago given up preliminaries with her. The sexual act with him gave her absolutely no pleasure, she felt vacant and used. She wondered vaguely if all men became like this after you married them. In courting days, anxious to please, thrilled to bits if they got to fondle you for half-an-hour. But after the marriage—a quick lay and that was that.

'That was marvellous,' he said, 'how was it for you?'

She simulated pleasure. 'Marvellous,' she repeated his adjective unable to think of anything else to say.

He turned the light out. 'Goodnight.'

She squeezed her eyes shut to keep in the tears, 'Goodnight.'

He lay there and thought about what a bitch Claudia was.

She lay there and thought about how virile and sensitive Paul was.

Finally, they both fell asleep.

CHAPTER TEN

'I WANT TO stay the night,' Claudia said, stretching languorously.

Conrad was on the 'phone to room service. He sat on the side of the bed, rolls of suntanned flesh around his middle, bald head shining slightly with sweat.

'This is Mr. Lee, suite 206—send me up six pieces of lightly buttered toast spread with caviar—and the best stuff I mean. Also send a bucket of ice, a glass of milk and a dish of chocolate ice cream,' he glanced over at Claudia—'You want anything, baby?'

She shook her head.

He spoke into the 'phone again, 'Also some chocolate cake and some cream—a jug of cream. O.K., that's all.'

'I'm going to stay the night,' Claudia announced.

'What do you want to do that for?'

' 'Cos I want to go to the studio with you tomorrow like you promised, I'm not letting you out of my sight!'

He laughed, 'Baby, you're too much! I've been married three times and I thought I knew broads pretty well, but you're something else!'

She laughed too, throwing her head back so that her hair spread out around her, 'Wouldn't you sooner I was honest?' she asked. 'I'm not some naïve little bit, you know. I dig you, I think you're the end. But, also, I don't see why you shouldn't help me.'

'I haven't promised you anything.'

'Oh, yes you have, you've promised me a test.'

'So I've promised you a test. So what if you're lousy?'

'I won't be lousy,' she smiled, 'I may not be able to act but I photograph like a dream! And in the sort of movie you're making I'm sure you can find something for me.'

There was a discreet knock on the bedroom door. 'Your order is here, sir,' a voice said.

Conrad lumbered off the bed and reached for a paisley silk dressing-gown.

God—you're old and fat, Claudia thought. 'I love your dressing-gown, darling,' she purred.

'Simpsons,' he said, pleased. He grabbed some change off the dressing-table and disappeared into the other room.

Claudia rolled across the bed twining herself round in the sheet. 'I'm going to get in his damn movie if it kills me,' she muttered to herself. 'I haven't screwed that for nothing!'

He came back into the bedroom munching on a piece of toast. 'This is lousy caviar—you want to go out somewhere?'

'What time is it?' she asked surprised.

He consulted a large gold watch. 'One thirty—what's open?'

She thought quickly if they went out she wanted to be sure that she came back to the hotel with him after. She was determined to stick with him until he got her a test.

'All the clubs stay open till around four,' she said, 'and we can stop by my apartment so I can get some clothes to wear to the studio tomorrow. Great idea.' She jumped out of bed.

He studied her figure. 'You know you really have a beautiful body, how would you feel about appearing on the screen nude?'

'I hadn't really thought about it.'

'Well, think about it. There's a part you might be right for. Of course you would only have your clothes off in the continental version.'

'So test me.'

They went to a new discotheque—Charlie Browns. It was jammed but they were squeezed on to an already full table due to the fact that Conrad slipped the head waiter five pounds.

The records were so loud you couldn't hear yourself speak and on the tiny dance floor couples were jammed together frantically shaking and surging and having a ball. There was a scattering of well known people, a lot of girls in mad gear with long straight hair and long straight fringes covering half their faces, and a few representatives of the latest swinging pop groups sporting hair almost as long as the girls.

It was very dark.

At their table there was a photographer Claudia knew. She greeted him with a kiss and introduced him to Conrad. He was with one of the top models of the moment, a tall slim girl who photographed out of this world.

Claudia couldn't sit still, the music swept over her in a great wave of loudness and beat.

'Can you shake?' she asked Conrad.

'Can I what?'

'Shake, dance, twist,' she screamed at him to be heard above the noise.

They struggled to the dance floor, where Claudia broke loose in mad wild sinuous gyrations. Conrad just sort of stood there jiggling about. It was hot and the sweat started to trickle down Conrad's bald head. God you think you're a swinger, Claudia thought, look at you making a fool of yourself—don't you know you're too old to do this. She said 'Darling, you're a peachy dancer!'

'Sweetie pie!' The voice was unmistakable. Right beside them on the dance floor was Shirley, complete with the Hon. Jeremy. 'Where's your divine boy-friend?'

Claudia smiled. 'Thought you were going to Windsor,' she yelled.

'Well sweetie, we did, but it was absolutely too dreadful. I mean it was almost empty. Can you imagine anything more ghastly?' The Hon. Jeremy nodded vehement agreement.

By this time Conrad was sweating profusely. 'Let's sit down,' he said weakly.

'Sweetie, we will come over in a minute. Where are you sitting?'

Claudia smiled and waved pretending she hadn't heard. She didn't relish the thought of being stuck with Shirley and Jeremy again.

When they got back to their table it was even more crowded, and there was a great squeezing up of people to make room for them. The model girl said to Conrad, 'I adored your last film. Will you be making your new one in this country?'

The photographer asked Claudia to dance. She accepted, not too eager to leave the skinny bird chatting up Conrad, but anxious to dance again, and Giles the photographer was a wild dancer.

Claudia had had a short affaire with him at one time, but they had decided it was much more fun to be mates. They were too much of a kind to be lovers. Occasionally, if one or the other was at a loose end they would call each other and spend an evening together and if they felt like it end up in bed. But it was purely a brother and sister relationship with a little sex thrown in. Giles was very good looking in a dark, almost Spanish way. Women were mad for him and his services as a fashion and society photographer were in demand.

'Who's the father figure?' he asked cynically. 'Cindy says he's a big Hollywood mogul and I think she fancies big Hollywood moguls.'

'Well, tell her to keep her false nails off this one, he's already been bagged!'

They did a ritual dance together—him standing very still and giving rhythmic sexy twitches and she almost bumping and grinding before him. 'Fancy a bit of pot?' he asked conversationally.

She glanced over at their table, some more people had joined it and Conrad seemed quite happy ordering drinks and talking loudly with a lot of arm waving. 'Yeah, great idea,' she said.

They slipped off the dance floor and out on to a balcony that extended along one half of the club. It was windy and surprisingly quiet as the windows and doors from the club were all soundproofed. Giles lit one cigarette and they took it in turns to drag deeply on it.

'I've got to get in the right frame of mind to screw that bag of bones,' he said. 'We're doing a big layout for *Vogue* and I want to have the right atmosphere between us. Christ, I tell you it's like banging a skeleton!'

They both giggled. 'Lots of luck,' laughed Claudia, 'how would you like mine? Attractive, isn't he?'

'I'd suggest a foursome,' said Giles, 'but I know we'd only end up doing it to each other, so what's the use.'

They both collapsed in gales of laughter at this, then Claudia said, 'C'mon, we'd better get back inside.'

'What's the scene?' Giles asked. 'You going to become a big movie starlet?'

'Star—baby—star.'

They walked back into the noise and heat and rejoined their table. Cindy was listening attentively as Conrad told a long boring story about how he first arrived in America at the age of fourteen. Shirley and the Hon. Jeremy had also joined the table.

'Sweetie—what a fascinating man!' gasped Shirley—'Such a history.'

'Hello, Giles poppet.'

'Hello, Shirley—how's business?'

'Business?'

He laughed. 'Forget it baby.'

'I say, old man,' stammered Jeremy, 'liked those photos you did of Shirley—jolly fine set.'

'Well, I'm a jolly fine photographer.'

Claudia and Giles both fell about at that and then Claudia decided it was about time she came between Cindy's adoring gaze and Conrad. She snaked her arm around his neck and whispered something in his ear—he looked surprised. 'Here?' he said, 'Now?'

She giggled. 'No one will see, want me to?'

He laughed hoarsely. 'You're a wild broad, save it for later, huh?'

For some obscure reason Conrad ordered champagne for the whole table, and everyone proceeded to get well and truly loaded.

'I'm going to throw a big party tomorrow night,' said Conrad.

Claudia was delighted—'For me, darling?'

'Yeah for you—anyone—you're all invited.'

'Oh goodie—how super,' trilled Shirley—'where and what time, sweetie?'

'Make it at my hotel—Plaza Carlton—I'll take over a big room there—about ten o'clock.'

'Crazy,' said Claudia, 'did everybody hear that—tomorrow at ten.' She kissed Conrad's ear. 'I'm just going to the loo—be right back.' She threaded her way through the crowded tables to reception. 'I want to make a quick 'phone call,' she said to the girl there.

'Go ahead,' said the girl passing over the house 'phone.

It was after three o'clock. She dialled the number slowly, a strange smile playing around her lips. A sleepy male voice answered the 'phone. 'Hello, David darling,' she whispered, 'I'm having a great time, how about you?'

She hung up immediately. 'Just letting my husband know everything's cool,' she said to the surprised girl and swept back inside.

Waking up the next morning was not too much fun. Seeing Conrad asleep beside her like a discontented slug made her stomach turn. Her head felt heavy and her skin like much used parchment. She made it to the bathroom and took an icy cold shower. It was absolutely freezing agony, but the after effects were worth it.

They had not returned to Conrad's hotel earlier that morning but instead had ended up in her flat.

After the shower she dressed carefully, and did a meticulous make-up, all ready to accompany Conrad to the studio. Then she made some coffee and finally shook him. He woke up badly.

Much coughing and foul sounds in his throat, blood-shot eyes, bad breath and B.O.

'Christ, what time is it?' he muttered, the universal cry of people waking up in other people's apartments.

'It's just ten o'clock." She handed him some coffee.

'Where's the 'phone?'

She groped around under the bed, where she had placed the 'phone off the hook.

He called his secretary and issued a list of instructions. 'I've got to get back to the hotel and get changed,' he said, struggling into his clothes.

'I'm coming with you.'

'Oh c'mon baby—what for?'

'For my test you promised me.'

He stared at her. 'I'm not going to forget your damn test— but it can't be done just like that, today, it's got to be set up.'

'So I'll come with you while you set it up.'

He shook his head. 'You don't give up, do you.' He picked up the 'phone and called his secretary again. 'Listen, I want a test fixed for a Miss Claudia—' he looked at her blankly—

'Parker,' she said quickly.

'Parker. Fix it up as soon as possible, her agent will call you later today to get the details.'

He hung up. 'O.K. baby?'

She kissed him. 'O.K. baby, listen you haven't forgotten the party tonight.'

'Party?'

'Yes, don't you remember you asked a whole group of people to a party tonight at your hotel.'

'Oh yeah—that's right, I'll get it in hand. All right baby, see you later then.'

'Yes, I'll come by a couple of hours early in case you need anything.'

'The way I feel right now I won't need anything—but you never know.' He gave a ribald laugh and left.

CHAPTER ELEVEN

LINDA 'PHONED PAUL at work as soon as the children had gone off to school and David to the office.

He was anxious to see her.

'I can't manage it,' she said.

He was most persuasive and eventually she agreed to meet him during his lunch hour. It was a crisp sunny day and they met in Green Park. She had never seen him in a suit before and it didn't look quite right somehow. She decided it was because it was ready made and ready made suits always managed to be just that little bit wrong.

They strolled along hand in hand but Linda didn't feel easy. She felt over-dressed in her matching coat and hat and crocodile shoes and bag. She knew she looked all wrong strolling hand in hand with Paul Bedford in Green Park. It wasn't that she felt old, or at least older than him—but she felt in spite of the fact that she didn't want to feel that way—she felt she was slumming.

'What's on your mind?' he asked. 'Something bothering you?'

'Oh, I don't know, Paul. You know this is all wrong. I'm not the sort of woman that can get involved in an affaire. I have my children and my home and I feel I must keep trying with my husband. It must be partly my fault that things have gone so wrong. I can't just give up and become involved with you. That's no answer at all.'

'What's the matter, Linda? Are you frightened of losing your security if David finds out?'

'No. I'm frightened of losing my self respect.'

They walked in silence for a while and then he said, 'What are you trying to say?'

'I'm trying to say that I can't lead two lives, I want to stop it now before it goes any further.'

His voice sounded weak. 'Don't leave me now that I've found you. I've been waiting and hoping to meet someone like you. You're a warm person. I need a warm person, I won't make any demands on you, just to see you when you're free.'

'It's not enough for either of us, I don't want to see you again.'

His mood changed. 'You're like all the others. I should have known you're just a hard bitch at heart, you're frightened of losing all your home comforts. Women have hearts like bloody adding machines. Look at Margarethe—dropped me for my father just because he had a few bob. My bloody mother killed herself to get away from him, and my bloody sister took off one day and vanished to get away from him, but then what happens? My girl friend marries him.'

'I'm sorry, Paul—but I'm not going to be a substitute for your mother, sister, or Margarethe. I'm too old for you. Forget the past and go and find someone you can be happy with.'

'Is that what you want?'

'That's what I want.'

He sneered at her, 'Well you were a bloody easy lay—and not bad for an old bird.'

She turned and started to walk quickly away.

'Who's going to stuff your crumpet now?' he yelled after her.

She felt the colour rise in her face, and she started to run, not stopping until she reached her car. She leaped in and started the car. He was nowhere in sight. She drove home, cold tears running down her face all the way.

The Grossmans were sitting in the bar of their hotel, Lori cool in pale lilac chiffon, silver hair swept back in elaborate curls, neckline plunging to show off two satin smooth white breasts.

Jay was wearing a well-cut black suit with a button down collar and a black knit tie. They made an extremely good-looking couple.

The Coopers arrived to meet them exactly on time. Linda was wearing a black silk dress and pale beige mink stole, her short auburn hair rather severe but very chic. David, conventional in a midnight-blue suit, white shirt, blue tie and big sapphire cuff-links.

They all had a drink and then moved on to the Savoy Grill.

Jay enlivened the evening with amusing tales about Hollywood. David chatted amicably about business and politics. The two women were mostly silent. Lori was obviously disappointed that Princess Margaret wasn't there. She complained about the lack of ice and checked her make-up a lot.

Jay finally said, 'For Christ sake stop looking in the mirror, we all know you're beautiful, it's the reason I married you, isn't it?'

She pouted a lot after that.

When they were on the coffee, Jay said, 'Hey—how about dropping by the party Conrad's giving tonight, we promised we would.'

'Well, I'm really feeling a bit tired,' Linda said, 'you know it was the children's first day at school, and what with all the preparation, I'm rather exhausted.'

'Oh, come on, Linda,' said David jovially. He was feeling rather pleased with himself due to the fact that he had avoided getting in touch with Claudia all day. Little tramp, teach her a lesson. And how about that 'phoning him up in the middle of the night to make him jealous. He would show her, she would have to come begging to be forgiven.

'Yes, Linda, you must come,' said Jay. 'It will be a laugh, I can promise you that.'

'Oh all right'

She accompanied Lori to the ladies' room, where between applying powder rouge, Lori drawled, 'That son of a bitch thinks I'm a damn idiot. He'll find out who's the idiot when I get half of everything he's got.'

'I beg your pardon?' said Linda politely.

'It's California law—I know it's California law.' At that Lori sank into silence, carefully applying another coat of lip gloss.

The party was in full swing when they arrived. There were sixty or seventy people there already and more arriving all the time. Huge buffets of good food covered one side of the room, and there were three bars strategically placed and a swinging six-piece group to which people were dancing.

They pushed their way through to the nearest bar and ordered drinks. Jay appeared to know quite a few people and he introduced everybody and soon David and Linda were involved with different groups chatting away.

'Come with me to find Conrad,' Jay said to Linda, 'I must at least let him know I put up an appearance.'

They found Conrad sitting at a table eating chocolate ice cream and drinking straight bourbon. Claudia was by his side —wearing a bright red ruffled dress and a lot of fake diamonds.

Conrad gave genial greetings and invited them to sit down, moving two other people to do so.

'You remember Mrs. Cooper—Linda,' Jay said.

'Sure, sure, what do you think of the party? I know how to do these things right, huh?'

'You certainly do,' Jay said admiringly.

'Hallo, Mrs. Cooper,' Claudia said, slurring her words slightly, she had been drinking steadily for several hours. 'Is Mr. Cooper about?'

'Why yes,' said Linda. 'Did you want to see him about something?'

'Yes, as a matter of fact I did.' She knocked a glass down on the table accidentally, the dark alcohol making a splashy stain on the tablecloth. 'I want to tell him what he could do with his bloody Beauty Maid campaign. Stuff it up his arse—that's what he can do with it,' she hiccoughed.

Linda stared at her coolly. 'I'll see he gets the message, dear,' she said and turned to talk to Jay.

Claudia stood up from the table. 'I think I'll give him the bloody message myself,' she said, and weaved unsteadily off.

'Well,' Linda was startled, 'what's the matter with her?'

Jay shrugged. 'I don't know. What's with your girl-friend, Con?'

Conrad laughed—'Oh, she's a cuke. I've promised her a bit in the movie and it's gone to her head.'

'What bit?'

'Well, for the Continental version, I thought it would be a cute idea to have a semi-naked broad standing beside the credits, sort of torn slave dress jazz. This kid's got a great body—and if she photographs O.K. we'll use her. O.K.?'

'Fine,' said Jay with a smile. 'Sounds like it has a lot of class!'

Linda arose from the table. 'Excuse me a minute,' she said. She walked hesitantly around the room looking for David, she couldn't see the drunken girl or him. She sighed, it was probably nothing, the girl was drunk.

She saw Lori surrounded by a group of admiring males. She went over. Lori was saying, 'Well where we come from, we just don't have any problems with negroes. They know their place and keep it. Why, some of my best maids were coloured.'

'Have you seen David?' Linda asked.

'Yeah,' she hardly glanced at Linda. 'He went out on the terrace.'

It's stupid, Linda thought, I shouldn't be tracking him down like this, it's childish. She made her way on to the terrace and found it deserted. Just as she was leaving she heard a low throaty chuckle, she looked again and saw over in the corner a couple in a close embrace.

She backed into the shadows and edged closer. The girl was pulling his head down to her breast which was popping out of the top of her dress, she was fondling him intimately.

'You're the craziest, Claudia,' he muttered, 'the best ever.' Now he was pulling her dress right down so it hung around her waist. 'I missed you so much, one night without having you was hell.'

Shocked and sickened, Linda backed away. They hadn't seen her. Dazed, she wandered back into the main room. She was heading for the door when Jay appeared and grabbed her arm. 'What's the matter, you look terrible, what happened?'

She looked at him with unseeing eyes. 'I've got to get out of here,' she mumbled, pushing his arm away and continuing to make for the door. He caught hold of her arm again firmly and steered her to the nearest bar.

'The lady wants a large brandy, and fast,' he said. 'Now tell me what the hell has happened, Linda.' He took her hand and held it tight. 'Tell me,' he said in a softer voice.

She looked at him, her eyes were full of shock. 'I suspected he played around—maybe—once in a blue moon, up in Manchester or something—but this . . . With me right here. It's horrible.'

The waiter brought the brandy and she took large gulps. 'I—I was looking for David. I wanted to warn him about that drunk tart. Lori said he was on the terrace. I went there and he was there with her, they were necking—she had half her dress off, they were saying these things to each other. . . .'

'Oh God!' said Jay, 'that stupid son of a bitch. Look—I mean the girl was drunk, maybe he was trying to get rid of her.'

Linda's eyes were scornful. 'With words like—one night without having you was hell.'

'What do you want to do?' asked Jay. 'Shall I take you home?'

She shook her head. 'What can I do? This is it for me. I can't go on after this. I'm finished with him. I want to divorce him. I hate him.' Her voice shook. 'I want to go home but I can't, I can't even speak to him again. What can I do?'

'Look—it's no good making decisions while you're upset. Let me take you home. I'll come straight back and talk to David, tell him not to go home tonight.'

She laughed bitterly—'Tell him not to ever come home again. Tell him to go off with his "best ever" little slut. Tell him he can do what he wants—'cos I don't care any more, I'm nothing to do with him any more, I'm through.' She took another large gulp of brandy. 'I'm going to start crying in a minute—please get me out of here.'

They got a taxi outside the hotel. Linda was worried that either Lori or David would miss them and that maybe David would come home, but Jay reassured her, 'I'll be back within an hour and if he does miss you he'll just be looking around. As for Lori, she won't even know I'm gone.'

'Oh Jay,' Linda sighed, 'I'm so embarrassed, dragging you away from the party and everything. The whole situation is so sordid and awful.'

'Don't be embarrassed,' he took her hand comfortingly. 'If it's any solace I was involved in exactly the same situation myself. In Hollywood at a real swinging party, my first wife Jenny vanished, I searched all over and eventually found her in bed with the host. So you see I do understand.'

'What did you do?'

'I was a schmuck, I gave her another chance, came home early one day and found her banging the delivery boy.'

They sat in silence for a while, then Jay said, 'I suppose for some people one woman or one man is enough—but not for any of the people I know. I guess one gets what one deserves out of life. I've been married three times—each time to a beautiful girl with about as much thinking power as a rabbit. It must be a sickness with me—I marry stupid dumb beautiful broads.'

Linda hesitated. 'I—I was unfaithful to David this week. The first time in eleven years of marriage. I'm so ashamed about it now. It was with a boy—a twenty-year-old boy—I don't know why . . .' She tailed off, 'David hadn't touched me in months, we were so far apart, he was never home. It just happened. I suppose I'm as guilty as he is.'

'Listen—never feel guilty. What good can that do? Sleep on things, and see how you feel in the morning. You've got young children, don't make any hasty decisions.'

The taxi arrived at the house.

'Goodnight, Jay—thank you for everything.'

'Linda, I'll call you tomorrow, rest easy—it will be all right.'

Claudia found David in a group with Lori. She edged quietly up behind him and pressing her body against his back she covered his eyes with her hands and said in a Marilyn Monroe type voice, 'Guess who, baby!'

There was no mistaking that body. He was surprised, and suddenly, sharply excited. She had the most incredible effect on him, he just had to know she was there to want her. He turned slowly, eyes looking around to see if Linda was anywhere about. She wasn't.

'Hello, Claudia.'

'Hello, Claudia,' she mimicked his voice. 'Don't I get a better greeting than that? By the way, you can stuff your Beauty Maid Campaign up your arse, Cha cha cha!'

The group he had been standing with were all listening interestedly, including Lori.

He took Claudia firmly by the arm, bruising her flesh. 'Let's go and find Linda,' he said, walking off and pulling her with him.

'Let's go find Linda!' she said incredulously. 'You've got to be joking!'

He marched her on to the terrace, finding a deserted dark corner. As soon as he let go of her she wound her arms around his neck and kissed him. 'Did you miss me?' she whispered. 'I was going to be so mad at you, but I couldn't,' she giggled, 'I'm smashed, you know.'

'You're a little bitch, leaving me sitting in that restaurant, 'phoning up in the middle of the night. *You* were going to be mad, what about me?'

She nibbled his ear, rubbing her body against him.

Her dress was held up by two thin shoulder straps, he peeled them off, pulling her dress down to her waist. She wore nothing underneath and she guided his mouth to her breasts.

All sense of reason was gone. He was with Claudia and had to have her, it didn't matter that they were on a public terrace, that his wife was somewhere around, that anybody could appear. It was dark. He pushed her down on to the cold concrete ground and lifted her skirt, she wore no panties and she was giggling. He took her quickly, it was all over in a minute. 'Christ!' he muttered. 'Christ.'

She lay there still giggling, her dress just a bunch around her waist. He pulled her up, looking around, relieved to see that no one had come out. She was unconcerned.

'We've got to go back inside separately,' he said.

'Screw you!' she replied.

'You just did.' He straightened his tie and wiped a hand-kerchief around his face to remove all traces of lipstick and make-up. 'Listen, I'll 'phone you tomorrow. I'll get away early from the office and come over. I've got a surprise for you.'

'You've always got a surprise for me. You're the man with the permanent hard on!' she laughed. 'What a title for a television series—I can see it now—The Man With The Permanent Hard On—starring Dick Hampton!'

He kissed her—'You go in first—go straight to the ladies' room, you look a mess.'

'Thank you, kind sir. Are you sure you're finished with me?'

'Go on, be a good girl. I'll try to 'phone you later.'

She stuck out her tongue at him—waggling it obscenely, and then sauntered off through the french windows completely at ease.

He took a deep breath—what a girl! After a safe five minutes he followed her in. The party was still in full swing. He grabbed a drink from a passing waiter and started to look around for Linda. This was becoming a dangerous habit, bumping into Claudia at parties.

He observed Lori dancing with a seedy, fairly well known actor. She was moving her hips in steady bumps and grinds and she smiled coolly at him. She certainly knew how to move. He edged closer. 'Seen Linda?' he said.

Lori looked deadpan—'Well, last I saw of her she was heading towards the terrace looking for you.'

'The terrace?' he said, stunned.

'The terrace, honey,' she swayed away from him.

He started to look for Linda seriously. He ploughed his way across the room, through groups of people laughing and chatting. A girl grabbed his arm, she was thin and pretty and he remembered her as a friend of Claudia's from the restaurant.

'Hello, ducky,' she cooed, 'fancy seeing you here.'

'Hello,' he looked around for her spotty boy-friend.

'Oh, Jeremy's gone to fetch me another drink.' She didn't leave go of his arm. 'Super party—but I didn't expect you to be here.'

'Why not?' he said patiently, she was far too thin for him to find attractive.

'Well, you know—I mean I know we're all very modern and everything, but you struck me as the jealous type.'

'What are you talking about?' He shook his arm free.

'Well after all—the party is being given by Conrad Lee for Claudia, and I shouldn't have thought you would come. I mean one shouldn't mix business with pleasure, should one? And you're obviously pleasure and he's obviously business,' she smiled blandly—'here comes Jeremy with my drink, see you again,' and she walked off to meet the approaching Jeremy.

'Bitch!' He stood there furious. Claudia hadn't mentioned Lee or the fact that the party was for her. Bitch! Bitch! Bitch!

The quest for Linda was forgotten, and a new one for Claudia began. He wanted to get a few facts straight.

Jay arrived back at the party. He was thoughtful. It was a tricky situation to handle, telling another man he couldn't go home to his own wife. It could easily end in a punch on the nose. He saw David across the room talking to a girl.

He was an attractive man, big and dark and the ladies obviously fell for him. Lori had said she thought he was probably fantastic in bed, but from talking to Linda it didn't sound that way. Lori had a habit of thinking most men were fantastic in bed, her way of letting Jay know that she didn't think he was. He approached David quickly, best to get it over with fast. He told him the situation. David was suitably flattened. He tried to deny it but when Jay told him word for word what Linda had told him, he was forced to admit it.

'You're an idiot,' Jay said. 'You've got a great wife, if you want to screw around why do it under her nose?'

'What is she going to do?'

'She mentioned divorce.'

'She can't talk like that, she's got no proof. So I kissed a girl at a party, what does that prove? I'm going home, I'm not going to be shut out of my own home.'

Jay shrugged. 'I can't stop you, I can only offer advice. She's in a state of shock, going home tonight will only make things worse. If you wait until morning, I'm sure you'll both see things a hell of a lot clearer.'

'I'm going home. I know Linda, she's upset but I can explain to her.'

Jay glared at him. 'I promised Linda you'd stay away tonight.'

David glared back. 'Well, that's tough because I'm going home now.'

They held the glare a few moments and then Jay said, 'Goodnight, schmuck, don't forget to say goodnight to your girl-friend, you'll probably find her kissing Conrad's arse.'

On that note they parted company.

CHAPTER TWELVE

WHEN DAVID ARRIVED at his house and put his key in the front door it wouldn't open. He lit a match to make sure he was using the right key, but although it turned smoothly, the door remained tight shut. Realization dawned, Linda had bolted it from the inside. He went around to the back door, but that also was tightly barred. A strong choked anger rose in him. He returned to the front door and pressed his finger firmly down on the bell push. The jangly sound of the buzzer was loud and insistent. There was no response. He tried it again, this time leaving his finger there for several minutes. A light went on in the upstairs window, it was the maid's room. He waited impatiently for her to come down and let him in, but nothing happened and after a while her light went out again.

He was furious—Linda was obviously up, and had told Anna to ignore the bell. He kicked savagely at the door but only succeeded in hurting his foot. This is incredible, he thought, who the hell does she think the bloody house belongs to!

'Listen, Linda,' he shouted, 'don't be such a fool—open the door or I'm going for the police.'

The house loomed still and dark before him. What to do? He banged on the door with his fists—nothing. He leaned on the bell push again—nothing. Then, faintly, from upstairs, there floated down the sound of a child crying. He stood there, undecided about what to do. He felt guilty about waking the children, but after all, it was really Linda's fault for not letting him in. He pushed the bell firmly and insistently for one final time and to his surprise the bolts were pushed back and the door opened a few inches. He went to push it further open but it clanged to a shuddering stop—the chain was on.

Linda peered out at him, white-faced and angry. 'Go away, you make me sick.' Her voice sounded flat and tired.

'Oh come on, let me in, we'll talk about it, it was nothing— I was drunk.'

'I don't want to talk to you, I don't want to see you. Go back to your little scrubber and leave me alone.'

She slammed the door in his face.

He swore, hammered on the door and shouted, 'You'll be sorry, Linda. I'll bloody go away and I won't come back!'

She didn't return to the door. Furious, he strode back to his car, got in and started it viciously.

When David left the party, Jay 'phoned Linda and warned her. He then got hold of Lori who was dancing sexily with a swarthy-faced Ambassador and sat her down firmly in a corner.

'You saw David take that broad to the terrace. What's with you, big mouth? Why did you tell Linda?'

She looked disinterested. 'I don't know what you're talking about, honey,' she drawled. 'Is something going on?'

'Yeah, something's going on,' he shrugged disgustedly. 'Are you really as drunk as you pretend to be?'

She looked sulky. 'You're so nasty to me, Jay, I don't know why I married you.'

'Would two mink coats, a chinchilla and a big house and pool jog your memory?'

She stood up, smoothing her hands down her body, ironing imaginary wrinkles in her dress. 'I'm going to dance again, you interrupted me before—that was a very sweet important guy I was dancing with.'

She walked off, beautiful, cool. Jay shook his head in despair, she was an idiot or a bitch or a clever combination of both.

The noise at the table that Conrad and his group were sitting at was becoming progressively louder. Shrieks of drunken laughter, spilt drinks, Claudia climbing on the table and dancing, with the men all peering up her skirt, becoming aware of the fact that she had no panties on. Egged on with screams of drunken encouragement, she started to peel her dress off.

Jay viewed the scene, he was horribly sober, they all seemed to be behaving like a bunch of wild monkeys. He felt disgusted.

A large crowd was gathering round the table goggle-eyed at Claudia's free show. The foreign Ambassador rushed over with Lori. It was a fast strip tease, as Claudia only had her dress to take off. She threw it off, kicking it from the table, and then proceeded to dance to the music of a slow hand clap from the crowd. Her body glistened proudly and the men in the crowd pressed closer and closer while the women, suddenly jealous at such perfection, started to try and move them away.

A very harassed-looking man in pin-stripe trousers and black jacket pushed his way towards the table. He represented the management, shocked and horrified he approached Conrad, who waved him drunkenly away. 'We shall have to call the police unless this—this—woman gets dressed at once.'

Claudia stuck her tongue out at him, the only part of her that hadn't been exposed to public view.

Eventually of course the police arrived, they wrapped Claudia in a blanket and hauled her off to the police station and booked her for indecent exposure.

The next morning it was headlines. Claudia was a star for the day that is. She was photographed and quoted, and Conrad immediately cashed in on her wave of publicity and announced that she would be appearing in his new film. He contacted her agent and signed her for two days' work at £60 per day.

She was delighted. She returned from the police station at lunch time, triumphant. She gave a press reception, posed for countless more pictures, and then was taken off to the studio in a chauffered car for make-up and hair tests. She didn't see Conrad, efficient crew-cut hairstyled young men took over. She was pleased, he had served his immediate purpose, and she hers. When she returned from the studio in the evening, David was propped outside her front door. Sober and giddy with her sudden success he didn't look so good to her. 'What do you want?' she said coldly, and then added with a burst of enthusiasm, 'Hey—did you see me in the papers today?'

He trailed her into the flat, and started immediately to mix a drink. She flitted around talking excitedly, forgetting her coldness of a moment before. After all, David did belong to someone else, and it was she he was coming to.

'I'm going to take you out to dinner tonight, where do you want to go?'

She laughed. 'Oh I see, all of sudden I'm a star, and you want to be seen with me! What about wifey tonight, then? Aren't you frightened one of her spies will see us?'

'You don't have to worry about her, I've left her.'

Silence hung heavy in the room until slowly Claudia walked over very close to him and kissed him hard. 'You've left her for me?'

'For you.' He ran his hands down her back enclosing them round her buttocks. 'I couldn't stand not being with you all the time any longer after last night and you doing that stupid strip with everybody ogling you. When I saw you in the paper this morning and I read what happened, I just knew we couldn't go on any longer unless it was together. So I told Linda, I said I wanted a divorce and here I am.'

She shook her head in disbelief. 'You really left her for me, isn't that wild!'

'I'm going to divorce her and marry you,' he said firmly.

She wandered round the room. 'I don't want to get married, but thanks for the thought anyway. Hey—baby we can do what we want, go where we want. It's too much!'

He followed her round the room—'Don't you understand, I said I'd marry you.'

She laughed. 'But I don't want you to. You don't have to.'

'But I want to,' he grabbed hold of her. She was wearing a clingy orange sweater, matching slacks and shiny white boots. She slipped away from him—'Listen, baby—let's get clear on the subject. I don't—do not have, I repeat, any desire to make the wedding bells scene—so don't keep on making the offer like it's such a damn big deal. I don't want to marry you!' She was almost shouting, and sensing her mood, he dropped the subject.

'Where do you want to go?' he said. 'We can go anywhere you want.'

She stretched, cat-like, in her orange outfit. 'Oh, I'm tired, I don't feel like getting dressed and going out!'

He looked surprised—'You're always complaining we never go anywhere—and now that we can go wherever you like—you don't want to go.'

She flopped in a chair, her legs thrown casually over the side. 'Ever heard the story of the kid that wanted some candy—moaned and cried and carried on till eventually it got candy, then ate so much it was sick?' She giggled. 'Get the message?'

'What the hell's the matter with you? Don't you understand what I've done for you today?'

She shrugged. 'For me? I should have thought it would have been for yourself. Where are you going to live?'

'I'm taking an apartment. I thought in the meantime I'd stay here with you, then we can move into the new place together.'

She studied her fingernails, admiring the pearly glow. 'Is it a penthouse?'

'Is what a penthouse?'

'The apartment you're taking.' There was a pause. 'Well, is it?'

'I don't know, what the hell does that matter? We'll find a penthouse if that's want you want.'

She smiled at last, pleased and purry. 'Yes, that's what I want. Can I start looking tomorrow? It's going to be too crowded for the two of us here.' She held out her arms to him, 'I'm sorry I've been bitchy, but it's been a busy day.'

He fell into her arms, and kissed her, feeling the familiar immediate desire rise in him.

She kissed him hard, running her tongue across his teeth and scratching the back of his neck with sharp nails. He started to reach for her body, but she pushed him away and leaped up. 'Not now, baby. Let's go to dinner and then think of it—we can come back home together. It will be a whole different scene.'

She switched on the record player and the sound of the 'Stones' filled the room. She danced around, throwing off her sweater and wriggling out of her slacks in time to the music. She wore a brief white bra and the shiny white boots.

He watched her, mesmerized. 'Why don't you ever wear pants?'

'Why spoil the line?' she laughed. 'Does it bother you? I've never had any complaints before!'

She vanished into the bathroom and he heard the sound of a bath running. He followed her in, she was bending over the bath, filling it with bubbles. She had discarded the bra, but the boots remained. He grabbed her from behind. She struggled weakly, half laughing. He tried to hold on to her and get out of his clothes at the same time, but she slipped and fell into the bath. By this time, she was helpless with laughter and very

wet and covered in bubbles, and she stuck her legs over the side
of the bath with her boots still on. He undressed hurriedly and
followed her into the bath. The water cascaded over the side.

'I think I'm going to like living here,' he said.

CHAPTER THIRTEEN

THE SUN was streaming into the bedroom and David couldn't
sleep any longer. Claudia lay sprawled beside him, taking up
more than half her share of the bed. She claimed she couldn't
sleep with the curtains drawn, which accounted for the fact that
every morning the light woke him too early. He glanced at his
watch, it was only half-past six and they hadn't got to bed until
four. He felt tired and dreadful and hungover. It was no use
getting up and drawing the curtains now, as he couldn't go
back to sleep once he was awake.

The spacious bedroom was a mess. Claudia had a habit of
stepping out of her clothes all over the place and just leaving
them. Therefore one had to pick one's way through the debris
in the mornings.

It's amazing, he thought, how my life has changed in such a
short period of only six months.

The new dress he had bought her lay in a crumpled ball at
the bottom of the bed. It was red pleated chiffon and she had
seen it in a window in Bond Street and he had surprised her
with it the next day. The surprise had cost him one-hundred
and fifty guineas. He picked it up. She had spilt a glass of wine
on it and there was a crumpled stain.

In the green marble bathroom leading off the bedroom the
mess continued. She had not emptied the bath and it was filled
with cold dirty water. Bottles of make-up and hairbrushes and
perfumes were scattered everywhere. The sink was clogged with
soap left to congeal beneath a dripping gold tap, and hair.
Beneath the mess it was a beautiful apartment. A penthouse as
she had wanted, in a new block of flats in Kensington. It cost
far too much money a week, a fortune in fact. But Claudia
loved it and didn't want to move.

He emptied the old water and picked up the bath towels on
the floor. He really wished she could learn to be tidy, but it
seemed impossible for her. With Linda, there had never been
a thing out of place.

He went through a small marble lined, mirrored hallway to
the kitchen. Here there were stale cups of half-drunk coffee,
dirty dishes piled up, filled ashtrays creating a bad smoky
atmosphere.

Fortunately it was Friday, which meant that they had a new cleaning woman starting. The last one had left in disgust when she found out they weren't married, leaving a cryptic note saying, 'I'm not used to such filth'. At first he thought she was referring to the state Claudia left things in, but the porter had told him what she really meant.

He made a cup of strong tea and managed to burn a couple of pieces of toast. Claudia had acquired a small yappy Yorkshire terrier which suddenly came bounding out, anxious to take a walk no doubt. It usually slept on the bed with them and would burrow beneath the covers at night. David hated it. He hated small dogs.

He left it sniffing around the kitchen and went into the huge open plan living-dining room. This was the pièce de résistance of the apartment, a beautiful spacious room, one wall completely glass, leading on to a landscaped patio, another wall marble and the rest of the wall space mirrored. The room was chaotic. They had had people in for drinks before going out the previous evening, and half-empty glasses seemed to be all over the place. Overflowing ashtrays, spilled nuts, magazines, photographs of Claudia, cushions on the floor. Thank God it would all be cleared up today.

He went to the front door and collected his papers, extracting his *Times* and *Guardian* from amongst the various film and fashion magazines Claudia seemed to have delivered daily.

He drank his tea, it was too strong, ate his toast, it was burnt, and read the papers through bleary eyes. Soon it would be time to get dressed and go off to work.

Linda woke early. The sun was shining and it was a lovely day. She felt good.

At last she was starting to enjoy the selfish pleasures of sleeping alone. Taking up the whole of the bed, waking and sleeping when she pleased, always being able to get into the bathroom.

It had been hard at first, the decision of getting a divorce terrible. She kept thinking of the children without a father. But the fact that David had moved out and set up home with Claudia had helped her to be strong; that he could do that was enough.

She found a good solicitor and put herself in his hands. It was quite simple really.

Today was the day, the day she was going to appear in court, stand calmly before a judge and state the facts. Her solicitor, a short stocky grey-haired man, would be by her side. An enquiry agent would be there to offer relevant information. Her counsel was tall and attractive and sympathetic, and they had all assured her it would go quite smoothly. It was undefended and clear cut.

She dressed, choosing her clothes carefully. A dark-brown neat suit, low-heeled shoes, not too much make-up. Surveying herself in the mirror, she thought she looked the part. An abandoned wife, sad, with feeling of courage.

The children were staying with her mother. She ate a solitary breakfast of boiled eggs and coffee, wishing that she hadn't sent them away, wishing that their noisy laughter was filling the house. However, after she was finished in court, she was going to leave by train and join them all for the week-end, and they would return to the house together on Monday. The house belonged to her now. Financial arrangements had been amicable. She got the house and fairly generous support for herself and the two children.

David visited the children every week-end either on Saturday or Sunday. Linda always managed to avoid seeing him. In fact, she hadn't seen him for three months and then it had been in her solicitor's office to make the financial settlement final.

She made only one stipulation about his seeing the children, and that was the fact that she didn't want them in Claudia's company at all. He didn't argue on that point.

She finished her coffee, soon it would be time to go to her solicitor's office and accompany him to court.

Claudia woke at eleven. There was someone ringing the door-bell. She groped her way to the front door, struggling into a flimsy négligée covered in make-up stains.

A short squat woman stood facing her. 'I'm Mrs. Cobb,' she announced, 'the agency sent me.' She had red heavy hands and a scrubbed old face.

'Oh, come in, Mrs. Cobb," Claudia said, stifling a yawn. 'I'm afraid it's a ghastly mess, but I'm sure you'll cope.'

She took her into the kitchen and gestured under the sink. 'You'll find everything you need under there. Excuse me if I leave you to it, I had a ghastly late night.'

Mrs. Cobb looked grimly around, and didn't say anything.

Claudia took a can of peaches from the fridge and tipped them into a dish—'My breakfast,' she said with a bright smile and, stopping to collect the magazines and papers from the living room, she went back to the bedroom.

Propped comfortably back in bed, she leafed idly through the papers, the *Daily Sketch* being her favourite. It was the show page that interested her. She scanned it eagerly, looking, as usual, for any mention of Conrad Lee. She was delighted, today there was a whole article on the location of his film in Israel.

It also stated that the company would be returning to England at the end of the week for studio work.

She made a big pencil ring around the article and 'phoned her agent on the shell-pink bedside telephone. She still had her two days' work to do on Conrad's film. Things had become rather complicated and the unit had gone on location before reaching Claudia's scenes. However the film company had given her agent constant promises that as soon as the unit returned she would be needed for her two days.

She gave her agent the good news and he promised to look into it immediately. She stretched languidly, the past few months since moving to the penthouse had been fun, although David was becoming a bit of a bore. The penthouse was too much! The most beautiful apartment. All her friends were very impressed. She had done lots of photographic assignments there, and she was always pleased when they appeared in various magazines—saying lovely young actress and model, Claudia Parker, relaxing in her penthouse apartment.

Giles was coming over at two o'clock to do a nude layout for a prominent men's magazine. She hoped David would be working late, as she disliked Giles intensely, in spite of the fact that he didn't even know she had had an affaire with him. Anyway, if he knew she was doing a nude layout he would be furious, he was very stuffy that way. The American magazine was paying her and Giles a lot of money, and anyway she didn't mind showing off her body, after all, it was certainly worth showing.

She lounged back in bed, yawning. Soon it would be time to start preparing herself, until then she could relax.

David arrived at the office tired and bad-tempered. His secretary greeted him with a worried face. 'Oh, Mr. Cooper your uncle wants to see you at once, his secretary asked me to get you to go straight to his office as soon as you arrived.'

What now? Being summoned by Uncle Ralph was never good news. His uncle had been most disapproving about his split with Linda. Divorce was a frowned-upon sin in the Jewish religion, and Uncle Ralph was very religious when it suited him.

He was sitting like a small, bald buzzard behind his desk in his early Victorian style office. His secretary, Penny, a wide-eyed blonde, ushered David in. He appraised her sexy long legs in her ultra short skirt. Trust Uncle Ralph to have the only good-looking secretary in the building.

'Good morning, David,' Uncle Ralph grunted. 'Sit down—sit down. Wanted to have a word with you about the Fulla Health Beans account.'

'We don't have it any more.'

'Exactly—exactly, that's what I wanted to talk to you about.' His uncle launched into a long lecture about the reason they had lost the account, which was because of David's un-enthusiastic attitude lately, and the fact that he didn't seem in good health and was always tired. He hinted that perhaps the job was too much for him.

David listened carefully, dissecting every word Uncle Ralph said, because every word Uncle Ralph said always meant something else. What he was actually saying was—'Don't come in here dragging your arse because you've been up with a hot piece all night. Either work or get the hell out.' He concluded the lecture with the information that Mr. Taylor of the Fulla Beans account was in town for one more night, and that he was prepared to reconsider his decision about withdrawing the account.

'Now you take him out to dinner,' Uncle Ralph said. 'Tell him our plans, lay it on thick. Get him drunk, entertain him. Take him to a night-club and fix him up with a hostess. Keep him happy, whatever happens, I want that account back.'

'Yes, sir.' David got up.

Penny was sitting behind her desk in the outer office, legs crossed neatly beneath her desk. She smiled at him, an open invitation in her innocent wide eyes. He wondered vaguely if she was sleeping with the ugly old buzzard, the rumour around the building said she was. He wouldn't mind knocking a piece of that off, get one over on Uncle Ralph. He leant over her desk. 'How come I only ever see you here?'

Her smile widened and she started to reply, but the buzzer rang on her desk and she jumped up quickly. Uncle Ralph had anticipated the pass and was summoning her to the safety of his office! She scampered off, sexy legs beneath a short skirt.

David returned morosely to his own office, and his own secretary who was pale and mousy and flat chested with a long skirt. She had a mad crush on him which she tried to conceal, making it all the more obvious.

'Oh, Mr. Cooper,' she said, 'is everything all right?'

'Everything's fine,' he sat glumly at his desk, the thought of entertaining Mr. Taylor of Fulla Beans to a gay evening out on the town was depressing.

'Oh dear, Mr. Cooper,' his secretary was almost wringing her hands. 'Oh dear, it had to happen today too.'

'What's so special about today?'

'Well, it's your divorce today.' She lowered her eyes. 'Well, I mean—'

So it was—he had forgotten all about it. It seemed strange that Linda could go into a court somewhere and divorce him and he didn't have to be there. It didn't seem right somehow.

His solicitor had written informing him of the date some time ago, and stated that they would send someone along purely as a formality.

His secretary stood nervously by his desk. 'Thanks for the cheerful reminder, Miss Field,' he said.

She flushed. 'Oh, I'm sorry—I thought you knew. . . .' Her words tailed off. 'Would you like some coffee, Mr. Cooper?'

'That would be nice, Miss Field.'

She fled gratefully and almost tearfully from his office.

'Sonovabitch!' he muttered. 'Sonovabitch!'

The entrance hallway into the courts was tall and sinister and huge. There were people scurrying in all directions, and long passages and stairs everywhere. The overall atmosphere was one of gloom. Linda's solicitor gripped her firmly by the arm and manœuvred her along up various flights of stairs and into a couple of old elevators. It seemed to take ages to get wherever they were going.

'I hope your case will be heard before the luncheon recess,' her solicitor said, 'chances are that it will be.'

'How long will it all take?' Linda asked nervously.

'Not too long, it's very straightforward, shouldn't take long at all.' They had arrived in a long hallway with benches along the walls, and this, Linda presumed, was where they were going to wait. It was crowded with people and there were a scattering of men in long white curled wigs and black gowns. Her solicitor called one of them over. 'This is your counsel, Mr. Brown.'

Mr. Brown was tall and distinguished looking, with a tanned crinkly face. He had a soothing hypnotic voice, and he discussed the questions he would ask Linda briefly. She felt sick. The whole thing was so awful. Her stomach was fluttering, she wondered if there was a ladies' room close at hand where she could go and collapse.

Her solicitor was saying, 'I think it might be a good idea if we go in and sit through a couple of cases before yours. It will give you a chance to see how things are done.'

She nodded bleakly. He led her through an ordinary door into an ordinary room, and she got a jolting shock. Instead of a huge stately-looking court room as she had imagined, it was a small plain room with about six rows of benches where onlookers sat, a small slightly raised desk where the judge sat, and a raised wooden dais where the witness stood. It was awful. Everyone was so close to everyone else. It was like someone's living-room converted into a court for a day.

She sat on a bench in horror. A slightly built man was standing on the witness dais being questioned.

'And did you know at that time that your wife had had intercourse with Mr. Jackson?'

'Yes, sir.'

'And it was the same day that she packed her bags and left?'

'Yes, sir.'

'Leaving you in the matrimonial home with the children of your marriage, Jennifer and Susan?'

'Yes, sir.'

The case droned on. The slightly built man expressionless as he was asked question after question.

The judge sat wisely on his bench, nodding occasionally and looking for all the world like a senile old owl. At the conclusion of evidence he said, in hardly more than a mumble, 'Divorce granted. Custody of the children. Maintenance referred to chambers. Next case, please.'

The expressionless slight man suddenly broke into smiles, his shoulders straightened and he left the room happily.

The next case was a mousy-looking blonde with a heavy Cockney accent who was out to divorce Joe—from the sound of it, a wildly attractive sex maniac. It's so unfair, Linda thought, we're the innocent ones, and we're the ones who have got to stand up in this stupid little room and reveal the most personal aspects of our lives.

'Were your marital relationships satisfactory at first?' Counsel asked.

'I should say so!' Mousy blonde replied, drawing a muffled ribald laugh from somewhere in the court room.

At last it was Linda's turn. She stood shakily in the witness stand, horribly aware of how close everyone was to her. She resented the rows of spectators, why should they be allowed to sit there and stare and listen. It wasn't fair. After she was sworn in her counsel began the questions. She answered in a muffled quiet voice, eyes staring straight ahead. A document was produced from an enquiry agent and the judge inspected it briefly. Her counsel continued with the questions which were really statements of fact which she had only to confirm. Eventually he indicated to the judge that he was finished.

The judge adjusted his glasses, peered for a few brief seconds at Linda, and then said, 'Divorce granted, custody of the two children and costs to be paid by the husband. Maintenance and access referred to chambers.'

It was all over. She left the stand in a daze. Her solicitor came and took her arm. 'Congratulations,' he whispered.

Giles was late of course, he was always late. He was strung with cameras and looked tired. 'Give me some strong black coffee.

darling,' he said. 'I've had a terrible morning shooting bras in the middle of the New Forest.'

He collapsed in a chair, stretching his legs out and yawning. 'Y'know, this is a great pad, almost worth putting up with your boy-friend.'

'Almost?' questioned Claudia. She had done a skilful make-up, pale creamy matt base, clever blended rouge, pale brown lipstick and huge fluttery eyes. She looked fabulous.

'Yeah, almost. I mean, darling, he's such·a square. Hey, you look divine, wish we were shooting this at night, how late can I stay?'

'Well, until my lord and master gets home, I guess—you know how jealous he is. I'll give him a buzz around five and see what time he'll be home.'

'I want to shoot some wild stuff on the terrace—sort of get you silhouetted against the view of London jazz. Lots of hair flowing about and all that gear.'

'Sounds cool.' She was wearing a pink denim shirt tucked into matching hipster pants with a huge gold buckled belt and white boots.

'Great outfit,' he said, 'we can start off with that, discarding it bit by bit.'

'So how's your love life?' she asked. 'Still with that skinny model?'

'Yeah, we break up about every two weeks regularly, but then it's back together again time.'

'I see her on the cover of every magazine I pick up, it's amazing, 'cos I mean she's not really that great-looking, but she photographs beautifully.'

'Well, she's got a camera face, y'know. She sees a camera and the face switches on, comes to life, otherwise it's just static! I guess our affaire keeps going because she's really screwing my camera and I love the results. She's making me a bomb. I can't miss with anything I shoot of her.'

The 'phone rang. It was Claudia's agent, excited and pleased. It was true, the unit was returning at the end of the week and Claudia would probably be needed the following week.

'The director is flying in today,' her agent said, 'and the company is going to try and pin him down to a definite date.'

'Oh, fabulous.' Claudia was delighted, she had waited six months for this.

'Let's get started, darling,' Giles said when she hung up, 'before I go to sleep.'

Giles worked fast, using three different cameras. He threw himself completely into it, becoming utterly absorbed in what he was doing. Claudia of course blossomed before a camera, pouting, smiling, giving a tiger snarl, big, big sexy eyes always innocently staring, lips open and glossy. She undid the pink shirt, letting it fall casually open. There was nothing underneath.

After a while Giles said, 'Take your shirt off and fold your arms across your boobies. That's it—great! Give me a snarl. That's beautiful, baby. One leg slightly bent—a surprised look, marvellous! Now cover your boobies with your hands, give me the big-eyed baby look—beautiful!'

Giles kept shooting picture after picture. 'You look divine, darling, turn your back to me and swing your head around quickly, let your hair fall—great! Hey listen, I've got a terrific idea if you don't mind getting wet. Put the shirt back on and I'll hose you down with water, it will look very effective.' He picked up the water hose used to water the plants, and turned it on her. She screamed and giggled. 'It's cold!' He dropped the hose and picked up his camera.

He was right, it was effective. Her clothes had moulded themselves to her body, and her nipples stood out firm and strong through the shirt.

After an hour on the terrace Giles said, 'Crazy, let's go inside, baby. I've got some beautiful stuff of you out here.'

She was shivering. 'Lead the way to the shower,' he said, 'I don't want you catching cold. Strip off slowly, I want to capture it all.'

He followed her into the bathroom with his cameras, watching every moment as she wriggled out of her wet clothes and secured her hair with a couple of pins. As she stood under the shower, her body gleamed as the rivulets of water hit her, he said, 'Lean back, close your eyes, just let the water fall over you. Great! Bring your arms up behind your head, lovely, darling, that's lovely.'

They finished in the bathroom and Giles said, 'Now for some jazz in the bedroom and then we should have it made.'

She put on a filmy black chiffon robe, trimmed with feathers, and let her hair down. The robe was transparent, casting a black haze over her body.

'Lie right in the middle of the bed, bring your head up, bend one knee ever so slightly, no, your left knee, darling—that's it. Wet your lips and give me the look. No, that's too hard, a soft look like you just made it.'

He took a few shots and then put his camera down. 'Listen, you want these pictures to look really good?'

'Of course I do—what's the matter?' She sat up, her perfect breasts falling free of the robe.

'Darling, you just haven't got the right look, you're trying too hard, more relaxed, please.'

She stretched. 'I'm relaxed.'

'Yeah, I know, but you know what I want, I want the cat that just got the cream look.'

'So give me the cream . . .' she reached for him.

'Just what I had in mind.'

They made love easily, slowly, almost offhandedly, and afterwards he got quickly up, and picked up his camera. 'Stay just as you are. That's perfect. *Now* you look authentic!'

David 'phoned Claudia at five o'clock. He had been trying to make up his mind whether to take her along with Mr. Taylor of Fulla Beans or not. Eventually he had decided it would be better not to take her, as he would pay more attention to her than to Mr. Taylor, and that would defeat the purpose of the whole outing. 'What are you doing, darling?' he asked.

She giggled, 'Oh, just lying around.'

He put her in the picture about the evening ahead and she said, 'That's all right, I'll find something to do.'

'Why don't you get an early night and I'll wake you when I get in?'

She suddenly laughed. 'Hey David, I feel like a wife. Are you sure you haven't got some dolly little bird standing by your side?'

'Honestly, Claudia, don't be so stupid.'

'Well, baby, don't worry about it. I don't mind, anything you can do I can do too.'

'Listen, it's a business dinner. Now what are you going to do?'

She paused, then said, 'The President of America.'

'What?'

She laughed. 'I'm only joking! Go on, I believe you. Have a nice dinner, I shall probably ask a few people over, and we'll sit around and wait for your esteemed return.'

'All right,' he said reluctantly, 'an early night would do you much more good.'

'You're beginning to sound so stuffy,' she mimicked his voice, 'an early night would do you much more good!'

He ignored her comment. 'I'll 'phone you later. Be good.'

'Yes, sir, anything else, sir?'

'Goodbye.' He put the 'phone down, annoyed at the way she spoke to him. Annoyed by the fact that he was still so jealous of her. Annoyed by the fact she was going to ask people over. He would have to try and find Mr. Taylor a randy hostess and get rid of him early. He went into his private bathroom to change his shirt and shave.

Miss Field knocked nervously to say goodnight, and he rewarded her with a glimpse of his naked chest. She blushed deeply and he wondered idly if she had ever been laid. He really couldn't imagine it. She wore long knee length pink bloomers which he had noticed when she sat opposite him taking dictation. Also she was flat-chested, and who would want to lay a flat-chested ugly girl? Once he had screwed the most horrifying-looking girl, cross-eyed, bad teeth, acne, but she had had the best and biggest knockers he'd ever seen and wild legs. She had been a great lay too, but he hadn't bothered to see her again, that face was too much.

David had met Mr. Taylor once before briefly. He was middle-aged and running to fat, he had thinning brown hair plastered neatly to his scalp to give the impression that it wasn't thinning at all, but just grew that way. He had a thick Lancashire accent and a thick Lancashire wife with two matching sons. He was a bore.

David met him in the bar of his hotel. He had been drinking lager beer but switched to scotch as soon as David arrived. David tried to be charming—but Burt Taylor's idea of charming was a person who drank fast and told an everlasting run of dirty stories. David tried to please, and Burt rewarded him with hearty guffaws and conspiratorial winks. By the time they arrived at the restaurant David was well on the way and Burt already there—drunk, that is.

David tried to insert a little business into the conversation, but Burt switched it neatly back to the subject of sex by remarking how he bet David had a lot of hot ones passing through his job. 'All those little model girls,' Burt said, 'that's how they get the job, by sleeping with you, isn't it?' David didn't argue.

Eventually they reeled out of the restaurant arm in arm, Burt singing snatches of old Rugby songs. David patted Burt on the back. 'Let's go and have some fun then.'

They went to a plushy night-club, filled with tired painted hostesses and jocular lecherous out of town businessmen on expense accounts. The Maitre'de, a smooth suave Cypriot, asked if they would care to meet two nice young ladies.

'Oh yes,' Burt boomed, 'only make sure they're not all that nice.' He roared with laughter.

A few minutes later two girls arrived at their table, one was tall and buxom, with red hair and a strapless green velvet dress, she was about thirty. The other was smaller and slightly timid-looking—in spite of a dress cut low enough to reveal almost all of her scrawny bosom. She was very young. They both tried to attach themselves to David, but he excused himself from the table, realizing he hadn't 'phoned Claudia. He tried to sound sober, but there was so much noise and music on the other end of the 'phone that it was difficult to hear anything. A man answered the 'phone and he was told to hang on while the mystery voice located Claudia.

David hung grimly on to the 'phone, feeling the alcohol pounded out of his body by a sudden mad anger. By the time she reached the 'phone he felt almost sober.

'Hi, darling,' she cooed, 'where are you? I'm having a marvellous time, it turned into a party.'

'Who answered the 'phone? Who's there?'

'Oh, I don't know, heaps of people. Hurry home, baby.' And she hung up. He stood in the 'phone booth a few minutes, then intent on getting rid of Burt Taylor, he hurried back to the table. Burt had ordered champagne naturally, since David would be paying the bill. The two hostesses were flanking him on either side and he looked blissfully happy.

David thought the best thing to do was to get hold of the big brassy redhead and proposition her to take Mr. Burt Taylor off somewhere, he obviously preferred her to the younger one.

There was a cheesy Latin American band playing. 'How about a dance?' he said directly to the redhead. She smelt heavily of cheap perfume, and pressed herself groin to groin with him.

He managed to push her away a little and said, 'Hey listen, you want to make yourself a few pounds?'

She looked interested. David explained the proposition. They bargained, reached an agreement, and sat down, David carefully slipping her the money beforehand.

Burt Taylor was a bit put out. He took him to one side and said, 'I saw her first, boyo, I don't want the skinny bit.'

David smiled, this was going to be easy. 'It's all right, she can't stop talking about you, you've got it made.'

'Well, in that case . . .' Burt leered, 'we won't be wasting too much more time here.'

David reckoned another half-an-hour and he would be home. He patted Burt on the shoulder—'I'll get the bill,' he said.

There were photographers outside the court waiting for Linda. The fact that Claudia Parker had been named as the other woman made the case almost newsworthy.

'Over here,' one of them called. Linda rushed ahead, her solicitor gripping her arm. The cameras clicked.

'What do they want?' she questioned. 'Can't they leave people alone. I'm nobody.'

Her solicitor hailed a passing taxi and pushed her in. 'It's best for you to get away from here. Congratulations again, we'll be in touch with you.'

'Well, can't I give you a lift?' she said, trying to delay being left on her own.

'No, no, my office is just round the corner. Goodbye, Mrs. Cooper.' He was gone and the taxi was moving off down the street.

'Where to, lady?' asked the cab driver. She sat there slightly dazed, it had all happened so quickly, it was like a dream. 'Where to, lady?' the cab driver repeated, slightly impatient.

She didn't feel like rushing straight to the station, she felt like a drink and a cigarette and a half hour of quiet relaxation. 'The Dorchester,' she said.

The bar was fairly crowded, mostly with businessmen, but she found a secluded table, ordered a sherry and sat back to enjoy it. She decided she would have lunch there. It was good to be on her own. She would order smoked salmon and boeuf strogonoff, fresh strawberries with cream maybe even drink champagne.

'It is Linda Cooper, isn't it?' She looked up, hesitated and then said, 'Jay—Jay Grossman. Why I would hardly have recognized you, what a wonderful tan.'

He sat down, smiling. 'I just got in from Israel. How are you? It's been months and months.'

'I'm fine,' she smiled back at him.

'And David?'

'David? I don't really know. I just divorced him about half-an-hour ago.'

Jay looked surprised. 'You really did it then. Was it about that night?'

She nodded. 'Yes, it was about that night. He's living with her now.'

'Wow, you certainly mean what you say.'

'How is Lori?'

'Lori is very happy. Lori is married to a Texas oil tycoon who buys her two mink coats a week, so she's very happy.'

'You mean you've divorced too?'

'Yes, I'm divorced yet again, we do these things quickly in the States. She went to Nevada and shed me in six weeks on extreme mental cruelty—then married this other man the very next day. The only good thing is she didn't knock me for any alimony or settlements so I was lucky. Supporting the other two ex's costs me enough.' He laughed. 'Are you meeting anyone?'

She shook her head.

'Well, what about having lunch with me?'

She smiled, she liked Jay. 'I'd love to.'

'Good.' He stood up. 'I've just got to rearrange a few things, I'll be right back.'

After he left Linda quickly took out her compact. She studied her face and added more lipstick. She wished she looked a bit more glamorous, but she had deliberately put on her dress-down clothes to appear in court. Jay was a very attractive man. Since separating from David, Linda had only been out with a man once, partly because her solicitor had warned her not to, and partly because she didn't want to. The episode with Paul had left its mark, and she preferred to stay at home or perhaps visit married friends. The evening she had gone out had been an utter bore, and to add insult to injury the man she had been with had immediately expected her to go to bed with him. Divorcees, she gathered from him, were supposed to include that in the evening's activities.

Jay returned to the table. 'Everything under control, where would you like to eat?'

They decided to stay where they were. They moved into the restaurant, and Jay entertained her with amusing anecdotes about the location and idle gossip about the people involved.

He took her hand over coffee and said, 'My God, it's nice to be with someone who has a brain and not just a body. You know, I really like you, Linda, you're a really nice person.' She smiled a little stiffly, she didn't want Jay to think of her as such a nice person. Nice was such a dull word, it conjured up twin-sets and sensible shoes.

He looked at his watch. 'Wow—it's nearly three o'clock, I've got to rush.' He called for the bill. 'Let me drop you at the station, I've got a studio car.'

'No, it's right out of your way, I can easily get a cab.'

'Oh, O.K., if you insist. I'll put you in the cab though.'

They left the restaurant and walked through the lobby where Jay was hailed by a couple standing there. The woman was tall, blonde and pretty, the man short, stocky and red-faced. The man said, 'Oh, Mr. Grossman, sorry you couldn't make lunch. This is my client, Miss Susan Standish.'

Miss Susan Standish smiled a direct smile at Jay, she had very small white teeth and she looked even prettier when she smiled. Jay smiled back. Linda saw his eyes flicker with interest as they swept over Miss Standish. Tall pretty blondes were obviously his type.

'I'll be right back,' he said, and took Linda to the entrance. He made no comment about the couple he had obviously stood up for lunch. He kissed her on the cheek, 'Linda, let's do this again sometime. When will you be back?'

'Thank you for a lovely lunch, Jay. I'll be back Monday.'

He saw her into a cab. 'I'll talk to you then,' he said.

The 'phone rang and Claudia stretched languorously across the bed and picked it up. She spoke briefly, and with a grin she hung up.

'Baby,' she said to Giles, 'tonight we can swing, Daddy won't be home till late!'

Giles said, 'What are we waiting for, let's have a party, get on the 'phone. Call the liquor store first.'

They picked out names at random. Giles would say, 'Remember that kooky little girl who always wore those terrible thigh length black boots . . .' and they would track her down, inviting another half dozen people en route. Claudia changed into a startling silver lamé cat suit. Giles snatched a nap, sprawled across her bed, and eventually people began to appear.

By the time David 'phoned again the party was in full swing. Claudia was completely stoned. She didn't even know half the people who were there. The music was so loud that the tenants in the flat below had complained three times. They had stopped 'phoning as the last time a beautifully spoken debutante had told them exactly what to do in explicit detail. She was now accommodating an out-of-work window cleaner on the sofa in full view of everyone.

'Swinging party!' Giles said. 'What happens when big daddy comes walking in?'

'Big daddy's going to have to join in the fun or big daddy can walk right out again.'

'Darling, sweetie-pie—how divine of you to invite me.'

Claudia blinked, focusing slowly. 'Shirley baby, how are you?'

'I'm fine, simply fine. Just got back from the most divine holiday.'

'You look great, just great—all that crazy suntan. Where's the Hon. what not?'

'Ditched him, darling. I've got the most divine man now simply a poppet. You'll be amazed.'

'Grab a drink, darling, and join in, it's all happening here. . . .'

Claudia trailed off as a Spanish-looking gentleman grabbed her from behind—'You is beautiful,' he said, 'I eat you up.'

'Really,' Shirley said, 'it looks like you're in good hands, I'll see you later, sweetie.'

She left Claudia struggling with the boy. Claudia had never seen him before. 'Leave me alone, you oaf,' she said. He was very strong. 'You beautiful,' he said proudly, obviously his English vocabulary was limited. He twisted her round in his arms and kissed her. 'Your breath stinks!' she exclaimed, still struggling. He held her even tighter and kissed her again. It was at this moment that David appeared. He stood, shocked, in the doorway of the apartment. He spotted Claudia immediately, and striding across the room he hauled the Spanish boy away from her—smashing his fist into his face. The boy slumped to the floor, blood seeping from his nose.

'You little tramp,' he said, and brought his arm back-handedly across her face. Nobody really noticed what was going on, the music was too loud and they were all too stoned.

'Get these dregs out of here,' David snarled at her. She rubbed her cheek, her eyes huge and filled with tears—more from pain than from anything else. 'You lousy sonofabitch,' she muttered, 'how dare you hit me—how dare you.'

'I'll do what I want to you, I bought you, didn't I? Now get this damned place clear.'

'You can go to hell,' she ran over to the Spanish boy and cradled his head in her arms.

'I'm warning you, Claudia, you're pushing me too far.'

She continued to cradle the boy's head and ignored him.

He stood for a few seconds, then said, 'Right.' He marched off into the bedroom. It was at this particular moment that Giles was reaching a hard fought for climax with a girl of dubious colour. It was unfortunate that it happened to be right in the middle of David's bed. David swore loudly, but nothing bothered Giles, and he kept on going, although the girl squeaked and attempted to object.

David grimly took a suitcase from the top of a cupboard, he methodically sorted his clothes from Claudia's, packing as much as he could.

Giles and the girl got up. She glared at David as she re-arranged her clothes. 'Some people don't care,' she muttered, 'they just barge in anywhere.'

Giles made a mock bow—'Performance over, next show at four o'clock.' They walked out of the bedroom.

David locked the door behind them and continued packing. He finally filled three suitcases. His mind was cold with anger. He unlocked the bedroom and strode to the front door with two of the cases—the party was still in full swing. He returned for the third suitcase.

' 'Bye 'bye, darling,' Claudia screamed above the noise, she was reeling across the room towards him, the front zipper on her cat suit was undone, almost to her waist, and her breasts pushed forward to escape. Her hair was wild and blood was smeared across her face.

'You look lovely,' he said, 'just like the drunken little whore you are.'

She laughed. 'Get stuffed,' she shouted, 'get lost—don't come back, you're a bloody bore.'

Giles joined her—'You tell him, darling,' he said, slipping his hand inside the open zipper. She made an obscene gesture and turned her back.

David left.

CHAPTER FOURTEEN

'WELL, LOOK DARLING, what is happening?' Claudia's voice was edgy and cold on the 'phone. 'I mean they have been back ten days now, and they should be able to tell us something.'

Her agent was noncommittal. 'I can't get any definite date out of them.'

'But I signed a contract for two days' work, a contract, remember?'

'Yes, I know, but they've paid you for the two days' work you were supposed to do. You got the £120 already, so they don't have to use you.' She snorted angrily. 'What kind of an agent are you? I'm supposed to be in that film. It's a big film and it will do me a lot of good—a lot more good than these walk-on bits you keep offering me. If you can't do it, tell me—tell me and I'll get someone who can!'

Her agent's voice was resigned. 'I'm doing my best.'

'Well, your best's not enough. Forget it, I'll do it myself, I'll call Conrad Lee.' She slammed the 'phone down. 'Stupid agents! They never do a thing for you except take your money.'

The flat was in a terrible mess. The new daily had walked out the day after the party. Actually, the party had still been going on the next morning when she arrived and she had taken one horrified look at the red-headed boy wearing Claudia's cat suit who answered the front door, and she left.

It had been a good party, lasted three days in all. Claudia didn't remember too much about it really—but Giles assured her it had been a gas.

David hadn't returned. He hadn't 'phoned and he hadn't communicated in any way, although a mousy secretary had arrived one day about a week later to collect his mail and request that in future it be forwarded to his office. Claudia didn't miss him. She was rather glad he had gone really. Life was too confining with someone watching every move you made.

Claudia was really a very independent girl. She had fallen in with David because it was easy and he had left his wife, and it just sort of happened. It was rather nice having all the bills paid and lots of new clothes and no problems. She would have to think about going back to work, a secret job she had which had always given her enough money to lead a comfortable independent life. It would be better though to be in Conrad's movie, and become a star and make lots more money that way.

The other way gave her a vicarious thrill though, and none of her friends, no one knew about it. She had always kept it a closely guarded secret and before she was living with David all her friends had wondered but never found out how she always managed to be so financially secure and independent. The job excited her, she wore wigs and did special creative make-up jobs completely disguising her own features. She starred in glorious technicolour in blue movies! In four years she had been in thirty of them, earning at least eight or nine hundred pounds per film. So successful was she at the disguise jobs that she was known as three completely different girls, all in constant demand by the voyeurs who got to see the finished product. If she wanted to work again, all it would take would be a 'phone call. This is Evette—or Carmen—or Maria, and arrangements would be made. She was paid cash, and she contacted them— they had no way of reaching her. It was a satisfactory arrangement.

However, she wasn't sure that she wanted to go back to doing that. Sometimes her co-stars left a lot to be desired, and of course if you weren't in the right mood, it could be pretty grim.

No—to appear in Conrad's movie would be the best thing, and if her agent couldn't fix it, she certainly would. Conrad would probably be delighted to hear from her again.

She 'phoned the hotel he had stayed at on his previous visit, but he wasn't registered there. She 'phoned the studio and spoke to a secretary who took her name and said she would pass Mr. Lee her message. She tried to find out where he was living, but the girl was polite but firm—'We're not allowed to disclose Mr. Lee's address,' she said, 'but I'll certainly see he gets your message.' It wasn't very satisfactory, Claudia wanted to get to him personally. Giles would be able to find out. Giles was working for the 'in' magazine of the moment and they seemed to be able to get hold of anyone. She called him at the studio, but there was no reply.

'Oh dammit,' she muttered, finally getting up. There was a stack of bills at the front door. David had stopped paying for everything since he had left, and the bills were steadily mounting. She couldn't stick him with any of them as the flat and everything was in her name. It was a question of getting hold of Conrad and becoming a star. 'Once I get hold of that old bald buzzard, no problem,' she laughed, 'he'll be putty in my hands.'

Linda stayed in the country with her parents and the children much longer than she expected to. It was so peaceful, the children were out playing all day and she sat in the house while her mother fussed around her. It was very relaxing, and knowing that to return to London was to be the beginning of a new life, she clung on to the limbo period of being with her parents.

Her mother wanted her to stay there permanently. 'Sell your house,' she urged Linda, 'there's plenty of room for you here.'

Linda rejected the offer. Her parents' home was just a temporary retreat, and tempting as the thought was, it would be a mistake to stay. She would be buried there, stifled. Her mother would take care of everything, even to bringing up the children. Linda would become the elder daughter of the family.

One Saturday afternoon David turned up. It was the first time she had seen him since they separated.

'I tried 'phoning the house, I was worried,' he said. 'I thought you'd be here.'

Her voice was stilted, cold. 'Why didn't you 'phone here? Why did you just come?'

He was ill at ease, it was strange to see David groping for words—he who was usually so sure of himself. 'I wanted to see the children,' a note of indignation crept into his voice, almost a whine, she thought. 'I'm supposed to see the children, you know.'

He looked thin and tired. 'I've left Claudia,' he blurted out.

She looked at him dispassionately. 'Oh!'

'You look marvellous,' he said.

She did look well. Her skin was glowing from long walks in the country and her hair was shining and unset, tied casually back with a ribbon, and she looked very slim in a pair of slacks and a loose shirt. 'Well,' she shrugged, 'the children are in the garden, I'll call them in.'

He put a hand on her arm. 'I said I've left Claudia.'

She brushed his hand impatiently away. 'I heard you the first time, David. I'll get the children.' She walked quickly from the room.

He stayed the whole afternoon, chatting amicably to her parents, entertaining Jane and Stephen with all sorts of games. David is turning on his well known charm, Linda thought miserably, I wish he'd go away.

He finally left at six. Her mother wanted to ask him to stay to dinner—but Linda hissed at her—'Don't you dare.' His charm had worked. 'He really wants you back,' her mother said after he had gone. She was really saying you should go back to him. Linda knew the signs. Her father was less direct.

'That boy needs a father,' he said, when Stephen played up before going to bed. Her mother said later in the evening, 'Poor David looks so unhappy.'

It was too much for Linda, they just didn't understand. They meant well, but she had had enough.

The next morning she told them she was going back to London, and on Monday morning she packed, and amidst tears from her mother, and gruff words of wisdom from her father, she and the children were put safely on a train.

She was glad to be back in her own house. The children were pleased and excited to be reunited with all their books and toys, and cries of 'super' and 'that's mine' rang through the house.

Anna gave her a list of 'phone messages, and amongst them were two calls from Jay Grossman. He had left his number. She didn't call back, she wanted to, but somehow felt if he really wanted to see her again he would try once more to 'phone her.

Monica had 'phoned her. They hadn't spoken since the separation, they were David's friends. She 'phoned Monica who was delighted. 'Dahling,' she exclaimed, 'I'm having a little dinner party—I'd love you to come.'

Linda was hesitant. 'When?'

'Tomorrow night, sweetie. I must see you, it's been such ages. Will you come?'

'Well, I don't know, Monica. I mean, have you invited David?'

'Dahling! What do you take me for? Of course not. I don't want any other excuses. I'll see you tomorrow, eight o'clock. Don't be late.'

That was settled then. It might be fun, Monica always invited interesting people. She would go to the hairdresser's, and then buy a new dress. It was about time she started going out again.

Claudia sprawled untidily on a sofa at the back of Giles' studio. He was hard at work photographing a languid brunette clad only in a silver bodystocking.

Claudia yawned. 'Why the hell don't you answer your bloody 'phone, you could have saved me a trip.'

Giles didn't look round, his concentration was completely on the model. After a few minutes he stopped, told the girl to take a break and wandered over to Claudia, lighting a cigarette. He stuck it in her mouth and she took a long drag. She spluttered and choked—'Jesus Christ! Smoking pot at this time of the day! You're too much!'

He laughed, took back his cigarette and said, 'What the hell do you want?'

'I came to see you,' she replied coyly.

'Cut the crap, I'm busy. What do you want?'

'Well, actually,' she stretched, 'I need Conrad Lee's number —I thought if you called your magazine they would have it.'

'Things must be tough if you're creeping back on that bandwagon.'

Her voice was irritable, sometimes she couldn't stand Giles. 'Things are not tough—and I'm not climbing back on any bandwagon.'

He laughed—'Don't forget it's me you're talking to, baby.'

'How could I possibly forget?'

They exchanged stares. 'All right,' he said, 'keep cool, I'll get it for you.' He 'phoned the magazine and they gave him the number. Claudia wrote it down and smiled. 'Thank you, darling,' she purred.

'That's all right, sweetheart—now get the hell out of here, I've got work to do.'

Claudia went shopping. She bought a white and gold silk jersey dress, and gold spikey-heeled shoes, unfashionable but sexy. She went to the hairdressers and had her hair elaborately piled on top of her head. Back home, she bathed, splashing half a bottle of musky oil into the bath. She took two hours with her make-up—making sure it was perfect. By the time she was dressed it was seven o'clock. She dialled the number Giles had given her. Conrad's unmistakably accented voice answered.

She smiled, it was all going to work perfectly. Her voice was cool and efficient. 'Mr. Lee?'

'Yes.' His voice was gruff.

'I am calling for *Star Magazine,* as you know we are featuring your photograph on our cover this week, and I wondered if you might answer a few short questions about yourself.'

His voice was now friendly—'My picture huh? Sure I'll answer a few questions.'

Conceited pig! 'Oh thank you, Mr. Lee, if you will just give me your address I'll be right over, and it will only take a few minutes.'

He was surprised, 'Can't I answer them now?'

'Oh no, Mr. Lee, it's important to get the personal reactions.'

'All right, all right.' He gave her his address, and, nearly laughing, she put down the 'phone. She admired her reflection in the mirror one last time and buzzed the doorman for a cab.

Conrad lived in an imposing house in Belgravia. The door bell was answered by a manservant in a white jacket and he ushered her into the library. She waited patiently for fifteen minutes until at last Conrad lumbered in. He hadn't changed. A fat cigar stuck from between his fleshy lips, and he was wearing the same green silk smoking jacket.

She arose, deliberately posing her body so that the thin silk dress clung even tighter. She knew she had never looked better. 'Hi,' she smiled provocatively.

He came to an abrupt standstill. She could see he didn't recognize her. He plucked the cigar from his mouth—'Are you the broad from *Star*?'

'Do I look like a lady journalist?'

His piercing eyes roved over her body. His memory stirred.

'Hey—you're the broad from the party I gave.' His voice changed 'Hey—what's going on here—what is this?'

'You're a difficult man to get hold of. I've left lots of messages for you.'

'So?'

'I thought it was about time we got together again. Don't tell me you've forgotten all the fun we had together last time.'

Interest flickered briefly in his eyes.

'Listen, I've got guests, you stay here and I'll see what I can do.'

He left the room and she smiled triumphantly. It was amazing what a fabulous body could do.

He was gone a long time and the manservant came in with a drink and left her some magazines. She leafed idly through them waiting, because eventually he would be back and then tomorrow morning, enter Claudia Star!

CHAPTER FIFTEEN

FROM THE DAY he walked out on Claudia, David felt depressed. It wasn't that he had wanted to stay, the whole situation had become impossible. Claudia was a slut, an out and out slut. She lolled around reading stupid magazines all day, only bothering with her appearance if they were going out. Staying in bed until noon or later, never tidying the flat. The only thing she seemed capable of was incessant love-making, and whereas before he had lived with her he had always been ready, now he was tired. She was insatiable—demanding, demanding and never getting enough. David had always prided himself on his sexual appetite, but this was ridiculous.

He was pleased to have an excuse to get out. He was depressed because instead of dismissing the whole Claudia mess from his mind and going home to his wife and children, he was an outcast, he had nowhere to go except to the coldness of a hotel room. There is nothing quite so bleak as living in a hotel. No privacy, no warmth, just four impersonal walls, a cold bathroom, and a Do Not Disturb sign.

He returned to work with a vengeance, and sat and brooded on the possibilities of getting back together with Linda.

He reasoned that she should take him back, after all there were the children to consider, they would want him back. A divorce could easily be rescinded, and everything could be like it was before, only this time he wouldn't be such a fool and get hooked up with a slut like Claudia. He would be more careful, pick and choose, short casual affaires, nothing that Linda could discover. He 'phoned his ex-home and the maid informed him that Linda and the children were in the country with her parents. He was pleased. Give Linda a little more time to get over it. She was a sensible woman, she would know it was right for them to be together. The first Saturday he was free he drove down to see her.

Linda looked surprisingly fresh and well. She was cold towards him, it was only to be expected. He told her about leaving Claudia, her reaction was strangely negative. Oh well, give her time. He was charming to her parents, he knew they were back on his side.

Later he drove back to London and called an old girl-friend, she was giggly and a bit stupid. They went to a movie and then back to her place. She was lousy in bed. She had none of the franticness of Claudia or the calmness of Linda. He left after an hour.

He woke early on Sunday, he had nothing to do. On an impulse he decided to go to his office and work. He had a backlog of letters and all sorts of odd things to sort out that he never had time for during the week. He wished his secretary was available, maybe she was, she looked the sort of mini-ann person who would never make any plans. Poor plain Miss Field. He telephoned her.

Her voice was timid, 'Chesterfield 4521.'

'Miss Field, Mr. Cooper here.'

'Oh!' her voice became a startled squeak as if she had been caught doing something she shouldn't have been.

'Miss Field, how do you feel about working today?'

'Oh Mr. Cooper—oh, really?'

'It's quite all right if you've already made other plans.'

'Oh no—oh no—Oh, Mr. Cooper, of course I can work today.'

'Good, I'll see you down at the office in about an hour.'

She was there before him, waiting like a pale white mouse outside the locked main door.

'You look very nice today, Miss Field,' he said.

She had brushed her thin stringy brown hair down instead of scragged back and she wore a harsh scarlet lipstick on her thin usually colourless mouth. Sunday clothes consisted of an off-white dress and blue woollen cardigan. She was a picture of plainness.

They worked efficiently through the day non-stop, until the light began to fade and David suddenly realized it was getting late.

'Well I suppose we should call it a day,' he said, yawning. 'You must be hungry.'

'Mr. Cooper,' her voice was hesitant, nervous, 'perhaps you

would care to have a little dinner with me.' A bright red flush was spreading up into her hairline. 'I make it my business to always prepare a Cordon Bleu dinner on Sundays—one of my little hobbies and I would be only too delighted if you would sample it.' She added quickly, 'Boeuf Stroganoff, with fresh green salad, followed by a lemon meringue pie.'

It sounded good, he had nowhere else to go. She kept blushing and he felt sorry for her. 'What a lovely idea, Miss Field. I'd be glad to.'

She lived in a tiny two-roomed flat. The sofa neatly festooned with crochet cushions, obviously did double duty as the bed.

She produced a half bottle of sherry—too sweet, and he sat and watched television while she pottered about in the kitchen.

He felt so sorry for her, poor lonely little spinster.

She prepared a delicious dinner and they drank a cheap Spanish wine. 'I brought it back from my holiday last year,' she said proudly.

After dinner she was obviously a little high. 'I don't usually drink,' she said with a giggle. He was also slightly high having drunk half of the wine and most of the sherry before dinner. His attention was riveted on the television screen. The Beauty Maid commercial was on and there was Claudia in her bath. Familiar sharp pull in his groin.

'Oh, Mr. Cooper, our commercial.' Miss Field sat quickly down beside him on the sofa. He felt the nearness of a leg beside him—he rested his hand on her thigh, Miss Field shrieked and before he knew it her arms were around his neck and she was pulling his mouth towards the thin red line. They kissed and as Claudia vanished from the screen so his desire vanished with her. But it was too late. Miss Field was already in action. All in the space of seconds she leaped up, turned the light off, wriggled out of her cardigan and was back beside him. 'My dearest, I am yours,' she said. 'I have waited for this moment too long.'

He couldn't believe it, the whole thing was so ludicrous.

She lay back expectantly, quivering.

What should he do? She was a good secretary, he didn't want to loose her. He didn't want to hurt her feelings.

She was getting impatient. 'David, my dearest, come to me: I am not afraid.'

Oh well, he took a deep breath and ran his hands tentatively across her bosom, there was no bosom! Coyly she said, 'I know I am not well endowed, but there is fire in my loins.'

Oh, my God! he thought. Tired of waiting she locked her hands behind his head and pulled his mouth down on hers.

This is a bloody nightmare, he thought, but as her tongue

worked on his mouth his body started to respond and soon he was ready again, she was angular and bony and surprisingly strong. She managed to get his trousers and pants off as he lay on top of her, then her mouth was travelling down his body and she was kissing him, and suddenly it was all over for him in a huge shaking furious bout of passion. He screamed but she didn't stop, sending him into a frenzy. A shudder enveloped her and at last she stopped, lying very still.

They lay in silence—his body sprawled across her at an angle. He could hardly believe what had just taken place. Placid, timid Miss Field Mouse certainly knew what she was doing.

He went and locked himself in the bathroom. His body was covered in red weals where her fingers had dug into him, she was a hot bitch!

When he returned to the room her cardigan was back on, and she was primly clearing the dishes. She avoided looking at him as he stepped into his shorts and trousers.

'Would you like coffee before you go, Mr. Cooper?' she said, her voice was even, only a slight flush across her cheeks indicating what had just taken place.

'Er, no thank you, Miss Field,' he took his cue from her. 'I really must get off.'

'Oh well, I do hope we can do this again.'

'Yes,' he hesitated. 'Well, goodbye then. See you at the office tomorrow.'

'Goodbye, Mr. Cooper, see you tomorrow.'

Out in the street David heaved a big sigh, he would have to get rid of her. To have her working with him at the office every day would be a horrible reminder.

Next time he would get a pretty secretary—just on the chance he should ever be thrown into an experience like that again.

He thought about Linda, about soft bosoms and warm lips. He was ready to go home.

'Linda dahling! You look positively stunning! So slim, so young! This divorce business certainly agrees with you.' Monica led Linda into the living-room. 'It's an interesting crowd to-night, no married couples, Jack and I decided that would be fun, now let me introduce you.'

There were perhaps twelve people sitting and standing around. Linda recognized Monica's brother, a dress designer, very swish. He was with a small short squat woman wearing a very unsuitable silk pyjama suit. 'That's Princess Lorenz Alvaro with Rodney,' whispered Monica, 'exciting isn't it?'

Linda had never heard of Princess Alvaro and she didn't see what was so exciting about it as Rodney was a well known queer.

She was soon chatting quietly to a doctor, tall, craggy faced, very pleasant. Before they had finished one martini he had invited her to dinner the following evening, and she thought why not? So she accepted. He was fairly attractive and seemed most taken with her. Definitely a nice man, not a David type at all.

More people arrived and Linda found herself wedged in a corner with the doctor telling her a long involved story about a patient of his with yellow jaundice. It was rather boring. She smiled politely and wished she hadn't accepted his dinner invitation. Doctor or not, he had a bad case of bad breath.

Idly she glanced around the room, then she saw Jay and she straightened up, smoothed down her dress and touched her hair. He hadn't seen her, he was talking to Rodney and Princess Alvaro and then he was joined by the blonde girl, who had been in the lobby of the hotel that day. She looked even prettier now in a crisp white trouser suit, her hair tied on top of her head with a white ribbon. He put his arm around her and she smiled up at him.

Linda pulled her eyes away, the doctor droned on.

Monica announced that a cold buffet was being served in the other room. 'I am hungry,' Linda said.

'Oh, good heavens,' said the doctor. 'I must have been boring you stiff, let's go and eat.' He took her possessively by the elbow and steered her into the other room where she bumped straight into Jay. He held two plates of food and they almost fell. 'Linda!' He sounded pleased.

'Jay,' she said, affecting the same tone.

'Where have you been?'

'Oh, in the country with the children.'

'You look terrific.'

Did I look so terrible before? she wondered. 'Thank you.'

They stood and smiled at each other, and then the doctor's grip tightened and he said, 'We'd better get in that queue before we're too late.'

'Oh, yes.' Linda's heart was beating fast.

'See you in a minute,' Jay said, he winked and imitated an English accent. 'You'd better get in the queue.'

When Jay was out of hearing distance, the doctor said, 'These American film types are all the same.'

'Oh?'

'You know—brash, vulgar, full of themselves.'

'Do you know Jay Grossman?' Linda asked crossly.

'Well, let's say we have a mutual friend.'

'Who?' Linda asked rudely.

'Name no names, Hear no pack drill.'

'What?' Suddenly she hated the doctor.

He smiled secretly, 'Well, as a matter of fact, it's one of his ex-wives.'

'Oh,' she tried to sound disinterested.

'A lovely woman,' the doctor continued. 'I believe she had a terrible time with him. She just remarried.'

'Is it Lori?' Linda asked coldly.

The doctor looked surprised. 'Yes, as a matter of fact, it is. She's here in London with her husband, he's very wealthy.'

'How interesting,' Linda said sarcastically. She quickly helped herself to food and rushed back into the other room, the doctor close behind her. There was nowhere to sit. Jay was with the blonde on a sofa. 'Linda,' he called. 'You can have my seat.'

'Excuse me,' she said to the doctor. Jay stood up and she sat down. The blonde glanced at her slightly annoyed.

'Susan,' Jay said, 'I want you to meet a very good friend of mine, Linda Cooper.'

'Hello,' Susan's smile was limp.

The doctor squatted on his haunches in front of Linda, eating from his crowded plate hungrily. Jay drifted away to the other side of the room. Susan suddenly got up and said to Linda, 'Perhaps your friend would like to sit here.' She moved across the room to join Jay, and the doctor quickly sat beside Linda. She was well and truly stuck, he obviously had no intention of leaving her side. 'Can I drive you home later?' he asked.

'I'm sorry I have my car with me.'

'Oh, pity,' he shook his head. 'Maybe I should follow you to see you get home safely,' he chuckled.

Linda could have screamed, he was such a bore! She didn't even bother to reply. She jumped up, he got up too.

'Excuse me,' she said firmly, 'I have to go to the ladies room.'

It was quiet upstairs in Monica's bedroom. She sat at the dressing-table and rearranged strands of her hair. Would Monica think her rude if she left? She didn't really care. She looked for her stole amongst the coats on the bed. What a waste buying the new black chiffon dress she was wearing. She found her stole and went downstairs, and slipped out quietly. She would call Monica tomorrow and explain that she had a headache and had thought it better not to bother with goodbyes. Monica would probably be insulted, not invite her again, but so what? It was much more fun staying at home with the children. Back home she undressed slowly, wondering why on earth three hours previously she had painstakingly applied such a careful make-up and looked forward so excitedly to Monica's dreary gathering. What had she expected? Prince Charming? Not a boring doctor with bad breath.

She felt depressed and old. Girls like Susan set the pace now, in their crisp trouser suits and lithe bodies. Face up to it, Linda, she thought, you've had your best years, you gave them to David. You've got two children, you're divorced, you have to settle for second best now.

She was lonely at night. Once, briefly, it had crossed her mind to 'phone Paul, but commonsense had prevailed. Maybe she had made a mistake divorcing David. Maybe she should have given him another chance, but no, she was right, this was better than living a lie with David.

She fell into a troubled sleep.

About an hour later the ringing of the 'phone woke her up.

'Hello,' her voice was sleepy.

'Are you trying to avoid me?'

'What?' her mind was still sleep-filled.

'I leave messages for you, you don't return my calls, you avoid me tonight and then just run off. I want dinner with you tomorrow night, no excuses.'

'Yes, Jay,' her voice was weak.

'I'll pick you up at eight, and no calls to say you can't make it. I've 'phoned you three times.'

She didn't know what to say.

'All right, tomorrow at eight,' he said after a short pause, 'and wear that black dress you had on tonight, it looks great.'

The 'phone clicked dead and she clung on to it. Suddenly everything seemed bright again. Jay Grossman was certainly not second best.

Eventually Conrad returned. He had been gone an hour and a half, and Claudia bored with the magazines and at being kept waiting was a little testy. She covered her irritation with a smile.

He was drunk, he grabbed hold of her, his fleshy hands feeling her body through her thin dress. She wriggled away, this wasn't the way she had it planned.

'Aren't we going upstairs?' she asked.

His breath, a mixture of strong garlic and scotch, enveloped her as he replied, 'Sure—sure. Just want a little preliminary.' He forced his hands inside the neckline of her dress, grabbing hold of her breasts with rough fingers.

'You're hurting me,' she complained, and then—'Hey—you're tearing my dress.' She pulled away from him again, furious at the torn dress, but still smiling provocatively. 'Let's go upstairs, lover,' she cooed, 'let's have a great scene upstairs.'

'All right take your dress off first—I want to take a look at the goods I'm getting.'

It was obviously no use arguing with him, she'd fix him when she got him in the sack. She peeled off sensuous folds of white jersey. Underneath she had on only a wisp of garter belt, and pale sheer stockings, her long legs emphasized by the exceptionally high heels she was wearing.

He lunged at her, falling to his knees and grabbing her around the waist. He sunk his teeth into her stomach and bit her hard.

She screamed with pain and kicked him away—'You son of a bitch!'

He laughed, hollow loud rumbles.

She rubbed her stomach, her eyes glinting dangerously, her mouth a tight smile. So he wanted to play games huh? Well, she knew a few of her own.

'Come on,' he lumbered to the door. She followed him. He pushed her up the stairs ahead of him, stroking her legs, trying to feel between them.

They reached the bedroom, it was very dark, she could hardly see a thing.

'Get on the bed,' he commanded.

She climbed on to a large circular bed, grimly thinking things were going to be different in the morning, when this big slob was sober.

He switched on the lights—bright glaring lights, that hit the bed at a hard angle. She noticed a huge mirror above the bed. He climbed on top of her not even bothering to remove his clothes, just unfastening his trousers.

'Open up, baby,' he said, 'let's have some action.'

He used her brutally—crushing and grinding her, and afterwards wanting it different ways, making her do it to him at every conceivable angle. She worked hard, this was something he had to remember. It was funny really, when she became famous everyone would say she was an overnight discovery. How right they would be!

At last he was finished. Her body ached from his pressures. She was bruised and worn. She lay spreadeagled on the bed, too limp to move.

He was surprisingly full of life. 'Got a little thrill for you,' he said, 'just stay where you are.' He got off the bed and pressed a switch by the door, the mirror above the bed parted and slid easily in two, leaving a huge gap in the ceiling. A ring of smiling faces peered down at her around the gaping aperture.

She sat up, horrified.

'Just a few of my friends,' Conrad said easily, 'these two way mirrors are a great gimmick for making a party go with a bang!' He guffawed. 'Pick out who you'd like next.'

A woman's face grotesquely made up and old said, 'How about me, Conrad. Can I have a turn with her. She seems to know what it's all about.'

A man's voice said, 'No, me next, let me give her a real piece!'

'Oh, God!' Claudia jumped off the bed.

'What's the matter?' Conrad asked. 'Don't you want to be in my movie?'

She stared at him, every instinct warning her to get out. But to leave now, what use was that. That wouldn't get her on the silver screen.

'All right,' she said. 'All right. I'll stay, but this time you'd better mean it.'

'I mean it,' he said blandly.

CHAPTER SIXTEEN

DAVID MANAGED to get through the early part of the next week without trouble. Miss Field was, as usual, the perfect quiet unobtrusive secretary. Neither of them made any reference to the previous Sunday, indeed, it was as if it had never happened. David felt that maybe it had all been a horrible dream, but some ghastly sense of foreboding warned him that it was true. The sooner he was rid of Miss Field, the better. Meanwhile their relationship was exactly the same as before. He decided to wait a couple of weeks then get her transferred to another department, maybe with a rise. She wouldn't object to that.

Mr. Taylor of the Fulla Beans account was in town. David didn't relish the thought, but as usual he was elected to entertain him. Did these poor out of towners *never* get tired of the inevitable clip joint night-club, and the pathetic blowsy hostesses? It seemed not. Once more David had to fix him up, this time with a big redhead called Dora. Dora laughed a lot, and suggested that it would be a lot of fun if Burt Taylor *and* David accompanied her back to her flat. Neither of them were too impressed with the idea, Burt because he didn't want to share her, and David because he didn't want to know! She was very insistent, and when Burt Taylor, eyes bulging at the thought of the show she was offering, started to think it wasn't such a bad idea after all, David became really fed up.

He managed to finally persuade them to go off on their own. How he hated this sort of entertaining, these night-club scrubbers weren't for him. He returned to his hotel room and went to bed.

The week dragged. Wednesday afternoon he 'phoned to speak to his children. They had just got home from school and were

having tea. Anna told him Mrs. Cooper was out. He was sure
Linda wouldn't mind if he popped in to see them, maybe she
would let him stay for dinner. It was all a question of time with
Linda, eventually she would realize the only sensible thing was
to take him back. He told Anna he would be right over, she
mumbled something in Spanish, he could hear the children's
excited squeaks in the background.

He left the office in high humour. He went to Hamleys and
filled his arms with toys. He stopped at Swiss Cottage and
bought flowers.

By the time he arrived at the house it was two hours later.
Linda answered the door tight-lipped and furious. She stood in
the doorway. 'The children are being bathed.'

'All right, I can wait.'

She didn't move. 'David, we have an agreement you visit the
children at the week-end.'

'Oh. What difference does it make? Are you going to penalize
me because I want to see my children?'

She stood back wearily, she didn't want to be unfair as far
as the children were concerned, after all, he was their father.
'Well, come in, but please don't do this again.'

'What do you mean? Please don't visit my own children
again?'

'No, David, I mean please keep to the agreed visiting times.'

'You surprise me, Linda,' he shook his head, 'I never thought
you would use Janey and Stephen as a weapon against me.'

Her eyes filled with tears at the injustice of what he was
saying. 'But I'm not, I'm just trying to do what's best.'

He looked at her coldly. 'And you think that it's best that
two innocent young children should not be allowed to see their
father.'

'Oh David, you're twisting what I'm saying.'

'I'm not twisting anything, I'm just repeating you.' He thrust
the flowers at her 'Take these—or perhaps you would prefer to
throw them out like you would me.'

She took the flowers. 'I'll see if bathtime is finished.'

'Can I have permission to go upstairs and see them in the
bath?" his voice was acid.

'Of course.'

Stephen stood at the top of the stairs, scrubbed and clean in
striped pyjamas. 'Daddy.'

Linda heard the cry of joy downstairs. She glanced at her
watch, it was six o'clock. Maybe she should call Jay and tell him
she couldn't keep their date. She felt so confused. David's
attitude towards her was so unfair, he acted as if the whole
thing was her fault. He came downstairs, Janey cuddled in his

arms, Stephen clinging to his hand. He fetched the packages from the car and the children yelled with excitement.

Linda shut the door of the living-room and left them all together. She went upstairs and lay down on the bed. She had thought the most painful part of divorce was over, but when you have children it's never over, there's always a small questioning voice—'Why doesn't Daddy live here any more? When can Daddy come back? Do you love Daddy?'

She 'phoned Jay. He was out.

After an hour she went downstairs. With a forced bright smile she said, 'Come along—time for bed, school tomorrow.'

Stephen glared at her, 'Oh, Mummy!' Janey started to cry.

David said, 'How about ten more minutes?'

'Please, Mummy,' Janey begged.

'Oh, O.K.—but no longer.' Linda glanced again at her watch, it was past seven and Jay was due at eight. She didn't want him and David to meet. She wished she could contact Jay and put him off. She didn't want to but she didn't feel like going out now.

After another twenty minutes the children were at last safely in bed, with David reading them stories. By the time he came downstairs it was a quarter to eight. His mood was cordial. 'I could do with a drink.'

She was nervous. She had a perfect right to go out on a date, but she instinctively knew David wouldn't like it.

David poured himself a scotch. 'You know Stephen's a very bright lad, we must have a serious talk about his future.'

She pulled herself together. 'Yes, we must, but not now. I have to get changed,' her voice became defiant. 'I'm going out.'

'That's nice.' There was a silence, then David added, 'Pretty cushy life you've got.'

Linda's voice was controlled, 'I beg your pardon?'

'Well, you know, no worries, nice house, I foot all the bills and you can just gad about doing what you like.'

'I don't gad about and you know it.'

'Oh come off it, Linda. You're an attractive woman, a divorcee. Any man knows he's on to a good thing—a bit of free crumpet is always popular, you must have dozens of offers, why I bet . . .'

Her face was blazing. 'Get out! Get out of here!'

He put his drink down calmly. 'What's the matter, don't try and tell me you're not getting it.'

'Please go, David, please go right now.'

He sauntered to the door. 'All right, all right, don't get excited. I won't hang around to mess up your date, I'll just get back to my hotel room—don't worry about me, just have a good time.'

He was at the front door and she slammed it in his face.

David climbed into his car. Thoughtless bitch! She was as bad as Claudia, they were all the same, all bitches trying to grab you by the balls and squeeze everything out of you. He drove around the block and then came back and parked a few houses away. May as well wait and see who she was going out with.

Jay was a few minutes late, but hardly late enough for Linda to have time to recover. He found her in tears.

'I can't go out,' she sobbed.

He put his arm around her and she leaned her head against his chest. She told him a jumbled account of what had happened. He was sympathetic. 'You talk to your lawyer first thing tomorrow. You can get a court order to stop him bothering you —he has set times to see the kids, and he'll just have to stick to them.'

'I just thought it would be so mean of me not to let him see the children.'

'That's how he wants you to feel. He's probably had enough screwing around and wants to come back. His only way of getting at you is through the kids.'

'Do you think so?'

'Sure, listen, Linda—I'm experienced in these things. He blew a beautiful set-up with you, you're not some little ding-a-ling, you're a lovely woman, and I bet he wants you back.' He paused and then asked casually, 'How do you feel about him?'

'I don't know. I mean I don't love him or anything like that. It's just that in spite of his insults I feel sorry for him, after all, I do have the home and children and what does he have?'

'Hey, whoa baby, you're starting to think like he wants you to think. He chose, didn't he?'

She nodded, 'You're right.'

'Good, at least you're starting to realize I'm always right!' He laughed. 'Now go upstairs, powder your nose, put on your black dress and let's go.'

She smiled. 'Yes, Jay.'

He took her to Annabels. They dined elegantly. Jay entranced her with amusing stories about the film and the location in Israel. He told her about his children, there were three of them, one by his first wife and two by his second.

'Beautiful blond Californians,' he said wryly. 'I don't get to see them too much, Lori hated children.'

'How old are they?'

'Well, Caroline's the eldest, she's fifteen—a real cukoo kid. Lives in San Francisco with Jenny, my first wife. Then there's Lee, he's ten, and Lance who's nine. They've got a great step-father now, and I see them whenever I'm in L.A.'

'I've never been to America. Is it as glossy as it all looks on the screen?'

Jay laughed, 'Well I guess you could say Hollywood is pretty glossy—personally the only thing I really dig there is the weather.'

After dinner they were joined by friends of Jay's, also in the movie business. It was a lovely evening. Jay took Linda home in his chauffeured studio car, he kissed her on the cheek.

'How about Saturday?' he asked.

'Yes,' she replied quietly.

'I'll call you tomorrow anyway. And don't forget, get on to your lawyer first thing.'

'I will.'

They smiled at each other. She let herself into the house and watched him through the window as he climbed back into the car. She liked him a lot.

Claudia buried herself into bed at her apartment. She huddled beneath the covers, bruised, used and frightened to face herself. She called her agent the day after the debacle with Conrad and told him everything was fixed, he should hear from the Studio in about a week. She took a variety of pills and slept, or tried to.

Claudia was not naïve, there had been many men, many different scenes, the blue movies, but never anything so degrading as the evening at Conrad's house. When she closed her eyes visions of evil smiling faces swept before her, all the things they had made her do raced through her thoughts. She could still feel their hands, her body screamed from the aches of sexual misuse. She stayed underneath the covers, not eating, ignoring the telephone, inert and numb for several days. Nobody cared, nobody came. If she died it would probably be months before they discovered her. Where were all her so-called friends? At last she forced herself to get up. She was thin and white. She dressed and went out. The people in the street disgusted her. She went to see Giles, he was away in Majorca. She returned home and hacked off all her tawny glorious hair with her nail scissors. She slipped back to bed, and this time, slept.

When she woke the next day she felt much better. She opened some cans and ate. She was horrified to see what she had done to her hair, it stuck out at all angles and looked a mess. She read the papers and magazines that had piled up by the front door. She called her agent. No, he hadn't heard yet. Had she read that Conrad was getting married? She grabbed the papers again, there it was—Conrad Lee—sixty-two years old, famous producer was to marry twenty-year-old model and ex-debutante Shirley Sheldon.

Shirley Sheldon! Claudia gasped in amazement. Shirley Sheldon! Ex-fiancée of the Hon. Jeremy Francis, ex-stripper. It couldn't possibly be true. Shirley was such a drag, a phoney debutante. She always had been interested in getting on in life. She had only hooked up with Jeremy because he was a Hon. Claudia supposed she was going for Conrad's loot, and also because he was fairly famous. But what on earth could he see in her? She wasn't *that* pretty, she had a lousy figure, and she was a dreary bore. The old schmuck must reckon she really was a debutante. What a laugh! Why, she had introduced them. She remembered Shirley coming to her party and having that great suntan, she must have got it in Israel. What a cow! Where had she been the other night? Didn't he involve his fiancée in his orgies? Why not?

Claudia read the article again. The wedding was set for that same day. She just couldn't believe it. Thin Shirley Sheldon, certainly not an ex-debutante, certainly not twenty.

'Ha,' Claudia snorted aloud. It was all too much.

On a sudden impulse she raced to the 'phone booth and looked up the Hon. Jeremy. She found his number and dialled quickly. He was home, stammering and unsure as ever. 'I s-s-say Claudia, how nice,' he said after she announced herself.

'Are you going to Shirley's wedding?' she asked bluntly.

'Oh, I should jolly well s-s-say so, wouldn't want to miss that— w-w-what?!' he chortled happily.

'Well, I thought we might go together,' she said casually. 'It's about time we got together.'

'I say, what a good idea, s-s-shall I fetch you?'

She smiled, it was all too easy. 'Terrific—what time?'

'Well if the reception s-s-starts at s-s-six, I think if I fetched you at about five-thirty.'

'Marvellous, Jeremy.' She gave him her address and hung up. What an idiot he was.

She spent the afternoon at the hairdresser, and emerged with a whole new look. Her hair, short like a boy's, sleek, with long sideboards. Fortunately it was the look of the moment anyway, all the top models were wearing it. It went well with the ultra short, skimpy gold shift she chose to wear.

Jeremy was impressed. 'I s-s-say, old girl, you look absolutely super!' he said when he called for her.

She fixed him with a strong martini and noticed his spotty complexion was still the same. She resisted a strong temptation to ask him if he ever got laid.

'Well, well, so good old Shirley's finally making the wedding bells scene,' she said, sipping at her martini and exhibiting a great deal of leg as she sat in the big armchair opposite Jeremy.

His eyes bulged. 'Yes, I'll s-s-say.'

'Whatever happened with you two?'

'Well,' he waved his long skinny arms about, 'she's a s-s-s-super girl, great fun and all that, but she s-s-said she needed someone more mature.' He took a few gulps of his drink, his Adam's apple bobbing rhythmically, 'We're s-s-still great pals,' he added lamely.

'Just as well,' Claudia said briskly, 'after all, she is much older than you.'

'She is?' Jeremy looked surprised.

'Well, I mean, I don't want to give away any secrets, I mean she looks after herself so well—but after all, how long can she go on fooling everybody?' Claudia shook her head wisely, and Jeremy stared at her, his mouth hanging open inanely. 'Shall we go?' Claudia asked brightly, jumping up and smoothing her dress down.

'Er—yes.' Jeremy got up too. He was very tall and ungainly—a real chinless wonder—Claudia thought, it was no surprise Shirley had ditched him for Conrad, at least Conrad was famous.

Jeremy drove a shiny red M.G. It was very uncomfortable, he had to cram himself behind the wheel.

'Why don't you get a bigger car?' Claudia asked. After all his parents were supposed to be loaded.

'Oh, this little bus really gets around,' he said proudly, 'wouldn't s-s-swop this one in.'

He drove badly, jerking the clutch, cutting up other drivers without even noticing and racing cars at the traffic lights.

Claudia felt sick by the time they arrived. She needed a fast drink. What a joy it would be to see Shirley's and Conrad's faces when they saw her. *Quel surprise!*

David sat in his car smoking a cigarette. He didn't have to wait long before a sleek black chauffeur-driven limousine glided to a halt in front of his house—well, Linda's house. A man emerged, David was too far away to recognize him. He swore under his breath and edged his car a little nearer, but it was too late. The man had already gone inside.

Well, Linda was certainly doing all right for herself, the man, whoever he was, obviously had money. Women were such bitches! They couldn't wait—here they were divorced only a few weeks, and there was Linda going out and living it up. Why she'd probably had this sucker all lined up! Cow! She was no better than Claudia. He waited impatiently for them to come out. They were certainly taking their time, probably having a quick one in the living-room. He contemplated going in and punching the man—whoever it was—on the nose. But she probably wouldn't let him in anyway. She would pay for this when he took her back. At the rate she was going maybe he wouldn't even want her back. He sat, immersed in his thoughts until they finally came out. The man, the bastard, had his arm around her. The chauffeur jumped out and opened the door for them. They climbed in, the chauffeur got back in the car and they slid off.

David set off in pursuit, keeping a discreet distance between the cars. It was unfortunate for him that at Swiss Cottage the chauffeur decided to skip through a yellow light, and David following him on red, was stopped by a policeman on a motor-cycle.

He had to produce his licence and insurance and the police-man gave him a lecture on dangerous driving. Of course, by the time he was free to go their car had long vanished into the night. Pangs of hunger didn't help his mood. He hated eating on his own, but at this hour there seemed no alternative. He decided to go somewhere cheerful and he headed for Carlo's. It was packed as usual. Lots of bright looking birds in their most startling outfits, and the actors, photographers and men about town who were their escorts for the night.

The head waiter told him with a phoney sad shake of his head that it would be at least two hours before he could squeeze a table for one in. David slipped him a pound and the waiter became a little brighter about the prospects. He asked David to wait at the bar, and he would see what he could manage.

David ordered a scotch on the rocks and surveyed the scene. He couldn't help thinking about the last time he had been here with Claudia. He wondered what she was doing now, but he didn't really care; if it hadn't been for her he would be at home with his wife.

A woman was staring at him. He stared back. She had mounds of silver-blonde hair piled on top of her head, and she wore a white mink coat. Her face looked familiar. She was with two men who were in deep conversation—loud old Americans—one had even gone as far as wearing cowboy boots. She sat there, cool, beautiful and remote from her companions.

Suddenly David remembered her. It was Lori Grossman. He put his drink down and went over to her table. 'Hello, Lori,' he said, and then by way of jogging her memory, 'it's David, David Cooper.'

Her smile was small, sensuous, she extended an elongated whiter than white hand. 'David, how nice.'

The two men stopped talking and she introduced the elder one, he must have been all of seventy, as Marvin Rufus—her husband. David looked surprised, whatever happened to Jay?

'Sit down—have a drink,' Marvin said, and immediately resumed his conversation with the other man.

Lori slipped off the white mink coat, revealing black lace, cut to a low V. She had small but perfect breasts. She was wearing no bra.

'I ditched Jay,' she said in answer to his unspoken question. 'He was a real cheap bastard.' She adjusted a fabulous diamond bracelet clamped around her thin wrist. 'Marvin knows how to treat a woman. . . .' She trailed off, her pale frosty aquamarine eyes staring hungrily into David's.

This one was ready! David congratulated himself on being so attractive to women. She was eating him up with her eyes! 'Linda and I are divorced,' he said, 'just didn't work out.'

'Yeah, I know,' she drawled.

'You know?' he said surprised.

She smiled. 'A little birdie told me and I suppose *you* know that my darling peachy ex is taking out your ex. Isn't that cosy?'

'Jay taking out Linda?' David couldn't believe it.

'That's right, honey.' She moved closer to him and he felt a sudden pressure from her leg under the table. His hand touched a silky thigh. She couldn't wait! Marvin and the other man talked on, something about market prices in London, and would the pound be devalued. 'How long are you here for?' David asked.

'Just a couple of days,' she drawled.

That would be long enough. If Jay was knocking off Linda he might as well grab a piece of Lori. She was obviously ready, willing and able.

Under the table his hand crept further up her leg, reaching smooth skin above the stocking top.

'Are you meeting someone?' Lori asked. David shook his head. 'Well, you must join us, Marve won't mind. He'll be talking business for hours.'

In a few minutes their table was ready. True to what Lori had said, her husband continued his marathon conversation with the other man, barely pausing to eat.

Lori ate like a sparrow, nibbling small pieces of steak, picking at a salad. Then the music started and David asked her to dance. She was very tall, her bird's nest of hair making her even more so.

'Well?' he said when they were on the dance floor. The prospect of messing up this spectacular piece of aloofness was exciting him. She felt his excitement and pressed closer.

'Marve will want to go gambling when we leave here, I'll say I'm too tired, and you'll offer to take me to the hotel. We have separate suites there, he won't disturb us.'

He gripped her to him hard, he could feel her bones, she ground her body to the sound of music sensually.

'What if it doesn't work?' he asked.

'It will work,' she gave a low laugh, 'it always has before.'

Jay 'phoned Linda on Thursday and Friday as he had promised. His 'phone call each day gave her a feeling of well being. He made her feel alive and attractive again.

She rushed around the shops searching for a suitable dress to beguile him with on Saturday night. Everything seemed to have been made for flat-chested seventeen year olds. She finally settled for a very simple white crepe shift, much too expensive, but beautifully cut. She spent the day absorbed in her children, taking them for a long walk on the Heath, and letting them ride on the donkeys. She loved her children, and with Jay in her life she seemed to love them even more.

She took her time getting ready for him—long hot scented bath, careful make-up, freshly combed hair, white crepe dress, few pieces of good jewellery. She couldn't stop herself from thinking about him making love to her. Did he want to? He obviously liked her a lot, would he make a pass at her tonight? Make a pass, what a juvenile thought. She was a divorced woman with two children, not a teenager on a second date. Would he want to sleep with her tonight. That was more like it. She wanted him, she needed him. It had been a long time. Finally she was ready and he was, as usual, on time.

'You look lovely,' he said, 'you don't mind if we stop at a party for a few minutes? Business.'

The party was in Belgravia, an elegant pre-Victorian house, complete with butler and maid at the door. Linda was immediately intimidated. She glanced around the luxurious living-room and recognized several well known faces. The place seemed to be filled with stars and beautiful young girls. Jay knew everyone. He moved around easily, greeting people and Linda trailed miserably behind him, feeling out of place and suddenly plain. To top it all, a gorgeous blonde whom Linda recognized as Susan Standish, put her arm around him intimately and whispered loud enough for Linda to hear—'You bastard! How dare you leave before I woke up this morning!'

Jay pushed her away, laughing easily.

Linda turned and walked away, nobody seemed interested in talking to her. It was one of those parties where everyone was a 'somebody' in the film industry and unless you were a 'somebody' or a beautiful young starlet, nobody wanted to know. She found a chair and sat down. What a fool she had been. Jay wasn't interested in her, he was probably just sorry for her. She sat brooding. After all, he was a big director, he had the pick of all the girls in London, what could she offer him that he couldn't get more brightly packaged elsewhere? He was heading for her across the room now, she turned on a bright smile, mustn't let him see she was upset—embarrass him, what for? There was nothing between them.

'Why did you rush off?' he asked, his eyes faintly amused, 'you left me in the clutches of a female would-be star—always in hot pursuit of us poor old directors. Why didn't you stay and protect me?'

She felt like saying—well you slept with her last night, what do you expect? Instead she just smiled and said, 'I don't know, I thought I'd sit down for a while.'

'We can go in a minute, I just had to put in an appearance otherwise Jan would have never let me forget it.' He pointed to a striking woman in her forties, their hostess.

They left soon after, and dined at a small French restaurant in Chelsea. Before they were half way through their meal, Jay asked her what was wrong. Linda was bad at concealing her feelings, and her manner with Jay had become almost stilted.

'Nothing.' Inexplicably she found her eyes filling with tears.

He changed the subject. 'Let's take the kids out tomorrow, I'm looking forward to meeting them.'

She couldn't think of an excuse. 'All right,' she nodded numbly, 'would you mind awfully if I went home now, I've got a ghastly headache?'

He looked surprised but didn't question her. He paid the bill and they left. Conversation was sparse travelling back to Finchley. Linda found the presence of the chauffeur sitting faceless in the front, a deterrent. At the door she offered Jay her hand and he shook it gravely. 'I'll see you and the kids about twelve tomorrow, we'll take them out to lunch.'

She nodded listlessly. In the morning she would 'phone and put him off.

The wedding reception was crowded.

'Steer me to the bar, I need a drink!' Claudia said at once.

'I s-s-say, shouldn't we try to find them first?' Jeremy stuttered, looking vacantly around.

'No, let's get a drink.'

They headed for the bar. Claudia had a fast glass of champagne, and felt a bit better. She surveyed the crowd, a lot of Shirley's pseudo society friends, rather a tatty-looking group. Here and there were gathered the Americans, the women noticeable in their mink coats or stoles, and the men for their loud voices.

'Dreary looking bunch,' Claudia commented.

Jeremy looked at her vaguely.

A waiter passed with a tray of canapés and Claudia grabbed a few. 'Ugh—lousy food!' she exclaimed, 'a bit of dried up old sausage meat, sort of like the bridegroom!' She giggled, and gulped down some more champagne.

Two tall, thin, slightly less spotty replicas of Jeremy approached them. 'J. Francis old chap,' one of them announced loudly, clamping his hand firmly on Jeremy's shoulder and surveying Claudia, 'how are we then?'

'Oh h-h-hello, Robin.'

Robin released his grip on Jeremy. 'Who's your lovely lady then?'

Jeremy waved his arms about, 'Er, Claudia P-p-Parker—this is Robin Humphries.'

'Lord Humphries, old boy, let the girl know who she's talking to.' He smiled at Claudia, revealing a line of crooked nicotine-stained teeth.

She smiled back. She was just starting her fourth glass of champagne.

The other young man pressed anxiously forward. 'I'm Peter Fore-Fitz Gibbons,' he said.

'I say C-c-Claudia,' Jeremy edged between her and Robin and Peter, 'we really should go and look for S-s-Shirley and her h-h-husband.'

'Whatever you say, lover,' Claudia winked at the two young men, 'see you later then. Keep it up.'

They exchanged puzzled looks.

'Funny girl, eh?' Robin said.

'Must be funny to be out with old Jeremy,' Peter agreed.

They watched her as she swayed across the room.

'Wouldn't mind a slice,' Robin said.

'Yes,' agreed Peter.

Claudia had spotted Shirley, and she made her way over to her.

'Shirley! You old dark horse!' She stood firmly in front of her, one hand balancing a glass of champagne, the other holding on to Jeremy.

Shirley didn't bat an eyelid. She smiled politely. 'Claudia darling, such a surprise! So glad you could make it, and Jeremy poppet,' she stood on tiptoe while he placed a sloppy kiss on her cheek, 'divine to see you both.'

'Where's the bridegroom?' Claudia asked, her words slurring slightly.

'Oh, he's around somewhere,' Shirley said brightly. 'Love your hairstyle, darling, wish I could get away with such a harsh cut.'

Claudia smiled. 'Oh, I'm sure you could.'

Jeremy stammered, 'Jolly good show this whole thing.'

Both girls ignored him.

'Conrad was telling me about the fun you had the other night,' Shirley said, her voice sugary.

Claudia gave her a sharp look. 'Yes, I thought *you* would be there.'

Shirley giggled softly, 'Why be there when I can see the film.'

'What film?' Claudia's voice became hard.

'Oh, Conrad always takes a film of those evenings.' Shirley smiled triumphantly, 'Didn't you know, it's his hobby actually, you must come over one night and we'll show it to you.'

Claudia stared at her, a horrible sinking feeling in her stomach. She knew Shirley wasn't lying.

'Well, darling,' Shirley continued, 'you did say you wanted to be in his movie.' With a tinkling laugh, she turned away to greet another guest.

Claudia stood there, furious and burning. The son-of-a-bitch!

Jeremy said, 'I say, old girl, everything s-s-super?'

She snatched her arm away. 'Oh shut up!'

'What,' Jeremy spluttered, looking hurt.

'Nothing,' she finished the last of her drink and handed Jeremy the empty glass, 'get me some more, will you?'

She had seen Conrad, he was joking and laughing with an elderly couple. She swayed over. 'Hey man,' she said in a loud voice, 'con-grat-ulations.'

His piercing eyes swept over her with disinterest. Shirley walked over and attached herself protectively to his arm.

Claudia smiled at Shirley. 'He's a lousy lay—but then I hear you are too, so that makes it cosy.'

The elderly couple exchanged glances and edged away. Jeremy appeared at that moment with a fresh glass of champagne for her. Claudia took it and held it up to them, 'Here's to a couple of beat-up old has-beens!'

People nearby were turning to stare.

Conrad said in a low controlled voice, 'Get the hell out of here, you little tramp.'

Claudia smiled. 'My pleasure, you old fart!' She took hold of a startled Jeremy's arm: 'Come on—let's get out of this.'

A scarlet Jeremy exited with her.

Outside she started to laugh. 'Wasn't that funny? Wasn't that too much?'

Jeremy stood there, his face still red, his spots standing out angrily. 'I s-s-say, Claudia, how could you. . . .'

'How could I what, man? It was only a giggle.' She suddenly flung her arms around him and kissed him, forcing his stiff lips open with her tongue. 'Come on, let's go back to my place and have some fun.'

Jeremy was reluctant to go, secretly wanting to go back to the wedding reception and apologize, but Claudia insisted. 'I'll show you what it's all about, baby,' she whispered.

Back at her flat she fixed strong drinks, and turned on the record player full blast. Jeremy sat rigid, unsure of himself, while she danced around the room undulating her body and peeling off her dress. She didn't take too much notice of him as she got carried away with the music, she danced and caressed her own breasts, then suddenly ready for him, she came over to where he sat. She began to pull his clothes off. He began to object.

'What are you—a faggot?' she screamed.

He got up and bolted for the door, running off down the stairs like a startled rabbit. Claudia followed him to the top of the stairs yelling after him but he didn't come back. In her drunken haze she was amazed, it was the first time a man—well whatever he was—had turned her down. He had to be queer, those chinless wonder types usually were. She went back into her flat and took a swig out of the scotch bottle. Lousy faggot! How dare he refuse her. Probably couldn't do it. She giggled, and then her eyes inexplicably filled with tears. What was her life all about? Where was she getting? It didn't seem to be very far.

All she wanted out of life was to be a star, was that asking so very much? Tears rolled down her cheeks. She turned the music even louder then lay on the floor by the Hi Fi speakers. The volume of the music excited her. She started to manipulate her own body—if that crazy skinny pansy couldn't satisfy her, then she would just have to do it herself. Before she could complete the job she fell into a deep drunken sleep, her snores mingling with the loud sounds of Charlie Parker.

True to what Lori had said after dinner Marvin immediately announced he wanted to gamble. The four of them stood in a huddle on the pavement in front of the restaurant.

'Wanna come and be my lucky charm?' Marvin asked Lori.

She wrapped her mink coat tightly around her and shook her head.

Cowboy boots, anxious to be off, stamped around.

'Well, I guess I'll just play a little craps then,' Marvin said.

'I'll see Lori back to the hotel if you like,' David said quickly, seizing the opportunity.

'That's mighty nice of you,' Marvin boomed. He kissed Lori on the cheek. 'All winnings for you sugar.' And with a brief handshake to David, he and Cowboy boots were away in a cloud

of cigar smoke and resonant Texan drawl. He was obviously a
trusting husband, either that or he didn't mind.

Lori laughed. 'Didn't I tell you?'

They walked around the corner to his car, and Lori whispered
to him, 'Are you big? I only like big men.'

In the car she acted like a bitch in heat, grabbing for him
immediately. He was proud of what he had to offer her. He
drove quickly to the hotel. Lori swept through the lobby,
haughty and imperial, her white mink drawing envious stares
from women. She stopped and greeted an actor she knew. The
man gave David an amused look.

Her suite was on the sixth floor, very luxurious, furnished in
opulent blue and silver. She threw her mink casually over a
chair—'Make yourself a drink, honey,' she drawled. 'I'm just
going to put on something more comfortable.' Her dialogue was
straight out of a Hollywood movie! He opened a bottle of
champagne that was conveniently on ice and poured two glasses.
This was the life! A beautiful woman in beautiful surroundings, champagne, what more could a man ask? She came back
soon—wearing a sheer black full length frilled négligée, her
hair still piled high. He handed her a glass of champagne and
she took a small sip, then lay down on the sofa, the négligée
falling back slightly revealing milky white thighs.

He didn't feel quite ready. She held out her arms to him.
'Come to baby, honey,' she drawled. He put his drink down and
went over to her.

'There's a silk robe in the bathroom,' she purred, 'why don't
you get out of your clothes and be comfortable like me.'

He did feel a bit restricted, and the setting did seem too perfect to start struggling out of his clothes all over the floor. He
kissed her on the mouth, tasting her lipstick and then he went
to the bathroom and put on the robe she had suggested. It was
paisley silk, probably her husband's. He admired his masculine
figure in the mirror, not bad for forty!

She was waiting for him, draped across the sofa looking like
a *Vogue* advertisement. He took her in his arms, she put her
hands inside his robe scratching his chest gently with talon-like
fingernails. He stroked her body, she was very thin with small
hard breasts and extended large nipples. An exciting body—not
soft and warm like Linda, nor curvy and exciting like Claudia.
But very sensuous all the same. Like a smooth white snake.

He parted her négligée. Her legs were exceptionally long,
crowned at the top by a small mound of silver-blonde hair,
matched perfectly to the hair on her head. She opened them
slowly, her hands moving round his back, digging her nails into
him pulling him closer.

With surprise he realized he wasn't yet ready. To distract her from this fact he moved his head to her breasts and started to kiss her there. She moaned softly, digging her nails even harder into his back. After a few minutes she grew impatient, and her hands travelled down his body. Her eyes were closed, but they snapped open suddenly when she felt him.

'What's the matter, honey?' she purred, a slight edge to her voice, 'this is real Georgia pussy!'

Embarrassed he said, 'It's nothing, just give me a moment.'

Annoyed she closed her eyes again, this time her hands working on him, pulling, stroking, kneading.

'Come on, sugar,' she pleaded, 'this little snatch is waiting for you!'

His physical reaction was nil. This was a nightmare, something that had never happened to him before. He grew panicky, conjuring up every erotic picture he could think of. Nothing, absolutely nothing. He tried to remember the last time he had had sex. Mousey Miss Field, his horrifying secretary. Desperately he thought of the evening he had spent with her.

Suddenly it was all right, he felt himself swelling, growing big, bigger.

Lori sighed with pleasure, 'That's beautiful, honey,' she wrapped her long pale legs around him, and he started to enter her, forcefully, powerfully, he would show her!

He drove into her, strong brutal thrusts, she squealed with delight, 'Ooh—ooh—that's great, honey—that's wild—ooh—don't stop—don't stop,' her voice changed, 'why have you stopped?'

He didn't reply, he was too overcome with embarrassment. He had heard about this happening to other men, but not to him.

She was getting angry, her sleek sexy drawl was turning shrill.

'What's the matter with you? Are we going to ball or not? If I want this sort of action I can get it with my husband!'

He rolled off her. 'I'm sorry.'

Furious she sat up—'You're sorry.' She stood up too, her hard breasts and exotic nipples staring accusingly at him. 'Get the hell out of here, I've got to find myself a real man.'

Humiliated, he went to the bathroom and dressed. When he came out she was on the 'phone purring, 'Sure, honey, in ten minutes' time will be fine.'

He let himself out. He was ashamed, what a terrible thing to happen, and why? He had fancied her, strongly fancied her, it wasn't her fault. Although maybe it was, after all she made no secret of the fact that there were many men other than her husband. He went to the bar and ordered a brandy. By the time he had finished it he had convinced himself it was all Lori's fault. Lousy bitch! She had castrated him with thoughts of all the other men. They were all the same, women were all the same. They all wanted to render you impotent in some way or other.

On a sudden impulse he decided to give it another try that night. Not with Lori of course, what about Miss Field Mouse? She was quiet and inoffensive, and he was going to get rid of her anyway, so what harm, one more bash? He didn't even fancy her so it would be real proof if he could make it with her.

He vaguely remembered where she lived. She was sure to be home. He had another brandy and set off.

Hammering on her door he found himself as hard as a rock. She got out of bed to answer the door, clutching a woollen dressing-gown around her, lank brown hair, sallow pinched face.

'Mr. Cooper!' she said surprised.

He pushed past her, taking his clothes off and dropping them on the floor. 'Get undressed,' he commanded.

Averting her eyes she obeyed him.

He took her savagely, pinning her puny body to the floor.

There was nothing wrong with him!

CHAPTER SEVENTEEN

LINDA NEVER DID 'phone and cancel Jay the next morning. He came and took them all out to lunch and the children were captivated. He told them stories, played with them and took them to a movie. In the evening he stayed at the house for a bacon and egg supper and Linda found herself unable to break off the relationship. She put Miss Susan Standish to the back of her mind and continued going out with Jay.

She liked him, the children liked him, Janey especially. He was wonderful with them. It became routine to spend every Sunday together. Jay always thought of new things for them to do, and they looked forward to their day out eagerly. It was a good thing, because since David's last visit he had not been heard from. Linda was furious, it was a pleasure as far as she was concerned, but she thought it selfish and mean of David to completely ignore the children. They were constantly asking, 'When's Daddy coming?' 'Where is he?' If it hadn't been for Jay at week-ends she was sure they would have been a lot more upset. 'Doesn't Daddy love us any more?' Janey asked sadly one afternoon.

'Of course he does, darling,' Linda replied, hugging her little girl to her. 'He's just very busy.'

'I love Uncle Jay,' Janey said solemnly, 'he's not too busy.'

So their relationship flourished, and at the end of a few weeks Linda found herself firmly in love with him. They went to the theatre, small intimate restaurants, large plush restaurants, movies, in fact they spent almost every night together, and regularly every week-end he would spend with her and the children.

Then they went to parties and museums and for drives in the country. He was amusing, attentive, interested in everything she did, but he never attempted more than a brief—almost brotherly —goodnight kiss.

It started to drive her mad. Her body screamed out for some sort of attention. Whenever they danced she would have to hold herself in tight check to prevent herself pushing her body intimately against him. When they kissed she was in suspense waiting for him to go further. But he remained the perfect gentleman. Never touching her.

It reached a point where she decided she could go on no longer. She resolved to bring it up at the next suitable moment. She rehearsed what she would say but it all sounded trite and horrible.

The opportunity came sooner than she expected. There was an end-of-film party at the studio, and Linda was chatting to Jay and Bob Jeffries, the assistant director, when up marched Miss Standish. She was wearing the same white trouser suit Linda had seen her in before. It suited her, complementing her glowing skin and tumbled blonde hair.

'Jay darling,' she murmured, 'can I have a little word with you?'

She had sly eyes, a secret smile always present.

'What is it, Susan?' his tone was pleasant.

'Privately.'

Jay shrugged his shoulders at Linda and Bob and walked away with Susan.

Linda said, 'Is she in the film?'

Bob laughed. 'At the moment she is but I've got a feeling she's going to land on the cutting-room floor.'

'Oh,' Linda quickly changed the subject, she didn't want Bob to think she was jealous.

Jay returned quite soon and didn't mention the incident, but Linda knew that as soon as they were alone she was going to bring it up.

After the party, joined by Bob Jeffries and his wife they went to Annabels. It was impossible to talk there, and on the drive home there was the ever present chauffeur.

'You're very withdrawn tonight,' Jay said, his tone light.

She nodded.

'What's the matter?' he was concerned.

'I don't want to talk now,' she said looking towards the chauffeur. 'Come in for coffee if you like.'

She had never invited him into her house when he took her home before, and she felt a little strange about it. She sat him down in the living-room and went into the kitchen. Now that she had him there what was there to say? It was all so difficult, there were no words that could really express the way she felt.

Absently she placed some chocolate biscuits on a plate, and filled the coffee jug. He was sitting reading the evening paper. She felt at a complete loss for words as she handed him his coffee. He solved the problem for her by speaking first.

'I have to go back to Los Angeles in two weeks.'

'Oh,' she felt deflated.

He hesitated and then said, 'How about coming with me?'

'With you?' For a few pleasant seconds she considered the possibility, then reality hit her, 'That's impossible, Jay, I couldn't leave the children.'

'Well, bring the children then, they'd love it there.'

She shook her head. 'I couldn't take them out of school, anyway. . . .'

He cut her short, 'Linda, I'm not very good at this sort of thing, I've only ever said it to idiots before,' he got up nervously, 'Linda, I'm asking you to marry me.' He rushed on, 'I love you very much, you're the most wonderful warm giving woman I've ever met. I know you've been burnt once and I know how you feel about men—but believe me I'll try to make you happy. I'm not perfect. I've been involved with a lot of stupid broads—I've got a weakness for tall blondes, I can't deny—but if you'll marry me I think everything will work and I think we could make a wonderful life together.' He paused, 'Well?'

'Jay,' she whispered his name. 'Yes, Jay, yes, yes.'

He kissed her. 'Let's do it soon, baby, like tomorrow. I can't wait for you much longer.'

She felt tears stinging her eyes. 'I love you.'

He stroked her hair then let her go. 'Go to bed, I'll call you first thing. I'll arrange everything, the sooner the better, huh?'

She nodded. 'The sooner the better,' she murmured.

Claudia spent the next few days after Shirley and Conrad's wedding in a drunken stupor. She drank a full bottle of scotch a day, occasionally cramming her mouth with sleeping pills or tranquillizers until she reached a sort of happy oblivion. She didn't eat, wash or dress but wandered around the apartment in a sordid naked splendour.

The 'phone rang but she never picked it up. One day the door buzzer rang so insistently that she was forced to answer it.

It was Giles—'Christ!' He was aghast at her appearance. He bundled her into a dressing-gown and made her drink black coffee until her eyes started to focus and she could talk.

'What kind of a trip have you been on?' he asked.

She shook her head. 'Man, I feel terrible.'

'You look terrible.'

'What day is it?'

'Oh, God, you've really been away, it's Monday.'

'Monday, I guess I went on a little bender.'

He surveyed the room, empty scotch bottles, broken records, overturned furniture. 'I guess so, who was the guy?'

She shrugged. 'No one. Just felt like getting stoned alone. What are you doing here anyway? Thought you were in Spain.'

'I've come bearing glad tidings. Your tits are world famous.' He produced a copy of *Man at Play*, one of the biggest selling men's magazines in the States. He opened it and showed her the centre fold-out. There was she in solid colour standing on her terrace with London silhouetted in the background, wearing the pink shirt which Giles had hosed with water. Her perfect rounded breasts standing out firm and full, the nipples rigid and pointed. He turned the page, there she was lying on her bed, black négligée filming around her, breasts escaping, mouth half open, eyes half closed. The next page and the next page were all of her. The caption said 'Beautiful London model and actress Claudia Parker shows us some of the better sights of Great Britain!'

'You're a big hit,' Giles said enthusiastically, 'they want us to do a whole new series of photos. They'll pay a bomb. Want us to fly to New York. Want you to meet Edgar J. Pool—owner of the magazine. This is your big chance, baby, this is successville.'

She studied the magazine, why, oh why, had she cut her hair? 'When do we go?' she asked, her face lighting up.

'As soon as we get you into shape. You look scrawny as hell and that hair, we'll have to get you a wig. Here, sign this.' He thrust a paper at her which she signed without so much as a glance. 'I'm going to book you into this health farm for a week, you really need it. I reckon about ten days from now we can go. I'll let them know. They're really wild for you—want you to be Miss Playgirl of the Year. Baby, you and I are going to be rich!'

Was it the fifth or sixth night David had spent with Miss Field? He couldn't remember. He only knew it had become a habit to leave the office, eat dinner, have a few drinks and then go hammering on her door.

She held a sort of morbid fascination for him. What was it about her that made sex so overpowering and exciting. It was certainly the most erotic sensation he had ever had. She always crept to the door clutching her woollen dressing-gown to her, he always had to command her to undress, and she took her clothes off reluctantly, revealing a thin white undernourished body. She was flat chested with flaccid nipples that didn't even harden to the touch.

However, when he was in her, pounding away, she held him in a grip of steel, squeezing and pumping the life out of him. Giving him no rest, holding him in her like a vice.

He tried to humiliate her by forcing her into ludicrous positions, but she took to them all with no argument. He hated her but he couldn't stop returning there night after night.

During the day at the office neither of them mentioned it. She crept around quietly going about her business mouse-like as usual.

He wanted to break the habit.

A busty provocative-looking girl called Ginny was doing an ad. for his company. He manœuvred an introduction to her. He found her very attractive, she reminded him of a much sexier more obvious version of Claudia.

He invited her out to dinner. She turned up in an almost topless startlingly red dress. She had very pink and white skin, and full pouty lips. This was going to be all right, he decided.

During dinner she drank frozen daquiris and giggled a lot. They danced, and her body was warm and bouncy. All the men in the restaurant were watching her, which made David feel good. At one point, during a vigorous shake, one full pink and white breast popped completely over the top of her dress, giving a full view of a pale brown nipple, wide and generous. She tucked herself back into her dress with an inane giggle.

David felt the time had come to take her back to his hotel. She put up little objection, and once there it was an easy job to peel her out of her red dress. She was wearing frilly pink panties underneath, and her body was like an overgrown cupid. Her breasts were so big and bouncy and unbelievable that he had a sneaky suspicion that they weren't breasts at all, just a lot of silicone injections put together.

He couldn't do anything, there was no excitement. Still giggling she was given money for a taxi and sent home.

He went to bed, couldn't sleep, until at last he was forced to get up and visit his Miss Field. By the time he got there his excitement was at such a peak that he hardly made it on top of her.

She had a strange power over him.

He tried with several other women, but each time the same result. His life began to revolve around Harriet Field.

He found out about her. She was thirty years old and had been with the firm for twelve years working her way up from the typing pool to become his private secretary. There was no gossip about her, she kept herself to herself, she was the office nonentity.

When he went to her at night they never talked, he just told her what to do and she did it, whatever it was. Sometimes, after, politely she would ask him if he would care for coffee or tea, he would always say no, and as soon as he could summon the strength he would get up and go.

He wondered what she thought about it all. Why did she never say anything? The whole thing was very unnatural. The next time, of course, was later that same evening. He went earlier than usual, and she was still up, clutching a skimpy cardigan around her non-existent bosom. Automatically she started to undress. It was the first time he had ever seen her get out of her clothes, usually it was just a nightgown and dressing-gown. There seemed to be layers of them, cardigan, jumper, a vest (one of the most unattractive garments he had ever seen), salmon pink bra, skirt slip, long woollen drawers, smaller pants, suspender belt and thick stockings. Shivering slightly she stood before him.

She was certainly a randy bitch, he thought, always prepared, always creamed up and ready to go. Probably been frustrated for years. Maybe he should make her wait for it tonight. She was already lying on the floor, opening pale sluggish legs. He couldn't make her wait, the burning desire he felt wouldn't let him, he ripped off his clothes hurriedly and crouched on top of her. She heaved a big sigh and they were away.

Afterwards she put on her dressing-gown and started to tidy his clothes, piling them neatly together, ready for him to put on.

He lay watching her, she really was plain, it wasn't that she made the worst of herself, it was just that there was nothing one could do to improve her. She noticed him looking at her and flushed.

'Tea or coffee, Mr. Cooper?'

'Both,' he said abruptly. She turned to go into the kitchen and he had a feeling she would bring him both if he didn't stop her. 'Sit down,' he said. She sat hesitantly, crossing her feet at the ankles, clasping her hands on her lap in front of her. 'I want to talk to you.'

They sat silently. After he had said he wanted to talk to her, he suddenly realized he didn't want to talk to her at all, he just wanted to go.

'It doesn't matter,' he said abruptly.

'Is something wrong, Mr. Cooper?'

'For God's sake don't call me Mr. Cooper.'

She lowered her eyes. 'Yes, David dear.'

Christ, she acted like a vestal virgin, she became so coy and retiring. He stood up, decisions filtering through his mind. He would fire her on Monday and this was positively the last time.

Maybe he should hammer it into her once more since this was the last visit. 'Get across the table,' he said wearily.

Linda and Jay were married a week later at Hampstead register office. Quietly with no fuss. Linda's parents were there, surprised but happy. The children dressed in their best clothes were strangely subdued. A few friends of Jay's and a few of Linda's.

Afterwards they all went back to Jay's hotel suite and ate wedding cake and drank champagne and chatted. It was very small, very informal. Soon Linda's parents said they should be starting the drive back to the country. They gathered together the children, who were going to stay with them, and all said goodbye.

Linda hugged Janey and Stephen to her. 'Mummy won't be away very long and then we're all going to live together in a beautiful big house with a swimming pool in America.'

'Wow—a swimming pool!' Stephen said delightedly.

Janey was fighting back tears, her little innocent chubby face concerned and worried. 'I hope the plane doesn't crash, Mummy.'

Linda laughed and hugged her. 'Don't be a silly baby.'

Jay picked up Janey and kissed her. 'You be a good little girl and Mummy will be back before you know it.'

Janey looked at him with big brown eyes. 'Are you my new daddy?'

Jay nodded solemnly. Janey kissed him and scampered off to her grandparents. Soon the rest of the guests departed and they were alone.

Linda took off her hat and sighed, 'I hate leaving the children.'

Jay laughed. 'It's only for a couple of weeks, you don't mind if I have a little time alone with my wife.'

'No I don't mind,' she smiled at him, 'I love you, Jay.'

There were several telegrams, one from Conrad and Shirley Lee honeymooning in Mexico—'Congratulations, English wives are best they don't want so much alimony. Love regards Conrad and Shirley.' A sarcastic one from his fifteen-year-old daughter Caroline, 'Best wishes Daddy on your fourth wife, Caroline.'

'She's a fresh kid,' Jay said grimly.

'Why do you say that?' Linda enquired.

'I don't know,' he shrugged, 'I guess it's my fault really. She's a tough little cookie—takes after her mother. I never spent any time with her, and Jenny never re-married, so I suppose it's affected her not having a father around.'

'I'd like to meet her,' Linda said quietly, 'maybe when we're settled she could come and stay with us for a while.'

'Forget it,' Jay laughed brusquely, 'her mother would never allow it, anyway, she's not a child any more, it's too late for me to start stepping in the picture.'

'She's only fifteen, Jay, I think we should try it.'

He kissed her. 'You're sweet.'

She smiled and changed the subject. 'I hope I've brought the right clothes for Jamaica, it's all been such a rush.'

'Are you sorry?'

'Sorry? What a ridiculous thing to say, of course I'm not.'

'Let's have dinner up here, the car will be picking us up at six a.m., we'd better get an early night.'

'That's a wonderful idea,' she yawned, 'I think I'll take a bath now.'

'Leave it to me, I'll order you something special.'

She went in to the bedroom. Her two suitcases and make-up case were stacked neatly at the bottom of one of the twin beds. Twin beds, how awful, she wondered how they'd manage.

She hoped she wasn't going to be a big disappointment to Jay. He was used to such beautiful women. She remembered elegant cool Lori. Perhaps it would have been better to have slept together before getting married. Then at least he would have known what he was getting. But he hadn't wanted that, although they hadn't actually discussed it she knew he didn't want that.

She unpacked a long blue silk nightdress and matching robe. It flattered her, plunging between her heavy breasts and swirling down to the floor clingingly. She took a long bath, carefully removing her daytime make-up and putting on a lighter one. She brushed her thick auburn hair, it was growing and reached almost to her shoulders. Her body and face were by no means perfect, but she was an attractive sensual-looking woman.

Jay had ordered more champagne, a delicious fish course, and thin slivers of perfectly white chicken in a cream wine and mushroom sauce on a bed of rice. Afterwards there were strawberries Romanoff and large goblets of Courvoisier brandy. After dinner Linda was bathed in a gloriously happy glow. Jay seemed to make everything perfect.

He took her to the bedroom and undressed her slowly, he made love to her beautifully. Nothing frantic, nothing rushed. He caressed her body as though there was nothing more impor-

tant in the world. He took her to the edge of ecstasy and back
again, keeping her hovering, sure of every move he made. Her
breasts grew under his touch, swelling, becoming even larger
and firmer. She floated on a suspended plane, a complete captive
to his hands and body. He had amazing control, stopping at just
the right moment. When it did happen it was only because he
wanted it to, and they came in complete unison. She had never
experienced *that* before, and she clung to him, words tumbling
out of her mouth about how much she loved him. Afterwards
they lay and smoked and talked. 'You're wonderful,' he said,
'you're a clever woman making me wait until after we were
married!'

'What?' She snuggled closer to him.

'Well, I wanted you very much, but I knew if I made a wrong
move I'd become just another guy on the make. You know I laid
Lori the first time I saw her. She came for an interview, we
locked the office door and made it then and there. Can you
imagine marrying a broad you screwed as soon as you met.
That's what kind of schmuck I was until I met you, and realized
what a real woman was like.'

She kissed him. 'But weren't you worried if we'd—well—like
each other in bed, I mean why didn't you try before?'

'Because I wasn't about to take no for an answer!'

'But I might not have said no!'

He agreed. 'No, you might not have, but you're not the sort
of woman to have an affair, you would have regretted it and I
would have become the bad one in your mind.'

'Oh,' she was amazed at how well he knew her. He was
probably right.

'What about Susan Standish?' she asked accusingly.

'I'm a man, Linda,' he said simply, 'don't expect me to make
excuses, she was a nice girl and I couldn't have you.'

Her eyes were closing. 'I love you, husband,' she murmured,
and soon she was asleep.

The health farm wasn't too bad. It was a place to relax, to think,
to take stock. Claudia submitted her body to the care of the
experts, and within a few days her physical appearance was back
to normal. She spent her days between massage and therapy,
sunning herself beside the luxurious swimming pool in the
grounds. The early English sun was weak but restful. She day-
dreamed a lot of the time, imagining herself a star, a success.
That was all she really wanted out of life, was it so much to ask?

Giles came to visit her.

'You look great!' he said enthusiastically. 'Just like the girl I
used to know.'

He had a lot of correspondence from the magazine, eagerly waiting her arrival.

'You've really made a big impression on *someone* there,' he said cheerfully, 'they can't wait. Planning promotions for you all over the place. They want to feature you as Miss Playgirl of the Year.'

Claudia was delighted. Maybe this was the opportunity she had been waiting for.

Soon she was ready to leave the farm. Giles took her back to his studio flat in Chelsea, 'I've moved all your things out of the penthouse,' he told her, 'it's not a good scene for you, you'll stay with me 'til we go.'

She was pleased. Giles was taking her over, and she liked it.

They slept in a big sprawling bed like brother and sister, and during the day Giles took her shopping for new clothes, and she bought a fabulous shiny ash-blonde wig to cover her own cropped hair until it grew back.

He paid for everything. 'An investment,' he told her airily.

Eventually he decided they were ready to go, and he wired the magazine. He received a lengthy cabled reply, they had already sent the tickets. The reply said, 'Be Prepared Big Welcome For Future Miss Playgirl. All Press alerted. Party planned for p.m. of your arrival.'

Claudia was delighted. New York awaited her.

It was just no good, David couldn't break the habit of Harriet Field.

He found it absolutely impossible to get an erection with any other woman. He tried religiously, even going so far as to take a girl to a pornographic show in the hope that that would excite him enough. The only result of that was that the girl got so worked up that when he couldn't satisfy her she called him every name under the sun.

He felt if he could only make it with anyone other than Harriet Field, the spell would be broken. But no, it remained an impossible feat, and sex with Harriet got better and better.

He took to staying at her apartment all night, and now he found he had to have her in the morning too. She became white and insipid-looking, and slowly she seemed to be draining the strength from him.

He would wake up in her cramped apartment, bad tempered and uncomfortable. It was obvious that if he was going to continue this relationship he would have to make other arrangements about her living quarters.

He didn't want to set her up in a flat, but it seemed the only answer.

She never said anything to him when they weren't having sex, she kept well out of his way. She sort of hovered, which infuriated him.

He usually drove her to the office dropping her about a block away, and she would huddle on her seat in the car, mouse-like and silent.

He hated her, but he couldn't leave her.

Was it never going to end, this mad animal desire he had for this wretched creature?

He hadn't seen his children, somehow he felt ashamed to face them.

His life was one long round of work, to which he threw himself into wholeheartedly, and sex with Harriet. Otherwise he slept.

He got very thin and haggard-looking. It's got to end soon, he reasoned with himself, I'll just keep going until I've had so much of her it will be over.

He ignored everything else and concentrated on getting Harriet out of his system. This involved sleeping with her at every possible opportunity, and now, even at the office he would sometimes lock the door and take her quickly on the floor or across his desk. It didn't help. It just seemed to make her more exciting.

He plodded on, determined to finish the affair.

At London airport Claudia was besieged by photographers.

'Look this way', 'Look over here', 'Pull your skirt up a bit', 'Let's see some leg.'

Claudia obliged, she was wearing a very short skirt with matching coat, and clingy silk sweater.

Giles stood by watching. He knew he had made a smart move getting her to sign the personal management contract. Now he had fifty per cent of her, and he had a hunch that fifty per cent was going to mean an awful lot of loot.

The Americans were about to discover a new sex symbol. She would bowl them over. Whereas in England she was just looked on as another little starlet, she had the potential to be a big star. Giles was sure of this. With the right exposure and the right publicity she had it made. He would have to watch her closely, see she didn't drink too much, didn't get laid by the wrong people. She was smiling sexily at the photographers, her head thrown back, lips parted, slanty green eyes shining. She blossomed even more in the spotlight. Her bosom strained to escape from the thin confines of her sweater, her legs were long and shapely.

'Come on baby, we'll miss the plane,' Giles said at last.

She gave the photographers one last provocative pose, then took Giles' hand, squeezing it firmly—'This is a ball!' she exclaimed.

In another part of the airport Linda and Jay sat in a V.I.P. lounge sipping coffee. Jay's was laced with a good stiff shot of whisky. He hated flying and found the only way he could climb on a plane was to be mildly stoned. Linda admired her wedding ring, a thin band of perfect diamonds. She could hardly believe how much she loved this man. After David the thought of being able to pick up the pieces and start again had seemed impossible. Now, the ten years with David seemed almost non-existent.

Jay took her hand. 'You look beautiful today.'

She smiled. 'Thank you.'

A stewardess arrived and told them it was time to board the plane. A lone photographer stopped them in the hall, 'Is it possible to have a picture, Mr. Grossman?'

'Sure,' Jay smiled amicably, and put his arm around Linda.

She was surprised. 'Why do they want your picture?' she whispered.

'The studio usually arranges it. Another plug for the movie.'

'Oh,' she nodded wisely.

They sat in comfort on the plane, Jay taking furtive swigs out of a silver hip flask. Then the great engines began to roar, and the plane taxied gently off down the runway.

One morning David woke up in a particularly foul temper. His head ached, and the room smelt of stale sex—Harriet never seemed to open any windows.

He reached for her immediately, his physical feelings overcame anything else.

After satisfying himself he felt even worse.

She made him coffee and gave him the morning paper. He smoked a cigarette and glanced at the paper. On the front page was Claudia. She faced the camera three-quarters on, bosom thrust out, hair long and wild, amused knowing smile. She looked gorgeous, shapely legs disappearing into a short skirt. 'Beautiful model and actress Claudia Parker (21) leaves for New York today. Miss Parker plans to discuss film offers. She is travelling with Giles Taylor, well known avant garde fashion and society photographer. Both deny a romance.' David felt anger—anger that she should look so good and appear so happy. After he had left her he had imagined she would go to pieces, vanish from his life.

But there she was on the front page, off to America, without apparently, a care in the world.

Little bitch! She had ruined his marriage. He turned the page in a fury, why couldn't she just have faded into oblivion?

There on the next page was a small picture of Linda with a man. She looked calm and smiling, and the man held her arm protectively.

'Mr. Jay Grossman, well known Hollywood director, and the new Mrs. Grossman leave for a honeymoon in Jamaica. Mr. Grossman has just finished making "Besheba" here and on location in Israel.'

Mrs. Jay Grossman—it was impossible. How dare she! He studied the picture intently, searching her face for signs of unhappiness, but there were none—she was serene and confident and very attractive. How could she do it without telling him? Then he remembered last week she had left three messages at the office for him to 'phone her, and he hadn't bothered to return her calls. He hadn't even seen the children for weeks.

'Blast.' He swore angrily. He had always imagined that Linda would be available when he did decide to settle down. She would take him back. Harriet Field had delayed his thoughts about getting back with Linda. He had drifted into this sordid affair with her, and everything else had been neglected. He hadn't even thought about seeing his children.

He felt trapped, what could he do? There was no Linda to save him now. The time had come to run. He thought of the words of a children's song—Run Rabbit—run rabbit—run run run—and they repeated in his mind with an insistent monotony.

There were retching sounds coming from the bathroom, soon Harriet came into the room. Unusual for her, she hadn't dressed yet, but was clutching her faded woollen robe around her.

She stood in front of him, white and wretched-looking. 'We are with child,' she stated blankly.

He stared at her in panic and slowly he realized it was too late to run, the trap was closing.

TO GLORY WE STEER

Alexander Kent

Come, cheer up, my lads! 'tis to glory we steer,
To add something more to this wonderful year;
To honour we call you, not press you like slaves,
For who are so free as the sons of the waves?
DAVID GARRICK: Heart of Oak

'To Glory We Steer' is published by
Hutchinson & Co. Ltd.

The Author

Alexander Kent has always had a great interest in naval affairs, particularly in the ships and men of the eighteenth century. At the outbreak of war in 1939, and in spite of his belonging to an army family, he joined the navy and served in the Battle of the Atlantic as well as in the campaigns in the Mediterranean and Normandy. After the war, while establishing himself as a full-time writer and self-taught naval historian, he became more determined to write an authentic story of the period which remained closest to his heart—of the ships, and the men who by choice or enforcement lived, served and died in them. As a keen yachtsman he takes every opportunity to visit the scenes of this great naval heritage, to collect and examine relics of a time which for him is still very much alive.

> 'To be sure I lose the fruits of the earth,
> But then I am gathering the flowers of the Sea.'
>
> ADMIRAL BOSCAWEN, 1756

1. THE *PHALAROPE*

THE NEW YEAR OF 1782 was only three days old but already the weather had made a decided change for the worse. Steady drizzle, pushed by a freshening southerly wind, explored the narrow streets of Portsmouth Point and made the stout walls of the old fortifications gleam like polished metal. Moving threateningly above the huddled buildings the cloud was unbroken and the colour of lead, so that although it was all but midday the light was feeble and depressing.

Only the sea was really alive. Across the normally sheltered expanse of the Solent the surface quivered and broke with each eager gust, but in the distorted light the wave crests held a strange yellow hue in contrast with the dull grey hump of the Isle of Wight and the rain-shrouded Channel beyond.

Captain Richard Bolitho pushed open the door of the George Inn and stood for a few moments to allow the drowsy heat to enfold him like a blanket. Without a word he handed his cloak to a servant and tucked his cocked hat beneath his arm. Through a door to his right he could see a welcoming fire in the coffee room, where a noisy throng of naval officers, interspersed with a few bright scarlet uniforms of the military, were taking their ease and keeping their worries and demands of duty beyond the low, rain-slashed windows.

In another room, grouped in contemplative silence around several small tables, other officers studied their playing cards and the faces of their opponents. Few even glanced up at Bolitho's entrance. In Portsmouth, and at the George Inn in particular, after years of war and unrest, only a man out of uniform might have warranted attention.

Bolitho sighed and took a quick glance at himself in a wall mirror. His blue coat and gold lace fitted his tall figure well, and against the white shirt and waistcoat his face looked unusually tanned. Even allowing for a slow voyage back from the West Indies, his body was still unprepared for an English winter, and he forced himself to stand a little longer to clear the aching cold from his limbs.

A servant coughed politely at his elbow. 'Beg pardon, sir. The admiral is waitin' on you in his room.' He made a small gesture towards the stairway.

'Thank you.' He waited until the man had hurried away to answer some noisy demand from the coffee room and then took a final glance at the mirror. It was neither vanity nor personal interest. It was more of a cold scrutiny which he might offer to a subordinate.

Bolitho was twenty-six years old, but his impassive features and the deep lines on either side of his mouth made him appear older, and for a brief instant he found himself wondering how the change had come about. Almost irritably he pushed the black hair away from his forehead, pausing only to allow one rebellious lock to stay in place above his right eye.

Neither was that action one of vanity. More perhaps one of embarrassment.

Barely an inch above his eye, and running deep into his hair-line, was a savage diagonal scar. He allowed his fingers to touch it momentarily, as a man will let his mind explore an old memory, then with a final shrug he walked briskly up the stairs.

Vice-Admiral Sir Henry Langford was standing, feet well apart, directly in front of the highest log fire Bolitho had ever seen. His glittering uniform shone in the dancing flames, and his thick shadow seemed to reach out across the spacious room to greet Bolitho's quiet entrance.

For several seconds the two men stood looking at each other. The admiral, in his sixties, and running to bulkiness, his heavy face dominated by a large beaked nose above which his keen blue eyes shone like two polished stones, and the slim, tanned captain.

Then the admiral stirred into life and stepped away from the fire, his hand outstretched. Bolitho felt the heat from the fire released across the room, as if a furnace door had been flung open.

'I am glad to see you, Bolitho!' The admiral's booming voice filled the room, sweeping away the years and replacing the image of an overweight old man with that of Bolitho's first captain.

As if reading his thoughts the admiral added ruefully, 'Four teen years, isn't it? My God, it doesn't seem possible!' He stood back and studied Bolitho critically like a plump bird. 'You were a scraggy midshipman, twelve years old, if I remember correctly. Hardly an ounce of flesh on you. I only took you aboard because of your father.' He smiled. 'You still look as if a good meal would not come amiss!'

Bolitho waited patiently. Those fourteen years of service had taught him one thing at least. Senior officers had their own ways of getting round to the reasons for their actions. And it usually took time.

The admiral moved ponderously to a table and poured two generous glasses of brandy. 'With most of the world against us, Bolitho, brandy has become somewhat of a luxury.' He shrugged. 'However, as I am more troubled by rheumatism than gout, I look upon it as a last remaining necessity.'

Bolitho sipped carefully and studied his superior over the rim of the glass. He had arrived back from the West Indies just three days earlier, as one year faded and gave way to the next. His ship, his beloved *Sparrow*, had been handed over to the dock-yard for a well-earned refit, while her less fortunate company were scattered through the every-hungry fleet to replace the growing gaps left by death and mutilation. Most of the sloop's crew had been away from their homeland for six years, and with a little well-earned prize money they had been hoping to see their loved ones again, if only for a short while. It was not to be, but Bolitho knew that his feeling of resentment and pity would be as useless as a ship without sails.

The pale eyes fixed suddenly on Bolitho's face. 'I'm giving you the *Phalarope*, Bolitho.' He watched the brief shaft of emotion play across the young captain's features. 'She's lying out at Spithead right now, rigging set up, yards crossed, a finer frigate never floated.'

Bolitho placed the glass slowly on the table to give his mind time to deal with the admiral's words. The *Phalarope*, a thirty-two-gun frigate, and less than six years old. He had seen her through his glass as he had rounded the Spit Sand three days ago. She was certainly a beautiful ship, all that he could ever have hoped for. No, more than he could have dreamed of.

He pushed the *Sparrow* to the back of his thoughts. It was part of yesterday, along with his own hopes of taking a rest at his home in Cornwall, and getting to know the firm feel of the countryside, of so many half-remembered things.

He said quietly, 'You do me a great honour, sir.'

'Nonsense, you've more than earned it!' The admiral seemed strangely relieved. As if he had been rehearsing this little speech for some time. 'I've followed your career, Bolitho. You are a great credit to the Navy, and the country.'

'I had an excellent teacher, sir.'

The admiral nodded soberly. 'They were great days, eh? Great days.' He shook himself and poured another brandy. 'I have told you the good news. Now I will tell you the other part.' He watched Bolitho thoughtfully. 'The *Phalarope* has been attached to the Channel Fleet, mostly on blockade duty outside Brest.'

Bolitho pricked up his ears. Being on blockade duty was no news at all. The hard-pressed fleet needed every frigate like gold in its constant efforts to keep the French ships bottled up in their

Channel ports. Frigates were maids of all work. Powerful enough to trounce any other vessel but a ship of the line in open combat, and fast enough to out-manœuvre the latter, they were in permanent demand. What caught his immediate attention was the way the admiral had stressed *has been attached* to the Channel Fleet. So there were new orders. Maybe south to help relieve the beleaguered garrison in Gibraltar.

The admiral continued harshly, 'Most ships go rotten from without. Wind and sea are cruel masters, even to the best timbers.' He stared at the rain splattering across the windows. '*Phalarope* has received her rot from within!' He began to pace angrily, his shadow crossing and recrossing the room like a spectre. 'There was almost a mutiny a month back, and then when her squadron was engaged in battle with some blockade runners she avoided action!' He halted and glared at Bolitho with something like shock. 'Can you believe that? A King's ship, and she failed to engage!'

Bolitho bit his lip. Mutiny was always a threat. Men pressed from life ashore, a handful of troublemakers, even one stupid officer, could turn a well-drilled ship into a living hell. But it rarely occurred with other ships in company. Usually this sort of madness broke out in a ship becalmed under a relentless tropical sun, with fever and disease the main instigators. Or during a long voyage out of sight of land, when a ship seemed to shrink in size with each dragging day, as if to force the men at each others' throats.

Sir Henry Langford added sharply, 'I've relieved her captain of his command, of course.'

Bolitho felt a strange warmth for this tired, irritable old man, whose flagship, a massive three-decker, was even now taking on stores in the harbour and preparing to carry her master back to his squadron off the hostile French coast. He had said '*of course*'. Yet Bolitho knew that many admirals would have backed up their captains even knowing them to be both guilty and incompetent.

The admiral gave a small smile. 'I am afraid your honour is double-edged! It is never easy to take over an unhappy ship, especially in time of war.' He pointed at a sealed envelope on his desk. Its seals glittered in the firelight like fresh blood. 'Your orders. They require you to take command forthwith and proceed to sea.' He weighed his words carefully. 'You will seek out Sir Samuel Hood's squadron and place yourself under his orders.'

Bolitho felt dazed. Hood was still in the West Indies whence he had just returned. He had a brief picture of the same thousands of miles of empty sea, in command of a strange ship, with a crew still seething in discontent.

'So you see, Bolitho, I am still a hard taskmaster!' The admiral shuddered as a squall hit the window. 'I am afraid you are nearly one hundred men under strength. I had to remove many of the troublemakers, and replacements are hard to come by. Some I will have to hang, as soon as a court martial can be convened. You have barely enough men to work the ship under way, let alone in action.' He rubbed his chin, his eyes glittering. 'I suggest you make sail at once and head for the West Country. I understand that the fishing fleets are mostly in port in Devon and Cornwall. The weather it seems is not to their liking.' His smile broadened. 'I see no objection to your visiting Falmouth, Bolitho. While your officers are ashore pressing some of these fishermen into the King's service, you might well find the time to call upon your father. You will give him my kind regards, I hope.'

Bolitho nodded. 'Thank you, sir. I will do that.' All at once he wanted to get away. There was so much to attend to. Stores and cordage to be checked, food and provisions for the long voyage. Above all, there was the *Phalarope*, waiting for him, ready to judge or condemn him.

The admiral picked up the canvas envelope and weighed it in his hands. 'I will not advise you, Bolitho. You are young, but have more than proved yourself. Just remember this. There are bad men and good men aboard your ship. Be firm, but not too hard. Do not regard lack of knowledge as insubordination, like your predecessor.' There was a bite to his tone. 'If you have difficulty in remembering all this, try and recall what you were like when you came to serve me as midshipman.' He was no longer smiling. 'You can give the ship back her rightful place by returning her pride. But if you fail, even I cannot help you.'

'I would not expect you to, sir.' Bolitho's eyes were hard grey, like the sea beyond the harbour.

'I know. That is why I held the command for you.' There was a murmur of voices beyond the door and Bolitho knew the audience was nearly over. The admiral added, 'I have a nephew aboard the *Phalarope*, he is one of your young gentlemen. His name is Charles Farquhar, and he might yet make a good officer. But do him no favours for my sake, Bolitho.' He sighed and handed over the envelope. 'The ship is ready to sail, so take advantage of this southerly wind.' He held Bolitho's hand and studied his face intently. 'We may not meet again, Bolitho, for I fear my days are numbered.' He waved down the other man's protest. 'I have a responsibility, and I have certain rewards for my duty. But youth I cannot have.'

Bolitho hitched up his sword and tucked his hat under his arm once more. 'Then I will take my leave, sir.' There was nothing more he could say.

Almost blindly he walked through the door and past the little group of whispering officers awaiting their admiral's pleasure.

One officer stood apart, a captain of about his own age. There the similarity ended. He had pale, protruding eyes and a small, petulant mouth. He was tapping his fingers on his sword and staring at the door, and Bolitho guessed him to be the man who had been taken from the *Phalarope*. But he seemed unworried, merely irritated. He probably had influence at Court, or in Parliament, Bolitho thought grimly. Even so, he would need more than that to face Sir Henry.

As he crossed to the stairway the other captain met his stare. The pale eyes were empty of expression yet vaguely hostile. Then he looked away, and Bolitho reached the foot of the stairs where a marine orderly waited with his cloak.

Outside the inn the wind howled in his face and the rain dashed across his skin like ice rime. But as he walked slowly towards the Sally Port he noticed neither.

When he reached the Hard, Bolitho noticed that the highwater garland of slime and weed was all but covered by the angry, hissing wavelets, and he knew that the tide was nearing the flood. With luck he could get his new ship under way on the ebb. Nothing made a ship's company settle down to a fresh master more quickly than routine and work.

As he left the shelter of the last line of buildings he caught sight of the boat which waited to carry him away from the land. The oars were tossed, and swayed like twin lines of bare trees as the small craft rocked uneasily in the swell, and he guessed that each man in the boat was watching his slow approach. At the top of the stone ramp, his thick body framed against the cruising wavelets, was the familiar shape of Stockdale, his personal coxswain. Aboard the *Phalarope* there would be one friend at least, he thought grimly.

Stockdale had followed him from ship to ship. More like a trusting dog than a man. Bolitho often found time to wonder at the bond which had held them together, a link which was beyond explanation in words.

As a young and very junior lieutenant Bolitho had been sent ashore with a recruiting party during the uneasy peace, when he had considered himself more than fortunate to be spared the indignity of so many of his fellows, that of being beached and unwanted on half-pay. Volunteers had been few, but when about to return to his ship to face the wrath of his captain Bolitho had seen Stockdale standing miserably outside a local inn. Stripped to the waist he had made a truly imposing figure, his thickset body a mass of muscle and power. A loudmouthed barker at his side had called to the small naval recruiting party that Stockdale was a prize-fighter of great repute, and that a golden guinea would be immediately awarded to any one of Bolitho's men who could lay him low. Bolitho had been weary, and the thought of a cool drink at the inn while his men tried their luck overcame his normal objections to what he thought to be a degrading spectacle.

As it happened, he had had in his party a gunner's mate who was not only a very proficient fist-fighter but a man quite used to maintaining discipline by that and any other means which came his way. He had thrown aside his jacket, and encouraged by the other sailors had gone to the attack.

Exactly what had happened next Bolitho was not quite sure. It was said that one of the sailors had managed to trip Stockdale, and that seemed likely, as Bolitho had never seen him beaten since that day, but the next instant, even as Bolitho had been reaching for his ale, there had been a scream of rage from the barker and a great bellow of laughter from the sailors.

Bolitho had found the gunner's mate pocketing his guinea while the infuriated barker had proceeded to beat Stockdale with a length of chain, interspersed with threats and curses.

It was then that Bolitho had discovered that Stockdale accepted loyalty like a manacle. He never flinched from the unjust beating, although he could have killed his tormentor with one blow.

Pity or disgust drove Bolitho to stop the beating, and the look of dumb gratitude on Stockdale's battered face only helped to make things worse. Watched by the grinning sailors and the flint-eyed barker he had asked Stockdale to volunteer for the King's service. The barker had raised a storm of protest at the thought of his living being removed for all time.

Stockdale had given a brief nod and picked up his shirt without a word. Even now he hardly ever spoke, his vocal cords having been damaged over the years of fighting in one town after another.

Bolitho had imagined that his angry gesture had ended the matter. But it was not so. Stockdale had settled down aboard ship in a manner born. For all his strength he was gentle and patient, and only one real object seemed to alter his placid way of life. Wherever Bolitho went, so did he.

At first Bolitho decided to ignore this fact, but when at length he had his own command and required a personal coxswain, Stockdale just seemed to be there, ready. As he was now.

He was staring emptily at the sea, his body motionless in the wind, his wide white trousers and blue jacket flapping around his limbs like pennants on a heavy ship of the line. He turned at Bolitho's approach and knuckled his forehead, his deep brown eyes watching his captain with silent concern.

Bolitho gave a tight smile. 'Is everything ready, Stockdale?'

The man nodded slowly. 'I've stowed your boxes in the boat, sir.' He glared at the waiting boat's crew. 'I've had a word with this lot about how things should be done from now on!'

Bolitho stepped down into the boat and gathered his cloak tightly around him. Stockdale grunted an order and the boat idled clear of the stonework.

'Out oars! Give way together!' Stockdale swung the tiller and squinted between the oarsmen as the boat turned and bit into the first angry swell.

Bolitho watched the oarsmen through narrowed eyes. Each man was careful to avoid his scrutiny. The new captain, any captain, was second only to God. He could promote and flog, reward and hang any man aboard, and when a ship was out of company, alone on the high seas, the powers were exercised according to a particular captain's temperament, as Bolitho well knew.

As the boat pushed into open water he forgot the straining seamen and concentrated his full attention on the distant frigate. Now that he was closer he could see the steady pitch and roll of the graceful hull as she strained at the taut cable in the freshening wind. He could even see the flash of bright copper as she showed her bilges, and then as she canted to the opposite side he could make out the busy activity on the maindeck below her tall, tapering masts and furled sails. Aft by the entry port there was a neat scarlet rectangle of marines already drawn up to greet him, and momentarily in the wind he caught the sound of twittering pipes and the hoarse bellow of orders.

She was a fine ship, he thought. One hundred and forty feet of power and living grace. From the high gilt figurehead, a strange bird mounted on the back of a dolphin, to her carved poop with the rippling ensign above she was the proof of a shipbuilder's art.

Now he could see the group of officers waiting on the quarter-deck, more than one with his glass raised and trained on the tossing boat. He set his face in an impassive mask, forcibly dampening down the excitement and the sense of challenge which the ship had given him.

'Boat ahoy!' The hail was caught by the wind and tossed to the screaming gulls above.

Stockdale cupped his hands and yelled, '*Phalarope*!' There was no doubt now for the waiting officers. No doubt at all that their new overlord was approaching.

Bolitho opened his cloak and threw it back across his

shoulders, the feeble light glinting on his gold lace and the hilt of his sword. Still the frigate grew bigger and bigger, until at last she towered above the boat, blotting out all else.

As the oarsmen manœuvred towards the entry port Bolitho ran his eye slowly along the masts and yards and the taut black rigging. There was no sign of slackness, everything was as it should be. The hull was well painted, and the amount of gold leaf around the figurehead as well as the broad-windowed stern was proof that her last captain had spent a good deal of his own money to make her so.

The thought of money well spent made him glance briefly at his boxes in the sternsheets. He had brought over a thousand pounds of prize money back from the Indies, yet apart from the new uniforms and a few small luxuries he had little to show for it. And now he was off to sea again, where a mutineer's knife might end his life as quickly as a French cannon ball, unless he was constantly vigilant. He suddenly recalled the admiral's warning, 'If you fail, even I cannot help you!'

The boat lurched alongside and almost threw him from his feet as he jumped clear of the gunwale and began to climb up the spray-dashed side.

He tried to shut his ears to the crash of sound which greeted him. The trilling pipes from the side party, and the slap of muskets as the marines presented arms; it was too easy and too dangerous to let his guard slip even for an instant. Even to allow himself to enjoy this moment to the full, for which he had been waiting for so long.

A tall, heavily built lieutenant stepped forward and removed his hat. 'Lieutenant Vibart, sir. I am the senior here.' He had a thick, rasping tone, and his face was unsmiling.

'Thank you, Mr. Vibart.' Bolitho stared past him along the full length of his ship. The gangways on either side of the hull which connected the forecastle with the quarterdeck were crowded with silent men, and others had climbed into the shrouds so that they could see their captain better. His eye moved on, across the neat lines of guns, firmly lashed behind closed ports, the spotless decks and well-flaked lines. Lieutenant Vibart was a good first lieutenant as far as smartness and outward appearance was concerned, he thought.

Vibart was saying gruffly, 'Mr. Okes and Mr. Herrick, the second and third lieutenants, sir.'

Bolitho nodded, keeping his expression noncommittal. He had a quick impression of two young officers, nothing more. Later the men would emerge from behind the strange faces. Right now it was more important that his own impression on them was made quite clear.

'Have the hands lay aft, Mr. Vibart.' He drew his commission from inside his coat and unrolled it as the men were urged towards him. They looked healthy enough, but their bodies were clad in rags, and some of them seemed to be dressed in the remains of what they had been wearing when pressed into service. He bit his lip. That would have to be changed, and at once. Uniformity was all important. It killed envy amongst the men, if only for poor remnants of clothing.

He began to read himself in, his voice carrying crisply above the sigh of wind and the steady thrumming of stays and rigging.

It was addressed to Richard Bolitho, Esquire, and required him forthwith to go on board and take upon him the charge and command of captain in His Britannic Majesty's frigate *Phalarope*. He finished reading and rolled the scroll in his hands as he looked down at the assembled faces. What were they thinking and hoping at this moment?

He said: 'I will address the men further, Mr. Vibart.' He thought he saw a gleam of resentment in Vibart's deepset eyes, but ignored it. The man looked old for his rank, maybe seven or eight years older than himself. It could not be pleasant to see a chance of command moved back another pace by his sudden arrival. 'Are you in all respects ready to proceed to sea?'

Vibart nodded, 'Yes, sir.' He sounded as if he meant to say 'of course'. 'We were warped out here a week ago, and the fresh water came aboard this forenoon by lighter. We are fully provisioned in accordance with the admiral's orders.'

'Very good.' Bolitho turned back to the crew. Sir Henry Langford had taken no chance, he thought dryly. With the ship fully provisioned and safely anchored away from the shore there was little chance of contaminating the fleet with her unhappiness. He longed for a few minutes alone so that he could read fully the extent of his orders. They might give him a further clue to the puzzle.

He cleared his throat. 'Now, men, I just want to tell you of our destination.' They would know he had had no time to inform his officers, and this immediate show of confidence might well help to bridge the gulf between quarterdeck and forecastle.

'England is fighting for her life! Even as we lie here, anchored and impotent, our country is at war with France and Spain, with the Dutch and the rebellious colonialists in the Americas. Every single ship is needed to win the day, each man amongst you is vital to our just cause!' He paused and waited a few seconds. In the *Sparrow* his men would have cheered, would have shown some animation. Suddenly, as he stared along the packed, expressionless faces he felt a pang of longing and loneliness. In his mind's eye he could see the little sloop's cheerful, tanned company, like a lot of carefree pirates. The healthy faces, the feeling of oneness which was totally absent here. He saw Stockdale standing by the lee rail and wondered what he thought about his new shipmates.

He allowed a note of hardness to creep into his voice. 'Today we sail for Falmouth.' He steeled himself. 'And from thence to the West Indies to join Sir Samuel Hood against the French and their allies!'

No individual called out, but something like a moan of pain transmitted itself through the packed figures below him. A petty officer snarled, 'Silence on deck! Keep quiet, you scum!'

Bolitho added flatly, 'I ask nothing but your loyalty. I will do my duty, and I would wish you to do the same!' He turned on his heel. 'Carry on, Mr. Vibart. We will make sail in one hour. See that all boats are secured, and then be so good as to have the anchor hove short.' His tone was cold and final, but the lieutenant blocked his way, his mouth working angrily.

'But, sir! The West Indies!' He struggled for words. 'God, we've been on the blockade for two years!'

Bolitho let his voice carry to the other officers. 'And I have been away for *six*, Mr. Vibart!' He walked aft where Stockdale soundlessly marked the cabin hatch for his retreat. 'I want all officers and senior warrant officers in my cabin in ten minutes!'

He ran lightly down the ladder, his head automatically bowed beneath the low deck beams. Right aft, below a spiralling lantern, a red-coated marine snapped to attention outside his cabin door. Beyond it would be his haven, the only place aboard a crowded ship where he could think and dream alone.

Stockdale held open the door and stood aside as Bolitho entered the cabin, which after *Sparrow*'s cramped and spartan quarters seemed almost spacious.

The sloping stern windows ran the whole width of the main cabin, and the thick glass gave a wide, panoramic picture of tossing water and the hostile, grey sky. The air was heavy and damp, and once again he was conscious of the cold in his limbs. It would be good to get back to the sun, he thought. To see blue and gold through those windows, and know again the peace of a friendly sea.

A partition hid his sleeping quarters, and another concealed the small chart room. The main cabin itself contained a good table and matching chairs, as well as a bulkhead desk and a hanging wardrobe for his uniforms which even now Stockdale was unpacking from the boxes.

The previous captain had done well for himself, Bolitho thought. On either side of the cabin, discreetly hidden in a canvas cover, was a big twelve-pounder, lashed down like some leashed beast, so that even here, in the captain's own domain, the air would be filled with smoke and death when action found the frigate.

He made himself sit quietly on the padded bench below the windows, and ignoring Stockdale's furtive movements and the shipboard noises above and beyond the door began to read his orders.

But apart from the usual directions the orders told him nothing. There were extra marines aboard, with a full captain in charge of them instead of the original sergeant. That was interesting. Sir Henry Langford obviously considered that if all else failed Bolitho could defend himself with the afterguard.

He slammed the thick papers on the table and frowned. He did not want protection. He had meant what he had said. He wanted loyalty. No, he *needed* loyalty!

The deck canted beneath him and he heard the patter of bare feet overhead. In spite of everything he was glad to be leaving the land. At sea you had room to think, and space to act. Only time was at a premium.

Exactly ten minutes after Bolitho had left the quarterdeck the officers filed through the door into his cabin.

Vibart, his head lowered beneath the deck beams, introduced each one in order of seniority in the same rasping tone.

Okes and Herrick, the two other lieutenants, and Daniel Proby, the master. The latter was old and weathered like carved wood, his body round-shouldered beneath his well-worn coat. He had a lugubrious, heavy-jowled face, and the most mournful eyes Bolitho had ever seen. Then there was Captain Rennie of the marines, a slim and languid young man with deceptively lazy eyes. Bolitho thought that he at least would guess that there might still be trouble in the offing.

The three midshipmen stood quietly in the background. Farquhar was the most senior, and Bolitho felt a small pang of uneasiness as he studied the youth's tight lips and haughty expression. The admiral's nephew might be an ally. He could equally be the admiral's spy. The other young gentlemen, Neale and Maynard, seemed pleasant enough, with the usual crumpled cheekiness which most midshipmen reserved as their defence against officers and seamen alike. Neale was minute and chubby, and could not be more than thirteen, Bolitho thought. Maynard, on the other hand, was keen-eyed and as skinny as a pike, and watched his captain with a fixed and intent expression which might mean anything.

Then there were the senior warrant officers. The professional men. Evans, the purser, a small ferret in a plain dark coat, dwarfed by Ellice, the surgeon, brick-red and perspiring, with anxious rheumy eyes.

Bolitho stood with his back to the windows, his hands clasped behind him. He waited until Vibart had finished speaking and then said, 'We shall get to know each other better very soon, gentlemen. For the moment let me say that I shall expect all of you to do your best to pull the ship's people together into one efficient company. When I left the Indies things were not going well for England. It is likely, indeed it is more than probable, that the French will take full advantage of our military commitments in that area for their own ends. Action will certainly seek us out, and when that happens I want this ship to give a good account of herself.' He watched their faces, trying to pierce their guarded expressions. His gaze fell on Herrick, the third lieutenant. He was a round-faced, competent looking officer, but there was an air of assumed attentiveness about him, like one who had been betrayed in the past and no longer trusted a first impression.

He dropped his eyes to the deck as Vibart said, 'May I ask if we're being despatched to the Indies because of the trouble we had aboard, sir?' He stared unflinchingly at Bolitho's grey eyes, his voice challenging.

'You may ask.' Bolitho watched him narrowly. There was something dominant about Vibart. A sense of inner force which seemed to cow all the others into mere spectators. He said calmly, 'I have studied the reports and the logs. I consider that the near-mutiny,' he let his voice hang on the last word, 'was caused as much by negligence as anything else.'

Vibart replied hotly, 'Captain Pomfret trusted his officers, sir!' He pointed to the books on the table. 'You can see from the log books that the ship did all which could be expected of her!'

Bolitho pulled a book from beneath the others and saw Vibart look momentarily off guard.

'I often find that this, the punishment book, is a better gauge of a ship's efficiency.' He turned the pages idly, forcibly hiding the disgust he had felt when he had first examined it. 'In the past six months over a thousand lashes were awarded to the crew.' His voice was cold. 'Some men received four dozen at a time. One apparently died after punishment.'

Vibart said thickly, 'You can't win men by weakness, sir!'

'Nor by senseless cruelty, Mr. Vibart!' His tone was like a whip. 'In future I will have more attention to leadership than to brutality in my ship!' He controlled his voice with an effort. 'Also, I want every man fitted out with proper clothing from the slop chest before we reach Falmouth. This is a King's ship and not a Spanish slaver!'

There was a sudden heavy silence, so that ship and sea intruded into the cabin. The clatter of deck gear, the sluice of the tide around the rudder, and the distant bark of commands added to Bolitho's sense of isolation.

He continued evenly, 'At Falmouth we will make efforts to increase our company to full strength. I will send parties of trusted hands ashore to press suitable men for service. Not cripples and young boys, but *men*. Do I make myself clear?'

Most of them nodded. Lieutenant Okes said carefully, 'I have often read of your exploits in the *Gazette*, sir.' He swallowed painfully and glanced quickly at Herrick. 'I think the whole ship will be happy to have you as captain.' His voice trailed away miserably and he fidgeted with his sword.

Bolitho nodded. 'Thank you, Mr. Okes.' He could not afford to add anything else. Okes might be seeking favouritism, or making haste to cover up some old misdemeanour. But still, it was a beginning.

He added, 'I cannot alter what Captain Pomfret did or did not do. I have my own ways, and I expect them to be considered at all times.' From the corner of his eye he saw the master shaking his head doubtfully. 'Do you wish to say anything, Mr. Proby?'

The old man looked up with a jerk, his jowls shaking. 'Er, no, sir! I was just thinking it will make a change to navigate in some deep water instead o' all these shoals an' mudbanks!' He smiled, the effort only adding to his mournful appearance. 'The young gentlemen will benefit from a long voyage, no doubt?'

It was meant in all seriousness, but the midshipman Neale nudged his companion Maynard and they both tittered. Then Neale saw Vibart's frown and hurriedly looked at his feet.

Bolitho nodded. 'Very well, gentlemen, prepare to get under way. I will come on deck in ten minutes.' He met Vibart's eye. 'I shall be interested to see the men at their stations, Mr. Vibart. A bit of sail drill might take their minds off their troubles for a while!'

The officers filed away and Stockdale firmly closed the door. Bolitho sat down and stared at the piles of books and papers. He had tried to find an opening and had failed. There was a barrier, a shield of resentment, or was it fear? He had to find out himself. He could trust no one, confide in nobody until he was sure of his ground.

He looked at Stockdale and asked quietly, 'Well, how do *you* like the *Phalarope*?'

The ex-fighter swallowed hard, as he always did to clear his maimed cords. 'She's a good craft, Captain.' He nodded slowly. 'But I don't care much for the meat inside the bones!' He placed Bolitho's sword carefully beside the pistol rack and added meaningly, 'I should keep these by you, Captain. Just in case!'

Richard Bolitho climbed the ladder to the quarterdeck and made himself walk slowly to the weather rail. The frigate was alive with fresh activity, and he could see men standing at the capstan bars, while others waited below the masts with their petty officers. He gauged the wind against his cheek and glanced quickly aloft at the masthead pendant. The ship tugged at her cable eagerly and fretfully, as if she too wanted to be free of the land once again, and Bolitho curbed his own impatience as he watched and waited the final preparations for sea.

The decks gleamed with blown spray and drizzle, and he realized with a start that he was already soaked to the skin. But perhaps it was just as well that his seamen should see him unshrouded in watchcoat and unprotected from the weather as indeed they were themselves.

He caught sight of the midshipman Maynard hovering by the lee rail, and again thanked God for his ability to remember names after hearing or reading them but once.

'You are in charge of signals, Mr. Maynard?' The youth nodded, his thin body looking like a scarecrow against the angry water alongside. 'Very well. Make a signal to the Flag. "Ready to proceed".'

He saw the flags soaring aloft and immediately forgot them as Vibart strode aft his face set in a grim frown. 'Anchor's hove short, sir!' He touched his hat. 'All stores secured!'

'Very well.' Bolitho lifted his glass and watched the flags blowing out from the shore signal tower. Maybe, just to the right, from his warm room at the inn, the admiral would be watching.

Maynard yelled, 'Reply, sir! "God speed and good luck"!'

Bolitho handed his glass to Stockdale and thrust his hands beneath the tails of his coat. 'Get the ship under way if you please. Lay a course to weather the headland.' He would take no part in it. He would watch each man. And every man would know it.

The boatswain's mates took up the cry, 'Hands aloft! Loose tops'ls!'

The rigging and shrouds were suddenly alive with swarming figures as the topmen ran aloft as surefooted as cats, the laggards urged on mercilessly by the petty officers with fists and ropes ends alike.

'Break out the anchor!' Mr. Quintal, the barrel-chested boatswain, swung his cane over the straining forecastle hands. 'Heave! Put yer backs into it, you whimperin' old women!' His cane whacked down and a man cried out. 'Heave! Heave!' The capstan jerked and then cranked steadily as the dripping cable came inboard.

'Loose heads'ls!' The cry was passed along the deck like a chant. High above, the released canvas flapped and banged in the wind, and the men strung out along the swaying yards like ants kicked and grappled with each growing area of rebellious sail.

Bolitho ignored the flying spray and watched the men dashing from one job to the next. The shorthandedness was all the more apparent now with the topmen aloft.

Herrick called from the bows, 'Anchor's aweigh, sir!'

Like a released animal the frigate paid off into the wind, her deck heeling sharply as the gust found and held her.

Vibart grated, 'Man the braces there! Look alive!'

The men at the braces laid back heaving and panting until the great yards began to squeak round. Then the wind filled the sails and the billowing canvas thundered out hard and full as the *Phalarope* went about and gathered way.

By the time the anchor was catted and made fast the land was already drawing away on the starboard quarter, the Isle of Wight quite invisible in a curtain of drizzle and spray.

Everything creaked and banged as the ship continued to swing on course, with shrouds and rigging whining like the strings of some mad orchestra.

Bolitho watched the unwanted men sliding down the stays and adding their weight to the men at the braces. 'Lay her on the port tack, Mr. Vibart.' He looked back across the taffrail and tried to recall what was so terrible about Captain Pomfret. He remembered the man's cold eyes, and the cowed faces of his men.

Proby was standing hump-backed beside the quartermaster, his battered old hat over his ears like a candle-snuffer. Bolitho said, 'Let her run freely, Mr. Proby. There may be need for reefing down later, but I want to reach Falmouth as soon as possible.'

The master watched the captain's slim figure beside the rail and sucked his teeth. Pomfret had never let the frigate have her head. Now she was flying like a mad thing as more and more canvas crept along her yards and exploded, full-bellied before the wind. When he looked at the spiralling mastheads he could almost imagine they were bending. But his eyesight was not so good now, so he made no comment.

Vibart stood at the quarterdeck rail one foot on a carronade slide, his eyes slitted as he watched the men at their stations. Once he looked back too, towards Portsmouth, where Pomfret had left the ship under orders. Where Bolitho had come aboard to replace him, and by so doing had killed Vibart's own chance of promotion.

He watched Bolitho's profile and felt the anger running through him like fire. It was five thousand miles to Hood's squadron. A lot could happen before that.

He awoke with a start as Bolitho said crisply, 'Dismiss the watch below, Mr. Vibart, and double the lookouts.' He gestured towards the open channel. 'Here, everyone is an enemy.' He gave Vibart a meaning glance and went below.

2. BEWARE THE PRESS!

THE GIG'S CREW pulled steadily towards the stone jetty and then gratefully tossed their oars as Stockdale growled an order and the bowman jabbed at a ringbolt with his boathook.

Bolitho turned his head to look back at the frigate and smiled slightly to himself. The *Phalarope* was anchored well out in Falmouth Bay, her sleek shape black and stark against the sea and watery sunlight which had at last managed to break through the scudding clouds. The ship had made a slow approach towards the headland, and he had no doubt that her presence had long since been reported, and every able-bodied man in the town would have taken full advantage of the warning to make himself scarce from the dreaded press.

By his side, huddled in his boat cloak, Lieutenant Thomas Herrick sat in silence, his eyes watching the rain-soaked hills beyond the town and the grey, timeless bulk of the castle above Carrick Roads. There were several small craft moored in the safety of the Roads, coasters and tubby fishing boats enjoying the shelter and the protection of the anchorage.

Bolitho said, 'A brisk walk will do us good, Mr. Herrick. It may be the last chance we get for a while.' He stepped stiffly from the boat and waited until Herrick had followed him up the worn steps. An ancient sailor with a grey beard called, 'Welcome, Captain! It is a fine ship you have out there!'

Bolitho nodded. A Cornishman himself, and a native of Falmouth, he knew well enough that it was unlikely any younger men would dare to stay and pass idle remarks to a King's officer. Frigates were too busy to enter port unless for one thing. To gather men.

Vibart had voiced that very thing as the *Phalarope* had swooped through the night, her sails thundering to the wind, her bow throwing back the spray in an unbroken white wake. But when Bolitho had outlined his plan even he had lapsed into silence.

As a boy Bolitho had often seen the approach of a ship of war, and had heard the news shouted down the narrow streets, the

cry carried from house to house like a distress signal. Young
men had dropped their work, bid hasty farewells to their friends
and families, and made for the safety of the hills, where they
could watch and wait until the ship had made sail and dipped
towards the horizon. There was a rough coast road above the
cliffs which led north-east away from Falmouth towards Gerrans
Bay and St. Austell. No press gang would take the time and
trouble to follow them. Hampered by weapons and the short
breath left by lack of exercise, they would know such efforts to
be wasted. No, there were few who were slow or stupid enough
to allow the King's men an easy catch.

In pitch darkness Bolitho had turned the ship inshore and
heaved to, the deck canting savagely to the stiff wind and the
swift offshore currents. Old Proby had been at first doubtful, and
then had openly showed his admiration. There were no beacons,
and apart from a dull shadow of land there was nothing to show
that Bolitho had found the exact point below Gerrans Bay
where the chart displayed a tiny crescent of beach.

A landing party had been detailed soon after leaving Portsmouth, and below the quarterdeck, their faces pale in a shaded
lantern, the selected men had listened to Bolitho's instructions.

'I am putting you ashore here in the two cutters. You will be
in two parties. Mr. Vibart and Mr. Maynard with one, and Mr.
Farquhar with the second.' He had sought out the severe face of
Brock, the gunner. 'Mr. Brock will also accompany the second
party.' Farquhar might be too eager if left alone, he thought.
Brock's experience and self-contained efficiency would make a
nice balance.

'If I know Falmouth, as soon as the ship appears in the Bay at
first light the sort of men we are after will make their way along
the coast road as fast as they can go. If your parties keep up a
steady march along that road as soon as you leave Pendower
Beach, they should run right into your arms. It saves selection, I
believe.' He had seen Brock nod his narrow head approvingly.
'The boats will return to the ship and you can march straight on
to Falmouth.' A few of the men sighed, and he had added
calmly, 'It is only five miles. It is better than tramping around
the town for nothing.'

With Herrick at his side he walked briskly up the sloping road
towards the neat houses, his shoes slipping on the well-remem-
bered cobbles. By now Vibart must have made some catches, he
thought. If not, if he had made his first misjudgement, it would
only help to add to the tension in the *Phalarope*.

Lieutenant Okes was still aboard in charge of the ship until
his return, and Captain Rennie's marines would be able to deter
anyone who still hoped to desert. Even a desperate man would

find it hard to swim the long stretch of tossing water from the anchored frigate.

He glanced sideways at Herrick and said abruptly, 'You have been aboard for two years, I believe?' He watched the guard drop behind the lieutenant's eyes. He had an open, homely face, yet there was this reserve, this caution, which seemed to symbolize for Bolitho the attitude of the whole ship. It was as if they were all cowed to a point where they neither trusted nor hoped. He added, 'According to the log you were officer of the watch when the trouble started?'

Herrick bit his lip. 'Yes, sir. We were beating up from Lorient. It was during the middle watch and quiet for the time of year.'

Bolitho watched the uncertainty crossing the man's face and felt a touch of pity. It was never easy to be the junior lieutenant in a ship of war. Promotion was slow and hard without either luck or influence. He thought of his own first chance, how easily it might have gone against him. One piece of luck had followed hard upon another. As a lieutenant in a ship of the line, at the very time of the American rebellion, he had been sent away in charge of a prize crew in a captured brig. While heading towards Antigua he had fallen upon a privateer and had fooled her captain into believing that his brig was still an ally. A rush of boarders, a swift and savage clash of steel, and the second ship had been his. Upon arrival at Antigua he had been welcomed by the Commander-in-Chief like a hero. Victories had been scarce, and reverses only too many.

So at the age of twenty-two he had been given command of the *Sparrow*. Again luck had guided his footsteps. The sloop's original commander had died of fever, and her first lieutenant was too junior for the coveted post.

He forced the sympathy to the back of his mind. 'How many men were in the mutiny?'

Herrick replied bitterly, 'No more than ten. They were trying to release a seaman called Fisher. Captain Pomfret had had him flogged for insubordination the previous day. He had been complaining about the foul food.'

Bolitho nodded. 'That is not uncommon.'

'But Captain Pomfret was not satisfied!' The words burst from his lips in an angry flood. 'He had him lashed to the bowsprit, without allowing the surgeon even to treat his back!' He shuddered. 'In the Bay of Biscay, with frost on the rigging, and he left him lashed there like so much meat!' He controlled himself with an effort and muttered, 'I am sorry, sir. I keep thinking about it.'

Bolitho thought back to Pomfret's neat, matter-of-fact recording in the log. The protesting seamen had rushed the quarter-

deck and overpowered the quartermaster and master's mate at
pistol point. Only Herrick, a man who obviously agreed with
everything the seamen had offered as a grievance, stood between
them and a full-scale mutiny. Somehow or other he had cowed
them with words. He had ordered them back to the forecastle
and they had obeyed because they trusted him. The next day
Pomfret's vengeance had broken over the ship in a wave of
ferocity. Twenty floggings, and two men hanged. He would not
wait until the *Phalarope* rejoined the fleet, nor would he wait
for higher authority to gauge his actions. Herrick's bitterness
was well founded, or was it? On the face of it, Pomfret was
within his rights. Perhaps Herrick should have shot down the
mutineers, or even have foreseen the coming danger. He could
have summoned the afterguard, given his life if necessary.
Bolitho chilled at the thought of what might have happened if
Herrick too had been overcome while he tried to reason with
the desperate seamen. The sleeping officers would have been
slaughtered, the ship thrown into chaos in enemy waters. It did
not bear thinking about.

He persisted, 'And then later, when you rejoined the fleet off
Brest and came to action with those French ships. Why was the
Phalarope not engaged?' Again he saw the wretched emotions,
the uncertainty and anger.

Then it dawned on him. Herrick feared him almost as much
as Pomfret. He was captain. He had taken over the ship where
Herrick's own misery and shame moved like a ghost between
decks. Gently he added, 'I take it that the crew were making
their own protest?'

Herrick sunk his chin into his neckcloth. 'Yes, sir. There was
nothing you could put a name to. Sails were badly set. Gun crews
slow in responding.' He laughed sharply. 'But it was wasted.
Quite wasted!' He looked sideways at Bolitho, a brief spark of
defiance in his eyes. 'Pomfret usually avoided action if possible!'

Bolitho looked away. You fool, he thought angrily. You have
allowed this man to act as a conspirator. You should silence him
now, before everyone aboard knows you have accepted an open
criticism of Pomfret, a selected captain, without a murmur.

He said slowly, 'When you have a command of your own,
Herrick, you may feel otherwise. The right course of action is
not usually the easiest.' He thought of Vibart's hostility and
wondered what *he* had been doing during the mutiny. 'I know
that every officer must *earn* his men's loyalty.' He hardened his
tone. 'But a captain has the loyalty of his officers as a right, do I
make myself clear?'

Herrick looked straight ahead along the street. 'Aye, aye, sir!'
The guard was restored. His expression wooden and controlled.

Bolitho halted below the church wall and looked up the familiar street which ran beside the churchyard. At the top of the road was the house, its square, uncompromising shape, the familiar grey stonework as enduring as his memory of it.

He stood looking up at it, suddenly apprehensive, like an intruder. He said, 'Carry on, Mr. Herrick. Go and see the garrison victualling officer and arrange to have as many fresh eggs and butter sent over to the ship as you can manage.'

Herrick was looking past him towards the big house, his eyes suddenly wistful. 'Your home, sir?'

'Yes.' Bolitho began to see Herrick in a different light again. Away from the order and discipline of the frigate and framed by the rain-washed building behind him he looked vaguely defenceless. Bolitho knew from his own methodical study of the ship's papers that Herrick came of a poor, middle-class Kentish family, his father being a clerk. For that reason he would be without influence when he most needed it, and unless he was very fortunate in battle his chances of advancement were slight.

The sight of his home, the confusion of judgement and ideas angered him, and he said sharply, 'After you have dealt with the Army perhaps you would care to join me for a glass of wine before we sail, Mr. Herrick?' He gestured up the road. 'My father will welcome you.'

Herrick opened his mouth, an unspoken refusal caught in mid-air. He tugged at his cross-belt and said awkwardly, 'Thank you, sir.' He touched his hat as Bolitho turned away towards the house. Herrick stood quite still, the wind tugging at his boat-cloak, until Bolitho reached the gates. Then, chin sunk on chest, he walked slowly towards the castle, his brow creased in a deep frown.

Lieutenant Giles Vibart cursed as his feet skidded on loose stones and a seaman cannoned into his back. The grey morning light showed the extent of the previous night's wind, and the long grass and gorse was flattened and glittering with rain. He pulled his watch from inside his coat and then held up his hand.

'We'll stop here for a bit!' He saw his order passing down the small party of men, and waited until they had squatted beside the crude track before he crossed to the two midshipmen and the gunner.

'We'll give these idlers ten minutes and then move off again.' He looked round as a shaft of frail sunlight touched his cheek. 'Then you can take a party further inland, Mr. Farquhar, in case of stragglers.'

Farquhar shrugged and kicked at a pebble. 'Suppose nobody comes, sir?'

Vibart snapped, 'Just do as you're told!'

Maynard, the other midshipman, readjusted his dirk and looked anxiously towards the resting seamen. 'I hope none of 'em try and desert. The captain would be very displeased!'

The gunner gave a lazy grin. 'I picked them myself. They're all old hands.' He picked up a piece of grass and pulled it between his uneven teeth. 'All pressed men, too. Much better than volunteers for this job!'

Vibart nodded. 'Quite right, Mr. Brock. There's nothing better to give an edge to the press. No sailor likes to think others are getting away with it!'

Brock frowned. 'An' why should they? It's not right that the fleet is expected to fight bloody battles and keep the country free of the Frogs without help from these lazy, pampered civilians! They make money and live happily with their wives while we do all the hard work!' He spat out the grass. 'To hell with 'em, I say!'

Vibart walked away from them and stared down at the rocky beach below the cliff. What did it matter what anybody said? They needed men, and the sooner the better.

He watched the wind hissing through the tangled grass and thought again of the frigate's dash through the night. How unlike Pomfret, he thought. He had always liked and expected a smart ship. But to him it had been more like a possession than a weapon of war. He lorded it in his fine cabin, enjoying his choice wines and well-stocked food store while he, Vibart, ran the ship and did all the things of which he was totally incapable. He moved restlessly on his thick legs as the old fire of resentment and injustice explored his mind like a drug.

Pomfret had been full of promises. A word in the right quarter and his first lieutenant would receive recognition and promotion when the time was right. All Vibart had to do was take care of the ship and her discipline and he would do the rest.

The captain had no interest in prize money. He was rich beyond Vibart's imagination. He was equally indifferent to glory. He was inefficient as he was cowardly.

Vibart would have been able to manage Pomfret's indulgences but for the captain's real weakness. Like many cowards he was a bully and a sadist. To Vibart harsh discipline was a necessity, but senseless cruelty seemed to be pointless. It weakened or maimed men who would be better employed on duty, it damaged the blind trust of men required to obey without question.

But Vibart was only a lieutenant, and was thirty-three years old. Unlike most of the other officers he had not entered the Navy as a boy, but had come the hard way, having served in merchant vessels the length and breadth of the world. His last three years at sea, prior to entering the Navy as a master's mate, had been aboard an African slaver where he had soon learned that senseless brutality had meant loss of profit at the end of a voyage, with stinking holds as full of useless carcasses as prime, saleable bodies.

He turned angrily and shouted, 'Right! We'll move off now!' He watched with brooding eyes as the men picked up their weapons and shambled down the track, while that arrogant young monkey Farquhar strode up the hillside to head inland. He was typical, Vibart thought viciously. Eighteen years old, pampered and well bred, with a powerful admiral to watch over his progress like a nurse. He glared at the lanky Maynard: 'Don't stand there gaping. Go ahead of the party!'

Well, in spite of their advantages of breeding and influence he, Giles Vibart, had shown them. He allowed the knowledge to stir his insides like rum. He had realized that Pomfret's weakness could not be changed, just as he had soon understood that to oppose him would have finished any hope he might have had left for personal reward. He had managed to overcome his own objections. After all, did it really matter that men were unjustly flogged? They might be flogged later for real cause, so where was the difference?

He had had one ally aboard the unhappy frigate. David Evans, the purser, had kept him fully informed of what was going on between decks. Evans was an evil man even by the standards of his trade. Whenever his ship touched land he would be ashore negotiating for stores and food, using his keen brain and ready tongue to purchase the very worst, the most rancid stock available, and adjusting the price to his own pocket. Vibart, as first lieutenant, was well aware of this trick, but used his knowledge to his own advantage. Evans had useful toadies on the lower deck, reliable men who would inform readily on their messmates for small reward.

Carefully and methodically Vibart had put ruthless pressure on the crew. But floggings were all in the captain's name, never in his own. He was always careful to show off his own seamanship and prowess at navigation whenever Pomfret was not there to see it. Whatever happened when the pressure broke through the men's resistance, Vibart had to be sure that he was ready and blameless at any enquiry.

Evans had told him about the proposed mutiny, and Vibart had known that the moment had at last arrived. When he had suggested to Pomfret that the flogged seaman, Fisher, should be lashed to the bowsprit like some flayed figurehead, he had known that it was the last thing needed to fan alive the flame of anger and mutiny.

The ringleaders had chosen their time well, he conceded. If Okes had been officer-of-the-watch he might have panicked and raised an almighty row which even Pomfret, half sodden with drink in his bunk, would have heard. But Herrick was a different matter. He was a thinker. He would be bound to reason with the men, to prevent an uprising rather than to crush it by brute force.

Knowing all these things, even to the chosen time, Vibart had waited breathlessly in his cabin. Squeezed in the wardroom had been the ship's full complement of marines, their sergeant another of Vibart's willing helpers. It was such a straightforward plan that Vibart had wanted to laugh at its simplicity.

The mutineers would rush the quarterdeck and overpower the watch. Herrick, rather than raise the alarm and drive Pomfret to another bloody frenzy, would try to quieten them, to listen to their complaints. But the men would kill him, and then Vibart would rush on deck and blanket the quarterdeck with musket fire. At the court of enquiry even the most biased admiral would not fail to see that Vibart had saved the ship, when one officer lay dead with his watch and the captain slept in a drunken stupor.

Even now on the wet hillside Vibart could remember the sound of his own breathing in that sealed cabin. Then the stealthy approach of the mutineers even as two bells pealed out from forward. But there were no shots, and no cries. No rasp of steel, or the sound of Herrick's last gasp for life.

When at last, unable to control his anxiety, he had crept on deck he had found Herrick at his post, the maindeck deserted.

The young lieutenant had reported the incident as a 'deputation' concerned with the welfare of the dying Fisher. That was all. When Vibart had pushed him further, Herrick had still stood his ground, his anger giving way to contempt as his eyes had fallen on Vibart's loaded pistols and the marine sergeant at the cabin hatch.

The next morning Pomfret had been almost as beside himself as if an actual mutiny had broken out. 'Complaints?' He had screamed at Vibart across the wide cabin. 'They *dare* to complain?' Even without much prompting he had seen the men's actions as a real challenge to his own authority.

When at last the frigate had been ordered to Portsmouth to face an enquiry, Vibart had known fresh hope. Things had moved fast. The ship had been stripped of known troublemakers and had been fitted out for another long spell of service. Pomfret had stayed in his cabin, sulky and brooding up to the time he was ordered from the ship. But no new commission had arrived for Vibart. No command of either the *Phalarope* or any other ship.

He was back exactly as he had been when he had first joined the frigate under Pomfret, except that the new captain, Bolitho, was another kind of person entirely.

He jerked from his thoughts as Maynard called breathlessly, 'Sir! One of the men is signalling from the hillside!'

Vibart drew his sword and slashed sharply at a small bush. 'So the captain guessed right, did he?' He waved his arm in a half circle. 'Right, you men! Get to either side of the road and wait for Mr. Farquhar's party to work round behind them. I don't want anyone to escape!' He saw the men nod and shuffle to the bushes, swinging their clubs and readjusting their cutlass belts. When the moment of contact actually came, even Vibart was taken off guard.

It was more like a carefree procession than a party of men avoiding the press gangs. Some fifty or more men tightly bunched on the narrow track, talking, some even singing as they strolled aimlessly away from Falmouth and the sea.

Vibart saw Farquhar's slim silhouette break the skyline and stepped out from the bushes. His appearance could not have affected them more deeply had he been something from another world. He held up his sword as his men stepped out across the road behind him.

'In the King's name! I charge you all to line up and be examined!' His voice broke the spell. Some of the men turned and tried to run back along the road, only to halt gasping at the sight of Farquhar's men and the levelled muskets. One figure bolted up the hillside, his feet kicking the grass like some terrified rabbit.

Josling, a bosun's mate, lashed out with his cudgel. The man screamed and rolled down the slope and lay in a puddle clutching his shin. Josling turned him over with his foot and felt the man's bleeding leg. Then he looked at Vibart and said off-handedly, 'No eggs broken, sir!'

Shocked and dazed the men allowed themselves to be pushed into line on the road. Vibart stood watching and calculating. It had been so easy that he wanted to grin.

Brock said, 'Fifty-two men, sir. All sound in wind and limb!'

One of the uneven rank dropped on to his knees and whimpered, 'Please, *please*, sir! Not me!'

There were tears on his cheeks, and Vibart asked harshly, 'What is so special about you?'

'My wife, sir! She's *ill*! She needs me at home!' He rocked on his knees. 'She'll die without my support, sir, in God's name she will!'

Vibart said wearily, 'Stand that man on his feet. He makes me sick!'

Another at the end of the rank said in a tight voice, 'I am a shepherd, I'm excused from the press!' He stared round challengingly until his eye fell on Brock. 'Ask him, sir. The gunner will bear me out!'

Brock sauntered across to him and held up his cane. 'Roll up your sleeve.' He sounded bored, even indifferent, and several of the watching men forgot their shocked misery to lean from the rank and watch. The man in question took a half-pace away, but not quickly enough. Like a steel claw Brock's hand fastened on his rough shirt and tore it from his arm to display an interwoven tattoo of crossed flags and cannon.

Brock stepped back and swayed on his heels. He looked along the rank. 'No man has a tattoo like that unless he is a seaman.' His voice was slow and patient, like a schoolmaster with a new class. 'No man would recognize me as a gunner unless he had served in a King's ship!'

Without warning his cane flashed in the weak sunlight. When it returned to his side the other man had blood on his face where it had cut almost to the bone. The gunner looked at him levelly. "Most of all, I dislike being taken for a fool!' He turned his back, dismissing the man from his mind.

A seaman yelled, 'Another signal, sir! One more group comin' down the road!'

Vibart sheathed his sword. 'Very well.' He looked coldly at the shivering line of men. 'You are entering an honourable service. You have just learned the first lesson. Don't make me teach you another!'

Maynard fell into step beside him his face troubled. 'It seems a pity that there is no other way, sir?'

Vibart did not reply. Like the man who had begged for his wife, such statements lacked both purpose and meaning.

Only aboard the ship did anything count for any of them.

Bolitho sipped at his port and waited until the servant girl had cleared away the table. His stomach had long grown used to meagre and poorly cooked shipboard food, so that the excellent meal of good Cornish lamb left him feeling glutted and uncomfortable.

Across the table his father, James Bolitho, drummed impatiently on the polished wood with his one remaining hand and then took a long swallow of port. He seemed ill at ease, even nervous, as he had been from the moment of his son's arrival.

Bolitho watched him quietly and waited. There was such a change in his father. From his own boyhood days to the present time Bolitho had seen his father only on rarely spaced occasions when he had returned here to the family home. From foreign wars and far-off countries, from exploits which children could only guess at. He could remember him as tall and grave in his naval uniform, shedding his service self-discipline like a cloak as he had come through that familiar doorway beside the portraits of the Bolitho family. Men like himself, like his son, sailors first and foremost.

When Bolitho had been a midshipman under Sir Henry Langford he had learned of his father's wounds whilst he had been engaged in fighting for the fast-advancing colonies in India, and when he had seen him again he had found him suddenly old and embittered. He had been a man of boundless energy and ideas, and to be removed from the Navy List, no matter how honourably, was more than the loss of an arm, it was like having his life cut from within him.

Locally in Falmouth he was respected as a firm and just magistrate, but Bolitho knew in his heart that his father's very being still lay with the sea, and the ships which came and went on the tide. Even his old friends and comrades had stopped coming to visit him, perhaps unable to bear what their very presence represented. Interest changed so easily into envy. Contact could harm rather than soothe.

Bolitho had a brother and two sisters. The latter had now both married, one to a farmer, the other to an officer of the garrison. Of Hugh, his older brother, nothing had yet been said, and Bolitho made himself wait for what he guessed was uppermost in his father's mind.

'I watched your ship come in, Richard.' The hand drummed busily on the table. 'She's a fine vessel, and when you get to the West Indies again I have no doubt you will bring more honour to the family.' He shook his head sadly. 'England needs all her sons now. It seems as if the world must be our enemy before we can find the right solution.'

It was very quiet in the house. After the pitch of a deck, the creak of spars, it was like another world. Even the smells were different. The packed humanity, and the varied aromas of tar and salt, of cooking and damp, all were alien here.

It felt lonely, too. In his mind's eye he could still picture his mother, young and vivacious as he remembered her. Again, he had been at sea when she had died of some brief but final illness. Now there was no companion for James Bolitho, and nobody to sit enraptured or amused by stories of the family's past exploits.

Bolitho glanced at the great clock. 'My men will have found new people for the crew by now or not at all,' he said quietly. 'It is a sad necessity that we have to get seamen like this.'

His father's face came alive from his inner thoughts. 'I believe that their duty is more important than their passing comfort! Every week I have to sign deportation orders for the colonies, or hang useless thieves. Life in a King's ship would have spared them the indignity of life ashore, would have saved them from petty greed and temptation!'

Bolitho studied his father's face and remembered himself as he had appeared in the mirror of the George Inn at Portsmouth. It was there in his father, as it was in the portraits along the walls. The same calm face and dark hair, the same slightly hooked nose. But his father had lost his old fire, and his hair was grey now, like that of a man much older.

His father stood up and walked to the fire. Over his shoulder he said gruffly, 'You have not yet heard about your brother?'

Bolitho tensed. 'No. I thought he was still at sea.'

'At sea?' The older man shook his head vaguely. 'Of course, I kept it from you. I suppose I should have written to you, but in my heart I still hoped he might change his ways and nobody would have known about it.'

Bolitho waited. His brother had always been the apple of his father's eye. When last he had seen him he had been a lieutenant in the Channel Fleet, the next in line for this house and for the family inheritance. Bolitho had never felt particularly close to Hugh, but put it down to a natural family jealousy. Now, he was not so sure.

'I had great hopes for Hugh.' His father was talking to the fire. To himself. 'I am only glad his mother is not alive to know of what he became!'

'Is there something I can do?' Bolitho watched the shoulders quiver as his father sought to control his voice.

'Nothing. Hugh is no longer in the Navy. He got into debt gambling. He always had an eye for the tables, as I think you know. But he got into *deep* trouble, and to end it all he fought a duel with a brother officer, and killed him!'

Bolitho's mind began to clear. That explained the few servants and the fact that over half the land belonging to the house had been sold to a local farmer.

'You covered his debts then?' He kept his voice calm. 'I have some prize money if . . .'

The other man held up his hand. 'That is not necessary. It was my fault for being so blind. I was stupid about that boy. I must pay for my misjudgement!' He seemed to become more weary. 'He deserted the Navy, turned his back on it, even knowing how his act would hurt me. Now he has gone.'

Bolitho started. 'Gone?'

'He went to America. I have not heard of him for two years, nor do I want to.' When he turned Bolitho saw the lie shining in his eyes. 'Not content with bringing disgrace on the family name, he has done this thing. Betrayed his country!'

Bolitho thought of the chaos and death at the disaster of Philadelphia and answered slowly, 'He may have been prevented from returning by the rebellion.'

'You know your brother, Richard. Do you really think it likely? He always had to be right, to hold the winning cards. No, I cannot see him pining away in a prison camp!'

The servant girl entered the room and bobbed in a clumsy curtsy. 'Beggin' pardon, zur. There's an officer to zee you.'

'That'll be Herrick, my third lieutenant,' said Bolitho hurriedly. 'I asked him to take a glass with us. I'll tell him to go if you wish?'

His father stood up straight and flicked his coat into position again. 'No, boy. Have him come in. I will not let my shame interfere with the real pride I have in my *remaining* son.'

Bolitho said gently, 'I am very sorry, Father. You must know that.'

'Thank you. Yes, I do know. And you were the one I thought would never make your way in the Navy. You were always the dreamer, the unpredictable one. I am afraid I neglected you for Hugh.' He sighed. 'Now it is too late.' There was a step in the hallway and he said with sudden urgency, 'In case I never see you again, my boy, there is something you must have.' He swallowed. 'I wanted Hugh to have it when he became a captain.' He reached into a cupboard and held out his sword. It was old and well tarnished, but Bolitho knew it was of greater value than steel and gilt.

He hesitated. 'Your father's sword. You always wore it!'

James Bolitho nodded and turned it over carefully in his hands. 'Yes, I always wore it. It was a good friend.' He held it out. 'Take it! I *want* you to wear it for me!'

His father suddenly smiled. 'Well then, let us greet your junior officer together, eh?'

When Herrick walked uncertainly into the wide room he saw only his smiling host and his new captain, one the living mould of the other. Only Bolitho saw the pain in his father's eyes and was deeply moved.

It was strange how he had come to the house, as he had always done in the past, seeking comfort and advice. Yet he had mentioned nothing about the difficulties and danger of his new command, or the double-edged responsibility which hung over his head like an axe.

For once, he had been the one who was needed, and he was ashamed because he did not know the answer.

At dawn the following day the frigate *Phalarope* unfurled her sails and broke out her anchor. There were no cheers to speed her parting, but there were many tears and curses from the women and old men who watched from the jetties.

The air was keen and fresh, and as the yards creaked round and the ship heeled away from the land Bolitho stood aft by the taffrail, his glass moving slowly across the green sloping hills and the huddled town below.

He had his ship, and all but a full complement. With time the new men would soon be moulded into sailors, and given patience and understanding they might make their country proud of them.

St. Anthony's Light moved astern, the ancient beacon which was the returning sailor's first sight of home. Bolitho wondered when or if he would see it again. He thought too of his father, alone in the old house, alone with his memories and shattered hopes. He thought of the sword and all that it represented.

He turned away from the rail and stared down at one of the ship's boys, a mere infant of about twelve years old. The boy was weeping uncontrollably and waving vaguely at the land as it cruised away into the haze. Bolitho asked, 'Do you know that I was your age when I first went to sea, boy?'

The lad rubbed his nose with a grubby fist and gazed at the captain with something like wonder.

Bolitho added, 'You'll see England again. Never you fear!' He turned away quickly lest the boy should see the uncertainty in his eye.

By the wheel old Proby intoned, 'South-west by south. Full and by, quartermaster.'

Then, as if to cut short the agony of sailing, he walked to the lee rail and spat into the sea.

3. BEEF FOR THE PURSER

TWENTY DAYS after weighing anchor the frigate *Phalarope* crossed the thirtieth parallel and heeled sickeningly to a blustering north-west gale. Falmouth lay three thousand miles astern, but the wind with all its tricks and cunning cruelties stayed resolutely with the ship.

As one bell struck briefly from the forecastle and the dull copper sun moved towards the horizon the frigate ploughed across each successive bank of white-crested rollers with neither care nor concern for the men who served her day by day, hour by hour. No sooner was one watch dismissed below than the boatswain's mates would run from hatch to hatch, their calls twittering, their voices hoarse in the thunder of canvas and the never ending hiss of spray.

'All hands! All hands! Shorten sail!'

Later, stiff and dazed from their dizzy climb aloft, the seamen would creep below, their bodies aching, their fingers stiff and bleeding from their fight with the rebellious canvas.

Now, the men off watch crouched in the semi-darkness of the berth deck groping for handholds and listening to the crash of water against the hull even as they tried to finish their evening meal. From the deck beams the swinging lanterns threw strange shadows across their bowed heads, picking out individual faces and actions like scenes from a partially cleaned oil painting.

Below the sealed hatches the air was thick with smells. That of bilge water mixing with sweat and the sour odour of seasickness, and the whole area was filled with sound as the ship fought her own battle with the Atlantic. The steady crash of waves followed by the jubilant surge of water along the deck above, the continuous groaning of timbers and the humming of taut stays, all defied the men to sleep and relax even for a moment.

John Allday sat astride one of the long, scrubbed benches and gnawed carefully at a tough piece of salt beef. Between his strong teeth it felt like leather, but he made himself eat it, and closed his mind to the rancid cask from which it had come. The deep cut on his cheek where Brock's cane had found its mark had healed in an ugly scar, and as his jaws moved steadily on the meat he could feel the skin tightening painfully where blown salt and cold winds had drawn the edges together like crude stitching.

Across the table, and watching him with an unwinking stare, sat Pochin, a giant seaman with shoulders like a cliff. He said at last, 'You've settled in right enough, mate.' He smiled bleakly. 'All that squit when you was pressed came to nothin'!'

Allday threw a meat bone on to his tin plate and wiped his fingers on a piece of hemp. He regarded the other man with his steady, calm eyes for several seconds and then replied, 'I can wait.'

Pochin glared through the gloom, his head cocked to listen to some of the men retching. 'Lot of bloody women!' He looked back at Allday. 'I was forgettin', you are an old hand at this.'

Allday shrugged and looked down at his palms. 'You never get rid of the tar, do you?' He leaned back against the timbers and sighed. 'My last ship was the *Resolution*, seventy-four. I was a foretopman.' He allowed his eyes to close. 'A good enough ship. We paid off just a few months before the American Revolution, and I was clean away before the press could lay a finger on me!'

An old, grey-haired man with washed-out blue eyes said huskily, 'Was you really a shepherd like you told 'em?'

Allday nodded. 'That, and other things. I had to stay out in the open. To keep away from the towns. I would choke to death under a roof!' He gave a small smile. 'Just an occasional run into Falmouth was enough for me. Just enough for a woman, and a glass or two!'

The old seaman, Strachan, pursed his lips and rocked against the table as the ship heeled steeply and sent the plates skittering across the deck. 'It sounds like a fair life, mate.' He seemed neither wistful nor envious. It was just a statement. Old Ben Strachan had been in the Navy for forty years, since he had first trod deck as a powder-monkey. Life ashore was a mystery to him, and in his regimented world appeared even more dangerous than the privations afloat.

Allday looked round as a hunched figure rose over the table's edge and threw himself across his arms amongst the litter of food. Bryan Ferguson had been in a continuous torment of seasickness and fear from the very moment Vibart's figure had appeared on that coast road. In Falmouth he had been a clerk working at a local boatyard. Physically he was not a strong man, and now in the swinging lantern's feeble light his face looked as grey as death itself.

His thin body was bruised in many places both from falling against unfamiliar shipboard objects and not least from the angry canes of the bosun's mates and petty officers as the latter sought to drive the new men into the mysteries of seamanship and sail drill.

Day after day it had continued. Harried and chased from one part of the ship to the next with neither let-up nor mercy. Quivering with terror Ferguson had dragged his way up the swooping shrouds and out along the yards, until he could see the creaming water leaping below him as if to claw at his very feet. The first time he had clung sobbing to the mast, incapable of either moving out along the yard or even down towards the safety of the deck.

Josling, a bosun's mate, had screamed up at him, 'Move out, you bugger, or I'll have the hide off you!'

At that particular moment Ferguson's tortured mind had almost broken. With each eager thrust of the frigate's stem, and with every passing hour, Ferguson's home fell further and further astern. And with it went his wife, sinking into the wave-tossed distance like a memory.

Over and over again he had pictured her pale, anxious face as he had last seen her. When the *Phalarope* had been sighted heading for Falmouth Bay most of the young townsmen had headed for the hills. Ferguson's wife had been ill for three years, and he had seen her get more frail and delicate, and on that day she had been more than unwell and he had begged to stay with her. But gravely she had insisted.

'You go with the others, Bryan. I'll be all right. And I'm not wanting the press to find you here!'

The nightmare became worse when he considered that if he had stayed with her he would still be safe and able to protect and help her.

Allday said quietly, 'Here, take some food.' He pushed a plate of dark meat across the boards. 'You've not eaten for days, man.'

Ferguson dragged his head from his forearms and stared glassily at the relaxed looking seaman. Unbeknown to Allday, Ferguson had almost jumped from the swaying mainyard rather than face another hour of torture. But Allday had run inboard along the yard, his feet splayed and balanced, one hand held out towards the gasping Ferguson. 'Here, mate! Just follow me an' don't look down.' There had been a quiet force in his tone, like that of a man who expected to be obeyed. He had added harshly, 'Don't give that bugger Josling a chance to beat you. The bastard enjoys making you jump!'

He stared now at the man's dark features, at the scar on his cheek, and at his calm, level eyes. Allday had been accepted immediately by the frigate's seamen, whereas the other newly pressed men were still kept at arm's length, as if on trial, until their merits or shortcomings could be properly measured. Perhaps it was because Allday was already hardened to a life at sea. Or from the fact he never showed his bitterness at being pressed, or boasted about his life ashore like some of the others.

Ferguson swallowed hard to bite back the rising nausea. 'I can't eat it!' He peered wretchedly at the meat. 'It's swill!'

Allday grinned. 'You'll get used to it!'

Pochin sneered. 'You make me spew! I suppose you used to take your wife up to the 'eadland and go moist-eyed at the sight of a King's ship! I'll bet you used to feel so holy, so almighty proud as the ships sailed safely past!' Ferguson stared at the man's angry face, mesmerized by his hate.

Pochin glared across the canting deck where the other crowded seamen had fallen silent at his outburst. 'You never had a thought for the poor buggers who manned 'em, nor what they was doin'!' He turned back to Ferguson with sudden malice. 'Well, your precious woman'll be out on the 'eadland now with some other pretty boy, I shouldn't wonder.' He made an obscene gesture. 'Let's 'ope she finds the time to be proud of *you*!'

Ferguson staggered to his feet, his eyes wide with a kind of madness. 'I'll kill you for that!'

He swung his fist, but Allday caught his wrist in mid-air. 'Save it!' Allday glared at Pochin's grinning face. 'His wife is sick, Pochin! Give him some rest!'

Old Ben Strachan said vaguely, 'I 'ad a wife once.' He scratched his shaggy grey head. 'Blessed if I can remember 'er name now!'

Some of the men laughed, and Allday hissed fiercely, 'Get a grip, Bryan! You can't beat men like Pochin. He envies you, that's all!'

Ferguson hardly heard the friendly warning in Allday's voice. Pochin's goading tone had opened the misery in his heart with renewed force, so that he could see his wife propped in her bed by the window as clearly as if he had just entered the room. That day, when the press gang had pushed him down the hill-side, she would have been sitting there, waiting for his return. Now he was never going back. Would never see her again.

He staggered to his feet and threw the plate of meat down on the deck. 'I can't!' He was screaming. 'I won't!'

A horse-faced fo'c's'leman named Betts jumped to his feet as if shaken from a deep sleep. 'Don't jeer at 'im, mates!' He stood swaying below one of the lanterns. 'He's 'ad enough for a bit.'

Pochin groaned. 'Lord save us!' He rolled his eyes in mock concern.

Betts snarled, 'Jesus Christ! What do you have to suffer before you understand? This man is sick with fear for his wife, and others here have equal troubles. Yet all some of you can do is scoff at 'em!'

Allday shifted in his seat. Ferguson's sudden despair had touched some hidden spring in the men's emotions. Weeks, and in some cases years at sea without ever putting a foot on dry land were beginning to take a cruel toll. But this was dangerous and blind. He held up his hand and said calmly, 'Easy, lads. Easy.'

Betts glared down at him, his salt-reddened eyes only half focusing on Allday's face. 'How can you interfere?' His voice was slurred. 'We live like animals, on food that was rotten even afore it was put in casks!' He pulled his knife from his belt and drove it into the table. 'While those pigs down aft live like kings!' He peered round for support. 'Well, ain't I right? That bastard Evans is as sleek as a churchyard rat on what he stole from our food!'

'Well, now. Did I hear my name mentioned?'

The berth deck froze into silence as Evans, the purser, moved into a patch of lamplight.

With his long coat buttoned to his throat and his hair pulled back severely above his narrow face he looked for all the world like a ferret on the attack. He put his head on one side. 'Well, I'm waiting!'

Allday watched him narrowly. There was something evil and frightening about the little Welsh purser. All the more so because any one of the men grouped around him could have ended his life with a single blow.

Then Evan's eye fell on the meat beside the table. He sucked his teeth and asked sadly, 'And who did this, then?'

No one spoke, and once more the angry roar of the sea and wind enclosed the staggering berth deck with noise.

Ferguson looked up, his eyes bright and feverish. 'I did it.'

Evans leaned his narrow shoulders against the massive trunk of the foremast which ran right through both decks and said, ' "I did it, *sir*." '

Ferguson mumbled something, then added. 'I am sorry, sir.'

Allday said coldly, 'It was an accident, Mr. Evans. Just an accident.'

'Food is food.' Evans' Welsh accent became more pronounced as his face became angrier. 'I cannot hope to keep you men in good health if you waste such excellent meat, now can I?'

Those grouped around the table stared down at the shapeless hunk of rancid beef as it lay gleaming in a patch of lamplight.

Evans added sharply, 'Now, you, whatever your bloody name is, *eat it*!'

Ferguson stared down at the meat, his mind swimming in nausea. The deck was discoloured with water and stained with droppings from the tilting table. There was vomit too, perhaps his own.

Evans said gently, 'I am waiting, boyo. One more minute and I'll take you aft. A touch of the cat might teach you some appreciation!'

Ferguson dropped to his knees and picked up the meat. As he lifted it to his mouth Betts pushed forward and tore it from his hands and threw it straight at Evans. 'Take it yourself, you bloody devil! Leave him alone!'

For a moment Evans showed the fear in his dark eyes. The men had crowded around him, their bodies rising and falling like a human tide with each roll of the ship. He could feel the menace, the sudden ice touch of terror.

Another voice cut through the shadows. 'Stand aside!' Midshipman Farquhar had to stoop beneath the low beams, but his eyes were steady and bright as they settled on the frozen tableau around the end table. Farquhar's approach had been so stealthy and quiet that not even the men at the opposite end of the deck had noticed him. He snapped, 'I am waiting. What is going on here?'

Evans thrust the nearest men aside and threw himself to Farquhar's side. With his hand shaking in both fear and fury he pointed at Betts. 'He struck me! *Me*, a warrant officer!'

Farquhar was expressionless. His tight lips and cold stare might have meant either amusement or anger. 'Very well, Mr. Evans. Kindly lay aft for the master-at-arms.'

As the purser scurried away Farquhar looked round the circle of faces with open contempt. 'You never seem to learn, do you?' He turned to Betts, who still stood staring at the meat, his chest heaving as if from tremendous exertion. 'You are a fool, Betts! Now you will pay for it!'

Allday pressed his shoulders against the frigate's cold, wet timbers and closed his eyes. It was all happening just as he knew it would. He listened to Betts' uneven breathing and Ferguson's quiet whimpers and felt sick. He thought suddenly of the quiet hillsides and grey bunches of sheep. The space and the solitude.

Then Farquhar barked, 'Take him away, Mr. Thain.'

The master-at-arms pushed Betts towards the hatch ladder adding softly, 'Not a single flogging since we left Falmouth. I knew such gentleness was a bad mistake!'

Richard Bolitho leaned his palms on the sill of one of the big stern windows and stared out along the ship's frothing wake. Although the cabin itself was already in semi-darkness as the frigate followed the sun towards the horizon, the sea still looked alive, with only a hint of purple as a warning of the approaching night.

Reflected in the salt-speckled glass he could see Vibart's tall shape in the centre of the cabin, his face shadowed beneath the corkscrewing lantern, and behind him against the screen the slim figure of Midshipman Farquhar.

It took most of his self-control to keep himself immobile and calm as he considered what Farquhar had burst in to tell him. Bolitho had been going through the ship's books again trying to draw out Vibart's wooden reserve, to feel his way into the man's mind.

Like everything else during the past twenty days, it had been a hard and seemingly fruitless task. Vibart was too careful to show his hostility in the open and confined himself to short, empty answers, as if he hoarded his knowledge of the ship and her company like a personal possession.

Then Farquhar had entered the cabin with this story of Betts' assault on the purser. It was just one more thing to distract his thoughts from what lay ahead, from the real task of working the frigate into a single fighting unit.

He made himself turn and face the two officers.

'Sentry! Pass the word for Mr. Evans!' He heard the cry passed along the passageway and then added, 'It seems to me as if this seaman was provoked.'

Vibart swayed with the ship, his eyes fixed on a point above the captain's shoulder. He said thickly, 'Betts is no recruit, sir. He knew what he was doing!'

Bolitho turned to watch the open, empty sea. If only this had not happened just yet, he thought bitterly. A few more days and the damp, wind-buffeted ship would be in the sun, where men soon learned to forget their surroundings and started to look outboard instead of watching each other.

He listened to the hiss and gurgle of water around the rudder, the distant clank of pumps as the duty watch dealt with the inevitable seepage into the bilges. He felt tired and strained to the limit. From the moment the *Phalarope* had weighed anchor he had not spared himself or his efforts to maintain his hold over the ship. He had made a point of speaking to most of the new men, and of establishing contact with the regular crew. He had watched his officers, and had driven the ship to her utmost. It should have been a proud moment for him. The frigate handled well, lively and ready to respond to helm and sail like a thoroughbred.

Most of the new men had been sorted into their most suitable stations, and the sail drill had advanced beyond even his expectations. At the first suitable moment he intended to exercise the guns crews, but up to this time he had been prevented from much more than allocations of hands to the various divisions by the unceasing wind.

Now this, he fumed inwardly. No wonder the admiral had asked him to watch young Farquhar's behaviour.

There was a tap at the door and Evans stepped gingerly into the cabin, his eyes flickering like beads in the lamplight.

Bolitho gestured impatiently. 'Now then, Mr. Evans. Let me have the full story.'

He turned to stare at the water again as Evans launched into his account. To start with he seemed nervous, even frightened, but when Bolitho allowed him to continue without interruption or comment his voice grew sharper and more outraged.

Bolitho said at length. 'The meat that Betts threw at you. What cask did it come from?'

Evans was caught off guard. 'Number twelve, sir. I saw it stowed myself.' He added in a wheedling tone, 'I do my best, sir. They are ungrateful dogs for the most part.'

Bolitho turned and tapped the papers on his table. 'I checked the stowage myself, too, Mr. Evans. Two days ago when the hands were at drill!' He saw a flicker of alarm show itself on

Evans' dark face and knew that his lie had gone home. A feeling of sudden anger swept through him like fire. All the things he had told his officers had been for nothing. Even the near-mutiny seemed to have made no impression on the minds of men like Evans and Farquhar.

He snapped, 'That cask was in the low stowage, was it not? And how many others were down there, do you think?'

Evans peered nervously around the cabin. 'Five or six, sir. They were some of the original stores which I . . .'

Bolitho slammed his fist on the table. 'You make me sick, Evans! That cask and those others you have suddenly remembered were probably stowed two years ago before you began the Brest blockade! They most likely leak, and in any case are quite rotten!' Evans looked at his feet. 'I—I did not know, sir.'

Bolitho said harshly, 'If I could prove otherwise, Mr. Evans, I would have you stripped of your rank and flogged!'

Vibart stirred into life. 'I must protest, sir! Mr. Evans was acting as he thought fit! Betts struck him. There is no way of avoiding that fact.'

'So it appears, Mr. Vibart.' Bolitho stared at him coldly until the other man looked away. 'I will certainly back my officers in their efforts to carry out my orders. But senseless punishment at this time will do more harm than good.' He felt suddenly too tired to think clearly, but Vibart's anger seemed to drive him on. 'In another two weeks or so we will join the fleet under Sir Samuel Hood, and then there will be more than enough to keep us all occupied.'

He continued more calmly, 'Until then, each and every one of you will translate my standing orders into daily fact. Give the men your leadership and try to understand them. No good will ever come of useless brutality. If a man still persists in disobedience, then flogged he will be. But in this particular case I would suggest a more lenient experiment.' He saw Vibart's lower lip quivering with barely controlled anger. 'Betts can be awarded extra duties for seven days. The sooner the matter is forgotten, the sooner we can mend the damage!' He gestured briefly, 'Carry on with your watch, Mr. Farquhar.'

As Evans turned to follow the midshipman Bolitho added flatly, 'Oh, Mr. Evans, I see no reason for me to mention your neglect in the log.' He saw Evans watching him half gratefully, half fearfully. He finished, 'Provided I can show that you purchased the meat for your own purposes, your own mess perhaps?'

Evans blinked at Vibart and then back to Bolitho's impassive face. 'Purchase, sir? Me, sir?'

'Yes, Evans, *you*! You can make the payment to my clerk in the forenoon tomorrow. That is all.'

Vibart picked up his hat and waited until the door had closed behind the other man. 'Do you require me any more, sir?'

'I just want to tell you one thing more, Mr. Vibart. I have taken fully into consideration that you were under considerable strain during your duty with Captain Pomfret. Maybe some of the things you had to do were not to your liking.' He waited, but Vibart stared woodenly across his shoulder. 'I am not interested in the past, except as a lesson to everyone of what can happen in a badly run ship! As first lieutenant you are the key officer, the most experienced one aboard who can implement my orders, do you understand?'

'If you say so, sir.'

Bolitho dropped his eyes in case Vibart should see the rising anger there. He had offered Vibart his due share of responsibility, even his confidence, and yet the lieutenant seemed to accept it like a sign of weakness, of some faltering uncertainty. The contempt was as plain in his brevity as if he had shouted it to the ship at large. It could not be easy for Vibart to take orders from a captain so junior in age and service. Bolitho tried once more to soften his feelings towards Vibart's hostility.

The latter said suddenly, 'When you have been aboard the *Phalarope* a little longer, sir, then maybe you will see it different.' He rocked back on his heels and watched Bolitho's face with a flat stare.

Bolitho relaxed his taut muscles. It was almost a relief that Vibart had shown him the only way to finish the matter. He eyed him coldly. 'I have read every log and report aboard this ship, Mr. Vibart. In all my limited *experience* I have never known a ship so apparently unwilling to fight the enemy or so incapable of performing her duty.' He watched the expression on Vibart's heavy features altering to shocked surprise. 'Well, we are going back to war, Mr. Vibart, and I intend to seek out and engage the enemy, *any* enemy, at every opportunity!' He dropped his voice. 'And when that happens I will expect to see every man acting as one. There will be no room for petty jealousy and cowardice then!'

A deep flush rose to Vibart's cheeks, but he remained silent.

Bolitho said, 'You are dealing with men, Mr. Vibart, not *things*! Authority is invested with your commission. Respect comes later, when you have earned it!'

He dismissed the first lieutenant with a curt nod and then turned back to stare at the creaming wake below the windows. As the door closed the tension tore at his body like a whip, and he gripped his hands together to prevent their shaking until the pain made him wince. He had made an enemy of Vibart, but there was too much at stake to do otherwise.

He slumped down on the bench seat as Stockdale pattered into the cabin and began to spread a cloth across the table.

The coxswain said, 'I've told your servant to bring your supper, Captain.' There was mistrust in his tone. He disliked Atwell, the cabin steward, and watched him like a dog with a rabbit. 'I don't suppose you'll be havin' any officer to dine with you, sir?'

Bolitho glanced at Stockdale, battered and homely like an old piece of furniture, and thought of Vibart's seething bitterness. 'No, Stockdale. I will be alone.' He leaned back and closed his eyes. Alone and vulnerable, he thought.

Lieutenant Thomas Herrick tightened the spray-soaked muffler about his neck and shrugged his shoulders deeper into his watch-coat. Above the black, spiralling masts the stars were small and pale, and even in the keen air he could sense that the dawn was not far away.

The labouring ship herself was in darkness, so that the shapes around the deserted decks were unreal and totally unlike they appeared in daylight. The lashed guns were mere shadows, and the humming shrouds and stays seemed to go straight up to the sky, unattached and endless.

But as Herrick paced the quarterdeck deep in thought, he was able to ignore such things. He had seen them all too often before, and was able to pass each watch with only his mind for company. Once he paused beside the ship's big double wheel where the two helmsmen stood like dark statues, their faces partly lit in the shaded binnacle lamp as they watched the swinging compass or stared aloft at the trimmed sails.

Three bells struck tinnily from forward, and he saw a ship's boy stir at the rail and then creep, rubbing his eyes, to trim the compass lamp and adjust the hour-glass.

Time and again he found his eyes drawn to the black rectangle of the cabin hatch, and he wondered whether Bolitho had at last fallen asleep. Three times already during the morning watch, three times in an hour and a half the captain had appeared momentarily on deck, soundless and without warning. With neither coat nor hat, and his white shirt and breeches framed against the tumbling black water, he had seemed ghostlike and without true form, with the restlessness of a tortured spirit. On each occasion he had paused only long enough to peer at the compass or to look at the watch-slate beside the wheel. Then a couple of turns up and down the weather side of the deck and he had vanished below.

At any other time Herrick would have felt both irritated and resentful. It might have implied that the captain was too unsure of his third lieutenant to leave him to take a watch alone. But when Herrick had relieved Lieutenant Okes at four o'clock Okes had whispered quickly that Bolitho had been on deck for most of the night.

Herrick frowned. Deep down he had the feeling that Bolitho had acted more by instinct than design. As if he was driven like the ship, by mood rather than inclination. He seemed unable to stand still, as if it took physical force to hold himself in one place for more than minutes at a time.

A figure moved darkly at the quarterdeck rail and he heard Midshipman Neale's familiar treble in the darkness.

'Able Seaman Betts has just reported, sir.' He stood staring up at Herrick, gauging his mood.

Herrick had to tear his thoughts back to the present with a jerk. Betts, the man who had apparently escaped a flogging or worse only at Bolitho's intervention, had been ordered to report at three bells for the first part of his punishment. Vibart had made it more than clear what would happen if he failed to execute the orders. He saw Betts hovering behind the small midshipman and called, 'Here, Betts. Look lively.'

The man moved to the rail and knuckled his forehead. 'Sir?'

Herrick gestured upwards towards the invisible topmast. 'Up you go then!' He kept the harshness from his tone. He liked Betts, a quiet but competent man, whose sudden flare of anger had surprised him more than he cared to admit. 'Get up to the main topmast, Betts. You will stand lookout until the first lieutenant orders otherwise.' He felt a touch of pity. One hundred and ten feet above the deck, unsheltered from the cold winds, Betts would be numb within minutes. Herrick had already decided to send Neale up after him with something warm to eat as soon as the galley fire was lit for breakfast.

Betts spat on his hands and replied flatly, 'Aye, aye, sir. Seems a fair mornin'?' He could have been remarking on something quite normal and unimportant.

Herrick nodded. 'Aye. The wind is dropping and the air is much drier.' It was true. Betts' instinct had grasped the change as soon as he had emerged from the packed, airless berth deck where eighteen inches per man was the accepted hammock space.

Herrick added quietly, 'You were lucky, Betts. You could have been dancing at the gratings by eight bells.'

Betts stood staring at him, unmoved and calm. 'I'm not sorry for what 'appened, sir. I'd do it again.'

Herrick felt suddenly annoyed with himself for mentioning the matter. That was his trouble, he thought angrily. He always wanted to know and understand the reason for everything. He could not leave matters alone.

He snapped, 'Get aloft! And mind you keep a good lookout. The dawn'll be awake soon.' He watched the man's shadow merge with the main shrouds and followed him with his eye until he was lost in the criss-cross of rigging against the stars.

Again he found himself wondering why Bolitho had acted as he had over a man like Betts. Neither Vibart nor Evans had mentioned the matter, which seemed to add rather than detract from the importance of the affair. Perhaps Vibart had over-stepped his authority again, he pondered. Under Pomfret the first lieutenant's presence had moved over the ship, controlling every action and day-to-day happening. Now he seemed hampered by Bolitho's calm authority, but the very fact that their disagree-ment was close to showing itself openly only made things worse. The ship seemed split in two, divided between the captain and Vibart. Pomfret had remained a frightening force in the back-ground, and Herrick had found his work cut out to stay impartial and out of trouble. Now it appeared as if such neutrality was impossible.

He thought back to the moment he had gone to the big house in Falmouth. Before he had imagined he would find only envy there. His own poor beginnings were hard to shake free. He recalled Bolitho's father, the great pictures along the walls, the air of permanence and tradition, as if the present occupants were merely part of a pattern. Compared with his own small home in Rochester, the house had seemed a veritable palace.

Herrick's father had been a clerk in Rochester, working for the Kentish fruit trade. But Herrick, even as a small child, had watched the ships stealing up the Medway, and had allowed his impressionable mind to build his own future accordingly. For him it was the Navy. Nothing else would do. It was odd because there was no precedent in his family, all of whom had been tradesmen, sprinkled with the occasional soldier.

His father had pleaded in vain. He had warned him of the pitfalls, which were many. Lack of personal standing and financial security made him see only too clearly what his son was attempting to challenge. He even compromised by suggest-ing a safe berth aboard an Indiaman, but Herrick was quietly adamant.

Quite by chance a visiting warship had been laid up near Rochester while repairs had been carried out to her hull. Her captain had been a friend of the man who employed Herrick's father, a grave senior captain who showed neither resentment nor open scorn when the eleven years old boy had waylaid him and told him of his desire to go to sea in a King's ship.

Faced by the captain and his employer, Herrick's father had given in. To do him full justice he had made the best of it by

using his meagre savings to send his son on his way, outwardly
at least, a young gentleman as good as any of his fellows.

Herrick was now twenty-five. It had been a long and arduous
journey from that time. He had learned humiliation and
embarrassment for the first time. He had faced unequal opposition of breeding and influence. The starry-eyed boy had been
whittled away and hardened like the good Kentish oak beneath
his feet. But one thing had not changed. His love of the sea and
the Navy stayed over him like a protecting cloak or some strange
religion which he only partly understood.

This timeless thing was the same to all men, he decided. It
was far above them. It controlled and used everyone alike, no
matter what his ambition might be.

He smiled at himself as he continued his endless pacing. He
wondered what young Neale, yawning hugely by the rail, would
think of his grave faced senior. Or the helmsmen who watched
the swinging needle and gauged the pull of the sails. Or Betts,
high overhead on his precarious perch, his own thoughts no
doubt full of what he had done and what might lie in store for
him behind Evans' vengeance.

Maybe it was better to be unimaginative, he thought. To be
completely absorbed in day-to-day worries, like Lieutenant Okes
for instance. He was a married man, and that was obstacle
enough for any young officer. Okes spent his time either fretting
about his distant wife or treading warily to avoid Vibart's eye.
He was a strange, shallow man, Herrick thought, unsure of himself, and afraid to unbend even with his own kind. It seemed as
if he was afraid of becoming too friendly, and nervous of express-
ing an opinion outside the necessities of duty. As if by so doing
he might awake suspicion elsewhere or give a hint of misplaced
loyalty.

Herrick moved his stiff shoulders inside his coat and pushed
Okes from his thoughts. He might after all be right. Aboard the
Phalarope it often seemed safer to say nothing, to do nothing
which might be wrongly interpreted later.

He stared at the weather rail and noticed with a start that he
could see the carved dolphin above the starboard ladder and
the fat, ugly carronade nearby. His thoughts had carried him
through another half hour, and soon the dawn would show him
an horizon once more. Would bring another day.

Harsh and clear above the hiss of spray he suddenly heard
Betts' voice from the masthead. 'Deck there! Sail on the starboard bow! Hull down, but it's a ship!'

Snatching his glass from the rack Herrick scrambled up into
the mizzen shrouds, his mind working on the unexpected report.
The sea was already gathering shape and personality, and there

was a finger of grey along where the horizon should be. Up there, high above the swaying deck, Betts would just be able to see the other ship in the dawn's cautious approach.

He snapped, 'Mr. Neale! Up you go and see what you can discover. If you give me a false report you'll kiss the gunner's daughter before you're much older!'

Neale's face split into a grin, and without a word he scampered like a monkey towards the main shrouds.

Herrick tried to stay calm, to return to his pacing as he had seen Bolitho do. But the newcomer, if there was indeed a ship, filled him with uncertainty, so that he stared at the dark sea as if willing it to appear. Betts called again. 'She's a frigate, sir! No doubt about it. Steerin' south-east!'

Neale's shrill voice took up the call. 'She's running before the wind like a bird, sir! Under all plain sail!'

Herrick breathed out noisily. For one brief instant he had imagined it might be a Frenchman. Even out here, alone and unaided, it was not impossible. But the French rarely sailed fast or far by night. Usually they lay to and rode out the darkness. This was no enemy.

As if to open his thoughts Betts yelled, 'I know that rig, sir! She's an English ship right enough!'

'Very well, keep on reporting!' Herrick lowered the speaking trumpet and peered back along the quarterdeck. Even in minutes the place had taken more shape and reality. The deck was pale and grey, and he could see the helmsmen again as familiar faces.

There might be new orders in the other frigate. Maybe the American war was already over and they would return to Brest or England. In his heart Herrick felt a sudden twinge of disappointment. At first the prospect of another long commission in the unhappy *Phalarope* had appalled him. Now, with the thought that he might never see the West Indies at all, he was not so sure.

Neale slithered straight down a backstay, disdaining shrouds and ratlines, and ran panting to the quarterdeck.

Herrick made up his mind. 'My respects to the captain, Mr. Neale, and tell him we have sighted a King's ship. She will be up to us in an hour, maybe much less. He will wish to prepare himself.'

Neale hurried down the hatchway and Herrick stared across the tumbling waste of water. Bolitho would be even more concerned, he thought. If the *Phalarope* was ordered home now, all his plans and promises would be without meaning. He would have lost his private battle before he had had time to begin.

There was a soft step beside him and Bolitho said, 'Now, Mr. Herrick, what about this ship?'

4. THE SIGNAL

BOLITHO steadied his glasses against the weather rigging and
waited for the other ship to leap into focus. In the time it had
taken him to walk from his cabin to the quarterdeck and listen
to Herrick's excited report, the dawn sun had slowly clawed its
way over the horizon so that already the endless waste of tossing
whitecaps was touched with pale gold, the shadows gone from
the short, steep waves.

The other vessel made a fine sight in the strengthening light,
he thought, with her tall pyramids of full sails and the unbroken
curtain of spray bursting around the high bow. She was moving
fast, her topmasts glittering in the weak sunlight like crucifixes.

Over his shoulder he called, 'You have a good lookout, Mr.
Herrick! He is to be complimented for such an early sighting.'

Even for a trained seaman it was not easy to pick out a ship
from the shadows of night and dawn and identify her. She was
English right enough, and there was a certain familiarity about
her. Vaguely in the background he could hear the boatswain's
mates calling the hands, the shrill twitter of pipes.

'All hands! All hands! Show a leg!'

He could imagine the sleep-dazed men tumbling from their
hammocks groaning and protesting, while from forward came
the usual mixture of smells from the galley. Another day, but
this time it would be different. The sea was no longer empty
and hostile. The other ship might make the men remember that
they were part of something real and important.

He saw the frigate's big yards begin to change shape and
heard Herrick say, 'She's going about, sir. She'll be up to us
shortly!'

Bolitho nodded absently. The stranger would swing round to
run parallel, keeping the *Phalarope* down to leeward. As Herrick
had suggested, it might mean new orders.

He climbed down from the rigging suddenly chilled and tired.
The keen spray had moulded his shirt to his body and his hair
felt wet against his cheek. He noticed that his ship had changed
yet again. The quarterdeck seemed thronged with figures, the
officers keeping to the lee side, but with their glasses raised and
watching the other frigate.

Midshipman Maynard looked anxiously towards the stranger
and strained his eye through his big telescope. As he was in
charge of signals he knew that Bolitho would be watching him.

The maindeck was also alive with newly awakened seamen,
and the bosun's mates had to use their ropes ends more than

usual to drive them away from the bulwark as they peered across the water at the frigate's approach. Chattering and excited they stowed their hammocks in the nettings and still staring abeam moved reluctantly towards the galley hatch.

Bolitho lifted his glass again as tiny black balls soared to the other ship's yards and broke out to the wind.

Vibart leaned against the binnacle and growled at Maynard, 'Come on then! Read it out!'

Maynard blinked the spray from his wet eyes and flicked rapidly through his book. She's made her number, sir! She's the *Andiron,* thirty-eight, Cap'n Masterman.'

Bolitho closed his glass with a snap. Of course. He should have known her immediately. When in *Sparrow* he had often seen her on patrol off the American coast. Masterman was an old hand at the game. A senior captain, he had chalked up many successes against the enemy.

The *Andiron* had completed her manœuvre and was settling down on the same course as the *Phalarope.* Her sudden wide turn had taken her across the *Phalarope*'s beam, but as her sails bellied and filled once more she began to overhaul to windward.

Bolitho watched Maynard's signal party hoisting the *Phalarope*'s number and wondered what Masterman would say when he eventually discovered that he was now in command. The signal books would still show Pomfret as captain.

Maynard shouted, 'Signal, sir! *Andiron* to *Phalarope.* Heave to, have despatches on board.'

The sunlight glittered along the *Andiron*'s closed ports as she swung slightly down on the other ship.

Herrick said, 'She'll not need to lower a boat, sir. She could drift a raft across.' He rubbed his hands. 'I wonder if she has any fresh vegetables aboard?'

Bolitho smiled. This was just what he had hoped for. A distraction to take their minds off themselves if only for a passing moment. 'Carry on, Mr. Vibart. Heave to, if you please!'

Vibart lifted his speaking trumpet. 'Main tops'l braces! Look alive there!'

Stockdale appeared at Bolitho's side holding his captain's blue coat and cocked hat. He squinted at the other ship and grinned. 'Like old times, Captain.' He peered forward as Quintal, the boatswain, let loose a stream of curses and obscenities. The men had been slow to respond to the sudden orders, and already there was chaos on the crowded deck where off-duty idlers collided with others who were struggling with spray-swollen braces.

Maynard said hoarsely, 'Signal, sir!' His lips moved slowly as he spelled out the message. 'Have you news of Hood's squadron?'

Quintal had at last got his men sorted out, and with sails

flapping and thundering the *Phalarope* began to swing heavily into the wind.

Bolitho had half slipped his arms into his coat, but pushed Stockdale aside as Maynard's words chilled his mind like ice. Masterman would never ask such a question. Even if he had lost his squadron he would certainly know that *Phalarope* was a stranger and had never served in these waters before. His mind rebelled, and he stared mesmerized as his ship continued to swing until the *Andiron*'s bowsprit seemed to point at right-angles across his own.

Vibart turned startled and confused as Bolitho yelled, 'Belay that order, Mr. Vibart! Stand by to go about!'

He ignored the surprised gasps and the fresh clamour of orders and concentrated his reeling thoughts on the other ship. Suppose he had made a mistake? It was too late now. Perhaps it had been too late from the moment the *Andiron* had appeared.

Then he saw the other frigate's bows beginning to swing round still further. With her yards turning as one she altered course and charged down towards the helpless *Phalarope*. A few more seconds and the way would have been lost from the *Phalarope*'s sails, and the *Andiron* would have crossed her un-protected stern, unchallenged and overwhelming.

Bolitho felt his ship labouring round, his ears deaf to the cries and curses from officers and men alike. The weeks of sail drill in all weathers were taking charge, and like puppets the seamen tugged at sheets and braces, their minds too dazed by their captain's behaviour to understand what was happening.

Vibart yelled, 'My God, sir! We'll collide!' He stared past Bolitho's tense figure towards the onrushing frigate. Still the *Phalarope* wallowed round, her bowsprit following the other ship like a compass needle.

Bolitho snapped, 'Steer south-east! Out second reefs!' He did not listen to his repeated orders but walked briskly towards the scarlet-coated marine drummer boy beside the cabin hatch.

'Beat to quarters!'

He saw the boy's dull expression giving way to something like horror. But again training and discipline took charge, and as the drum began to stutter its warning tattoo the tide of men on the maindeck swayed, faltered and then surged in opposite directions as gun crews rushed madly to their weapons.

Vibart gasped, 'Her ports are opening! My God, she's running up her colours!'

Bolitho saw the striped flag breaking to the crosswind and followed Vibart's shocked stare as the frigate's ports opened and the concealed guns trundled outwards like a row of shining teeth.

He said harshly, 'Clear for action, Mr. Vibart! Have the guns loaded and run out immediately!' He checked Vibart as he ran to the rail. 'It will take all of ten minutes. I will try to give you that amount of time!'

The deck canted as the ship steadied on her new course around and away from the other frigate. But the *Andiron* was already turning on the same circle, her sails flapping as she headed into the wind in an effort to close the range. From her peak the new American flag made a patch of bright colour against the tan sails, and Bolitho had to tear his mind back to the present to stop himself thinking of what would have happened but for that one stupid signal.

Andiron would have crossed the *Phalarope*'s unprotected stern and her gunners, hitherto concealed behind the bulwark and sealed ports, would have poured shot after shot through the big cabin windows. The balls would have screamed and torn the full length of his command, and with half the men still below, helpless and unprepared, the disaster would have been over within minutes.

Even now it might be too late. *Andiron* was a bigger ship, and her deep keel was better for this sort of handling. Already she was cutting across the *Phalarope*'s stern and beating rapidly up to windward to regain her first advantage. In another fifteen minutes she would try the same manœuvre again, or she could be content to close the range from the larboard quarter. With the wind in her favour action could not be avoided.

He made himself walk to the taffrail and stare back at the other ship. The pretence had gone now, and he could see the crouching gunners, the clusters of officers on the canting quarterdeck. What had happened to Masterman? he wondered. He were better dead than know his proud ship to be a privateer.

He turned his back on the *Andiron*'s dark hull and looked along his own command. The chaos had gone, and to the unpractised eye the ship looked ready and eager for battle.

On both sides the guns had been run out and the gun captains were testing their trigger lines and passing hoarse orders to their men. Boys ran the length of the deck throwing down sand to give the gunners a firm grip when the time came, while others scuttled from gun to gun with water buckets for the swabs and to damp down any sudden fire.

Vibart stood below the quarterdeck rail and yelled, 'Cleared for action, sir! All guns loaded with double shot and grape!'

'Very well, Mr. Vibart.' Bolitho walked slowly towards the rail and ran his eye along the larboard side guns. They would be the first to engage. His heart sank as he picked out faults in the pattern like flaws in a painting.

At one gun a captain was even having to put a rope fall into the hands of one of his men, as the poor wretch stared at it without comprehension. His mind was too full of fear, his eyes too mesmerized by the overtaking frigate with her long row of guns to heed what the petty officer was saying. At each gun there were men like this. With so many new hands, pressed from unwarlike jobs ashore, this danger was inevitable.

Given time, he could have trained each and every one of them. Bolitho banged his fist slowly on the rail. Well, there *was* no more time. *Andiron* not only had more guns, but they were eighteen-pounders against *Phalarope*'s twelve-pounders. Most of her crew would no doubt be made up of English deserters and seasoned sailors who were no strangers to battle. Any crew which could take the *Andiron* from Captain Masterman was a force to be feared.

At his back Captain Rennie stood nonchalantly by the hammock nettings, his sword looped to his wrist with a gold lanyard, as he watched Sergeant Garwood dressing his men into neat scarlet ranks. There was something very reassuring about the marines, Bolitho thought grimly, but their muskets would not be much use against eighteen-pounders!

All at once the remorse and despair he had been enduring since the *Andiron*'s first treachery had shown with her flag gave way to something like blind rage. It was too late for the 'if onlys' and the 'maybes'. He had brought his ship and his men to this. His was the sole responsibility. He had recognized the American's trap just in time to save them all from the first blow, but he should have seen it earlier.

He walked to the rail and shouted along the deck, 'Now listen to me, men! In a few moments we are going to give battle to that ship!' He saw every face turned towards him, but already they had lost meaning and personality. They were a crew. Good or bad, only time would show. But that they should all trust him was essential.

'Just take your time and obey orders, no matter what is happening around you! Each gun is fitted with the new flintlock, but make sure there is a slow-match at hand in case of failure!'

He saw Okes look across from the starboard battery to where Herrick waited by his own guns. A quick exchange of glances which might have meant anything.

He felt Stockdale slipping the coat over his shoulders and then the firm clasp of the swordbelt around his waist. He watched the powerful frigate plunging over towards the larboard quarter, his eyes gauging the speed and the distance.

'One more thing!' He leaned forward as if to will them to listen. 'This is a King's ship! There will be no surrender!'

He thrust his hands beneath the tails of his coat and walked slowly to the weather rail. It would not be long now. He looked across to Proby's shabby outline beside the wheel. 'In a moment we will beat to windward, Mr. Proby.' He heard a mumbled assent and wondered what the master would make of his order.

The American captain would no doubt expect the smaller ship to turn again and try to slip downwind, and as soon as she turned he would pour a full broadside into the *Phalarope*'s stern, as he had first intended. Bolitho's manœuvre would bring the *Phalarope* round towards the other ship, and with luck Herrick might be able to get in the first blood.

He saw the flash of sunlight on a telescope from the *Andiron*'s quarterdeck and knew the other captain was watching him.

'Stand by, Mr. Proby!' He lifted his hat and yelled along the maindeck, 'Right, lads! A broadside for old England!'

With a protesting groan the yards came round, while overhead the canvas thundered like a miniature battle. Bolitho found that his mouth was as dry as sand, and his face felt chilled into a tight mask.

This was the moment.

John Allday crouched beside the second gun of the larboard battery and stared fixedly through the open port. In spite of the cool morning breeze he was already sweating and his heart pumped against his ribs like the beating of a drum.

It was like being a helpless victim of a nightmare, with every detail clear and stark even before it happened. Somehow he imagined it would be different this time, but nothing had changed. He could have been sailing into battle for the first time, new and untried, with the agony of suspense tearing him apart.

He tore his eyes from the open square of water and glanced back across his shoulder. The same men who had jeered Ferguson or ringed Evans in menacing silence now stood or crouched like himself, slaves to their guns, their faces naked and fearful.

Standing a little apart from the battery, his back to the foremast, Lieutenant Herrick was watching the quarterdeck, his fingers resting on his sword, his bright blue eyes unwinking and devoid of expression.

Allday followed the officer's stare and saw the captain at the quarterdeck rail, his palms resting on the smooth wood, his head jutting slightly as he watched the other ship. The latter was almost hidden from Allday by the high bulwark and gangway and the other guns, but he could see her topmasts and straining sails as she bore down on the larboard quarter, until she seemed to hang over the *Phalarope* like a cliff.

Pryce, the gun captain, slung the powder horn over his hip

and squatted carefully behind the breech, the trigger line in his hands. Through his teeth his voice sounded strange and taut. 'Now, lads, listen to me! We'll be firing a broadside first.' He looked at each man in turn, ignoring the other gunners at the next port. 'After that it will all depend on how quickly we load and run out. So move sharply, and as the cap'n said, take no notice of the din about you, got it?'

Ferguson clung to the rope tackle at the side of the gun and gasped, 'I can't take it! God, I can't stand this waiting!'

Pochin on the opposite side of the breech sneered, 'Just as I said! It takes more than pretty clothing to make men of the likes o' you!' He jerked savagely at the tackle. 'If you'd seen what I've seen you'd *die* of fear, man.' He looked around at the others. 'I've seen whole fleets at each others' throats.' He let his words sink in. 'The sea covered in masts, like a forest!'

Pryce snapped, 'Hold your noise!'

He cocked his head as Herrick called, 'Gun captains! As soon as we engage on the larboard side send your best men to back up the other battery under Mr. Okes!'

The captains held up their hands and then turned back to watch the empty sea.

Allday looked across at Okes and saw the officer's face gleaming with sweat. He looked white. Like a corpse already, he thought.

Vibart's voice rang hollowly through his speaking trumpet. 'Braces there! Stand by to wear ship!'

Allday ran his fingers along the cold breech and whispered fervently, 'Come *on*! Get it over with!'

The *Phalarope* was outclassed and outgunned, even he could see that. With half her men already too terrified to think it was just a matter of how soon her colours would fall.

He glanced down at his legs and felt a chill of terror. It never left him, and the years on the quiet Cornish hillside amongst the sheep had done nothing to dispel it. The fear of mutilation, and the horror of what followed.

Old Strachan called softly from the next gun, ''Ere, you lads!' He waited until his words had penetrated the minds of the new men. 'Wrap a neckscarf around yer ears afore we start to blow! You'll 'ave no eardrums else!'

Allday nodded. He had forgotten that lesson. If only they had been prepared and ready. Instead they had stumbled out from their hammocks and almost at once the nightmare had begun. First the excitement of a friendly ship, fading instantly in the drummer's roll as the men ran gasping and wide-eyed to quarters. He could just see the same little drummer boy beside one rank of marines. He was staring across at the captain as if to read his own fate.

Pryce muttered, 'Never bin in a fight like this afore.' He looked up at the billowing sails. 'Too much wind. It'll be hit hard an' run, you mark my words!'

There was a rasp of steel as Herrick drew his sword. He lifted it above his head, the blade holding the sun like firelight.

'Stand by in the larboard battery!'

Ferguson moaned softly, 'Oh, Grace! Where are you, Grace?'

From aft Vibart bellowed, 'Put the helm down! Hard down there!'

They all felt the deck begin to cant further as the seamen forward let go the headsail sheets and allowed the plunging frigate to swing wildly across the wind.

Allday swallowed hard as the gunport suddenly darkened and the other ship's raked bow pushed across his vision. She filled the port, her guns and spray-soaked hull leaning at an angle as if to reach out and smash the *Phalarope* as she swung impudently towards her.

Herrick dropped his sword. *'Fire!'*

The captains jerked their lines and the whole world fell apart in the staggering, uneven broadside. Choking smoke billowed back through the ports, rasping the lungs and filling every eye as the guns lurched angrily back on their tackles. It was like hell, too terrible to understand.

But already the gun captains were yelling like fiends, urging and hitting at their stunned gunners as the powder monkeys ran forward with fresh cartridges and new, gleaming balls were lifted from the racks.

Pryce knocked down a man's arm and screamed, 'Sponge out, you bastard! Remember what I taught you! You'll blow us all up if you drop a charge into a burning gun!' The man mumbled dazedly and obeyed him as if in a trance.

Herrick shouted, 'Reload there! Lively, lads!'

Allday waited a few more minutes and then threw his weight on the tackles. Squealing like angry pigs the gun trucks rumbled forward again, the muzzles racing each other to be first through the ports.

But the *Phalarope* was almost into the *Andiron*'s bow. A few more feet and it seemed as if both ships would smash into each other, to die together in locked combat.

'Fire!'

Again the savage roar of a broadside, the deck yawing away beneath them with its force. But this time more ragged, less well aimed. Through the din of shouts and groaning spars Allday heard some of the balls strike home, and saw Maynard, one of the midshipmen, waving his hat in the streaming smoke and yelling to the sky, his words lost in the guns' roar.

The *Andiron* must have fired simultaneously with the *Phalarope*, her gunfire lost in the general thunder of noise. There was more of a feeling than a sound, like a hot wind, or sand blasted across a parched desert.

Allday looked up as the sails jerked and twisted as if in agony. Holes were appearing everywhere, and from high aloft came a falling tangle of severed halyards and ropes. A block dropped on to the breech with a loud clang, and Pryce said without looking up from his priming, 'The bastards fired too soon! The broadside went right over our 'eads!'

Allday peered through the port, still dazed, but understanding at last what Bolitho had done. The *Phalarope* had not turned away, had not offered her stern for punishment. Her sudden swing to attack had caught the enemy off balance, and rather than risk a senseless collision he had hauled off so that his first broadside had failed to make real contact.

He heard Herrick call across to Lieutenant Okes, 'By God, Matthew, that was a close thing!' Then in a wilder tone, 'Look at the masthead pendant! The wind's veering!'

There was bedlam as the enemy ship swung rapidly clear of the charging *Phalarope*. But so sudden or so unexpected was the attack that the *Andiron*'s captain had failed to notice what Bolitho must already have seen even as he steered towards possible disaster.

Instead of beating back to windward the *Andiron* met the full wind hard across her larboard bow. For a moment it looked as if she would rally and at worst come crashing back alongside.

Herrick was jumping with excitement. 'My God, she's *in* irons! She's in irons!'

Men were standing beside their guns calling the news along the deck while across the water, framed in a rolling bank of gunsmoke, the *Andiron* rolled helplessly up wind, unable to pay off on either tack. Already men were running along her yards, and across the shadowed water they could hear the blare of commands through a speaking trumpet.

Herrick controlled himself. 'Over to the starboard battery. Jump to it!' Pryce touched the men he needed and scampered across the deck.

From aft came the call, 'Stand by to go about! Man the braces!'

Allday threw himself down beside the opposite gun and showed his teeth to the crouching men.

Old Strachan croaked, 'The cap'n can certainly 'andle the ship well enough.'

Okes shouted, 'Silence there! Watch your front!'

Herrick walked to the centre of the deck and watched the carpenter and the boatswain hurrying to repair the brief damage.

Men were already climbing aloft to splice the severed lines, and others were at last rigging nets above the maindeck to give some protection from falling blocks or spars.

Round came the yards once more, sails thundering, braces screaming through the blocks as the men ran like goats to obey the constant demands from the quarterdeck.

It did not seem possible. Caught and surprised one instant, and the next moment they were not only attacking, but hitting the enemy again and again.

Bolitho must have thought it all out. Must have planned and schemed during his lonely walks up and down the night-darkened deck, waiting for just an eventuality.

He could see him now, calm-eyed and stiff-backed behind the rail, his hands behind his back as he watched the other ship. Once during the waiting Herrick had seen him wipe his forehead, momentarily brushing away the lock of dark hair and displaying the deep, savage scar. He had seen Herrick watching him and had jammed on his hat with something like anger.

Herrick ran his eye along his own guns, now manned by depleted crews and blind to the enemy as the *Phalarope* tacked round to close the range. He had heard Pochin's bitter remarks and had seen the way Allday had rallied to help the new men. It was strange how they all forgot their other worries when real danger was close and terrible.

It was true that the ship was different under Bolitho. And it went deeper than the uniform clothing now worn by all hands, issued on Bolitho's order to replace the stained rags which had been commonplace in Pomfret's time. There was this violent uncertainty instead of sullen acceptance, as if the men wanted to draw together to match the young captain's enthusiasm, yet had forgotten how to go about it.

Okes said sharply, 'She's under way again! She's swinging round!'

The *Andiron*'s sails were flapping and banging in apparent confusion, but Herrick could see the difference in her outline and the new angle of her yards.

Bolitho's voice cut through their speculations. 'Another salvo, lads! Before she completes her turn!'

Herrick breathed out sharply. 'He's going to try and cross her stern! He'll never make it. We'll be broadside to broadside in minutes!'

The wild confidence which their successful attack had brought him changed to the chill of uncertainty as the *Phalarope* gathered way, her masts and spars quivering under the press of sail. He gripped his sword more tightly and gritted his teeth as once more the enemy topsails showed above the hammock nettings.

The masts were no longer in line, she was swinging fast and well. There was nothing else for it but to take what had to come.

Okes could only stare at the oncoming ship, his jaw open as the distance was swallowed up in the gap of tossing water between them. He held up his sword. 'Stand by starboard battery!' But his voice was lost in a savage ripple of gunfire from the other ship as gun after gun belched fire and smoke from aft to forward as each one came to bear.

This time there was no mistake.

Herrick felt the hull shudder beneath his feet and reeled against the foremast as smoke blotted out the deck and the air became full of splintering woodwork and falling rigging. Above and around him the air quivered and shook with the crash of guns, and the nerve jarring scream of cannon balls as they whipped through the smoke like things from hell.

The scream of passing shots mingled with closer, more unearthly sounds as flying splinters ripped into the packed gunners and bathed the smooth decks with scarlet. Herrick had to bite his lip to retain control of himself. He had seen men bleed before. In an occasional skirmish, and under the cat. From a fall or a shipboard accident. But this was different. It was all around him, as if the ship was being painted by a madman. He could see specks of blood and gristle across his white breeches, and when he looked across at the nearest gun he saw that it had been upended and one of its crew had been pulped into a scarlet and purple mass. Another man lay legless, a handspike still gripped and ready, and two of his companions were clinging together screaming and tearing at each other's terrible wounds in the insane torment.

The enemy frigate must have reloaded almost at once, and another ragged volley thundered and crashed in the *Phalarope*'s side. Men cried and yelled, cursed and fumbled blindly in the choking smoke, while above their heads the nets jerked and danced madly to the onslaught of falling gear from aloft.

A powder monkey ran weeping towards the magazine hatch, only to be pushed away by one of the marine sentries. He had dropped his cartridge carrier and was running below, to the safety of darkness. But the sentry yelled at him and then struck at him with his musket. The boy reeled back and then seemed to come to his senses. With a sniff he picked up his carrier and made for the nearest gun.

There was a scream of shot, and Herrick turned biting back vomit as the eighteen-pound shot cut the boy in half. The head and shoulders remained upright on the planking for several seconds, and before he turned away Herrick saw that the boy's eyes were still open and staring.

He cannoned into Okes who still stood with upraised sword, his eyes fixed and glassy as he gaped at the remains of his battery. Herrick shouted, 'Fire, Matthew! Give the order!'

Okes dropped his sword and here and there a gun lurched back adding its voice to the dreadful symphony.

Okes said, 'We're done for! We'll have to strike!'

'Strike?' Herrick stared at him. All at once the reality was cruel and personal again. Death and surrender had always been words, a necessary but unlikely alternative to victory. He looked towards the quarterdeck at Bolitho's tall figure and the marines beyond. The latter must have been firing their muskets for some while, yet Herrick had not even noticed. He saw Sargeant Garwood with his half-pike dressing one rank where two red-coated bodies had left gaps in the line, while he called out the time and numbers to his men as they reloaded and fired another volley into the smoke. Captain Rennie had his back to the enemy and was staring across the other rail as if seeing the sea for the first time.

Pryce, the gun captain, gave one long scream and fell backwards at Herrick's feet. A long splinter had been torn from the deck and had embedded itself in the man's shoulder. Through the blood Herrick could see the thick stump of jagged timber sticking out like a tooth, and knew that the other end would be deep inside. The splinters were always the most dangerous and had to be cut out from the flesh in one piece.

Herrick gestured towards the men by the main hatch. 'Take this one below to the surgeon!' They had been staring at a pulped corpse beside the hatch, its teeth white against the flayed flesh, and Herrick's harsh tone seemed to give them strength to break the spell.

Pryce began to scream. 'No!' Leave me here by the gun! For God's sake, don't take me below!'

One of the men whispered, ''E's a brave 'un! 'E don't want to leave 'is station!'

Pochin spat on the gun and watched the spittle hissing on the barrel. 'Squit! 'E'd rather die up 'ere than face the butcher's knife.'

There was a splintering crack, like that of a coach whip, high overhead, and as Herrick squinted up through the drifting smoke he saw the maintopgallant quiver, and then as the wind tore jubilantly at the released canvas it began to slide forward.

Herrick cupped his hands. 'Look alive, you men! Get aloft and cut those shrouds! It'll foul the foremast otherwise!'

He saw Quintal and some seamen running up the shrouds and then winced as another cannon ball ploughed along the deck by his feet and smashed into two wounded gunners beside the lee bulwark. He looked away, sickened, and heard Vibart yell, 'Heads below! The t'gallant is falling!'

With a jarring crash the long spar pitched over the bulwark and remained trapped and tangled in a mass of rigging, the torn sail ballooning in the water alongside and dragging at the ship like a sea anchor. To add to the horror, Herrick could see the man, Betts, the one who had first sighted the other frigate, pinned in the trailing rigging like an insect in a web.

Vibart yelled, 'Axes there! Cut that wreckage adrift!'

Betts stared up at the frigate with glazed eyes, his voice short and painful between his teeth. 'Help me! Don't let me go to the bottom, lads!'

But already the axes were at work, the men driven half mad by the din, too dazed to care for the suffering of one more seaman.

Okes seized Herrick's arm. 'Why doesn't he strike? For Christ's sake *look* what he's doing to us!'

Herrick's mind was dulled and refused to work clearly any more. But he could see what Okes was trying to show him. The heart had gone out of the men, what heart there had been. They crouched and whimpered as the enemy balls thundered all around them, and only occasionally did a single gun reply. Then it was usually a small handful of men led by one seasoned and dedicated gun captain which kept up a one-sided exchange with the enemy.

Herrick shut his ears to the screaming wounded as they were dragged below and closed his eyes to everything but the small open patch of quarterdeck where Bolitho stood alone by the rail. His hat had gone and his coat was stained with powder and blown spray. Even as he watched Herrick saw a messenger run towards the captain, only to be cut down by musket fire from the other vessel as she loomed sideways out of the smoke. Musket balls were thudding against the hammock nettings and biting across the deck, yet Bolitho never budged, nor did he alter his expression of detached determination.

Only once did he look up, and then to glance at the large scarlet ensign which streamed from the gaff, as if to reassure himself that it still flew. Herrick shook his head. 'He'll not strike! He'll see us all dead first!'

5. RUM AND RECRIMINATIONS

THE DECK slewed over as the *Phalarope*'s helm went hard down and she swung blindly on to her new course. Bolitho had lost count of the number of times his ship had changed direction, or even how long they had been fighting.

Of one thing he was sure. The *Andiron* was outmanœuvring him, was still holding to windward and keeping up a steady barrage. His own gunners were hampered by yet another hazard. The wind was falling away, and his men were now firing blindly into an unbroken bank of thick smoke which rolled down from the other ship and mingled with their own intermittent firing. The smoke seemed to writhe with many colours as the American privateer continued the attack. Once, when a freak wind had blown the smoke skywards like a curtain Bolitho had seen the *Andiron*'s battery belching long orange flames as each gun was trained and fired singly across the bare quarter mile between the two frigates. They were firing high, the balls screaming through the rigging and slashing the remaining sails to ribbons. Ropes and stays hung from above like weed, and every so often heavy blocks and long slivers of wood would fall amongst the labouring gunners or splash in the clear water alongside.

She intended to dismast and cripple the *Phalarope*. Maybe her captain had plans for using another captured ship, just as he had the *Andiron*.

The long nine-pounders on the quarterdeck recoiled as one, their sharp, barking detonations penetrating the innermost membranes of Bolitho's ears as he stared through the smoke and then back at his own command. Only on the quarterdeck was there still some semblance of unity and order. Midshipman Farquhar stood by the taffrail, his eyes bright but determined as he passed his orders to the gun captains. Rennie's marines were standing fast, too. From their smoke-blinded positions behind the hammock nettings they kept up a steady musket fire whenever the other ship showed herself through the choking fog of powder smoke.

But the maindeck was different. Bolitho let his eyes move slowly over the chaos of scarred planking and grisly remains which marked every foot of deck space. The guns were still firing, but the intervals were longer, the aim less certain.

At first Bolitho had been amazed at the success of that opening broadside. He had known that later the lack of training would slow down the barrage, but he had not dared to hope for such a good opening. The double-shotted guns had fired almost as one, the ship staggering from the combined recoil. He had seen the bulwarks jump apart on the other frigate, had watched the balls tear through the packed gunners and gouge into her spray-dashed hull. It had seemed momentarily that the battle might still be contained.

Through the streaming smoke he saw Herrick moving slowly aft along the starboard battery checking the gunners and aiming each weapon himself before allowing the gun captain to jerk his trigger line. It should have been Okes on the starboard side, but perhaps he was already dead, like so many of the others.

Bolitho made himself examine each part of the agonizing panorama which the *Phalarope* now represented. His body felt sick and numb from the constant battering, but his eye and mind worked in cold unison, so that the pain and suffering was all the more apparent.

Small pictures stood out from the whole, so that wherever he looked there was a pitiful reminder of the cost and the price still to be paid.

Many had died. How many he had no way of knowing. Some had died bravely, serving their guns and yelling encouragement and curses up to the moment of death. Some died slowly and horribly, their mutilated and broken bodies writhing in the blood and flesh which covered the deck as in a slaughterhouse.

Others were less brave, and more than once he had seen men shamming death, even cowering in the stench and horror of the discarded corpses until dragged and kicked back to their stations by the petty officers.

Some had escaped below in spite of Rennie's sentries, and would now be covering their ears and whimpering in the bilges to face drowning rather than the onslaught from the *Andiron's* guns.

He had seen the little powder monkey cut in half, and even above the roar of battle he had heard his own words to that same boy just three weeks ago:

'You'll see England again! Never you fear!'

Now he was wiped away. As if he had never been.

And there had been the seaman Betts, trapped and writhing on the severed topgallant. The man he had used to try to prove his authority. The axes had cut the spar away, and with a sigh it had bobbed clear of the ship before moving away in the smoke in a trail of rigging. The spar had idled past the quarterdeck, and for a brief instant he had seen Betts staring up at him. The man's mouth had been open like a black hole, and he had shaken his fist. It was a pitiful gesture, but it felt like a curse from the whole world. Then the spar had rolled over, and before it had faded astern Bolitho had seen Betts' feet sticking out of the water, kicking in a futile dance.

He tore his eyes from the carnage as more balls slapped through the main course and whined away over the water. It could not last much longer. The *Andiron* had hauled off slightly to windward. He could see her upper yards and punctured sails moving above the smoke bank as if detached from the hidden ship beneath, and guessed she was drawing clear to pound the *Phalarope* into submission with slow, carefully aimed shots.

He did not recognize his own voice as he gave his orders automatically and without pause. 'Tell the carpenter to sound the well! And pass the word for the boatswain to send more men aloft to splice the mizzen shrouds!' There was little point any more, but the game had to be played out. He knew no other way.

His eye fell on an old gun captain at the nearest twelve-pounder below the quarterdeck. The man showed fatigue and strain, but his hoarse voice was unhurried, even patient as he coaxed his crew through the drill of reloading. 'That's right, my boys!' He peered through the haze as one of his men rammed home the cartridge and another cradled the gleaming ball into the gaping muzzle. A splinter flew from the gunport and laid open his arm, but he merely winced and tied a filthy rag around his biceps before adding, 'Ram that wad well home, bucko! We don't want the bugger to fall out again!' He saw Bolitho watching him and showed his stained teeth in what might have been either pain or pride. Then he bawled, 'Right then! Run out!' The trucks squeaked as the gun lumbered up the canting deck and then roared back again as the old man pulled his trigger.

Vibart loomed across the rail, his figure like a massive blue and white rock. He looked grim but unflinching, and waited for the nine-pounders to fire and recoil before he shouted, 'No water in the well, sir! She's not hit below the waterline!'

Bolitho nodded. The American obviously felt sure of a capture. It would not take long to refit a ship in one of the dockyards left by the British retreating from the American colonies.

The realization brought a fresh flood of despairing anger to his aching mind. The *Phalarope* was fighting for her life. But her men were failing her. *He* was failing her. He had brought the ship and every man aboard to this. All the hopes and promises were without meaning now. There was only disgrace and failure as an alternative to death.

Even if he had contemplated flying from the *Andiron*'s attack it was too late now. The wind was falling away more and more, and the sails were almost useless, torn like nets by the screaming cannon balls.

A marine threw up his hands, clawing at the gaping scarlet hole in his forehead before pitching back into his comrades.

Captain Rennie drawled, 'Fill that space! What the hell do you think you're doing?' To Sergeant Garwood he added petulantly, 'Take the name of the next man who dies without permission!'

Surprisingly, some of the marines laughed, and when Rennie saw Bolitho looking at him he merely shrugged, as if he too understood it was all part of one hideous game.

The ship staggered, and overhead the sails boomed in protest as the fading wind sighed against the flapping canvas. Bolitho snapped, 'Watch your helm, quartermaster! Steady as you go!'

But one of the helmsmen had fallen, a pattern of scarlet pouring from his mouth and across the smooth planking. From somewhere another seaman took his place, his jaw working steadily on a wad of tobacco.

Vibart growled, 'The starboard battery is a shambles! If we could engage the opposite side it would give us time to reorganize!'

Bolitho eyed him steadily. 'The *Andiron* has the advantage. But I intend to try and cross her stern directly.'

Vibart peered abeam, his eyes cold and calculating. 'She'll never allow it. She'll pound us to shavings before we get a cable's length!' He looked back at Bolitho. 'We will have to strike.' His voice shook. 'We can't take much more.'

Bolitho replied quietly, 'I did not hear that, Mr. Vibart. Now go forrard and try and get the full battery into action again!' His tone was cold and final. 'When two ships fight, only one can be the victor. I will decide on the course of action!'

Vibart seemed to shrug. As if it was not his concern. 'As you say, sir!' He strode to the ladder adding harshly, 'I *said* that they did not respect weakness!'

Bolitho felt Proby shaking his arm and turned to see the anxiety etched on his mournful face. 'The wheel, Captain! It don't answer! The yoke lines have parted!'

Bolitho stared dully over Proby's rounded shoulders to where the helmsmen pulled vaguely at the wheel, the squeaking spokes responding in empty mockery as the ship paid off and began to sidle sluggishly downwind.

The sudden movement brought more cries from the maindeck as the frigate rolled her gunports skyward in a dizzy, uncontrollable elevation.

Bolitho ran his fingers through his hair, realizing for the first time that his hat had been knocked from his head. The masthead pendant was barely flapping now, and without power in her sails the ship would drift at the mercy of the sea until her surrender or destruction. It would take all of an hour to re-rig the rudder lines. By then . . . he felt a cold shudder across his spine.

He cupped his hands. 'Cease firing!'

The sudden silence was almost more frightening than the gunfire. He could hear the chafe and creak of spars, the gurgle of water below the counter, and the swaying clatter of loose rigging. Even the wounded seemed quelled, and lay gasping and staring at the captain's still figure at the quarterdeck rail.

Then across the water, drifting with the smoke like a final insult, he heard a wild cheering. It was more like a baying, he thought bitterly. Like hounds closing for the kill.

A V-shaped cleft broke in the smoke, and through it came the *Andiron*'s raked bow and the long finger of her bowsprit. Filtered sunlight played across her figurehead and glinted on raised cutlasses and boarding pikes. As more and more of the other ship glided into view Bolitho saw the press of men running forward to the point where both ships would touch. Others were crawling out along the yards with grapnels, ready to lash the two enemies together in a final embrace. It was nearly finished. He heard Stockdale mutter at his elbow, 'The bastards! The *bastards*!'

Bolitho saw that there were small tears in the man's eyes, and knew that the battered coxswain was sharing his own misery.

Above his head the flag whipped suddenly in a small breeze, and he knew that he dare not look at it. A defiant patch of scarlet. Like the red coats of the marines and the great glittering pools of blood which seeped through the scuppers as if the ship herself was bleeding before his eyes.

A new wildness moved through his mind, so that he had to lock his fingers around his swordbelt to prevent his hands from shaking. 'Get Mr. Brock! At the double!'

He saw Midshipman Maynard lope forward, and then forgot him as his glance strayed again to the watching men. They were exhausted and smashed down with the fury of battle. There was hardly a spark amongst them. His fingers settled on the hilt of his sword and he felt the painful prick of despair behind his eyes. He could see his father, and so many others of his family, ranked with his crew, and watching in silence.

Proby said hoarsely, 'I've sent a party to splice the yoke lines, Captain.' He waited, plucking the buttons of his shabby coat. 'It were not your fault, sir.' He shifted beneath Bolitho's unwavering stare. 'Don't you give in, sir. Not now!'

The gunner reached the quarterdeck and touched his hat. 'Sir?' He was still wearing the felt, spark-proof slippers he always wore in the dark magazine, and he seemed dazed by the sudden silence and the litter of destruction about him.

'Mr. Brock, there is a task for you.' Bolitho listened to his own voice and felt the strange wildness stirring him like brandy. 'I want every starboard gun loaded with chain shot.' He watched the *Andiron*'s slow, threatening approach. 'You have about ten minutes, unless the wind returns.'

The man nodded and hurried away without another word. His was not to question a meaningless order. A command from the captain was all he required.

Bolitho looked down at the maindeck, at the dead and wounded, and the remaining gunners. He said slowly, 'There will be one final broadside, men.' The words swept away his own illusion of making a last empty gesture. He continued, 'Every gun will have chain shot, and I want each weapon at full elevation.' They began to stir, their movements brittle and vague like old men, but Bolitho's voice seemed to hold them as he added sharply, 'Load, but do not run out until the word!' He saw the gunner's party carrying the unwieldy chain shot to each gun in turn. Two balls per gun, and each ball linked together with thick chain.

Captain Rennie said quietly, 'They're getting close, sir. They'll be boarding us very soon now.' He sounded tense.

Bolitho looked away. All at once he wanted to share the enormity of his decision, but at the same instant he knew the extent of his own loneliness.

His last effort might fail completely. At best it would only drive the enemy to a madness which only the death of the whole of his crew would placate.

Herrick looked aft, his eyes steady. 'All guns loaded, sir!' He seemed to square his shoulders, as if to project some strange confidence over his battered men.

Bolitho pulled out his sword. Behind him he heard the marines fixing their bayonets and shuffling their booted feet on the stained planking.

He called, 'Stand by the starboard carronade, Mr. Farquhar! Is it ready?' He watched narrowly as the other ship's bowsprit swung over the *Phalarope*'s bulwark, her forechains and rigging alive with shouting men. Her captain must have stripped his guns to get such a large boarding party. Once aboard, they would swamp the *Phalarope*, no matter how desperate the resistance.

Farquhar swallowed hard. 'Loaded, sir. Canister, and a full charge!'

'Very good.' The *Andiron* was barely twenty feet clear now, the triangular patch of trapped water between them frothing in a mad dance. 'If I fall, you will take your orders from Mr. Vibart.' He saw the young officer's eyes seeking out the first lieutenant. 'If not, then watch for my signal!'

The *Andiron*'s bow nudged the main shrouds and a great yell of derision broke from the waiting boarders.

Bolitho ran down the ladder and leaped on to the starboard gangway, his sword above his bare head. A few pistols banged across the gap and he felt a ball pluck at his sleeve like an invisible hand.

'Repel boarders!' He saw the gunners staring up at him, uncertain and shocked, their guns still inboard and impotent.

Herrick jumped up beside him, his eyes flashing as he shouted, 'Come on, lads! We'll give the buggers a lesson!'

Somebody voiced a faint cheer, and the men not employed at the guns surged up to the gangway, their cutlasses and pikes puny against the great press of boarders.

Bolitho felt a man drop screaming at his side, and another pitched forward to be ground between the hulls like so much butcher's meat. He could see the privateer's officers urging their men on and pointing him out to their marksmen. Shots banged and whistled around him, and the cries and jeers had risen to one, terrifying roar.

The hulls shuddered once more and the gap began to disappear. Bolitho peered back at Farquhar. The quarterdeck with its dead marines seemed a long way away, but as he waved his sword in a swift chopping motion he saw the midshipman jerk the lanyard and felt the gun's savage blast pass his face like a hot wind.

The canister shot contained five hundred closely packed musket balls, and like a scythe the miniature bombardment swept through the cheering boarders, cutting them down into a bloody tangle of screams and curses. The boarders faltered, and a young lieutenant who had climbed up on the *Andiron*'s bowsprit dropped unsupported on to the *Phalarope*'s gangway. His scream was cut short as a big seaman lashed out and down with an axe, and then his body was pinned between the hulls and forgotten.

Bolitho shouted wildly, 'Come on, you gunners! Run out! *Run out!* He held out his sword like a barrier in front of his men. 'Back there! Get back!'

His small party fell back, confused by this turn of events. They had faced certain annihilation, and had accepted it. Now their captain had changed his mind. Or so it seemed.

But Herrick understood. Almost choking with excitement he yelled, '*All guns run out!*'

Bolitho saw the survivors from the carronade's single blast falling back towards their guns, shocked and dismayed as the *Phalarope*'s muzzles trundled forward and upwards towards them.

'Fire!' Bolitho almost fell overboard, but felt Stockdale catch his arm as the whole battery exploded beneath his feet.

The air seemed to come alive with inhuman screams as the whirling chain shot cut through sails and rigging alike in an overwhelming tempest of metal. Foremast and maintopmast fell together, the great weight of spars and canvas smashing down the remaining boarders and covering the gunports in a whirling mass of canvas.

The recoil of *Phalarope*'s broadside seemed to drive the two ships apart, leaving a trail of wreckage and corpses floating between them.

Bolitho leaned against the nettings, his breath sharp and painful. 'Reload! Carry on firing!' Whatever happened next, the *Phalarope* had spoken with authority, and had hit hard.

The frigate's proud outline was broken and confused in tangled shrouds and sails. Where her foremast had been minutes before there was only a bright-toothed stump, and the resonant cheers had given way to screams and confusion.

But she pushed forward across the *Phalarope*'s bows, followed by a further ragged salvo and a single angry bark from a forecastle nine-pounder. Then she was clear, gathering her tattered sails like garments to cover her scars, and pushing downwind into the rolling bank of smoke.

Bolitho stood watching her, his heart thumping, his eyes watering from strain and emotion.

The minutes dragged by, and then the insane realization came to him. The *Andiron* was not putting about. She had taken enough.

Half stumbling he returned to the quarterdeck where Rennie's marines were grinning at him and Farquhar was leaning on the smoking carronade as if he no longer trusted what he saw.

Then they started to cheer. It was not much at first. Then it gathered strength and power until it moved above and below decks in an unbroken tide.

It was part pride and part relief. Some men were sobbing uncontrollably, others capered on the bloodstained decks like madmen.

Herrick ran aft, his hat awry, his blue eyes shining with excitement. 'You did for them, sir! My God, you scuppered 'em!' He clasped Bolitho's hand, unable to stop himself. Even old Proby was grinning.

Bolitho controlled his voice with one last effort. 'Thank you, gentlemen.' He looked along the littered decks, feeling the pain and the blind exultation. 'Next time we will do better!'

He swung round and pushed through the whooping marines towards the dark sanctuary of the cabin hatch.

Behind him, as if through a fog, he heard Herrick shout, 'I don't know about *next* time, lads! This will do me for a bit!'

Bolitho stood breathing hard in the narrow passageway listening to their excitement and laughter. They were grateful, even happy, he realized dully. Perhaps the bill would not be too high after all.

There was so much to do. So many things to prepare and restore before the ship would be ready to fight again. He fingered the worn sword hilt and stared wearily at the deck beams. But it would wait a moment longer. Just a short moment.

Herrick leaned heavily on the forecastle rail and wiped his forehead with the back of his hand. Only the slightest breeze ruffled the calm sea ahead of the gently pitching bows, and as he watched he saw the sun dipping towards the horizon, its glowing reflection already waiting to receive it and allow night to hide the *Phalarope*'s scars.

Herrick could feel his legs shaking, and again he tried to tell himself it was due to fatigue and the strain of a continuous day's working. Within an hour of the privateer's disappearance Bolitho had returned to the quarterdeck, his hair once more gathered neatly to the nape of his neck, his face freshly shaved, and the dust of battle brushed from his uniform. Only the lines at the corners of his mouth, the grave restlessness in his eyes betrayed any inner feelings as he passed his orders and began the work of repairing the damage to his ship and crew.

At first Herrick had imagined the task impossible. The men's relief had given way to delayed shock, so that individual sailors lay aimlessly about the stained decks like marionettes with severed strings, or just stood and stared listlessly at the aftermath of the nightmare.

Bolitho's sudden appearance had started a train of events which nobody could really explain. Every officer and man was too spent, too dulled by the brief and savage encounter to spare any strength for protest. The dead had been gathered at the lee rail and sewn into pathetic anonymous bundles. Lines of kneeling men had moved from forward to aft working with heavy holystones to scrub away the dark stains to the accompaniment of clanking pumps and the indifferent gurgle of sea-water.

The tattered and useless sails were sent down and replaced with fresh canvas, while Tozer, the sailmaker, and his mates squatted on every available deck space, needles and palms moving like lightning as they patched and repaired anything which could be salvaged and used again.

Ledward, the carpenter, moved slowly around the splintered gun battery, making a note here, taking a measurement there, until at length he was ready to play his part in restoring the frigate to her original readiness. Even now, as Herrick relived the fury of the bombardment and heard the screams and moans of wounded men, the hammers and saws were busy, and the whole new areas of planking were being tamped neatly into place to await the pitch and paint of the following morning.

He shivered again and cursed as his knees nearly gave under him. It was shock rather than mere fatigue. He knew that now.

He thought back to his impressions of the battle, to his own stupid relief and loud-voiced humour when the enemy had hauled away. It had been like listening to another, uncontrollable being who had been incapable of either silence or composure. Just to be alive and unharmed had meant more than anything.

Now as the sky grew darker astern of the slow moving ship he examined his true feelings and tried to put his recollections into some semblance of order.

He had even tried to regain some of the brief contact he had made with Bolitho. He had crossed the quarterdeck where the captain had been staring down at the labouring sailors and had said, 'You saved us all that time, sir. Another minute and she'd have been into us with a full broadside! It was a clever ruse to ask us to heave to. That privateer was a cunning one and no mistake!'

Bolitho had not lifted his gaze from the maindeck. When he had replied it had been as if he was speaking to himself. '*Andiron* is an old ship. She has been out here for ten years.' He made a brief gesture towards the maindeck. '*Phalarope* is new. Every gun is fitted with the new flintlock and the carronades are almost unknown except in the Channel Fleet. No, Mr. Herrick, there is little room for congratulations!'

Herrick had studied Bolitho's brooding profile, aware perhaps for the first time of the man's constant inner battle. 'All the same, sir, she outgunned us!' He had watched for some sign of the Bolitho he had seen waving his sword on the starboard gangway while shots had hammered down around him like hail. But there had been nothing. He had ended lamely, 'You'll see, sir, things will be different after this.'

Bolitho had straightened his back, as if throwing off some invisible weight. When he had turned his grey eyes had been cold and unfeeling. 'I hope you are right, Mr. Herrick! For my part I was disgusted with such a shambles! I dread to contemplate what might have happened in a fight to the finish!'

Herrick had felt himself flushing. 'I was only thinking . . .'

Bolitho had snapped. 'When I require an opinion from my third lieutenant I will let him know! Until that moment, Mr. Herrick, perhaps you will be good enough to make your people get to work! There will be time later for suppositions and self-adulation!' He had swung on his heel and recommenced his pacing.

Herrick watched the surgeon's party carry another limp corpse from the main hatch and lay it beside the others. Again, another picture of Bolitho sprang to his mind.

Herrick had been between decks on a tour of inspection with

the carpenter. There were no shot holes beneath the water-line, but it had been his duty to make sure for his own satisfaction. Still dulled by the noise of battle he had followed Ledward beneath the massive, curved beams, his tired eyes half mes-merized by the man's shaded lantern. Together they had stepped through a screen and entered a scene from hell itself.

Lanterns ringed the dark space, to allow none of the horror to escape his eyes, and in the centre of the yellow glare, strapped and writhing like a sacrifice on an altar, was a badly wounded seaman, his leg already half amputated by Tobias Ellice, the surgeon. The latter's fat, brick-red face was devoid of expression as his bloody fingers worked busily with the glittering saw, his chins bouncing in time against the top of his scarlet-daubed apron. His assistants were using all their strength to restrain the struggling victim and pin his spreadeagled body on top of the platform of sea chests, which sufficed as an operating table. The man had rolled his eyes with each nerve-searing thrust of the saw, had bitten into the leather strap between his teeth until the blood had spurted from his lips, and Ellice had carried on with his amputation.

Around the circle of light the other wretched wounded had awaited their turn, some propped on their elbows as if unable to tear their eyes from the gruesome spectacle. Others lay moan-ing and sobbing in the shadows, their lives ebbing away and thereby spared the agony of knife and saw. The air had been thick with the stench of blood and rum, the latter being the only true way of killing the victim's senses before their turn came.

Ellice had looked up as the man had kicked out wildly and then fallen lifeless even as the severed limb had dropped into a waiting trough. He had seen Herrick's face stiff with shock and had remarked in his thick, tipsy voice, 'A day indeed, Mr. 'Errick! I sew an' I stitch, I saws an' I probes, but still they rushes to join their mates aloft!' He had rolled his rheumy eyes towards heaven and had reached for a squat leather bottle. 'Maybe a little nip for yerself, Mr. 'Errick?' He had lifted it against the light. 'No? Ah well then, a little sustenance for meself!'

He had given the merest nod to his loblolly boy, who in turn had pointed out another man by the ship's rounded side. The latter had been immediately seized and hauled screaming across the chests, his cries unheeded as Ellice wiped his mouth and had then ripped away the shirt from the man's lacerated arm.

Herrick had turned away, his face sweating as the man's scream had probed deeper into his eardrums. He had stopped in his tracks, suddenly aware that Bolitho was standing slightly behind him.

Bolitho had moved slowly around the pain-racked figures, his voice soothing but too soft for Herrick to comprehend. Here he had reached to touch a man's hand as it groped blindly for comfort or reassurance. There he had stopped to close the eyes of a man already dead. At one instant he had paused beneath a spiralling lantern and had asked quietly, 'How many, Mr. Ellice? What is the bill?'

Ellice had grunted and gestured to his men that he had completed his ministrations with the limp figure across the sheets. 'Twenty killed, Cap'n! Twenty more badly wounded, an' another thirty 'alf an' 'alf!'

It was then that Herrick had seen Bolitho's mask momentarily drop away. There had been pain on his face. Pain and despair.

Herrick had immediately forgotten his anger and resentment at the captain's remarks earlier on the quarterdeck. The Bolitho he had seen on the ship's side waving his sword had been real. So, too, was this one.

He stared down at the canvas-shrouded corpses and tried to remember the faces to fit against the names scrawled on each lolling bundle. But already they were fading, lost in memory like the smoke of the battle which had struck them down.

Herrick started as he caught sight of Lieutenant Okes' thin figure moving slowly along the shadowed maindeck. He had hardly seen Okes at all since the action. It was as if the man had been waiting for the hard-driven sailors to finish their work so that he could have the deck to himself.

There had been that moment immediately after the sound of the last shot had rolled away in the smoke. Okes had staggered up through a hatchway, his eyes wild and uncontrolled. He had seemed shocked beyond understanding as he had looked around him, as if expecting to see the enemy ship alongside. Okes had seen Herrick watching him, and his eyes had strayed past to the smoking guns in the battery which he had left to fend for themselves. He had clutched Herrick's arm, his voice unrestrained and desperate. 'Had to go below, Thomas! Had to find those fellows who ran away!' He had swayed and added wildly, 'You believe me, don't you?'

Herrick's contempt and anger had faded with the discovery that Okes was terrified almost to a point of madness. The realization filled him with a mixture of pity and shame.

'Keep your voice down, man!' Herrick had looked round for Vibart. 'You damn fool! Try and keep your head!'

He watched Okes now as the man skirted the corpses and then retraced his steps to the stern. He too was reliving his own misery. Destroying himself with the knowledge of his cowardice and disgrace.

Herrick found time to wonder if the captain had noticed
Okes' disappearance during the battle. Perhaps not. Maybe Okes
would recover after this, he thought grimly. If not, his escape
might be less easy the next time.

He saw Midshipman Neale's small figure scampering along the
maindeck and felt a touch of warmth. The boy had not faltered
throughout the fight. He had seen him on several occasions,
running with messages, yelling shrilly to the men of his division,
or just standing wide-eyed at his station. Neale's loss would have
been felt throughout the ship, of that Herrick was quite sure.

He hid a smile as the boy skidded to a halt and touched his
hat. 'Mr. Herrick, sir! Captain's compliments and would you lay
aft to supervise burial party!' He gulped for breath. 'There's
thirty altogether, sir!'

Herrick adjusted his hat and nodded gravely. 'And how are
you feeling?'

The boy shrugged. 'Hungry, sir!'

Herrick grinned. 'Try fattening a ship's rat with biscuit, Mr.
Neale. As good as rabbit any day!' He strode aft, leaving Neale
staring after him, his forehead creased in a frown.

Neale walked slowly past the bow-chasers, deep in thought.
Then he nodded very slowly. 'Yes, I might try it,' he said softly.

Bolitho felt his head loll and he jerked himself back against his
chair and stared at the pile of reports on his table. All but
completed. He rubbed his sore eyes and then stood up.

Astern, through the great windows he could see moonlight on
the black water and could hear the gentle sluice and creak of
the rudder below him. His mind was still fogged by the countless
orders he had given, the requests and demands he had answered.

Sails and cordage to be repaired, a new spar broken out to
replace the missing topgallant. Several of the boats had been
damaged and one of the cutters smashed to fragments. In a week,
driving the men hard, there would be little outward sign of the
battle, he thought wearily. But the scars would be there, deep
and constant inside each man's heart.

He recalled the empty deck in the fading light as he had stood
over the dead men and had read the well-tried words of the
burial service. Midshipman Farquhar had held a light above
the book, and he had noticed that his hand had been steady and
unwavering.

He still did not like Farquhar, he decided. But he had proved
a first-class officer in combat. That made up for many things.

As the last corpse had splashed alongside to begin its journey
two thousand fathoms deep he had turned, only to stop in surprise as he had realized that the deck had filled silently with men

from below decks. Nobody spoke, but here and there a man coughed quietly, and once he had heard a youngster sobbing uncontrollably.

He had wanted to say something to them. To make them understand. He had seen Herrick beside the marine guard, and Vibart's massive figure outlined against the sky at the quarter-deck rail. For a brief moment they had all been together, bound by the bonds of suffering and loss. Words would have soiled the moment. A speech would have sounded cheap. He had walked aft to the ladder and paused beside the wheel. The helmsman had stiffened. 'Course south-west by south, sir! Full an' by!'

He had returned here. To this one safe, defended place where there was no need for words of any sort.

He looked up angrily as Stockdale padded through the door. The man studied him gravely. 'I've told that servant o' yours to bring your supper, Captain.' Stockdale peered disapprovingly at the litter of charts and written reports. 'Pork, sir. Nicely sliced and fried, just as you like it.' He held out a bottle. 'I took the liberty of breaking out one o' your clarets, sir.'

The tension gripped Bolitho's voice in a vice. 'What the hell are you jabbering about?'

Stockdale was undaunted. 'You can flog me for sayin' it, sir, but today was a victory! You done us all proudly. I think you deserve a drink!' Bolitho stared at him lost for words.

Stockdale began to gather up the papers. 'An' further, Captain, I think you deserves a lot more!'

As Bolitho sat in silence watching the big coxswain laying the table for his solitary meal, the *Phalarope* plucked at the light airs and pushed quietly beneath the stars.

From dawn to sunset she had given much. But there would be other days ahead, thanks to her captain.

6. A SIGHT OF LAND

BOLITHO walked to the starboard side of the quarterdeck and rested his hands on the sun-warmed hammock netting. He did not need either chart or telescope now. It was like a home-coming.

The small island of Antigua had crept up over the horizon in the dawn's light, and now sprawled abeam shimmering in the forenoon sunlight.

Bolitho felt the old excitement of a perfect landfall coursing through his limbs, and he had to make himself continue in his interrupted pacing, if only to control it. Five weeks to a day since the *Phalarope* had showed her stern to the mist and rain

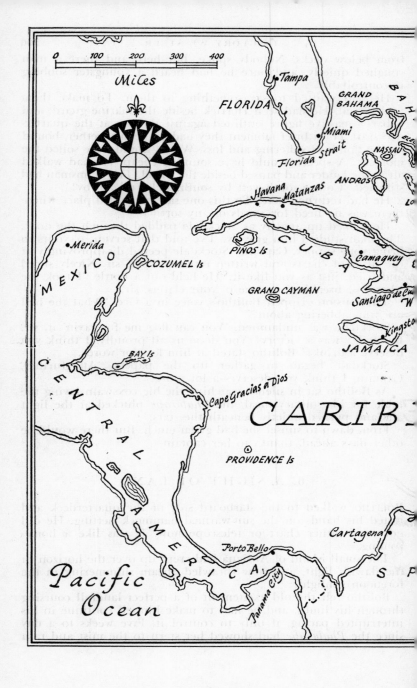

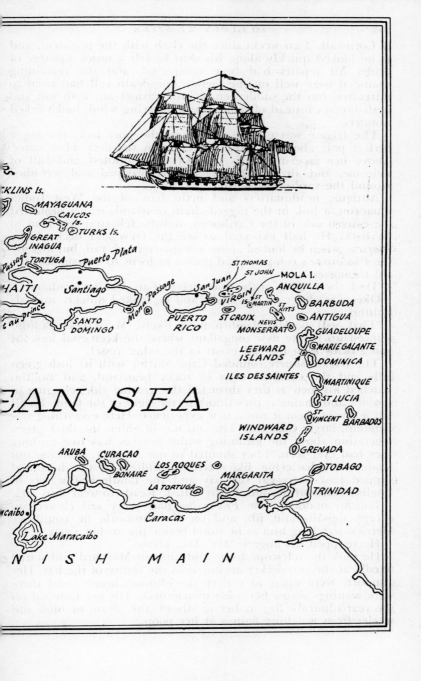

of Cornwall. Two weeks since the clash with the privateer, and
as he looked quickly along his ship he felt a quick upsurge of
pride. All repairs had been completed, and the remaining
wounded were well on the mend. The death roll had risen to
thirty-five, but the sudden entry into warmer air, with sun and
fresh breezes instead of damp and blustering wind, had worked
wonders.

The frigate was gliding gently on the port tack, making a
perfect pair above her own reflection in the deep blue water.
Above her tapering masts the sky was cloudless and full of
welcome, and already the eager gulls swooped and screamed
around the yards with noisy expectancy.

Antigua, headquarters and main base of the West Indies
squadron, a link in the ragged chain of islands which protected
the eastern side of the Caribbean. Bolitho felt strangely glad to
be back. He half expected to see the crew and deck of the
Sparrow when he looked across the quarterdeck rail, but already
the *Phalarope*'s company had grown in focus to overshadow the
old memories.

'Deck there! Ship of the line anchored around the headland!'

Okes was officer of the watch and he looked quickly towards
Bolitho.

'That will be the flagship most likely, Mr. Okes.' Bolitho
glanced up to the new topgallant where the keen-eyed lookout
had already seen the tall masts of the other vessel.

The frigate slowly rounded Cape Shirley with its lush green
hills and the tumbled mass of rocky headland, and Bolitho
watched his men as they thronged the weather side, clinging to
shrouds and chains as they drank in the sight of the land. To all
but a few of them it was a new experience. Here everything was
different, larger than life. The sun was brighter, the thick green
vegetation above the gleaming white beaches was like nothing
they had ever seen. They shouted to one another, pointing out
landmarks, chattering like excited children as the headland
slipped past to reveal the bay and the landlocked waters of
English Harbour beyond. Proby called, 'Ready to wear ship, sir!'

Bolitho nodded. The *Phalarope* had every sail clewed up
except topsails and jib, and on the forecastle he could see
Herrick watching him as he stood beside the anchor party.

He snapped his fingers. 'My glass, please.'

He took the telescope from Midshipman Maynard and stared
fixedly at the two-decker anchored in the centre of the bay. Her
gunports were open to collect the offshore breeze, and there
were awnings across her wide quarterdeck. His eye fastened on
the rear-admiral's flag at her masthead, the gleam of blue and
scarlet from watching figures at her poop.

'Mr. Brock! Stand by to fire salute! Eleven guns, if you please!' He closed the glass with a snap. If he could see them, they could see him. There was no point in appearing curious.

He watched the nearest point of land falling away and then added, 'Carry on, Mr. Proby!'

Proby touched his hat. 'Lee braces there! Hands wear ship!'

Bolitho glanced quickly at Okes and waited patiently. At length he said evenly, 'Clear those idlers off the side, Mr. Okes. That is a flagship yonder. I don't want the admiral to think I've brought a lot of bumpkins with me!' He smiled as Okes stuttered out his orders and the petty officers yelled at the unemployed men by the rail.

The salute began to pound and re-echo around the hills as the frigate swung slowly towards the other ship, and more than one man bit his lip as the saluting guns brought back other more terrifying memories.

'Tops'l sheets!' Proby mopped the sweat from his streaming face as he gauged the slow approach to the anchorage. 'Tops'l clew lines!' He looked aft. 'Ready, sir!' Bolitho nodded, only half listening to the salutes and the staccato bark of orders.

'Helm a' lee!' He watched the quartermaster pulling steadily at the polished spokes and saw the nearest hillside begin to swing across the bows as the *Phalarope* turned into the wind and began to lose way. Now there was no sound but for the gentle lap of water as the ship glided slowly towards the shore.

Bolitho called, 'Let go!'

There was a splash from forward followed by the jubilant roar of cable as the anchor plunged into the clear water.

Maynard said excitedly, 'Signal, sir! From *Cassius* to *Phalarope*. Captain to repair on board.'

Bolitho nodded. He had been expecting it and was already changed into his best uniform. 'Call away the gig, Mr. Okes, and see that its crew is properly turned out!' He saw the harassed lieutenant hurry away and wondered momentarily what was worrying him. He seemed strained. His mind only half on his duty.

Vibart came aft and touched his hat. 'Any orders, sir?'

Bolitho watched the boat being swayed out, the petty officer in charge using his cane more than usual, as if he too was well aware of the watching flagship.

'You can stand by to take on fresh water, Mr. Vibart. We will no doubt be warping through into English Harbour directly, and the men can go ashore and stretch their legs. They've earned it.'

Vibart looked as if he was going to argue but merely replied, 'Aye, aye, sir. I'll see to it.'

Bolitho looked across at the two-decker. The *Cassius*, seventy-four, flagship of Rear-Admiral Sir Robert Napier. He was said to be a stickler for promptness and smartness, although Bolitho had never actually met him before.

He climbed down the ladder and walked slowly towards the entry port. It was strange to realize that he had been in command for only five weeks. It seemed as if he had been aboard for months. The faces of the side party were familiar now, and already he was able to pick out the personalities and the weaknesses.

Captain Rennie saluted with his sword and the guard presented arms.

Bolitho removed his hat and then replaced it as the gig idled alongside with Stockdale glaring from the tiller. The pipes twittered and shrilled, and as he stepped into the gig he looked up at the ship's side, at the fresh paint and neat repairs which hid the clawing scars of battle. Things might have been a lot worse, he thought, as he settled himself in the sternsheets.

The oars sent the little boat scudding across the calm water, and when Bolitho looked astern he saw that his men were still staring after him. He held their lives in his hands. He had always known that. But before the short battle some might have doubted his ability. They might even have thought him to be like Pomfret.

He thrust the thought to the back of his mind as the flagship grew and towered above him. They did not have to like him, he decided. But trust him they must.

Rear-Admiral Sir Robert Napier did not rise from his desk but waved Bolitho towards a chair by the broad stern gallery. He was a small, irritable-looking man with stooping shoulders and sparse grey hair. He seemed bowed down by the weight of his dress coat, and his thin mouth was fixed in an expression of pernickety disapproval.

'I have been reading your reports, Bolitho.' His eyes flickered across the younger man's face and then returned to the desk. 'I am still not quite clear about your action with the *Andiron*.'

Bolitho tried to relax in the hard chair, but something in the admiral's querulous tone sparked off a small warning.

Bolitho had been met at the flagship's entry port with due ceremony and greeted courteously by the *Cassius*'s captain. The latter had appeared uneasy and worried, as well he might with a man like Sir Robert aboard, Bolitho thought dryly. The first sign that all was not well had been when he had been ushered into a cabin adjoining the admiral's quarters and told to wait for an audience. His log and reports had been whisked away, and he had stayed fretting in the airless cabin for the best part of an hour.

He said carefully, 'We made a good voyage, in spite of the engagement, sir. All repairs were carried out without loss of sailing time.'

The admiral eyed him coldly. 'Is that a boast?'

'No, sir,' Bolitho replied patiently. 'But I imagined that the need for frigates is still acute out here.'

The other man ruffled the documents with a wizened hand. 'Hmm, quite so. But the *Andiron*, Bolitho? How did she manage to escape?'

Bolitho stared at him, caught off guard. 'Escape, sir? She nearly laid us by the heels, as I have stated in my report.'

'I read that, dammit!' The eyes glowed dangerously. 'Are you trying to tell me that she ran away?' He looked aft through a window to where the *Phalarope* swung at her anchor like a carved model. 'I see little sign of combat or damage, Bolitho?'

'We were well supplied with spare spars and canvas, sir. The dockyard foresaw such an eventuality when they fitted her out.' The admiral's tone was getting under his skin and he could feel his anger smouldering, ignoring the warning in the man's eyes.

'I see. Captain Masterman lost *Andiron* after engaging two French frigates four months back, Bolitho. The French gave the captured ship to their new allies, the Americans.' The contempt was clear in his voice. 'And you state that although your ship was disabled and outgunned she made off without attempting to press home her advantage?' There was anger in his voice. 'Well, *are* you?'

'Exactly, sir.' Bolitho controlled his answer with an effort. 'My men fought well. I think the enemy had had enough. If I had been able to give chase I would have done so.'

'So you say, Bolitho!' The admiral put his head on one side, like a small, spiteful bird. 'I know all about your ship. I have read Admiral Longford's letter and all that he had to say about the trouble there was aboard when with the Channel Fleet. I am not impressed, to say the least!'

Bolitho felt the colour rising in his cheeks. The admiral's insinuation was obvious. In his view the *Phalarope* was a marked ship and unacceptable, no matter what she achieved.

He said coldly, 'I did not run away, sir. It happened just as I stated in the report. In my opinion the privateer was unwilling to sustain more damage.' He had a sudden picture of the crashing broadside, the chain shot ripping away the enemy's sails and rigging like cobwebs. Then another picture of the silent dead being dropped overboard. He added, 'My men did as well as I had hoped, sir. They had little time to defend themselves.'

'Please don't take that tone with me, Bolitho!' The admiral stared at him hotly. '*I* will decide what standards your people have reached.'

'Yes, sir.' Bolitho felt drained. There was no point in arguing with this man.

'See that you remember it in future.' He dropped his eyes to the papers and said, 'Sir George Rodney has sailed to reorganize his fleet. He will be returning from England at any time. Sir Samuel Hood is away at St. Kitts, defending it from the French.'

Bolitho said quietly, 'St. Kitts sir?' It was barely one hundred miles to the west of his chair aboard the flagship, yet the admiral spoke as if it was the other side of the world.

'Yes. The French landed troops on the island and tried to drive our garrison into the sea. But Admiral Hood's squadron retook the anchorage, and even now is holding all the main positions, including Basseterre, the chief town.' He glared at Bolitho's thoughtful face. 'But that is not your concern. I am in command here until either the Commander-in-Chief returns or Admiral Hood sees fit to relieve me. You will take your orders from *me*!'

Bolitho's mind only half attended to the other man's irritable voice. In his mind he could see the tiny island of St. Kitts and knew exactly what its safety meant to the harassed British. The French were strong in these waters, and had been more than instrumental to the British defeats at the Chesapeake the previous year. Driven from the American mainland, the British squadrons would depend more and more on their chain of island bases for supplies and repairs. If they fell, there would be nothing to prevent the French or their allies from swallowing up every last possession in the Caribbean.

The French fleet in the West Indies was well trained and battle hardened. Their admiral, Count de Grasse, had more than once out-guessed and outfought the hard-pressed ships of the British. It had been de Grasse who had driven a wedge between Admiral Graves and the beleaguered Cornwallis, who had assisted the rebel general, Washington, and had organized the American privateers into useful and deadly opponents.

Now de Grasse was testing the strength of individual British bases with the same sure strategy which had made him his country's most valuable commander. Using Martinique to the south as his main base, he could attack every island at will or, the thought brought a chill to Bolitho's mind, he could speed to the west and fall upon Jamaica. After that there would be nothing to sustain the British. They would have the Atlantic behind them, and nothing to keep them from complete destruction.

The admiral was saying smoothly, 'I will require you to carry out patrols to the westward, Bolitho. I will draft my orders immediately. The enemy may try and transport more troops down from the American mainland to the Leeward Islands, or even further south to the Windward Islands. You will keep contact with the rest of my squadron, and with Admiral Hood at St. Kitts *only if absolutely necessary!*'

Bolitho felt the cabin closing in on him. The admiral had no intention of trusting *Phalarope* with the fleet. Once again the frigate seemed doomed to isolation and suspicion.

He said, 'The French will be reinforced by privateers, sir. My ship would be well employed closer inshore, I would have thought.'

The admiral smiled gently. 'Of course, Bolitho, I had almost forgotten. You are no stranger out here. I think I read somewhere of your little exploits.' His smile vanished. 'I am sick and tired of hearing stories of privateers! They are nothing but scavengers and pirates, and no match for one of *my* ships! You will do well to remember that, too! *Andiron*'s capture was a disgrace which should have been forestalled! If you meet her again, I would suggest you summon help to avoid another lamentable failure to capture or destroy her!'

Bolitho stood up, his eyes flashing. 'That is unfair, sir!'

The admiral studied him bleakly. 'Hold your tongue! I am tired of young, hot-headed officers who cannot understand strategy and discipline!' Bolitho waited for his breathing to return to normal. 'Privateers are just one part of the pattern. The French are the real danger!'

There was a long silence, and Bolitho heard the distant thud of marine's boots and the muted blare of a bugle. The two-decker was like a small town after a frigate, but Bolitho could not wait to get away from it and the admiral's insulting remarks.

The latter said offhandedly, 'Keep a close watch on your patrol, Bolitho. And I would suggest you watch your fresh water and supplies very closely. I cannot say exactly when you will be relieved.'

'My men are tired, sir.' Bolitho tried once more to get through the admiral's cold rudeness. 'Some of them have not been ashore for years.' He thought of the way they had watched the green hills and gasped at the sight of the smooth, deserted beaches.

'And I am tired of this interview, Bolitho.' He rang a small bell on the desk. 'Just do your allotted duty, and remember that I will brook no deviation from it at any time. Foolhardy schemes are useless to me. See that you do not allow your apparent sense of self-importance to mar your judgement.' He waved his hand and the door opened silently behind Bolitho.

He stood outside in the passageway, his hands shaking with suppressed anger and resentment. By the time he had reached the entry port his face was again an impassive mask, but he hardly trusted himself to reply to the quiet words of the *Cassius*'s captain as the latter saw him over the side.

The older man said softly, 'Watch your step, Bolitho! Sir Robert lost his son aboard the *Andiron*. He will never forgive you for letting her get away, *whatever* the reason, so you must try and ignore his words, if not his warning!'

Bolitho touched his hat to the guard. 'I have had a lot of warnings of late, sir. But in an emergency they are rarely of any use!'

The flagship's captain watched Bolitho step into the gig and move clear of the *Cassius*'s long shadow. In spite of his youth, Bolitho looked as if he might make trouble for others as well as himself, he thought grimly.

'Deck there! The cap'n's returnin'!'

Herrick moved out of the shade of the mizzen mast and hurried towards the entry port. He brushed some crumbs from his neckcloth and hastily tugged his cross-belt into position. He had always been able to tolerate the dull and badly prepared food aboard ship in the past, but with the *Phalarope* riding at her anchor and the ample provisions of English Harbour lying within cannon shot, it had been all that he could do to swallow his lunch. He squinted across the glittering water, his keen eyes immediately picking out the returning gig, its small crew clean and bright in their check shirts, the oars rising and falling like gulls' wings. Herrick stiffened as Vibart joined him by the rail.

The first lieutenant said, 'Well, now we shall see!'

'I'll wager the admiral was delighted to see our captain.' Herrick darted a hasty glance to make sure that the side party was properly fallen in. 'It will do a power of good for our people.'

Vibart shrugged. 'What do admirals know about anything?' He seemed unwilling to talk and unable to drag his eyes from the approaching gig. Herrick could see Bolitho's square shoulders in the stern-sheets, the glitter of sunlight on his gold lace.

A master's mate said suddenly, 'Two water lighters shovin' off from the shore, sir. Deep laden by the looks of 'em!'

Herrick glanced in the direction of the man's arm and saw the two ugly craft moving clear of the land. They crawled ponderously towards the frigate, their great sweeps making heavy work of the journey.

Herrick muttered, 'I thought we would wait until we warped through into the harbour?'

Vibart slammed his hands together. 'By God, I knew this

would happen! I just *knew* it!' He moved his heavy body violently and pointed towards the blue sea. 'That's for us, Mr. Herrick. No cream for the *Phalarope,* either now or ever!' He added angrily, 'Not until the ship is used as she was meant to be used!'

A boatswain's mate called, 'Stand by!'

Again the pipes shrilled their salute and the sweating guard slapped their muskets to the present.

Herrick touched his hat and watched Bolitho's face as he climbed up through the port. His features were calm and empty of expression, but his eyes as he glanced briefly along the main-deck were cold and bleak, like the North Atlantic.

Vibart said stiffly, 'Water lighters making for us, sir.'

'So I see.' Bolitho did not look round, but stared instead at the newly scrubbed decks, the quiet atmosphere of order and readiness. He added after a moment, 'Carry on with immediate loading, and tell the cooper to prepare extra casks.'

Herrick asked cautiously, 'Are we to sea again, sir?'

The grey eyes fixed him with a flat stare. 'It would appear so!'

Vibart stepped forward, his eyes hidden in shadow. 'It's damned unfair, sir!'

Bolitho did not answer, but seemed entirely preoccupied in his thoughts. Then he said sharply, 'We will be making sail within two hours, Mr. Vibart. The wind seems light, but good enough for my purpose.' He looked round as Stockdale padded on to the quarterdeck. 'Oh, tell my servant I will require some food as soon as possible. Anything will do.'

Herrick stared at him. Bolitho had been away for the best part of two hours, yet the admiral had not even bothered to entertain him or offer him lunch. What the hell could he be thinking of? A young, courageous captain, fresh from England with news, as well as a fine addition to the fleet, should have been welcomed like a brother!

He thought of his own feelings while he had eaten his meagre meal in the wardroom. Each mouthful had nearly choked him as he had imagined Bolitho dining with the admiral and enjoying the full fare which a flagship could provide in harbour. Poultry, fresh lean pork, even roast potatoes perhaps! The climate was unimportant to Herrick where good, familiar food was concerned.

Now he realized that Bolitho had received nothing. The same feeling of shame and pity moved through him that he had earlier felt for Okes. A slur on Bolitho was an insult to every man aboard, yet the captain carried the full brunt of it. It was so unfair, so calculated in its cruelty that Herrick could not contain himself.

'But, sir! Did the admiral not congratulate you?' He fumbled for words as Bolitho shifted to watch him. 'After all you have done for this ship?'

'Thank you for your concern, Herrick.' For a brief moment Bolitho's expression softened. 'Things are not always what they first appear. We must be patient.' There was not a trace of bitterness in his answer, nor was there any warmth either. 'But in war there is little time for personal understanding.' He turned on his heel adding, 'We will have gun drill as soon as we get under way.' He disappeared down the cabin hatch and Herrick looked round in dull amazement.

So Vibart had been right. *Phalarope* was a marked ship, and would remain one.

The master's mate came aft. 'Boat shovin' off from the *Cassius,* sir!'

Herrick felt suddenly angry. It was all so pointless, so stupid. 'Very well. It will be bringing despatches. Man the side, if you please.'

He was still angry when a debonair lieutenant climbed up through the port and after removing his hat stood and stared curiously around the deck, as if expecting to see some sort of spectacle. 'Well?' Herrick scowled at the visitor. 'Have you had a good look?'

The officer blushed and then said, 'My apologies, sir. I was expecting something rather different.' He held out a bulky canvas envelope. 'Orders for Captain Bolitho from Sir Robert Napier, Rear-Admiral of the Red.'

It sounded so formal after their first exchange that Herrick could not help smiling. 'Thank you. I'll take 'em aft in a moment.' He studied the officer's tanned face. 'How goes the war out here?'

He shrugged. 'A hopeless muddle. Too much sea and too few ships to cover it!' He became serious. 'St. Kitts is under siege, and the rebels are consolidating up in the north. Everything will depend on how much the French can bring to bear.'

Herrick turned the heavy envelope over in his hands and wondered if he would ever be opening his own orders. In command of his own ship.

'If the privateers are as good as the one we fought then the battle will be a hard one.' Herrick studied the man's face intently, just waiting for some sign of doubt or amusement.

But the lieutenant said quietly, 'We heard about the *Andiron.* A bad business to lose her so. I hope you get a chance to even the score. What with that renegade John Paul Jones playing hell with our communications, it is only to be expected that others will follow his example.'

Herrick nodded. 'I don't see why it should be a disgrace for Captain Masterman to lose his ship in combat.'

'You have not heard?' The officer dropped his voice. 'She fought two French frigates at once. At the height of the battle the *Andiron* was hailed by some American officer aboard one of the enemy ships. He called on the *Andiron*'s people to go over to his side.'

Herrick's jaw dropped. 'And you mean that is what happened?'

He nodded. 'Exactly! They would never surrender to Frogs, but this American made it sound like a new life, so what did they have to lose? And of course they will fight all the better *against us*! Every man-jack knows it will be flogging round the fleet and the gibbet if they are caught now.'

Herrick felt sick. 'How long had *Andiron* been in commission?'

'I'm not sure. About ten years, I believe.' He saw Herrick's mind working and added grimly, 'So *watch* your own people. Out here, thousands of miles from home and surrounded by the King's enemies, emotions play a big part in a man's loyalty.' He added meaningly, 'Especially in a ship where trouble has already felt its way!'

He broke off as Vibart strode back from the maindeck. He touched his hat to the first lieutenant and said formally, 'I have twenty-five men for you in my cutter, sir. The admiral requested they be used as replacements for the ones killed in battle.' He watched as Vibart climbed down to the port where the marines were already mustering a growing rank of lean-looking sailors.

The officer said quickly, 'I have already spoken enough, my friend. But these men are outcasts. Nearly all have been in serious trouble of one kind or another. I think Sir Robert is more concerned in ridding his flagship of their influence than he is of helping your captain.' With a hurried glance at the distant two-decker he made towards his waiting boat. He whispered finally, 'Sir Robert watches everything. No doubt it will soon be common knowledge that I have spent ten minutes in conversation with *you*!' Then he was gone.

Vibart clumped aft, his face wrinkled in a scowl! 'We will read in those men immediately, Mr. Herrick. I suppose the captain will want them dressed like the rest of his precious company?' He sniffed. 'In my opinion they look more at home in rags!'

Herrick followed his angry glance and felt his spirits drop even further. These replacements were not men raw from the press. They were hardened and professional, and at any other time would have been worth their weight in gold. But now they stood idly and insolently watching with all the arrogance of wild

animals as the master's mate and Midshipman Maynard sorted
them into order and seniority. Curses and beatings would not
impress their sort. Even floggings had changed them little,
Herrick thought.

Vibart muttered, 'We'll see how the captain deals with this
pretty bunch!'

Herrick did not speak. He could imagine the difficulties which
seemed to be piling up hour by hour. If the captain tried to
separate these troublemakers from the rest of the crew he would
lose any respect he had gained. If he did not, their influence
could wreak havoc on the crowded berth deck.

On patrol, out of touch with help, the *Phalarope* would need
all her resources and skill to stay intact and vigilant.

Herrick had a sudden picture of the *Andiron* as she must have
been when Masterman's crew had surrendered. He stared round
the sunny quarterdeck and felt chilled in spite of the glare. He
imagined himself, suddenly alone, in a ship where disciplined
and loyal seamen had become strangers and mutineers.

Midshipman Maynard was watching him anxiously. 'Signal,
sir. Flag to *Phalarope*. Complete lightering and proceed to sea
with all despatch.'

Herrick said wearily, 'Acknowledge, Mr. Maynard.'

Herrick stared over the rail where the seamen toiled with the
fresh-water casks and then across at the tall-masted flagship.
Almost to himself he muttered, 'You bastard! You just can't
wait, can you.'

Grumbling and cursing, the duty watch climbed down the
various ladders and into the already crowded berth deck. Both
air and lighting came through the central hatchways, and in
addition several canvas chutes had been rigged to help ventilate
the overpopulated living spaces. At each scrubbed mess table
men sat and made use of their time to their own best advantage.
Some repaired clothing, heads bent to catch the filtered sunlight
on their needles and coarse thread. Some worked on small model
ships, and others merely sprawled yarning with their companions.

There was a brief lull in the buzz of speculation and rumour
as some of the new men pattered down a ladder followed by
Belsey, the duty master's mate. All of the men had been read in,
had taken the regulation shower under the deck pump, and now
stood blinking in the shadows, their bodies pale and naked
against the ship's dark sides. Each man carried a new shirt and
a rolled pair of trousers, as well as his own small possessions.

Belsey spun his cane and pointed to the corner mess table
where Allday and old Strachan watched the procession in silence.
He barked, 'You two! You'll be in this mess, got it?' He glared

into the dark corner of the berth deck. 'You've been given your watch and action stations, so just get settled in, and look sharp about it!' He raised his voice. 'Show these replacements where to sling their hammocks, and then get this deck cleared up!' He wrinkled his thick nose. 'It's like a bloody pigsty down here.'

One of the men detailed dropped his bundle on the table and looked down at Strachan and the others. He was tall and well muscled, and his broad chest was covered in a deep mat of dark hair. He seemed quite unconcerned about his nakedness and the rasp in Belsey's introduction.

He said calmly, 'Harry Onslow is the name, mates.' He looked over his shoulder. 'An' this is Pook, another good topman from the *Cassius*!' He spat out the name of the flagship, and Belsey who was hovering nearby strode across to the crowded table.

'Pay attention!' He stared round the watching faces. 'Don't you start thinking that you've got a real fine fellow here, my friends!' He gave a short grin. 'Turn round, Onslow!' He moved his cane menacingly. 'Just get a bit o' sunlight over you!'

Onslow turned his body obediently so that the light played across his back. Something like a hollow groan came from the packed sailors, and Belsey added coldly, 'Take a good look, afore you start listening to the like o' this scum!'

Allday tightened his lips as he saw the savagely mutilated skin on Onslow's body. He could not imagine how many times the man had been flogged, but that he had survived was surely a miracle. The whole of his back, from the nape of the neck to the top of his buttocks was ugly with broken and uneven weals, pale and obscene against his tanned arms and legs.

Ferguson looked away, his mouth quivering.

Even Pochin, a hard spectator at many floggings, said thickly, ' 'Ere, mate, put yer shirt on!'

The other man, Pook, was thin and wiry, and although his back also displayed the clawing embrace of the cat, it was nothing compared with Onslow's.

Belsey sauntered away followed by the other new seamen.

Onslow pulled the shirt over his head and shook out the clean new trousers. Calmly he remarked, 'What is so different about your captain? Does he like his men to look pretty?' He had a lazy Norfolk accent, and seemed quite unmoved by the horror his scars had unleashed.

Ferguson said quickly, 'He's different. He stopped Betts being flogged.' He tried to smile. 'You'll be all right aboard this ship, Onslow!'

Onslow looked him over without expression. 'Who asked *you* then?'

'All captains are swine!' Pook was tugging on his trousers,

and then strapped a wicked-looking knife around his waist.
'We've had a bellyful in the *Cassius*!'

Onslow said, 'Betts, did you say? What happened to him?'

'He attacked the purser.' Pochin looked thoughtful. 'Cap'n
Bolitho refused to 'ave 'im flogged.'

'Where is he know?' The man's eyes were dark and unwinking.

'Dead. Went over the side with the main t'gallant!'

'Well, then.' Onslow pushed Ferguson off the bench and
squatted in his place. 'It didn't do him much good, did it?'

Old Strachan folded his carving in a piece of sailcloth and
said vaguely, 'But the lad's right. Cap'n Bolitho promised that
he would see us fair if we pulled our weight. We'll be taking a
run ashore soon.' He squinted towards the hatch. 'Just think of
it! A walk through them hills, and maybe a drop o' somethin'
from a friendly native!'

Ferguson tried again. As if he had to believe in somebody to
retain his own sanity. 'And Mr. Herrick said he would try and
get a letter put aboard the next homebound ship for me. Just to
tell my wife I'm alive and well.' His expression was pitiful.

'You can read and write, can you, little man?' Onslow studied
him calmly. 'You could be very useful to me.'

Allday smiled to himself. Already the noise and rumble of
voices was returning to the messes. Maybe Ferguson was right.
Things might be better from now on. He hoped so, if only for
Ferguson's peace of mind.

Pochin asked sourly, 'How did you get the lash, Onslow?'

'Oh, the usual.' Onslow was still watching Ferguson, his face
deep in thought.

Pook said ingratiatingly, ' 'E kicked a bosun's mate! An' afore
that he . . .'

Onslow's mouth opened and shut like a trap. 'Stow it! It's
what happens from now on that counts!' Then he became calm
again. 'I was a boy when I came out here ten years back. For
years I've been waiting for that last voyage home, but it never
comes. I've been shipped from one captain to the next. I've stood
my watches, and I've faced broadsides more times than I can
remember. No, mates, there's no let-up for our sort. The only
way out is sewn up in a hammock, or take our own course like
the lads in the *Andiron*.'

He had every man's attention now. He stood up, his face set
and brooding. 'They chose to leave the King's service. To make
a new life for themselves out here, or in the Americas!'

Strachan shook his grey head. 'That's piracy!'

'You're too old to matter!' There was a bite in Onslow's voice.
'I've yet to find a fair captain, or one who thought beyond prize
money and glory for himself!'

At that moment shadows darted across the hatches and the air was filled with twittering pipes.

Pochin groaned. 'Blasted Spithead nightingales! Do they never get tired of blowin' 'em?'

The voices of the bosun's mates echoed round the berth deck. 'All hands! All hands! Stand by to make sail! Anchor party muster on the fo'c's'le!'

Ferguson stared blankly at the sunlight on the ladder, his mouth hanging open. 'He promised! He promised me I could get a letter home!'

Onslow clapped him on the shoulder. 'And he'll promise a lot more, I shouldn't wonder, lad!' He faced the others, unsmiling. 'Well, mates! Do you understand now what I was saying?'

Josling, a bosun's mate, appeared on the ladder, his face running with sweat. 'Are yew deaf? Jump to it there! A taste of my little rope for the last on deck!'

There was a stampede of running feet as the men came to their senses and surged up to the sunlight.

'Stand by the capstan!' The orders clouted their ears. 'Hands aloft! Loose tops'ls!'

Allday saw Ferguson staring wildly at the green, inviting island with its low, undulating hills. He felt a lump in his own throat now. It was not unlike Cornwall in the summertime, he thought. Then he touched Ferguson's arm and said kindly, 'Come on, lad. I'll race you aloft!'

Vibart's booming voice filled the air. 'Loose heads'ls! Man the braces!'

Allday reached the mainyard and ran quickly along the foot-rope to join the others lying across the thick spar. Below him he could see the busy deck, and over his shoulder he could identify Bolitho's tall figure by the taffrail.

From forward Herrick yelled, 'Anchor's aweigh, sir!'

Allday dug his toes into the footrope as the sail billowed and filled beneath him and the great yard moved ponderously to catch the wind. Already the land was sliding away, and by the time the sails were set and trimmed it would be lost in the haze. Perhaps for ever, he thought.

7. A SPANISH LUGGER

HERRICK moved slightly around the mizzen mast in an effort to remain in the shadow cast by its thick trunk. He found that his eyes were constantly slitted against the harsh glare, his tongue continually moving across his parched lips as the forenoon watch dragged slowly to its conclusion.

Above his head the sails hung limp and lifeless, and there was not a breath of wind to ruffle the flat, empty expanse of sea, upon which the becalmed frigate lay motionless and hushed.

He plucked at his grubby shirt, immediately irritated by the futility of his action. It felt sodden with sweat, yet his whole being seemed to cry out for moisture. He could feel the deck seams gripping stickily at his shoes, and once when he had inadvertently rested his hand on one of the quarterdeck nine-pounders he had almost cried out with pain. The barrel had been as hot as if it had been firing without pause. His lip curled bitterly at the thought. There had been no action, nor was there likely to be under these impossible conditions.

After leaving Antigua the *Phalarope* had sailed directly to her allotted station, but apart from sighting another patrolling frigate and then later the bulky shape of the *Cassius*, she had kept the sea to herself.

And now, to top it all, the frigate was becalmed. For twenty-four hours she had idled aimlessly above her reflection, carried at will by the sluggish currents, the lookouts worn and weary from staring hopefully for a squall to break the spell. Seven long days since they had sailed with such haste from Antigua, seven days of watching the burnished horizons and waiting.

Herrick glanced forward where the duty watch lay like dead men below the dark shadow of the bulwark. Their half-naked bodies had already lost their pallor, and more than one un-seasoned sailor bore savage burns on his skin from the sun's relentless glare.

Midshipman Neale leaned against the nettings, his round face for once devoid of mischief or interest. Like the rest, he seemed crushed and defeated by the inactivity and heat.

It was hard to believe that anything else existed outside their own enclosed world. St. Kitts lay some fifty miles to the south-east, and the Anegada Passage which separated the Virgin Islands from the disputed Leewards was spread in an eye-searing haze across the motionless bowsprit.

Of Hood's efforts to hold St. Kitts they had heard nothing, and for all Herrick could guess even the war might have ended. When they had met the flagship, Bolitho had made a signal requesting the latest information, but the reply had been unhelp-ful to say the least. The *Phalarope* had been carrying out gunnery practice, using several old and useless casks as targets. Herrick knew that Bolitho had done it more to break the monotony than with any hope of improving the standards of marksmanship by such methods.

Cassius's flags had soared angrily to her yards, and soon Maynard had reported warily that the admiral was demanding an immediate cease-fire. 'Conserve powder and shot', the signal had ordered curtly. So that was that.

Bolitho had made no comment, but Herrick knew his captain well enough now to understand the sudden anger in his grey eyes. It was as if the admiral had gone out of his way to isolate the *Phalarope,* as a doctor would separate a leper from his fellow humans.

He jerked from his thoughts as Bolitho's head and shoulders appeared through the cabin hatch. Like the other officers, he was dressed in shirt and white breeches, and his dark hair was clinging to his forehead with sweat. He looked strained and edgy, and Herrick could almost feel the restlessness which was making Bolitho fret at the inaction around him.

Herrick said, 'Still no wind, sir.'

Bolitho shot him an angry glance and then seemed to control himself. 'Thank you, Mr. Herrick. So I see.' He walked to the compass and glanced at the two listless helmsmen. Then he moved to the starboard rail, and Herrick saw him wince as the sun smote his shoulders like a furnace.

Bolitho said quietly, 'How are the men?'

Herrick replied vaguely, 'Not happy, sir. It is bad enough out here, without short water rations!'

'Quite so.' Bolitho nodded without turning. 'But it is necessary. God knows how long we will be pinned down like this.'

His hand moved vaguely to the scar beneath the rebellious forelock of hair. Herrick had seen him touch the livid mark on several previous occasions, usually when he appeared to be entirely wrapped in his own thoughts. Once Herrick had questioned Stockdale about it, and learned that it had happened when Bolitho, as a junior lieutenant, had been sent ashore to an island with a small party of seamen to refill water casks.

Unknown to the captain or anyone else, the island had not been uninhabited, and almost as soon as the launch had grated up the beach the party had been ambushed by a horde of yelling natives. One had snatched up a cutlass from a dying sailor and attacked Bolitho as he had tried to rally his out-numbered men. In his thick, jolting voice Stockdale had described the scene around the launch, with half the sailors butchered or dying and the others falling back desperately in a frantic effort to regain the safety of the sea. Bolitho had fallen, separated from his men, his face masked in blood from the cutlass slash which should have killed him. The sailors who survived were all for leaving their officer, whom they supposed to be dead anyway, but at the last minute they rallied, and as more boats pulled to their aid Bolitho was dragged to safety.

Herrick knew there was a lot more to it than that. Just as he guessed that it had been Stockdale's massive right arm which had held the men from panic and had saved the man he now served like a devoted dog.

Bolitho walked forward to the quarterdeck rail and stared towards the bows. 'The haze, Mr. Herrick. It looks not unlike a Channel mist.'

Herrick's dry lips cracked into a rueful smile. 'I never thought I would miss the Channel Fleet, sir. But how I would like to hear the wind and feel the cold spray again.'

'Maybe.' Bolitho seemed lost in his thoughts. 'But I have a feeling the wind will return soon.'

Herrick stared at him. It was not a boast or an empty statement of hope. It was like another small picture of the man's quiet confidence, he thought. There was a step on the deck behind them and Vibart said harshly, 'A word, Captain.'

Bolitho replied, 'What is it?'

'Your clerk, Mathias, sir.' Vibart watched Bolitho's impassive face as he continued, 'He's had a bad fall in the hold, sir.'

'How bad?'

Vibart shook his head. 'He'll not see another day, I'm thinking.' There was no pity in his voice.

Bolitho bit his lip. 'I sent him down there myself to check some stores.' He looked up suddenly, his face clouded with concern. 'Are you sure nothing can be done for him?'

'The surgeon says not.' Vibart sounded indifferent. 'Apart from his ribs, which are badly stove in, he's got a split in his skull you could put a marline-spike through!'

'I see.' Bolitho stared down at his hands on the rail. 'I hardly knew the man, but he was a hard worker and tried to do his best.' He shook his head. 'To die in action is one thing, but this . . .'

Herrick said quickly, 'I will get another clerk, sir. There is a new man, Ferguson, one of those pressed in Falmouth. He can read and write, and is more used to that sort of work.' Herrick recalled Ferguson's wretched expression as the ship had left Antigua. He had promised to help him get a letter away to his wife. Perhaps this release from the heavy duties of seamanship and the harsh control of the petty officers would make up for the omission in some way.

Herrick watched Bolitho's grave face and wondered how the captain could find the time to grieve over one man when he himself was burdened with such bitter responsibility.

Bolitho said, 'Very well. Detail Ferguson and tell him his duties.'

A yell came from the maintopmast. 'Deck there! Squall comin' from the starboard bow!'

Herrick ran to the rail, one hand shading his eyes. Incredulously he saw the gentle ripple pushing down towards the becalmed ship and heard the rigging stirring itself as the inert sails moved slowly into life.

Bolitho stood upright and clasped his hands behind him. 'What are you all staring at? Stir those men, Mr. Herrick, and get the ship under way!'

Herrick nodded. He had seen the excitement beneath Bolitho's outburst. As the sails filled and flapped overhead Bolitho's expression was almost boyish with pleasure.

It was not much of a wind, but sufficient to get the *Phalarope* moving once more. The water gurgled around her rudder, and as the braces squeaked in the blocks the sails swung to embrace every last ounce of air, eager for the life it had given them.

Bolitho said at length, 'Keep her north-west by north, Mr. Herrick. We will remain on this leg until sunset.'

'Aye, aye, sir.' Herrick watched him walk back to the taffrail and peer down at the small wake. There was no sign of the anxiety he must be feeling, he thought. The wind was a small respite and no way a recompense for the endless, meaningless patrol, yet Bolitho acted as if everything was normal, outwardly at least.

Again the masthead lookout was to prove that nothing could be taken for granted.

'Deck there! Sail fine on the starboard bow!'

Herrick lifted his glass but Bolitho snapped, 'You'll not see anything from here! The haze is like a blanket to the north of us!'

Vibart muttered, 'Mr. Neale, get aloft!'

'Belay that!' Bolitho sounded dangerously calm. 'You go, Mr. Herrick. I want an experienced eye at this moment!'

Herrick ran to the main shrouds and began to climb. He quickly realized how out of condition his body had become, and by the time he had reached the topmast trestle and cross-trees his heart was pounding like a drum. The bearded lookout moved over for him and pointed with a tarry hand.

'Over yonder, sir! Can't make her out yet!'

Herrick ignored the ship swinging like a toy beneath his legs and opened his glass. At first he could see nothing but bright sunlight across the low-lying haze with the million glittering mirrors of the sea beneath. Then he saw the sail and felt a tinge of disappointment. The hull was well shrouded in mist, but from the sail's strange dorsal shape he guessed it was small, probably a coasting lugger of some sort. Not worth taking as a prize, and hardly worth sinking, he decided angrily. He yelled the information to the deck and saw Bolitho staring up at him.

'A lugger, you say?' Bolitho sounded interested. 'Keep watching her!'

'She's not seen us.' The lookout squinted towards the sail. 'Reckon us'll be up to 'er afore she spots us.'

Herrick nodded and then looked down as Vibart called, 'Pipe all hands! Stand by to wear ship!'

So Bolitho was going to close her anyway. Herrick watched the sudden burst of activity on the decks below. He had not seen such a sight since he was a midshipman. The scampering, apparently aimless figures, which surged from between decks and then merged as if by magic into recognizable patterns of discipline and purpose. He could see the petty officers checking their watch bills as they bawled names and orders. Here and there the officers and warrant officers stood like little isolated rocks amidst the surging tide of running seamen.

Again the yards moved round, flapping indignantly as the frigate altered course two points to starboard. Herrick felt the mast tremble, and tried not to think of the time it would take to fall to the deck.

But the breeze which had found the *Phalarope* had reached the other sail, and as the mist glided away in its path the lugger gathered way and heeled jauntily, another tan sail already creeping up her stumpy mainmast.

The lookout champed on a wad of tobacco and said calmly, 'Her's a Spaniard! Oi'd know that rig anywhere.'

Bolitho's voice cut through his speculation. 'You may come down now, Mr. Herrick! Lively there!'

Herrick reached the deck gasping and sweating to find Bolitho waiting for him, his face deep in concentration.

'She'll have the edge on us, Mr. Herrick. She can make better use of these light airs than we can.' He gestured impatiently towards the forecastle. 'Clear away the two chasers and fire across her bows!'

Herrick got his breath and gasped, 'Aye, aye, sir! It would only take one ball to shatter her timbers!'

He saw something like amusement in the grey eyes as Bolitho replied, 'She may have the most precious cargo of all time, Mr. Herrick!'

Herrick stared at him dazedly. 'Sir?'

Bolitho had turned to watch the gunners scampering forward towards the two long nine-pounders on the forecastle. '*Information*, Mr. Herrick! Out here, the lack of it could lose a war!'

One shot was enough. As the tall waterspout fell in a splatter of spray beyond the lugger's bows, first one sail and then the other crumpled and fell, leaving the boat rocking dejectedly to await the *Phalarope*'s pleasure.

Bolitho's wide cabin seemed almost cold after the furnace heat of the quarterdeck, and he had to force himself to stand quite still by the stern windows to steady his racing thoughts and plan the next move. With real effort he closed his ears to the muffled shipboard noises and distant shouts as a boat was dropped alongside to take a boarding party to the lugger, which now rode uneasily under the frigate's lee. It had been all Bolitho could do to remain outwardly unruffled as his orders were passed and carried out, so that in the end he could no longer face the watchful glances of his officers or avoid the buzzing speculation of the upperdeck idlers.

His casual guess about the coming of a wind had seemed like a miracle, and when the lookout had reported the lugger in the haze he had felt his pent up emotions churning around like raw alcohol. The waiting and petty irritations were momentarily put to one side, even the shame he felt for the admiral's attitude to *Phalarope* could be overlooked, if not forgotten.

There was a tap at the door, and he swung round, caught off guard. 'Enter!'

He stared for a few seconds at the pale-faced seaman who hovered uncertainly in the doorway. He wrenched his mind away from the lugger and nodded towards the desk by the bulkhead.

'You must be Ferguson? You will be working here when I require you.' His tone was terse, his thoughts still following the invisible boarding party.

Ferguson stared round the cabin and blinked. 'Yes, sir. I mean —aye, aye, sir.' He seemed confused and nervous.

Bolitho studied him kindly. 'I will tell you more of your duties later. At the moment I am rather busy.' He looked round with a jerk as little Neale panted up to the door.

'Captain, sir!' He fought for breath. 'Mr. Okes has taken the lugger!'

'So I should hope!' Bolitho added dryly, 'Her skipper has a whole broadside staring down his throat.'

Neale considered the point. 'Er, yes, sir.' He stared up at Bolitho's calm face, obviously wondering how the captain could bear to leave the upperdeck when something was at last happening. He added, 'The boat is returning now, sir.'

'That was what I wanted to hear, Mr. Neale.' Bolitho looked through the stern windows towards the empty sea, its surface still ruffled by a small but steady breeze. 'When the boat comes alongside tell Captain Rennie with my compliments to keep the lugger's officers apart until I can question them. Mr. Okes can carry on with his search of the lugger and report when he finds anything.'

'The lugger's *officers*, sir?' Neale's eyes were like saucers.

'They may be dressed in rags, boy, but they are still officers!' Bolitho watched the midshipman patiently. 'And make no mistake, they will know these waters like their own faces.'

The midshipman nodded and scurried away. Bolitho paced restlessly around the cabin and then paused by his table where his personal chart of the Caribbean lay in readiness. The complex mass of islands and soundings, the vague surveys and doubtful descriptions were like the clues of a giant puzzle. He frowned and tugged at his chin. Somewhere amongst the tangle of scattered islands lay the key to the whole campaign. The first to find it would win the day. The loser would be driven from the Caribbean for ever.

With the points of his brass dividers he traced the *Phalarope*'s course and halted at the small pencilled cross. Out here he was doing no good. Fifty miles away St. Kitts might still be fighting a siege, whilst just over the horizon Count de Grasse's great fleet could be mustering for a final attack on the scattered British naval units. With the British driven from these islands, the French and their allies would unroll the South Americas like a chart. Would command the North and South Atlantic and reach for the rich rewards of Africa and beyond.

He pushed the apprehension from his mind as he heard the clatter of feet above and the thuds of muskets on the deck planks.

Vibart appeared in the dorway. 'Prisoners aboard, sir.' He glared at Ferguson who seemed to be trying to curl into a ball beside the desk. 'The lugger is Spanish well enough. Twenty men aboard all told, but no resistance. I have the master and two mates under guard outside, sir.'

'Good.' Bolitho stared at the chart. 'Twenty men, you say? That is a large crew for such a small craft. The Spaniards are usually more sparing when they man a vessel of any kind!'

Vibart shrugged. 'Mr. Farquhar says that the lugger has been used for coastal trading. Not much use for us.'

'I'll see the master first. You can go on deck and keep an eye on Mr. Okes' progress in the lugger. Let me know if he has found anything.'

The lugger's skipper was small and swarthy, dressed in a tattered shirt and wide canvas trousers. Two gold ear-rings bobbed from beneath his lank hair, and his dirty, bare feet completed the picture of neglect and poverty.

Beside him, Midshipman Farquhar seemed elegant and unreal.

Bolitho kept his eyes on the chart, conscious of the Spaniard's uneven breathing and the shuffling movements of his bare feet on the deck. He said at length, 'Does he speak English?'

'No, sir.' Farquhar sounded impatient. 'He just gabbles.'

Still Bolitho kept his eyes on the chart. Almost offhandedly he said, 'Then take him on deck and tell the master-at-arms to run a halter up to the mainyard.'

Farquhar fell back startled. 'Halter, sir? Do you mean to hang him?'

'Of course I do!' Bolitho put a rasp in his tone. 'He is no further use to me!'

The Spaniard's legs buckled and he pitched forward at Bolitho's feet. Sobbing and weeping he pulled at Bolitho's legs, the words flooding from his lips in a wild torrent.

'Please, Captain! No hang, *please*! I am a good man, sir, I have wife and many poor children!' His cheeks were running with tears. 'Please, sir, no *hang*!' The last word was almost a shriek.

Bolitho stepped from the man's grasp and said calmly. 'I had an idea that your knowledge of English might return.' To Farquhar he added crisply, 'You may try that ruse on the two mates. See what you can find out!' He turned back to the whimpering man on the deck. 'Now stand up and answer my questions, or indeed I *will* hang you!'

He waited a few more moments, his mind half dwelling on what might have happened if the Spaniard really had been unable to speak English. Then he asked, 'Where were you heading and with what cargo?'

The man stood swaying from side to side, his grubby hands clasped as if in prayer. 'I go to Puerto Rico, Captain. I take small cargo of timber, a little sugar.' He wrung his hands. 'But you can take it all, excellency! Just spare my life!'

'Hold your tongue!' Bolitho peered at the chart. The story was possible. These small trading boats were as common as fleas in the Caribbean. He asked sharply, 'From where did you come?'

The man smiled ingratiatingly. 'I go all around, Captain.' He waved his hands vaguely. 'I carry only small cargoes. I reap a living where I can. It is a hard, hard life, excellency!'

'I will ask you once more!' Bolitho fixed him with a hard stare.

The man shifted wretchedly. 'Martinique, Captain. I has small work there. But I *hate* the French, you understand?'

Bolitho dropped his eyes to hide the excitement he now felt. Martinique, the headquarters of all French naval operations, the most heavily protected fortress in the whole Caribbean.

'You hate the French? Your gallant allies?' Bolitho's sarcasm was not lost on the Spaniard. 'Well, never mind that. Just tell me how many ships were there in the anchorage.' He saw the man's eyes glitter with fright and guessed that he understood which anchorage he meant.

'Many ships, excellency!' He rolled his eyes. 'Many *big* ships!'

'And who commands these many big ships?' Bolitho could hardly keep the anxiety from his voice now.

'The French admiral, excellency!' The Spaniard puffed out his cheeks as if to spit on the deck, but caught sight of the marine sentry watching from the doorway and swallowed noisily. 'He is a French pig, that one!'

'The Count de Grasse?'

The man nodded violently. 'But you know everything, Captain! You are blessed by the Almighty!'

Bolitho looked up as Farquhar entered the cabin. 'Well?'

'Only a little English between them, sir.' He seemed angry with himself. 'But I gather they were heading for Puerto Rico.'

Bolitho gestured at the sentry. 'Take this prisoner out and keep him closely guarded.' Then he said absently, 'He was lying. He sailed from Martinique. The French would never allow him to carry on trading when they too might be under siege at any time!' He tapped the chart. 'No, Mr. Farquhar, he was at Martinique well enough, but his destination is elsewhere!'

Vibart entered and bowed his head beneath the deck beams. 'Mr. Okes reports that the cargo is much as you already know, sir. But there are new ship's spars and casks of salt meat stowed beneath the main load.' He sounded doubtful. 'There is also a great deal of spare canvas and cordage.'

'As I thought!' Bolitho felt strangely relieved. 'The lugger was taking supplies from Martinique'—his finger moved along the charted islands—'to where?' He looked from Vibart's brooding face to Farquhar's baffled one. 'Get that Spanish skipper back here at once!'

Bolitho walked slowly to the stern window and leaned out over the water as if to clear his brain. The Spaniard had seemed pleased to tell him about the French ships at Martinique, when he must have known that patrolling British ships would already know this information. He must have imagined that Bolitho had missed the main item.

He swung round as the man was pushed through the door. 'Now listen to me!' His voice was still controlled, but the harshness made the lugger's master start to quiver uncontrollably. 'You lied to me! I warned you what would happen, did I not?' He dropped his voice still further. 'Now just once more. Where were you bound?'

The man swayed. 'Please, excellency! They kill me if they know!'

'And I will kill you if you keep me waiting!' He saw Herrick's face watching him from the doorway with fixed fascination.

'We sail for Mola Island, Captain.' The man seemed to have shrunk in size. 'The cargo was for ship there!'

Herrick and Farquhar exchanged mystified glances.

Bolitho bent over his chart. 'Mola Island is Dutch.' He measured the distance with his dividers. 'Thirty miles to the nor'-east of our present position.' He looked up, his eyes hard and devoid of pity. 'How many such voyages have you made?'

'Many, excellency.' The Spaniard looked as if he wanted to be sick. 'There are soldiers there. French soldiers. They come from the north. They have ships also.'

Bolitho breathed out slowly. 'Of course! De Grasse would never attempt to move his ships against Jamaica or anywhere else unless he could be sure of a diversion elsewhere and full support from the military!' He stared at the others. 'Our fleet watches Martinique to the south and waits for the French to move, and all the time they are filtering down from the American mainland, gathering for a big, final assault!'

Vibart said bleakly, 'We must inform the *Cassius*, sir.'

Herrick spoke from the doorway, his voice eager. 'We could send the lugger to find the flagship, sir, and stay here in readiness!'

Bolitho did not seem to hear them. 'Sentry, take this prisoner and lock him up with the others. My compliments to the boatswain, and tell him to select any of the lugger's crew he thinks could be sworn into our company. I would imagine that even the *Phalarope* would seem better than a prison hulk!'

The marine grinned. 'Aye, aye, sir!' He jabbed the Spaniard with his musket and hustled the man away.

'It will be two days before we meet up with the *Cassius* again.' Bolitho was thinking aloud. 'By then it may be too late. That Spaniard has told us a good deal, but he cannot know the whole truth. If the French have been gathering a force of men and ships in this small island they must be expecting to move, and soon. I consider it our duty to investigate, and do our utmost to stop them.'

Vibart swallowed hard. 'Do you intend to leave the patrol area, sir?'

'Do you have any objections, Mr. Vibart?' Bolitho eyed him calmly.

'It is not *my* responsibility, sir.' Vibart dropped his gaze before Bolitho's cool stare.

Herrick said quickly, 'It is a great risk, if I may say so, sir.'

'As is everything worthwhile, Mr. Herrick.' Bolitho straightened his back and added briskly, 'My compliments to Mr. Proby. Tell him to wear ship and steer north-east. We will be sailing close to the wind so it will be nightfall before we reach Mola Island. Before that time there is much to be arranged, gentlemen!'

He looked around their faces and continued, 'Put a prize crew aboard the lugger, and ask Mr. Okes to search for the recognition signals. It is my guess that this island will be heavily guarded. The lugger will be too useful to spare for finding the admiral.'

Vibart said sulkily, 'The admiral will not be pleased by your acting like this, sir.'

'And my conscience would never rest if I allowed my own prestige to come before this obvious duty, Mr. Vibart!'

His eyes moved to Herrick and Farquhar. 'This will be a good opportunity for each of you.' He paused and looked around the cabin. 'For the ship, too.'

He waited until the cabin had emptied and then walked to the windows again. For one more minute he allowed the nagging doubts to play havoc with his thoughts. He had acted impetuously and without pausing to consider the possible consequences. Skill and ability were only half the battle. There always had to be a good amount of luck. And if he was mistaken now, there would not be that amount of luck in the whole world.

He saw Ferguson watching from the desk like a mesmerized rabbit and realized that he had forgotten all about his being there. But the story he might repeat on the berth deck might do good for the ship's dwindling morale, he thought vaguely. If the *Phalarope* was lucky this time it would make all the difference.

And if not? He shrugged. There would be few survivors to dispute the matter.

Above his head he heard the afterguard tramping with the braces and felt the deck canting slightly as the frigate went about. Momentarily framed in the stern windows he saw the small lugger swinging round to keep station on the quarter, and wondered how many men had already cursed the keen-eyed lookout for sighting her.

Aloud he remarked, 'You will have something to tell your wife now, Ferguson. She will be proud of you perhaps?'

Bolitho heaved himself from the cutter's sternsheets and allowed groping hands to pull him unceremoniously up and over the lugger's low bulwark. For several seconds he stood swaying on the unfamiliar deck to allow his eyes to get accustomed to the gloom and the packed figures around him.

Already the cutter had shoved off, and apart from the gleam of white spray around the oars it was lost in the enfolding darkness. Bolitho tried to see where the *Phalarope* now lay, but she, too, was well hidden, with not one glimmer of light to betray her presence. He tried to hold on to the mental picture of the chart and of the island which now lay somewhere across the lugger's blunt bows.

Captain Rennie loomed out of the darkness and said in an unnecessary whisper, 'I've packed the marines below, sir. Sergeant Garwood will keep 'em quiet until they are required.'

Bolitho nodded and tried to remember once again if he had left anything to chance. 'You have made sure that all muskets and pistols are unloaded?'

Rennie nodded. 'Yes, sir.' He sounded as if he meant, 'Of course, sir'. A primed musket exploding at the wrong moment, a trigger pulled by an over-excited marine, and their lives would be worth even less than they were now.

'Good.' Bolitho groped his way aft where Stockdale stood straddle-legged beside the crude tiller bar, his head cocked towards the loose flapping sails. Midshipman Farquhar squatted by a shapeless bundle on the deck which Bolitho managed to recognize as the luckless Spanish skipper. He had been brought along as both guide and surety.

Rennie asked flatly, 'Do you think we will get inshore without trouble?'

Bolitho glanced up at the high, bright stars. There was the merest sliver of silver for a moon floating above its reflection in the flat water. The night was dark enough to hide anything. Maybe too dark.

He said, 'We shall see. Now get under way, and make sure the compass light is well shaded.' He walked clear of Rennie and his questions and brushed past the crouching sailors whose eyes gleamed like marbles as they watched him pass. Occasionally he heard the rasp of a cutlass or a dull clink from the bows where McIntosh, a gunner's mate, was making a last-minute examination of his hastily rigged swivel gun. It was loaded with canister, and at close range would be quite deadly. It had to be perfect, Bolitho thought grimly. There might be no time for a second shot.

He wondered what Vibart was thinking, left in charge of the frigate, with hours to wait before he could play his part in the raid. He thought, too, of Herrick's face when he had told him he was taking Lieutenant Okes with him in the lugger. Herrick had known there was no other choice in the matter. Okes was his senior, and it was only fair that he should get the chance of making a name for himself. Or dying before Herrick, Bolitho thought dryly. Vibart's position and seniority made him the obvious choice for taking charge of the *Phalarope*, and if both Bolitho and Vibart were killed, Herrick could still move his way up the chain of command.

Bolitho scowled in the darkness and cursed himself for his

morbid thoughts. Perhaps he was already too tired, too worn out by planning and preparation to think any more. All day long, while the frigate had beaten her way towards Mola Island, things had moved at a swift pace. Men and weapons had been transferred to the lugger, and the latter's cargo had been either dropped overboard or rowed across to the *Phalarope* for their own use. The lugger's cramped hold was now packed with marines, each man too busy fighting back the nausea thrown up by the stench of fish oil and sour vegetables to care much about what might lie ahead.

Mathias, Bolitho's clerk, had died and had been dropped overboard with a brief prayer, his death and passing hardly making a break in the frantic preparations. Looking back, it was hard even to recall his face.

Lieutenant Okes stumbled along the side deck, his shoulders hunched as if he expected to be struck by some unseen object. He peered at Bolitho's watchful shape and muttered, 'All—all the men are ready, sir.' He sounded taut and nervous.

Bolitho grunted. Okes' behaviour had been worrying him for some time. He had even offered to stay aboard the frigate in Herrick's place, which was odd, in spite of the danger. Okes, he knew, was not a rich man, and any extra promotion, a glowing report in the *Gazette*, would make all the difference to his career. He was probably frightened. Well, so was anyone but a raving maniac, Bolitho thought.

He replied, 'We shall see the headland soon. There should be plenty of surf to show its position.' He screwed up his eyes to will himself to see the picture he had built of the island in his mind.

It was shaped something like a rough horseshoe, with the deep anchorage lying snugly between the two curved headlands. But the village was on the seaward side of the nearest headland, that being the only beach on the whole island. According to the chart and what he had wrung from the lugger's skipper, the village was connected to the anchorage by a rough road which crossed a steep ravine by way of a wooden bridge. The tip of the headland was therefore isolated by the ravine, and on its highest point there was said to be a powerful battery of guns, probably twenty-four-pounders, which could easily defend the whole anchorage. A sandbar and several isolated reefs completed the hazardous approach. In fact, the approach was impossible without consent from both battery and good daylight. No wonder the French had chosen this place as their strongpoint.

' 'Eadland, sir!' A seaman pointed abeam. 'There, sir!'

Bolitho nodded and walked aft again. 'Steer close, Stockdale. There is a beach about a quarter of a mile ahead, and a wooden pier, if this Spaniard's word is worth anything!'

From the bow a seaman dropped his leadline overboard and then said hoarsely, 'By the mark two, sir!'

Two fathoms under the keel, and still a long way to go. There was no chance of a surprise attack here either, except by craft as small as the lugger. The only thing in their favour was surprise. Nobody in his right mind would expect a single small boat to approach a heavily guarded island in total darkness.

Belsey, the master's mate, said gruffly, 'I can see th' pier, sir. Look, over yonder!' Bolitho swallowed hard, conscious of a prickling in his spine. He readjusted his sword and made sure that his pistol was ready at his waist.

'Get the Spaniard up here!' The tension was making his voice harsh, and he heard the prisoner's teeth chattering like dice.

He gripped the man's arm, smelling his fear. Now was the time to make the Spaniard more afraid of *him* than of anything the enemy could do. 'Listen to me!' He shook the man slowly with each word. 'When we are challenged, you know what to do?'

The Spaniard nodded violently. 'Show lantern. Give the signal, excellency!'

'And if they ask why you are coming in at night tell them you have despatches for the garrison commander.'

'But, excellency! I never get despatches!'

'Hold your tongue! *Just tell them!* If I know anything about sentries, they'll be satisfied for long enough!'

The pier crept out of the darkness like a black finger, and as the sails were lowered swiftly and the lugger glided gently towards the tall piles a lantern flickered into life and a voice yelled, '*Qui va la?*'

The Spaniard opened the shutter of his own lantern. Two long flashes and two short ones. In a quavering voice he began to stutter his message, his words broken up by great gulps for breath. He was shaking so badly that Farquhar had to hold him upright against the mast like a corpse.

The sentry called something to another man, as yet hidden by a small hut in the middle of the pier, and Bolitho heard him laugh. There was a click of metal and then another as the sentries uncocked their muskets.

The bow swung against the pier, and Bolitho saw the sentry leaning forward to watch the lugger bump alongside. He had slung his musket over his shoulder, and his tall shako shone briefly in the glow from a long clay pipe. Bolitho held his breath. This was the time to see if he had chosen his men correctly.

He saw a sailor, moving with elaborate calm, climb nimbly up the nearest wooden ladder, the mooring rope in his hand. The sentry called after him, his voice muffled as he turned his back to watch the man looping the rope's eye over a bollard.

The next sailor, who had been crouching on the stem, leapt straight upwards like a cat. For a moment the two figures swayed together in a macabre dance, but there was hardly any sound. Only when the sailor released his grip and lowered the dead sentry carefully on the pier did Bolitho realize it was time to act.

He snapped, 'Next man up!'

Belsey, the master's mate, slipped over the bows, and followed by the other seaman who was wiping his knife blade on his trousers, disappeared around the side of the hut.

This time there was a little more noise. A clatter of a falling musket, and something like a gurgle. But nothing more.

Bolitho scrambled up to the pier, his body shaking with suppressed excitement. 'Right, Mr. Okes, get your party ashore and up to the end of the pier at the double!' He stopped an onrushing seaman with the back of his hand and snarled, 'Quietly there! There's a guardhouse at the far end!'

Rennie's marines were already pouring gratefully from the hold, their white crossbelts bright and eerie against their uniforms. Rennie had not forgotten his part, and within minutes he had split his men into two parties, and with a single command had both files trotting briskly along the pier towards the silent village.

Stockdale was the last to leave the lugger, his cutlass swinging from his hand like a toy.

Bolitho took a last look round and checked his bearings. 'Very well, Stockdale, let us go and take a look!'

8. THE RAID

BOLITHO lifted his hand, and behind him the file of sailors shuffled to a standstill. 'We will wait here for ten minutes! Pass the word down the line!'

He waited until silence had again fallen over the steep roadway and then added quietly to Lieutenant Okes, 'We'll push on a bit further and have a look at the bridge. We can't help Rennie's marines by standing here worrying, and it's already near two o'clock. There is a lot to do before dawn finds us.'

He walked on without waiting for Okes to comment. He could feel the loose stones crunching beneath his shoes, and was conscious of a new sense of light-headedness. Everything had gone so well that the strain was all the more telling. Surely the luck could not last?

It had been less than an hour since the lugger had tied up to the pier. After killing the two luckless sentries, Captain Rennie's marines had gone on to capture the small guardhouse at the end of the coast road with hardly a scuffle. The sleeping soldiers, all ten of them, had been gleefully clubbed into deeper slumber, or worse, and the duty N.C.O. had been seized and trussed like a terrified chicken.

Bolitho had left Rennie to spread his men along the roadside and occupy the high ground above the village. From there they should be able to withstand anything but a really heavy assault until the raiding party had completed its work.

Bolitho dropped on one knee and strained his eyes into the darkness. He could just see the spidery outline of a high wooden bridge and the isolated headland beyond, where the sleeping gun battery lay as yet unaware of what was happening. It was quite a solid bridge, Bolitho thought. Wide and heavy enough for guns and stores, for shot, and all the materials for building breastworks and embrasures. It would take a long time to replace once destroyed.

A boot crunched at his side and Sergeant Garwood peered down at him. 'Cap'n Rennie's respects, sir. The marines is all in position. We've 'ad the lugger warped to the end o' the pier so that we can cover our withdrawal with the swivel gun.' He stared towards the bridge. 'I'd like to 'ave a crack at that lot, sir!' He sounded envious.

'You get back to Captain Rennie and tell him to hold the road until we fall back.' Bolitho smiled in the darkness. 'Don't worry, Sergeant, you'll get your pennyworth of fighting before the night's done!'

He saw the man's white crossbelt fading in the shadows and then said sharply, 'Right, Mr. Okes, call up the rest of the party and keep them quiet! A flogging for the first man to make a sound!' He turned back to the bridge. There was probably a sentry at one end, if not both. It would all have to be very quick.

Okes returned breathing heavily. 'All here, sir.'

Farquhar was close behind him, his face pale in the faint moonlight. He said, 'I have picked Glover for the job, sir.'

Bolitho nodded. He recalled that the seaman in question was the one who had so neatly killed the first sentry.

'Very well. Send him forward.' He watched the man slide over the rim of stones and bushes and fade immediately into the deep patch of shadow before the bridge. Then he added slowly, 'Now remember, men, if Glover fails to find that sentry and the alarm is given, we will have to make a rush for it.' He drew his sword and saw the lethal glitter of cutlasses along the roadside.

To Okes he whispered, 'Mr. Farquhar will take five men to deal with the guns and magazine. McIntosh, the gunner's mate, will lay a good charge to blow the bridge when we fall back, understood?'

Okes nodded. 'I—I think so, sir!'

'You must be *sure*, Mr. Okes!' Bolitho eyed him keenly. Suddenly he wished it was Herrick at his side. Should he be killed before the raid was finished, how would Okes manage? He continued evenly, 'According to our captive Spaniard, there is a rough track down from the battery to the inside of the anchorage. I intend to go down there as soon as the battery is taken and see what can be done about the ships in the harbour. I will try and set fire to one or more of them, and *Phalarope* can deal with any which make a dash for it!' He swung round as Stockdale, dragging the whimpering Spaniard behind him, strode through the bushes, his teeth white in his face.

'Sir! Glover's just whistled! 'E's done for the sentry!'

Bolitho stood up. If only he had a thousand men instead of sixty, he thought vaguely. They could take and hold the whole island intact until help arrived. He tugged his hat down firmly over his eyes and glanced back at his men. He was thankful that every one of them was hand-picked. There had not been a single incident so far to warrant either punishment or anger.

'Now then, lads! Quickly and quietly, and no fuss!' He waved his sword, aware suddenly that his face was fixed in a wild grin. 'Follow me!'

In two files the sailors padded towards the bridge. Bolitho kept just ahead of the nearest men, his eyes straining ahead towards the deserted bridge, which all at once seemed a long way off and vulnerable.

Pad, pad, pad went the feet, and Bolitho knew without turning his head that the orderly approach was already changing into a charge. Then his shoes were booming hollowly on the wooden boards of the bridge, and from the corner of his eye he saw the angry swirl of surf, and heard the roar of a tide-race between the steep walls of the ravine. He almost fell over the spread-eagled corpse of a uniformed sentry, and saw Glover waiting to greet him, a captured musket in his hands.

Bolitho did not pause but gasped, 'Well done, Glover! Now follow me!'

A semi-circular wall pitted with square gunports ran around the far side of the headland, and as his feet slipped on the stubble of gorse and dried grass Bolitho counted seven or eight large guns facing seaward. A high mound was built well behind the guns, and he guessed that these earthworks had been thrown up to protect the magazine.

There was a startled cry from the shadows below the wall and a soldier seemed to rise out of the ground at Bolitho's feet. He saw the bared teeth and heard the man's quick intake of breath as he lunged forward and upward with his bayonet.

Glover, who was pressing close on Bolitho's heels, gave a terrible scream and fell back pinioned on the blade like a slaughtered pig. Bolitho slashed out wildly and felt the shock jar up the sword blade and along his arm like a blow. The soldier seemed to crumple, his arm almost severed from his body by the force of the stroke.

He was lost and forgotten underfoot as the sailors surged wildly along the flattened ground, their eyes staring like madmen as they looked for further victims.

There were only six more French soldiers sleeping in a small stone hut beside a great earth furnace, which even now glowed malevolently and cast an eerie light across the garlands of bright round shot and the cutlasses of the jubilant sailors.

One soldier sat up gaping, as if he no longer trusted what he saw. A cutlass cut him down before he could even cry out, and two more died screaming even as they struggled for their weapons.

Bolitho ignored the gruesome sounds from the hut and leaned across the breastworks to stare down at the great shimmering mirror of the anchorage. There were two big ships anchored well out in the centre and two smaller ones near the foot of the cliffs. He could see the riding lights like fireflies on the still water. There was no alarm. Nothing to break the quiet night watch. Bolitho felt the sweat cold on his brow and realized that his body was shaking uncontrollably.

Farquhar climbed up beside him, his dirk glinting faintly against his dark coat. 'The battery is ours, sir.' He sounded less controlled than usual, and Bolitho knew that he was suffering the same insane wildness as the rest of them.

Farquhar added in a calmer tone, 'Eight guns, sir. Two of them are thirty-two-pounders!' He sounded impressed. 'If they heated the shot in the furnace the Frogs would be able to sink any attacker with ease. A ship would be ablaze in no time from that sort of hammering!'

Bolitho nodded and pointed at the anchored ships. 'I'd like to use the guns on them! But the din would bring the whole island down on us!' He gestured towards the two large craft. 'They'll be troopships, but the soldiers will be sleeping under canvas ashore somewhere. The French would have no use for soldiers too cramped and seasick to march when the time came!'

Okes ran up to him, his sword held across his body like a shield. 'What now, sir?'

Bolitho glanced at the stars. 'It will be getting light in two hours. By that time I want every gun either spiked or pushed over the edge of the cliff. The latter if at all possible. The last thing will be to blow the magazine.'

Farquhar nodded. 'I have put my men to work with hand-spikes already. I think all the guns will go over the edge well enough, sir.'

'Very well.' Bolitho watched Okes' quick breathing. 'You take charge of the bridge and deal with that, Mr. Okes. Seize anyone who comes down the road, although I imagine it would take an eager spy to get past Rennie's pickets!'

Belsey, the master's mate, said, 'I've found the cliff path, sir. It leads right down to the sea. There are two longboats moored at the foot.' He waited. 'Shall I carry on, sir? I got my men ready.'

Bolitho nodded and watched the man lope away. Belsey had already shown he was well able to manage his part in the proceedings.

He walked back past the hut and then said sharply, 'Get those men out of there. There's a lot to be done yet!' The sharpness in his tone was more to cover his disgust than his anger. He had seen three of his men gleefully stripping the butchered corpses and crowing together like ghouls at a sacrifice.

He continued quietly, 'Get everything ready, Mr. Okes, but do not pull back until I give the signal. If I fall, then you must take command and use your own discretion.' He tapped the ground with his sword. 'But the guns must be destroyed and the battery blown, no matter what else is happening. Have a good fuse put on the bridge, and make sure the men know what they are doing.' He clapped Okes across the shoulder, and the man all but fell to his knees. 'It has been well worth our visit, Mr. Okes! Those two troopships alone could carry enough men to storm Antigua itself if necessary!'

Bolitho walked quickly towards the edge of the cliff where Stockdale waited for him, leaning on his cutlass. He paused and looked back. He felt a sudden surge of pride at the way things had gone so far. Men were working busily in the darkness, and already one of the giant guns had been trundled clear of its mounting. He could see Farquhar and McIntosh stooping over the box of fuses, entirely absorbed in their work of destruction, and other men loading their muskets and watching the captured bridge.

He turned on his heel and followed Stockdale down the steep, roughly hewn steps. If only he could enlarge this feeling of pride and purpose to the rest of the *Phalarope*'s company, he thought. It could be done. He had shown these men *how* it could be done.

It was dark and very cold at the foot of the steps, and he saw the small group of armed seamen already squatting in one of the longboats. He said to Belsey, 'Mark how the nearest ship swings at her anchor, Belsey!' He pointed at the small sloop which was riding less than two cables from the crude jetty below the cliff. Her stern was pointing towards the centre of the anchorage, her bowsprit towards the narrow span of water between the headlands.

Belsey nodded and rubbed his chin. 'Aye, sir! The tide's a-comin' in!' He stooped and dipped his arm underwater along the edge of the steps. 'I can feel no weed 'ere, sir. It must be well on the make.'

'It is.' Bolitho squinted his eyes in concentration. 'We'll go for the sloop there. There'll not be much of a watch kept. They'll think themselves safe enough below the battery. I know *I* would!'

Belsey nodded doubtfully. 'An' *then*, sir?' He sounded as if he would accept anything now.

'We'll set fire to her and let her drift into the nearest troop transport. She'll burn like dry grass!'

The master's mate bared his teeth. 'That'll raise the alarm well enough, sir!'

Bolitho laughed shortly. 'You can't get *everything* without payment!'

He clambered over his men and into the sternsheets. 'Get those oars muffled and be sharp about it! Use your shirts, anything!' He glanced quickly at the stars. Was it imagination, or were they paler than the last time he had looked? He snapped, 'Shove off! And pull handsomely!'

The oars rose and fell, the men holding their breaths as the boat sidled clear of the cliffs. The current gurgled impatiently around the counter and sent the hull swinging crazily into the mainstream.

Bolitho laid his hand on Stockdale's arm. 'Let her run. The tide is an ally tonight.'

He could see the sloop clear across the longboat's bow now, her slender bowsprit pointing directly above his head. He whispered, 'Easy, lads! *Easy!*' He could see a lantern aft by the taffrail and another small glow beside the foremast. That was probably the crew's hatch left open because of the warm night.

'Boat your oars!' He gritted his teeth as the heavy oars were laid carefully across the thwarts. Every sound seemed like a thunderclap. 'Steer with the current, Stockdale.' He leaned forward. 'You, in the bow! Have a grapnel ready!' To himself he added, 'The noise won't matter once we get aboard!'

'*Sir!*' The stroke oar was pointing wildly. 'Look, sir! A guard-boat!'

Bolitho cursed himself for his over-confidence. When he swung his head he saw the white splash of oars and heard the creak of rowlocks barely twenty yards away.

There were gasps of surprise from some of his men, but Bolitho said harshly, 'Now, bowman! The grapnel!'

The longboat swung clumsily across the sloop's stem even as the pronged grapnel soared up and bit into the bulwark.

Everything seemed to be happening at once. There were shouts and cries from the prowling guardboat, followed by a ragged volley of musket shots. The stroke oarsman beside Bolitho screamed and fell writhing over the gunwhale, his arms thrashing as he vanished below the dark water. Bullets thudded into the boat and into the sloop's side beyond.

The men faltered as a face appeared overhead and the longboat was briefly lit in the angry flash of a pistol. Belsey ducked and swore savagely, and another man fell whimpering, blood gushing from his shoulder.

Bolitho ran along the slewing boat and leapt for the sloop's rail. For a moment his feet kicked above the water and then he was up and over, the breath knocked out of him as a seaman followed him across the bulwark and fell on top of him.

He struggled to his feet as the rest of his depleted party scrambled up beside him. The sloop's one misguided defender lay open mouthed and staring in a widening pool of blood, and a second man who suddenly appeared naked at the open hatch gave a shriek of terror and fled below, slamming the hatch behind him.

Bolitho sheathed his sword and said calmly, 'It will save us the trouble of seeking them out.' Then as a further volley banged out from the guardboat he shouted, 'You know what to do, Belsey! Cut the cable, and put a hand at the wheel!'

His men were yelling and shouting like madmen as they scampered about the darkened deck as if it was an everyday occurrence. From astern Bolitho heard the raucous blare of a trumpet and then the strident rattle of a drum. He could imagine the panic and pandemonium as the sleep-fuddled crews tumbled from their hammocks in response to the call to arms.

'Cable's cut, sir!' A voice yelled from the bows.

'Very well, let the current take her!' Bolitho ran to the rail and peered through the gloom towards the nearest transport. There were more lights now, and he thought he could see the gunports being raised along the upperdeck. Their anger will give way to prudence in a moment, he thought wildly.

'Fire the ship, Belsey!' He pointed at the foremast. 'Start from there!'

Fascinated he watched Belsey's busy seamen as they upended the riding light across a deadly mixture of oil, loose cordage and spare canvas. The result was as swift as it was frightening. With a savage roar the flames soared up the shrouds and engulfed the whole forepart of the deck. Great tongues of fire lit up the whole anchorage, so that the other ships stood out stark and tall in the inferno. Rigging and cordage flamed and crackled as the fire reached through the tarred ropes and found the neatly furled sails. Spars and planking, sun-dried and well painted, flared like tinder, so that the roaring heat reached still further, consuming the sloop greedily as the men fell back, stunned by the extent of their destruction.

Bolitho clawed his way aft through the choking smoke and away from the searing heat. He was glad that Belsey had remembered to open the hatch, and noticed that most of the sloop's crew had already jumped over the side and were either swimming or drowning while their world burned above them.

He leaned coughing on the taffrail and stared across at the big transport. Gone was the belligerence and awakened anger. Her decks seemed to be swarming with stampeding figures as officers and men dashed wildly to their stations, colliding with each other as they stared in horror at the approaching fireship.

The second transport was already slipping her cable, but the nearest ship stood no chance at all. Some of her men must have realized the inevitability of the collision, and Bolitho saw several small white splashes alongside as they jumped overboard. There were pistol shots too, and he guessed that the French officers were busy trying to restore calm and order to the last.

Belsey led his choking, wheezing men to the poop and yelled, 'Time to go, sir!' He was grinning, and his eyes were streaming from the smoke.

Bolitho pointed down. 'The quarter boat is tied under the counter! Down you go, lads, and sharp about it! The magazine will blow before long!'

One by one the sailors slithered down the rope and into the small boat below the poop. Bolitho went last, his lungs seared from the advancing fire, his eyes all but blinded.

Stockdale bawled, 'Out oars! Give way together!'

The boat pulled clear, each man's eyes white in the cruel glare as the burning sloop drifted past. Several French sailors were swimming nearby, and one tried to pull himself aboard the overcrowded boat. But Stockdale pushed him away, and Bolitho heard the man's cries fading piteously astern.

A seaman yelled, 'They've struck, by God!'

Sure enough, the sloop had reached the other vessel, and already the flames were racing up the transport's tall masts where the half-loosed sails vanished like ashes in a strong wind.

'Keep pulling, lads!' Bolitho turned to watch, satisfied but awed by the terrible success of his attack.

The sloop's magazine exploded, the shockwave making the

little boat jump beneath Bolitho's chattering seamen. The little ship, which thirty minutes earlier had been riding quietly at her anchor, folded amidships and dipped spluttering and hissing below the surface. But the work was done. The transport was ablaze from stem to stern and with fore and main-masts already down in a welter of flame and dense smoke.

Of the second transport nothing was visible through the pall. But Bolitho knew that she had only two choices. To try to warp clear and risk the fate of her sister, or drift ashore to be left a useless ruin when the tide retreated.

Belsey said, 'There are lights at the end of the bay, sir! That must be where the troops are camped!'

Bolitho wiped his smoke-blackened face and nodded. 'There will be a hornet's nest about our ears shortly!' With their ships destroyed and no battery to protect them, the French soldiers would be all the more willing to die to avenge their disgrace, he thought grimly.

But it was done. And done far better than he had hoped. In future, people might remember this when they spoke the name of the *Phalarope*.

Lieutenant Matthew Okes stared down from the gun battery shocked and dazed by the raging holocaust and the echoing thunder of exploding powder. He could feel the hot breath of the burning ship across his sweating face, and his nostrils rebelled against the stench of charred timbers and other horrors he could only guess at.

Farquhar said sharply, 'Time to send the guns over!'

Okes nodded dumbly, his eyes still fixed on the blazing transport as it rolled slowly on to one side. Men were swimming and floating amongst the great mass of fragments and charred flotsam, and the glittering water was constantly pockmarked by falling wreckage from muffled explosions within the shattered hull. Faintly through the drifting smoke he could see the second transport already hard aground, her masts leaning at a dangerous angle.

Behind him he heard the rumble of chocks and then a ragged cheer as the sailors sent the first gun careering over the cliff edge and on to the rocks below. A second and then a third gun crashed after it, and he heard McIntosh yelling at his men to throw their weight against the others.

Okes could feel the strength draining from his limbs, and wanted to run from the scene of hell and destruction which lit the whole anchorage in a panorama of red flames and spark-dappled smoke. It was all sheer madness, something which none of them could control.

There was no sign of Bolitho, and even if he had succeeded in escaping from his drifting fireship he would have a much longer passage to make back to the headland.

Farquhar said, 'Look, sir! There are troops coming over the hill!'

As Okes tore his eyes away the transport took a final roll and plunged beneath the surface. Immediately the fierce light was extinguished like a candle and the anchorage was once more plunged into deep shadow. Okes blinked through the smoke and realized for the first time that the sky was already brighter and there was a tinge of grey along the ridge of hills beyond the anchorage. The fierceness of the blazing ships had hidden the dawn's stealthy approach, and now as he followed the direction of Farquhar's arm he saw with rising panic the faint glint of bayonets and the bright colours of a raised standard moving inexorably over the rim of the nearest hill like a mechanical caterpillar.

His eyes darted from the marching troops to the bridge. From his own position on the battery to the end of the coast road. In a voice he no longer recognized he shouted, 'Prepare to blow the magazine, Mr. Farquhar!' He stared round like a trapped animal. 'I must see Rennie at once. You carry on here!'

He started to walk quickly away from the battery, ignoring the curious stares of the seamen and Farquhar's look of questioning contempt. His racing thoughts seemed to take over his feet, so that all at once he was running, his breath gasping painfully, his shoes skidding across stones and gorse alike as he ran blindly across the bridge, past the armed sailors on the far side and out along the open road. Here and there he could see the scarlet patches of crouching marines amongst the hillside bracken, and he was horrified to realize that he could already see the beach below and the jumble of houses beyond the pier. The growing daylight added to his sense of nakedness, and in his imagination he thought he heard the tramp of French soldiers as they marched steadily to cut his escape to the sea.

He rounded a bend in the road and almost fell on top of Captain Rennie, who was sitting comfortably on a small mound of grass, his cocked hat and sword lying neatly beside him. Cradled on his knees was a half-eaten pie, and even as Okes staggered to a halt Rennie glanced up at him and dabbed at his mouth with a handkerchief.

'Delicious.' He looked curiously past Okes. 'They sound busy back there.'

Okes stared round wildly. This was almost too much. He wanted to scream, to shake Rennie, to make him realize the enormity of the danger.

Rennie's eyes narrowed, but he said calmly, 'A chicken pie. I had almost forgotten what it was like.' He gestured over his shoulder, but kept his eyes on Okes' stricken face. 'Some Dutch folk from the village brought it for me during the night, y'know. Damn nice people really. It's a pity we're at war, isn't it?' He stood up and wrapped the remainder of the pie carefully in his handkerchief. Then he said quietly, 'You'd better tell me what is happening.'

Okes controlled his breathing with a savage effort. 'The French are coming! Over there, behind the hill.'

'I know. My men have already spotted them.' Rennie regarded him calmly. 'What did you expect them to do?'

The marine's obvious indifference gave Okes the little extra strength he still needed. 'You can start falling back. I've given orders to fire the magazine.' He dropped his eyes. 'I'm blowing the bridge as soon as McIntosh is ready!'

Rennie stared at him. 'But the captain! How in hell's name can he get back to us without the bridge?' He clapped on his hat and reached for his sword. 'I'd better go and have a look back there.'

Okes blocked his way, his eyes blazing. 'You know the orders! I'm in charge if anything happens to the captain! Your duty is to cover the withdrawal!'

Sergeant Garwood trotted round the bend, his half-pike glittering in the growing light. 'Sir.' He ignored Okes. 'The Frogs is comin'! There's best part of a company movin' down on our flank. I think the rest will try and work round the village and take us from the rear.'

Rennie nodded, his face suddenly grave. 'Very well. I'll come at once.'

He turned back to Okes and said slowly, 'You'll wait a bit longer surely? It takes time to get a boat back to the headland!'

Okes swung on his heel as a ragged volley of musket fire echoed around the hills. 'Get back to your men, Captain Rennie. I hope I know *my* duty!'

Rennie shrugged and walked quickly up the sloping hillside towards the firing. When he looked back he could see the smoke from the anchorage drifting across the headland in a solid wall, and tried to picture the devastation beyond.

Against the hillside and the glittering water below the cliff Okes' running figure looked frail and lost. 'I hope you *do,* Mr. Okes!' Rennie spoke aloud to the empty hillside. Then he turned and began to run to his prepared positions and his men.

Okes found McIntosh already squatting on one side of the bridge, craning his head to peer down at one of the massive wooden trestles.

'Ready?' Okes could hardly stop himself from shouting. 'Well, are you?'

McIntosh nodded. 'Aye, aye, sir. A two-minute fuse. And a four-minute fuse to the magazine.' He rubbed his hard hands. 'Mr. Farquhar is waiting atop the battery to light it as soon as the cap'n gets back.'

Okes swayed and then controlled himself. 'Wait here!' He started to run again, and as soon as he had reached the outskirts of the battery he blew his whistle and yelled, 'Clear the headland! Fall back there!'

Startled, the seamen gathered up their weapons and began to hurry towards the bridge. Most of them had seen the approaching soldiers and needed no second order. A petty officer, his face stained with dirt and smoke, strode across to the panting lieutenant. 'Beggin' yer pardon, sir! The cap'n ain't come yet!'

'Yes, yes, I know that!' Okes glared at him glassily. 'You go with the others and get them across the bridge. Wait for me there, and be ready to move!' He peered through the smoke. 'Where is Mr. Farquhar?'

The man shrugged. 'Gone down the steps, sir. He said he'd get a better chance of seeing through the smoke from there.'

Okes strode to the battery wall and leaned against it for support. With the sailors gone and the gunports unoccupied and empty the place seemed strangely dead. He made himself walk to the top of the steps. There was no sign of Farquhar, of anybody in fact.

There was a fresh burst of firing, intermingled with wild cheering, and his limbs started to move as if he had already lost control of them. He walked to the open door of the magazine and stared for several seconds at the waiting fuse and the smouldering slow match beside it. It was not his fault, he told himself. There was nothing else he could do. He sank to his knees, his eyes filled with the fuse and the mental picture of Bolitho hurrying away towards the anchored sloop.

Damn them! Damn them all! He had to steady his wrist with his other hand as he took the match and held it against the fuse.

He felt the nausea hard in his throat as he staggered to his feet and ran quickly towards the bridge.

McIntosh stared up at him, his eyes uncomprehending.

'Light it, you fool!' Okes was already halfway across the bridge. 'Or stay there and go up with the magazine!'

McIntosh fired the fuse and scrambled on to the bridge. He caught Okes up around the curve in the road and gasped, 'Where's Mr. Farquhar, sir? An' what happened to the captain?'

Okes snarled, 'Back to the beach! All of you!' To McIntosh he added, 'All dead! Like you'll be if the French catch you!'

There was a thunderous roar, followed almost immediately by a second, sharper explosion. The force of the detonations seemed to quell the musket fire and distant shouts, so that the whole island appeared to be stunned by the noise.

The growling rumble went on, and Okes heard a splintering crash as the bridge fell into the ravine like so much kindling wood.

Strangely, he found that he could walk now, his feet moving almost steadily as he followed his men down the road towards the pier and safety. He had acted in the only way possible. He kept his eyes fixed on the pier. The *only* way. Others would soon see that, too. He pictured his wife's face when she read the announcement in the *Gazette*.

'Lieutenant Matthew Okes, who carried the brunt of the responsibility of this daring raid after the death of his commanding officer, is to be congratulated on his valour and his keenness to press home an attack against impossible odds!'

He slowed to a halt as a group of marines burst through the gorse and took up positions on the road itself.

A marine yelled, 'Here they come, lads!'

Sergeant Garwood's voice boomed from beyond the hilltop. 'Hold your fire, my darlings! Ready, now! *Fire!*'

His last order came as a charging line of blue uniformed soldiers rose above the skyline and started to run down towards the beach. As the musket smoke drifted clear Okes saw the soldiers falling back, leaving others screaming and kicking in the low gorse.

'Reload! Take yer time!' Garwood sounded calm. 'Aim low, lads!'

Another sharp volley, but this time there were more soldiers, and they came on with fresh determination in spite of losses. And here and there a marine lay dead, and several others crawled slowly down the hillside after their comrades.

Okes could see Rennie standing imperturbably on a hillock, ignoring the sharpshooters as he controlled his thin line of retreating men. He felt his envy giving way to hatred. Rennie would never have acted as *he* had done! He would have waited for Bolitho and allowed everyone to die for nothing!

Okes shouted, 'To the lugger! Lively there!'

The sailors ran wildly to the pier, carrying their wounded companions and yelling encouragement to the marines. It seemed to Okes that another age passed before all his men were aboard and the last of the marines were falling back along the pier. There was a fresh morning breeze to fill the lugger's sails, and as the last marine scrambled gasping over the bulwark the boat idled clear.

With a maddened roar the French soldiers charged from cover and headed for the pier. From individual uniformed blobs they converged into a solid force, and as they surged on to the pier itself they merged into a single enemy.

McIntosh crouched in the bows and looked along the swivel gun. He ignored the sporadic musket fire, and waited until the soldiers were packed into a yelling, tangled throng before he jerked back the lanyard. 'There, my beauties!' He stood up wildly in the pitching boat as the canister shot cut through the screaming soldiers like a scythe. 'That's fer the cap'n! An' all the others!'

Before the second wave of soldiers had reached the bloody, threshing carnage on the pier the lugger had gone about and headed out to sea. Aboard there was silence now, and even when the *Phalarope*'s raked masts rounded the headland and bore down on the small boat like a protective parent, the exhausted men could not even muster a cheer.

Okes looked back at the island, at the smoke, and the vague outline of the headland battery. It was over.

The lugger was to be abandoned after the raid, so Okes had it laid alongside the *Phalarope*, where many hands reached down for the wounded and the silent victors.

Captain Rennie stood aside to allow Okes to climb up the frigate's side. He said, 'After *you*, Mr. Okes. I'd not want to spoil your entrance this morning!'

Okes stared at him, his mouth hanging open to reply. Then he saw the cold hostility in Rennie's eyes and decided against it. He must expect jealousy, he told himself firmly. He must be prepared to deal with it.

He reached for the main chains and swung himself up and over the frigate's side. For a moment longer he stared around the familiar deck. He had survived.

9. DEFEAT

BOLITHO did not actually remember hearing the exploding magazine. It was more like a sensation, or the ending of a nightmarish dream when a man awakes even more afraid of the waiting reality. He recalled sitting in the stern of the crowded and half-swamped boat, staring back at the hissing, writhing water where the transport had made her last dive to the bottom. His eyes ached from the blaze, and were now dulled by the ship's sudden disappearance and the shadow which reached across the high-sided anchorage to hide the pain and terror beneath.

His men were laughing and chattering with relief and excitement, but as Bolitho turned back to search for the treacherous rockfalls at the foot of the cliff the whole world seemed to explode in one gigantic tremor. Rocks rained down into the water, and as the men pulled desperately at the oars one large piece of splintered stone struck the stem like a hammer, and Bolitho staggered to his feet as the sea surged jubilantly into the listing boat.

It seemed as if the bombardment from above would never cease. He saw one man swept underwater by a complete section of cliff even as he tried to scramble up on to the rocks. Belsey, the master's mate, fell cursing into deep water, and when Stockdale heaved him bodily up on to the rocks he yelled in anguish, 'Me arm! God, me arm's broken!'

Bolitho's dazed thoughts were slowly returning to normal, and as he called encouragement to his half-drowned men his mind rebelled against what he knew to be true. Someone had fired the magazine without waiting for him and his party. He could find only small gratitude for the fact that had his boat returned minutes earlier they would have all been blasted skyward with the magazine and the battery.

He called, 'Follow me, lads! We'll climb along the water's edge on these rocks. The tide's dropping, so we should be able to reach the steps well enough.' He groped his way forward, knowing that they would follow. There was no choice. At the far end of the anchorage he could hear the frantic cries and the urgent notes of a trumpet. The French were too busy saving their own to care about the raiding party. But it would not last. Then the vengeance would be swift and final.

He staggered to a halt and blinked through the haze of acrid smoke. In the pale morning light which filtered down the steep ravine he could clearly see the remains of the bridge. There was no point in climbing the steps now. There was no way back to the beach.

A seaman ran dazedly past him and stared open mouthed at the wreckage. 'You bastards!' His voice shook with despair. 'You damn, cowardly *bastards!*'

'Silence!' Bolitho pushed the man back with the others. 'No doubt there was a good reason for blowing the bridge this early.' But he saw the look on Stockdale's face and knew that he had seen the lie in his eyes.

Belsey moaned and leaned against Stockdale for support. 'They left us to die! Ran to save their precious skins!'

Bolitho held up his hand. 'Quiet!' He cocked his head. 'Listen!'

A seaman said sharply, 'Over there, sir. I heard somethin' too.'

They scrambled over the smoking, splintered timbers until the first seaman fell back with a gasp of horror. Midshipman Farquhar was sitting propped against the ravine's rough wall, his body pinned in position by a great baulk of timber, and lying close by his side was a neatly severed leg.

Farquhar opened his eyes and croaked, "Thank God, sir! I thought I was going to die alone!" He saw their expressions and managed a painful grin. 'It's not *my* leg, sir! It belongs to our Spanish prisoner!'

Bolitho glanced around him and then up at the brightening sky. 'Right. Lift that timber off him, and be very careful!' He knelt beside the midshipman and ran his hands swiftly beneath the massive beam, keeping his eyes on Farquhar's taut features as his fingers probed at his trapped body.

Farquhar said between his teeth, 'Nothing broken it seems!' He lay back and closed his eyes as the beam quivered and began to move. 'I was looking for you, sir. Then I returned to the magazine and saw that the fuse was almost burned through!' He sounded near breaking. 'I seized our Spaniard and ran for the bridge, but just as we reached it the whole thing blew up and dropped into the ravine.' He winced. 'And us with it!'

The beam was dragged clear, and Bolitho tightened his jaw as he saw the smashed remains of their prisoner. He asked harshly, 'How did it happen?'

Farquhar allowed himself to be lifted to his feet. Immediately his legs buckled, and Stockdale said gruffly, ' 'Ere, I'll take the young gentleman, sir!'

Farquhar clung to Stockdale's shoulder and said, 'Sorry about all this, sir. I'll be all right in a while.' He remembered Bolitho's question and said vaguely, 'I can't understand it, sir. I still can't believe it happened.'

Bolitho pulled the dirk from Farquhar's belt and handed it to one of the seamen. 'Here, make a good splint with this for Mr. Belsey's arm. It will suffice until we get back to the *Phalarope*.'

Belsey watched the men's awkward fingers and groaned. 'Watch what yer doin'! You're like a pair of blind whores!'

Bolitho walked slowly along the weed-encrusted stonework. Fourteen men including himself. One with a broken arm, and one already half delirious from a ball in his shoulder. Farquhar looked as if he might fall unconscious, too.

He tried to push the bitterness and suspicion to the back of his mind. That would keep. Right now he had to get these men to safety. No doubt the rest of the raiding party was already embarked in the lugger. He suddenly felt calmer. Whatever else happened, he had succeeded in his work. Two transports destroyed and a valuable sloop with them. And without a battery

Mola Island would be useless to the French and their allies for a long while to come.

Stockdale called throatily, 'The second longboat, sir! It'll still be tied to the jetty where we left it!'

Bolitho scrambled across the wet stones and stared down at the remaining boat. It was not much of a craft. Patched and well used, and with only four oars and a mere scrap of canvas furled around the mast for every purpose. But no doubt the garrison had only used it for visiting the ships in harbour.

He said grimly, 'Get them aboard, Stockdale. We'll have to make the best of it.'

A ray of yellow sunlight lanced suddenly across the headland and glittered in the deep water. Without effort Bolitho could see the gleaming barrel of one of the battery's cannon almost below the swinging boat. A few feet this way and there would be no way out at all! 'Four of you man the oars! The rest of you take turns in baling and keeping a sharp lookout!'

Belsey struggled into a sitting position and peered at his splinted arm. The limb was tightly wrapped in an assortment of rags and strips of clothing, and stuck out in front of him like a club. He shook his head. 'Gawd! If I ever use this flipper agin I'll be surprised!'

'Shove off! Give way together!' Bolitho squatted on the gun-wale and pushed the tiller hard over. As the boat moved swiftly with the current he stared up at the blackened crest of the headland and wondered what had happened in those last minutes before Farquhar had been flung to almost certain death.

Farquhar moved weakly against the boat's side and snapped, 'Pull lively, Robinson! I'll flay you alive if you don't do your share!' In spite of his misery Bolitho smiled to himself. Farquhar's experiences had not softened his attitude to duty.

The oars rose and fell steadily, and the boat moved further and further from the jutting headland with its attendant pall of drifting smoke.

A man in the bows spoke Bolitho's thoughts for him, and for once he could find no words to rebuke him. The sailor stared back along the labouring men and snarled, 'Gone! Look round, lads! The bloody ship's gone without us!'

Farquhar said bitterly, 'She must have gone around the island, sir. We'll never catch her now.'

'I know.' Bolitho shaded his eyes against the glare and looked thoughtfully at the stumpy mast. 'Get that sail broken out, lads. We'll get clear of Mola Island and make for the nearest friendly one.' His crisp tone hid the doubt and the anger.

Stockdale wiped the wounded seaman's forehead with a wet rag and muttered, 'A miracle would come in 'andy, sir!'

Bolitho stripped off his tattered coat and regarded him calmly. 'I'm afraid that is not my province, Stockdale, but I will bear it in mind.' He settled against the tiller bar and steered towards the rising sun.

Lieutenant Thomas Herrick listened to the bell as it announced the end of the first Dog Watch and then resumed his pacing back and forth across the quarterdeck.

With a warm but fresh breeze from her quarter the *Phalarope* had made good time back to her patrol area, yet Herrick could find nothing but apprehension and a sense of loss at the speedy passage. He still could not accept what had happened, and felt the same inner anguish he had experienced when the weary raiding party had clambered up the frigate's side.

Even then he had been unwilling to accept that Bolitho was missing. Then he had seen Rennie's grim features and had felt the nervous uncertainty of the other returning sailors and marines. Only Okes had appeared unmoved by the disaster. No, Herrick frowned as he tried to relive exactly the moment Okes had stepped aboard, unmoved was not the proper description. There had been a sort of guarded jauntiness about him which was totally out of character. Herrick had gone to question him, but Vibart had summoned Okes to the quarterdeck where he had been brooding in silence since the landing party had left for the shore.

Rennie had been unusually reticent. But when Herrick had persisted, the marine had said shortly, 'It was a dangerous mission, Thomas. We must always expect such things to happen!' He had been watching Okes speaking jerkily to the first lieutenant and he had added bitterly, 'I was sent to this ship with my detachment to reinforce the discipline. To protect the officers from any new threat of mutiny.' His eyes had blazed with sudden anger. 'It now appears that the *Phalarope*'s officers must be protected from each other!' Rennie had ended, 'I must attend to my wounded. They at least have nothing of which to be ashamed!'

Herrick had then cornered McIntosh, the gunner's mate. The latter had looked nervously at the quarterdeck before replying, 'How can I tell, sir? I just did my duty. Mr. Farquhar was the only one who must have seen what happened.' He had gestured wearily astern. 'And he's back there, dead with the rest!'

'But you think something went wrong, don't you?' Herrick's voice had been harsh.

'You know I can't afford to answer that, Mr. Herrick?' The man had looked back at the wounded and exhausted seamen from the lugger. 'It took a lot of pain and sweat to get where

I am now. You know what would happen to me if I made accusations.'

Herrick had let him go, his eyes contemptuous, yet knowing in his heart that McIntosh was speaking the truth.

He stiffened as he heard Vibart's heavy step beside him.

'Pipe the hands aft, Mr. Herrick. I will tell them what is to be done.' Vibart looked composed and calm. Only his eyes betrayed a certain glitter which could be either excitement or triumph.

Herrick said, 'Are you sure there is nothing more we can do?'

Vibart stared past him at the ruffled water. 'I told you this morning, Mr. Herrick, just as I voiced my fears to the captain. The venture was dangerous and foolhardy. That it was a success is fortunate for all of us. But Bolitho knew the risk he was taking. There is nothing more to be said.'

Herrick persisted. 'But is Lieutenant Okes *sure*?'

'I am satisfied with his report.' There was a new edge to Vibart's tone. 'So that is enough!' He walked ponderously to the weather rail and sniffed loudly. 'At least we are back in our proper area. Now we can contact the flagship.'

Herrick spoke swiftly to Midshipman Neale and watched him scamper forward. Then he heard the boatswain's mates shouting, 'All hands! All hands! Lay aft!'

As the men poured up from below he crossed to Vibart and said slowly, 'He was a good officer. I still think he could have escaped.'

'Then I will trouble you to keep your opinions to yourself, Mr. Herrick!' The deepset eyes were flecked with anger. 'You may have considered yourself one of his favourites, but I will have no such behaviour now.'

He turned away from Herrick's taut features as Quintal, the boatswain, touched his hat and rumbled, 'All present, sir.'

Vibart strode to the quarterdeck rail and stared down at the upturned faces. Herrick stayed by the helmsmen watching Vibart closely. Vibart said, 'We are back on our patrol. We will shortly make contact with the admiral, and I will in due course tell him of our great success!'

Herrick felt himself tremble with anger. So it was a great success now, was it? When Bolitho was alive it had been foolhardy and dangerous, but now that Vibart stood to reap the full credit it was already a different picture.

'I am not satisfied with the recent slackness of discipline aboard, and I intend that this ship will return to a proper state of efficiency as of now!'

Vibart was staring round the assembled crew, his face flushed. Herrick felt sick. He is enjoying it, he thought. He is actually glad Bolitho is dead!

Herrick turned as Okes stepped through the cabin hatch and walked uncertainly towards him. Herrick took his sleeve and whispered fiercely, 'What did you tell Vibart, Matthew? For God's sake, what is the matter with you?'

Okes drew back. 'I told him nothing but the truth! Am I to be blamed for Bolitho's misfortunes?'

'And what of young Farquhar? Did you *see* him die?'

Okes looked away. 'Of course I did. What the devil are you trying to imply?' But there was a shake in his voice, and Herrick was suddenly reminded of Okes' behaviour during the battle with the privateer. His fear, his complete terror. A man could not change overnight.

'I want to know, Matthew. You had better tell me now.'

Okes seemed to have recovered himself, and when he looked at Herrick his eyes were opaque and expressionless. 'I told the truth, damn you!' He tried to smile. 'But you should not worry too much. You'll be moving up to second lieutenant!'

Herrick stepped back and looked at him with disgust. 'And *you* will be first, no doubt! And both you and Vibart will be the heroes of the day!'

Okes' face drained of colour. 'How dare you! You were not there, so it is easy to be jealous and insulting! Bolitho was *only* a man!'

'And *you* are not fit to polish his shoes!' Herrick swung round as Vibart stepped between them.

'I will have no quarrelling aboard my ship, Mr. Herrick. Any more of it and I will make an entry in the log!' He looked hard at Okes. 'Come to the cabin. I have a few things to say to you.'

Herrick watched them go, sickened and helpless.

Little Neale asked quietly, 'What does it all mean, sir?'

Herrick looked down at him, his face grave. 'It means that we must watch our step in the weeks ahead, my boy. With the captain gone I feel no security here.'

He stiffened as he saw Evans, the purser, hurrying aft, an aggrieved expression on his ferret face. Behind him Thain, the master-at-arms, ushered two frightened-looking seamen, his face leaving Herrick in no doubt as to what would happen next. Floggings, and more floggings. All the old scores kept hidden while Bolitho had been in command would break into the open like festering sores.

He faced Evans and said sharply, 'Well? What is it now?'

Evans smiled nervously. 'Caught these men red-handed! Stealing rum they were!'

Herrick's heart sank and he called the men forward. 'Is that right?' He realized that both seamen had taken part in the raiding party.

One of the men said sullenly, 'Aye, sir. The rum was for one of our mates. 'E was wounded. We reckoned it would 'elp 'im.' His companion nodded in agreement.

Herrick took Evans aside. 'It could be true.'

'Of course it is true!' Evans stared at him in amazement. 'But that is hardly the point! Stealing is stealing. There is no excuse, and you know it.' He eyed Herrick with little disguised glee. 'So you had better inform Mr. Vibart.' He drew himself up importantly. 'Or I will, Mr. Herrick!'

'Don't you get stroppy with me, Evans!' Herrick's face was a mask of fury. 'Or I'll have you broken, believe me!' But it was only anger. There was nothing else he could do but inform Vibart.

He handed over the watch to Neale and went wearily below. The sentry opened the cabin door for him before he had reached it, and Herrick guessed that the marine had correctly foreseen his surprise. Vibart had moved into Bolitho's quarters already. It only added to Herrick's sense of nightmarish unreality.

Vibart looked up from the desk and stared at him.

'Two men for punishment.' Herrick saw Okes leaning against the stern windows, his face lost in thought.

Vibart leaned back in the chair. 'Say "sir" when you address me, Mr. Herrick.' He frowned. 'I can't imagine why you make such a point of worsening your position?' He continued coldly, 'Make a report in the log, Mr. Herrick. Punishment at eight bells tomorrow morning. Two dozen lashes apiece.'

Herrick swallowed. 'But I have not told you their offence yet, sir!'

'No need.' Vibart gestured towards the open skylight. 'I happened to overhear your nonsensical conversation with Mr. Evans just now. And I must warn you I do not approve of your apparent wish to toady with men who lie and steal!'

Herrick felt the cabin closing in around him. 'Is that all?' He swallowed again. 'Sir?'

'For the present.' Vibart looked almost relaxed. 'We will alter course to the south'rd in one hour. Try and make sure that the men do not slacken off during your watch.'

'Aye, aye, sir.' Herrick contracted his stomach muscles into a tight knot.

Outside the cabin he turned momentarily and looked back. The door was shut again and the marine sentry stared blankly in front of him beneath the swinging lantern. It was just as if Pomfret had returned and now sat back there in the big cabin. Herrick shook his head and mounted the ladder to the quarter-deck. It was all moving so much to a pattern again that he found himself wondering if Pomfret *had* been the controlling influence which had made the *Phalarope* into a living hell!

When he returned to the deck he saw that the sun had already moved closer to the horizon. The sea was empty, a great desert of silver and purple hues, with an horizon like a knife edge.

Out here a ship's captain was God indeed, he thought bitterly. Only under Bolitho had he felt the meaning of purpose and understanding, and after Pomfret it had seemed like a new chance of life.

He looked aft to the taffrail as if expecting to see Bolitho's tall shape watching the trim of the sails or just waiting for the sun to reach the horizon. Herrick had never disturbed Bolitho at those moments, but had drawn on each occasion to better his own understanding of the man. In his mind's eye he could still see the strong profile, the firm mouth which could be amused and sad almost at the same instant. It did not seem possible that such a man could be wiped out like something from a slate.

He resumed his slow pacing, his chin low on his chest. In this world, he thought, you could never depend on anything.

To the tired men in the longboat the night seemed cold and cheerless, and even those who had cursed the blazing sunlight and bemoaned their urgent thirst found no comfort from the darkness.

Bolitho groped his way aft to where Farquhar was sitting beside the tiller. With Stockdale's assistance he had just dropped a dead seaman over the side while the other men had watched in silence. The sailor in question had been spared the worst of his wound and the suffering of pain and thirst by remaining almost unconscious from the moment he had been shot down by the sloop's deck watch. The longboat was moving so slowly under her small sail that it seemed to take an age for the corpse to bob astern. There was not even an anchor to weight the man's body. In fact there was not much of anything. Just a cask of rancid water, little more than a day's ration of a cup per man.

Bolitho sank into the sternsheets and stared up at the glittering ceiling of stars. 'Keep her due south if you can.' He felt dry and aching with fatigue. 'I wish we could get a bit more wind in this wretched sail.'

Farquhar said, 'I think the boat would sink, sir! It feels rotten and worm-eaten!'

Bolitho eased his legs and thought back over the long, slow passage of time. If that was only the first day, he pondered, what would happen in the next? And the next after that?

The men were quiet enough, but that too could be dangerous. The first relief at escaping from the French could soon give way to mistrust and recriminations. The misery of being a prisoner of war might soon appear comfort itself compared with a living death without food or water.

Farquhar said absently, 'In Hampshire there will be snow on the hills now, I expect. All the sheep will be brought down to their feed, and the farm workers will be drinking good ale by their firesides.' He licked his lips. 'A few will be thinking of us maybe.'

Bolitho nodded, feeling his eyelids droop. 'A few.' He thought of his father in the big house and the row of watchful portraits. After this there would be no heir to carry on the family's name, he thought dully. Maybe some rich merchant would buy the house when his father died, and would find time to wonder at the portraits and the other relics of deeds and men soon forgotten. He said, 'I am going to try and sleep for an hour. Call me if you need anything.'

He closed his eyes and did not even hear Farquhar's reply.

Then he was aware of his arm being tugged and of the boat swaying and rolling as the listless seamen came to life and crowded excitedly in the bows. For a moment longer he imagined that he was dreaming. Then he heard Farquhar shout, 'Look, sir! She came to look for us after all!'

Bolitho staggered to his feet, his sore eyes probing over the heads of his men as he tried to pierce the darkness. Then he saw it. It was more an absence of familiar stars than an actual outline, but as he stared he began to see the contours of something darker and sharper. A ship. He snapped, 'Make a light, Stockdale! Fire some of those rags!'

The sliver of moon struck silver from the distant sails, and against the night's dark backcloth Bolitho could see the darker tracery of raked masts and rigging. It was a frigate right enough.

The makeshift flare sizzled and then burst into flames, so that once more the eyes were blinded and limited to the small confines of the boat. Some men were cheering, others merely hugged each other and grinned like children.

'Now we shall get an answer to the mystery, Mr. Farquhar.' Bolitho pushed the tiller over as the ship changed shape and moved silently above them. He could hear the creak of yards, the sudden flurry of canvas as the frigate started to back her sails and heave to. He thought he heard a distant hail and the sound of running feet. He said. 'Lower the sail, Stockdale! You men forrard, get ready to catch a line!' But nobody needed any encouragement from him.

The bowsprit swung dizzily barely feet away, and as Stockdale lit another crude flare Bolitho felt the grip of ice around his heart. The frigate's figurehead danced and flickered in the light as if it was alive. A gilt-painted demon wielding a pair of furnace irons like weapons of war.

Stockdale threw the flare into the water and turned to stare at Bolitho. 'Did you see, sir? Did you *see*?'

Bolitho let his arm go limp. 'Yes, Stockdale. It is the *Andiron*!'

The cheers and jubilation in the longboat died as suddenly as the flare, and the men stood or sat like stricken beings as lanterns shone down from the frigate's deck and a grapnel bit into the boat's gunwale.

His men stood aside to let Bolitho pass as he made his way to the bows and reached out for the dangling ladder which had suddenly appeared. He was still too fatigued and too stunned by the change of events to mark a clear sequence of what was happening. His mind would only record brief, unreal images, magnified and distorted by patches of light from the circle of lanterns. Glittering bayonets, and pressing, curious faces.

As he stepped into the lamplight he heard a mixture of gasps and comments. An Irish voice called, 'It's an English officer!' Another with a twangy colonial accent broke in. 'Hell it is! It's a *captain*!'

One by one the *Phalarope*'s men climbed up the side and were pushed into line against the ship's gangway. An officer in a dark coat and cocked hat pushed through the packed crowd and regarded Bolitho with amusement.

'Welcome aboard, Cap'n! A real pleasure!' He turned and shouted, 'Put the men under guard and drop a round shot through that coffin of a boat!' To a massive Negro he added, 'Separate any officers amongst them and take 'em aft!' Then to Bolitho he made a mock bow. 'Now if you will come with me, I am sure the captain will be glad to make your acquaintance.'

Even in the uncertain light of the lanterns Bolitho was able to distinguish the old, familiar details of the privateer's maindeck. He recalled with sudden clarity the last time he had visited the ship to see his friend Captain Masterman, a grave but friendly officer, who unlike many of his contemporaries had always been willing to share his knowledge and experience, and pleased to answer Bolitho's constant stream of questions.

The memory helped to drive back some of the gnawing despair, so that he automatically straightened his shoulders and was able to feel some bitter satisfaction at the scars and crudely repaired damage left from the *Phalarope*'s broadsides. The *Andiron*'s captain must have been heading for Mola Island to complete the repairs, he thought. Maybe the captured lugger's contents of spars and canvas had been earmarked for the *Andiron* alone.

He ducked his head as the officer led the way below the wide quarterdeck. At each step of the way he saw curious groups of the frigate's crew as they gathered to watch him pass. They were a mixed crew sure enough, he decided. Some were openly hostile and called insultingly as he strode by. Others dropped their eyes or hid their faces, and Bolitho guessed that they were probably English deserters, some even members af the *Andiron*'s original crew. There were Negroes and olive-skinned Mexicans. Loud-mouthed Irishmen and dark faced sailors who must have breathed their first breaths by the Mediterranean. But it was obviously a close-knit company, if only because of their mutual danger and the hazards of their chosen trade.

The officer opened a heavy door and stood aside to let Bolitho enter a small, sparsely furnished cabin.

'You can wait here. We have to get under way now, but I guess the captain'll want to see you soon.' He held out his hand. 'I'll take the sword.' He saw Bolitho's look of resentment and added, 'And in case you start getting ideas of glory, there is a guard right outside the door.' He took the sword and turned it over in his hands. 'A pretty ancient blade for an English captain?' He grinned. 'But then I imagine things are getting a bit difficult for you all round?'

Bolitho ignored him. The officer was goading him. There was no point in pleading or asking favours. He watched the lamplight shining dully on his father's sword and then deliberately turned his back.

He was a prisoner. He must save his energy for later. The door slammed and he heard the officer's feet moving away.

Wearily Bolitho slumped down on a sea chest and stared at the deck. Farquhar and Belsey would be kept apart like himself. No doubt the *Andiron*'s commander would wish to question each one separately. As he himself would have done. It was strange to realize that it was only two days since he had been questioning the terrified Spaniard aboard his own ship. And in the following period so much had happened that it was almost impossible to trace the pattern of time and events.

One thing was sure. He had lost his ship, and for him the future was an empty ruin.

The stuffy air in the cabin aided by the heavy fatigue in his body eventually took effect. As the deck canted slightly and the ship once more gathered way, Richard Bolitho leaned back against the cabin bulkhead and fell instantly asleep.

He was awakened by someone shaking his arm, and for a few more moments he found himself hoping it was all part of a terrible dream. Perhaps he could go back and take up reality again, even in the cramped uncertainty of the longboat. But it was the same officer who had escorted him to the cabin, and as Bolitho sat up on the chest he said, 'I thought you were dead!'

Bolitho realized with a further start that there was daylight in the passage outside the door, and as his mind accepted the reality of his position he heard the busy sounds of holystones and the sluice of water across the upperdeck.

'What time is it?'

The officer shrugged. 'Seven bells. You've been asleep for nearly seven hours at that!' He beckoned to a seaman in the passageway. 'There is some water for shaving and a razor.' He eyed Bolitho coldly. 'My man here will stay with you to make sure you don't cut your throat!'

'You are very considerate.' Bolitho took the bowl of hot water and ignored the seaman's look of fascinated interest. 'I would hate to die and miss seeing you hang, Lieutenant!'

The officer grinned calmly. 'You sure are a little firebrand, I'll say that for you.' He spoke sharply to the seaman. 'Just watch him, Jorgens! One false move and I'll expect you to deal with him, got it?'

The door slammed and the sailor said, 'The cap'n wants to see you when you's ready.' He licked his lips. 'He's havin' your breakfast got ready.' He sounded amazed at such treatment.

Bolitho continued with his shaving, but his mind was as busy as his razor. Perhaps it would be better to do as the officer had implied, he thought bitterly. One slash with the razor and his captors would be left with neither a ready victim nor a possible source of information.

He remembered Herrick's face when he had told him, 'Information. Out here the lack of it could lose a war.' Now his own words were coming back to mock him.

Then he thought of Farquhar and the others, and the look on Stockdale's battered face when the privateer's men had pulled them apart. It had been an expression of trust and quiet confidence. At that terrible moment it had done more to hold back Bolitho's final despair than any words or deeds imaginable.

He wiped the razor and laid it on the chest. No, there was more to living than a man's own private hopes, he decided.

He pulled his torn uniform into shape and brushed the dark hair back from his forehead. 'I'm ready,' he said coolly. 'Perhaps you will lead the way?'

He followed the seaman along the passageway, and in the filtered daylight he saw more evidence of the brief battle. Smashed timbers shored up with makeshift beams, and telltale red blotches which so far had defied weeks of scrubbing.

An armed sailor stood aside and opened the main cabin door, and as Bolitho entered the once familiar place he was momentarily blinded by the dazzling reflections from sea and sky as the morning sunlight blazed across the wide stern windows.

The *Andiron*'s captain was leaning out over the stern bench, his body a dark silhouette against the glittering water, but Bolitho's eyes fastened instead on his own sword which lay in the centre of the polished table.

He waited, standing quite still, his feet automatically braced against the ship's easy plunge and roll. Even this cabin was not spared from the *Phalarope*'s wounded anger. More scars, and deeply gouged gaps left by flying splinters. *Andiron* must have spent little time in harbour, he thought.

The officer at the window turned very slowly, so that the light played across his face for a few moments before becoming once more a dark silhouette. For the second time in twenty-four hours Bolitho's reserve almost broke. It took all his strength to keep him from crying out in disbelief, but when the other man spoke he knew that this too was no fantasy.

'Welcome aboard the *Andiron*, Richard! When my second lieutenant brought me this sword I knew it had to be you!'

Bolitho stared at his brother, feeling the years dropping away, his brain reeling with a thousand memories. Hugh Bolitho, the son about whom his father had spoken so bitterly, yet with so much anxiety. Now commanding an enemy privateer! It was the culmination of every worst possible belief.

His brother said slowly, 'It had to happen of course. But I hoped it might be otherwise. At some other place perhaps.'

Bolitho heard himself say, 'Do you know what you have done? What this will do to . . .?' He faltered, even unable to accept that they were both sons of the same man. He added quietly, 'So you were in command when we fought your ship last month?'

Hugh Bolitho seemed to relax slightly, as if he considered the worst was now over. 'Yes. And that was a real surprise, I can tell you! We were just closing for the kill when I caught sight of you through my glass!' His face crinkled as he relived the moment. 'So I hauled off. You were lucky that day, my lad!'

Bolitho tried to hide the pain in his eyes and said shortly, 'Are you saying that my being there made a difference?'

'Did you think you had won the day, Richard?' For a moment longer Hugh Bolitho studied his brother with something like amusement. 'Believe me, in spite of your chain shot I could still have taken the *Phalarope*!' He shrugged and walked to the table and stared at the sword. 'I was taken off guard. I had no idea you were returning to the Indies.'

Bolitho watched his brother closely, noting the grey streaks in his dark hair, the lines of strain about his mouth. He was only four years older than himself, but there could have been ten years between them. He said, 'Well, I am your prisoner now. What do you intend to do with me?'

The other man did not answer directly but picked up the sword and held it against the sun. 'So he gave it to *you*!' He shook his head, the gesture both familiar and painful. 'Poor Father. I imagine he believes the worst of me?'

'Are you surprised?'

Hugh Bolitho placed the sword on the table and thrust his hands deeply into his plain blue coat. 'I neither asked for nor expected this encounter, Richard. You may think as you please, but you know as well as I do that events out here are moving too quickly for a display of sentiment.' He watched his brother narrowly. 'When I saw you standing on your deck with that wretched crew of yours going to pieces around you, I could not bring myself to close the combat.' He waved one hand vaguely. 'Just like the old days, Richard. I could never find it easy to take what you thought was yours.'

Bolitho replied evenly, 'But you always did, didn't you?'

'Those days are past.' He pointed at a chart spread across another table. 'We are sailing for St. Kitts. We will make a landfall before night.' He watched the doubt in Bolitho's eyes. 'I know you so well, Richard. I can see the same old look of mistrust there!' He laughed. 'St. Kitts has already fallen to our ally. Sir Samuel Hood has pulled out to lick his wounds!' He waved across the chart. 'It will soon be over. Whether your government believes it or not, America will be an independent nation, perhaps sooner than they think!'

Bolitho felt his fingers locking together behind his back. While he was here being confronted with his past, his own world was falling apart. St. Kitts gone. Perhaps the French were already massing for an attack elsewhere. But where? They had the whole Caribbean to choose from.

His brother said quietly, 'If you are trying to make some scheme to foil my own plans you can forget it, Richard! For you the war is over.' He tapped the table with his fingertips. 'Unless?'

'Unless what?'

Hugh Bolitho walked round the table and stared him in the face. 'Unless you come in with us, Richard! I am well considered by the French. I am sure they would give you a ship of sorts! After what you did at Mola Island I am sure they would not deny your tenacity!' He smiled at some secret thought. 'It might even be the *Phalarope*.'

He studied Bolitho's unsmiling face and then walked back to the window. 'These are *our* waters now. We get our intelligence from many sources. Fishermen, trading boats, even slavers when

we get the chance. With St. Kitts fallen your ships will draw
further south to Antigua and beyond. There are not many
patrols in this area now. It is too wasteful for your admiral, am
I right?' He smiled sadly. 'Just one ship perhaps. Just one.'

Bolitho thought of the *Phalarope* and tried to imagine what
Vibart would do.

'Your ship, Richard. The *Phalarope*! We need every frigate
we can get. It is the same in all navies. And I have made sure
that your admiral, that pompous fool, Sir Robert Napier, will
be *informed* of our movements. I am quite sure that he will be
so drunk with your success at Mola Island that he will soon
despatch the *Phalarope* to find us! The admiral will surely be
eager to avenge the loss of the *Andiron* from his command, eh?'

'You must be mad!' Bolitho watched his brother coldly.

'Mad? I think not, Richard. I have interrogated your men.
They have told me how their ship was punished by Admiral
Napier for letting *Andiron* escape. They told me also of the
trouble there was aboard before you took command.' He spread
his hands. 'I am afraid that most of your men have thrown in
their lot with me. But do not distress yourself, it was wise of
them. There is a whole new world opening up out here, and
they will be part of it. When the war is over I will sail for
England just to claim my inheritance, Richard. Then I will
return to America. I have proved my worth out here. The past
holds nothing for me.'

Bolitho said calmly, 'Then I pity your new nation! If it
depends on traitors for existence it has a difficult course to steer.'

His brother remained unmoved. 'Traitors or patriots? It
depends on a point of view! In any case, the *Andiron* will
anchor off St. Kitts tonight. Not in the main harbour, but in a
quiet little bay which I think would be considered quite ideal
for recapturing her!' He threw back his head and laughed.
'Except that the *Phalarope* will be the one to step into the net,
my brother!'

Bolitho stared at him without expression. 'As far as you are
concerned I am a prisoner. I do not wish to tarnish either the
name of my family or my country by being called a *brother*!'

Just for an instant he saw the barb go home. Then his brother
recovered himself and said flatly, 'Then you will go below.' He
picked up the sword again. 'I will wear this in future. It is mine
by right!'

He banged the table and a sentry appeared in the doorway.
Then he added, 'I am glad you are aboard my ship, Richard.
This time, when the *Phalarope* comes creeping under my guns,
I will have nothing to forestall me!'

'We will see.'

'We shall indeed.' Hugh Bolitho walked across to his chart. 'If I have the temper of your crew rightly, Richard, I think they will soon be eager to follow *Andiron*'s orders!'

Bolitho turned on his heel and walked back past the guard.

Behind him the *Andiron*'s captain stayed watching the door, his hand still holding the tarnished sword like a talisman.

10. THE RED BAIZE BAG

FOR RICHARD BOLITHO each day of captivity seemed longer than the one before, and the daily routine aboard the *Andiron* dragged into a slow torture. He was allowed the comparative freedom of the frigate's poop, from where he could watch the regular comings and goings of shore boats, the casual routine of a ship at anchor. At night he was returned to the solitude of a small cabin, and only joined Farquhar and Belsey for meals. Even then it was difficult to talk freely, because one of the privateer's warrant officers always waited close at hand.

It was a week since the *Andiron* had dropped her anchor, but to Bolitho it felt like an eternity. As each day passed he seemed to withdraw more and more into himself, going over his predicament again and again until his mind felt as if it was bursting.

From his small piece of deck he could see Belsey sitting gloomily on a hatch cover beside Farquhar, both apparently engaged in staring at the empty sea. Like everyone else aboard they were waiting, he thought bitterly. Waiting and wondering when *Phalarope* would approach the island and fall into the trap. He noticed that Belsey had a fresh bandage on his arm, and thought back to that first and only petty triumph when he had been allowed to join the other two after his meeting with his brother.

It was obvious at the time that both Farquhar and Belsey had already been told who the *Andiron*'s captain really was, just as it was equally plain to see their pitiful relief at his reappearance. Did they really believe that he would desert them and give his allegiance to the enemy? Even now he was surprised and faintly pleased to find that he was angry at the idea.

Belsey had been moving his bandaged arm painfully and had said, 'The ship's surgeon is goin' to have a look at it, sir.'

It had been then, and only then that Bolitho had remembered Farquhar's dirk which still lay hidden and used as a splint beneath the crude bandages. Hardly daring to speak, and watched by the others, he had broken a piece of wood from the cabin chair, and with Farquhar's help had replaced the dirk with a piece of polished mahogany. Once Belsey had yelped aloud and Bolitho had snapped, 'Keep quiet, you fool! We may have use for this later on!'

The dirk now lay hidden in his own bedding below decks, but after the agonizing passing of days he could no longer view the possession of such a puny weapon with much hope.

He had seen little of his brother, and for that he was thankful. Once he had caught sight of him being rowed ashore in his gig. And on other occasions he had watched him staring at the tall mass of headland which towered above the anchored ship.

Bolitho had examined and thought over that one conversation in the stern cabin until he could see meanings where there were none. But he was sure of one thing. Hugh Bolitho was not bluffing. He had no need to.

The *Andiron* was anchored off the southern tip of the Island of Nevis, a smaller subsidiary of the main island, St. Kitts. Bolitho knew from experience that this small, oval-shaped island was separated by The Narrows a mere two miles or so from St. Kitts itself and a full fifteen miles from the main town of Basseterre where Hood had successfully stood siege until forced to cut his cables and retire to Antigua.

Nevis had been a good choice, Bolitho conceded grimly. During his endless walks up and down the poop he had watched the rapid preparations, the careful cunning which had gone into laying a perfect trap for any ship attempting to seize the *Andiron*.

The sheltered piece of water was commanded by the jutting promontory of Dogwood Point, while inland and towering like a miniature volcano was the bare outline of Saddle Hill. From either position even a wall-eyed lookout could quickly spot any unusual or suspicious approach and send a report down to both ship and shoreline.

It was so simple that Bolitho had to admit he would have used the same method himself. Perhaps it was because it was his own flesh and blood which was working out the plan, and a mind like his own was laying the snare.

If Sir Robert Napier had been informed of *Andiron*'s presence here, it was not unreasonable to expect him to take some sort of offensive action. A swift frigate attack would not match up to the smarting loss of St. Kitts, but it would do much for the morale of the embattled British fleet. It did not have to be the *Phalarope*, of course.

Bolitho discounted the idea immediately. His brother had been right about that, too. Admiral Napier would have few ships at his disposal now that Hood was back in the saddle, In addition, he would see *Phalarope*'s success as an act of justice to purge her name and avenge the memory of his own son.

He tried again to put himself into the position of an attacking captain. He would make a slow approach, just to make sure that the information about the *Andiron* was not suspect, and in order that the lookouts ashore should not see any sign of a masthead before sunset. Then under cover of darkness he would close the shore and drop a full boarding party of perhaps three or four boats. It would not be easy, but a ship foolish enough to anchor away from the defended base might be expected to fall after a swift struggle. He closed his eyes tightly and tried to blot out the picture of the attacking ship at the moment of truth and realization.

There was a hidden battery of artillery already sighted and ranged across the whole area below the headland. And although to all outward appearances the *Andiron* was resting confidently below a friendly island, Bolitho had seen the preparations and the care his brother had gone to, to make sure of a victory.

Guns were loaded with grape and depressed behind their closed ports. Boarding nets were already slung, suitably slack to prevent a quick inrush of any who lived through the first holocaust of fire. The *Andiron*'s men slept at their stations, each one armed to the teeth and eager to complete his captain's strategy.

Rockets were rigged on the quarterdeck, and as soon as the boarders were engaged the rockets would be fired. From further inshore the signal would be passed to a waiting French frigate and the battle would be all but over. The attacking ship would stand no chance if caught without the best part of her crew. And if she closed to give the boarding party support the shore artillery would pound her to fragments before she realized her mistake.

And if it was the *Phalarope* there was one further despairing thought. Vibart would be in command. It was hard to see his mind working fast enough to deal with such a situation.

Bolitho gritted his teeth and walked slowly to the side. The island looked at peace. The defenders had settled down now and were waiting like himself. Except that when the time came *he* would be battened below, helpless and wretched as he listened to the death of his own ship. Or worse, her capture, he thought for the hundredth time.

He felt a fresh pang of inner pain as he saw one of the *Andiron*'s cutters unloading fruit alongside. There was no mistaking the bulky shape of Stockdale straddle-legged on the gunwale tossing up the nets of fruit as if they were weightless.

Strangely, that had been almost the hardest thing to bear. Stockdale of all people. Whether he had been eager or reluctant, Bolitho did not know, but he had gone over with the privateer's crew, and like sheep the other men from his raiding party had followed suit. He knew he could not blame them. If Stockdale, the captain's trusted coxswain, could change colours, why not they?

Stockdale looked up, squinting against the sun. Then he threw a mock salute, and some of the men laughed delightedly.

The American officer of the watch said dryly: 'Sometimes I think there's no such thing as loyalty, Captain! Just a *price*!'

Bolitho shrugged. 'Perhaps.'

The officer seemed glad of a chance to break Bolitho's brooding silence. 'I can't get over your being our captain's kin. It makes it kind of unnerving. But then I guess it's that way with you?'

Bolitho glanced quickly at the officer's tanned features. It was a friendly face. And that of a man lonely and tired by war, he thought. He said evenly, 'Have you been with him long?'

'A year or so.' The man frowned. 'It seems longer now. He came aboard as first lieutenant, but soon got command when the skipper was killed in a fight with one of your ships off Cape Cod.' He grinned. 'But I hope I'll be able to go home soon. I've a wife and two boys waiting for me. I should be tending my farm, not fighting King George!'

Bolitho recalled his brother's firm promise that he was returning to Cornwall to claim his rightful inheritance, and felt the same savage bitterness as when he had heard the words the first time. He controlled his rising emotion and asked quietly, 'Do you really think it will be that simple?'

The man stared at him. 'What could happen now? I don't mean to add insult to injury, Captain, but I don't really think the British stand much of a chance to regain America.'

Bolitho smiled. 'I was thinking more of the French. If as you say American independence will be ratified by all those concerned, do you imagine the French will be prepared to sail away and leave you alone? They have done most of the fighting remember. Without their fleet and supplies do you think you would have succeeded thus far?'

The American scratched his head. 'War makes strange allies, Captain.'

'I know. I have seen some of them.' Bolitho looked away. 'I think the French will want to stay out here, as they tried to do in Canada.' He shook his head. 'You could easily exchange one master for another!'

The officer yawned and said wearily, 'Well, it's not for me to decide, thank the Lord!' He shaded his eyes and peered towards the dark shadow below Saddle Hill. A white and blue dot was moving rapidly down the rough track from the summit in a cloud of dust.

The officer looked meaningly at Bolitho and said briefly,

'Horse and rider! That means one thing, Captain. The bait has been accepted. It will be tonight, or not at all!'

There was a shout from the forecastle as a blinding needle of light stabbed out from the bleak headland. Someone was using a heliograph, and from further inland Bolitho heard the eager beating of drums.

He asked, 'How did they get a signal?'

The officer closed his mouth and then said not unkindly, 'There is a chain of fishing boats out there, Captain. They pass the sighting reports from boat to boat. The nearest one is well in sight of the hill lookouts.' He looked embarrassed. 'Why not try and forget it? There's nothing you can do now. Any more than *I* could do if the situation were reversed!'

Bolitho looked at him thoughtfully. 'Thank you. I will try to remember that.' Then he resumed his pacing, and with a shrug the officer returned to the opposite side of the poop.

The short truce was over. They were no longer fellow sailors. The flashing heliograph had made them enemies once more.

'It'll be sunset in one hour!' Daniel Proby, the *Phalarope*'s master, scribbled slowly on his slate and then ambled across to join Herrick by the weather rail. 'But in all my experience I've not seen one like this!'

Herrick brought his mind back to the present and followed Proby's mournful gaze across the vast glittering waste of open sea.

For most of the afternoon and early evening the frigate had pushed her way steadily north-east, and now as she lay close-hauled on the port tack, every mast and spar, every inch of straining canvas shone with the hue of burnished copper. The sky, which for days had remained bright blue and empty, was streaked with long cruising clouds, streaming like trails of glowing smoke towards the far horizon. It was an angry sky, and the sea was reacting to the change in its own way. Instead of short, choppy whitecaps the surface had altered to advancing lines of hump-backed rollers, one behind the other in neatly matched ranks which made the ship heave and groan as her figurehead lifted to the sky and then plunged forward and down in drawn-out, sickening swoops.

Herrick said, 'Maybe a storm is coming through from the Atlantic?'

The master shook his head, unconvinced. 'You don't get much in the way of storms at this time of year.' He glanced aloft as the sails thundered as if to mock his words. 'All the same, we will have to take in another reef if it don't improve a bit.'

In spite of his gloom Herrick was able to smile to himself. He could not see Vibart being happy about that. For two days, since he had received his new orders, he had been driving the ship like a madman. He thought back again to the moment a lookout had sighted the distant sail. For an instant they had all imagined it was a patrolling frigate or the *Cassius* herself. But it had been a fast-moving brig, her low hull smothered in spray as she had gone about and run down towards the *Phalarope*.

Her arrival had been an unexpected but welcome diversion as far as Herrick was concerned. The tension aboard the frigate was getting bad enough to *feel*, like something with a soul of its own. In a matter of days there had been seven floggings, but instead of settling the crew into dumb servility it had only helped to drive a firm wedge between quarterdeck and forecastle. There was little chatter or laughter any more between decks, and when an officer passed close by a group of seamen, the latter would lapse into sullen silence and turn their faces away.

Midshipman Maynard had reported, 'The brig is *Witch of Looe*, sir! She has despatches for us!'

Vibart had waited importantly on the quarterdeck, alone and aloof, saying nothing and watching everything.

A boat had skipped across the choppy water, and soon a young lieutenant had climbed aboard carrying the inevitable canvas envelope. Herrick had been standing nearby, straining his ears, trying to imagine what was happening. He had heard Vibart asking about the flagship and the lieutenant's brief reply.

'These orders are from the admiral, sir. I have nothing to add.'

The reply had been too brief, almost insolent, and Herrick had guessed that the young lieutenant was high enough on the admiral's list of favourites to afford such rudeness.

Vibart had started to tell the brig's messenger about the raid on Mola Island and had then clamped his jaw tightly shut. He had turned on his heel, merely adding for Herrick's benefit, 'Get the ship under way, again, Mr. Herrick. I have work to do!'

He was always the same now, Herrick pondered. Fluctuating between ponderous self-importance and fits of blind rage. From one hour to the next you could never be sure of his reactions, and it was doubly bad because he was always in evidence. Watching and criticizing and bawling out fresh orders to overrule those of his subordinates.

Herrick had stopped the lieutenant at the entry port and had tried to get more information.

The officer had regarded him thoughtfully. 'St. Kitts has fallen. The fleet is falling back and regrouping. I am on my way to Antigua now.' He had stared across at his own ship. 'But Rodney is said to be on his way back from England with twelve ships of the line. I hope to God he will be in time.' Then he added quickly, 'Where is your captain?'

'Dead.' Herrick's tongue had lingered on the word. 'We lost him at Mola Island.'

'Well, I don't care much for your new commander, my friend.' The lieutenant had paused above his swaying boat. 'We have been searching for the *Phalarope* for two days! The admiral will not be pleased that you were off your station, Mola Island or not!' He had rolled his eyes. 'Sir Robert is a stickler for routine.'

Herrick's mind shifted to the next part in the sequence of events which had sent the *Phalarope* on her new course towards the islands. Vibart had called a meeting in the stern cabin. Every officer and warrant officer had been present, and it was somehow typical of Vibart that while he sat comfortably in his chair, all the others were kept standing.

'Sir Robert Napier has received information that the *Andiron* is lying off Nevis.' He had plunged into what sounded very like a carefully rehearsed speech. 'She is apparently carrying out repairs and awaiting fresh orders, but there is no saying how long she will remain there.' He had looked slowly around their faces. 'Sir Robert requires that we make our way to Nevis forthwith to sink or cut-out the *Andiron*.' His words had dropped in the cabin like stones in a pool. 'We will make as quick a passage as possible.' He had glared meaningly. 'So make sure there are no mistakes, Mr. Proby!'

Herrick had been studying Vibart during his announcement, and had been surprised by his apparent eagerness to begin the operation. It might be a false piece of intelligence, but if not, it would not be an easy matter to cut-out an anchored ship close inshore to a hostile island.

Then, as Vibart had droned on about details and timing, he had realized that Vibart's demeanour owed much to his own uncertainty. So far, although he had been in command since Bolitho's loss, Okes stood in the best position to gain full credit for past successes against the enemy. He still had to ensure the firmness of his own control, and this new operation was the obvious opportunity.

It was odd that he had sent no despatches across to the *Witch of Looe*, Herrick thought. It was just as if he wanted to save the whole record for the admiral's ear alone. Sir Robert might be angry about *Phalarope* being off station, but the destruction of the Mola Island battery and transports, and a victory over the privateer *Andiron* would do much to placate anyone but the devil himself.

But now that Vibart had had time to consider the full implications of his orders he had changed yet again. As the ship drove towards the chosen rendezvous he had grown nervous and edgy, and more than once had let his impatience get the upper hand. Only that morning he had had a man flogged for letting a marline-spike fall from the foreyard. It had struck quivering in the deck within feet of Packwood, a boatswain's mate. Vibart had been brooding on the quarterdeck, watching the boats being checked and moved ready for instant lowering. Packwood's startled shout had given him yet one more outlet for his unpredictable temper.

'Get that man down here!' His voice had stopped all work on the maindeck. 'I saw what he did! That was meant to fall on Packwood!'

Even the boatswain's mate had voiced a protest. 'It's lively aloft today, sir. It was an accident.'

Vibart's face had gone scarlet. 'Silence! Or I'll see your backbones, too!'

Again the dread pipe. 'All hands lay aft to witness punishment!' Again the agonizing passage of time while the grating was rigged and the marines had made a scarlet rectangle on the quarterdeck.

The seaman in question was a man called Kirk. He was a thin, hollow-eyed sailor who had gone almost deaf after the encounter with the *Andiron*, his ears apparently permanently damaged by the thundering crash of broadsides.

Mr. Quintal, the boatswain, had walked slowly aft, the familiar red baize bag swinging from his wrist as the silent company parted to allow him through.

Up to the last moment, even as Vibart closed the Articles of War and announced harshly, 'Four dozen, Mr. Quintal!', Herrick doubted if Kirk had heard a single word.

Only when the boatswain's mates seized him and stripped his thin body and spread-eagled him across the grating like a writhing crucifix did he start to scream and protest.

Most men took their punishment in silence. The tremendous force of a single blow from the cat-o'-nine-tails was enough to drive the wind from the lungs and left little to cry on.

Kirk's cries continued as his wrists were tied in position so that his feet were only just touching the deck, and the boatswain's mates exchanged quick glances, momentarily unnerved by the man's terror.

Quintal drew the lash from the red bag and handed it to Packwood. Gruffly he had said, 'Two dozen. Josling can do the other two.' Under his breath he added, 'If he lives that long!'

Vibart had replaced his hat and nodded curtly. 'Carry on!'

Herrick had seen plenty of floggings, and had steeled himself to accept what was part of naval life. But this one had seemed different, and unfair because of Vibart's obvious eagerness.

The marine drummer had struck into a quick roll, and Packwood had drawn back his thick arm.

'One!' The lash came down with a swishing crack.

As usual Herrick had been sickly fascinated by the time it took to show its mark. For a moment there was nothing on the man's naked back, not even a bruise, but even as the lash swung back for the second stroke the whole area of taut skin from the shoulder to the waist opened and shone in a criss-cross mass of fine cuts.

'Two!' Kirk screamed and wriggled helplessly on the grating, and Herrick saw blood on his chin and knew that he had bitten through his tongue.

'Three!' Packwood faltered and hit again, his eyes glassy as Kirk's back began to shred into a tangle of bloody flesh.

Vibart's voice had cut through the roll of the drum. 'Harder, Packwood! Don't go easy on the scum, unless you wish to change places with him!'

And so it had continued. Stroke by stroke, to the inhuman rattle of the drum. Kirk had fallen silent and limp after the first dozen, but when Ellice, the surgeon, had pronounced grimly, ''E's still alive, sir, but not takin' it well!', Vibart had snapped, 'Carry on with punishment!'

Herrick had seen Midshipman Neale holding Maynard's sleeve as if for support as the grisly flogging had continued.

Kirk had little flesh to begin with, and after eighteen strokes Herrick thought he could see the gleam of bone and muscle through the man's butchered skin.

Josling had taken the lash from his fellow boatswain's mate and had run it through his fingers to clear it of flesh and gristle. With a quick glance upwards at Vibart's expressionless face he had carried on with the second two dozen.

At the twentieth stroke Mr. Quintal had knocked up Josling's arm and had said firmly, 'That's enough, sir! He's dyin'!'

Kirk's bloodied body had been cut down and carried below, but only after Ellice had backed up the boatswain's quick intervention. He had muttered vaguely, 'Might live. Can't say. I think his kidneys have burst.'

Herrick had looked for some sign of pity or even triumph on Vibart's heavy features. But there had been nothing but stony indifference. Captain Pomfret had watched floggings like a man will watch a spectacle of sport, and at each bloody conclusion he was almost elated, as if he had just experienced some perverted sexual act. But not Vibart. There was nothing at all which Herrick could recognize as feeling of any sort.

He turned away swiftly as Vibart appeared at the cabin hatch and sniffed at the wind. Vibart studied the strange copper sky and remarked slowly, 'Wind's freshened. We'll shorten sail in ten minutes.' He glanced at Proby. 'Now, are you sure of our position? Our *exact* position?'

Proby nodded gloomily. 'Aye, sir. Nevis bears nor'-east, near on fifteen miles.'

Vibart regarded him searchingly. 'I hope for your sake that is so, Mr. Proby.' He contented himself with another quick bark at the helmsman, 'Watch her head, you fool! Keep her close to the wind!'

Herrick glanced aloft and knew that the ship was running perfectly. Vibart was obviously getting more and more on edge as they drew nearer the island. Not afraid. He had never shown a sign of fear at any time. No, it went far deeper, to the lurking possibility of failure.

Vibart saw Herrick watching him and snapped, 'Have you detailed the cutting-out parties?'

'Aye, sir. All the boats except the gig are prepared. The gig is unsuitable for this work.'

'I know that, Mr. Herrick!' Vibart's eyes were flecked with red. 'You will take over-all charge of the boarders with Maynard, Packwood and Parker in charge of the other three boats.' He looked darkly at the men working on deck. 'As a master's mate, Parker will be ideal for getting sail on the *Andiron* if you succeed in your attack.'

'Yes, sir.' Herrick knew all this. He had detailed each man personally, and had already decided on his set plan. He asked, 'Do you expect much opposition, sir?'

'We are committed now. It doesn't matter what I think!'

Proby consulted his massive watch and said, 'Call all hands! Prepare to shorten sail!'

Herrick wondered why Vibart had left it so long. Several times he had seen fishing boats in the far distance. There was no point in advertising the *Phalarope*'s haste by her obvious press of sail.

The seamen were already climbing the shrouds and pulling themselves out along the swaying yards. With the ship's uncomfortable motion the business of taking in sails was all the more dangerous to the unwary.

Vibart growled, 'This will make us harder to see. And with the wind rising all the time it will save us the trouble of shortening later on.' He seemed to be thinking aloud.

Proby cupped his hands and yelled hoarsely, 'Tops'ls and jib's all we need! Lively there!'

Followed by Vibart's eyes and the urgent shouts of their petty officers the men aloft fought at the thrashing canvas, cursing the wind and the treacherous sails which tried their utmost to hurl the men from the yards to the deck beneath.

Herrick felt the ship's motion ease slightly as topgallants and courses contracted and finally submitted to the struggling seamen. He watched the long cruising rollers and gauged the distance between them. It would be more sheltered below Nevis's lee, he thought, but even so it would not be easy to keep the raiding boats together. He caught sight of Okes standing at the lee rail, and found himself wondering why Vibart had not chosen him for the cutting-out expedition. If Okes was so changed and reliable, he was the obvious choice.

Captain Rennie sauntered across the quarterdeck and remarked quietly, 'Congratulations, Herrick. I hope you do well tonight. I wish I could come with you, but marines are hardly suitable for falling about in boats!'

Herrick smiled. 'Thank you.'

Rennie gestured towards Okes. 'It would seem that our commanding officer knows more than we thought, eh? He will not trust this attack to a man who is as weak as water!'

Herrick glanced quickly at the open skylight. 'Keep your voice down! Your remarks might be taken seriously!'

Rennie shrugged but dropped his voice. 'I feel past caring. Like a man walking on ice. It can only take so much!'

He walked away, and Herrick stood watching the seamen shinning down from the work aloft. If only Bolitho were here to inspire and carry them all, he thought heavily. He could imagine the *Phalarope* sailing into Antigua with Vibart expanding with pleasure as cheers and congratulations marked their return to the fleet and to glory. It would make victory all the more bitter, he thought. But for Bolitho the *Phalarope* would never have got this far, and if Vibart retained his command the future was bleak indeed.

Tobias Ellice rolled aft and mounted the quarterdeck ladder, touching his shabby hat and belching simultaneously. 'Kirk's dead,' he grunted abruptly. 'I'm having him sewn up nice an' neat like!'

Herrick replied, 'Very well. I'll put it in the log.' He could smell the rum on the surgeon's breath and wondered how the man was able to perform his duties.

Ellice said, 'You can also put in the log that I'm sick of this ship and the whole bloody lot of you!' He swayed tipsily and would have fallen but for Herrick's arm. He muttered, 'Treat 'em like dogs!' He shook his head vaguely. 'No, not dogs, they live like kings by comparison.'

Herrick regarded him wearily. 'Have you finished?'

Ellice took a giant red handkerchief from the tail of his coat and blew his nose loudly. 'You can sneer, Mr. Herrick! You're off to gain glory tonight and to test your steel against the enemy.'

He bared his teeth and tried to focus Herrick in his rheumy eyes. 'But you'll change yer tune when you're down below waiting for the saw to lop off your pretty arm or take away a leg or two!'

'Only two?' Herrick eyed him with sad amazement.

Ellice became suddenly serious as his rum-sodden mind grappled with Herrick's question. 'You can live without 'em, boy! I've seen it many a time.' He dropped his voice. 'But watch out for your wedding-tackle! A woman'll forgive much, but lose that lot and you might as well be food for the fish!'

Herrick watched him go and then strode aft to the taffrail. Another man dead. Whose turn would it be next?

Bryan Ferguson took another cutlass from the deep chest and handed it to old Ben Strachan. The latter peered quickly along the heavy blade and then bent over the grindstone and began to run the cutlass back and forth across the spinning stone, his eyes gleaming brightly in the flying sparks.

Ferguson looked at the berth deck and at the leaping shadows cast by the madly swinging lanterns as the ship rolled and staggered beneath his feet. It was strange how he was now able to retain his balance, and even his stomach seemed able to resist the lurking agony of seasickness.

The low-beamed berth deck was strangely deserted by comparison with its usual appearance of crowded humanity, he thought. Apart from the men selected for the boarding parties, all other available hands were on deck preparing the ship for action. As he watched Strachan concentrating on his sharpening he could hear the menacing rumble of gun trucks as the main armament was carefully loaded and then lashed once more behind sealed ports. The decks were already sanded, and he could hear Mr. Brock, the gunner, yelling some last-minute instructions to his magazine party.

There was a strong smell of neat rum pervading the berth deck, and he turned to stare at the huddled groups of seamen who remained below enjoying a small moment of rest before taking to the boats. He said quietly to Strachan, 'What will happen, do you think?'

Strachan tested the blade and laid it carefully on the pile beside him. 'Hard to tell, mate. I've been on a few cuttin' out raids myself. Sometimes it was all over with a few prayers and a few "Oh my Gods" an' afore you knew what 'ad 'appened you was back aboard none the worse! An' other times you was shocked to be still alive!'

Ferguson nodded, unable to picture the nerve-wrenching horror of a raid in total darkness. His new duties as clerk kept him away from that sort of danger and had somehow thrown him further apart from his companions.

It was all he could do to stay clear of trouble with the first lieutenant. Vibart read every order and account at least twice, and he never failed to follow up a complaint with a threat of punishment.

Ferguson thought back to the floggings and the last one in particular. He had wanted to hide his face, yet was stricken and mesmerized by the relentless punishment so that he had watched it to the end. Kirk had died in the sickbay, but his sobbing cries still seemed to hover in the space which had once been his home.

Strachan remarked, 'It's gettin' pretty rough up top. I wouldn't like to be takin' part!' He shook his grey head. 'It was as black as a pig's belly when I last took a look!'

Onslow, the big seaman from the *Cassius,* sauntered across and stared thoughtfully at Ferguson for several seconds. In his checked shirt and tight canvas trousers he looked even taller and more formidable than usual, and his thick hair was tied to the nape of his neck with a piece of red ribbon.

He said, 'You'll be staying aboard then?' He smiled. 'And quite right, too.' He rested his hand on Ferguson's thin shoulder. 'You save your energy, my lad. I'll want to be knowing what is happening down aft in the cabin.'

Ferguson stared at him. 'I—I don't understand?'

Onslow yawned and spread his arms. 'It's always just as well to know what the officers are planning next, y'see. That's what stops men like us staying rabble. With knowledge,' he tapped his forehead meaningly, 'we are equal to them, and *ready*!'

Lugg, a gunner's mate, ran down a ladder and squinted through the gloom. 'Right, you lot! On deck and lively about it! Each man take a cutlass and muster aft!'

Onslow eyed him calmly. 'What, no pistols?'

Lugg replied coldly, 'I'll pistol you if you don't learn some manners!'

There was a rasp of steel as each hurrying figure took a cutlass, and once or twice Ferguson spoke to a passing familiar face, but each time he received no answer.

Strachan wiped his hands and muttered, 'Save yer breath, mate. They're thinkin' of what lies ahead. There'll be talk enough later, I shouldn't wonder!'

John Allday hung back to the last. Then he picked up a cutlass and swung it slowly in the lamplight. Quietly he said, 'Be careful of Onslow, Bryan. He is a born troublemaker. I don't trust him an inch!'

Ferguson studied his friend with surprise and something like guilt. Since his unexpected change of jobs to captain's clerk he had seemingly drifted away from Allday's quiet protection, and whenever he had returned to the berth deck it had always been Onslow or his friend Pook who had dragged him into a tight circle of chatter and speculation.

Allday saw the uncertainty on Ferguson's face and added, 'You saw the flogging, Bryan. Be warned!'

'But Onslow is on our side, surely?' Ferguson wanted to understand. 'You heard him talking today. He was as sickened as the rest of us!'

'I heard him.' Allday's mouth twisted in a grim smile. 'But he only talks. He is never the one who goes to the gratings!'

Old Strachan mumbled, 'I seen a lad like 'im in the old *Gorgon*. Stirred up the men till they never knew which way ter jump. They 'anged 'im in the end!'

'And they'll hang all of us if he keeps up this mutinous talk!' Allday's eyes flashed. 'We are here, and we must make the best of it!'

Lugg peered down the ladder and bellowed, 'Come up on deck, you idle bugger! You're the last as usual!' But there was no real anger in his voice. He was as tense and jumpy as everyone else aboard.

Ferguson called, 'Good luck!' but Allday was already running on deck, his eyes momentarily blinded in the darkness which enclosed the pitching hull like a cloak.

Overhead there were few stars, and then only occasionally visible between the low scudding clouds.

Petty officers were bawling names, and slipping and cursing the seamen pushed into separate parties near the boats which were already clear of their chocks, ready to be swayed outboard.

Allday saw the white lapels of Lieutenant Herrick's coat gleaming faintly against the dark sky and was strangely glad he was going with his boat. Midshipman Maynard seemed a likeable enough youngster, but he lacked both experience and confidence. He could see him now whispering furtively to his small friend Neale below the quarterdeck.

Herrick said sharply, 'Now listen to me, lads! I will lead in the launch. The cutter will follow close astern and then the pinnace. Mr. Parker will stay last in the jolly boat.' He had to shout above the moaning wind, and Allday glanced uneasily at the creaming water alongside and the rising spectres of blown spray. It would be a hard pull, he thought, and automatically spat on his hands.

He pricked up his ears as Parker, the master's mate, reported, 'All present, Mr. Herrick. Sixty-six men all told!'

'Very good. I will inform the . . .' He faltered and added harshly, 'I will tell Mr. Vibart!'

Allday bit his lip. There was no love lost between Herrick and the new captain, he thought.

He saw Onslow leaning negligently against a pike rack and remembered Ferguson's uneasiness. It was odd how eager Onslow had been to see Ferguson appointed as clerk, he decided. And how convenient it had been that Mathias, Bolitho's original clerk, had died in the hold.

'Sway out the cutter!' Mr. Quintal groped his way towards the tackle. 'Hoist away there!'

Allday faltered, his mind suddenly filled with one, stark picture. He had been masthead lookout the morning Mathias had fallen to his death. It was strange how he had not thought of the connection before. He had seen the clerk climbing through the small inspection hatch shortly before he had been found unconscious and dying. But there had already been someone else in the hold *before* that! He looked quickly at Onslow, remembering the exact moment and the fact that it had been Onslow who had reported the clerk's fall.

He felt Quintal's hard hand on his shoulder and threw his weight against the tackle with the others. All at once the sea seemed to become rougher and the *Phalarope* seemed to shrink by comparison.

Through his racing thoughts he heard Onslow say casually, 'We'll give the buggers a taste of steel!'

But who did he mean? Allday wondered.

11. FORTUNE OF WAR

THE *Phalarope's* heavy launch, packed as she was with additional men for the cutting-out raid, began to ship water within minutes of leaving the security of the frigate's side.

Herrick wedged himself in one corner of the stern and peered over the heads of the straining oarsmen, his vision hampered by both darkness and a continuous stream of bursting spray. He tried to concentrate on the set plan of attack, but as time dragged by and the boat's swooping motion became more pronounced he found that half of his mind dwelt on the realization that things were already moving against him. The wind had gained in force, and he didn't need to consult his small compass to know that it had also veered more to the east, so that what cover there might have been from the island was lost in an angry welter of tossing whitecaps and great swirling patterns of backwash from partially hidden rocks.

Every so often he looked astern and was thankful to see the cutter riding in his wake, her banks of oars slashing one moment at wave crests and then buried to the rowlocks as the boat dropped into another sickening trough.

Ryan, a seasoned quartermaster, swung the tiller bar and yelled, 'She'm takin' it poorly, sir! The lads are all but wore out!'

Herrick nodded but did not reply. It was obvious from the slow, laboured stroke that the men were already exhausted and in no shape for carrying out any sort of attack. More and more Herrick was nagged by the thought that Vibart had dropped the boats too soon. Nevis Island was still only a darker patch in the night's angry backcloth, and there was no sign at all of the chosen landmarks.

He felt a surge of anger when he remembered Vibart's brusqueness when he had last seen him. All he had wanted was to get the boats away. No second plan, no arrangements for possible discovery had even been discussed.

The *Andiron* was supposed to be anchored below Dogwood Point, but even allowing for better shelter inshore, it was still likely that her captain had called extra hands to watch for possible dangers in the rising wind. Herrick had a sudden picture of his exhausted boats' crews arriving at the ship's side to be met with a murderous fire from the awakened and eager gunners.

Ryan was shouting again. 'There's a strong drift, y'see! It'll carry us clear of the 'eadland, sir!' He sounded bitter. 'It'll be a long pull to clear the point at this rate.'

As if to back his words there was an anonymous rumble of voices from the darkened boat. Someone muttered, 'We should turn back. There's no chance now!'

Herrick glared down the boat. 'Silence! Do you want the whole island to hear us?'

Ryan whispered, 'Could we not lie beneath the point, sir?' He sounded slightly ashamed. 'We could rest the men a bit an' then try again.'

Herrick nodded, another plan forming in his brain. 'Good idea. Signal the cutter, Ryan.' He took the tiller as the quartermaster opened the shutter of his lantern and blinked it twice astern. To the oarsmen he snapped, 'Keep the stroke! *Together*, now!' There was no muttering, but he could sense them all watching him in the darkness. He added, 'The rest of you keep baling, and watch the oars. I want 'em muffled at every pull!'

Ryan said, 'Cutter's turning', sir. I can see the pinnace back there, too.'

'Well, thank God for that!' Herrick forgot the grumbling seamen as the skyline hardened into a jagged overhanging cliff. It was Dogwood Point well enough, but they had drifted further than he had feared. They were not below it, but on the wrong

side altogether. As he stared wretchedly at the land's hostile outline he felt the boat's motion begin to ease and heard the oars
pick up a steadier time as the launch thrust into more sheltered
water. He said quietly, 'Oars! Easy with those blades now! You
sound like a lot of damn cattle!'

The boat rode uneasily in the inshore swell while the weary
sailors fell across their oars and sucked gratefully at the damp
air. The pinnace moved out of the gloom and lay close by, and
then the cutter crossed to the other side and paddled nearer so
that Midshipman Maynard could make himself heard.

'What shall we do, Mr. Herrick?'

'Lie here for a bit!' Herrick spoke slowly to give himself time
to sort out his hazy ideas. He wished Maynard would not sound
so lost and bewildered in front of his men. Things were already
bad enough. He added, 'Where is Mr. Parker and the jolly boat?'

Maynard shrugged, and Packwood, the boatswain's mate,
called quickly from the pinnace, 'We've lost sight of him long
since, Mr. Herrick!'

Herrick controlled his reply with an effort. 'Maybe he turned
back!'

A seaman murmured, 'Sunk more likely!'

Herrick made up his mind. 'Come alongside! But get some
fenders out!'

He waited, holding his breath as the two boats sidled against
the launch. At each creak and thud he expected to hear shouts
from ashore, or the ominous rattle of musket fire. But only the
wind and the hissing spray interrupted his words as Maynard
and Packwood craned to hear him.

'If we pull around the point we shall be too late to make an
attack.'

Maynard muttered petulantly, 'We were given too far to row
in my opinion. It was impossible from the start!'

Herrick snarled, 'No one is asking for your opinion, so just
listen to me will you?' Herrick was surprised at the savagery in
his own voice but hurried on, 'There should be a bit of fore-
shore below the point, so we'll head for it now. Mr. Packwood
will wait with half a crew per boat and lie as close as possible
to the rocks.' He waited, feeling the tension dragging at his
patience. 'Understand?'

They nodded doubtfully and he continued, 'Mr. Maynard will
accompany me ashore with thirty men. If we scale the point we
should be able to see down the other side. If the *Andiron* is still
there we might try an attack even now, especially if she looks
peaceful enough and is close to the headland. Otherwise we will
head back to the picking-up area.' He had a brief picture of
Vibart's scorn and rage when he returned to announce the

failure of the attack. He again felt the same unreasonable anger at the mission. The admiral should have sent a heavier force. Even the *Cassius* would have helped just by adding her strength and availability for the final withdrawal.

Perhaps it was his own fault after all. If he had not trusted Vibart's complacency and had checked the distance from the shore more carefully. If only he had allowed for the change of wind and the savage offshore drift. He shook himself angrily. It was too late now. The present was all that counted.

But he still found time to imagine Bolitho in these circumstances. The mental picture of that impassive face helped to steady him and he said in a level voice, 'Bear off and head for the rocks. But not a sound, *any* of you!'

One by one the boats moved inshore, and when almost hemmed in by dark-fanged rocks the first men leapt slipping and cursing into shallow water.

There was no point in trying to split the party into groups now, Herrick decided. It would take too long, and they had taken enough chances already. He watched the three boats move clear and then snapped, 'Mr. Maynard, come with me. McIntosh will take charge down here.' He groped through his mind to remember the carefully listed names. 'Allday and Martin follow me!'

Allday seemed a capable man, and Martin, who had once earned a rare living as a Dorset poacher, was as nimble and quiet as a rabbit.

As they climbed in silence up the steeply sloping cliff Herrick again thought of Bolitho and his dashing attack on Mola Island. There he had had to deal with every sort of danger, yet he had succeeded at the cost of his own life. Compared with Mola Island this escapade was nothing, he thought grimly.

And why had he made a point of suggesting an alternative to the attack? Was he perhaps already preparing to slip away to the waiting *Phalarope* without even attempting to complete the mission?

He stumbled and almost fell to the rocks below, but a hand seized his wrist and he heard Allday say, 'You must watch this sort of cliff, sir! It feels secure, but the stones are only caked in soil. There's no real grip in them.'

Herrick stared at him. Of course, Allday had been a shepherd as well as a sailor. After Cornwall's rocky cliffs and hills this was probably child's play to him.

As if reading his thoughts Allday murmured. 'Many's the time I've been down this sort of thing after a wandering lamb.'

They froze into silence as Martin hissed, 'Sir! There's a sentry up yonder!'

Herrick stared. 'Where? Are you sure, man?'

Martin nodded vehemently. 'Thirty yards or so over there! I heard his boots. *There!*' His eyes gleamed excitedly. 'Did you hear 'em?'

'Yes, I did.' Herrick sank down on a ledge of wet grass. A sentry up here. What was the point of it? No man could see much beyond the edge of the cliff at night-time. He said, 'We'll crawl closer and take a look!'

Holding their weapons clear of the treacherous stones they wriggled across the side of the headland, their eyes smarting from straining and watching.

Herrick said at length, 'Martin, get away to the left. Allday, take the seaward side.' He watched them crawl away. 'We'll push on up this slope, Mr. Maynard. I feel that something is not quite right here.'

Allday came back first, his body bent double as he ran quickly from bush to bush. 'The *Andiron*'s there right enough, sir! She's just on the other side of the point. She's in complete darkness. Not a light or a sound from her!'

Maynard muttered, 'They must be damn confident!'

Allday said, 'The crew could be ashore, sir.'

'Unlikely.' Herrick tried to find the cause of his uncertainty. 'Their anchorage must be a good one.' He stiffened and then relaxed as Martin slithered down the slope on his scrawny buttocks. Martin waited to regain his breath.

'Them's soldiers up there, sir!'

'What are they doing?' Herrick forced himself to remain calm.

'Sleepin' by the looks of it, sir!' Martin picked a thorn from his bare foot. 'They'm got a sentry at each end, but the rest is just lyin' about.' He shrugged. 'Sleepin' like I said!' He sounded scornful.

Herrick asked sharply, 'What did you mean, Martin, "at each end"?'

'Oh, I forgot, sir.' Martin grinned. 'They've got six pieces of artillery along the side of the cliff.'

Herrick felt strangely relaxed. Not knowing the odds was always worse than actually facing them. Almost to himself he said, 'Just two sentries, you say?'

Martin nodded, 'Aye, sir. An' about thirty men lyin' beside the guns.' He chuckled. 'I could'a cut their throats easily!'

Herrick said, 'You may have to.' Suddenly it was quite clear what he had to do. The *Andiron* slept at anchor because she was well protected by firmly mounted field pieces. No doubt each gun was already loaded and ranged to cover the whole anchorage. It was not an uncommon arrangement where no proper harbour was available.

He felt suddenly cold at the thought of what would have happened if his boats had made their planned attack. The casualties and the noise would have killed any chance of success.

He said flatly, 'Get to the beach, Mr. Maynard. Send every available man up here as fast as you can. Anchor the boats and let the remaining men swim ashore. Tell McIntosh and the others that I intend to rush the guns and put 'em out of action. Then we'll take to the boats and go for the *Andiron* as planned!'

They all watched him in silence. Then Maynard said, 'And you, sir?'

Herrick patted Martin's shoulder. 'Our poacher is going to earn his keep tonight, Mr. Maynard!'

Martin pulled a knife from his belt and handed his heavy cutlass to Allday. He said cheerfully, 'Easy, sir! It don't seem fair, do it?'

When Martin and Maynard had slithered back into the darkness Herrick said quietly, 'Those soldiers must be silenced as they sleep. Killed or clubbed, I don't care. But they must be kept from raising the alarm!'

Allday winced as Maynard's dirk clattered on a rock below and then said, 'It's them or us, isn't it, sir?'

'How is your arm, Mr. Belsey?' Bolitho heard the master's mate move somewhere in the pitch darkness and knew he had asked the question merely to break the nerve-jarring silence. With Belsey and Farquhar he had been hustled below and locked unceremoniously in a tiny unused storeroom somewhere beneath the *Andiron*'s forecastle, and after a short attempt at conversation each man had lapsed into silence and the apprehension of his own thoughts.

Belsey said, 'Fair enough, sir. But this motion is makin' me sweat!' The ship's uneasy movement had certainly increased even during the last hour. The storeroom was below the *Andiron*'s water-line, and the savage jarring of the anchored hull was all the more apparent. The crew had already paid out more hawse to compensate for the sudden change of wind which now swept across the once protected anchorage with mounting ferocity.

Belsey added, 'Maybe the *Phalarope* will stand out to sea agin, sir? Surely they'll not send boats out in this lot?'

Bolitho was glad the others could not see his face. A change of weather would make little difference to Vibart's determination to produce a victory, he thought. From the moment the signal had been flashed down the hillside to the hidden defenders he had felt a growing despair, the fretting certainty of calamity and destruction for the *Phalarope* and her company. And he was powerless to help a single man.

He felt a sudden pressure at his shoulders as the ship heeled in a deep swell. She was snubbing at her cable at regular intervals now, and he could feel the deck lifting and then sliding back with each shuddering jerk.

He found himself thinking again of his brother, and wondered what he was doing at this moment. His earlier eagerness at the proposed massacre of *Phalarope*'s boarding party must have given way a little to the anxiety for his own ship's safety. At any other time he would have made sail and headed for the more sheltered side of the island. It was strange how the unexpected change of weather had taken part in the game. Not that it could have any final effect. It merely prolonged the misery of waiting.

Farquhar said absently, 'I wish something would happen! This waiting is getting on my nerves!'

Bolitho shifted his position to stare at the brightly lit crack in the storeroom door. Occasionally a shadow blotted out the tiny sliver of light as a sentry moved his position in the narrow passageway beyond. As he rearranged his cramped limbs Bolitho felt the warm touch of steel against his leg and remembered the hidden dirk. For all the use it was now he could have left it in the cabin, he thought wearily.

It was strange that the guards had not bothered to search him. But they were so openly confident, and with such good reason, that it was only to be expected. Even his brother had found time to see him just as he was being led below to the storeroom.

Hugh Bolitho had been wearing their father's sword, as well as a brace of pistols, and seemed to have gained new life and excitement from the impending battle.

'Well, Richard. This is your last chance.' He had stood easily on the swaying deck, his head on one side as he had watched his brother with something like amusement. 'Just one decision, and it is yours to make!'

'I have nothing to say to you. Not now. Not ever!' Bolitho had tried not to stare at the sword. It had been like a final insult.

'Very well. After this I may see little of you. I will have much to do.' He had stared up at the angry sky. 'The wind is rising, but I expect to have visitors none the less!' He had added in a harder tone, 'You will have to take your chances with the French authorities. I must take *Andiron* to join the combined fleets.'

He had seen his brother's immediate caution and had continued calmly, 'I can tell you now, Richard. For you will be unable to take part. The French admiral, de Grasse, will join with a Spanish squadron. Together with our ships they will attack Jamaica.' He had made a curt gesture as if to demonstrate the finality of the campaign. 'I am afraid King George will have to find fresh fields to conquer elsewhere!'

Bolitho had said to his guard, 'I wish to go below.'

His brother had called after him, 'You are foolish, Richard. And what is worse, you are *wrong*!'

As he sat in the swaying storeroom Bolitho found plenty of time to relive the bitterness and the sense of defeat.

There was a scraping of metal as the bolts were drawn from the door, and Belsey groaned. 'Comin' to gloat again! God rot their bloody souls!'

But as the lamplight flooded the storeroom and seared their eyes Bolitho could only stare with surprise. Stockdale stood blinking in the doorway, a heavy boarding axe swinging from his hand.

Bolitho struggled to his feet and then caught sight of the sentry sprawled below the swinging lantern, the back of his head smashed in like an eggshell.

Stockdale said humbly, 'I am sorry it took me so long, Captain! But I had to win their confidence.' He grinned sheepishly. 'Even now I'm not sure I done as you expected.'

Bolitho could hardly speak. He gripped the man's massive arm and muttered, 'You did rightly, Stockdale. Have no fear of that!' To the others he said, 'Are you with me?'

Farquhar replied dazedly, 'Just tell me what to do, sir!'

'Quick, Stockdale!' Bolitho stepped into the passageway and peered into the darkness beyond the lantern. 'Tell me what is happening!'

The ex-prizefighter answered thickly, 'They're getting worried up top, sir. No sign of an attack, an' the ship's taking the wind badly.' He thought for a moment. 'Maybe we could swim for the beach, sir?' He nodded with rare excitement. 'Yes, we could do it with luck!'

Bolitho shook his head. 'Not yet. They will be watching like hawks. We must not think of ourselves. We must try to save the *Phalarope* before it is too late!'

Stockdale glanced at the corpse by his feet. 'They change the guard in half an hour, sir. There's not much time!'

'I see.' Bolitho tried to stifle the excitement and urgency in his mind and think more clearly. 'We cannot fight the whole crew, but with luck we might still surprise them!'

Belsey said, 'I'd like to take a few of the buggers with me!'

Bolitho drew the dirk from his breeches and held it glinting in the lamplight. 'Lead the way, Stockdale. If we can get to the forecastle there is something which we can do to provide a diversion!'

Farquhar picked up the dead guard's cutlass and murmured bleakly, 'Are you thinking of the cable, sir?'

Bolitho shot him a swift glance of approval. 'The ship is

already dragging hard at her anchor. If we could cut the cable she would be in serious danger. Our men are out there somewhere, and they will soon pull clear when they see *Andiron* drifting towards the point!'

Belsey broke in excitedly, 'The *Andiron*'ll have to make sail, sir! Even then she might not be in time! She'll run hard aground with the wind in this quarter.'

'Begging your pardon, sir.' Stockdale looked at Bolitho sadly. 'They've already got a strong anchor party in the bows looking out for trouble!'

Bolitho smiled coldly. 'I'm not surprised.' He gestured to the others. 'Come, we have little time.' As they crept along the passageway he added, 'Remember that nine-pounder on the forecastle, Mr. Farquhar?'

Farquhar nodded, his eyes gleaming. 'Yes, sir. One of the bow-chasers!'

Bolitho paused below a narrow ladder, straining his eyes towards the hatch above. It might just work. They would all die for their efforts, but he knew that each man now understood that well enough.

He said quietly, 'The gun was lashed there while the rail was being repaired from *Phalarope*'s mauling. If it were cut loose now, in this gale, it would run amuck like a maddened bullock!'

Belsey sucked his teeth. 'My God! A nine-pounder weighs well over a ton! It'd take a bit of holding down!'

Bolitho said, 'If I cut the lashings, Stockdale, could you . . .?'

The man grinned down at him. 'Say no more, Captain!' He swung the heavy axe. 'Just a few minutes is all I'd need!'

'A few minutes are all you'll get, my lad!' Bolitho eased himself up the ladder and peered through the hatch. Again the whole deck area was deserted. He stared up the next and final ladder and then said, 'You can stay behind, Belsey. You can't fight with one arm.'

'Nor can I sit an' do nothin', sir!' Belsey eyed him stubbornly. 'Never mind me, sir. I can still do a bit.'

Any sound made by their stealthy footsteps was drowned by the creak of spars and the thrumming rattle of shrouds and rigging. Bolitho peered quickly at the nearest line of lashed guns and the shadowed shapes of their crews. Most of the men were lying on the deck or resting against the bulwark, and only a few were still on their feet. And they were watching outboard, their eyes only just raised above the hammock nettings.

Bolitho saw the solitary nine-pounder, its long outline jutting aft towards the maindeck. He could hear it creaking gently, as if angered by the lashings which held it tethered and impotent beside the capstan.

Bolitho brushed the sweat from his eyes and cursed the painful beating of his heart against his ribs. It was now or never. At
any moment they would be seen for what they were and the
gesture would have been in vain. While the others watched him
with fixed fascination he stood up and sauntered openly towards
the gun. Then he seated himself noisily on the deck and folded
his arms across his chest as if trying to sleep.

Farquhar said between his teeth, 'God, look at him! Surely
one of those men will realize who he is?'

But the very openness of Bolitho's movements seemed to have
killed any immediate interest, and while the *Andiron* rolled
from one sickening arc to another the ship's forecastle remained
quiet and undisturbed.

Belsey turned on his side by the hatch coaming and croaked,
'Look! There's an officer coming!'

They watched in stricken silence as the blue and white shape
of a ship's lieutenant made its way slowly forward from the maindeck towards the forecastle ladder. The officer had to pause half-
way up the ladder as a heavier squall than usual struck the ship's
side with a crash of spray which made the foremast vibrate like
a young tree.

Then Stockdale who had turned his gaze back to Bolitho said,
'He's done it!'

As the frigate's bows lifted and yawed against her anchor cable
the nine-pounder began to move. At first the movement was
hardly noticeable, then with its small chocks squealing it
thundered down the full length of the forecastle to smash with
shivering force against the foot of the foremast.

Everyone was yelling and shouting at once. Some of the shouts
changed to cries of fear as the gun swung malevolently as if
controlled by invisible hands and then charged crazily back
across the sloping deck.

The lieutenant called, 'You men! Get handspikes and fresh
lashings! Lively there, or it'll smash through the side!'

The anchor watch rose from their concealed positions and ran
back from the bows to join the stampede of men at the break
of the forecastle. In the centre of the confusion, jubilant and
deadly, the long nine-pounder turned its muzzle as if to sniff
out new havoc, and then careered squeaking and rumbling towards the opposite side. It crashed against another gun and
scattered a shot rack like loose pebbles. The rolling cannon balls
added to the pandemonium, and some could be heard thudding
on to the deck below.

A braver seaman than some leapt across the gun's breech, his
hands already fastening a rope's eye around the muzzle. But as
the gun trundled back again he screamed and fell against the

bulwark to receive the twenty-six hundredweight of wood and metal full on his chest.

Bolitho seized Farquhar's arm and snapped, 'Look! They've got a wedge under the carriage! We've not long now.'

Even as he spoke some of the seamen around the gun turned and stared, their expressions of shock and disbelief changing to cold fury. Bolitho and his two companions slowly retreated towards the bows, the wind and sea at their backs, a converging mass of men driving towards them, all the more terrible because of their complete silence.

Then, to break the spell, a man bellowed, 'Kill them! Cut the bastards down!'

Pressed on by the men behind, the whole mob swept forward, only to sway to an uncertain halt as something like a gunshot echoed around the deck, followed instantly by Stockdale's great shout of triumph.

'It's parted! The cable's cut!'

For a moment longer the *Andiron*'s seamen stared at one another, and then as the realization of their unexpected peril dawned on their minds they hesitated no longer. An officer was yelling from the maindeck, and the cry was carried forward by men who had still managed to keep their heads.

'Hands aloft! Hands aloft! Loose tops'ls!'

From aft Bolitho heard his brother's voice magnified and hardened by his speaking trumpet. 'Man the wheel there!' And then as the ship trembled from stem to stern like a released animal he shouted, 'Mr. Faulkner! Drive those men to the braces!'

Bolitho leaned against the rail, the dirk still held across his body as the frigate heeled still further and began to fall away. Men were running wildly up the shrouds, and already a small patch of canvas was billowing and flapping against the dark sky.

The speaking trumpet called again. 'Cover those men on the fo'c's'le! Shoot them down if they try to escape!'

Belsey wiped his forehead and muttered, 'If our lads *is* out there they'll not want to try an' board!' He peered at Bolitho's tense face. 'I can die in peace now, sir! I reckon we did right well tonight!'

Bolitho saw his face light up with a bright orange glow, and as he turned in surprise the air around him seemed to come alive with the searing whine of gunshot. Stays and halyards parted, and beyond his feet the deck planking splintered and cracked as a thousand balls swept across the forepart of the ship.

Farquhar pointed. 'Look! The battery has fired on us!' He waved his hat. 'The stupid fools have fired on their own men!'

Bolitho pulled him down. 'And us! So keep your head lowered, Mr. Farquhar. You may have use for it still!'

There was no further gunfire, but the one, carefully loaded salvo was sufficient. The prompt action by the *Andiron*'s officers and the quick response of her more level-headed sailors might have taken her clear of danger. But as the whining barrage of grapeshot swept her shrouds and yards free of men and cut down some of the hands still cramming her maindeck, the last opportunity was lost. The black outline of Dogwood Point appeared to grow double in size until the ship was dwarfed beneath it. Even then it looked as if the wind and tide would carry her clear, but as Bolitho pulled his gaping companions to the deck the *Andiron* gave a long-drawn-out shudder, followed instantly by a tremendous crash which threw the remaining seamen from their feet.

Belsey stared up at the sky and crossed himself. 'The main-mast is fallin'! My God, so is the mizzen!'

Fascinated, Bolitho watched the two great masts shiver and then bow very slowly towards the starboard side. Then as stays parted and the angle became more acute the masts thundered down in a flapping tangle of spars and torn sails to plunge eventually into the white-crested water alongside.

Another crash and yet another shook the hull, and while the deck tilted more and more towards the sea Bolitho dragged himself to his feet and shouted, 'She's hard on the sandbar! She'll break her back and capsize in minutes!'

He could hear guns tearing themselves from their lashings and charging across the deck to carve through the screaming, struggling remnants of their late masters. There was no hope of lowering a boat, and nobody even attempted it. Already some were leaping overboard, to be swept away instantly in the strong current. Others ran below as if to find safety in the darkness, and all around voices cried and pleaded, threatened and cursed as their ship broke up beneath them.

The foremast splintered some four feet from the deck and followed the rest into the sea. From a trim frigate the *Andiron* was changed into a lolling, dismasted hulk, already a thing of ugliness and horror.

Belsey shouted above the din, 'There's a hatch cover, sir! Look, floating by the bowsprit!' He watched Bolitho wildly. 'We could jump for it!'

Bolitho turned to watch as the deck shivered yet again and another released gun charged through a group of crawling seamen. Then he saw his brother standing alone by the quarterdeck rail, his body appearing to be at a forty-five-degree angle on the heeling deck. He was not calling any more, but was standing quite motionless, as if to share the agony of his ship to the last.

For a moment longer Bolitho stared towards him, separated

from the other man by far more than a length of deck. He could feel a sudden surge of understanding, even pity, knowing full well how he himself would have felt at such a time.

Then he said sharply, 'Over you go, lads! Jump well clear!'

Belsey and Farquhar leaped together, and he saw them struggling towards the listing square of timber. Stockdale said hoarsely, 'Here, Captain, I'll jump with you!'

As he gripped the rail Bolitho heard a cry behind him and got a vague glimpse of an officer dragging himself up the canting deck towards him. He saw blood on the man's face and recognized him as the lieutenant who had shared his lonely captivity on the poop. The man who had spoken of his farm and the impossible freedom of peace.

Then he saw the pistol in the lieutenant's hand, and even as he tried to pull himself over the rail the deck lit up with a blinding flash, and something like a white-hot iron exploded across his ribs.

Stockdale tore his eyes from Bolitho and gave a short, animal cry. It was as if it had been torn from his very soul. With all his strength he cleaved outwards with his axe, the force of the blow almost decapitating the American officer, so that the man seemed to bow forward in a grisly salute.

Bolitho was vaguely aware of being gathered bodily in Stockdale's arms and then falling through the air. His lungs were bursting and his throat was filled with salt water, and when he tried to open his eyes there was only stinging darkness.

Then he was being hauled up and across the little raft, and he heard Belsey gasp, 'Oh the bloody bastards! They've done for the captain!'

Then Farquhar's voice, shaking but determined. 'For God's sake watch out! There's a boat! Keep down and stay silent!'

Bolitho tried to speak, but could only stare up at Stockdale's misty face framed against the low, scudding clouds. He could hear oars, the swish of a boat cutting through water. But captivity or death were not in vain. Not this time! He listened to the distant boom of surf across the wrecked frigate, the small cries of those who still clung to the shattered hull.

Then, as if from right overhead he heard a sharp cry followed instantly by the click of a flintlock. It was still a dream, and nothing seemed to affect him personally. Only when a loud, English voice called, 'Them's some of the devils down in th' water, sir!' did the slow realization begin to break through the mist and the pain.

Farquhar stood up yelling, 'Don't shoot! Don't shoot, we're English!'

Then everyone seemed to be shouting at once, and as another

boat pulled nearby Bolitho heard one familiar voice as if from far away.

'Who have you got there, Mr. Farquhar?' Herrick's question was shaking with emotion, as if he still mistrusted what he saw.

Farquhar replied, 'It's the captain!'

Bolitho felt hands lifting him up over the gunwale, and saw distorted faces swooping above him in vague, unreal patterns. Hands moved across his ribs, and there was the stabbing fire of fresh pain. Then the muffling comfort of a bandage, and all the time the excited chatter of the men around him. . . . His men.

Herrick had his face very close, so that Bolitho could see the brightness in his eyes. Somehow he wanted to say something, to reassure Herrick, to make him understand.

But he could no longer find the strength even for that. Instead he squeezed Herrick's hand, and then allowed the waiting darkness to gather him in like a cloak.

12. 'CONFUSION TO OUR ENEMIES!'

THE HIGH AFTERNOON SUN blazed down on the sheltered water and threw a dancing pattern of reflections across the deckhead above Bolitho's small desk. Just by turning his head he could see the lush green hillsides of Antigua and a few scattered dwellings around the smooth stretch of St. John's harbour. He had to force himself back to his task of completing his report in readiness for the admiral's scrutiny.

He leaned his forehead against the palm of his hand, feeling the weakness moving through his veins, willing him to rest, to do anything but attend to the waiting duties and orders. Beneath his shirt he could feel the stiff embrace of the bandage, and allowed his mind to move back in time, as he had done so often since his unexpected return to the *Phalarope*.

Like everything else which had happened, it was difficult to separate fact from vague delirious pictures which had come and gone with the stabbing agony of his wound. By the merest chance the pistol ball had passed cleanly between his ribs, leaving a deep and ragged scar which made him wince with every sudden movement.

From the moment he had been dragged aboard the frigate and the boats had been hastily hoisted on deck his memory was blurred and disjointed. The savage and unheralded storm had only helped to add to the nightmare quality of his recollections, and for two weeks the ship had driven south-west ahead of the screaming wind, unable to do other than run before it under all but bare spars. Then as he had struggled to avoid the surgeon's clumsy care and the vague comings and goings of his officers, the wind had moderated and *Phalarope* had at last gone about to beat her way back to Antigua and make her report.

He stared down at the carefully listed descriptions and the mentions of individual names. Nothing must be left out. There was never time for second thoughts.

Each name brought back a different memory and gave him the strange sensation of being an onlooker.

Midshipman Charles Farquhar, who had behaved in a manner far exceeding his actual experience and authority and in the best interests of the Service. A sea-officer who would one day merit senior command.

Arthur Belsey, master's mate, who in spite of his injured arm did everything possible to assist the final destruction of the *Andiron*.

Bolitho tapped his pen thoughtfully against Belsey's name. That last wild leap to safety from the *Andiron's* shattered hull had finished any hope he might have had for return to proper duty. His broken arm was now beyond repair, and he would be a weakened cripple for the rest of his life. With luck, a good mention in the report, plus Bolitho's commendation, might ensure his quick discharge with some suitable recognition for his long service. He would probably return to Plymouth and open a small inn there, Bolitho thought sadly. Every seaport was full of such men, broken and forgotten, but still clinging to the fringe of the sea which had discarded them.

Of Lieutenant Herrick's assault on the artillery there was little to add to the bare facts. If he had tried to embroider the truth, to give Herrick more of the praise which he so richly deserved, the admiral would be quick to see the other side of the coin. That it was largely luck, added to a goodly portion of impudence.

There were so many 'ifs', Bolitho thought moodily.

If the cutting-out party had been dropped closer inshore every man would be either dead or imprisoned. If the tide had not been too strong for Herrick's oarsmen he would have pressed on with his impossible mission, instead of taking the secondary path of his own making.

And what of Stockdale? Without his aid and unshaken loyalty none of these things would have come about at all. In his fight-dulled brain he had worked out each careful move, unaided and without guidance of anyone. And again his last action had been to save Bolitho's life.

But what could he do for him? There was no promotion open to him, no reward which made any sense. Once when he had pattered into the cabin to tend to Bolitho's wound he had asked the giant seaman what he would most cherish as payment for his bravery and his devotion.

Stockdale had not even hesitated. 'I'd like to go on serving you, Captain. I don't have no other wish!'

Bolitho had been considering the idea of getting Stockdale discharged ashore as soon as the ship returned to an English port. There with a little help he might be able to settle down to live his life in peace and security. But as what? Stockdale's prompt and simple reply had driven the suggestion from his mind. It would only have hurt the man.

He wrote: 'And of my coxswain, Mark Stockdale, I can only add that without his prompt action the entire mission might have ended in failure. By cutting the *Andiron*'s cable and thereby allowing her to drift beneath Lieutenant Herrick's fire he ensured the total and complete destruction of the ship with a minimum loss to our own side.' He signed his name wearily across the bottom and stood up. Pages of writing. It was to be hoped that they would be read by those unbiased against the *Phalarope*'s name.

At least Farquhar's uncle, Vice-Admiral Sir Henry Langford, would be pleased. His faith would be sustained, and given time his hopes for his nephew would certainly materialize.

Bolitho leaned out of the stern window and let the warm air caress his face. He could hear the creak of tackles and the steady splash of oars as boats plied back and forth to the shore. The ship had dropped anchor in the early morning, and all day the boats had been busy gathering fresh stores and taking the wounded to more comfortable quarters in the town.

He watched the impressive line of anchored ships, the growing might of the West Indies fleet. Perhaps their presence had dwarfed what might have otherwise been a triumphant return for the *Phalarope*. He frowned at his recurring thought. Maybe the *Phalarope* was still to be treated with shame and mistrust?

Bolitho let his eyes move slowly along the great ships with their towering masts and lines of open gunports. There was the *Formidable*, ninety-eight, fresh out of England with Sir George Rodney's flag at her truck. There were others too, their names already well known in the face of war. *Ajax* and *Resolution, Agamemnon* and *Royal Oak,* and Sir Samuel Hood's flagship *Barfleur*. And there were some he did not recognize at all, no doubt reinforcements brought by Rodney from the Channel Fleet. And they were all gathering for one purpose. To seek out and destroy the great French and Spanish fleet before it in turn drove the British from the Caribbean for good.

He turned his head to look towards his own small squadron on the other side of the anchorage. The elderly *Cassius* dwarfing the little *Witch of Looe*. And one other frigate, the *Volcano*, a vessel very similar to the *Phalarope*.

There was still no summons from the admiral. Just a brief message brought by a pink-faced midshipman to state that Bolitho's report was required before sunset. The frigate was to complete reprovisioning and await further orders. Nothing more.

Nothing more until something even stranger had happened.

Halfway through the forenoon a boat had put off from the *Cassius* and within minutes a dapper lieutenant had reported himself to Bolitho. He had said, 'Rear-Admiral Sir Robert Napier sends his compliments, sir. He wishes to inform you that he will be willing to accept an invitation for dinner tonight aboard your ship. He will be bringing our captain as an additional guest.' The officer had watched the consternation on Bolitho's features and had added helpfully, 'Is there anything I can do to help, sir?'

Bolitho had been stunned by the wording of the message. It was unusual for flag officers to dine aboard their less impressive ships. It was *unknown* for them actually to word their own invitations! Bolitho had thought of his dwindling provisions and the crude results produced from the galley.

The lieutenant from the *Cassius* had obviously been well briefed. 'If I may make a suggestion, sir?'

Bolitho stared at him. 'Anything you can say would be a great help at this moment.'

'My captain is sending some stores from his own pantry, sir. In addition there will be some quite drinkable wine arriving within the hour.' He had ticked off the items on his fingers, his face wrapped in thought. Bolitho had guessed that the young man was not unused to the strange behaviour of his admiral. 'If I may suggest some lean pork, sir? It is in goodly supply in St. John's, and the cheese is newly arrived with Admiral Rodney's ships from England.'

Bolitho had sent for Vibart and the purser, Evans, and explained what was due to happen. For once Vibart seemed too surprised to make any comment, and Bolitho had said curtly, 'See to it, Mr. Vibart. And tell my servant to clean out the cabin and lay a full table.' He had felt suddenly reckless. 'Sir Robert Napier must not expect a flagship's fare aboard a mere frigate!'

Now, looking back, he knew that the momentary recklessness was more likely to have been a result of too much sun on the open quarterdeck and the weakening pain of his wound.

Well, it could not be helped. It was more than obvious what the admiral intended. With Rodney back at the reins he would not wish to lambast *Phalarope* in public. He would not even risk an open argument aboard his own flagship. No, he would come to the *Phalarope* in person, like God coming down to smite a sinner, Bolitho thought bitterly. No success would wipe away his first displeasure or recompense his son's death. If the *Andiron* lay under guard beneath the guns of his own flagship the admiral might have felt differently. But the privateer was now less than nothing. A mere pencilled mark on a chart.

Bolitho sat down heavily on the stern bench, suddenly tired and irritable. He stared at the waiting report and then called, 'Sentry! Pass the word for Mr. Herrick!'

The report could go across to *Cassius* now, he thought angrily. Whatever else happened, he wanted to make sure that his men received recognition and had their efforts properly recorded.

Herrick entered the cabin and stood alertly beside the desk. 'Take this envelope over to the flagship.' Bolitho saw the immediate concern on Herrick's open face and became more irritated. Try as he might he could not keep the dullness from his voice, and knew that in spite of all his efforts his fatigue was wearing him down, so that every word seemed to drag from his lips.

Herrick said carefully, 'May I suggest that you take a rest, sir? I think you have been doing too much.'

'Kindly attend to your duties, damn you!' Bolitho looked away, angry with Herrick but more so with himself for the unfairness of his attack.

'Aye, aye, sir.' Herrick seemed unmoved and said, 'May I ask if this is the full report about the *Andiron*, sir?'

Bolitho turned coldly. 'Of course it is! Were you afraid I'd not included your efforts in this escapade?'

Herrick eyed him steadily. 'I am sorry, sir. It's just that——' He swallowed hard. 'Well, we feel, those of us who took part,' he began to stammer. 'You are the one who should take all the credit, sir!'

Bolitho looked at the deck, the blood singing in his ears. 'You have a happy knack of making me feel ashamed, Mr. Herrick. I would be obliged if you would refrain from doing so in the future!' He looked up sharply, remembering with sudden clarity the sound of Herrick's voice in the darkness, the touch of his hands on his wound. 'But thank you.' He walked slowly to the desk. 'The attack on the *Andiron* was a series of lucky occurrences, Mr. Herrick. The end result may seem to some to justify this. But I must admit that I am still dissatisfied. I believe in luck, but I know that no man can *depend* upon it!'

'Yes, sir.' Herrick watched him closely. 'I just wanted you to know how we all feel.' His jaw jutted stubbornly. 'Whatever lies in store for us, we'll feel all the better for your being in command, sir.'

Bolitho ruffled the papers on his desk. 'Thank you. Now for God's sake go to the *Cassius*, Mr. Herrick.' He watched Herrick duck through the door and heard his voice calling for the quarter boat. It was odd how easy it was to tell his fears to Herrick. Stranger too that Herrick was able to listen without taking advantage of this confidence.

His eye fell on the punishment book, and again he felt the tired glow of anger. While he had been a prisoner of his own brother the old disease had broken out again. Floggings and more floggings, with one man dying of his agony under the lash. Maybe there would be time to heal the damage, he thought grimly. He must accept Vibart's sullen explanations, just as he had had to recognize Okes' report on the attack on Mola Island. He must back up his own officers. And if they were weak and stupid, then *he* must take the blame for that also.

He thought too of Vibart's attitude since his return to command. Due to his wound and the swirling darkness of pain and sickness he had not seen his face at the actual moment of return. But in the days which had followed, the days and nights of creaking timbers and thundering seas against the hull, he had seen him several times. Once when he had been delirious and sweating in his swaying cot he had seen Vibart standing over him and had heard him ask, 'Will he live? Tell me, Mr. Ellice, will he *live*?'

Perhaps he had only imagined it. It was hard to tell now. But for a brief moment he was sure he had heard the true resentment in Vibart's voice. He wanted him to die. Just as his return from the dead was still leaving him resentful and bitter.

The door opened and Stockdale said throatily, 'I've told Atwell to lay out your best uniform, sir. And he'll be in here shortly to prepare the table.' He stared at Bolitho's worn features and then said flatly, 'You'll be taking a rest now, I expect?'

Bolitho glared at him. 'I have *work* to do, damn you!'

Stockdale said, 'I'll just turn your cot down. A couple of hours until the Dog Watches will do you a power of good.' He ignored Bolitho's expression and added cheerfully, 'I see the *Formidable*'s here, sir! She's a fine big ship an' no mistake! But then you'd need a big ship to hold an admiral like Rodney!' He stood for a moment longer, one hand resting on the cot. 'Are you ready now, sir?'

Bolitho gave in. 'Well, just two hours. No more.'

He allowed Stockdale to help him into the cot and felt the tiredness closing in on him once more. Stockdale picked up his shoes and said to himself, 'You rest there. We'll need a good captain tonight to meet the bloody admiral!'

As he turned Stockdale's eye fell on Bolitho's empty rack

above the cot, and for a moment he felt strangely unnerved. The sword was back there somewhere in the wrecked *Andiron*. If only he could have got it back. If only . . .

He stared down at Bolitho's face relaxed in sleep. And he wanted to do something for *me*! He pulled the curtain to shade Bolitho's face from the reflected sunlight and then ambled slowly towards the door.

The tall stone jetty threw a welcome rectangle of dark shade across the *Phalarope*'s cutter as it rested easily alongside the steps. Packwood, the boatswain's mate, paused at the top of the steps and looked down at the lolling seamen in the boat. 'You can take a break. But nobody leaves the cutter, got it?'

Onslow squatted comfortably on the gunwale and pulled a short clay pipe from his shirt. Under his breath he murmured, 'Right, Mr. bloody Packwood! We do all the work, and you go off an' fill your belly with rum!'

Most of the other men were too weary to comment. All day they had pulled the cutter back and forth to the anchored frigate, the first excitement of seeing a friendly port again soon giving way to grumbling complaint.

Packwood was in charge of their party, and although a capable man and considered to be fair in his allocation of work, was plagued by a complete lack of imagination. If he had told the men that the work was essential, not only to the *Phalarope*'s efficiency, but more important, to the welfare of the crew once she returned to sea, some of the bitterness might have been dulled. As it was, Packwood had been too long in the Navy to seek for unnecessary explanations to anything. Work was work. Orders would be carried out at all times without question.

Pook, Onslow's constant companion, raised himself on his scrawny legs and peered towards the distant houses. He breathed out slowly. 'Mother of God! I kin see women!'

Onslow grimaced. 'What did you expect? Bloody clergymen?' He watched the men from beneath lowered lids. 'The officers will be doing themselves well enough. You see if I'm not right, lads!' He spat over the side. 'But just one of you try an' lay a little foot on the shore an' see what happens!' He gestured towards a red-coated marine who was leaning contentedly on his grounded musket. 'That bloody bullock'll place a ball between your eyes!'

John Allday lay across the oars and watched Onslow thoughtfully. Every word the man spoke seemed to be carefully weighted and fashioned before it was uttered. He turned as another seaman named Ritchie spoke up from the bow.

Ritchie was a slow-thinking Devon man, with an equally slow

manner of speech. 'When we was at Nevis Oi didn't see yew runnin' off, Onslow!' He blinked his mild eyes against the glittering water. 'Yew had plenty of time to go an' join your rebel friends!'

Allday watched Onslow, expecting a flash of anger. But the tall seaman merely eyed Ritchie with something like pity. 'An' what good would that do? If I went over to the rebels or to the Frogs, do you think we'd be any better off?' He had their full attention now. 'No, lads. We'd be exchanging one master for another. A fresh flag, but make no mistake, the lash feels the same in any navy!'

Ritchie scratched his head. 'Oi still don't see what yew'm gettin' at!'

Pook sneered, 'That's because you're stupid, you great ox!'

'Easy, lads.' Onslow dropped his voice. 'I meant what I said. Out here or in the Americas a man can live well. A new life, with a chance to make something for himself!' He gave a small smile. 'But to start off right a man needs more than hope. He needs money, too!'

Nick Pochin stirred himself and said uneasily, 'If the war ends an' we gets paid off, we can go back to our homes.'

'And who'll want to remember you there?' Onslow looked down at him coldly. 'You've been away too long, like all the rest of us. There'll be nothing for you but begging on the streets!'

Pochin persisted. 'I was a good ploughman once. I could do it again!'

'Aye, maybe you could.' Onslow watched him closely, his eyes full of contempt. 'You can push your furrow for the rest of your stupid life. Until the furrow is deep enough for some fat squire to bury you in!'

Another voice asked cautiously, 'Well then? What's the point of arguing about it?'

'I'll tell you the point!' Onslow slid from the gunwale like a cat. 'Soon we'll be at sea again. You've seen the fleet mustering here. There'll be no rest for the likes of us. The buggers always need an extra frigate!' He pointed at the *Phalarope* as she swung gently at her anchor. 'There is our chance, lads! The price of our future!' He lowered his voice again. 'We could take the ship.' He spoke very slowly to allow each word to sink in. 'Then we could use her to bargain for our own price!' He looked around their grim faces. 'Just think of it! We could parley with the other side and name our own amount! Then with the money and a free passage we could split up and go our own ways, every one of us richer than he ever thought possible!'

Pochin sat up with a jerk. 'That's mutiny! You mad bugger, we'd all be caught and hanged!'

Onslow grinned. 'Never! After the war is over, who will have time to care about us?'

Pook added gleefully, 'He's right! We'd be rich!'

Allday said, 'And we'd never see England again!'

'And who cares about that?' Onslow threw back his head. 'Do you think we have any chance at present? You saw what they did to Kirk? You've seen men die week by week from disease or the lash. From battle or falling from aloft! And if you escape all that, it's more than likely that you'll get shipped off in some other ship, as *I* was!'

Allday felt a chill at his spine as the uneasiness and resentment moved through the boat like a threat. He said quickly, 'Do you think Captain Bolitho would stand for your ideas?' He looked at the others. 'I've been through the mill, but I trust the captain. He's a brave and fair man. He'll not let us down!'

Onslow shrugged. 'Suit yourself.' He added tightly, 'Just so long as you keep your thoughts *to* yourself, mate! If what I said gets out, we'll know where to come a'hunting!'

There was a scattered murmur of assent from the boat, and Allday realized with sudden shock that Onslow's little speech had already gone deep. It was strange that nobody had noticed before how Onslow had persisted in his efforts to rouse the men to mutiny. Perhaps because his words were carefully chosen and without the blind malice of a wronged sailor. The latter was too common to rouse much more than jeers.

He thought too of Mathias's death in the hold and Onslow's careful manœuvring to get Ferguson the job as captain's clerk. The pattern was like a slow but deadly disease. When the symptoms came to light the victim was already beyond hope.

He said, 'You'll find me ready enough, Onslow! Just you keep out of *my* way!'

Pochin muttered, 'Watch out! 'E's comin' back!'

Packwood stood at the top of the steps, his face sweating profusely from a hasty tankard of rum. 'Right, my babies! Stand by to take on some more casks!' He swung his rattan casually. 'After this trip you can go to your sty and get cleaned up. The admiral is coming to see you all this evening!'

Pook nudged his friend. 'That Allday! Is he safe?'

Onslow ran his fingers around the loom of his oar. 'The men like him. It must be handled carefully. It needs thinking about.' He watched Allday's naked back rippling in the sunlight. 'But *handled* it must be!'

Punctual to the minute, Rear-Admiral Sir Robert Napier stepped through the *Phalarope*'s entry port and removed his hat to receive his due respects. As the shrill pipes faded into silence

and the marine guard presented arms the frigate's small
drummer, accompanied by two reedy fifes, broke into a frail
but jaunty march, and with a final glance around the upperdeck
Bolitho stepped forward to meet his admiral.

Sir Robert nodded curtly to the assembled officers, and as the
marines banged their muskets to the deck he carried out a brief
but searching inspection of the guard, followed at a discreet
distance by Rennie and Captain Cope of the *Cassius*.

Bolitho tried to gauge the admiral's mood or his real reason
for his visit from the man's profile, but Sir Robert's pinched face
remained sphinxlike and unchanging, even when he fired the
occasional question or comment to Rennie about the bearing of
the marines.

At the end of the double line of men he paused to survey the
maindeck. 'You keep a smart ship, Bolitho.' There was nothing
in his dry tone to suggest either praise or suspicion.

'Thank you, sir.' Bolitho wished that he was alone aboard the
flagship in the great stern cabin. There he could face and deal
with anything Sir Robert chose to say. These circumstances kept
every comment on a formal and controlled level which made his
nerves raw with uncertainty.

Whatever the admiral really thought of the ship, Bolitho was
certainly satisfied with her appearance. Long before a frantic
messenger had reported a flurry of activity aboard the flagship
and the smartly crewed barge had pulled swiftly towards the
Phalarope's side, Bolitho had been round his ship to make
absolutely sure that Sir Robert would find no fault with her at
least.

The ship's company had manned the side, every eye on the
small, gold-laced figure in the stern of the barge, and now as the
admiral stood in silent contemplation there was an atmosphere
of nervous expectancy which defied even the fifes and drum on
the quarterdeck.

The admiral said, 'You may dismiss the hands, Bolitho.'

At the prearranged signal the men poured from the maindeck,
and with a clash of weapons the marines wheeled and followed
suit.

Then he said, 'I have read the report, Bolitho. It had a great
deal to say.' His wintry eyes drifted across Bolitho's set features.
'I was particularly interested in the part about the *Andiron*'s
captain.' He saw Bolitho stiffen and continued calmly, 'As a
matter of fact I had received information as to his identity, but
I thought it best to let you carry out your task.' He shrugged,
the movement painful beneath his heavy uniform. 'Of course,
what I did not know was that you were in fact already a
prisoner at his hands.'

'And if you had known, sir?' Bolitho tried to keep his tone relaxed.

'I am not sure. Your first lieutenant is apparently capable in many ways, but I fear he will always be a man who takes orders. A *born* subordinate!'

From the corner of his eye Bolitho saw Captain Cope being ushered below by his own officers, and waited for the admiral to continue. He did not have long to wait.

'*Andiron* is finished. Her very existence was a challenge and an insult to every man in our fleet. I have already passed my views on the matter to the Commander-in-Chief, and I have no doubt you will receive due recognition.' He faced Bolitho squarely. 'However, the fact that your own brother once commanded her and is obviously still alive may in some quarters be taken as some sort of connivance on your part.' He walked to the side and stared at the *Cassius*. 'I do not happen to take that view myself, Bolitho. I gave you the task, not in spite of the *Andiron*'s captain but because of him! You and your ship behaved very well indeed. I have told Sir George Rodney as much.' He added slowly, 'But had your brother been killed it might have been better all round.'

'I think I understand, sir.'

'Of course you do!' The admiral's old testiness was breaking through. 'To be killed is to be forgotten. But if he is taken in the future, he will have no defence. A public trial and hanging will follow. And I think you realize that such disgrace can smear a whole family!'

'Yes, sir.'

Sir Robert rubbed his hands. 'Well, enough of that. You carried out your orders as best you could. That will have to suffice for the present. You did in fact find out about the enemy's intentions. If it is true, it will weigh heavily in your favour.'

He looked up at the gently moving flag and murmured, 'We could do with a little good fortune at the moment!'

Sir Robert lapsed into silence until Bolitho had guided him below to his cabin where the other officers were already seated. With the table fully extended and ten officers already crammed round it, the cabin seemed to be full to capacity, and Bolitho found time to wonder why the admiral had bothered to make this journey away from the comparative luxury of his own quarters. The officers rose to their feet and then sank expectantly into their seats again as Bolitho and the admiral squeezed around the head of the table.

Bolitho also realized for the first time that this was the only occasion he had sat down to dine with all his officers. As Atwell and two hastily recruited messmen began to serve dinner he glanced round the table marking the strange difference which seemed to have come over the familiar faces. They were like embarrassed strangers, he thought vaguely.

Apart from his lieutenants and Captain Rennie he had arranged for the three midshipmen to be present also. As representatives of the ship's warrant officers Proby, the master, and Tobias Ellice, the surgeon, sat in stiff discomfort, their eyes on their plates.

Still the admiral gave no sign of relaxing. In almost complete silence the dinner went on. But with it came the wine, this time brought by the admiral's personal steward, a tall, disdainful man in a scarlet jacket. It was then that Bolitho began to realize what Sir Robert was doing. Coupled with the tension and the unaccustomed richness of the excellent dinner, the wine began to take effect. When Bolitho noticed that the admiral had hardly eaten more than a bird's share of the food and made a point of keeping the same glass of wine at his elbow, he fully understood.

Voices grew louder, and while Sir Robert sat calmly at Bolitho's side the officers began to talk more freely. Bolitho did not know which he felt more. Annoyance or admiration. Not content with a bald report, no matter how concise, Sir Robert was here to hear for himself. From the men who until now had been mere names from Bolitho's pen.

Some of the strain seemed to drain out of him. Right or wrong, the admiral's sly methods were now beyond his control.

Slowly the story began to unfold. Each phase being taken up and polished by a different officer. The attack on Mola Island and the taking of the battery. The more eloquent elaborated on the plan as a whole, the less capable ones contenting themselves on painting the smaller parts to the overall picture.

There was humour too in some of the recollections. Like the story of Parker, the master's mate, who had commanded the jolly boat during the attack on the *Andiron*. Separated from the other boats by the rising sea, he had returned to the *Phalarope* only to have his discomfort further increased by a volley of musket fire from some vigilant marines. And the story of Captain Rennie conducting the retreat from Mola Island with his sword in one hand and half a chicken pie in the other. But this sort of reminiscence did not last.

Sir Robert snapped suddenly, 'And you, Mr. Farquhar, were left behind with the Spanish prisoner?'

Farquhar eyed him carefully, and for a moment Bolitho felt the tension returning to the crowded table. But Farquhar kept his head. Even the fact that it was well known that Sir Robert normally made a point of never addressing anyone below the rank of lieutenant failed to ruffle him.

'Yes, sir. I joined the captain and together we went into captivity.'

The admiral swung round in his chair and peered at Okes, who until now had remained almost silent. 'Your part in this business seems to have kept you very busy, Mr. Okes?'

The lieutenant looked up startled. 'Er, yes, sir. I did what I had to do. There was no other way!'

Sir Robert sipped his wine and eyed him coolly. 'For an officer who has gained nothing but glory you sound remarkably guarded, Mr. Okes. A modicum of modesty is welcome these days, but not when it sounds remarkably like guilt!' For a second longer he held Okes' pale face with his cold eyes, and then he laughed. It was a humourless sound, but it helped to break the sudden and unhappy silence.

'And you, Mr. Herrick?' Sir Robert craned round his own captain to stare along the table. 'Your exploits at Nevis seem a trifle haphazard? But against that you obtained the result you intended no doubt?'

Herrick gave a broad grin. 'Captain Bolitho has already pointed out to me the pitfalls of too much luck, sir!'

'Did he indeed?' The admiral's eyebrows rose slightly. 'I am gratified to hear it.'

And on it went in the same vein. The admiral would question and listen, or when that failed would openly provoke the luckless officer into some excited and unguarded reply.

The loyal toast was called for by the junior officer present. Midshipman Neale, dwarfed on either side by Proby and Ellice, squeaked, 'Gentlemen, the King!' and then sank into a blushing silence.

Bolitho noticed that the admiral's right hand was curled like a claw around his goblet, and when the latter saw him looking at it the admiral snapped petulantly, 'Damned rheumatism! Had it for years!'

For a few moments Bolitho took time to appreciate the man sitting by his side. Not the admiral, with all his petty foibles, his unfair uses of privilege and rank, but the actual man.

He was old, probably in his sixties, and to Bolitho's knowledge had not set foot ashore for more than a few days at a time in the last ten years. He had shifted his flag from ship to ship, dealing with problems and strategy which Bolitho could only half imagine.

The admiral was looking at him unwinkingly. 'Are you still wondering why I came, Bolitho?' He did not wait for an answer. 'I commanded a frigate myself many years ago. The happiest time in the Navy for me. Life was easier in many ways then. But the stakes were not so high.' The shutter dropped again. 'I

came because I wanted to see what you have *made* of this ship.'
He tugged at his chin as if to seek some way of avoiding a
compliment. 'What I find does not displease me entirely.' He
dropped his voice, so that it was almost lost in the newly
awakened conversation around the table. 'Most of your officers
appear to have great respect for you. I know from experience
that it is very hard to come by!'

Bolitho gave a small smile. 'Thank you, sir.'

'And you can remove that stupid smile from your face!' The
admiral shifted beneath his coat. 'I like to know the men whom
I command! When I see a sail on the horizon I don't wish to
know the size of her guns or the state of her paintwork. I want
to know the mind of the man in control, see?' He stared over
the heads of the lolling officers. 'England is fighting for her life.
It is a war of defence now. The attack will come later, perhaps
years later, after I am dead and buried! But until that time
England depends on her ships, maybe only a couple of hundred
ships which are in a position to act to full advantage!' He
tapped on the table, so that the others fell silent and turned to
listen. 'And those ships depend on their captains and no one
else!'

Bolitho opened his mouth to speak but the admiral said
testily, 'Hear me out! I know your reputation now. You are an
idealist in many ways: You have hopes for better conditions for
your men, so that they can make the sea an honourable career
again.' He waved a finger. 'When I was younger I wanted all
those things and more beside. But a good captain is the one who
accepts all these difficulties as they stand and still manages to
run an efficient ship, one worthy of honour and praise!'

He glared round the table. 'Well, gentlemen, did I make
myself understood?'

Bolitho followed his gaze. Vibart, flushed and unsmiling.
Herrick, still grinning and unquenched by the admiral's earlier
sarcasm. Rennie, stiff-backed but with eyes so glassy that they
were beyond focus. Old Daniel Proby, humbled by being with
such illustrious company, yet whose face was stiff with sudden
pride, as if he had heard a deeper meaning in the admiral's
words. And Ellice, the bucolic surgeon, who had been drinking
without pause since they had arrived at table. Bolitho could find
time to pity Ellice. Poorly paid, like all ships' surgeons, it was
no wonder he was more of a butcher than a doctor. It was a race
which would win. Drink or a fatal mistake, it was merely a
matter of time.

Okes, still smarting from the admiral's keen appraisal of the
half-remembered attack on Mola Island. Bolitho noticed how
he kept darting quick, desperate glances towards Farquhar, who

by comparison was calm and impassive, his thoughts perhaps far away. Maybe still back there below the shattered bridge where he had been left to die by the man who now sat watching him. The fact that Farquhar had made neither comment nor complaint must be all the more worrying for Okes, Bolitho thought grimly.

And the two other midshipmen, Maynard and Neale. Excited and untouched by the deeper channels of comment and thought around them. Bolitho was suddenly very aware of his responsibility to all of them.

The admiral stood up and lifted his glass. 'A toast!' His pale eyes flashed below the low beams. 'Death to the French!'

The glasses came up as one and the voices rumbled the reply, 'And confusion to our enemies!'

The admiral called to his captain, 'Time we were going, Cope!'

Bolitho followed him to the upperdeck, only half listening to the scamper of feet and the hurried creak of oars alongside. It was over. The admiral would never admit a mistake, but Bolitho knew that the worst was behind him. *Phalarope* was free of disgrace at last.

He lifted his hat as the admiral crossed to the port and waited until he had vanished to the waiting barge. Then he clamped on his hat and began to pace the deserted quarterdeck, his hands clasped behind him.

The admiral had also made it plain in his own way that if the ship was free of disgrace it was up to her captain to keep her so.

He looked at the riding lights dancing across the water and listened to the plaintive scrape of a violin and the accompanying sadness of an old shanty. If the men could still sing there was hope for all of them, he thought.

13. DANGER FROM WITHIN

THE PIPES SHRILLED in salute as Richard Bolitho stepped through the ornate entry port and on to the *Formidable*'s wide deck. Automatically he doffed his hat to the quarterdeck, and as he returned the greeting of the flagship's officer of the watch he allowed his eyes to move swiftly up and around him, taking in the busy activity, the seemingly endless deck space and the long lines of gleaming guns.

An impeccable midshipman in white gloves crossed the deck at a trot, and under the beady eye of the duty officer led Bolitho aft towards the great stern cabin, to which every available captain had been summoned at an hour's notice.

Bolitho had been toying with his lonely breakfast, pondering on the previous night's strange dinner party and Sir Robert Napier's persistent questions, when Maynard had hurried into his cabin with news of the signal. As he had hurriedly changed into his best uniform Bolitho had wondered why Sir Robert had not mentioned this meeting with the Commander-in-Chief. He must have known about it. As Bolitho had stared unseeingly at his reflection in the bulkhead mirror he had wondered if Sir Robert was making just one more private test. He probably kept his glass trained on the *Phalarope*'s deck from the moment *Formidable* had hoisted her general signal.

He almost cannoned into the midshipman and realized that they had reached the great cabin. The youngster called, 'Captain Richard Bolitho of the *Phalarope*!'

But only those officers standing near the door took any notice, and soon returned to their own busy conversation. For that Bolitho was grateful. He made his way to one corner of the cabin, and as one messman took his hat another placed a tall glass of sherry in his hand. Neither spoke a word, and Bolitho guessed that it was no easy matter to remain calm and unruffled when serving the Commander-in-Chief.

He sipped at his glass and carefully studied the other officers. There must be about thirty captains present, he decided. Captains of every size and shape, of every age and seniority. After the first scrutiny Bolitho decided that he must be the most junior, but just as he had reached this conclusion he felt a movement at his elbow and turned to meet the gaze of a tall, gangling lieutenant whom he vaguely remembered as the commander of the little brig, *Witch of Looe*.

The latter raised his glass and said quietly, 'Your health, sir! I was coming across to see you and tell you how glad I am of your safe return.'

Bolitho smiled. 'Thank you.' He shrugged. 'I am afraid your name has escaped me.'

'Philip Dancer, sir.'

'I will remember it in future.' Bolitho saw the lieutenant loosening his neckcloth with one finger and suddenly realized that he was actually nervous. It was not easy to be so junior in such an illustrious gathering. He said quickly, 'I expect this seems a bit luxurious after your little brig?'

Dancer grimaced. 'Just a bit!'

They both looked at the great stern windows with the wide gallery beyond where the admiral could take an undisturbed walk above the ship's own wake. There were long boxes of potted plants too, and on the handsome sideboard Bolitho caught a glimpse of gleaming silver. Then the buzz of conversation died away, and every man turned to face a side door as the small procession entered the cabin.

Bolitho was shocked to see the change which had come over Sir George Rodney since he had last seen him some two years earlier. Beneath the resplendent uniform with its bright ribbon and decorations the admiral's once upright figure appeared bent and drooping, and his mouth, now set in a tight line, betrayed the illness which had plagued him for so many months. It was hard to picture him as the same man who had overwhelmed a powerful enemy force only two years ago to break through and relieve the besieged fortress of Gibraltar, or who had attacked and sacked St. Eustatius and taken over three million sterling back to England as a prize.

But the eyes were the same. Hard and steady, as if they drew and contained all the energy of his being.

At his side his second in command, Sir Samuel Hood, made a sharp contrast. He looked calm and composed as he studied the assembled officers, his features dominated by his large, arrogant nose and high forehead.

Behind his two superiors Sir Robert Napier looked almost insignificant, Bolitho thought.

Sir George Rodney lowered himself into a tall chair and folded his hands on his lap. Then he said curtly, 'I wanted you all here to tell you that it now seems likely the French and their allies will attempt a final overthrow of English forces in this area.' He coughed shortly and dabbed his mouth with a handkerchief. 'Comte de Grasse has assembled a strong force of ships of the line, the most powerful vessels ever gathered under one flag, and were I in his fortunate position I would have no hesitation in preparing to do battle.'

He coughed again, and Bolitho felt a tremor of uneasiness transmit itself through the watching officers. The strain of years of planning and fighting were paring Rodney away like a knife blade. When he had sailed for England there was not an officer in his fleet who did not believe it was his last journey and that another would return to take his place. But somewhere within that tired body was a soul of steel. Rodney intended to see no replacement in the West Indies to take either the fruits of his hard and unsparing work or the shame and misery of possible defeat.

Sir Samuel Hood said evenly, 'Intelligence has reached us that there is more to de Grasse's intentions than a mere sea victory. He has been gathering seasoned French troops, as well as supplying arms and assistance to the American colonials. He is a shrewd and dedicated strategist, and I believe he intends to exploit whatever successes he has already made.' He looked suddenly across the nearest heads and fixed his heavy lidded eyes on Bolitho.

'The captain of the frigate *Phalarope* has added to this information in no little amount, gentlemen!'

For a few seconds every head in the cabin turned to stare at him, and caught off guard by this turn of events Bolitho felt a tinge of confusion.

In those few seconds he got a vague impression of faces and the reactions of their owners. Some nodded approvingly, and some merely eyed him with barely masked envy. Others studied his face as if to search out some deeper meaning from the admiral's comment. A small item of praise from Hood, and therefore condoned by the great Rodney himself, could immediately mark Bolitho as a firm rival in the ladder of promotion and reward.

Hood added dryly. 'Now that you all know each other, we will continue! From this day forward our vigilance must be stepped up. Our patrols must make every effort to watch each enemy port and spare no efforts to pass information back to me. When de Grasse breaks out it will be swift and final. If we cannot call his challenge and close him in battle we are done for, and make no mistake about it!'

His deep, booming voice filled the crowded cabin, so that Bolitho could almost feel the import of his words like a physical force.

The admiral went on tirelessly and methodically to outline the known whereabouts of supply ships and enemy forces. He showed neither strain nor impatience, and there was nothing at all in his manner to betray the fact that he had only recently returned to Antigua after holding St. Kitts against the whole French military force and their attendant fleet.

Sir George Rodney interrupted, 'I want every one of you to study and familiarize yourselves with my signal requirements.' He looked sharply around the cabin. 'I will not tolerate any officer misunderstanding my signals, any more than I will accept excuses for failing to execute same!'

Several captains exchanged quick glances. It was well known that when Rodney had tried to close the French admiral de Guichen off Martinique, and had not succeeded because some of his captains had failed either to understand or react to his signals, he had been quite ruthless. More than one captain now lived on miserly half-pay in England with nothing but disgrace and bad memories for comfort.

Rodney continued in a calmer tone, 'Watch for my signals. Wherever, and on whatever ship my flag flies, *watch for my signals!*' He leaned back and stared at the deckhead. 'This time there will be no second chance. We will win a great victory, or we will lose everything!'

He nodded to Hood, who added briefly, 'Orders will be issued immediately to senior officers of squadrons. From the moment you leave here the fleet will be in all respects ready for sea. It is up to our patrolling frigates and sloops to watch the enemy's lairs like hounds.' He pounded the table with his fist. 'Give the Commander-in-Chief the scent and the kill is assured!'

There was a murmur of approval, and Bolitho realized that the meeting was over.

Lieutenant Dancer said quietly, 'I wonder where our squadron will be sent? I would hate to miss the final scene when it comes!'

Bolitho nodded, mentally smiling at the picture of the tiny *Witch of Looe* engaging de Grasse's three-deckers. Aloud he said, 'There are never enough frigates. In every war it is the same story. Too little too late!' But he could say it without bitterness. *Phalarope* would be needed more than ever now. With the vast sea areas, the complex hiding places amongst the lines of scattered islands, every frigate would have more than enough to do.

He realized with a start that a sharp-faced flag-lieutenant had crossed the cabin to stop him leaving with the others.

'Sir George Rodney wishes to speak to you.'

Bolitho hitched up his sword and walked across the thick carpet. By the table he halted, half listening to the retreating scrape of footsteps. He heard the door close and the distant shrill of pipes speeding the exit of the fleet's captains, and for a terrible moment he thought he had misunderstood the flag-lieutenant's words.

Rodney was still sitting in his chair, his eyes half closed as he stared at the deckhead. Hood and Sir Robert Napier were completely engrossed in a chart on a nearby desk, and even the messmen seemed busy and oblivious to the young captain by the table.

Then Rodney lowered his eyes and said wearily, 'I know your father, Bolitho. We sailed together, of course. A very gallant officer, and a good friend.' He let his gaze move slowly across Bolitho's tanned face and down the length of his body. 'You have a lot of him in you.' He nodded. 'I am glad to have you under my command.'

Bolitho thought of his father alone in the big house, watching the ships in the bay. He said, 'Thank you, sir. My father wished to be remembered to you.'

Rodney did not seem to hear. 'There is so much to do. So few ships for the task.' He sighed deeply. 'I am sorry you had to meet your only brother in such a fashion.' His eyes were suddenly fixed and unwavering.

Bolitho saw Sir Robert Napier stiffen beside the chart and heard himself reply, 'He believes what he is doing is right, sir.'

The eyes were still hard on his face. 'And what do *you* believe?'

'He is my brother, sir. But if we meet again I will not betray my cause.' He hesitated. 'Or your trust, sir.'

Rodney nodded. 'I never doubted it, my boy.'

Sir Samuel Hood coughed politely, and Rodney said with sudden briskness, 'Return to your ship, Bolitho. I hope that both you and your father will be spared further hurt.' His eyes were cold as he added, 'It is easy to do your duty when there is no alternative. Yours was not an easy choice. Nor will it be if your brother is taken!'

He lapsed into silence, and the flag-lieutenant said impatiently, 'Your hat, sir! And I have just called for your boat!'

Bolitho followed the harassed officer into the sunlight, his mind still dwelling on the admiral's words. So the whole fleet would now know about his brother. In the confined, monastic world of ships permanently at sea he would be discussed and measured against past exploits and future events.

He ran down the gangway to the waiting boat and stared across at the anchored *Phalarope*. Once she had been on trial. Now it was the turn of her captain.

On the evening of the same day that Bolitho had attended the conference aboard the *Formidable,* and with a minimum of fuss or ceremony, the *Phalarope* weighed and headed for the open sea.

The following morning found her a bare fifty miles to the south-west, her full set of sails drawing on the gentle breeze which did little to ease the growing power of the sun.

But this time she was not completely alone. Even from the deck it was possible to see the *Cassius,* her tall pyramids of canvas golden in the early sunlight as she moved on a ponderous and slow parallel course. Somewhere beyond her, hidden below the lip of the horizon, was the frigate *Volcano*. Invisible, and ahead of the slow-moving formation, Lieutenant Dancer's tiny *Witch of Looe* alone enjoyed a certain freedom of movement beyond the scrutiny of her admiral.

Lieutenant Herrick had just taken over the forenoon watch and stood relaxed by the quarterdeck rail as he idly watched the men at work on the maindeck. Earlier the swabs and holystones had made the planking wet and pliable, but now as the heat slowly mounted above the gently swaying hull the decks shone in shimmering whiteness while the normal business of splicing and running repairs was carried out.

It was a peaceful scene, and the combination of warmth and a good breakfast left Herrick drowsy and at ease. Occasionally he cast an eye towards Midshipman Neale to make sure he had his glass trained on the distant flagship, and *Phalarope* was keeping as good a station as the wind allowed.

He could see Lieutenant Okes inspecting the starboard battery of twelve-pounders with Brock, the gunner, and wondered, not for the first time, what was going on behind his strained features. Ever since the raid on Mola Island Okes had been a changed man. And the admiral's casual comments across the dinner table had made him withdraw even more into himself.

As for Farquhar, it was quite impossible to tell what he was thinking. Herrick was not sure if he envied the midshipman's aloof reserve or admired him for it. It was strange how Farquhar's manner had always made him feel on the defensive. Perhaps it was because of his own humble beginnings, he decided. Even here, cooped up in a small frigate, Farquhar retained his distance and individuality.

Herrick tried to imagine what he would have felt if, as Rennie had suggested, Okes had retreated from the raid without care or interest, and had left *him* to die. He pictured himself reacting as Farquhar had done, but instantly in his heart he knew he was deceiving himself. More than likely it would have ended in an open conflict, with a court martial to round it off.

The helmsman coughed warningly, and Herrick turned quickly as Bolitho came up the cabin hatch. He touched his hat and waited as Bolitho walked first to the compass and then stood looking up at the masthead pendant. Then he relaxed slightly as Bolitho crossed to his side and looked down at the busy seamen on deck.

'Another fifty miles to our patrolling station, Mr. Herrick. At this speed we will need another day!' There was impatience in his tone, and a touch of irritation which Herrick was now able to recognize immediately

Herrick said, 'But still it is comforting to see the *Cassius* abeam, sir. If de Grasse ventures out this way we will not be alone!'

Bolitho stared at the distant gleam of sails, but there was no response to Herrick's forced cheerfulness. 'Ah yes, the flagship.' He gave a bitter smile. 'Forty years old, and so much weed on her bottom that she crawls even in a strong gale!'

Herrick looked quickly at the *Cassius*. Up until this moment size and seniority had represented safety and a ready shield He replied, 'I did not know, sir.'

'She was a Dutch prize, Mr. Herrick. Look at the rake of her beakhead!' Then as if realizing that he was speaking from memory of things which were of no importance he added harshly, 'My God, this crawling makes me sick!'

Herrick tried another tack. 'Our orders, sir. May I ask what is expected of us?'

He immediately regretted his impulse and checked himself as Bolitho turned his head away to watch a slowly circling gull. But from the set of the captain's shoulders and the way his hands were locked on the rail he knew that he had struck on something uppermost in Bolitho's mind.

But Bolitho's voice was calm as he answered, 'We will take up our station fifty miles to the west'rd of Guadeloupe and keep contact with our'—he waved his hand towards the open sea—'with our squadron!'

Herrick digested this information slowly. The excitement and frantic preparations at Antigua had left him in little doubt of an impending battle, and he knew that even now most of those proud ships he had watched with an undiminished fascination would have weighed and set sail to complete Rodney's plan to seek out and confront the Comte de Grasse.

Bolitho continued absently, 'There is a chain of ships up and down the Caribbean. One good sighting and the chase will be on.' But there was no excitement in his voice. 'Unfortunately, Martinique is another hundred miles to the south of our patrol area, Mr. Herrick. De Grasse will be there with the bulk of his ships. He will bide his time and then make a dash for Jamaica.' He turned swiftly and stared at Herrick's frowning face. 'And when Rodney's frigates report that the French have sailed, the fleet will attack him!' He shrugged, the gesture both angry and despairing. 'And we shall still be on our station, as useless as a signpost in a desert!'

'But the French may come this way, sir.' Herrick felt Bolitho's bitterness changing his own eagerness to gloom. As he spoke he realized the reason for Bolitho's earlier scorn of the elderly *Cassius*. It was obvious that Rodney was using Admiral Napier's small squadron for the least important part of his overall plan.

'And pigs may lay eggs, Mr. Herrick!' said Bolitho evenly. 'But not in our day!'

'I see, sir.' Herrick was at a loss for words.

Bolitho studied him gravely and then touched his arm. 'Cheer up, Mr. Herrick. I am bad company this morning.' He winced and fingered his side. 'I am thankful that ball missed anything vital. But I could well do without its reminder.'

Herrick watched him thoughtfully. 'You should take more rest, sir.'

'I find it hard even to sit down, Mr. Herrick.' Bolitho shaded his eyes to watch the set of the sails. 'There is so much happening. History is being made all around us!' He suddenly began to pace, so that Herrick had to fall in step to keep up with him. 'De Grasse will come out, I'm sure of it!' He was speaking quickly in time with his steps. 'You saw that freak gale which gave you your chance to rake the *Andiron*? Well, it was rare indeed for this time of year. But later,' he smiled grimly at some hidden memory, 'later in the year the hurricanes hit the West Indies in profusion. From August to September they follow one another like messengers from hell itself!' He shook his head firmly. 'No, Mr. Herrick, de Grasse will come out soon. He has much to accomplish before that time.'

Herrick said, 'But which way will he go?'

'Maybe through the Martinique Passage. But either way he will head straight for the central Caribbean. There are a thousand miles between him and Jamaica. You could lose a whole fleet in such an area. If we fail to make contact when he sails we will never catch him again until it is too late!'

Herrick nodded, at last understanding the full reason for Bolitho's apprehension. 'He has troops and guns. He can occupy any territory he chooses to take.'

'Quite so. The men and stores we dealt with at Mola Island were just a part of his strength. He had hoped to tie down the fleet while he drove on to Jamaica unimpeded. Now he knows we are alerted. His urgency will be all the keener.'

He stopped in his tracks and stared fixedly at the naked horizon. 'If only we knew! If only we could go and find out for ourselves!' Then he seemed to realize that he was showing his own despair and he added briefly, 'You may return to your watch, Mr. Herrick. I have some thinking to do.'

Herrick walked back to the rail, but as the sun beat down on the tinder-dry decks, he was constantly aware of Bolitho's shadow. Back and forth, up and down.

When Herrick had been a midshipman he had dreamed of the time when he might attain the impossible heights of a lieutenant. From then on he had watched the slow path to promotion, gauging his own progress by the experience or the incompetence of his superiors. And all the time, nursed in the back of his mind like some precious jewel, was the idea that one day he might at last hold a command of his own.

But now, as he watched Bolitho's restless shadow and imagined the fretting thoughts which kept it company, he was not so sure.

Halfway through the forenoon the pipes shrilled, 'Stand easy!' With varying degrees of relief the frigate's seamen threw themselves into patches of shade to make the most of the short break in routine.

John Allday stayed where he had been working, with his legs astride the larboard cathead, his bronzed body sheltered from the sun by the jibsail. In the foremost part of the ship he had been engaged in cleaning and scraping one of the great anchors, and as he squatted comfortably above the small bow wave he rested one foot on the anchor's massive stock, feeling its warmth against the bare skin. At his back the other members of the working party lounged in various stages of abandon, while above their heads the air was tinged with a slow-moving vapour of smoke from their long pipes.

Old Ben Strachan picked up a new rope and examined the eye-splice which one of the ship's boys had just completed. 'Not bad, youngster. Not bad at all.' He sucked noisily at his pipe and peered aft the length of the *Phalarope*'s deck. 'Is that the cap'n pacin' up an' down?'

Pochin, who was lying with his head cradled on his thick arms, muttered, 'Course it is! Must be mad to be in this 'eat when 'e could be down in 'is cabin!'

Allday swung one leg and stared thoughtfully at the clear water below him. Pochin was still worried about Onslow's words in the cutter. He was edgy, as if he realized his own guilt. Just listening to such talk made a man liable to be labelled a conspirator.

He turned slightly to look aft, and across the length of the ship he saw Herrick, watching him from the quarterdeck. The lieutenant gave him a brief nod of recognition before returning to his own contemplation, and Allday suddenly remembered that moment on the crumbling cliff when he had stopped Herrick from falling to the rocks below. In spite of his original intention to stay apart from internal affairs in the *Phalarope,* and to keep clear of loyalty to either faction, Allday was beginning to realize that such neutrality was impossible, even dangerous.

Allday liked Herrick, and recognized what he was trying to do. He was always ready to listen to complaints from his division, and was never quick to award punishment. But he was no fool, and few took advantage of his humane manner a second time.

Allday could see the captain still pacing the quarterdeck at the weather rail, coatless with his shirt open to his chest and his dark hair pulled back to the nape of his neck. He was a harder man to know, Allday thought, but it was strangely reassuring to see him back at his familiar place on the poop. Allday, perhaps better than most, knew the reputation of the Bolitho family. On his visits to Falmouth he had often heard them discussed in the taverns, and had even seen the house which was the captain's home. It was strange to realize that he had a brother fighting on the other side. Allday wondered how he would have felt. Not only that, but Bolitho's brother was said to have deserted from the Navy, a crime which could only be wiped out at the end of a rope.

He came back from his thoughts as Ferguson climbed up from the maindeck and walked across to the rail. He looked strained and self-conscious in his clean clothes, a marked contrast to the tired and sweating seamen who had once been his companions.

Ferguson fidgeted for a few moments and then said, 'Do you think we will see any more fighting?'

Pochin turned his head and growled, 'You should know! Aren't you in the captain's pocket?'

Allday grinned. 'Don't pay any attention to Nick.' He dropped his voice. 'Has Onslow been after you again?' He saw Ferguson's pale eyes flicker.

'Not much. He just passes the time with me sometimes.'

'Well, remember my warning, Bryan!' Allday studied him closely. 'I've not told a living soul aboard, but I believe he had a lot to do with Mathias's death.' He saw the disbelief on Ferguson's face and added sharply, 'In fact, I'm sure he had!'

'Why should he do a thing like that?' Ferguson tried to smile, but his mouth remained slack.

'He's a bad one. He knows no other life but this. He came to the fleet as a child. His world is bounded by the sides of a wooden hull.' He ran his hands along the carved cathead. 'I've met a few of his kind before, Bryan. They're as dangerous as wolves!'

Ferguson said, 'He'll not make trouble. He wouldn't dare!'

'No? And why do you think he keeps asking about the cabin? He's biding his time. His sort have a lot of patience.'

'The captain'd not stand for any more trouble!' Ferguson showed his agitation in the quick movement of his hands. 'I've heard him telling Mr. Vibart about taking care of the men. About how he wants them treated.'

Allday sighed. 'You see? You're even telling me what you've heard. If you want to stay safe you'd better keep what you know to yourself.'

Ferguson stared at him. 'You don't have to tell me!' He tightened his mouth with sudden anger. 'You're just like the others. You're jealous because of my job!'

Allday turned away. 'Suit yourself.'

He waited until he heard Ferguson moving aft again. Then he turned to watch as Onslow stepped from beside the mainmast

to stop his passing. He saw Onslow grinning and patting Ferguson on the shoulder.

Pochin's hard voice interrupted his thoughts. 'What d'you
reckon? D'you think Onslow is right?' He sounded worried. 'If
there is more trouble aboard this ship we'll all be in it. We'll
have to take sides!'

Allday replied flatly, 'You'd be a fool to pay heed to that
one!' He tried to put some value to his words. 'Anyway, the
captain'll make short work of him if he tries anything!'

Pochin nodded doubtfully. 'Maybe. Dyin' under a French
broadside is one thing, but I'll not cough out blood for 'im or
the buggers like Onslow!'

The pipes shrilled again, and the men stirred themselves back
to work.

Allday kept his eyes down to his task as Quintal, the boatswain, and Josling, one of his mates, walked forward to inspect
the forecastle. He heard Josling say, 'I see that the old *Cassius*
was signalling just now, Mr. Quintal?'

Quintal replied in his deep voice, 'Aye, lad. We'll be hauling
off shortly to our own little patrol area. It'll be a long job, I
wouldn't wonder, so see that you keep the hands busy. There's
nothing worse for discipline than too much free time.' The rest
of his comments were lost to Allday as the two men moved up
towards the bowsprit, but he had heard enough.

Phalarope was to be alone again, and out of sight of the flagship. The boatswain was right. With the heat and the dull
monotony of an empty patrol, Onslow would find a good breeding ground for more trouble if he could.

He looked sideways at his silent companions, each man
apparently engrossed in his own task, yet each no doubt thinking of that green patch of land which they had just left behind.

No ordinary seaman had set foot ashore. Some of the crew had
not left a deck for years. It was hardly surprising that men like
Onslow could find a ready audience.

He shaded his eyes and stared towards the horizon. Already
the distant two-decker seemed smaller, her hull lost in the heat
haze below the clear sky. Her sails had merged into one shining
pyramid, and as he watched she appeared to sink lower in the
glittering sea. Another hour and she would have vanished
altogether.

After that, he thought coldly, you could trust no man.

Deep below the forecastle deck where Allday sat immersed in
his own thoughts was the *Phalarope*'s cable tier. In harbour it
was a spacious, empty place, but now, as the frigate moved listlessly on the calm water, it was packed to the deckhead with the

massive anchor cables. Coil upon coil, the great, salt-hardened ropes added to the sour stench of the bilges and the richer smells of tar and hemp. Stout upright pillars on either side of the shelving hull held the cables clear of the timbers to allow easy access to the ship's fabric at all times. These 'carpenter's walks' as they were named ran the full length of the hull below the water-line to afford inspection and, if necessary, repairs in time of battle. Little wider than a man's body, they were usually in total darkness.

But now, as the bow wave swished dully against the timbers and furtive rats continued their endless search for food, a small, shaded lantern cast an eerie light against the piled cable and threw a distorted reflection back to the faces of the men squeezed in the narrow passageway.

Onslow held the lantern higher and peered at the waiting men. He only had to count them to be sure. He knew each man's face and name without need for further examination.

'We must be quick, lads! We'll be missed if we stay too long!'

Like an echo he heard Pook's voice. 'Just pay heed to wot 'e says!'

Onslow's teeth gleamed in the darkness. He could feel his legs shaking with wild excitement, like the effect of rum on an empty stomach. 'We're pulling away from the other ships. I think the time has almost come to carry out our plan.'

He heard a dull murmur of agreement and grinned even broader. Just by saying *our* instead of *my* acted on these men like the crack of a whip.

'From what Ferguson has told me Bolitho intends to run to the south'rd. The *Phalarope*'ll be on the end of the patrol line. No chance of meeting any of the others, y'see?'

A voice asked from the darkness, ' 'Ow can we take the ship on our own?' He broke off with a yelp as Pook drove his elbow into his ribs.

Onslow said calmly, 'Leave that part to me. I'll tell you how and when.' He looked at the crouching line of dark figures. All the ones who had come with him from the *Cassius,* and several more recruited in the *Phalarope*. It was far more than he had dared to hope. 'We must get rid of the bloody bullocks. Without their red coats athwart the quarterdeck it'll be easy.'

Pook asked, 'Wot about Allday an' the like?'

'Ah yes.' Onslow smiled crookedly. 'Master John Allday.'

Pook added gloomily, 'The lads *listen* to 'im!'

'And if anything happened to Allday we'd get a lot more on our side, eh?' Onslow's brain was moving ahead of his words. 'But it has to be clever. If it looks like our doing we might as well hang ourselves!'

They all froze as heavy footsteps sounded overhead. Then as they died away Onslow continued easily, 'I think Allday guesses what happened to Mathias. He's too clever to live, is that one!' He reached out and gripped Pook's arm. 'So we'll make him a bloody martyr, shall we?' He gave a rumbling laugh. 'Now we can't do fairer than that!'

The same uncertain voice tried again. 'We'll be cut down afore we can raise a finger, I say!'

'*I'll* cut you down, you bugger!' For a moment Onslow's good humour retreated. Then he added more calmly, 'Now listen to me, all of you! We must wait a bit longer to get the lads more worried. Then when the time's ripe I'll tell you what I want. That fool Ferguson can keep an eye on the captain's log for me, just so that I know where we are. When we get a bit nearer some land, I'll be ready.'

He snapped his fingers. 'Those weapons we brought off from Mola Island. Have you got 'em safely stowed?'

Pook nodded. 'Aye, they'll not be discovered!'

'Right then. Get back to your work now, lads. And stay out of trouble. You're all marked men anyway, so don't give the bastards a chance to nail you!'

He watched them creeping away into the darkness beyond the dim lantern and felt satisfied. Now, just as he had told those poor sheep, it was just a matter of time.

14. BLOOD AND FRESH WATER

TOBIAS ELLICE, the *Phalarope*'s surgeon, arose wheezing from his uncomfortable stooping position and threw the sweat-stained bandage out of the open stern window. 'Right, sir. You kin stand up now if you like.' He stepped away from the bench seat as Bolitho threw his legs over the side and lifted himself to his feet.

Ellice mopped his streaming face and peered closely at the rough scar across Bolitho's ribs. 'Not a bad job of work, if I says so meself!' He beamed and licked his lips. 'It's thirsty work, an' no mistake!'

Bolitho touched the scar with his fingertips and then stood facing the open windows to allow the tiny breeze to play across his bare skin. It was good to be rid of the bandage, he thought. Its very embrace was a constant reminder of the *Andiron* and all that had gone before. It was well to leave it all in the past. There were troubles enough to deal with today and the next day after that.

It was a full fourteen days since they had sailed with the squadron from Antigua, and almost every one of them had been like this one. Hardly a lick of air which could seriously be called a breeze to fill the hungry sails or even to ventilate the ship. And all the time a broiling sun which seemed to bleach the colour from the sky itself. The nights brought little respite. Between decks the air remained humid and heavy with damp, and the seamen were further wearied by the constant calls to trim sails, only to be dismissed cursing and despairing as the wind died before a single sheet could be handled.

It was enough to break even the sturdiest heart, Bolitho thought heavily. And coupled with the fact that they had not sighted a single sail, and knew nothing of events beyond the mocking horizon, he found it was all he could do to restrain his own mounting impatience.

'How are the men?' He reached for a clean shirt and then relented. The old one would have to do. There was little point in badgering his servant to wash more clothes than necessary.

Ellice shrugged. 'Not happy, sir. 'Tis bad enough as it is without hungering after a drink all the time.'

'Water is precious, Mr. Ellice.' It was now reduced to a pint a day per man, which was less than adequate. But there was no telling how long it would be before their senseless vigil was broken. He had increased the daily ration of *Miss Taylor*, as the rough white wine from the victualling yard was named, but its satisfaction was only temporary. Within a few hours the drinker would be left as dry as before. He added as an afterthought, 'They must get as much fresh fruit as we can spare. It is the only thing to keep down disease out here.'

It was odd how much clamour and argument there had been in Antigua when he had insisted on a full cargo of fruit to be shipped for his crew. Maybe that was what the admiral had meant when he had said, 'You are an idealist in many ways!' But to Bolitho's practical mind it was only being sensible. Even though he had paid for the fruit from his own pocket he knew it was more of a good investment than a method of arousing favouritism with his men. A fit and healthy sailor was worth far more than a basket of fruit. In fact, the normal wastage did not stop there. Other men were used to care for their sick comrades, and their work had to be taken on by still more men. And so it went on, yet there were still plenty of captains who could see no further than their prize money as a measure of success.

He tucked his shirt into his breeches and said, 'Take a glass if you will, Mr. Ellice.' He looked away ashamed as the big, untidy man shambled quickly to the sideboard and slopped a generous portion of brandy into his goblet. Ellice's hand shook as he poured and downed a second glass before mumbling, 'Thankee, sir. That's the first today!'

Bolitho glanced at the shadow of the stern, close to the barely moving wake. The sun was high in the sky. It was more than likely that Ellice had already consumed a goodly portion from his private store.

'I did not see you go ashore in Antigua, Mr. Ellice? You had only to ask.'

Ellice licked his lips and shot a quick glance at the decanter. 'I never go on land now, sir, thankee all the same. At first I used to wander like a lovesick girl amongst the grass and weep when the shoreline dropped over the sea's edge.' He saw Bolitho nod towards the decanter and hurriedly poured another drink. 'Now when the ship sails I hardly looks up.' He shook his head as if to restore some broken memory. 'Anyway, I've seen it all!'

There was a tap at the door, but before Bolitho could call it burst open and Lieutenant Vibart stamped into the cabin. He looked strained and angry, and wasted no time in breaking his news.

'I have to report that we are almost out of fresh water, sir.'

Bolitho studied him for a few seconds. 'What do you mean?'

Vibart glanced round the cabin. 'I have the cooper outside, sir. It might save time if *he* told you!'

Bolitho ignored Vibart's insolent manner. 'Send him in.' He was glad that the sea's reflected glare kept his face in deep shadow. At every turn events seemed to twist and mock at his efforts. Now this, the one predominant worry, had been fanned alight even as he had been openly discussing it with Ellice.

Mr. Trevenen, the *Phalarope*'s cooper, was an undersized warrant officer who was known for his extremely bad eyesight. Too long in too many darkened holds had left him half blind, like some creature of the night. Now, as he stood blinking and shifting uneasily under Bolitho's stare he looked small and defenceless.

Bolitho stifled his usual feeling of pity which inevitably arose on the rare occasions of meeting the cooper. 'Well, spit it out, man! What the hell have you discovered?'

Trevenen gulped miserably. 'I've been doin' my rounds, sir. You see I always does 'em on a Thursday. If you build up a system of inspections you can . . .'

Vibart bellowed, '*Tell* him, you old fool!'

The cooper said in a small voice, 'Two thirds of me casks are foul with salt water, sir.' He peered at his feet. 'I don't understand it, sir. In all my years afloat I never seen nothin' like it.'

'Hold your damned tongue!' Vibart looked as if he would strike the wretched man. 'Admit that you made a mistake at

Antigua. You're so bloody blind you don't know the difference! If I had my way I'd . . .'

Bolitho made himself speak slowly to give his mind time to recover from the shock. 'If you please, Mr. Vibart! I think *I* can evaluate the extent of this information!' He turned again to Trevenen. 'Are you sure now?'

The wrinkled head nodded violently. 'No mistake about it, sir!' He looked up, his faded eyes filling his face. 'In all my years, sir, I never . . .'

'I know, Mr. Trevenen, you just told us.' Bolitho added to Vibart sharply, 'Have the casks checked for yourself, Mr. Vibart. Separate the fresh ones from the others, and see that the salt water is drained away and the wood cleaned off.'

He strode to the chart and leaned across it, his face set in a deep frown. 'We are here.' He tapped the chart with the heavy dividers. 'Fifty miles south-west of Guadeloupe, give or take a mile.' He picked up his ruler and ran it across the thick parchment. 'There are some small islands to the south of us. Uninhabited and useless except for wrecking the unwary sailor.' He made a small cross on the chart and stood up. 'Call the hands and prepare to wear ship, Mr. Vibart. This breeze, slight though it is, will suit our purpose.'

He looked across at Trevenen. 'Whatever the reason for this, be it seepage or sheer carelessness, we must have water, and quickly! So prepare your party to take on a fresh supply.'

Trevenen blinked at him. He looked like a man who had just heard of a miracle at first hand.

Bolitho continued, 'We should make a landfall within two days, sooner if the wind finds us again. I have visited these islands before.' He touched the scar beneath the dark forelock of hair. 'There are streams and reliable pools on some of them.'

Vibart said heavily, 'The admiral gave no orders about leaving our station, sir.'

'Would you have the men die of thirst, Mr. Vibart?' Bolitho stared down at the chart again. 'But if you are worried I will have my clerk make an entry in the patrol report today.' He smiled wryly. 'Should I vanish again, you will have the necessary shield from Sir Robert's anger!'

Ellice said dreamily, 'I was in a ship once when this 'appened. Two of the seamen ran amuck for want of water!'

Vibart snarled, 'Well you at least will be untroubled by *that*, I imagine!'

Bolitho smiled in spite of his troubled thoughts. 'Carry on, Mr. Vibart. Have the hands mustered to their stations. I will be up directly.' He watched the door quiver in its frame and then said to Ellice, 'You asked for that, Mr. Ellice!'

The surgeon was unmoved. 'With all due respect to the first lieutenant, sir, but he was too long aboard a slaver, if you ask me. To 'im men is just bloody extra cargo!'

'That will do, Mr. Ellice.' Bolitho glanced at the decanter. As if by magic it had emptied during his talk with Trevenen. 'I suggest you take a turn around the maindeck.'

Ellice peered at him uncertainly. Then he grinned. 'Aye, sir. So I will. It'll give me a fair appetite!' He ambled away, his shabby coat hanging around him like a sack. Rain or fine, sun or sheeting squalls, Ellice was never dressed differently. Some had even suggested he slept in his clothes.

Bolitho dismissed him from his mind as the pipes shrilled and the decks thudded with bare feet as the men ran to their stations for wearing ship.

Within an hour the *Phalarope* had gone about, her sails flat and listless in the relentless glare. But in spite of the outward stillness there was enough power in the breeze to cause a small ripple beneath her gilt figurehead, and at the mainmast truck the commissioning pendant flapped and whipped with lonely agitation, as if it commanded the only strength the wind had to offer.

Lieutenant Herrick walked slowly aft along the maindeck, his eyes moving from side to side as he watched the men flaking down ropes and putting a last tautness in sheets and braces. He knew that they were discussing the news about the contaminated water, and other things beside, but as he passed even the usually friendly ones fell silent. The past two weeks of heat and dull discomfort were showing their teeth now, he decided. No one complained or grumbled any more. That was the worst sign of all.

He halted as Midshipman Maynard appeared below the quarterdeck and leaned heavily on a twelve-pounder. Beneath his tan his thin features were as pale as death, and his legs looked as if they were near collapse.

Herrick crossed to his side. 'What is it, lad? Are you ill?'

Maynard turned and stared at him, his eyes opaque with fear. For a moment he could not speak, then the words poured from his dry lips in a flood.

'I've just come from below, sir.' He screwed up his face. 'I was sent down to the orlop to fetch Mr. Evans.' He swallowed hard and tried to speak coherently. 'I found him in his cabin, sir.' He retched and swayed against the gun.

Herrick gripped his arm and whispered fiercely, 'Go on, lad! What the hell is wrong?'

'Dead!' The word was wrung from his lips. 'My God, sir! He's been cut to pieces!' He stared at Herrick's grim features, reliving the nightmare of his discovery. He repeated faintly, 'Cut to pieces.'

'Keep your voice down!' Herrick struggled to control his shocked thoughts. In a calmer tone he called, 'Mr. Quintal! Take Mr. Maynard aft and see that he is kept alone!'

The boatswain, caught in the act of reprimanding a seaman, stared from one to the other. He touched his forehead and said gruffly, 'Aye, aye, sir.' Then he asked quietly, 'Is somethin' up, sir?'

Herrick looked at Quintal's broad, competent face and answered flatly, 'It seems that the purser is dead, Mr. Quintal!' He saw the quick start of alarm in the man's eyes and added, 'Show no sign! This ship is like a tinderbox as it is.'

Herrick watched the boatswain leading the young midshipman into the shadow of the quarterdeck and then glanced quickly around him. Everything looked as it had two minutes earlier. Lieutenant Okes had the watch and was standing at the quarterdeck rail, his eyes up at the topsails. Further aft Herrick could just see the captain in conversation with Vibart and Rennie, while at the wheel the two helmsmen looked as if they had been at their posts since time began.

Herrick walked slowly towards the lower cabin hatch. He made himself move calmly, but his heart felt as if it was in his throat.

With all hands employed trimming sails the lower deck was deserted and strangely alien. A few lanterns swung on their hooks, and as he began to climb down the second and last ladder Herrick could sense an air of menace and danger. Even so, he was totally unprepared for the sight in the purser's tiny cabin.

Deep in the hull of the ship the stillness was all the more apparent, and the solitary lantern on the low deckhead cast a steady circle of light on a scene which made Herrick's throat choke with bile. Evans, the purser, must have been secreting a bag of flour for his own private uses when his assailant had struck him down. He lay spread-eagled on the upended sack, his eyes bright in the lamplight, while from his severed throat a great torrent of dark blood seeped and congealed in the scattered flour. There was blood everywhere, and as Herrick stared with fixed horror at the corpse at his feet he saw that Evans had been stabbed and slashed as if by some crazed beast.

He leaned again the door and touched his face with his hand. His palm felt cold and clammy, and he thought of young Maynard alone with this appalling spectacle. No one could have blamed him if he had rushed screaming to the upperdeck.

'My God!' Herrick's voice hung in the gloom in a mocking echo. He almost cried out again as a foot rasped on the ladder behind him, but as he groped blindly for his pistol he saw that it was Captain Rennie, his scarlet coat like a reflection of the blood on the cabin deck.

Rennie brushed past him and stared fixedly at the corpse. Then he said coldly, 'I'll put two of my best men on guard here. The cabin must be sealed until there has been an investigation.' He eyed Herrick meaningly. 'You know what this means, don't you?'

Herrick felt himself nod. 'I do.' He pulled himself together. 'I'll go and tell the captain.'

As he climbed up the ladder Rennie called quietly, 'Easy, Thomas. There will be at least one guilty man watching your face on deck!'

Herrick glanced back at the open cabin door, making himself form a final picture of the murdered man. 'I suppose I was expecting something like this.' He bit his lip. 'But when it comes, it's still a shock.'

Rennie watched him go and then stepped carefully over the glaring corpse. Ignoring the thing by his polished boots he began to search methodically amongst the scattered souvenirs of the purser's life.

Herrick's face was like stone as he crossed to the weather side of the quarterdeck to where Bolitho was still speaking with Vibart. He touched his hat and waited until Bolitho turned to face him.

'Well, Mr. Herrick?' Bolitho's smile of welcome faded. 'Is it more trouble?'

Herrick looked quickly around him. 'Mr. Evans has been murdered, sir.' He spoke in a tight, clipped voice which he no longer recognized. 'Maynard found him a few minutes ago.' He ran his hand across his face. It was still cold, like the mark of death.

Bolitho said slowly, 'What have you done so far, Mr. Herrick?' There was nothing in his question to betray what he must be feeling, and his features were composed in an impassive mask. 'Take your time. Just tell me what you saw.'

Herrick moved closer to the rail, his eyes on the glittering water. In a slow, flat voice he described the events from the moment Maynard had appeared on deck to the actual second of realization.

Bolitho listened in complete silence, and at Herrick's side Vibart stood swaying with the ship, his hands opening and closing from either anger or shock at Maynard's discovery.

Herrick concluded heavily, 'He had not been dead long, sir.' He found himself repeating the midshipman's words. 'He has been cut to pieces!'

Captain Rennie marched across the deck and said crisply, 'I have put some men on guard, sir.' He saw Bolitho looking at his boots and bent quickly to wipe a bright stain from the polished leather. He added calmly, 'I've had a good look round, sir. Evans' pistols are missing. Stolen most likely.'

Bolitho eyed him thoughtfully. 'Thank you, gentlemen. You have both behaved very well.'

Vibart said vehemently, 'What did I tell you, sir? Softness with these scum is no use! They only understand a hard hand!'

Bolitho said, 'His pistols, you say?'

Rennie nodded. 'He had two small weapons. He was very proud of them. Gold-mounted and quite valuable, I believe. He said he got them in Spain.' He fell silent, as if he, like the others, was thinking of the dead man as he had once been. One of the most disliked men in the ship. A man with grudges and hates more than most. It was not difficult to understand that he would have an equal number of enemies.

Proby climbed the ladder and touched his hat. 'May I dismiss the watch below, sir?' He seemed to realize that he was intruding and muttered, 'Beggin' your pardon, sir!'

Bolitho said, 'Have the hands stay at their stations, Mr. Proby.' They all looked at him. There was a new coldness in Bolitho's voice and an unfamiliar hardness in his eyes. To Rennie he continued, 'Post sentries at every hatch. Nobody will go below.'

Vibart murmured, 'So you'll see it *my* way, sir?'

Bolitho swung round. 'Someone is guilty, Mr. Vibart. But not the whole ship! I don't want this man to escape, or his actions to contaminate the rest of our people!' In a calmer tone he said, 'Mr. Herrick, you will take the berth deck with Mr. Farquhar and the boatswain. Captain Rennie will search the rest of the ship with his own men.' He looked down at the waiting seamen on the decks and gangways. 'Mr. Vibart, you will take the upper-deck yourself with Mr. Brock. Look in every locker and beneath each gun, and be as quick as you can!'

He watched them troop down the ladder and then returned his attention to the crowded maindeck. Every sailor was now fully aware that something was wrong. He saw one nudge his companion, and another fell back fearfully as Vibart and the gunner pushed through the watching men.

Perhaps Vibart was right after all? He gripped his hands together behind him with such force that the pain helped to control his whirling mind. No, he must not think like that. Without faith there was nothing. Nothing at all.

As the minutes dragged on a growing wave of apprehension moved across the crowded maindeck like smoke from an uncontrollable fire. The seamen at the foot of the mainmast parted to allow Vibart and the gunner to move through and then shuffled together as if for mutual support.

Pochin rubbed his tarry hands on his trousers and glared angrily after Vibart's bulky figure. 'What the hell's happenin'?' He reached out as a boatswain's mate made to pass him. 'Do *you* know, Mr. Josling?'

Josling darted a quick glance at the quarterdeck. 'The purser. 'E's dead!'

A new ripple of uneasiness broke over the waiting men, and Pochin stared across at Allday who was leaning watchfully against the mast. 'Did you hear that, man?'

Allday nodded and then slowly turned his head to look at Onslow. He was standing a bit apart from the others, his legs relaxed, his brown arms hanging loosely at his sides. But there was an air of animal watchfulness about the man, betrayed in the flat hardness of his eyes and the excited dilation of his nostrils. Allday released his breath very slowly. In his own mind he had no doubt as to where the finger of accusation would point.

Old Strachan muttered, 'Looks bad, don't it? I got a feelin' that we're in for another squall!'

There was a sudden burst of activity from the quarterdeck, and as every head turned aft Captain Rennie's marines trooped up the ladders and formed a solid scarlet barrier athwart the deck. Sergeant Garwood dressed the ranks and then took his place beside the small drummer. Captain Rennie stood coolly ahead of his men, one hand resting on his sword hilt, his face empty of expression.

From the side of his mouth the sergeant rasped, 'Fix bayonets!' Every hand moved as one, the blades rippling along the swaying front rank before clicking into place on the long muskets.

On deck the tension was almost unbearable. Every man watched transfixed, afraid to speak or turn his head for fear of missing some part of this new drama. Here and there a hand moved to dash away the sweat, and somewhere in the packed throng a man began to cough nervously.

Allday saw the captain speaking with Lieutenant Herrick and the boatswain, and watched as Bolitho shook his head at something one of them said. It might have been anger or disbelief. It was impossible to tell.

Vibart had realized that the search was over, and moved slowly aft, his hands pushing the silent men aside like reeds, his red-rimmed eyes fixed on the little group behind the marines.

Pochin whispered, 'We'll soon know now!'

Allday darted another glance at Onslow. For a moment he felt something like pity for him. He had been so long penned up in a ship he had known no other life but the ceaseless battle of the lower deck.

Captain Bolitho's voice broke into his thoughts, and when he looked aft again he saw him at the quarterdeck rail, his hands resting on the starboard carronade as he stared down at the assembled seamen.

'As most of you know by now, Mr. Evans the purser is dead. He was killed in his cabin a short while ago, without pity, and without reason.' He broke off as Herrick descended one of the ladders to speak to the first lieutenant. Then he continued in the same even tone, 'Every man will stand fast until the culprit has been taken!'

Pochin's scarred face was streaming with sweat. He said in a hoarse voice, ''E's got some 'opes! Every bastard in the ship 'ated the bloody purser!'

But no one responded or even gave him a glance. Every eye was on Vibart as he moved purposefully along the maindeck with Brock at his back.

Even the sound of sea and canvas seemed stilled, and as Vibart halted below the mainyard Allday could hear his heavy breathing and the squeak of his sword belt.

For a few seconds longer the awful suspense continued. Then, as Vibart ran his eye slowly around the watching faces, Brock stepped forward and lifted his cane.

'That's him, sir! That's the murderous cur!'

The cane fell in a tight arc, and Allday reeled back, half stunned from the blow.

The weeks and months dropped away, and he was back on the cliff road with Brock lashing out at his face with the same cane while the other members of the press gang crowded round to watch. He could feel the blood stinging the corner of his mouth, and there seemed to be a great roaring in his ears. Voices were calling and shouting all around him, yet he felt unable to move or defend himself as Brock struck him once more across the neck with his cane. Vibart was staring at him, his eyes almost hidden by his brows as he watched Brock pull him from the mast and away from the other men.

Old Strachan croaked, ''E was with me! 'E never done it, Mr. Vibart!'

At last Vibart seemed to find his voice. But his words were strangled, as if his body was so taut with insane anger that he could hardly get himself to speak. 'Silence, you stupid old fool!' He thrust the man aside. 'Or I will take you, too!'

Some of the men had recovered from the first shock and now

surged forward, pressed on by those at the rear. Instantly there was a barked command from the quarterdeck, and a line of muskets rose above the rail. There was no doubting their intent, or the gleam in Sergeant Garwood's eyes.

Bolitho was still at one side of the rail, his figure dark against the pale sky. 'Bring that man aft, Mr. Vibart!'

Old Strachan was muttering vaguely, ''E was with me, I swear it!'

Brock pushed Allday towards the quarterdeck and snapped, 'Were you, Strachan? *All* the time?'

Strachan was confused. 'Well, all but a minute, Mr. Brock!'

Brock's voice was harsh. 'It only takes a minute to kill a man!'

Allday made another effort to clear his dazed mind as he was pushed up a ladder and past the grim-faced marines. He felt like another person, someone on the outside untouched by the cruel reality of events. Even his limbs felt numb and beyond his control, and the cuts from Brock's cane had neither pain nor meaning. He saw Lieutenant Herrick watching him like a stranger, and beyond him Proby, the master, looked away, as if he could not bear to meet his eye.

Captain Bolitho seemed to appear from nowhere, and as they faced each other across three feet of deck Allday heard him say, 'John Allday, do you have anything to say?'

He had to move his numb lips several times before the words would come. 'No, sir.' An insane voice seemed to cry from the depths of his soul. Tell him! Tell him! He tried again. 'It wasn't me, sir.'

He tried to see beyond the shadow which hid the captain's face. He could see the lines at the corners of his mouth, a bead of sweat running from beneath the dark hair. But there was no reality. It was all part of the same nightmare.

Bolitho said, 'Do you recognize these?'

Someone held out a pair of small pistols, bright and evil looking in the sunlight.

Allday shook his head. 'No, sir.'

'Or this?' Bolitho's voice was quite empty of emotion.

This time it was a knife, the tip broken off by the force of savage blows, its worn handle dark with congealed blood.

Allday stared. 'It's mine, sir!' He clapped his hand to his belt, his fingers brushing against an empty sheath.

Bolitho said, 'The pistols were found amongst your possessions below. Your knife was discovered beneath Mr. Evans' locker.' He paused to let the words sink in. 'Where it was dropped after the struggle.'

Allday swayed. 'I didn't do it, sir.' The words seemed to hang in his throat. 'Why would I do such a thing?'

As if from a long way off he heard Vibart's harsh voice. 'Let me run him up to the yard now, sir! It will give others of his sort something to think about with him dancing from a halter!'

Bolitho snapped, 'I think you have said enough, Mr. Vibart!' He turned back to Allday. 'After your behaviour since you first came aboard, I had high hopes for you, Allday. Mr. Herrick has already spoken on your behalf, but on this occasion I can find no reason for leniency.' He paused. 'Under the Articles of War I could have you hanged forthwith. As it is, I intend that you should be tried by court martial as soon as the opportunity arises.'

There was a low murmur of despair from the maindeck, and Allday knew that in everyone's eyes he was already a dead man.

Bolitho turned away. 'Place him in irons, Mr. Vibart. But any unnecessary brutality will be answerable to me!'

Dazed, and stumbling like a drunken man, Allday allowed himself to be led below.

Deep below the maindeck there were two tiny cells, each just large enough to contain one man. Allday watched dumbly as the rough manacles were snapped around his wrists and ankles, but only when the door was slammed and bolted behind him and he was left in total darkness did the true realization close on him like a vice.

By the time the *Phalarope* returned to port, and a necessary number of officers was available for a court martial, no one would remember or even care if he was guilty or not. He would be used as an example to others. A dancing, kicking puppet on the end of a rope as he was hauled slowly to the mainyard to the accompaniment of a drum's mournful beat.

He smashed his fists against the door, and heard the sound echo and vibrate in the stillness of the hull. Again and again, until he could feel the blood running across his fingers and taste the angry tears on his lips.

But when he fell exhausted and gasping behind the door, there was nothing but silence.

The deep, empty silence of a tomb.

Lieutenant Herrick rested his shoulder against an empty hammock netting and stared moodily along the frigate's deserted decks. An hour of the middle watch had passed, and in the bright moonlight the sails and rigging gave off an eerie glow, like those of some phantom vessel.

Try as he might, he could not put the thought of Allday and the murdered purser from his mind. He should have been able to tell himself that it was over and done with. Just one more item in the log to be talked over for a time and then forgotten.

Evans was dead, and his killer was penned below in irons. That at least should be some small satisfaction to everybody. An undetected murderer, at large to terrorize the lower deck or to strike again, would have been far more to worry about.

He tried to picture Allday standing over that hideous corpse, crazed enough to rip at the man's body until it was hardly human, yet calmly able to steal a pair of pistols and secrete them in his own quarters. It did not make any sense at all, but Herrick knew that had it been anyone else but Allday he would never have questioned such evidence.

Just before coming on watch Herrick had made his way below to the darkened cells, and after sending the marine sentry to the top of the ladder, had opened the door and held a lantern inside.

Allday had crouched against the opposite side, his hands shading his eyes from the light, his feet skidding in his own filth. Any disgust or anger Herrick may have felt faded in that instant. He had expected loud denials of guilt, or dumb insolence. Instead there was only a pathetic attempt at pride.

He had asked quietly, 'Have you anything more to tell me, Allday? I have not forgotten that you saved my life on the cliff. Perhaps if you tell me the full circumstances I will be able to do something to attract clemency on your behalf?'

Allday had made as if to brush his long hair from his eyes, and then looked down at the heavy manacles. In a barely controlled voice he had replied, 'I did not do it, Mr. Herrick. I cannot find a defence for something I *did not do!*'

'I see.' In the silence Herrick had heard the scampering of rats, the strange, unknown creaks of a ship at sea. 'If you change your mind, I . . .'

Allday had tried to step towards him and had fallen forward on Herrick's arm. For a few seconds Herrick had felt the touch of his bare skin, damp with fear, had smelt his despair, like the odour of death.

Allday had said thickly, 'You don't believe me either! So what's the point?' His voice had gained some small inner strength. 'Just leave me alone! For God's sake leave me *alone!*'

But as Herrick had been about to rebolt the door Allday had asked quietly, 'D'you think they'll send me home for court martial, sir?'

Herrick knew that the Navy would have other ideas. Justice was swift and final. But as he had stared at the heavy studded door he had heard himself reply, 'Maybe they will. Why do you ask?'

The answer had been muffled, as if Allday had turned his face away. 'I would like to see the green hills again. Just once. Even for a few minutes!'

The sadness and despair of those last words had dogged Herrick for the rest of the day, and now during his watch they were with him still.

'Damn!' He spoke aloud with sudden anger, and the two helmsmen jerked upright by the wheel as if he had struck them.

The senior man watched anxiously as Herrick walked towards the wheel and said quickly, 'Full an' bye, sir! Course south by east!' Herrick stared at him and then at the gently swinging compass card. Poor devils, he thought vaguely. Scared sick because I swore aloud.

A dark figure moved from the lee rail and walked slowly towards him. It was Proby, his heavy jowls glowing faintly from his short clay pipe.

Herrick said, 'Can't you sleep, Mr. Proby? The breeze is slight but steady now. There'll be nothing for you to attend to tonight.'

The master sucked noisily at the stem. 'It's the best time of the night, Mr. Herrick. You can look into the wind's eye and think about what you've done with your life!'

Herrick looked sideways at Proby's crumpled features. In the pipe glow his face looked like a piece of weatherworn sculpture, but there was something reassuring about him all the same. Timeless, like the sea itself.

He said at length, 'Do you think we have heard the last of Evans' death?'

'Who can say?' Proby shifted on his flat feet. 'It takes time to clean such a deed from a man's memory. Aye, it takes a long time.'

The pipe glow suddenly vanished in the palm of Proby's beefy hand, and he said tersely, 'The captain is on deck, Mr. Herrick!' Then in a louder, matter-of-fact tone he said, 'We should make a good landfall tomorrow if this wind holds. So I'll bid you good night, Mr. Herrick!'

Then he was gone, and Herrick moved towards the lee rail. From the corner of his eye he could see Bolitho standing straight against the weather rail, the moonlight sharp across his white shirt as he stared at the glittering reflections beyond the ship.

Bolitho had not left the quarterdeck for more than an hour at a time, and ever since Allday's arrest he had been seen by the taffrail, either pacing the deck or just staring out to sea, as he was now.

Earlier Herrick had overheard the master speaking to Quintal, the boatswain, and now as he watched Bolitho's motionless figure the words came back to him. Quintal had said in a hoarse whisper, 'I didn't know he felt like that about Evans. He seems fair troubled by it all!'

Old Proby had weighed his words before replying. 'It's the deed which bothers the captain, Mr. Quintal. He feels betrayed, that's what is wrong with *him*!'

Herrick saw Bolitho touch the scar on his forehead and then rub the tiredness from his eyes. Proby was right, he thought. He feels it more than we realize. Whatever any of us does, he shares it like his own burden.

Before he realized what he was doing, Herrick had crossed the deck to Bolitho's side. Instantly he regretted his action. He half expected Bolitho to turn and reprimand him, and even that might have been better than the complete silence. He said, 'The wind is holding well, sir. The master has prophesied a quick landfall.'

'I think I heard him.' Bolitho seemed deep in his own thoughts.

Herrick saw that the captain's shirt was dark with thrown spray and clung close to his body like another skin. There were deep shadows beneath his eyes, and Herrick could almost feel the inner torment which was keeping Bolitho on deck instead of the privacy of the cabin.

He said, 'Would you like me to call your servant, sir? Perhaps a hot drink before you turn in for the night?'

Bolitho twisted round at the rail, his eyes bright in the moonlight. 'Spare me this small talk, Mr. Herrick! What is it which bothers you?'

Herrick swallowed hard and then blurted out, 'I have been speaking with Allday, sir. I know it was wrong, but I feel partly responsible for him.'

Bolitho was watching him closely. 'Go on.'

'He is one of my men, sir, and I think there may be more to what happened than we think.' He finished lamely, 'I know him better than most. He is not the sort to change.'

Bolitho sighed. 'Only the stars never change, Mr. Herrick.'

Herrick said stubbornly, 'Even so, he may be innocent!'

'And you think this is important?' Bolitho sounded tired. 'You believe that the life of one man, a man almost certain to be found guilty, is worth consideration?'

'Well, as a matter of fact, I do, sir.' Herrick felt Bolitho's eyes fixed on his face in a cold stare. 'The authorities will not listen to half a story . . .'

Bolitho shifted with sudden impatience. '*We* are the authority out here, Mr. Herrick! And I will decide what is to be done!'

Herrick looked away. 'Yes, sir.'

'As it happens, I entirely agree with you.' Bolitho pushed the lock of hair back from his forehead, ignoring Herrick's open astonishment. 'But I just wanted to hear it from one other person!'

He became suddenly brisk. 'I think I will go below now, Mr. Herrick, *without* a hot drink. Tomorrow we will search for fresh water and attend to the matter of fighting a war.' He paused momentarily by the rail. 'I will also think about what you have said tonight. It may be important for all of us.'

Without another word he turned on his heel and descended the cabin stairway. Herrick stared after him, his jaw hanging open.

'Well, I'll be damned!' He shook his head and grinned. 'Well, I'll be *double*-damned!'

15. THE STORM BREAKS

SURPRISINGLY the wind did hold, and twenty hours after Proby's prophecy the *Phalarope*'s anchor splashed down into deep, clear water amidst a huddle of low, desolate islets.

Apart from lowering boats and filling them with water casks in readiness for the following morning, it was pointless to attempt a landing with night so close at hand, but at the first hint of daylight, long before the sun was able to burnish an edge to the horizon, the first boatloads of men grated up the narrow shelving beach of the nearest islet.

Bolitho climbed through the tangle of dark scrub at the top of the beach and stared round at the busy preparations behind him. The boats had already shoved off to collect more men, and the ones already landed were standing huddled together, as if conscious of the island's bleak inhospitality. One or two of the sailors were staggering like drunken revellers, their legs so used to the pitch and toss of a ship's deck that the unfamiliar land destroyed their sense of balance.

Petty officers bawled orders and checked their lists of names, and as the next batch of men arrived to join the swelling mass of sailors at the water's edge the first parties picked up their casks and tools and began to stumble inland.

Lieutenant Okes appeared on the ridge and touched his hat. 'All working parties ready, sir.' He looked harassed.

Bolitho nodded. 'You have your orders, Mr. Okes. Just follow the rough map I made for you and you should find fresh water without difficulty. Keep the men moving fast before the sun comes up. You'll need every available man to carry the full casks down to the beach, so see they don't wander off.'

He saw Trevenen, the cooper, scurrying ahead of another party accompanied by Ledward, the carpenter, the latter ever hopeful of replenishing his stock of spare timber. He'd not find much here, Bolitho thought grimly. These islets were useless and left well alone, but for occasional fresh-water parties. Underfoot the ground was hidden by layer upon layer of rotten vegetation, its heavy stench well mixed with seagull droppings and small bright patches of fungus. Further inland there were a few hump-backed hills, from the top of which a man could see the sea in every direction.

Okes walked off after his men, and Bolitho caught sight of Farquhar's slim figure outlined against the green scrub, before he too vanished over the far side of the ridge. Bolitho had deliberately ordered the midshipman to join Okes in command of the main party. It would do them both good to work together, if only to break down the strange air of watchful tension be-tween them. It seemed as if Farquhar was playing some sort of game with Okes. Ever since his escape from the *Andiron* Farquhar had made a point of not speaking to Okes, but his presence alone seemed more than enough to reduce the lieutenant to a state of permanent agitation.

Okes had acted hastily during the retreat from Mola Island, but unless he made an open admission there was little point in pursuing the matter, Bolitho thought. He could sympathize with Farquhar, and wondered what he himself might have done under the same set of circumstances. Farquhar's built-in sense of caution had obviously taught him that there was more to a career than gaining petty triumphs. Also his breeding, the security of a powerful family, as well as his own self-confidence, gave him the ability to bide his time.

Herrick strode up the slope and said, 'Shall we return to the ship, sir?'

Bolitho shook his head. 'We'll walk a little further, Mr. Herrick.'

He pushed through a line of sun-scarred bushes and headed away from the beach. Herrick walked beside him in silence, no doubt thinking of the strangeness of the land around him. The sea's gentle hiss was gone and the air was heavy with alien smells and a thick, clinging humidity.

Bolitho said at length, 'I hope Okes can get the men working quickly. Every hour may be precious.'

'You are thinking of the French, sir?'

Bolitho wiped the sweat from his face and nodded. 'De Grasse may have sailed by now. If he behaves as Sir George Rodney believes he will, his fleet will already be striking west for Jamaica.' He looked up fretfully at the limp leaves and cloud-less sky. 'Not a breath of wind. Nothing. We were lucky it held long enough for us to reach here!'

Herrick was breathing heavily. 'My God, sir, I'm feeling this!' He mopped his face. 'I have not set foot ashore since Falmouth. I had almost forgotten what it was like.'

Falmouth. Again the name brought back a flood of memories to Bolitho as he strode unseeingly through the thick scrub. His father would still be waiting and wondering, nursing the hurt which Hugh had left with him. Bolitho wondered momentarily what would have happened if he had seen and recognized his brother on the *Andiron*'s poop on that first savage encounter. Would he have pressed home his attack with such fervour? If he had caused Hugh's death it might have eased the minds of the Navy, but in his heart Bolitho knew that it would only have added to his father's grief and sense of loss.

Perhaps Hugh already had another ship. He dismissed the idea at once. The French would not trust another prize to a man who had allowed *Andiron* to fall into her own snare. And the American rebel government had few ships to spare. No, Hugh would have his own problems in plenty at this moment.

He thought too of Vibart, left behind in charge of the frigate. It was strange how Evans' murder had affected him. Bolitho had always thought Evans to be more of a toady than a friend of the first lieutenant. Yet his death seemed in some way to have deprived Vibart of something familiar and reliable, the last outlet from his own isolation. Bolitho knew that Vibart blamed him for Evans' death, as much as he hated Allday for the deed. Vibart viewed humanity like sentiment. To him both were useless hindrances to duty.

He also knew that he would never see eye to eye with Vibart whatever happened. To Bolitho the humane treatment of his men, the understanding of their problems, and the earning of their loyalty, were as precious as gold. Equally he knew he must uphold this difficult and bitter man, for commanding a ship of war left little room for personal animosity amongst officers.

Bolitho halted with a jerk and pointed. 'Is that a marine?'

Herrick stood beside him breathing deeply. A red coat flashed between the dull foliage and then another, and as Bolitho started forward, Sergeant Garwood appeared at the head of a file of sweating marines.

Bolitho asked sharply, 'What are you doing ashore, Sergeant?'

Garwood stared fixedly over Bolitho's shoulder. 'Mr. Vibart 'as sent all the marines across, sir.' He swallowed hard. 'The prisoner Allday 'as escaped, sir. We've been sent to catch 'im again!'

Bolitho heard Herrick catch his breath and glanced quickly at his streaming face. He could see the shock and disappointment plain on the lieutenant's features, as if he was personally involved.

'I see.' Bolitho controlled the sudden rise of anger and added calmly, 'Where is Captain Rennie?'

'T'other side of the island, sir.' Garwood looked unhappy. 'The relief sentry found the cell guard clubbed senseless an' the prisoner gone, sir. 'Is manacles 'ad been struck off too, sir.'

'So someone else was involved?' Bolitho stared hard at the sergeant's bronzed features. 'Who else is missing?'

The marine gulped. 'Yer clerk, Ferguson, sir!'

Bolitho turned away. 'Very well, I suppose you had better carry on now that you are here.' He watched the man clump gratefully away and then said tightly, 'Mr. Vibart was over hasty to send all the marines ashore. If the ship was surprised at her anchor by another vessel, there would be insufficient men to repel an attack.' He turned abruptly. 'Come, we will go back to the beach.'

Herrick said wretchedly, 'I am sorry, sir. I feel to blame more than ever. I trusted Allday, and I was the one who chose Ferguson as your clerk.'

Bolitho replied flatly, 'It has proved that we were both wrong, Mr. Herrick. An innocent man does not run!' He added, 'Mr. Vibart should not have allowed his anger to blind his judgement in this matter. Allday will surely die if he is left here. He will go mad on this island once the ship has sailed, and will not thank Ferguson for his rescue from a cell!'

They hurried across the beach, and the drowsing gig's crew jerked into life as the two officers climbed aboard.

Bolitho shaded his eyes to look at the anchored frigate as the gig moved slowly across the placid water. The sun was only just showing above the nearest hump of land, and the *Phalarope*'s yards and topmasts were shining as if coated with gilt.

Herrick asked quietly, 'If the marines catch Allday, sir. What will you do?'

'I will hang him this time, Mr. Herrick. For the sake of discipline I have no choice now.' He glanced back at the land. 'For that reason I hope they do not find him.'

The bowman hooked on to the chains, and Bolitho pulled himself through the entry port.

At his elbow Herrick snapped, 'Why did you not hail the gig, man?' His own unhappy thoughts put an unusual edge to his voice.

The seaman at the entry port blinked and stammered, 'I'm sorry, sir. I—I . . .' His voice trailed away as he stared up at the quarterdeck.

There was a tight group of seamen beneath the quarterdeck, and as the cold realization seeped into Bolitho's brain, they pushed out into the growing sunlight which shone and reflected on their raised muskets.

Herrick thrust Bolitho aside and reached for his sword, but a giant sailor with a pistol snapped, 'Stay where you are, Mr. Herrick!' He pointed up at the quarterdeck rail. 'Otherwise it will go hard with that one!'

Two more men appeared from behind the cabin hatch, between them carrying the small, struggling figure of Midshipman Neale. One man drew a knife from his belt and laid it across Neale's throat, grinning down at the two officers as he did so.

The tall seaman, whom Bolitho now recognized as Onslow, stepped slowly across the maindeck, his pistol trained on Herrick. 'Well, Mr. Herrick? Do you drop your sword?' He grinned lazily. 'It's all the same to me!'

Bolitho said, 'Do as he says, Mr. Herrick.' He had seen the brightness in Onslow's eyes, and knew that the man was eager, desperately eager to kill. He was only just keeping his pent up madness in check. One false move and there would be no more time left to act.

The sword clattered on the deck. Onslow kicked it aside and called sharply, 'Take the gig's crew forrard and batten 'em down with the other pretty boys!' He tapped his nose with his pistol. 'They'll all join us later, or feed the fish!'

Some of the men laughed. It was a wild, explosive sound. Brittle with tension.

Bolitho studied Onslow, the first shock giving way to sudden caution. Every captain dreaded such a moment. Some had earned it, others had fallen foul of uncontrollable circumstances. Now it had happened to him. To the *Phalarope*.

It was mutiny.

Onslow watched as the gig's crew was bundled below deck and then said, 'We'll up anchor as soon as a likely wind blows. We have the master below, and either he or you will take the ship to open waters.'

Herrick said hoarsely, 'You're mad! You'll swing for this!'

The pistol barrel came down sharply, and Herrick dropped to his knees, his hands across his forehead.

Bolitho saw the blood bright across Herrick's fingers and said coldly, 'And if the wind fails to arrive, Onslow? What will you do?'

Onslow nodded, his eyes searching Bolitho's face. 'A good question. Well, we have a good little ship beneath us. We can sink any boat which tries to board us, do you not agree?'

Bolitho kept his face impassive, but realized that Onslow had good reasons for confidence. Outnumbered by the rest of the crew and Rennie's marines, Onslow was still in the position of king. Even a handful of men could keep boats at bay with the frigate's guns loaded with grape. He glanced at the sun. It would be hours before Okes started the long march back to the beach.

He said slowly. 'So it was you all the time.'

Another man, small and stinking of rum, capered round the two officers. 'He done it all! Just as 'e said 'e would!'

Onslow snarled, 'Stow it, Pook!' Then more calmly, 'Your clerk told me when the ship was nearing land. All I had to do was foul the fresh-water casks with salt.' He laughed, amused by the very simplicity of his plan. 'Then, when you headed this way, I killed that rat Evans.'

Bolitho said, 'You must have been very afraid of Allday to incriminate him with murder!'

Onslow glanced along the deck and then said calmly, 'It was necessary. I knew if the bullocks were still aboard some of my white-livered friends might not be so willing to seize the ship!' He shrugged. 'So I had Allday released, and the bullocks went charging off after him. Just as I *knew* they would!'

'You've damned yourself, Onslow!' Bolitho kept his voice level. 'But think of these other men with you. Will you see them hanged?'

Onslow shouted, 'Shut your mouth! And think yourself lucky I've not had you strung up at the mainyard! I'm going to barter the ship for our freedom! No bloody navy'll catch us after that!'

Bolitho hardened his tone to hide his rising despair. 'You are a fool if you believe that!'

His head jerked back as Onslow struck him across the face with the back of his hand. *'Silence!'* Onslow's shout brought more men pressing around. Herrick was dragged to his feet and his hands were pinioned behind him. He was still dazed, and his face was streaming with blood. Bolitho said, 'You can send the officers ashore. They are nothing to you, Onslow.'

'Ah now, Captain, you're wrong there!' Onslow's good humour was returning. 'Hostages. You may fetch a good price, too!' He laughed. 'But then you must be getting used to that!'

Pook yelled, 'Why not kill 'em now?' He waved a cutlass. 'Let me have 'em!'

Onslow looked at Bolitho. 'You see? Only I can save you.'

'What have you done with the first lieutenant?' Bolitho saw Pook nudge another seaman. 'Have you killed him, too?'

Pook sniggered. 'Not likely! We're savin' 'im for a bit o' sport later on!'

Onslow flexed his arms. 'He's flogged enough of us, Captain. I'll see how he likes the cat across *his* fat hide!'

Herrick muttered between his clenched teeth, 'Think of what you're doing! You are selling this ship to the enemy!'

'You're my enemy!' Onslow's nostrils flared as if he had been touched with a hot iron. 'I'll do what I like with her, and with you, too!'

Bolitho said quietly, 'Easy, Mr. Herrick. There is nothing you can do.'

'Spoken like a true gentleman!' Onslow gave a slow grin. 'It's best to know when you're beaten!' Then sharply he called, 'Lock them below, lads! And kill the first bugger who tries anything!'

Some of the men growled with obvious disapproval. Their lust was high. They were all committed. Bolitho knew that Onslow's careful plan was only half clear in their rum-sodden minds.

Onslow added, 'As soon as the wind gets up, we're off, lads! You can leave the rest to Harry Onslow!'

Herrick and Bolitho were pushed along the deck and down into the dark confines of a small storeroom. A moment later Midshipman Neale and Proby, the master, were thrust in with them and the door slammed shut.

High up the side of the cabin was a small circular port, used to ventilate the compartment and the stores it normally contained. Bolitho guessed that the mutineers had already dragged the contents elsewhere for their own uses.

In the darkness Neale sobbed, 'I—I'm sorry, sir! I let you down! I was on watch when it all happened!'

Bolitho said quietly, 'It was not your fault, boy. The odds were against you this time. It was just ironic that Onslow stayed aboard because he could not be trusted *off* the ship!'

Neale said brokenly, 'Mr. Vibart was in his cabin. They seized him and nearly killed him! Onslow stopped them just in time!'

Herrick said bleakly, 'Not for long!' Then with sudden fury, 'The fools! The French or the Spanish will never bargain with Onslow! They won't have to. They'll seize the *Phalarope* and take the whole lot prisoners!'

Bolitho said, 'I know that, Herrick. But if the mutineers began to think as you do, they'd have no reason for sparing our lives!'

'I see, sir.' Herrick was peering at him in the gloom. 'And I thought . . .'

'You imagined that I had given up hope?' Bolitho breathed out slowly. 'Not yet. Not without a fight!'

He stood up on an empty box and peered through the small vent hole. The ship had swung lightly at her cable and he could see the far end of the little beach and a low hill beyond. There was no sign of life. Nor had he expected any.

Proby muttered, 'Two of the mutineers I know well. Good men, with no cause to follow scum like Onslow and Pook!' He added thickly, 'It'll do 'em no good. They'll be caught and hanged with the rest!'

Herrick slipped and cursed in the darkness. 'Damn!' He groped with his fingers. 'Some old butter! Rancid as bilge water!'

Bolitho cocked his head to listen to the sudden stamp of feet and a wave of laughter. 'They've taken more than butter, Mr. Herrick. They'll be too drunk to control soon!' He thought of the knife's glitter across Neale's throat. Soon the second phase would be enacted. The mutineers would get bored with merely drinking. They would have to prove themselves. To kill.

He said, 'Can you come up here beside me, Neale?' He felt the midshipman struggling on to the box. 'Now, do you think you could get through that vent?'

Neale's eyes flickered in the shaft of sunlight. He replied doubtfully, 'It's very small, sir.' Then more firmly, 'I'll try!'

Proby asked, 'What do you have in mind, sir?'

Bolitho ran his hands around the circular hole. It was barely ten inches across. He controlled the rising excitement in his heart. It *had* to be tried.

He said, 'If Neale could slip through . . .' He broke off. 'The butter! Quick, Neale, strip off your clothes!' He reached out for Herrick. 'We'll rub him with butter, Herrick, and ease him through, like a sponge in a gun barrel!'

Neale pulled off his clothes and stood uncertainly in the centre of the storeroom. In the faint glow from the vent hole his small body shone like some discarded statue. Bolitho took a double handful of stinking butter from the deck and ignoring Neale's cry of alarm slapped it across his shoulders. As Herrick followed suit Bolitho said quickly, 'The loyal men, Neale, where are they?'

Neale's teeth were beginning to chatter uncontrollably but he replied, 'In the cable tier, sir. The surgeon and some of the older hands as well.'

'Just as I thought.' Bolitho stood back and wiped his palms on his breeches. 'Now listen. If we get you through this hole, could you climb along the forechains?'

Neale nodded. 'I'll try, sir.'

'The others will be locked in the tier by staple. If I can distract the guards you open the door and release them.' He rested his hand on the boy's shoulder. 'But if anyone sees you, forget what I said and jump for it. You could swim ashore before anyone could catch you.'

He turned to the others. 'Right, lend a hand here!'

Neale felt like a greasy fish, and at the first attempt they nearly dropped him.

Herrick suggested, 'One arm first, Neale, then your head.'

They tried again, with the room plunged into total darkness as the struggling, wriggling midshipman was forced into the vent hole. The boy was gasping with pain, and Proby said, 'Lucky he ain't no fatter.'

Then, with a sudden rush he was through, and after a few agonizing seconds, while they all waited for a shouted challenge from the deck, his eyes appeared outside the vent hole. He was scarlet in the face and his shoulder was bleeding from the rough passage. But he was strangely determined, and Bolitho said softly, 'Take your time, boy. And no chances!'

Neale vanished, and Herrick said heavily, 'Well, at least he's out of it if the worst happens.'

Bolitho looked at him sharply. It was almost as if Herrick had read his own thoughts. But he replied calmly, 'I'll blow this ship to hell before I let it fall to the enemy, Mr. Herrick! Make no mistake about it!'

Then, in silence, he settled down to wait.

John Allday leaned against a tall slab of rock, his chest heaving from exertion as he fought to regain his breath. A few paces away, lying like a corpse with his head and shoulders in a small pool, Bryan Ferguson drank deeply, pausing every so often to give a great gasp for air.

Allday turned to look back through the tangled mass of small trees through which they had just come. There was still no sign of pursuit, but he had no doubt the alarm was now under way.

He said, 'I've not had time to thank you, Bryan. That was a rash thing you did!'

Ferguson rolled on to his side and stared at him with glazed eyes. 'Had to do it. Had to.'

'It's your neck as well as mine now, Bryan.' Allday studied him sadly. 'But at least we're free. There's always hope when you have your freedom!'

He had been lying in his darkened cell listening to the familiar sounds of boats filling with men and pushing off from the frigate's hull. Then, as the emptied ship had fallen into silence, there had been a cry of alarm and the thud of a body falling against the door.

Ferguson had wrenched it open, his mouth slack with fear, his fingers trembling as he had unlocked the shackles and gabbled out some vague ideas of escape.

The dawn was still a dull smudge in the sky as they had slipped quietly over the side into the cool water. Like many sailors Allday could hardly swim a stroke, but Ferguson, driven by the desperation of fear, had helped him, until choking and gasping they had both staggered on to the safety of the beach.

Hardly speaking they had run or crawled through dense brush, had climbed over fallen rocks, never pausing to either look back or listen. Now they were between two low hills, and exhaustion had pulled them both to a halt.

Allday said, 'Come on, we'd better get ourselves moving again. Up this hill. We'll be safe there. You should be able to see miles from the top.'

Ferguson was still staring at him. 'You were right about Onslow. He is a bad man!' He shuddered. 'I thought he was just trying to be friendly to me. I told him things about the captain's log. About what the ship was doing!' He staggered to his feet and followed Allday slowly up the side of the hill. 'No one will believe me now. I'm as guilty as he is!'

'At least you know I didn't kill the purser!' Allday squinted up at the sun. It would soon be time to stop and hide.

'Onslow boasted about it!' Ferguson gave another shudder. 'After you had been taken to the cells I overhead him talking with some of the others, Pook and Pochin. He boasted how he had killed Evans!'

Allday pulled him into a bush. 'Look!' He pointed across to a distant hillside at a slow-moving line of red dots. 'The bullocks are out looking for us already.'

Ferguson gave a low cry. 'I'll never get back home! I'll never see Grace again!'

Allday looked at him gravely. 'Hold on, Bryan! We're not finished yet. Maybe another ship will call here one day, and we'll pretend we're shipwrecked!'

He turned to watch the distant marines as they moved away to the right. Marines in their heavy boots and equipment were no match for this sort of game, he thought. Even on a bare Cornish hillside he could have evaded them. Here it was easier, because of the heavy tangle of scrub all around them.

He said, 'It's all right. They're over the other side now. Come on, Bryan!'

They continued up the hillside until Allday found a sheltered clump of bushes which jutted from a great fallen slide of rock. He threw himself down and stared out at the great empty waste of water.

'We'll be safe here, Bryan. When the ship puts to sea we'll build a shelter like I had outside Falmouth. Don't worry about it.'

Ferguson was still standing, his eyes wide as he peered down at his friend. 'Onslow intends to take the ship!' His mouth quivered. 'He told me. He knew I couldn't do anything. He said that I was as guilty as the rest of them!'

Allday tried to grin. 'You're tired!' He tried again. 'Look, how can Onslow seize a frigate?' His grin faded into a look of shocked horror as the true implication dawned on him. He jumped to his feet and seized Ferguson's arm. 'Do you mean Onslow planned all of this? The fresh water, the murder, and my escape?' He did not wait for a reply. The expression on the other man's face was enough.

He gave a hollow groan. 'My God, Bryan! What are we going to do?'

Ferguson said weakly, 'I wanted to tell you. But there was no time! They'd have killed you anyway.'

Allday nodded heavily. 'I know, Bryan. I know.' He stared at the ground. 'I warned them about this.' He ran his fingers through his hair. 'Mutiny! I'll have no part of it!' He looked at Ferguson with sudden determination. 'We must go back and warn them.'

'It'll be too late!' Ferguson clasped his hands together. 'Anyway, I couldn't go! Don't you see? I'm one of them now!' Tears began to pour down his face. 'I couldn't take the lash, John! Please, I *couldn't*!'

Allday turned his back to hide his face from the other man. He stared out to sea, at the hard horizon line which seemed to represent the impossibility of distance. You poor little bugger, he thought. It must have cost a lot of pluck to knock down the sentry and open the cell. Over his shoulder he said calmly, 'I know, Bryan. But give me time to think things out.'

So it was all wasted after all. The determination to take life as it came, to accept danger and hardship in order that he should one day return home, had all come to nothing. It was curious that Ferguson, the one man aboard who had the most to lose, had been the one to spring off the disaster of mutiny.

And disaster it would be, he told himself grimly. They never gave up a search for a mutineer. No matter how long it took. He remembered seeing some of them hanging in chains at Plymouth. Rotting, eyeless remnants left to the gulls as a warning to others.

Far out on the flat, glittering water something moved to break the calm emptiness of the horizon. Allday dropped on one knee and shaded his eyes with both hands. He blinked to clear the moisture and then looked again. Months at sea as a masthead lookout had given him the sailor's instinct to interpret more than was merely visible to the naked eye. He turned his head very slightly. There was another one. Much smaller. Probably a mile beyond the first.

Ferguson seemed to realize something was happening. 'What is it?'

Allday sat down on the rock at his side and stared at him thoughtfully. 'There are two frigates out yonder, Bryan. Big ones, probably Frogs by the look of 'em.' He let the words sink in and then asked quietly, 'Tell me about your wife back at Falmouth. Grace, isn't that her name?'

Ferguson nodded dumbly, still not understanding.

Allday reached out and took his hand firmly in his own. 'She'll not want to remember you as a mutineer, Bryan?' He saw the quick shake of the head, the unheeded tears on his sun-burned cheeks. Then he continued, 'Nor will she want to remember you as the man who let his ship fall to the enemy without lifting a finger to help her.' He stood up slowly and pulled Ferguson to his feet. 'Take a look at those ships, Bryan, and then tell me what to do. You saved my life. I owe you that at least!'

Ferguson stared at the dancing reflections, too blinded with tears to see beyond Allday's quiet words. 'You want me to go back with you?' He spoke in a small voice, yet unable to stop himself. '*To go back?*'

Allday nodded, still keeping his eyes on Ferguson's agonized face. 'We have to, Bryan. You can see that, can't you?'

He touched Ferguson's arm, and after a momentary hesitation began to walk down the side of the hill. He did not have to look back to know that Ferguson was following him.

Bolitho felt the hair stirring against the nape of his neck, and stood up to face the small vent hole. After a moment he said, 'Do you feel it? The wind is returning!'

Herrick replied uneasily, 'Okes will never be back in time. And even if he is . . .'

Bolitho touched his lips. 'Quiet! Someone's coming!' He bent down and with a quick jerk thrust Neale's clothes out through the vent hole.

The door grated back and Pook peered in at them. He gestured with a heavy pistol. 'On deck! All of you!' His eyes were very bright, and his shirt was well stained with neat rum. Then he stared past Bolitho and shouted, 'Where's that brat gone, for Christ's sake?'

Bolitho said calmly, 'Out through the port. He swam ashore.'

Pook muttered, 'It'll do 'im no good! 'E can stay with the others to starve!'

Cursing and muttering to himself he drove the three officers on deck, where Onslow and some of his trusted men were assembled beside the wheel.

Bolitho whispered to Herrick, 'Don't provoke him. He looks too dangerous to trifle with!'

Onslow was certainly showing signs of strain, and as Bolitho and the others reached the quarterdeck rail he snapped, 'Right then! You can get the ship under way!' He levelled his pistol at Herrick's stomach and added meaningly, 'I shall shoot him if you try and trick me!'

Bolitho glanced along the maindeck, feeling his spirits sinking. There were some twenty men staring up at him. All the ones who had been sent from the *Cassius* and some others he recognized as old and trusted men of the original *Phalarope* crew.

As he had remarked to the unhappy Neale, it was just bad luck that all these men had stayed together aboard the frigate while other, more reliable elements had been sent ashore with the water casks. Normally it would not have mattered. He bit his lip and stared beyond the bowsprit where a small islet seemed to be swinging on its own momentum as the wind tugged at the anchored ship. Now it made the difference between life and death to all of them.

He nodded to Proby. 'Tops'ls and jib, Mr. Proby.' To Onslow he said, 'We will need more men to break out the anchor.'

Onslow showed his teeth. 'A good try, but not good enough. I will cut the cable!' He waved the pistol. 'I have enough men here for the sails!' He hardened his jaw. 'Try that sort of trick again and I will kill the lieutenant!' He cocked the pistol and pointed it again at Herrick. 'Carry on, *sir*!'

Bolitho felt the sun beating down on his face and tried to shut out the overwhelming sensation of defeat. There was nothing he could do. He had even put young Neale's life in danger now.

Quietly he said, 'Very well, Onslow. But I hope you live long enough to regret this.'

A man yelled from forward, 'Look! There are some men on the beach!'

Onslow swung round, his eyes glinting. 'By God, there's a boat shoving off!'

Bolitho turned to watch as the *Phalarope*'s jolly boat idled clear of the sand and began to move across the water. There were only two men in it, and he guessed that the landing party must have broken into panic at the sight of the frigate preparing to sail without them. Several mutineers were already aloft, and a jibsail flapped impatiently in the rising breeze. He could see many more men further along the green ridge and the glint of metal on a drawn sword.

Onslow said slowly, 'Let the boat get near enough to rake with a nine-pounder!' He was grinning. 'And fetch up Mr. bloody Vibart! We'll give those bastards something to remember us by!' To Bolitho he said, 'It will be a hanging after all, and who better?'

It took four men to drag the first lieutenant from the cabin hatch. His clothes were in ribbons, and his face was scarred and battered almost beyond recognition. For several seconds he stared up at the running noose which was already being passed down from the mainyard to eager hands on deck. Then he turned and looked up towards the quarterdeck, seeing Bolitho and the others for the first time. One of his eyes was closed, but the other stared straight at Onslow with neither fear nor hope.

Onslow called, 'Now, Mr. Vibart! Let us see you dance to our tune!' Some of the men laughed as he added, 'You'll get a good view from up there.'

Bolitho said, 'Leave him! You have *me*, Onslow, isn't that enough?'

But Vibart shouted, 'Save your pleadings for yourself! I don't want your damn pity!'

Suddenly a voice shouted, 'Look! In the jolly boat! It's Allday and Ferguson!'

Several men ran to the side, and one even started to cheer.

Onslow rasped, 'Stand by that gun! We don't need them here!'

Bolitho watched narrowly as another big seaman, the one called Pochin, pushed past the wheel and growled, ''Old on! It's Allday! 'E's a good mate, an' always 'as bin.' He looked down at the maindeck. 'What d'you say, lads?'

There was a rumble of agreement from some of the watching men, and Pochin added, 'Call the boat alongside.'

Bolitho could feel his heart pounding against his ribs as the boat bumped against the hull, and in sudden silence Allday and Ferguson climbed up through the entry port.

Pochin leaned over the rail and shouted, 'Welcome back, John! We'll sail together after all!'

But Allday stayed where he was below the starboard gangway, the sunlight bright across his upturned face. Then he said, 'I'll not sail with him!' He pointed straight at Onslow. 'He killed Evans and put the blame on me! I would have ended on a gallows but for Bryan here!'

Onslow replied calmly, 'But now you're free. I never intended you to die.' There was sweat on his forehead, and the knuckles around the pistol were white. 'You can stay with us, and welcome.'

Allday ignored him and turned to the men on deck. 'There are two French frigates out yonder, lads! Will you let the *Phalarope* fall to them because of the word of that murdering swine?' His voice grew louder. 'You, Pochin? Are you such a fool that you cannot see your own death?' He seized another seaman by the arm. 'And you, Ted! Can you live with this for the rest of your life?'

A babble of voices broke out, and even the men from aloft swarmed down to join the others in noisy argument.

Bolitho shot a glance at Herrick. It was now or never. He had seen two armed seamen walk aft to see what was happening. They had to be the sentries guarding the rest of the prisoners.

But it was Vibart who acted first. Broken and bleeding, his head sunk dejectedly in his shoulders, he was momentarily forgotten by the men around him.

With a sudden roar he lashed out and knocked his guards sprawling.

Bolitho yelled, 'Neale! *Now*, for God's sake!'

As he shouted he threw himself bodily sideways into Onslow, and together they rolled kicking and fighting across the deck.

Pook screamed with fury and had his feet kicked from under him by Herrick, who scooped up his pistol, cocked it and fired in a matter of seconds. The force of the shot lifted Pook from his knees and smashed him back against a carronade, his jaw and half his face blown to bloody fragments.

Somehow Onslow managed to fight himself free, and with one great bound cleared the rail to land amidst the other seamen. The sudden pistol shot had left the men standing like statues, but as Onslow hit the deck he snatched up a cutlass and yelled, 'To me, lads! Kill the bastards!'

Bolitho seized Onslow's pistol and fired point-blank at a man by the wheel, and then gasped, 'Go aft, Mr. Proby! Get weapons!'

There was a ragged volley from the forecastle, and the stunned mutineers reeled back across the maindeck as another handful of seamen surged up from below led by Belsey, the master's mate, his injured arm strapped across his body, but wielding a boarding axe with his good hand.

Herrick shouted, 'The boats are coming, sir!' He hurled his empty pistol at another shadowy figure and grabbed a cutlass from Proby. 'My God, the boats are coming at last!'

Bolitho snapped, 'Follow me!' Swinging the unfamiliar cutlass like a scythe he dashed down the ladder, hitting out with all his strength as a man charged across the deck with a long pike. He felt the hot blood spurt across his face as the massive blade sliced through the man's bulging neck artery as if it had been thread.

Faces loomed up, ugly and distorted, but faded into screams as he slashed his way across the deck to where Vibart was fighting with his bare hands against three mutineers. As he drove his cutlass into the nearest man's shoulder he saw the sun gleam on a knife, and heard Vibart's great bellow of agony. Then he was down, and as the released men from the cable tier charged into the fray, some of the remaining mutineers dropped their weapons and held up their hands.

Bolitho slipped in some blood and felt someone lifting him to his feet. It was Allday.

He managed to gasp, 'Thank you, Allday!'

But Allday was staring past him, to the far side, where encircled by levelled weapons and abandoned by his fellow conspirators, Onslow stood with his back against a gun, his cutlass still held in front of him.

Allday said, 'He is *mine*, sir!'

Bolitho was about to answer when he heard Vibart calling his name. In three strides he reached the man's side and knelt on the stained planking where Ellice and Belsey were holding Vibart's shoulders clear of the deck. There was a thin ribbon of blood running from the corner of Vibart's mouth, and as he lay staring up at Bolitho's grave features he looked suddenly old and frail.

Bolitho said quietly, 'Rest easy, Mr. Vibart. We'll soon have you comfortable.'

Vibart coughed, and the blood dribbled down his chin in a growing flood. 'Not this time. They've done for me this time!' He made as if to move his hand, but the effort was too much. From behind his shoulders the surgeon gave a quick shake of his head.

Bolitho said, 'It was a brave thing you did.'

There was a clash of steel across the deck, and Bolitho turned to see Allday and Onslow circling each other with bared cutlasses. The other men stood watching in silence. This was no court martial. This was the justice of the lower deck.

Bolitho looked again at Vibart. 'Is there anything I can do for you?'

The dying man grimaced as a fresh agony ran through his body. 'Nothing. Not from you. Not from anybody!' He coughed again, but this time the torrent did not stop.

As the returning boats ground alongside and the gangways became alive with breathless men, Vibart died.

Bolitho stood up slowly and stared at the dead man. It was somehow typical and right that Vibart had remained unflinching and unshaken to the end.

He saw Captain Rennie and Midshipman Farquhar stepping over some wounded seamen, their faces drawn and ashen by what they saw. He clasped his hands behind him to hide his emotion from them.

'Put these men under guard, Mr. Farquhar. Then carry on at once with loading the fresh water. We sail as soon as it is completed.' He walked slowly across to the opposite side, and as the men parted to let him through he saw Onslow staring up at him, his eyes already glazed in death.

All at once Bolitho felt sick and unclean, as if the mutiny had left him with another, deeper scar.

He said harshly, 'I hope we can match the French as well as we can fight each other!' Then he turned and strode aft.

16. A SPECIAL SORT OF MAN

MIDSHIPMAN MAYNARD tapped on the door of Bolitho's cabin and reported breathlessly, 'Mr. Herrick's respects, sir, and we have just sighted two sail on the starboard bow.' He darted a quick glance at the other officers who were standing beside Bolitho's desk. 'It's the flagship, and the frigate *Volcano*.'

Bolitho nodded, his face thoughtful. 'Thank you. My compliments to Mr. Herrick. Tell him to tack the ship to intercept.' He paused. 'And have the prisoners ready to be sent across to *Cassius*.'

He listened to Maynard's feet scurrying up the cabin ladder and then turned back to the other officers. 'Well, gentlemen, at last we have found the flagship.'

It had been two days since the *Phalarope* had crept away from the small islets. Two long days in which to think back on mutiny and murder. Bolitho had broken his normal practice of appearing regularly on the quarterdeck, and had spent long, brooding hours in his cabin, reliving each moment, torturing himself with regrets and recriminations.

He looked down at the chart and said slowly, 'From what Allday described, I would say that the French are out in force. The two frigates were probably feelers from de Grasse's main fleet. If so, they have changed their plans.' He tapped the chart with one finger. 'De Grasse would never waste frigates at a time like this. It looks to me as if he intends to avoid all the main channels and will use the Dominica Passage. That way he might well bypass our patrols.'

He stopped thinking aloud, and with sudden briskness rolled up the chart and laid it to one side.

He said, 'I shall go over to the *Cassius* and speak to the admiral.' He glanced at the neat pile of reports on the desk. 'There is much that Sir Robert will wish to know.' How trite it sounded, he thought bitterly. Like items in the ship's log, bald of feeling or humanity. How could he describe the atmosphere on the maindeck when he had spoken a prayer before the shrouded corpses had slid over the side?

Lieutenant Vibart's body, alongside those of the dead mutineers. The rest of the crew had gathered round in silence

Not just a silence of respect or sadness, but something much deeper. It was like an air of shame, a combined feeling of guilt.

He stared at the watching officers beside him. Okes and Rennie. Farquhar and Proby.

Bolitho continued in the same curt tone, 'You all showed great resource and courage. I have made a full report and I trust it will receive proper attention.' He did not add that without such a report from the ship's captain the story of the brief, savage mutiny would overshadow all else with the admiral and his superiors. As it was it might still be insufficient to save the ship's name from further harm.

He looked hard at Okes. 'You will take over as first lieutenant of course, and Mr. Herrick will assume your duties forthwith.' He switched his gaze to Farquhar. 'I do not have to add to what I have put in my report about you. You are appointed acting lieutenant immediately. I have no doubt whatever that it will be confirmed with equal speed.'

Farquhar said, 'Thank you, sir.' He looked round as if expecting to see an immediate change in his surroundings. 'I am very grateful.'

Okes said nervously, 'I still can't believe Mr. Vibart is dead.'

Bolitho eyed him impassively. 'Death is the only thing which is inevitable, Mr. Okes. Yet it is the one thing we can never take for granted!'

There was a tap at the door and Stockdale peered in. 'Flagship is signalling, Captain. For you to report on board as soon as possible.'

'Very well, Stockdale. Call away my boat's crew.' He added to the others, 'Remember this, gentlemen. The *Phalarope* was nearly lost by mutiny.' He allowed his tongue to linger on the word. 'What we have to decide now is whether we have gained anything by a reprieve.' He saw their quick exchange of glances and continued, 'The ship is either cleansed of evil or smeared by shame. The choice is ours. Yours and mine!' He looked around their grave faces. 'That is all. You may go.'

Stockdale reappeared as the officers filed out, and busied himself getting Bolitho's hat and sword. He said, 'Allday is waiting to see you, Captain.' He sounded disapproving.

'Yes, I sent for him.' He listened to the squeal of blocks as the gig was hoisted out, and remembered Stockdale's stricken face as he had returned with the rest of the shore party. He had stared round the stained deck at the corpses and then at his captain. He had said brokenly, 'I should never have left you, Captain! Not for an instant!' It was as if he believed he had failed Bolitho. He seemed to think that if he had stayed aboard the mutiny could never have happened.

Bolitho said quietly, 'Send him in. He is a good seaman, Stockdale. I wronged *him*, not the other way about!'

Stockdale shook his head, but shambled away to fetch the man who had broken the mutiny.

And what a risk he had taken, Bolitho thought. He had walked back towards the searching marines, knowing full well that they were unaware of his innocence, and that any man might shoot him down without waiting for an explanation. Allday had found Okes and Farquhar, and together it seemed they had decided it best for Allday to try to reach the ship unsupported by anyone but Ferguson. It was a right decision, and a brave one. If Onslow had seen a boatload of men approaching the ship the balance would have tipped in his favour.

There was a tap at the door and Allday stepped into the cabin. Dressed in white trousers and checked shirt, his long hair tied back with a length of codline, he looked every inch the landsman's idea of a sailor. On his cheek and neck there were two diagonal scars where Brock had struck with his cane.

Bolitho faced him for several seconds. Then he said, 'I called you here to thank you properly for what you did, Allday. I wish I could say something which would help clean away the wrong which was done you.' He shrugged. 'But I know of no such reward.'

Allday relaxed slightly. 'I understand, sir. As it was, it all turned out for the best.' He grinned self-consciously. 'I was a bit scared, I can tell you, sir.' His eyes hardened. 'But when I saw Onslow, that was enough! I'm glad I was able to kill him!'

Bolitho studied Allday with new interest. He had a clean-cut, intelligent face, and but for his total lack of education might have gone far and done well by himself.

'Onslow should be a lesson to all of us, Allday.' Bolitho walked to the stern windows, his mind going back over the thought which had nagged him most since the mutiny. 'He was doomed by his life and circumstances. It is up to us not to make any more Onslows through cruelty or lack of understanding.' He swung round. 'No, Allday, I failed with Onslow. He was just a man like the rest of us. He never stood a real chance from the day he was born!'

Allday stared at him with surprise. 'There was nothing *you* could have done for him, if you'll excuse me saying so.' He spread his hands. 'He was a bad one, and I've seen a few in my time!'

Maynard peered in the door. 'Closing the flagship now, sir. Ready to lower the gig.'

'Very good.' Bolitho looked at Allday. 'Is there anything I can do for you?'

Allday shifted uncomfortably. 'There is one thing, sir.' Then he lifted his chin, his eyes suddenly clear and determined. 'It's about Ferguson, your clerk, sir. Are you sending him over with the other mutineers?'

Bolitho spread his arms to allow Stockdale to buckle on his sword. 'That was the intention, Allday.' He frowned. 'I know he came back with you, and did much to repair the damage he had done by his complicity with Onslow. But,' he shrugged, 'there are several charges against him. He aided the mutineers with confidential information, without which any sort of uprising might have been impossible. He attacked a sentry and released a prisoner, the guilt or innocence of whom had not been decided.' He picked up his hat and stared at it. 'Do you think he should warrant complete pardon?'

Allday said quietly, 'Remember what you said about Onslow, sir? Ferguson's no real sailor, and never will be.' He smiled sadly. 'I've looked after him since we were pressed together. If you do this to him I shall feel I've let him down. I shall feel as you do now over Onslow!'

Bolitho nodded. 'I will have to think about it.' He walked to the ladder, ducking below the beams. Then he said, 'Thank you, Allday. You put a forceful argument.'

He ran up into the sunlight and looked quickly across at the *Cassius*. She looked big and reliable against the blue water, and he could see the other frigate hove to beyond her.

Herrick touched his hat. 'Gig ready, sir.' He glanced questioningly at the silent group of manacled men by the entry port. 'Shall I send 'em over while you're with the admiral?'

'If you please, Mr. Herrick.' Bolitho caught sight of Allday's tall figure beside the cabin hatch and added sharply, 'But have Ferguson kept aboard. I will deal with him myself.'

Herrick looked mystified. 'Ferguson, sir?'

Bolitho eyed him coldly. 'He *is* my clerk, Mr. Herrick! Have you forgotten so soon that you chose him for me?' He gave a brief smile and saw the relief flooding across the other man's face.

'Aye, aye, sir!' Herrick strode to the rail. 'Man the side there! Stand by for the captain!'

The pipes trilled and Bolitho vanished down into the boat.

Herrick looked round as old Proby mumbled, 'How old is he? Twenty-five or six?' He gave a deep sigh. 'I'm twice his age and more beside, and there are others like me aboard the *Phalarope*.' He watched the little gig skimming through the whitecaps towards the swaying ship of the line. 'Yet he's like a father to all of us!' He shook his head. 'Have you seen the way the crew look at him now, Mr. Herrick? Like children caught out doing wrong. They know how he *feels* what has happened, how their shame is more'n doubled for him!'

Herrick stared at him. It was rare for the master to say so much all at once. 'I never realized that you admired him, too!'

Proby pouted his pendulous lower lip. 'I'm too old for admiration, Mr. Herrick. It's deeper'n that. Our captain is a special sort of man.' He frowned and then added, 'I'd die for him, and willingly. I can't say more'n that!' He turned with sudden anger. 'Blast me, Mr. Herrick! How can you let me go on like that?' He shuffled noisily across the quarterdeck like an untidy spider.

Herrick crossed to the rail, his mind still dwelling on Proby's words. Below, watched by armed marines, the remnants of Onslow's conspirators stood awaiting passage to the *Cassius*. Herrick did not share Bolitho's shame on their behalf. He would willingly have hanged each one of them single-handed, if only to lift the despair from Bolitho's shoulders.

He remembered his own exultation when Okes and Rennie had boarded the frigate and he had realized that the mutiny's sudden fire had been quenched. It was then that he had seen through Bolitho's careful mask and had penetrated to the man within. Yes, Proby was right. He was a very special sort of man.

Midshipman Neale crossed to his side and trained his glass on the flagship. Herrick glanced down at the small midshipman and remembered his frantic struggles as they thrust his greased body through the vent hole. Neale's sudden appearance had made quite a sensation when he had flung open the doors of the cable tier. As Ellice, the surgeon, had said later, 'There we all was, Mr. 'Errick, thinkin' of death or worse, an' suddenly the doors come flyin' open like the gates of 'eaven itself!' The surgeon's crimson face had crinkled into a grin. 'When I saw this little naked cherub with the sun behind 'im I thought I was already dead without knowin' it 'ad 'appened!'

Herrick smiled to himself. Neale seemed to have grown in stature since the dreadful day. He said, 'In a few years you'll be getting promoted like Mr. Farquhar if you go on like this.'

Neale considered the suggestion and then replied, 'I never doubted it, sir.' He flushed and added quickly, 'Well, not often!'

Sir Robert Napier walked stiffly to a small gilt chair and sat down. For several seconds he stared at Bolitho's tense features and then said dryly, 'You are a very erratic and unpredictable young man, Bolitho.' He tapped his fingertips together. 'But there is one thing to be said in your favour. You are never dull!'

Bolitho did not trust himself to smile. It was still far too early to know exactly how his ideas had been received. With fretting impatience he had waited in an adjoining cabin while the admiral read his reports, and after what seemed like an hour he was ushered into the great man's presence. There were two other captains already present. Cope of the *Cassius,* and a thickset, unsmiling man Bolitho recognized as Fox of the frigate *Volcano.*

The admiral said, 'It seems to me that you are getting unnecessarily excited about the French frigates which one of your men sighted.' He waved one hand across his big coloured chart. 'Look for yourself, Bolitho. The Leeward and Windward Islands are like a broken chain running from north to south. If the French fleet is out in force, and I say *if,* Sir George Rodney's frigates will have reported the fact, and both sides will have engaged already. That being so, what further can I do in the matter?' He leaned back, his eyes fixed on Bolitho's face.

Bolitho glanced quickly at the other officers. Cope, being Sir Robert's flag captain, would naturally stay non-committal until he knew his master's intentions. Fox was the man to convince. He was said to be a hard man, and as he was somewhat old for his rank, inclined to be over-cautious.

Bolitho took his own chart and laid it carefully across the admiral's. He started quietly. 'The whole plan to contain and engage the French fleet is based on one main theme, sir. We know that de Grasse has his strongest force at Martinique to the south. To meet with his Spanish ally and to reach Jamaica, his first necessity is to *avoid* any damaging action with us.'

The admiral said irritably, 'I know that, dammit!'

Bolitho continued, 'I believe that the two frigates were part of a scouting force, ahead of the main fleet.' He ran his finger along the chart. 'He could sail north from Martinique, and if necessary deploy his ships amongst the scattered islands en route. Then, at his most suitable moment he could swing west to Jamaica as planned.' He looked at Fox who met his eyes without expression. He added urgently, 'Sir George Rodney is depending on a quick engagement, sir. But suppose de Grasse avoids that first contact, or, even worse, he makes a feint attack on our ships and *then* heads north?' He waited, watching the admiral's pale eyes moving across the chart.

Sir Robert said grudgingly, 'It could happen, I suppose. De Grasse could skirt any hostile land and then keep close inshore of more friendly territory, Guadeloupe for instance.' He puckered his lower lip. 'He would thereby avoid a running battle in open water, like the Martinique Passage.' He nodded, his face suddenly grave. 'Yours is a dangerous supposition, Bolitho.'

Captain Cope said uneasily, 'If the French can get ahead of Rodney we're done for!'

Bolitho asked, 'Could I suggest something, sir?' He tried to gauge the extent of his own forcefulness. 'If I am wrong, there can be no real harm in my idea.'

The admiral shrugged. 'I cannot find it in my heart to dampen such rare enthusiasm, Bolitho.' He wagged one finger. 'But I do not promise to abide by it!'

Bolitho leaned across the chart. 'My ship was down here in search of fresh water . . .'

The admiral interrupted, 'And well off her allotted station incidentally!'

'Yes, sir.' Bolitho hurried on. 'Allowing for perhaps a day without wind, and a further two days to regain contact with their admiral, the two French frigates would have had ample time to examine the full extent of *this* Channel.' He stood back slightly as the other two captains craned over to look. 'There is a whole cluster of small islands to the north of the Dominica Passage.' He paused. 'The Isles des Saintes. If I were de Grasse, that is where I would make for. From that point he could swing west to Jamaica, or run for safety at Guadeloupe if Rodney's fleet is too close on his heels.' He swallowed and added, 'If our squadron moved south-east we might be in a better position to observe, and if necessary to report to Sir George Rodney what is happening!'

Sir Robert rubbed his chin. 'What do you think, Cope?'

The flag captain shifted uncomfortably on his feet. 'It's hard to say, sir. If Bolitho is right, and I am sure he has considered the matter most carefully, then de Grasse will have chosen the most unlikely route to slip past our blockade.' He added unhelpfully, 'But of course, if he is wrong, then we will have left our allotted station without good cause!'

The admiral glared at him. 'You do not have to remind me!' He turned his gaze on Fox, who was still leaning over the chart. 'Well?'

Fox straightened his back. 'I think I agree with Bolitho.' He paused. 'However, there is one point which he seems to have overlooked.' He jabbed at the pencilled lines with his finger. 'If Sir George Rodney flushes de Grasse away from the Dominica Passage the Frogs will certainly have the advantage. The wind is too poor to allow our fleet time to re-engage before de Grasse dashes for open water.' He drew his finger slowly across the chart in a straight line. 'But our squadron might be right across their line of escape!'

The admiral stirred in his chair. 'Do you think I had not considered this?' He glared at Bolitho. 'Well, what do you say?'

Bolitho answered stubbornly, 'I still say we shall be in a better position to report and, if necessary, shadow the enemy, sir.'

The admiral stood up and began to pace with sudden agitation. 'If only I could get some real news! I sent the brig *Witch of Looe* away days ago to try and gain intelligence, but with this damn climate what can you expect?' He stared through the open stern windows. 'Sometimes we are becalmed for days on end. The war could be over for all I know!'

Bolitho said, 'I could take the *Phalarope* to the south'rd, sir.'

'No!' The admiral's voice was like a whipcrack. 'I will have no captain of mine taking what should be my responsibility!'

He gave a frosty smile. 'Or was it your intention to force me into this decision?' He did not wait for a reply. 'Very well, gentlemen. We will make sail and proceed south-east immediately.' He stared at each of them in turn. 'But I want nothing foolhardy! If we sight the enemy we will retire and report our findings to Sir George Rodney.'

Bolitho masked his disappointment. He must be content. He had not even expected Sir Robert Napier to agree to leaving the present area, let alone to commit himself to what might well be a pointless and time-wasting venture.

As he turned to follow Fox the admiral added sharply, 'And as to that other matter, Bolitho.' He rested his hand on the open envelope. 'I will deal with that in my own way. I do not wish the reputation of my ships to be tarnished by mutiny. I intend that it should stay within the squadron.' He was looking impatient again. 'As for Lieutenant Vibart, well, I suppose it cannot be helped now. A dead officer is no use to me, no matter how he died!'

Bolitho tried to think of a suitable reply. 'He died bravely, sir.'

The admiral grunted. 'So did the Christians in Rome! And damn little good it did anybody!'

Bolitho backed from the cabin and then hurried on deck to summon his boat. The sea was still speckled with small white-caps, and the admiral's flag was streaming bravely in the freshening breeze. It was good sailing weather, he thought. And that was too rare to waste at any time.

With the ponderous two-decker between them, the frigates spread their sails and hauled off on either beam. By nightfall the wind had fallen slightly, but was still sufficient to make the sails boom with unaccustomed vigour as the yards were braced round to keep all three ships on a slow starboard tack.

Before the night fell completely to hide one vessel from another there was a final unhappy incident. Bolitho had been striding up and down the weather side of the quarterdeck when he heard Okes snap, 'Mr. Maynard! Lively there! Train your glass on the flagship. She seems to be hoisting a signal.' Bolitho had crossed the deck to watch the midshipman fumbling with his long telescope. It was strange for the admiral to be sending signals in such poor visibility. A flare would have been more effective.

Maynard had lowered his glass and looked round at the two officers. He had looked sick, as he had on the day he had discovered Evans' body. 'It's no signal, sir!'

Bolitho had taken the glass from the youth's hands and trained it across the hammock netting. Coldly, he had watched the small black dot rising towards the *Cassius*'s mainyard. It had twisted as it made its slow journey. Twisted and kicked, so that in his imagination Bolitho had thought he could hear the drum's staccato roll and the steady tramp of bare feet as the selected men had hauled the choking mutineer slowly up to the yard.

Maynard was wrong about one thing. It *was* a signal to every man who saw it.

Bolitho had returned the glass and said, 'I am going below, Mr. Okes. See that you have the best lookouts aloft, and call me if you sight *anything*.' He had glanced quickly at Maynard and added quietly, 'That man, whoever he was, knew the price of his folly. Discipline demands that it be paid in full!'

He turned on his heel and walked below, despising himself for the cold unreality of his words. In his mind he seemed to hear Vibart's thick, accusing voice, still jeering at him for his weakness. What did one more death matter? Fever and unaccountable accident, the cannon's harvest or the end of a rope, it was all the same in the end.

He threw himself across his cot and stared at the deckhead. A captain had to be above such things, to be able to play God without thought for those who served him. Then he remembered Allday's words and the blind trust of men like Herrick and Stockdale. Such men deserved his attention, even his love, he thought vaguely. To use power as a tyrant was to be without honour. To be without honour was to be less than a man.

With that thought uppermost in his mind he fell into a deep sleep.

'Captain, sir!' Midshipman Neale rested his hand anxiously on Bolitho's arm and then jumped back in alarm as the cot swayed violently to one side.

Bolitho swung his legs to the deck and stared for a long moment while his mind sought to recover from the nightmare. He had been surrounded by screaming, faceless men, and his arms had been pinioned while he felt a noose being tightened around his neck. Neale's hand had only added to the nightmare's reality, and he could still feel the sweat running across his spine.

He said harshly, 'What is it?' The cabin was still in darkness, and it took him several more seconds to recover his composure.

Neale said, 'Mr. Herrick's respects, sir. He thinks you should know we've heard something.' He fell back another pace as Bolitho lurched to his feet. 'It sounded like gunfire, sir!'

Bolitho did not pause to find his coat but ran quickly to the quarterdeck. It was almost dawn, and already the sky was painted in a pale blue strip beyond the gently corkscrewing bows.

'What is it, Mr. Herrick?' He moved to the rail and cupped his hands to his ears.

Herrick stared at him uncertainly. 'I could be mistaken, sir. It might have been thunder.'

'Most unlikely.' Bolitho shivered slightly in the cool dawn breeze. 'Can you see the *Cassius* yet?'

'No, sir.' Herrick pointed vaguely. 'There's a mist coming up. It'll be another hot day, I'm thinking.'

Bolitho stiffened as a low rumble echoed sullenly across the open water. 'Maybe hotter than you think, Mr. Herrick.' He glanced up at the jerking canvas. 'The wind seems to be holding.' He was suddenly aware that there were several figures already standing on the maindeck. Everyone faced forward, listening and wondering.

Bolitho said, 'Call the hands.' He peered upwards again. In the dim light he could just see the masthead pendant whipping out like a pointing finger. 'Take out the second reef, Mr. Herrick. And set the fores'l and spanker.'

Herrick called for a boatswain's mate, and seconds later the ship came alive to the call of pipes and the stamp of running feet.

Then Herrick said, 'I still can't see the flagship, sir.'

'We won't wait for her!' Bolitho watched the men swarming aloft and listened to the harsh bark of commands. 'That is gunfire ahead. Make no mistake about it!'

Proby came on deck buttoning his heavy coat. He seemed half asleep, but as the big spanker filled with wind and the deck canted obediently to the wind's eager thrust he contained any comment he might have felt and crossed to the wheel.

Bolitho said calmly, 'Alter course two points to larboard, Mr. Proby.' The ship's sudden response to wind and sail had swept away the strain and sleep from his mind. He had been right. The waiting was almost over.

He looked sideways at Herrick and saw that his face was clearer in the growing light. He looked worried and not a little startled by the swift chain of events.

Bolitho said quietly, 'We will investigate, Mr. Herrick.' He pointed at the men swarming back along the yards. 'I want chain

slings fitted on every yard. If we are called to action our people
have enough to contend with at the guns. I don't want them
crushed by falling spars.' He halted the lieutenant in his tracks.
'And have nets spread above the maindeck, too.' He made himself stand quite still by the rail, his hands resting on the worn
and polished wood. He could feel the ship trembling beneath
his palms, as if his thoughts were being transformed into new
life, and the life was flowing through the *Phalarope* even as he
watched.

From newly awakened chaos the ship had already settled down
into a purposeful rhythm. All the weeks of training, the hours
of persistent instruction were giving their rewards.

Stockdale joined him by the rail. 'I'll get your coat, sir.'

'Not yet, Stockdale. That can keep for a moment longer.' He
turned as Okes appeared at the ladder, his face still crumpled
from sleep. 'I want the hands to eat well this morning, Mr. Okes.
I have a feeling that the galley fire will be out for some time to
come.' He saw the understanding spreading across the officer's
face. '*This* time we will be ready!'

Like a living creature the *Phalarope* lifted her bows and
smashed jubilantly into each succeeding rank of low waves, the
spray bursting back over her forecastle in long white streamers.

Herrick reported, 'Chain slings rigged, sir.'

'Very well.' It was an effort to speak calmly. 'Have the boats
swung out for towing astern. If we fight today there will be
enough splinters flying without the boats adding to them!'

Okes managed to ask, 'The gunfire, sir? What do you make
of it?'

Bolitho saw several men pausing to listen to his reply. He said
slowly, 'Two ships. One much smaller than the other by the
sound of the firing. We can be sure of one thing, Mr. Okes.
They cannot both be enemies!'

Herrick was back again. 'What now, sir?'

'I am going down to shave and wash. When I return I will
expect to hear that the men have been fed.' He smiled. 'After
that, we shall have to see!'

But once back in his cabin it was almost more than he could
bear to take time to shave and change his clothes. The breakfast
which Stockdale hurriedly laid on the cabin table he could not
even face. By tonight, or perhaps within the next few hours, he
might be dead. Or even worse, screaming for mercy under the
surgeon's knife. He shuddered. It was pointless even to think of
it. More, it was harmful.

Stockdale said, 'I have laid out a fresh shirt, sir.' He looked
searchingly at Bolitho. 'I think you should wear your best
uniform, too.'

'For heaven's sake why, man?' He stared at the coswain's battered face in surprise.

Stockdale replied gravely, 'This is the day, sir. I have the same feeling I had with you once before.' He added stubbornly, 'And the men will be looking to you, sir. They'll want to *see* you.' He nodded as if to settle the matter. 'After all that's happened they'll need to know you're with them.'

Bolitho stared at him, suddenly moved by the man's halting, broken voice. 'If you say so, Stockdale.'

Ten minutes later a voice echoed faintly above the sounds of sea and canvas. 'Deck there! Sail on the starboard bow!'

Bolitho made himself wait just a few more seconds as Stockdale buckled on his sword, and then walked to the cabin ladder. The quarterdeck seemed crammed with figures, all pointing and speaking at once. Every voice fell silent as Bolitho walked to the rail to take a telescope from Maynard.

Through the frigate's criss-cross of rigging he could see the distorted patterns of tossing whitecaps beyond her bows. The sky was already clear, but the water seemed to writhe in the grip of a slow-moving sea mist, and for once the new day felt drained of warmth.

Then he saw them. Two ships close together, their hulls hidden in a dense cloud of smoke and mist, their tattered sails hanging disembodied above the hidden battle below.

But the flags were easily visible. One blood red, like that which flew above him. The other clear and white. The flag of France.

He closed the telescope with a snap. 'Very well, Mr. Okes. Beat to quarters and clear for action!'

His eyes held them a moment longer. 'We must give well of ourselves today, gentlemen. If our people see us doing our best, they will be willing enough to do *their* duty!'

He half listened to the distant thunder of gunfire. 'Carry on, Mr. Okes!'

They all touched their hats and then looked at one another, as if each man realized that for some, maybe for all of them, it would be the last time.

Then the drum began to rattle, and the small moment was past.

17. FORM LINE OF BATTLE!

WITHIN TEN MINUTES of the drum's urgent tattoo the *Phalarope* was cleared for action. Decks were sanded and buckets of water stood within reach of every gun. Over the whole ship there had fallen a strange, gripping stillness, broken only by the uneasy slap of canvas and the steady sluice of water around the stem.

Bolitho shaded his eyes and watched the sun's unearthly orange glow as it tried to filter through the unending wall of sea mist. The bang and clatter of gunfire had become more uneven and sporadic with each dragging minute, and now as the distance fell away between the *Phalarope* and the other ships there came new sounds, more vicious, and somehow more personal. Bolitho could hear the sharp cracks of muskets and pistols, the jarring scrape of steel against steel, and above all the mingling cries of men fighting for their lives.

Okes wiped his face with the back of his hand and said quickly, 'This damn mist! I can't see what's happening!'

Bolitho glanced at him briefly. 'It is a godsend, Mr. Okes. They are too busy to see us!' He lifted his hand to the quartermaster. 'Starboard a point!' Then he walked to the rail and looked down at Herrick's upturned face.

'Have the guns loaded, but do not run out until I tell you.'

He saw the gunners push the fresh charges down the gaping muzzles, followed by the round, gleaming shot. The more experienced gun captains took time to fondle each ball, weighing it almost lovingly to make sure that the first salvo would be a perfect one.

He heard Herrick shout, 'Double-shotted and grape, lads! Let 'em *feel* it this time!'

A stronger breath of wind rolled aside the mist around the entangled ships, and Bolitho tightened his lips into a thin line. Almost stern on to the *Phalarope*'s swift approach was a French frigate, and alongside, listing and battered almost beyond recognition, was the little brig, *Witch of Looe*. One mast was already gone, and the other seemed to be held upright only by the remaining stays. He thought of her commander, the young Lieutenant Dancer he had met aboard the flagship, and marvelled at the man's pluck or wasted courage which had made him match his ship against this powerful opponent. His little pop-guns against the still-smoking twelve-pounders.

Okes said, 'They've seen us, sir!' He swallowed hard as something like an animal growl floated across the water. 'My God, look at them!'

The *Witch of Looe*'s shattered deck seemed to be swamped in French sailors, and as the drifting gunsmoke parted momentarily to allow the sunlight to play across the carnage, Bolitho saw the small knot of defenders, still fighting back from the brig's small quarterdeck. In a few more minutes they would be swamped completely.

The gunports along the French frigate's disengaged side suddenly opened, and to the steady rumble of trucks the guns appeared like a line of bared teeth.

Bolitho shut his ears and mind to the victorious shouts from the French frigate and concentrated his thoughts on the narrowing strip of water between them. Less than a cable's length to go, with neither ship able to fire. *Phalarope* was almost dead in line with the other ship's stern, so that if she held her course her bowsprit would drive straight through the stern windows. On one side of the enemy frigate lay the listing, riddled brig, and on the other the guns waited to claim another victim.

Bolitho called sharply, 'Run out the starboard battery!'

He watched as his men threw themselves against the tackle falls, and in a squealing, protesting line the guns trundled up the slight slope of the deck and out through the open ports.

There was a great bellow of noise from the French ship, wild and inhuman. The sound gained from killing and madness. *Phalarope*'s own men remained tense and cold, their eyes unblinking as the enemy's pockmarked sails grew higher and higher above the bows.

Bolitho placed his hands on the rail and said slowly, 'Now send your men across to the larboard battery, Mr. Herrick!' He saw the quick, mystified glances and added harshly, 'In another minute I am going to turn to starboard and go alongside the *Witch of Looe*. She is low in the water, our broadside should pass right above her!'

Herrick's frown gave way to a look of open admiration. 'Aye, aye, sir!'

Bolitho's voice stopped him in his tracks. 'Quietly there! I don't want the Frogs to see what we're doing!'

Crouching almost on their knees the gunners scuttled across to the opposite side, their excitement instantly quelled by hoarse threats from the gun captains.

Nearer and nearer. A few musket balls whined harmlessly overhead, but for the most part the French captain was prepared to wait. He could match gun for gun, and as *Phalarope*'s bows and foremast would take the first punishment he could afford to feel confident. His own ship was drifting slowly downwind and his gunners could thank the *Witch of Looe*'s weight alongside for a steadier platform beneath their feet. There was a faint ripple of cheering, drowned instantly by a fresh outburst of musket fire.

Proby muttered, 'The brig's people are cheering us, sir!'

Bolitho ignored him. One error now and his ship would change into a shambles. Fifty yards, thirty yards. Bolitho lifted his hand. He saw Quintal crouching like a runner, one beefy hand resting on the nearest seaman at the braces.

Bolitho shouted, '*Now!*'

At his side Proby added his weight to the wheel, as with a scream of blocks the yards began to swing, the sails flapping in protest, but answering the challenge of wind and rudder.

'Run out!' Bolitho felt ice cold as the larboard battery squealed across the sanded planks. 'Fire as your guns bear!'

He pounded the rail, counting each frantic second. For a moment he thought that he had mistimed the change of course, but even as he waited, holding his breath and hardly daring to watch, the bowsprit swung lazily across the French ship's high stern, almost brushing away a small group of sailors which had gathered above the hammock nettings.

Herrick ran from gun to gun, making sure that each successive shot went home. Not that he need have troubled. As the French gunners ran dazedly from the opposite side the first shots went crashing home. The *Phalarope* shuddered as she ground against the little brig, but maintained her way steadily down the ship's side, her guns belching fire and death above the heads of the stunned boarders and the remaining members of the brig's crew.

Bolitho winced as the quarterdeck nine-pounders joined in the din. But still there was no answer from the French ship. Bolitho had guessed correctly that the guns which stared impotently at the *Phalarope*'s smashing attack would have been in action right up to the moment of grappling and boarding the little brig.

He watched as great pieces of the frigate's bulwark caved in and fragments of torn planking rose above the smoke as if thrown from an invisible hand. An axe flashed dully, and Bolitho yelled, 'He's trying to free himself!' He drew his sword. 'Over you go, lads! Boarders away!'

As the *Phalarope* ground to a sluggish halt, her bows locked into the brig's fallen rigging and spars, Bolitho ran down the port gangway and clambered on to the *Witch of Looe*'s tilting deck. For a moment nobody followed him, and then with a great roar, half cheer and half scream, the waiting seamen swept over the bulwark behind him.

Most of the French sailors, caught between the *Phalarope*'s savage gunfire and the revived members of the brig's crew, threw up their hands in surrender, but Bolitho thrust them aside, his sword raised high towards his own men. 'Come on, lads! We'll take the frigate!' There would be time enough for the boarders later, he thought vaguely.

Once up the frigate's shot-pitted side the resistance became fierce and deadly. Wild, crazed faces floated around Bolitho as he hacked his way aft towards the poop, and his feet barely supported him in the heel-thick layer of blood which seemed to cover the deck like fresh paint. The enemy's upperdeck had been crammed with men. Some were boarders recalled from the *Witch of Looe,* and others were gunners caught off guard by the *Phalarope*'s sudden change of course. This tangled, momentarily disorganized mass of men had received the full force of the broadside. All the *Phalarope*'s larboard twelve-pounders and the quarterdeck battery as well, every one double-shotted and loaded with grape for good measure. It looked as if a maniac had been throwing buckets of blood everywhere. Even the lower edges of the sails were speckled in scarlet, and fragments of men hung from upended guns and splintered bulwarks alike.

A French officer, hatless and bleeding from a scalp wound, leapt in front of Bolitho, his thin sword red almost to its hilt. Bolitho lifted his own sword, but felt it parried aside, and saw the French officer's expression change from anxiety to sudden exultation. Bolitho tried to draw back, but the struggling press of figures prevented it. He could not lift his sword in time. He saw the man's arm come round, heard the swish of steel, and waited for the shock of the thrust.

Instead the Frenchman's face twisted with alarm as a battle-crazed marine burst through the throng, his fixed bayonet held in front of him like a spear. The sword swung round yet again, but it was too late. The momentum of the marine's charge impaled the officer on the bayonet and threw them both against the poop ladder. The marine screamed with wild delight and stamped his boot on the Frenchman's stomach, at the same moment wrenching out the dripping bayonet. The French officer sank slowly to his knees, his mouth opening and shutting like a dying fish.

The marine stared at him as if for the first time and then thrust the bayonet home again.

Bolitho caught his arm. 'That's enough! For God's sake, man!' The marine did not seem to hear him, but after a brief startled look at his captain's face he charged off into the battle once more, his expression one of concentration and hatred.

The frigate's captain lay on the poop, his shoulders supported by a young lieutenant. Someone was tying a crude tourniquet around the shattered stump of one leg, and the captain was only just hanging on to his senses as fighting, stabbing seamen reeled and staggered across his body.

Bolitho shouted, 'Strike! *Strike,* Captain! While you still have some men left!' He did not recognize his own voice, and his hand around the hilt of his sword was wet with sweat. He thought of the crazed marine and knew that he too was in danger of giving way to the lust of battle.

The French captain gestured faintly, and the lieutenant gasped, 'We strike! M'sieu, we strike!'

But even after the white flag had fluttered to the deck and men had been hauled bodily from the work of killing, it took time to make the *Phalarope*'s men realize they had won.

The first to congratulate Bolitho was Dancer of the *Witch of Looe*. Bleeding from several wounds, his arm tied across his chest with a piece of codline, he limped over the splintered bloodstained deck and held out his good hand. 'Thank you, sir! I was never more pleased to see any man!'

Bolitho sheathed his sword. 'Your own ship is sinking, I fear.' He looked up at the frigate's tattered sails. 'But you sold her dearly.'

Dancer swayed and then gripped Bolitho's arm. 'I was trying to warn Sir Robert! The French are out, sir!' He squinted his eyes as if to restore his dazed thoughts. 'Three days ago de Grasse met up with Rodney's fleet, but after a quick clash at long range, broke off the battle.' He pointed vaguely through the smoke. 'I have been trying to shadow the Frogs, and this morning I saw the whole fleet nor'-west of Dominica!' He shook his head. 'I think Sir George Rodney has managed to engage them again, but I cannot be sure. I was caught by this frigate before I could get back to the squadron.' He smiled ruefully. 'Now I have no ship at all!'

Bolitho frowned. 'Have you enough men to take this frigate as prize?'

Dancer stared. 'But she is *your* prize, sir!'

'We can discuss the share of financial reward at a later and more convenient time, Lieutenant!' Bolitho smiled. 'In the meantime I suggest you herd these prisoners below and make as much speed as you can with these rags for some port of safety.' He peered up through the smoke. 'The wind has veered slightly to south-east. It should carry you clear of any impending battle!'

Herrick blundered through the mess and tangle of corpses, his sword dangling from his wrist. He touched his hat. 'We have just sighted the *Cassius*, sir!'

'Very well.' Bolitho held Dancer's hand. 'Thank you for your news. At least it will justify Sir Robert's leaving his proper station!' He turned on his heel and climbed back across the sinking brig towards his own ship.

Still deep in thought he clambered over the bulwark and walked along the gangway. The gunners were standing below him, their faces upturned as he passed. The marine marksmen high in the tops and the little powder monkeys by the magazine hatch, all stood and stared at the slim solitary figure framed against the torn sails of the vanquished Frenchman.

It had been a swift and incredible victory. Not a man injured let alone killed in the attack, and no damage to the *Phalarope* at all. Some good men had died in the fight aboard the enemy ship, but the success far outweighed any such loss. A frigate taken as a prize, the *Witch of Looe* revenged if not saved, and all within an hour.

Yet Bolitho thought of none of these things. In his mind's eye he could see his well-worn chart, and the enemy's fleet moving in an irresistible tide towards the open sea, and Jamaica the prize.

Then a voice yelled out from the maindeck and Bolitho turned startled and caught off guard.

'Three cheers, lads! Three cheers for our Dick!'

Bolitho stared round at the quarterdeck as the air was split with wild, uncontrollable cheering. Herrick and Rennie were openly grinning at him. Neale and Maynard waving their hats to the men on deck below. Bolitho felt confused and entirely unprepared, and as the three cheers extended to a frenzied shouting Herrick crossed to his side and said, 'Well done, sir! Well *done!*'

Bolitho said, 'What is the matter with everyone today?'

Herrick replied firmly, 'You've given them more than a *victory*, sir! You've given 'em back their self-respect!'

The cheering died away as if from a signal, and Herrick said quietly, 'They want you to tell them, sir.' He dropped his eyes.

Bolitho moved to the rail and stared slowly around the familiar faces. These men. His men. The thoughts chased one another through his mind like shadows. Starve them, beat them. Let them face scurvy and disease, and death a hundred different ways. But still they could cheer. He gripped the rail hard and stared above their heads. When he spoke his voice was quiet, and those men furthest away leaned forward to hear it better.

'This morning we fought and beat a French frigate!' He saw some of the men nudging each other and grinning like children. 'But more important to me is the fact that we fought as a single unit, as a King's ship should, and must fight!' A few of the older seamen nodded soberly, and Bolitho tried to steel himself for what he had to tell them.

It was no use just telling men to fight. They had to be led. It was an act of mutual trust. He cleared his throat. 'When you see an enemy abeam and the balls begin to fly overhead, you all fight for many reasons.' He looked around their tanned and expectant faces. 'You fight out of comradeship, to protect each other, and avenge well-loved friends who have already laid down their lives. Or you fight out of fear, a fear which breeds a power of hatred for the enemy who is always faceless yet ever present. And above all we fight for our ship!' He waved his arm around him. 'This is our ship, and will remain so, as long as we have the will to live and die for what is right!'

Some of the men started to cheer again, but he held up his hand, his eyes suddenly sad. 'But this short fight today was only a beginning. I cannot tell you how our small deeds will fit into the great pattern of battle, for I do not know. I only know that it is our common duty to fight today, and to fight as we have never done before!'

He had their full attention now, and he hated himself for the truth which had to be told. 'This morning we had luck on our side. But before this day dies we will need much more than that.'

As he paused the air seemed to give a sullen shudder, which as every man turned to stare across the captured ship alongside extended into a low, menacing rumble, like thunder across distant hills.

Bolitho continued steadily, 'Over there, lads, lies the enemy.'

He watched each man in turn, his heart suddenly dreading what was to come. He had brought them all to this. For no matter what reason, or how justified his efforts might be seen by others, he had committed his ship and his men to the inevitable.

He felt a sudden gust of warm wind at his neck, and as he watched the low, writhing bank of morning mist began to move clear. One minute the two frigates with the sinking wreck of the *Witch of Looe* between them made up their own small world. To one beam lay the sun-tinted mist, and to the other the open sea, where night had already crossed the hard horizon, and the topsails of the labouring *Cassius* showed above its edge, gleaming in the sunlight like a pink shell. Then, as the mist rolled away that small world broke up for ever.

Shrouded in haze to the south-east Bolitho could see the low wedge of Dominica, while away to the north the scattered islands which were called the Saintes. But between these two there was no horizon. It was a sight so vast and so terrible that nobody said a word. From side to side, as far as the eye could reach, the blue water was topped with an unbroken line of ships. There seemed to be no gap between each towering crop of sails, and as the growing sunlight reflected across the apparently motionless panorama of armed might, Bolitho was reminded of an old painting he had seen as a child. The armoured knights at Agincourt, their great horses bedecked in standards and glittering mail, the proud pennants and banners streaming from lances as they gathered to charge the flimsy line of English archers.

Almost desperately he looked down at his spellbound men. 'Well, lads, what do you say?' He pointed towards the great shimmering line of ships. 'Beyond that fleet lies England, across five thousand miles of open sea. At our back is Jamaica.' He pointed down between his feet. 'And below us is a thousand fathoms to the bottom!' He leaned forward, his eyes flashing with sudden urgency. 'So which is it to be, lads?'

The new sound of distant gunfire was drowned in the sudden wave of wild and uncontrolled cheering which swept across the *Phalarope*'s maindeck, to be caught and carried by those aboard the captured frigate. Even wounded men who were being carried below shouted with the rest, some not knowing why, or even having heard Bolitho's words. It was as if all the bitterness and pent-up frustrations were being swept away by their great chorus of voices.

Bolitho turned away, and Herrick who was nearest saw the strange sadness and disbelief in his eyes. He said quickly, 'There's your answer, sir!' He was excited like the others, even jubilant.

When Bolitho turned to look at him he studied the lieutenant as if he was a stranger. 'Tell me, Mr. Herrick, have you ever seen a sea battle?' He waved towards the horizon. 'Like this one will be?' He did not wait for a reply. '*I* have. There is no dash and madcap victory. No hit-and-run when the game gets too rough.' He gripped his hands behind him and stared unseeingly past the other officers. 'The sky is so dark with smoke that it is like hell. Even the ships cry out, did you know that?' His voice became harsher. 'They cry because they are being torn apart, like the fools who man them!'

He swung round as Midshipman Maynard said hoarsely, 'Flagship's signalling, sir.'

Bolitho walked to the weather side and stared down at the listing brig. The water was already lapping over her bulwark, and only discarded corpses lolled on her battle-torn deck. He snapped, 'Do not acknowledge, Mr. Maynard!' To Herrick he added, 'Cast off from the brig and get under way.' He looked up at the masthead. 'We will steer due east!'

Herrick asked, 'What of the flagship, sir?'

'Sir Robert is a gallant gentleman, Mr. Herrick. But his seniority will have made him more careful than I.' He gave a short smile. 'And *his* men may not be so keen to die on this fine day!' His smile vanished. 'Now get those men to their stations, and stop this damn cheering!'

The *Phalarope* idled clear from the wreckage, and as the captured frigate cast off her grappling irons the little brig rolled slowly on to her beam, the bursting air bubbles tinged with scarlet as the creeping water surged triumphantly across her battered hull.

Bolitho lifted his glass as the yards went round and the deck canted slightly to the wind. He could see the frigate *Volcano*'s topmasts beyond the *Cassius,* and wondered how her captain would react to this awesome sight. Sir Robert Napier still had time to retire. One definite signal would take them all out of danger, mute witnesses as the French burst from the battle and headed for their goal.

Bolitho made up his mind. 'Mr. Maynard, make a signal to the *Flag.*' He saw Herrick look at Rennie and shrug, as if his captain's actions were now quite beyond his ability to keep up. 'Enemy in sight!'

He did not watch the flags soaring up the yards, but made himself walk back and forth across the quarterdeck, followed by the eyes of Rennie's square of marines. This was the decisive moment. Sir Robert was an old man, and past his best. To try to delay the French ships would give him nothing but glory he would never see. It might even be so futile that his action would be remembered with a scorn which could overshadow and despoil his whole career.

Maynard called, '*Flag* has acknowledged, sir!'

Bolitho bit his lip and continued his pacing. He could imagine the admiral's rasping voice as he dictated his signals, the uncertainty of the flag-captain, and the cautious confidence of Fox in the *Volcano.*

Maynard said suddenly, 'I can just make out her hoist, sir!' His eye was pressed to the end of the big telescope. '*Flag* to *Volcano*. Prepare for battle!'

The word flashed along the quarterdeck and down to the men waiting by the guns. Again the cheering, and again the cheer taken up across the water aboard the French ship. Bolitho waved absently as he saw Lieutenant Dancer's limping figure by the taffrail as the captured ship braced her yards and spread her tattered sails abreast the low wind.

Herrick said excitedly, '*Cassius* is making all sail, sir! My God, what a sight!' He seemed more impressed by the flagship's sudden activity than the fleet at his back.

Bolitho said, 'Have every man armed, Mr. Herrick. Put cutlasses and tomahawks at each gun. There will be plenty of fighting before long!'

Maynard lowered his glass, his voice shaking as he stared across at his captain. 'From *Flag*, sir! General signal.' He sounded as if he was trying to feel each word. '*Form line of battle!*'

Bolitho nodded slowly. 'Shorten sail, Mr. Herrick. We will bide here and allow the *Cassius* to meet up with us.' He sniffed the air. 'I feel we will lose the wind very soon. Dominica will act as a lee, I am afraid.'

He moved to the weather side and raised his glass across the nettings. Very slowly he moved the lens from side to side. In the small magnified picture he could see the dull flash of cannon fire, the brave flags and the gleam of sails as ship after mighty ship wheeled ponderously into line. He could feel the sweat at his spine, as he had after his nightmare. But this was real, yet harder to comprehend. God, there were three-deckers in plenty, perhaps sixty sail of the line, British and French, gliding together for a first, inexorable embrace.

He said sharply, 'Pass the word for Mr. Brock!' He did not lower his glass until the gunner reached the quarterdeck.

'Mr. Brock, I want both carronades taken to the forecastle. Put your best hands in charge of them, and see that their slides are freshly smeared with tallow.' He closed the glass and studied the gunner's dour face. 'The carronades are the only weapons we possess which the French lack.' He stared down at the nearest weapon, snub-nosed and ugly, and lacking either the grace or the proportion of a proper deck gun. Yet a carronade could throw a massive sixty-eight-pound shot at short range, the power of which was devastating. Each circular shot burst on impact to deluge everything nearby with murderous cast-iron balls. One shot had the lethal quality of grape, added to which was the weight of a much heavier weapon.

He walked slowly to the rail and looked down at the neat decks. Had he forgotten anything? He ignored Brock and his stripped working party struggling and cursing the heavy carronades. He had to concentrate his full being on the task ahead. He must trust each officer and man. If they failed now, it was his fault for some earlier lapse in judgement.

Suddenly the restless, crowded figures below each gangway took on another meaning. Bolitho felt the pain of loss, as if he was looking at faces already dead. Quintal, the boatswain, spitting on his hands and pointing aloft for the benefit of the men who waited to sail the ship into action. Farquhar, slim and self-contained, walking abreast his battery of guns, his eyes moving over each weapon and every man in its crew. And the seamen themselves. Tanned and healthy in spite of their discomforts. Some faces standing out more than others. Here a man who had done well at Mola Island. There another who had fled from his station when they had met the *Andiron*.

He let his eyes move up the shrouds, to the men like Allday still at work aloft, and the marines kneeling in the tops with their long muskets loaded and ready.

Then aft, here to the quarterdeck. With its nine-pounders, and Neale's tiny figure dwarfed by that of a pigtailed gunner's mate. And Proby, old Proby, waving his arms like some fat scarecrow as he gave his instructions to the helmsmen. One of the men at

the wheel Bolitho recognized as Strachan, the oldest sailor in
the company. Too old to work a gun to Brock's satisfaction, he
was still keen enough to stand his trick at the helm, and when
the hell of battle swept this very deck, Bolitho knew a man like
Strachan would never falter. Not because he was brave or stupid,
but because it was part of his life. The only life he had known,
and had been trained for.

Bolitho saw Okes watching him, his fingers playing nervously
with the scabbard of his sword. Inwardly he wished it was
Herrick at his side, but the latter would have his work cut out
handling the ship's firepower. And anyway, Bolitho thought with
sudden irritation, Okes was now first lieutenant. Vibart was
dead. Not even a memory any more.

By the cabin hatch Stockdale saw Bolitho's grave face and
gave a slight nod. He saw the captain's eyes catch the gesture
and then move. But Stockdale was satisfied. Bolitho knew he was
there. And that was enough.

Close-hauled, and making heavy weather of the faltering
breeze, the three ships tacked into line. Just as they had
rehearsed it so many frustrating times under the pitiless sun and
beneath the eye of this same querulous admiral.

Bolitho raised his hat as the *Volcano*'s sails billowed with
sudden power and the lean frigate took her station in the lead.
Cassius followed heavily in her wake, and as more flags soared
aloft, Bolitho said sharply, 'Take station astern the *Flag*, Mr.
Okes!'

He watched the men scampering to the braces, and then
looked at the two-decker, as like an elderly but experienced
warrior she opened her double line of ports and ran out her
guns.

A voice pealed out suddenly, 'Deck there! Ships on the starboard bow!' A pause while every eye peered up at the tiny
figure in the main crosstrees. 'Two ship o' the line! An' two
frigates!'

Bolitho tried to control his impatience. At the rear of the
small line *Phalarope* would engage last. By then, it might all be
decided, he thought bitterly.

The sails flapped dejectedly, and he heard the helmsmen curse
as the wheel went slack. 'Wind is backing to the east, sir!' Proby
looked mournful.

'Very well.' Bolitho lifted his glass and tried to see the nearest
enemy ships. The gunfire was louder and unending, but the
main battle fleets seemed stationary as before. It was of course
an illusion.

Beyond the *Cassius*'s flapping main course he saw a brief picture of the ships indicated by the lookout. Two big ones, very

close in line. With two smaller sails, one on either beam. But the falling wind was playing havoc with his own men, he thought angrily. They had cheered, expecting to fight or die in glory. But this waiting, this agonizing waiting, while all the time that slowly advancing fleet grew and grew, until the once exuberant seamen seemed too stunned to move, or drag their eyes from the smoke-shrouded ships.

Bolitho said, 'I am going aloft, Mr. Okes.' Without a glance at the sweating lieutenant he strode to the starboard gangway and made his way to the main shrouds. Even as a young midshipman Bolitho had never achieved a good head for heights, but after a quick look at the listless sails he started on the long climb to the main topmast.

As he swung through the lubber's hole of the maintop the waiting marines stared at him without speaking, and then turned their eyes back to the embattled fleets. The air was dinning with noise, and Bolitho's nostrils seemed full of the smell of powder and burned wood.

He found a solitary seaman perched in the crosstrees, and waited to regain his breath before opening his glass to stare over and beyond the slow-moving *Cassius*.

It was impossible to tell one line of battle from the other. The main British and French squadrons were practically ship to ship, yardarm to yardarm, their masts and sails enveloped in a dense pall of trapped gunsmoke.

He shifted the glass and tried not to look at the deck far below his dangling legs. Then he stiffened. The ships which this lookout had reported minutes earlier were breaking away from the main battle. The two ships of the line were in fact linked by a stout cable, and as he peered through the forerigging he realized that the furthest vessel, a big three-decker, was partially disabled and without either bowsprit or foremast.

The towing ship, hampered by her massive consort, yawed from side to side, her sails puffing and then falling slack in the sluggish wind. As she swung the sunlight threw strange shadows on her tall side, and on the gleaming rows of guns already run out and prepared to fight.

Bolitho nodded to the lookout. 'Keep a good eye on them.'

The man grinned. 'Got nothin' else to do, zur!' He leaned over to watch Bolitho's careful descent and then settled down at his post. As Bolitho made his way down the rough, vibrating ratlines he heard the man humming.

He found Okes and Rennie waiting for him beside the wheel. Bolitho said flatly, 'Two big ships right enough. But one of them is disabled. Probably in a collision during the night.' He rubbed his chin. 'The towing ship is flying a command flag. White over blue.' He forced a smile and called to Maynard, 'What do you make of that, my lad?'

The midshipman lowered his glass for a moment. 'Part of the French van, sir.' He looked uneasy.

'Right.' Bolitho walked to the rail. 'De Grasse will be worried about his transports. To mount an attack on Jamaica he will need more than fighting ships. He'll have troops and supplies in other craft, like the ones we burned at Mola Island.'

Okes said, 'While the fleet is engaged, de Grasse will try and force his transports this way!'

Bolitho nodded grimly. 'Right again.' He snapped his fingers. 'Part of the French van has been detached to clear the way for them!' He looked up at the listless sails. 'And three ships only bar their way.' He turned to Rennie who was swinging his sword idly against his polished boots. 'If we can turn the enemy's van, gentlemen, Sir George Rodney will do the rest!' He slapped his palms together. 'Like rabbits in a trap!'

Okes stared at the slow-moving ships ahead of the *Cassius*. 'In this case the rabbits are bigger than the hunters, sir!'

But Bolitho had already moved away. He paused beside the minute drummer boy and asked calmly, 'Give us a tune on your fife, boy.' He spoke loudly, so that the men at the nine-pounder could hear him.

The boy peered up from beneath his shako and swallowed hard. His lips were pale, and Bolitho could see his hands shaking against his tunic. 'Wh-what shall I play, sir?'

Bolitho looked around at the strained, watchful faces. 'What about "Hearts of Oak"? We all know that, eh, lads?'

And so with the overwhelming roar of battle drumming in their ears, the *Phalarope*'s sailors picked up the fife's feeble lilt.

Bolitho walked back to the weather side and lifted his glass. Even aboard the *Cassius* the men might hear the *Phalarope*'s sailors singing the well-used words and gain some slight confidence.

> 'Come cheer up my lads,
> 'Tis to Glory we steer . . .'

Bolitho watched the great rolling bank of black smoke as it moved steadily towards the three British ships. It was like a living thing, he thought coldly. Writhing, and alight with angry red and orange flashes. Yet he was grateful for its presence. At least it hid the horror and the gruesome scenes beyond.

He looked down at his men, their faces momentarily engrossed in their singing. *They* would not have much longer to wait.

18. A TRADITION OF VICTORY

JOHN ALLDAY tied his neckerchief tightly around his head and ears and then dashed the sweat from his face with one forearm. Right forward on the frigate's tapered forecastle he had an uninterrupted view of the *Cassius,* and ahead of her he could just see part of the *Volcano*'s upper rigging. Deliberately he turned his back on them and on the smoke-shrouded tangle of ships beyond. He looked down at McIntosh, the gunner's mate, who was on his knees beside one of the carronades as if in prayer.

As Allday had slithered to the deck from the mainyard, Brock, the gunner, had halted him with a sharp, 'Here you!' For a moment they had faced each other once again. Allday, the pressed seaman, whose skin still bore the scars of Brock's cane, and who had nearly hanged because of another's treachery and cunning. And the gunner, hard-faced and expressionless, who rarely showed any trace of his inner feelings, if he had any.

Brock had gestured with his cane. 'Up forrard, you! Join the crews on the carronades!'

Allday had made to run off but Brock had added harshly, 'I was wrong about you, it seems!' It was not an apology. Just a statement of fact. 'So get up there and do your best!' His thin mouth had moved in what might have been a smile. 'My God, Allday, your sheep would be proud of you today!'

He smiled at the recollection and then looked round with surprise as Ferguson scrambled up beside him. His eyes were bright with fear, and he clung to the hammock nettings as if he would fall without their support.

McIntosh grunted, 'What do *you* want here?'

'I-I was sent, sir.' Ferguson licked his lips. 'I'm no use for anything else.'

McIntosh turned back to his inspection of the training tackles. 'Christ Almighty!' was his only comment.

'Don't look at the ships, Bryan.' Allday picked up his cutlass and ran it through his belt. The hilt felt warm against his naked back. 'Just don't think about 'em. Keep down behind the nettings and do as I do.' He forced a grin. 'We have a fine view from here!'

Ritchie, the stolid Devon seaman, ran his fingers over the shot rack and asked vaguely, 'Wot are we to shoot at, Mr. McIntosh?'

The gunner's mate was edgy. 'The captain hasn't told me yet! When he does, I'll tell *you*!'

Ritchie shrugged. 'Us'll roast they devils!' He peered at the *Cassius.* 'The Frogs'll turn an' run!'

Kemp, one of the loaders, grimaced. 'When they sees *you* they will!'

Ferguson lowered his head against his arm. 'It's madness! We'll all be killed!'

Allday studied him sadly. He is right, he thought. Nothing can live against such a force. He said kindly, 'It's April, Bryan. Just think how it looks in Cornwall, eh? The hedgerows and the green fields . . .'

Ferguson stared at him. 'For God's sake, what are you talking about?'

Allday replied calmly, 'Have you forgotten already what nearly happened to us, Bryan?' He hardened his voice, knowing that Ferguson was at breaking point. 'Remember Nick Pochin?' He saw Ferguson flinch, but carried on. 'Well, he's dead, hanged aboard the *Cassius* with the other fools!'

Ferguson hung his head. 'I-I'm sorry.'

Allday said, 'I know you're afraid. And so am I. And so is the captain, I shouldn't wonder.'

At that moment Lieutenant Herrick stepped on to the fore-castle and walked briskly to the carronades. 'Everything well, Mr. McIntosh?'

The gunner's mate stood up and wiped his palms on his trousers. 'Aye, sir.' He studied the lieutenant and then added, 'Mola Island seems a long time ago now, Mr. Herrick.'

Herrick stared aft along the maindeck to the raised quarter-deck where Okes stood stiffly beside the captain. Would Okes crack this time? he wondered. Which way would his private shame make him react? He replied, 'It does indeed.'

Okes' voice, distorted by his speaking trumpet, echoed above the rumble of gunfire. 'Another pull on the weather forebrace there! Mr. Packwood, take that man's name!'

Herrick hid his dismay from McIntosh. Okes was so much on edge that he had to say something. Anything.

McIntosh said dryly, 'Promotion does not seem to solve *everything*, Mr. Herrick!'

Herrick swung round as flags broke from the *Cassius*'s yards. A moment later he heard Maynard yell, 'Engage the enemy, sir!' Then, in a slightly steadier voice, 'Tack in succession!'

The pipes trilled. 'Lee braces. Jump to it!'

Keeping time with the ponderous two-decker the frigates tacked slowly to the south-east. Herrick shaded his eyes as the sun lanced down between the sails, and saw the nearest enemy ships less than a quarter of a mile away. They were in no apparent order, but with their yards braced round were tacking on a converging course with the British squadron. The big three-decker hid her gaping ranks of guns in deep shadow as she swung slightly up wind. The tow had been cast off, and the leading ship of the line, unhampered by her massive consort, heeled easily in the breeze, her command flag pointing directly at the *Cassius*.

Herrick tried to clear the dryness from his throat. 'Carry on, Mr. McIntosh. I must attend my duties!'

He had to force himself to walk slowly down to the maindeck. As he passed an open hatch where a marine sentry leaned on his musket he saw the surgeon's scarlet face grinning up at him.

'Yer 'ealth, Mr. 'Errick!' He waved a tankard.

Herrick felt slightly mad. 'Damn you, Tobias! You'll not have my body today!'

Some of the men at the nearest guns chuckled. 'That's right, sir! You tell 'im!'

Herrick strode on to take up his position in the centre of the deck. Farquhar was below the quarterdeck, his haughty features slightly pale but determined. Herrick gave him a nod, but Farquhar did not seem to see him.

There was a crashing boom, all the more startling because every man had been expecting it. It was followed instantly by a ragged salvo, and another.

Bolitho's voice broke through Herrick's stricken thoughts. 'Note it in the log, Mr. Proby! We have engaged the enemy!' His voice was muffled as he turned away. 'Cut those boats adrift, Mr. Neale! They'll act like a damn sea anchor in this poor wind!'

Herrick looked at his hands. They were quite steady, yet he felt as if every bone and muscle was quivering uncontrollably. He could imagine the *Phalarope*'s boats drifting astern, and thought of Bolitho's earlier words to the crew.

'. . . below us it is a thousand fathoms to the bottom!' Herrick winced as another thunderous broadside sent a dull vibration through the planks at his feet. A thousand fathoms, and now not even a boat to save the survivors!

He looked up and saw that Bolitho had returned to the quarterdeck rail and was staring at him. He did not speak, but gave a strange, lingering smile, as if he was trying to convey some personal message to him.

Then Bolitho called sharply, 'Mr. Neale, do not run like that! Remember our people are watching you today!'

Herrick turned away. The message could have been for him, he thought. He felt strangely calmed by this realization and walked to the larboard battery and looked down the line of guns. In a few minutes every one of them would be firing. In a few minutes. He studied the faces of the men beside them and felt suddenly humble.

'Well, lads, this is better than practice, eh?'

Surprisingly they laughed at his stupid joke, and in spite of the cold fingers around his stomach Herrick was able to join them.

Bolitho blinked in the reflected sunlight and peered across the weather rail. Ahead of the *Phalarope* the flagship was holding her course, but the frigate *Volcano* which had been leading the line was pulling away to larboard, breaking the pattern as two French frigates drove down towards her.

Rennie gasped, 'He's done for! We cannot give him any help!'

The sea's surface shimmered as another crashing broadside rippled along the *Volcano*'s gunports. Gun by gun, each one carefully aimed and fired in rapid succession.

Undeterred the two frigates, with the wind in their favour, swept down on either beam.

Proby said sharply, '*Volcano*'s luffing!'

Bolitho breathed out painfully. Fox was no fool, and as wily as his name. As the two enemy frigates swept downwind for a quick kill the *Volcano* swung lazily into the wind, her sails flapping in violent protest. The nearest French ship realized her mistake just too late. As her yards started to swing, the *Volcano* presented her opposite side and fired a full salvo. The French ship seemed to stagger as if dealt a body blow. Across the water Bolitho could hear the crash of falling spars and the sliding thunder of overturned cannon. All else was hidden in the billowing clouds of smoke, but above it he could see *Volcano*'s ensign and all three masts still standing.

'Flagship signalling! "Close on *Flag*!"' Maynard ran to hoist an acknowledgement.

Bolitho tore his eyes from Captain Fox's lithe frigate as it went about to take the wind advantage from the two Frenchmen. *Cassius* was heading straight for the powerful two-decker with the command flag. She would need all the help she could get. Fox would have to manage for himself for a while.

'Starboard a point!' Bolitho ran to the rail and leaned out as far as he could. Then he saw the towering sails of the ship of the line as it drove down on a converging course with the flagship. They should pass port to port, he thought. He shouted to the maindeck, 'Stand by, Mr. Herrick!'

Okes yelled, 'The Frenchman's changing his tack, sir!' He was jumping with agitation. 'God in hell, sir! He's turning across the *Cassius*'s bows!'

Either the French captain was unwilling to face a gun for gun contest, or he hoped to rake the *Cassius*'s bows and masts as he crossed her course, Bolitho was not quite sure which. But either way he had not allowed for the extra sail carried by Admiral Napier's elderly flagship.

Instead, the two ships crossed their bowsprits and then met at right-angles with a sickening crash. As they locked together both ships opened fire, the arrowhead of water between them erupting in a great sheet of flame and black smoke.

Bolitho watched in chilled silence as *Cassius*'s foremast and main topgallant leaned drunkenly and then crashed down into the all-enveloping smoke. He could see rigging and spars ripping away the sails and scattering men from the tops like dead fruit.

Another broadside split the air apart, and Bolitho knew that the *Cassius*'s forward guns were within feet of the enemy's. Yet still they stayed locked together, their splintered bowsprits and jib-booms entangled like the tusks of two crazed beasts from a nightmare.

Bolitho cupped his hands. 'Both carronades to starboard!' He waved his hand at Proby. 'We will put her across the enemy's stern, if we can!' He half ducked as a ball screamed overhead and slapped through the driver leaving a ragged tear. A stray shot from the giants, but just as deadly, he thought grimly.

All around him men were coughing and wiping their eyes as the smoke reached out and over the frigate's decks.

The helmsman cursed as the *Cassius*'s torn sails loomed over the fog like some great spectre. But Bolitho gauged the set of the flagship's masts and knew he was on the right course. The fog closed in again, and he saw the double lines of flashes as both fired salvo after salvo at pointblank range. He could hear the two hulls grinding together, the screams and cries of the wounded and dying, mingled with the unbelievable sound of the admiral's drum and fife band. It was impossible to tell what they were playing, or how a man could live, let alone think of an empty tune in that holocaust.

But Bolitho shouted, 'A cheer, lads! Give a cheer to the *Flag*!' Muskets banged through the smoke, and Bolitho heard the balls thudding into the bulwarks and whining against the nine-pounders.

Rennie bellowed, 'Marksmen! Shoot down those bastards!' And from aloft came an answering volley.

The wind seemed to have gone altogether, although in the dense smoke it was impossible to gauge either speed or distance. Then out of the flickering, choking fog Bolitho saw the stern of the two-decker. It seemed to hang above the *Phalarope*'s starboard bow like an ornate cliff, and he could see the flash of musket fire from her stern windows as marksmen directed their attention to the frigate's forecastle.

Bolitho banged the rail with his hands, ignoring the whining balls and the cries from forward. In his mind he was picturing the enemy ship's lower gundeck. Cleared for action it was one long battery which ran from one end of the ship to the other. Bolitho had been a midshipman in a ship of the line, and he knew that there must be upwards of three hundred men in there, stooping in semi-darkness, choking in the acrid fumes, and firing their guns more from familiarity than accuracy.

He shouted, 'The carronades, Mr. McIntosh! Fire as we cross her stern!'

Rennie grinned and wiped his face with his sleeve. 'That'll kill a few, sir!'

Bolitho bit his lip as the sound of a mast thundering across smashed and broken rigging broke through the roar of combat. *Cassius* was a very old ship. Much more of this punishment and she would either break up or sink as she fought!

He wondered what had happened to the *Volcano*, and worse, the crippled three-decker. If the latter was able to engage, it would be over in minutes. Her lower gundeck was crammed with thirty-two-pounders. One of those could smash through two and a half feet of solid oak at maximum range. Bolitho tried not to picture what would happen to the *Phalarope*'s frail timbers.

'Ready, sir!' McIntosh was yelling like a madman.

Bolitho drew his sword. 'Larboard a point, Mr. Proby!' He watched the jib flapping and dropped his sword.

'*Fire!*'

Herrick felt the deck shudder beneath him as both carronades fired almost together. As the thick muzzle smoke eddied clear he stared up at the French ship's stern, momentarily forgetting the battle which raged around him. A few seconds earlier he had watched the tall stern emerge from the fog of gunfire and had seen the great cabin windows with their life-sized figures on either quarter, full-breasted nymphs carrying tridents with the vessel's name, *Ondine,* in scarlet and gilt across the wide counter between them, and had marvelled at the ship's overpowering appearance of grandeur and indestructibility. As the smoke moved clear he gaped at the black jagged holes which left the stern like the entrance of a fire-scarred cave. At the horror and chaos beyond he could only briefly imagine, for as a fresh gust of wind moved busily through the *Phalarope*'s sails the deck tilted, and with her helm hard over she swung in a tight arc around the enemy ship's larboard quarter.

He shouted hoarsely above the din, 'Ready, lads!' He peered along the crouching line of gun captains. 'Fire as you bear!'

The first guns of the starboard battery fired as one, and in ragged succession the others followed as lanyard after lanyard was pulled taut, and the double-shotted charges crashed into the trapped smoke alongside.

A few men were cheering, their cries broken by coughs and curses as the smoke swirled back through the open ports.

Herrick yelled, 'Reload! Reload and run out!' He watched narrowly as the frigate moved down the other ship's beam, barely twenty yards clear. He could see the crowded heads on the high bulwark, the stabbing yellow flashes of muskets from her tops, but from the lower gundeck with its line of powerful guns there was not a single shot in reply. The carronades' lethal attack must have swept through the crowded gundeck like a scythe through a field of standing corn.

But as he watched he saw the first guns on the upperdeck lurch back at their ports, and then in the twinkling of an eye the whole upper battery erupted in one deafening broadside.

Herrick fell back, half stunned by the volume of the combined sounds of exploding guns, following instantly by the demoniac screams of balls above his head. The nets which Bolitho had ordered to be placed over the maindeck jumped and vibrated to falling wreckage, blocks, severed rigging and whole strips of blackened canvas. But Herrick stared up with amazement as he realized that the ill-aimed broadside had missed everything vital to *Phalarope*'s movements. Not a mast or spar had fallen. Had it been the lower battery, he knew that the frigate's starboard side and gunports would now be a shattered ruin.

He heard the gun captains shouting like demons. 'Run out! Heave on the tackles! Stand clear!' Then with the jerk of trigger lines the guns rumbled back to the full extent of their tackles.

A musket clattered by Herrick's feet, and as he stared upwards he looked into the dead eyes of a spreadeagled marine who had pitched down from the maintop on to the net below.

But he forgot the marine immediately as something more terrible took his attention. Through the smoke, falling like a giant tree, he saw the *Ondine*'s mizzenmast. It was impossible, but it was happening. Mast, top and topgallant, with all the attendant weight of sails, rigging and yards, hung in the air as if caught in a strong wind. Then, amid the screams and desperate cries of those men caught like flies in the shrouds, it crashed down across the *Phalarope*'s quarterdeck. The hull quivered as if the frigate had hit a reef, and as Herrick ran aft to the ladder he felt the *Phalarope* shake from truck to keel and then begin to swing slowly to starboard. Like an unyielding bridge the *Ondine*'s severed mast held both ships together, and as a fresh

burst of musket fire struck foot-long splinters from the deck,
Herrick fought his way up the ladder and stared with dismay
at the destruction around him.

A complete yard had fallen amongst Rennie's marines, and
he turned away from the smashed, writhing remains as Sergeant
Garwood roared, 'Stand to! Leave those men alone!' He was
glaring at the remainder of his marines. 'Rapid fire on her poop,
my lads!' He vanished in a fresh cloud of smoke as the frigate's
guns fired again, the shots crashing into the *Ondine*'s hull, which
at the nearest point was ten feet clear.

Herrick pushed past the struggling seamen who were trying
to hack away the French rigging and dropped on one knee
beside Bolitho. For a moment he thought the captain had been
hit by a musket ball, but as he slid his arm beneath his shoulders
Bolitho opened his eyes and struggled into a sitting position.
He blinked at Herrick's anxious face and said, 'Keep the guns
firing, Herrick!' He peered up at the enemy ship alongside and
pulled himself to his feet. 'We must stop them boarding us!' He
groped for his sword and shouted harshly, 'Cut that wreckage
away!'

Okes staggered through the smoke, his breeches and coat
splashed with blood and torn flesh. His eyes seemed to fill his
face, and although he appeared to be shouting, Herrick could
hear nothing.

Bolitho pointed with his sword. 'Mr. Okes, clear the larboard
battery and prepare to repel boarders!' He reached out and
shook the lieutenant like a dog. 'Do you hear me, damn you?'

Okes nodded violently, and a long thread of spittle ran down
his chin.

Bolitho pushed him to the ladder, but Herrick said quickly,
'I'll do it, sir!'

'No you won't!' Bolitho looked wild. 'Get your guns firing!
It is our only chance!'

At that moment the *Ondine*'s guns banged out once again,
and Herrick flinched as the salvo seared his face like a hot wind.
He saw a party of sailors hacking away a length of broken
shrouds. In the next instant there was nothing but a squirming
mass of pulped flesh and bones, with a gaping gash in the lee
bulwark beyond.

Bolitho shouted in his ear, 'We'll not be so lucky next time!'

Herrick ran down the ladder, closing his eyes and ears to the
horror beside him as more great blows shook the frigate's hull
like hammers on an anvil. He walked through the smoke, his
eyes streaming, his throat like sand, as he shouted wild and
unheeded encouragement to the powder-blackened gunners.

Farquhar caught his arm and shouted, 'They'll never cut that mast away in time!' He pointed towards the *Ondine*'s lower gundeck. 'They'll not be silent for ever!'

Herrick did not reply. With the wind at her beam, and held aft by the broken mast, the *Phalarope*'s bows were starting to swing inwards towards the *Ondine*'s hull. Through the smoke he could see men running along the two-decker's side towards the point of contact, the filtered sunlight playing on raised weapons.

He saw Okes groping towards the forecastle, his sword still in its sheath. He snapped, 'Go with him, Mr. Farquhar! He looks in a bad condition!'

Farquhar's eyes gleamed coldly. 'It will be a pleasure!'

Herrick flinched as a complete section of the starboard gangway splintered skyward and one of the twelve-pounders lurched on to its side. A seaman screamed as a severed head landed at his feet, and another ran from the gun, his eyes blinded by flying splinters.

Herrick called, 'Take those men below!' But as he shouted he heard the sudden clank of pumps and knew that it was probably just as safe on deck.

He tried to shut it all from his mind and made himself walk back along the line of guns. Men were falling all around him but he knew he must not falter, and shouted, 'Keep hitting 'em, lads!' He waved his hat. 'If you want to see England again, keep those guns firing!'

On the forecastle the men from the unemployed guns gathered below the nettings, their hands gripping cutlasses and boarding axes as the bowsprit quivered against the enemy's forerigging. Okes croaked, 'Over you go, lads! Keep those swine off our bows!'

Some of the men cheered and began to scramble out along the bowsprit, others fell back as a flurry of musket shots cut through the eager sailors and sent their corpses spinning into the water below.

Farquhar said urgently, 'You must lead them! My God, you're asking the impossible!'

Okes swung round, his mouth slack. 'Hold your tongue! *I'll* give the orders!'

Farquhar eyed him coolly. 'I have said nothing in the past, *Mr.* Okes! But I will say it now as it seems we will all die today!' His hat was plucked away by a musket ball but he did not drop his eyes. 'You are a cheat, a coward and a liar! If I thought you were worth it, I would discredit you here and now in front of these men, whom you are too squeamish to lead!' He turned his back on Okes' stricken face and shouted, 'Follow me, you ragged heroes!' He waved his sword. 'Make way for a younger man!'

They laughed like lunatics and slapped his shoulders as he crawled over the nettings and clambered on to the smooth bowsprit. Shots whined all around him, but he was breathless with a mixture of relief and madness. All this was worth it, if only for telling Okes what he thought of him for his cowardice at Mola Island.

Okes stared back at the quarterdeck and chimpered as a seaman crawled past him, half disembowelled by a great sliver of torn planking. Bolitho was still at the quarterdeck rail, a speaking trumpet in one hand, his sword in the other. His uniform seemed to shine in the frail sunlight, and Okes could see the hammock nettings jumping as hidden marksmen tried to find the *Phalarope*'s captain.

Okes cried, 'I hope they kill you! I hope they kill all of you!'

He sobbed and groped for his sword. Nobody listened to his wild words, or even heeded his presence on the blood-spattered forecastle. He thought of the stinging words and the contempt in Farquhar's eyes.

'*Never!*' He pulled himself towards the bowsprit where already some of the men were clashing steel with the enemy seamen. 'I'll show the lot of you!' Heedless of the curses and screams he pulled himself over the clinging sailors and hacked at a French petty officer with his sword. He saw the man's shocked surprise as a great gash opened across his neck and he fell between the grinding hulls. Then he was up and over, pushing Farquhar aside in his frenzied efforts to reach and strike at the enemy.

Farquhar saw the madness on Okes' face and tried to pull him back. But it was useless. Encouraged by the apparent bravery of their officers the British sailors swarmed on to the *Ondine*'s bulwark.

Okes snarled, 'Are you afraid, Mr. Farquhar?' He threw back his head and emitted a shrill laugh. 'Your uncle won't like that!'

Farquhar parried a thrusting pike and followed Okes down on to the wide deck. It was every man for himself now.

Bolitho strained his eyes through the smoke and watched his men changing from defenders to boarders. Whoever had decided to board the *Ondine* had made the right guess, he thought grimly. He heard the axes ringing on the tangle of wreckage behind him and knew it was impossible to free *Phalarope* from its embrace before the *Ondine*'s heavy guns were brought back into action.

He crossed the deck and said to Rennie, 'We must board her from aft, too!' He saw the marine nod. 'Get some men together immediately!'

He heard someone sobbing and saw Neale on his knees below the lee rail. Midshipman Maynard was lying on his back, one hand held upright entangled in a signal lanyard, his eyes wide and unseeing and strangely peaceful. Neale was holding his hand and rocking back and forth, oblivious to the crash of gunfire and the slapping musket balls which had already claimed his friend.

Bolitho reached down and pulled Neale to his feet. The boy's last reserve seemed to collapse, and with a frantic cry he buried his face in Bolitho's coat, his body shaking with convulsions of grief. Bolitho prised him away and lifted his chin with the hilt of his sword. For a moment he stared down at him, then he said gravely, 'Take a grip of yourself, Mr. Neale!' He saw the stunned look in Neale's eyes and shut his mind to the fact that he was talking with a terrified thirteen-year-old child who had just lost his best friend. 'You are a King's officer, Neale!' He softened his voice. 'I said earlier, our people are watching you today. Do you think you can help me now?'

Neale brushed his eyes with his sleeve and looked back at Maynard's body by the bulwark. As the halyard jerked in the breeze his arm moved as if he still held on to life. Then Neale turned back to Bolitho and said brokenly, 'I'm all right now, sir!'

Bolitho watched him walk back to the shouting gunners, a small figure half hidden in the smoke and flame of this savage battle.

Rennie reappeared, a cut above one eye. 'Ready, sir!' He swung his curved sword. 'Shall I take 'em across?'

Bolitho looked around the battered quarterdeck. There seemed to be more corpses than live men, he thought wearily. He faltered as a shot crashed against the quarterdeck ladder and tore into the planking like a plough. With disbelief he saw Proby put his hands to his face and watched his fingers clawing at the sudden torrent of blood. The master staggered against the wheel, but as Strachan left the spokes to hold him he fell moaning on to his side and lay still. His hands thudded on the planking, and Bolitho saw that his face had been torn away.

'We must take the *Ondine*!' The words were wrung from his lips. 'If the French see their command ship strike, they'll . . .' He faltered and stared again at Proby's body. I've done for the lot of them! He felt the anguish changing to helpless anger. I have sacrificed the ship and every man aboard just for *this*!

But Rennie eyed him evenly and said, 'It is the right decision, sir!' He straightened his hat and said to his sergeant, 'Right, Garwood, do you feel like a little walk?'

Bolitho stared at him. It was as if the marine had been reading his mind. He said, 'The *Cassius* will support us.' He looked at the waiting marines. They crouched like animals, wild and beyond fear or even anger. 'It's us or them, lads!'

Then, as the men shouted and cheered he jumped on to the *Ondine*'s broken mast and began to claw his way across. Once he looked down at the water below him. It was littered with broken woodwork and sodden corpses, French and British alike.

As he reached the *Ondine*'s poop he felt the balls whining past him and heard screams at his back as men fell to join the waiting corpses below. Then as he reached the scarred bulwark he hacked away the remains of the French boarding nets and leapt down on to the deck. Dead and dying lay everywhere, but when he glanced quickly across the far side he felt a further sense of shock as he saw the *Cassius*. She was not alongside anymore, but drifting away in the smoke of her own wounds, a mastless hulk, battered beyond recognition. From every scupper he could see long, glistening streams of blood, which poured down the ship's side to colour the water in one unbroken stain. It was as if the ship herself was bleeding to death. But from the stump of her mizzen the ensign, pitted and torn with shot holes, still flapped in defiance, and as Rennie's yelling marines swept across the *Ondine*'s poop there was a burst of cheering from the *Cassius*'s deck. It was not much of a cheer, for there could not be many left to raise it, but to Bolitho it acted like the stab of a spur.

He ran across the littered deck, cutting down two seamen with hardly a pause, propelled on by the cheering and the battle-crazed men at his back. He could see his men on the *Ondine*'s forecastle, almost encircled by an overwhelming mass of French seamen, their stubborn resistance faltering as they were forced back towards the rail.

Bolitho yelled, 'Hold on *Phalarope*'s!' He saw the Frenchmen falter and turn to face this new threat. 'To me, lads! Cut your way through 'em!'

More men were swarming from the frigate now, and he saw Herrick's uniform through the smoke as he waved his men forward.

He turned as Okes slashed a path for himself in the press of figures, his sword gleaming red as he cut down a screaming midshipman and went on towards a man who was reloading a swivel gun beside the quarterdeck. Okes was bleeding from a dozen wounds, and as he reached the ladder the swivel gun exploded with a dull roar. The packed grapeshot lifted Okes like a rag doll and flung him lifeless into the fighting men below the ladder. The gunner fell a second later, cut down by a swinging cutlass.

Then, all at once, it was over. The deck clattered with the weapons thrown down by the *Ondine*'s seamen, and Bolitho realized that their cries of defiance had changed to pleas for quarter. He knew he could not hold his men back if they wanted to complete the slaughter. It fell to some unknown sailor to break the spell of destruction and killing.

'A cheer for the *Phalarope*!' The voice cracked with relief and jubilation. 'An' a cheer for Mad Dick!'

Bolitho climbed down the ladder, past the dazed Frenchmen and the mangled litter of entwined corpses.

'Captain Rennie!' He paused beside the remains of Lieutenant Okes. 'Hoist our flag above the French ensign!' He felt his hands shaking. 'Let them all see what you have done today.'

Sergeant Garwood said gruffly, 'The cap'n is dead, sir!' He unrolled the flag carefully. 'But I will do it!'

'Dead?' Bolitho stared after him. 'Rennie, too?' He felt Herrick pulling his arm and asked heavily, 'What is it?'

'The ships is ours, sir!' Herrick was shaking with excitement. 'The gundeck is like a slaughterhouse! Our carronades did more than . . .' He broke off as he saw Bolitho's face.

'Very well, Mr. Herrick. Thank you.' His voice shook. 'Thank *all* of you!' He turned away as more cheering echoed round the bloody decks.

Herrick shook his head as if he was beyond understanding. 'A two-decker, sir! What a victory!'

Bolitho replied quietly, 'We have a tradition of victory, Mr. Herrick.' He seemed to be speaking to himself. 'Now gather our people and send them back to the ship. They have cut the wreckage away.' He stared dully at the *Phalarope* and let his eyes move slowly along her length. There were great gaping holes in her once-trim hull, and she was well down by the head. It sounded as if the pumps were only just containing the inrush of water. All three topmasts had gone, and the sails flapped in the breeze in long canvas streamers. He could see bodies hanging in the tops, the great patches of scarlet across the smashed and buckled planking below. Intruding for the first time since their battle had begun came the distant thunder of that other great fight. Still far away and impersonal.

Bolitho made another effort to pull himself together. 'Lively, Mr. Herrick! The battle is still not over!'

If only his men would stop cheering. If only he could get away and be with himself.

Herrick waved his arm. 'Clear the ship, lads! We can take this wreck later in our own good time!'

Bolitho walked to the bulwark. Across the gap he could see Neale standing just where he had left him beside the wheel. He said, 'Tell my coxswain to take Mr. Okes and Captain Rennie over to the ship.' He saw Herrick's sudden anxiety and felt despair closing in again. 'Not Stockdale, Mr. Herrick?'

Herrick nodded. 'He fell as you were fighting on the poop, sir. He was defending your back from the marksmen.' He tried to smile. 'I am sure that was what he would have wished!'

Bolitho stared at him. Stockdale dead. And he had not even seen him fall.

Farquhar pushed forward, his features wildly excited. 'Captain, sir! The lookouts report that our fleet has broken the enemy's line in two places!' He stared round the stained, watching faces. 'Rodney has broken the French line, do you hear?'

Bolitho felt the breeze across his cheek, feeling its way through the battle's stench like an awed stranger. So de Grasse was beaten. He stared at the listing frigate below him, feeling the prick of emotion behind his eyes. Was all this sacrifice for nothing after all?

Herrick took his arm and said thickly, 'Look, sir! Over yonder!'

As the freshening wind pushed away the curtain of smoke from the embattled and shattered ships, Bolitho saw the tall outline of the big three-decker. Her guns were still run out, and her paintwork was gleaming and unscarred by any cannon. Throughout the fighting she had lain impotent or unwilling to face the holocaust of close combat, and no British blood had been given to her massive armament.

Yet in spite of all these things there was another flag flying above her own. The same that flew on the dismasted *Cassius* and aboard the *Ondine*. The same as the *Phalarope*'s own ensign and the victorious *Volcano* which now pushed her way through the last rolling bank of smoke.

Herrick said soberly, 'Do you need more than that, sir? She's struck to *you*!'

Bolitho nodded and then climbed over the bulwark. 'We will get the ship under way, Mr. Herrick. Though I fear she may never fight again!'

Herrick said quietly, 'There'll be other ships, sir.'

Bolitho stepped down on to the *Phalarope*'s gangway and walked slowly above the spent and sweating gunners.

'Other ships?' He touched the splintered rail and smiled sadly. 'Not like this one, Mr. Herrick.' He tilted his head and looked up at the flag.

'Not like the *Phalarope*!'

EPILOGUE

LIEUTENANT THOMAS HERRICK pulled his boat cloak closer around his shoulders and picked up his small travelling bag. The houses around the cobbled square were thickly covered in snow, and the wind which blew strongly inland from Falmouth Bay and seemed to pierce his bones to the marrow, told him that there was more to come. For a moment longer he watched the ostlers guiding the steaming horses into the inn yard, leaving the slush-stained coach which Herrick had just vacated isolated and empty. Through the inn windows he could see a cheerful fire and hear voices raised in laughter and busy conversation.

He was suddenly tempted to go inside and join these unknown people. After the long journey from Plymouth, and four days on the road before that, he felt drained and weary, but as he looked up at the mist-shrouded hump of Pendennis Castle and the bleak hillside beyond he knew he was only deluding himself. He turned his back on the inn and started up the narrow lane from the square. Everything seemed smaller than he remembered it. Even the church with its low wall and the leaning stones within the graveyard appeared to have shrunk since that last and only visit. He stepped sideways into a mound of muddy snow as two shouting children dashed past him dragging a home-made sledge. Neither gave Herrick a glance. That too was different from the last time.

Herrick ducked his head as a strong gust whipped the snow from a low hedgerow and across his face, and when he looked up again he saw the old house, square and grey, facing him like a picture from all those past memories. He quickened his pace, suddenly nervous and unsure of himself.

He heard the bell jangling within the house, and even as he released the heavy iron handle the door swung open, and a neat fair-haired woman in a dark dress and white cap stood aside to greet him.

Herrick said uncertainly, 'Good day, ma'am. My name is Herrick. I have just driven from the other side of England.'

She took his cloak and hat and stared at him with a strange, secret smile. 'That's a long journey, sir. The master is expecting you.' At that moment the door at the far side of the hall swung open and Bolitho stepped forward to meet him. For a long moment they both stood quite still, their hands clasped in an embrace which neither wanted to break.

Then Bolitho said, 'Come into the study, Thomas. There is a good fire waiting!'

Herrick allowed himself to be placed in a deep leather chair, and let his eyes stray over the old portraits which lined the panelled walls.

Bolitho watched him gravely. 'I am glad you came, Thomas. More glad than I can say.' He seemed nervous and ill at ease.

Herrick said, 'How it all comes back to me as I sit here. It is a year and a month since we weighed anchor from Falmouth and sailed for the West Indies together.' He shook his head sadly. 'Now it is all finished. The peace is signed at Versailles. It is over.'

Bolitho was staring into the fire, the dancing reflections playing across his dark hair and his grey, steady eyes. He said suddenly, 'My father is dead, Thomas.' He paused as Herrick jerked upright in his chair. 'And so is Hugh, my brother!'

Herrick did not know what to say. He wanted to find some word of comfort, something to ease the pain from Bolitho's voice. Without effort he could throw his mind back over the months, to the aftermath of the battle when the listing, battered *Phalarope* had limped painfully to Antigua for repairs. Herrick had known that Bolitho was offered an immediate passage home to England, for a better and bigger command. But he had stayed with the frigate. Nursing her through every indignity of the dockyard, and watching over the care and treatment of her sick and wounded men.

October had arrived, and with her refit only half completed the *Phalarope* was ordered home to England. The Battle of the Saintes, as it was soon to be known, was the last great struggle of that unfortunate war. As the frigate dropped her anchor at Spithead, England rejoiced to the sounds of peace. It was an unsatisfactory agreement, but for England the war had been too long on the defensive. And as Pitt had remarked to the House of Commons, 'A defensive war can only end in inevitable defeat.'

Bolitho had left the ship at Portsmouth, but only after every man had been properly paid off and letters of credit had been sent to the dependants of her many dead. Then with hardly a word he had left for Falmouth.

As first lieutenant, Herrick had stayed to hand over the ship to the dockyard, then he too had gone to his home in Kent.

Bolitho's letter had arrived within a few days, and Herrick had set off for Cornwall, hardly knowing if the invitation was genuine or just common courtesy.

But as he looked at the big, shadowed room and Bolitho's slim figure before the fire, he began to understand for the first time. Bolitho was now completely alone.

He said quietly, 'I am sorry. I had no idea.'

Bolitho said, 'My father died three months ago.' He gave a

short, bitter smile. 'Hugh went a few months after the Saintes battle. He was killed by accident. A runaway horse, I believe.'

Herrick stared at him, 'How do you know all this?'

Bolitho opened a cupboard and then laid a sword on the table. In the firelight it gleamed with sudden brightness which hid the tarnished gilt and well-worn scabbard.

Bolitho said quietly, 'Hugh sent this to my father. To give it back to me.' He turned back to the fire. 'He wrote that he considered it to be mine by right.'

The door opened, and the fair-haired woman entered with a tray of hot punch.

Bolitho smiled. 'Thank you, Mrs. Ferguson. We will dine directly.'

As the door closed again Bolitho saw the question on Herrick's face. 'Yes, that is the wife of Ferguson, my clerk. He works for me, too.'

Herrick nodded and took one of the goblets. 'He lost an arm at the Saintes. I remember.'

Bolitho poured himself a drink and held it to the firelight. 'His wife did not die after all. And Ferguson is quite a hero in the town!' It seemed to amuse him, and Herrick saw the old smile playing at the corners of his mouth. Bolitho added, 'Now the war is done, Thomas. You and I are on the beach. I wonder what lies ahead for those like us?'

Herrick replied thoughtfully, 'This peace will not last.' He lifted his goblet. 'To old friends, sir!' He paused, seeing the memories all over again. 'To the ship, bless her!'

Bolitho drained his drink and gripped his hands behind him. Even that unconscious gesture stabbed Herrick's memory like a knife. The screaming shot, the crash and thunder of battle, with Bolitho pacing the quarterdeck like a man deep in thought.

'And you, sir? What will you do now?'

Bolitho shrugged. 'I have the chance to become a landowner, I suppose. And a magistrate like my father.' He looked up at the portraits. 'But I can wait. For another ship.'

The door opened, and a man in a green apron asked, 'Will you be requiring any more wine from the cellar, Captain?'

Herrick jumped to his feet. 'My God! Allday!'

Allday grinned self-consciously. 'Aye, Mr. Herrick. 'Tis me right enough!'

Bolitho looked from one to the other. 'After Stockdale died, Allday here said he wanted to change his mind about leaving the Service.' He smiled sadly. 'So if the chance comes we will go back to sea together.'

Bolitho picked up the sword and held it in both hands. Over his shoulder he added quietly, 'When that time comes I will want a good first lieutenant, Thomas.' He turned and looked straight into Herrick's eyes.

Herrick felt the warmth flooding back through his body, sweeping away the doubt and the sense of loss. He raised his goblet. 'It is not far to Kent, sir. I'll be ready when you give me the word!'

Bolitho turned his face away and watched the snow whipping across the windows. For a while longer he looked at the grey sky and scudding clouds, and imagined he could hear the wind whining through shrouds and taut rigging, with the hiss of thrown spray rising above the lee bulwark.

Then he faced his friend and said firmly, 'Come, Thomas, there is much to talk about!'

Allday watched them go into the dining room, and then with a quiet smile he placed the sword carefully back in the cupboard.

A WIND OF DEATH

Gavin Black

'A Wind of Death' is published by
William Collins, Sons & Co. Ltd.

The Author

Gavin Black was born in Japan and lived in the East for his first twenty years. His home is now in Scotland. He has been a professional writer all his adult life: 'Never had a job,' he says, 'never wanted one.' And so he is not among the ranks of those writers who have filled in by being, at various times in their lives, cloakroom attendants, deckhands, club chuckers-out or garage hands. He has written straight novels, suspense thrillers, radio plays, a TV play, and many short stories which have appeared in North America in the *Saturday Evening Post*, *Woman's Day* and the *Toronto Star*. Much of his work is eminently filmable material, too.

To Felix Marti-Ibáñez

GULF OF SIAM

Cape Cambodia

N

THAILAND

Isthmus
of Kra

Kangar

Alor
Star

Kota Bharu

SOUTH

CHINA

SEA

KEDAH

KELANTAN

Kuala Krai

Penang
Island

George Town

To Europe

INDIAN

OCEAN

PERAK

Linguin

Kuala Lipis

Kampar

MALAYSIA

Kuantan

KUALA
LUMPUR

PAHANG

Strait of Malacca

Seremban

MALACCA

Malacca

JOHORE

Singapore

To Vietnam, Hong Kong etc.

SUMATRA
(INDONESIA)

Red guerilla areas

0   50   100   150

Miles

CHAPTER ONE

WHEN I WAS RECRUITED no one had told me that swollen feet were one of the occupational hazards of spying. I'd had a rough two weeks. The isthmus of Kra, that thin, long strip of southern Thailand which separates the Indian Ocean from the South China Sea, is rough country on the whole, sizeable portions of it still primary jungle. It had been my business to walk through this jungle in areas adjacent to the Malaysian frontier. The visit was highly unofficial and no one had rubber stamped a passport with permission for me to be there. A long, hot snoop had proved totally unrewarding because I hadn't found a trace of what I was looking for, or rather, what other people were looking for.

The only things which seemed active in that area were the elephants. There were a lot of these, totally uninhibited by man, thrashing around on tracks they make for themselves which tend to run in great fifty mile loops. We came on three herds of elephants, all minding their own business and expecting us to mind ours, which we did. Minding your own business is the law of survival in the jungle and if you stick to it you can move around in the daytime through the clutter almost as safely as you can in Westminster Abbey. That is, except for the snakes. Snakes have their own regulations and no one seems to have found out what they are. We were always watching for snakes.

I had travelled with two guides carrying sharp choppers. Sometimes we made as much as seven miles a day, but more often it was around five. I lost ten pounds in weight, became de-salinated in spite of salt tablets, and at several points came near to the heat exhaustion which is a factor to contend with on this type of excursion. Also, I didn't trust my guides all that much, and they showed no signs of becoming fond of me, only liking my money, and wanting more of it than they were likely to get. It was a situation which made for slightly unhappy travel.

But I got out all right, into Kelantan, and very glad indeed to be there. Kelantan is the state up north where the Japanese first landed in their attack on Malaysia, but before and after this event it has existed in a condition of amiable and relaxed torpor. It has a pleasant climate, cool beautiful mornings tending towards mist, and nights conditioned by sea breezes. There is a special breed of large grey monkeys trained to climb the palm trees as nut collectors, and these beasts sit chained at the edges of all villages looking more intelligent than the other locals, which they probably are. The humans, both male and female, are nearly all beautiful until they begin to get fat, which is early on. Nobody moves too much, and world crises, even Malaysian crises, don't get recorded in worry wrinkles on any face. The Sultan has a considerable number of wives but, in spite of this, and having no foreign commitments, manages to keep taxation down. The rich grow richer and the poor don't give a damn so long as their working monkeys stay in good health.

A state of this kind hasn't got a lot of need for its airfields. The one I was on had last seen scheduled use at the end of November 1941. On December 6th of that year the Japanese came over and scored direct hits on three parked lease-lend Buffalos, one Wildebeest, and one Blenheim, and that was the end of the R.A.F. in north eastern Malaysia for some time. The strip was evacuated by road transport and the Nipponese came past it at such speed on their travels south that it never had any tactical use again until an American called Clement P. Winburgh took it over privately, very privately.

With feet still puffy even after twenty-four hours in bed I stood by the ruins of what had probably been the officers' mess, but there wasn't much of the building left after a quarter of a century and steady overtime from white ants. The view, however, was splendid. To my left, looking north, was the spine of the main mountain ridge, bumpy in moonlight, formidable country into which a lot of people have ventured who have never come out again. It is tenanted by the hill people, the Sakai, as well as by another even more primitive lot who are rarely seen and are reputed to travel through trees using their hands and arms just like their simian near relations. The area also contains a jungle fortress in that section which eases down into Thailand, this occupied by Lum Ping the former Red leader during the Malaysia civil war which was played down locally into an emergency.

Lum Ping is now apparently quiescent, but not in exile. So far as anyone knows he has never been on a refresher course in Peking, just sits quietly in his hideout amongst monster anthills listening to the radio or watching television. Every now and then someone like Clement P. Winburgh remembers about Lum Ping and can't believe that such an active man has mellowed in his maturer years and is now quite content with his pension. In Kota Bharu, Kelantan's one street capital, I have heard it said that Lum comes down to the local race meeting disguised as a Chinese commercial traveller, but I've never met anyone who has had a tip on a horse from that retired butcher of helpless villagers.

I have always had a deep respect for those mountains. It has seemed to me nice country to stay out of, and for all my long residence in these parts I've never allowed idle curiosity to prod me into mounting an exploratory expedition. The locals leave that to crackpots out from tame Europe, giving these characters hospitality and good advice before they go in and—on the rare occasions when they come out again—gently packing up what's left for a return to source. I once had quite a lot to do with a man who had spent two months alone in the Malaysia ridge jungles and I don't want ever to look anything like that myself.

The fact that I had begun to was one of the reasons why I couldn't warm to this impending meeting with Clem. I had agreed to serve him in a certain limited capacity suited to my role as a business man in the country, but this would never again be stretched to taking on the job of border scout which in no way fitted my years, position in society, and more than slightly sybaritic temperament. On that decayed airstrip I was keeping my anger over a hot flame.

I wasn't even curious about who had cleared grass and scrub growth sprouting through tarmac on a section of a runway, this for American interests and at the expense of the U.S. taxpayer. That it had been done at all in a country which is touchy about outside interference was perhaps surprising, but I had seen stranger things. And someone had certainly been working here, quite hard, and within the last few days, and to pretty precise instructions.

I had the two-hour wait, with my feet continuing to ache, which is somehow nearly always closely associated with air travel. Then there was a drone of engines in the distance. I pushed down through long *lalang* to the cleared area and stood by it with my head up, watching for a light which blinked.

Nothing blinked, even when the noise came close, international regulations smashed by no in-flight flicker. The sound wasn't from light engines either, props of some kind, and big ones. Then moonlight hit a shape coming from north west to avoid passing over Kota Bharu, at about three thousand, and certainly no small plane.

A landing here in anything larger than a tycoon's plaything was lunacy. The cleared strip ended in black jungle which seemed just waiting to claim another wreck. I could now make out a solid fuselage and dumpy wings, and hear a power cut back. I was going to send up a warning flash from a pocket torch when something about the bulk coming straight at me, matronly and fat bellied, kept my finger from the button.

It was a twin engine Prestwick Pioneer, built in Scotland, at least fifteen years old, and once the work horse of these parts. The plane has a seventy mile an hour landing speed and the kind of brakes they don't seem to fit any more, these able to cut from touchdown to a dead stop in seconds. If it had to that plane could drop sideways like an old cow gone skittish, and the heavily built undercarriage was reinforced to take astonishing punishment from a landing surface.

With all the resources of American production behind him it seemed ludicrous that Clem had to bump around Asia in an antique British model. And yet I could see that the thing might be an answer to his needs. It could land on a clay laterite road if there was wing clearance. Further, it didn't begin to suggest anything remotely military. A few jobs like this were still in use by local contractors and mining engineers, and their lumbering, deliberate flight made them highly suited to aerial surveys. For Clem that commercial-seeming innocence might be a big attraction, the last thing you would expect to see jumping out of a Pioneer's cabin door were men armed with tommy-guns.

I got out of the way and not before time. The pilot came in to land on what I thought was a run over, apparently deciding to suddenly, putting down the nose sharply. She made contact, bounced, levelled out from this, settled, trundled and then stopped. There was a distance of twenty yards to the first of the big trees.

I didn't hurry and the door was open by the time I reached the plane, a set of folding steps dropped. At the top of them, moonlight on his face, was my old friend from a little revolution.

'Hallo,' he said at the start of what I hoped wasn't going to be another. 'Glad you could make it.'

'So am I. After your assignment.'

'Rough up there?'

'Only part of me got out. The rest belongs to Thai leeches.'

I climbed gleaming aluminium stairs. The plane had originally been a twenty-five seater, but was now a travelling office, with desk, filing cabinets, and a typewriter for reports which at once went into a top secret folder. The chairs, four of them, were of the executive suite type which could rock you into the position most restful for your ulcer and didn't appear to be bolted to the floor. Two of these were occupied by silent shapes wearing U.S. Army uniform, but with rank tabs invisible. The back end of the cabin had been partitioned off, perhaps to accommodate a double brass bedstead. Light was poor, from a single anglepoise which stretched its neck out over the desk and had a cloth on the shade to create semi-blackout. From the smell of cigar smoke no one had observed fire precautions during a landing.

I would have appreciated a warmer note of cordiality after all my sufferings for a dubious cause, but Clem did remember basic duties as a host.

'Like a drink?'

'Very much. Any ice?'

'Yes.'

'Then bourbon on the rocks.'

It was a shade surprising to find the plane not dry, in view of U.S. official service temperance. Clem's area, of course, avoided the ostentation of insignia and could probably please itself about detail, but there were still a couple of what might be high-ranking officers sitting in their chairs as though they belonged, too.

I had an impression of being under surveillance from the military, almost close scrutiny in fact, as much as the dim light permitted. There was some natural illumination coming through the door and in this I saw that one of the seated gentlemen had grey hair clipped tight into his head. Clem went beyond the partition without any introductions, which left me standing in something of a social vacuum, being observed by a couple of characters whose present roles had obviously rusted their skill in small talk. A door to the pilot's cell opened just beyond me and two figures, these in civilian white shirts, went wordless down the aluminium steps as though they had been told to do that.

'Had a nice flight from wherever your base is?' I asked.

Clipped grey hair cleared his throat but he didn't get beyond this before Clem came back with a glass, one glass. It wasn't going to be a party.

I drank standing up because no one had offered me a chair and there is still a lot of British diffidence in my make up. Clem didn't sit down either, but stood waiting, as though a minimal politeness demanded he held off the interrogation until I had quenched my thirst. I could see his face better now, remembering how a kind of durable boyishness had once pleased me, as had agate coloured eyes when they were warmed by laughter. My first impression of him, some time ago now, had been of a man whose head neatly declined to acknowledge the years which burdened mind and body, and in this light he still looked rather like a high school cheerleader who didn't make the first basketball team so went for the next best thing from the point of view of getting the girls.

'What have you to tell us about the Thailand frontier, Paul?'

His question was almost solemnly formal.

'It's still there, richly populated with natural fauna.'

'Nothing else?'

'Not that I saw.'

'You think your search was effective?'

That nettled.

'It's a big area and I may have missed a snake or two. But I did notice a population explosion of elephants.'

One of the military moved in his chair, the other pulled up the cloth of trousers baggy at the knees. The puffing of cigars continued.

I tried to assess the plane's passenger list. There was Clem, the Brass, the two men who had got off and there could be anything behind that partition. The lack of open candour in my reception was starting to irk just slightly. I felt I had earned the right to handshakes all round and some smiles.

'Our information,' Clem said, 'was practically positive.'

'So your courier told me. Which all goes to show that a lot of positive information about these parts still has to be classified unreliable. You can take it from me there is no major supply route from Malaysia into Thailand through that jungle. Or even a minor one. If there had been I'd have walked across it. I was going east-west. Which doesn't mean there isn't infiltration from time to time. There's no means of keeping tabs on that. But steady coming and going would mean a defined track, and there isn't one. I know.'

'You say,' Clem corrected. To make that slightly less bald he added. 'We never take as gospel anything from one source.'

'Fine. Are you going up there to look for yourself? You can have my route maps. They're in the car I've got parked up on the highway. And I should think my guides are still hanging around in Kota Bharu, if you'd like to use them.'

Clem was looking past me.

'Had you thought that those guides might have been a special issue to you?'

'I took fairly adequate precautions, I think.' My voice was crisp. 'I didn't chat about why or when I was leaving home. And I arrived in the village where I picked up my guides without any advance notice. They were neither of them lovable fellows. But then a man who knows his jungle rarely is. It's not a gracious life. I'd remind you that picking men for my junk crews is something I've been at now for a good many years. The right men, too.'

Clem stayed the dogged interrogator.

'No chance you were steered around anything you weren't wanted to see?'

'Let me repeat, I travelled east-west across the whole peninsula. Any Red track would have to be north-south.'

'They could be using water part of the way. You were down where the rivers are navigable in places, even stretches of a few miles where boats are practicable. Did you swim any rivers?'

'Two.'

'Rapids?'

'No. Gentle water. If you think this is a possibility why didn't your courier warn me about it?'

Clem didn't answer that. I wished I could see him better. There was enough light to show shape and features of a man I thought I knew fairly well but in that semi-blackout he stayed totally remote. The hiding could have been deliberate, a planned screen, because there was change in him he didn't want me to see. I was liking less and less those two seated figures representing another authority, this related to Clem's but still not his.

'What the hell's happened to you?' I asked.

It wasn't a particularly discreet question. Discretion isn't one of my portable virtues, and what I do carry about wears very thin under any kind of stress. The stress was real enough now. I had come on to this plane meaning to protest vigorously about an assignment I thought both unnecessary and unsuited to my talents. I had expected a heated interchange as a result of my candour, but nothing like this, nothing like a court of inquiry in a cabin under doused lights.

'How about taking the cloth off that shade?' I suggested. 'Or are you expecting attack at any moment?'

'You never know, do you?'

'I'd like some introductions.'

'This is Colonel Hackett, here. And that is General Winsdale.'

I had been right in my guess about seniority. Brass had come to see me, and gone to considerable trouble and perhaps some risk in an old plane to do so, which isn't something Brass does without good reason. From the two seats I got the kind of grunts you might expect from an Englishman in his club who wants to be allowed to get on with his *Times* in peace. If I'd been in a position to buy them a drink they wouldn't have accepted. And they wouldn't have lunched with me, either.

Quite a number of Americans in high places beyond their own borders are these days tending to take on the airs and graces of Britannia's old pro-consuls. They are obliged to run sizeable areas of the world, and it's a total headache, and the least you can get out of it is a little personal dignity. The British haven't a scrap of dignity left and are having fun for the first time in at least a century, going about like imminent bankrupts who have got everything tucked away in their wives' names, which leaves them astonishingly light on responsibility. And positively gay.

We haul down the flag at midnight, with a band playing, and the Queen's representative talking about a secure future for democracy in a former colony, knowing damn' well that the next morning—and a good thing, too—the Americans will be jetting into the place with a great deal of money to bolster up the shaky economy we've left behind, against Red infiltration. At times I feel very sorry for Americans in this half of the century, but these minutes in the plane weren't one of the times.

I took a long, deep breath.

'Clem, I rather gather you don't think a lot of my powers of observation. In view of this I hereby offer my resignation. And it gives me a great deal of pleasure to do it. Primarily I'm a business man. And for the last two weeks I have been the world's most uncomfortable business man.'

It seemed a long time before Clem got around to words.

'We don't accept resignations.'

'All right, then, let me claim my pension. Even though six months isn't exactly long service.'

He should have smiled, but didn't, even with all those good teeth. And quite suddenly I got a feeling of his hurt, of betrayal and damage done of which I was totally innocent. I was now certain that his travelling companions weren't the ones he would have chosen for this excursion, and that in some manner he was on the mat himself before these two men.

'How about sitting down, Paul?'

'Thanks, but I'm on my way back to Kota Bharu. It doesn't look as though a detailed report is going to get us anywhere.'

'Just sit down,' he said.

I went to the cabin door. At the bottom of steep steps were the two crewmen in white shirts. One of them looked up, then the other. Both gave a sharp impression of having received their orders and being quite ready to act on them. I was still staring down when Clem moved after me, quickly flipping my Luger from its hip holster.

He had made a football pass to the colonel with the gun even before I could swing around.

'What the hell is going on?'

Clem answered right away.

'We were interested in what you had to say about picking your crews. How you always got the right man. . . .'

'Give me back my gun!'

'Later. Maybe you ought to meet someone.'

Clem went through the door at the back of the cabin. It was the general who reached out for the anglepoise, pulling the cloth off it, and spinning the lamp around as a spot on the door. Clem appeared again acting as escort to a Chinese who kept his head bent low on a squat neck. Then, while I stared, the man's chin came up.

I found myself looking into the eyes of Kim Sung, my oldest and favourite junk captain. He is practically the commodore of my fleet, a man with all the instincts of a pirate who has gone through life with a shaky set of moral values. But I would have backed his loyalty to me against all comers.

Now he looked sick. He had the complexion colour of a Javanese wood carving from which the deep brown dye has been bleached by sun exposure. The core of his personality, an unassailable impudence, seemed to have been drained away, too.

I didn't say anything, neither did Kim. I was conscious of the colonel holding my gun and of his fingers probing it gently, as though the Luger had an unfamiliar feel which demanded this professional exploration. The muzzle was also more or less pointing at me.

'Is this the captain of your junk, the *Anwei*?' Clem asked finally.

'You know damn' well it is.'

'When did you last see this man?'

'About two months ago. And what's it to you? Why the hell is Kim Sung here and not in my ship doing his job?'

'I'm asking the questions, Paul.'

'On what authority?'

Officially he didn't have any, not on Malaysian soil, but this was a quibble over which he didn't waste time. Clem's authority was uniquely portable, and took small notice of national frontiers.

'Tell us your last orders to Kim Sung as captain of one of your junks?'

I glared. The light was now bright enough to show Clem's face, his eyes. I didn't like his eyes. They had been cold quartz like that once before in our contacts, and it hadn't been a particularly nice moment.

'Paul, what were your last orders to this man?'

'I don't remember. I don't think there were any last orders.'

'And yet he made a special trip to Kuala Lumpur to see you?'

'It was a routine trip. My base is in Kuala Lumpur.'

'Not many of your other captains seem to visit you there.'

A few people have opened files on my activities, but Clem's dossier would appear to offer pretty comprehensive and detailed coverage. I had suspected this before, and it had been something of an irritation that in spite of very positive efforts to identify Clem's man in Kuala Lumpur I hadn't been able to do so. Probably he had half a dozen contacts in this increasingly important Asian capital, all laying trip wires for each other on separate orders from on high. And, of course, I had been one of these wire layers myself, on an unpaid, honorary basis.

Clem wasn't enjoying my pauses. He knew perfectly well that pauses on the part of the man you are interrogating, if permitted allow him space in which to organize his own defence.

'Why didn't your other captains come to your Kuala Lumpur office? Why just Kim Sung?'

'It wasn't just Kim Sung. Only him more often than the others. He was really my fleet admiral.'

I used the past tense for my captain, and a realization of this made me look at him again. He wasn't trying to send me any message, just standing there in the extraordinary passivity of Chinese defeat, which seems like a total acceptance of what has happened. All the fires of resistance were out, doused, without even an ember sparking. Kim looked now like a wax effigy of the ruffian to whom all the piratical genes in my own blood had once responded.

'As your fleet admiral Kim Sung had a position of special trust and responsibility?'

'You could say that.'

'So that any orders issued to him would really be orders to the rest of Harris and Company's junk fleet?'

'No, they would not. My junks don't operate under orders from head office, except initially. They're tramps. They go where they can pick up cargoes. You could say they freelance. There are no specific signals sent from Kuala Lumpur saying move from A to B. I don't give that kind of order.'

'Kim Sung says you did, in this case.'

'What case?'

General Winsdale coughed. It might have been something he was holding until the movement of a symphony was over, a small spasm eruptive into a sudden silence. In a way it was seniority making its presence felt and we all waited, though in my case not from any deference. In those seconds I was still trying to make myself believe that Kim Sung had merely got himself into another of the recurring awkward situations which had starred his living, this time in some way tangling with American authority in South East Asia. It could happen so easily. American authority fans out now over these parts and in one way or another touches nearly all my trading areas. If Kim had broken somebody's new rules he had a right to my support, provided, that is, that he hadn't succumbed to any temptation to get in on a quick profits venture like the slave trade in indentured labour. This goes on quietly still, and I dislike it very much, something Kim knows well.

More than once in the past my commodore's zeal for increased turnover—from which he got his cut—had caused me considerable trouble and put the man on the mat in my office. But even at these times of real stress between us Kim had never lost his grinning impudence or the self-confidence behind it. His face now frightened me. It said fear, stark fear, and I had never believed he could feel this.

'Shall we stop playing cat and mouse?' I suggested. 'You know something and you intend to hit me with it hard. Supposing we have the blow right now?'

There was silence in the cabin. No one moved. The colonel had even stopped that finger inventory of a piece of my property.

'All right, Paul, here it is.' Quartz eyes held mine. 'A U.S.

destroyer picked up your junk the *Anwei* in the Amphitrite Group. It was trying to use cover in the atoll of Lin Tao. You know where the Amphitrite Group is?'

I nodded. The Amphitrite Group is south-east of the huge Red Chinese island of Hainan. It is also about on a parallel with the southern portion of Red Vietnam. At no time have any of my junks ever had any business in the area, which is at least eight hundred miles from our nearest point of regular trading. There are no cargoes to be had in those atolls and there is the very sharp danger of running foul of portions of the U.S. fleet patrolling the Gulf of Tonkin, the last thing I wanted to happen to one of my ships.

'You're astonished?' Clem's voice was gentle.

'Yes.'

'I expected you to be. The *Anwei*'s cargo will astonish you even more.'

'I'm sure.'

'It was copra. But we dug down through that to what I suppose you could call the ballast. This was arms.'

I didn't say anything. It was my hope that my face showed nothing. Clem watched me for a moment, then went on with that verbal gentleness.

'Forty British brens with thirty thousand rounds of ammo. Eighty-four Czechoslovak repeater rifles, with forty thousand rounds of ammo. There were a dozen French mortars as well, for which presumably they have the shells. Or these could be coming on another junk. It all seems rather like your old business, but to a new market.'

There was a large ice clot moving towards my heart.

'Where is this stuff supposed to have come from?'

'We know it came from Malaysia.'

I tried to smile. It didn't feel as though it were sitting on my face too well.

'You think I was getting rid of old stock?'

'No. The Czech rifles were made last year. We think the *Anwei* was being paid to do the transport job. Highly paid.'

'No one was paying my firm. All I know about this is that the *Anwei* was supposed to sail from Kuantan some twelve hours or so after I saw Kim Sung in my office. It was bound for Bintulu in Sarawak for normal trading.'

Clem broke his stare at me. He gave my captain the treatment I had been getting, using the same cool voice.

'What do *you* say, Kim Sung?'

The sailor looked at the floor. He swallowed. Then he used English, damningly simple English.

'Mr. Harris tell me to go to Kuala Marang in Tregannu when

I sail from Kuantan. This one hour sail. I must anchor five mile south of the town, near small river. Not show light. In night time there are two boats coming. We all working to lift guns into *Anwei*. I am to take to Dong Hoi in Vietnam. There is much money for me, Mr. Harris say. Also for crew.'

CHAPTER TWO

I HAD asked for Clem's blow. It destroyed a major illusion. I had believed that in a violent part of the world, where brother's hand is too often against brother, Harris and Company was a sound business with a steadily increasing turnover because internally we had achieved a partnership in sharing. I had bought loyalty at first, offering a big cash return for it, but was sure that I had seen this loyalty confirmed into something real through increasing common interest.

Kim Sung's defection meant that I had been a damn' fool. This man had for ten years been getting a swelling cut of trading profits. By local standards, and even western ones, he was moderately rich. Money couldn't be the motivation behind what he had just done, which meant that, like so many others who owed their original motherland nothing, he had gone over to Mao's China because he had come to believe that she held all the cards for the future.

It is, of course, a perfectly reasonable point of view. I shouldn't have been so winded, and I don't think I would have been with any of my other junk captains. I watch them. And Kim Sung had been one of my means of doing this. He knew more about the way my company operated than anyone else outside of head office. And if Kim had been playing his own game behind my back it meant almost certainly that other captains had been doing it, too, probably under the fleet commodore's orders. Instead of presiding over a nicely oiled trading concern stretching south from the Philippines I was only the front man for a dirty shambles. And a big laugh for the crews nominally in my employ, who took in Harris and Company's bonuses along with payola from old mother China. At that moment I could have knocked in all of Kim Sung's beautifully white front teeth.

'Mind if I take over the interrogation?" I asked.

After a minute Clem said:

"Okay."

The general cleared his throat again, as though he was about to intervene with a protest against irregularity in court martial proceedings, but thought better of it, and didn't say a word. I stepped closer to Kim Sung.

'Look at me.'

He didn't want to. But slowly that ugly mug came up. I had shared a lot of laughter with this man, on his ship and off it, and quite a few bottles as well. His sins, which I had thought redeemed by a large area of surprising honesty, had put deep seams in a sea-burnished face. What was visible of his eyes now seemed rigidly focused on my Adam's apple.

I used Cantonese. I told Kim that his mother had been the whore of his native village of Chi'in-k'an and his father an itinerant pedlar of unspeakables, but that even their coffined bones were now twitching at what their by-blow had been up to.

'Say, what's all this?' the colonel asked loudly.

'It's all right,' Clem said. 'I can follow.'

The C.I.A. give their top boys a good grounding in the Oriental Classics when that is the sphere of their operations, not to mention the local dialects. But my southern Chinese was acquired during a somewhat unconventional boyhood in Singapore, with about forty per cent of it idiomatically pressing close to the gutter. I was using all of that percentage, and if Clem was staying with me it says a lot for contemporary intensive study methods.

When I stopped the only sound in that plane cabin was Kim Sung's breathing. I have never thought of him as ever wanting to see me dead, but that was now his wish. And not quickly dead, either. His chin came up just a little further and he widened those concealing slits, letting me have a real look into his eyes. I knew then that wild anger had served me badly, that a little deliberate, controlled stirring up of shame just might have strengthened my position.

'Who paid you to take these arms to Vietnam?'

'You,' he said.

'When were you to get payment?'

'I got it in advance. Over your desk in Kuala Lumpur.'

'How much?'

'Five thousand dollars to me. Each of the crew got a thousand.'

'You've thirteen men. That means I handed over eighteen thousand dollars risk money. Together with another twenty thousand for normal cash trading, for which you had to account to me?'

'Yes.'

'You went back to your junk and paid out your men?'

'Yes.'

I turned to Clem.

'What sort of money did you find on the *Anwei* when you took her?'

'Around forty-two thousand dollars.'

'Each man carrying a fat roll?'

'There'd been a lot of gambling. I wouldn't say it was evenly distributed. But your twenty thousand trading money was in the safe untouched. There hadn't been any time for normal business.'

A little breeze came in the open door of the plane, bringing with it a smell of jungle, a movement of air that wasn't really refreshing because it was vitiated by all that vegetable use of oxygen. I was sweating. There was a fan on the desk but no one had switched the thing on, perhaps to conserve batteries. I turned back to my captain, to an impression of a man waiting, ready to return strike for strike.

'Did I tell you where the arms had come from, Kim Sung?'

'No.'

'But you got precise sailing instructions from me?'

'Yes.'

'What were they?'

'I was to sail in darkness for the Anabas islands, where I was to pick up a cover load of copra. It was left over from our voyage home to Kuantan. After that I was to go to Great Natoena. At night. You told me to anchor during the day. We were to work north through the Luconia Group, keeping in reefs so we didn't run into other shipping. You were nervous about the open passage between Thitu and the Amphitrites. You suggested we wait for bad weather before crossing this. And that's what I did.'

The statement was beautifully groomed. It could have been a direct product of Clem's Saigon office.

'Kim, you know perfectly well I never give you detailed sailing orders, which isn't surprising since you know the seas around here ten times better than I do.'

'This time you were worried about me running risks.'

'You're a rotten liar.'

'You say that now, *Tuan*. When I'm caught.'

The respect in that *Tuan* was sardonic.

'Did we talk about what you were to do if you did get caught?'

'No. But then I never have been before. Not like this.'

The implication behind that was naked. And Clem could have picked it up even if his Cantonese hadn't won him all 'A's at the training college. Kim Sung had never been caught on any of the other jobs, like this one, which he had done for me. I had the feeling that at his interrogation in some U.S. base up in Vietnam Kim had driven this home, deliberately, to destroy me because he had been brought down himself. There might have been strong inducements to do this, possibly a promise of leniency if he would dig a pit deep enough to trap and hold his boss. Clem had been thorough.

And yet the military were along in this plane, which could mean that some knives had been sharpened up for Clem, too.

It looked very much as though he had put a foot badly wrong somewhere, perhaps by recruiting me. There was a somewhat complex multiple trial going on in the belly of an old airplane, with the proper authority not too clearly defined.

I looked at Clem.

'So you planned that trip across Kra as a check on me? Litmus test. You *know* there is Commie traffic up there. If I came back and said there was no sign of it that shows me up bright Red?'

He shook his head.

'Not bright red. Just working for your own interests. As you were when you sold those diesel engines to China.'

My voice went loud.

'I might have known those diesels would be coming into it. Look, Clem, I sold my engines in competition with the Japanese, the Germans, the Czechs, and one Italian firm manufacturing under licence from a company in Jersey City. If you don't call that open competition I don't know what the hell it is. Just because you have a trade embargo on China doesn't mean that the rest of us who don't go along with you here are criminals. We're capitalists trying to survive in a market area which has to include selling to communism. I'd sell more diesels to China to-morrow if I got the chance, but I won't, and never have, done secret deals with them. Any sales I've made in that area have taken gold away from the Reds because I was paid in outside currency. With the diesels they got an engine that couldn't conceivably have anything but a commercial use.'

This wasn't strictly true, and I wished, the moment it was over, that I hadn't said it.

Clem's eyebrows lifted.

'I'd say your diesels have an interesting variety of uses. They give an average junk five knots an hour more speed than any engine they're mass producing themselves.'

'All right, granted. But they're still a power plant for junks. They can't be developed to get anything like the thrust needed for a patrol boat, and you know it.'

'A fast junk is a useful supply medium in war.'

'If you're going to produce that kind of argument you could say that plastic toothbrushes are war potential because soldiers use them.'

Clem's expression checked me. It hadn't changed much, it rarely did, but the little was enough. I was being manoeuvred on to the defensive and once there faced the hard task of producing a credible apologia for fairly normal business ethics. It's not something that the sensible executive attempts, and in my case—possibly slightly more than in most cases—commercial morals mightn't always launder snow white. You need a stable order for a pristine effect and that kind of society was totally unavailable where I lived.

Clem folded his brown hands together in front of his hips and looked down at them. He was wearing trousers and shirt of military drab, both in a slightly shiny material which looked like service issue. His hands somehow drew attention to an older body functioning under orders from that boy's head. There was a slight thickening at the waist, not really any suggestion of too much weight, just a hint of a general slackening in youth's muscles, of sags here and there which would only come tight as a result of conscious effort. He asked a question still looking at his hands.

'So Kim Sung here is a flat liar?'

'From a long line with unique talent at the job. He's fooled me for ten years, and with a happy grin on his face.'

'You didn't give him eighteen thousand dollars as a down payment to carry out a special assignment?'

'I gave him his trading money, that's all.'

'You knew nothing about the arms he was taking from Malaya?'

'I did not.'

'And now you have no second thoughts about what you saw up there in the border jungle?'

He looked up at me. And as certainly as though I could see into Clem's mind I knew he was checking down the list of other things he could throw at me if he wanted to. There were quite a few. Behind us the still neutrality of the military Brass was somehow positively officious. No chairs creaked and there was no wheeze of breathing, but they were there, and as big brothers with almost ultimate power.

'I've told you what I saw in the border jungle. Elephants, gibbons and the sweating backs of my guides. Those guides could have been a clever plant, I suppose. Though I still don't see how. And it's possible, too, that I was deliberately steered past what I wasn't meant to see. If the Reds are using navigable water then maybe I slipped up. But a water route would put them out in the open. Air reconnaissance ought to have picked up any movement of men in boats.'

'Air reconnaissance has,' Clem said softly.

While I was absorbing this I noticed a smile sketched on Kim Sung's lips. Anger at me had completely eliminated an earlier apathy of defeat. The stretched skin of fear had gone. The man seemed suddenly to be almost enjoying himself. Because of Kim I was going to have to call in the wreckers for the job of smashing down my entire organization and then start it all again from scratch. The sooner I got moving on this the better. The first move was to escape from Clem.

Once clear of the plane I would be running free. The jungle

was near, ready with all the prodigal hospitality it offers to fugitives until they get lost in it. I wouldn't get lost. I believed, too, that back in Kuala Lumpur I would be fairly safe from the long arm of the C.I.A. As a British subject I probably wouldn't have been safe at all, but as a Malaysian, and carrying a new nation's passport, I came under the umbrella of that nation's sensitivity about any rough stuff metered out to its citizens from foreign agencies. Friends in high places in the capital could be alerted on my behalf and Clem would have to walk softly, even though he continued to watch every move I made.

The general outlook for the escaper, however, wasn't too bright. It is just not good for a business man in tropic Asia these days to fall out with the United States of America. And the trader who does this is liable to find himself up against the kind of economic quarantine which can play hell with company dividends. Also, that freezing order on my junk movements would at once cut off two-thirds of my operations, something to send a cold trickle down a managing director's spine even without any threat to his personal freedom.

The alternative to making a sudden bolt for it was to go on proclaiming my innocence. This hadn't done me much good and I didn't feel that it was likely to do more at my trial, or court of inquiry, or whatever was scheduled. It was obvious that I was now under some kind of arrest, however illegal this might be. Clem had flown over here, accompanied by his unwanted guests, with the sole object of picking me up. Round one had been a preliminary questioning in which I had scored badly. Round two would now almost certainly be over in Saigon to which I would be flown in this plane, these decidedly formal proceedings, but still with no one in the least worried about having to explain away my sudden appearance in custody in Vietnam. In time of war little points like this don't have to be explained, even when they involve civilians. And possibly, as a registered sub-agent, I wasn't technically a civilian any longer.

I hadn't seen guns in the hands of those two young men in white shirts at the bottom of the aluminium steps. Clem wasn't armed. The colonel had the Luger, but it is a heavy weapon if you haven't fired one before, with a trigger kick upsetting to aim.

Even Clem, usually watching for everything, wasn't ready for that right to his jaw. He had been standing between me and the exit, but the blow spun him back to the curved cabin wall, with both hands out against it. He snapped forward again to grab my shirt, blocking the colonel's line of fire. I went through a moonlit opening like a man whose back hairs have been singed by huge flame, hands clutching for a low rail, but feet not bothering overmuch about steps. There was a lot of shouting, none of it too coherent. I hit the ground. One of the white-shirted boys went into a routine subsidiary to his basic training in flying machines and landed a chop at the base of my skull. I went flat on to cracked tarmac.

When machine-gun clatter started I wondered why anyone was bothering with such heavy armament against a prone escaper. There was a scream. The man who had hit me pitched forward. The other scrambled up metal steps. I caught this movement without really turning my head, a visual message that came dully, along with another saying that the firing wasn't from anywhere in the plane, but directed at it, passing over me. Bullets struck metal struts to whine again in ricochets, but most of them were getting into the cabin. Human noise said they were finding targets.

The man on the steps folded in two. He came down to a crumpled heap two feet from one of my outstretched hands, his head jerked back. I could see his face in moonlight. His mouth was open as though he had something to say that would now never be pushed into words.

The cut sword grass ended on a line ten feet ahead of me. I started to crawl towards the cover of tall *lalang,* very slowly, pushing fingers into fissures in asphalt, pulling weight forward that way, scarcely moving my legs at all, expecting at any second to be caught by a lowered trajectory of bullets.

The plane stayed the target. I thought there was return fire from it, but couldn't be sure. I heard a loud cry from somewhere ahead of me, in the open.

My hands touched the uncut *lalang,* fingers at once sliced by its sharp blades. I edged in, trying to avoid making a betraying ripple up above, suddenly feeling screened, almost sheltered from a killing. I lay still, head down.

The attackers weren't being careful about expenditure of ammunition. They might have had a special issue for this job, to make certain it was thorough. It was thorough all right. I was sure now that the attack had been from both sides of the plane, a sweeping crossfire carelessly dangerous to the attackers themselves.

The din eased, becoming a series of explosive postscripts before silence. Echoes were absorbed by a padding of thick jungle and into a tight stillness came the sudden squawking of frightened monkeys.

I couldn't seem to organize a coherent reaction to what had happened, or find my place in it. I was alive when a lot of others were dead, and from this came only ego controlled relief. I had started along a line of escape and might make the rest of the distance, and had no real concern for anything else.

Human voices took over from the monkeys, first an order

shouted, then a reaction to it, an excited jabbering followed by the crackle of trampled grass. A tide of men came sweeping through the *lalang*, and my ear against the ground picked up a vibration of their feet.

'Surround the plane!' That was in Cantonese. 'But watch that door. They mayn't all be dead yet.'

Grass rustled. A man coughed. Another called out something and there was a laugh. They passed by on either side, leaving me in my nest, safe in it. They made a row which provided cover for my movement. No one would see grass moving now. It was the plane they were all watching.

I sat up and looked at it, too, through my screen. A bright glare from torches hit the open cabin door, glittering on the steps, a hard supplement to moonlight. A man came forward into the whiteness, left arm lifted. His trousers were tucked into heavy boots and his shirt was splashed with camouflage. He wore a tin hat with netting over it.

The man's arm swung back, something heavy left fingers. He spun about and ran, shouting. The darkened cabin erupted, explosive light briefly contained by smashed windows, but suddenly expanding through these, shattering the suspended frame of the plane, severing its heavy belly, and bringing this to the ground in a rending of torn metal. For seconds the pilot's cockpit and the heavy wings continued to be supported by the landing gear, then the nose swung upwards as though for a frantic climb clear, like a disembowelled bird jerked into the reflex action of flight. The wing nearest me crumpled, ripped from the fuselage, and smacking down on tarmac. A collapsing undercarriage sent the cockpit sagging back on to the main wreckage. There was a shower of sparks. I waited for fire, but this didn't come, the fuel tanks somehow not ruptured. Only the tail portion of the plane had hit the ground almost intact, sliced from the main cabin and slightly spaced away from it, with rudder fin still firmly erect and a window of unbroken glass continuing to reflect moonlight.

The entire disintegration of that plane had perhaps taken half a minute, but it seemed to have been run before my eyes in a kind of deliberate slow motion, a half speed play-back to get detail, starting with an arm lifted for a throw, then a pause while the unseen grenade travelled into a close darkness, and a wait again before the hideous flowering of the explosion. I was still remote from the reality of the moment, as though held in a mental breathlessness by the sheer miracle of my own escape. And somehow the dead in that wreckage meant nothing, the men who had been watching a ladder, the colonel and the general in chairs watching me, Clem staring at his hands, and Kim Sung with just the hint of a smirk on his face.

Smell reached me, the thin, acrid air taint from discharged firecrackers immediately overpowered by the strong, half sweet odour of barbecued meat. I found myself again, behind staring eyeballs. I wanted to be sick.

In a war there isn't often time for the elation of total triumph, action runs on to the next phase. But a successful ambush is something isolated, remote from that continuing action, allowing time for an almost orgiastic celebration of sudden relief from tension. In a total and complete victory the men out there shook off discipline. They shouted and leaped about, not listening to a voice warning them back from wreckage, surging towards the plane, flashing light on it. And then someone began to sing, a bellow triumphing over a leader's screeched orders, the song taken up by other voices, amplified, the men prodding at debris with automatic rifles as they sang. It was like the chorale finish to some repulsive Red propaganda documentary, the tune a war march imported from China. I knew then that the three hundred miles of sea between Vietnam and Malaysia buys no immunity from the thing which is sweeping down through the whole of South East Asia.

But it was a moment for survival, nothing more. Din offered cover. I went up on hands and knees to crawl, and had been at it for minutes, sweating nearer that jungle wall, when noise died. Sword grass crackles under assault and I wasn't at once aware of that dribbling away of sound beyond me, just suddenly of total stillness again in possession of a forgotten airstrip. There were no voices and no orders. I had the hideous feeling that my movement through *lalang* had been spotted, reviving battle tension, putting men back into discipline. I could imagine them turned now in my direction, rifles lifted, all waiting for the command which would send out a blast of lead hail.

I had one chance in ten of making the jungle even under concentrated fire, but I'd have to run to do it. I stood, then had a look over my shoulder.

No one was turned towards me. Out on the cleared runway men were as motionless as in a frozen still when the projecting machine has broken down. It took me a minute to see why. A man had come out from the tail portion of the plane. He was leaning back against a torn edge of fabric, sagging against it, as though near to collapse. His head was bent. Moonlight fell over him. He held his right arm in his left hand. One arm had been shattered. It was Clem.

He moved slightly. The projector started again. Stillness broke. A creaking voice gave an order. Rifle lifted. Others swung to target. I yelled in Cantonese:

'Don't shoot! He's important!'

One gun did go off, but the aim was wild. The noise of it jerked Clem's head up, as though to look at death. Then he was looking at me.

So were half a hundred others, swinging around to do it, an order totally forgotten, but automatic guns still at the ready in their hands. I had seconds in which to exploit total surprise, with a fractional tide in my favour, a new tension for action not quite achieved. And frenzy had been spent.

'We surrender! We're your prisoners!'

I blundered through long grass, throwing words at them in the thin hope I was throwing confusion too.

The battle itself doesn't have room for the taking of prisoners, just sometimes the lull after it. No actor has ever held his audience more completely than I did in those seconds. I was inspired by a stark fear of the kind of death which smashes down a total, abject helplessness. My shouts were a kind of commentary on that death.

They listened. I even gained a certain confidence from this, conscious of the demands made by my role and at the same time submerged in it. I was putting on a display of anti-heroics which came near to the whimpering terror of complete defeat. The men with guns were watching what they could never believe would strike at them, a moral death in cowardice. And there was a pleasure in allowing the performance to go on which kept their fingers from the triggers. The single enemy frenziedly begging for life was basically comic. If I got a laugh the scene was totally mine.

The laugh came. It was loud and a cue for massed support. Laughter dispelled residual fear and replaced it with contempt. Sound roared out, relief, delight even. When I reached cleared ground it was seconds before anyone touched me and my arms were then seized without any real roughness. Only their leader had to remind his men that there was a war on. He came up to hit me in the face with a closed fist.

That ended laughter. I was propped up from behind for the beating. It was administered slowly, an oriental correction, something the occasion demanded automatically. There was no running commentary. The only really loud sounds were my grunts from blows and more than a grunt when I got a knee in the groin. Then I was thrown down and the leader used his boots, heavy boots. He was the man who had tossed a grenade into the cabin.

They rolled me over on to my back. A distant seeming face peered down. The interrogation began, in Cantonese.

'Did you come on that plane?'

'No.'

'Then you were the man waiting?'

'Yes.'

'You're Harris from Kuala Lumpur?'

'Yes.'

Broad lips separated. I saw teeth.

'Good. We're pleased to meet you.'

Someone tittered. The leader snapped that into silence.

There had been no gun fired. Clem was still alive. I couldn't turn my head to see him and anyway there was sweat stinging in my eyes. I answered questions fast to keep that boot from my mouth.

Those questions went on for a long time. It was an interrogation to confirm what they already knew, a cross checking of the kind Clem went in for. The man above me had been informed about my excursion into Thailand and its probable purpose. That purpose had been foiled from the outset by my guides, just as Clem had suggested. It gave the leader pleasure to tell me this. In fact the whole scene was giving him pleasure.

An actor's moment of triumph was over. I was a bit player with a new lead at the stage's centre. And the bit player was down for a bullet when his lines had been said. So was Clem. In the circumstances I should have tried to save one man, not two. We all take on more than we can cope with.

'Who's that man over there?' the leader asked.

'American.'

'I know that, you fool. But what does he do?'

'Intelligence.'

I got a kick, but not in the head.

'How big?'

'Very. Top.'

'Getting your orders from him here?'

'Yes.'

'Why here?'

'I don't know. I was told to come. After Thailand.'

'Answer me, you!'

'I have. I just don't know.'

'But you were working for them?'

'Yes.'

'How long?'

'Only months.'

The boot came in, to my ribs. I didn't seem to have any broken bones as yet, but couldn't expect my luck to hold. When I curled my body at all it just tempted him. I kept it straight.

'Liar. We know all about you. You've been at it for years. You were caught in Sumatra once. Only you got away then. You won't this time.'

'I've only worked a few months for the Americans.'

'Why? Your own country too feeble these days to make it worth your while?'

'I'm a Malaysian.'

He laughed.

'You won't be for long, Harris. We're going to cremate you in the plane, along with the rest.'

'You ought to take the American and me to Lum Ping.'

He reached down then and pulled me up by the front of my shirt, which ripped, but left me sitting.

'Who told you anything about Lum Ping?'

'We all know he's in those mountains.'

'Do you? How?'

'There's been no news of his leaving.'

'Get up, Harris. Get on your feet.'

This was to give him the pleasure of knocking me down again. I got up.

'Well, come on. What do you know about Lum Ping?'

'He's been seen in Kota Bharu.'

'Who by?'

'I don't know. It could have been bazaar talk.'

The blow came and I went with it, down again on to one inch stubble spikes which would have made a nice fakir's mattress.

'Who saw Lum Ping in Kota Bharu?'

'I don't know,' I said, spitting out blood.

The boot came in to my collar bone, which was a new area for it. But I had a small satisfaction. The Gauleiter was worried. And hope stirred that his worry would expand to the point where a rushed decision to cremate Clem and me might seem unwise.

My interrogator took time to light a cigarette, but without offering the pack to his men. He had removed the tin hat earlier to get comfortable for question time, and I saw his face clearly in the match flame. It was almost a pleasant face, the broad lips part of a bony, outsize cast of features together with a special issue in large fleshy ears which made their owner look unoriental. But he was Chinese all right, born to good feeding and those imported sports which tend to alter physique wherever they are practised. He went up to at least five feet eleven and I made him about thirty. A slight turn of the chance wheel in another direction could have had us as partners at one of those all male *towkays'* Singapore parties, both with sore palms from applauding imported Hong Kong striptease.

It is a comfort in war to be offered a clearly defined viciousness in your adversary, the simian Nip, the Mongolian wog, the slant-eyed Slav, but this was a man I'd have happily bought a drink at the bar of the swimming club and gone to dine with later up on the roof under the tropic stars while he told me all about the trouble he was having with women. As a friend he would be a comforting reserve for those occasions which do crop up fairly frequently out East, when you need some solid support for the rough stuff.

He was now looking down at me as though not totally dissimilar thoughts had popped into his mind, and it suddenly made for one of the oddest interludes in brutality I have experienced. I wasn't really surprised when he turned away, leaving me on the ground for his men to watch, but apparently not to touch, for none of them did. The half circle remained, men staring but now almost neutral, and to stretch out this blessed state I did nothing to provoke them. I didn't turn my head to see where their leader was going. I could guess anyway.

There was no sound of another interrogation over there by the plane. It seemed likely that Clem had now collapsed and was unconscious. I shut my eyes and thought about Kim Sung, now dead along with his captors.

It was quite possible that the leader of the attack had known that Kim was inside the plane, and why. In a sense my captain was an ally but that fact, even if understood, hadn't moderated the viciousness of the assault. Kim had been killed by bullets from his own side. It happens to their lesser operators who become expendable, and happens so often you would think that the word would get about and lesser operators become difficult to recruit. But the mystique of mother China is powerful. It has a potent, emotional appeal which even pulls in the emigrant children to that great bosom, and quite often to their deaths. It is the hardest of all mystiques to fight because its demands are totally beyond reason. Converts to Communism in our time are rarely landed by the dialectic, but much more often because what is offered fills a vacuum, an emptiness of no faith. God is dispensed with under Marxism, but not the chanted prayers, not the sermons, and not the vast relief from any personal need to cerebrate which is the direct result of a total subjection to a disciplined conformism.

The man who had been kicking me was educated, this plain from his voice. Very probably he was a younger son from a rich Singapore family, his loss to capitalism never mentioned at clan reunions, but not forgotten either. It was possible that this eccentric was being discreetly pensioned as a kind of quiet insurance against coming days of change. The idealist crops up now and then even in the best regulated families and it is unrealistic to attempt to keep him from his cause. This leader's cause, the only major one available in his environment, had turned him into a killer, and a killer for a truth which seemed to him as totally whole and complete as the one the Moslems once took with them on their assaults against Southern Europe. For Allah read Mao Tse Tung and you have it.

I lay on the ground knowing perfectly well that no latent humanity in my captors was going to save my life or Clem's. If we were able to survive it would be the direct result of intelligence brought to bear on a situation which, for all the temporary lull, still indicated just about maximum danger. I rated our chances as thin indeed. Round one was perhaps mine, in that thirty minutes after standing up in the grass I was still alive, but there were more rounds to come. It mightn't be long before I was fighting with blood in my eyes and more than half punch drunk, resistance neutralized by sheer fatigue more than fear. Under stress you can reach the point where the bullet is longed for as the ultimate escape. Also, I can take a beating, but have a terror of deliberate planned torture. Anticipation of this scares me right down to the soles of my feet, perhaps because I have had the course.

I heard boots coming back to the circle round me, and opened my eyes. The leader stared down.

'Your friend is dying, Harris,' he said in English acquired at university level. 'He may have been worth keeping. You're not.'

There was a revolver in his hand, a Smith and Wesson. It is remarkable how they manage to get ammunition for all the assorted makes they pick up.

'Let me go to him.'

'What for?'

'He could have fainted. Loss of blood.'

'All right.' That was almost mild.

My legs were still. The guerrillas moved with us, in a shuffling mob just behind. Over in the jungle the monkeys had gone back to sleep. The full moon, carefully chosen by Clem, put almost harsh light over his defeat and the tumbled wreckage of his transport. He lay just beyond where I had seen him standing, clear of the plane, one arm flung out, the other, which had stopped the bullets, folded under his body. The dark tarmac showed a darker stain of blood. His face was in shadow.

I bent down and turned him over, carefully, watched by a silent and almost quiescent audience. Clem's mouth was open and his eyes shut. In the moonlight his face looked drained beneath tan, like the victim of a car accident who may in moments be dead. His breathing was audible in a way I didn't like.

'There ought to be a first-aid box in the plane.'

No one was interested. A guerrilla cleared his throat and spat.

'Can I go for it?'

'All right.'

The leader came with me, torch in one hand, revolver in the other. We crunched over wreckage into the tail of the plane where it was dark, into a passage along one side of the fuselage, this flanking the stern compartment. Sudden light fell on a body in the corridor, folded down into a natural seeming position, buttocks on the floor, back against one wall, legs propped against the other. The colonel was dead, though his head somehow looked still supported by living muscle.

'Get over him,' the leader said.

I stepped across the body, sickened into one of those moments of sharp awareness which are the most unbearable detail of any war. You forget the actual violence quickly enough, but not its punctuation.

A door was half wrenched from its hinges by bullets but the cabin showed little damage. Two bunks had neatly folded blankets on them. Under the lower one was a large box marked with a red cross.

I was shaking by the time I got that box out on to the tarmac near Clem. I didn't at once lift the lid but when I did torches probed the contents. The container for morphia had phials and the syringe intact in cotton wool. I broke an ampoule and managed to put a measured amount in the cylinder, guessing at what I was doing, wondering if a much larger dose mightn't be the humane thing. Someone noticed the trembling of my fingers and said in Cantonese:

'He's scared.'

The leader asked a question.

'You know medicine?'

'This much.'

It hadn't seemed to occur to him yet that medical supplies were valuable. I put a needle in Clem's good arm, taking time to find a vein, then pushed the plunger. I got scissors and cut blood-sodden cloth away from that other arm. There seemed to be three centres to a viscous coagulation, three drilled wells into flesh and bone between wrist and elbow. There was no way to wash the wounds and a sponging with alcohol and lint would have taken too long. I turned the arm gently to see if there were egress holes and made out one. Two bullets were still in there.

Clem had nearly bled to death, but not quite. And if I said he couldn't be moved they would finish him and me.

'Is he dying?'

'No. Just arm hits. His legs are all right.'

'He can walk?'

'In a little, yes.'

I put on emergency dressing pads and bandages, using two rolls which dampened under my hands as I worked. I made a sling from the broadest roll and eased the shattered arm into this, while all the time that accelerated breathing went on, now possibly from the drug taking effect. It was pain which had knocked Clem out and he would have partial relief from this, for a time.

My enemies were now engaged in what was happening, an involved audience which had no other distraction from that involvement. When I asked that Clem be carried away from the plane to the long *lalang* the leader detailed men for this, and without comment. My idea was to dissociate the two survivors from the wreckage which contained the dead. If they were going to make a pyre of the aircraft there would still be the strong temptation to add us to it, especially if we were obvious during the excitement.

In the grass there was a four-foot anthill against which to prop Clem. I arranged the body, trying to make it seem not too near death, then sat down alongside. When I groped for cigarettes a couple of guns came up, but dropped again. I took out a cigarette and held up the pack to the nearest man. This was taken, but I wasn't offered a light. I had matches of my own.

It may have been the heat which stirred Clem from coma, or the strong red light of twenty-foot flames. Oil black smoke went straight up, blurring a complacent moon. Investigators might eventually find traces of bullet holes in melted metal fragments on an old airfield, but I didn't think they would. What was left would only suggest a night crash and instant, enveloping fire. Even identification of the plane was improbable. They had used four more grenades to make certain of this and to start the blaze.

The fact that Clem and I hadn't yet been added to the fire didn't mean much. The leader might experiment with prisoners, starting off with us, but he could change his mind at almost any point on the trek. The Malayan jungle is probably the best place in the world in which to leave bodies you don't want traced. Wild life scavengers get to work almost at once, even scattering the bones. And there is absolutely no danger that weeks later someone is going to stumble on something nasty at a picnic and yell for the police.

We had only one guard now, but his job had been made easy in that my hands were strapped back and held at the wrist by adhesive tape. I could still move legs and head.

Clem's lids lifted. His eyes were extremely bloodshot, suggesting a massive hangover, and the red light even spoiled blue irises. His mouth was open a little wider than he had been keeping it and his tongue pushed at the corners of his lips. He didn't seem to notice me at all, his stare focused on the big attraction. Then he looked down, lashes dropping, inspecting his own condition and taking some time over this assessment.

My reaction was a kind of joy at no longer being alone. I knew then how lonely I had been. Under acute stress a sentient friend permits an easing of terror in a sharing, and this was something I suddenly wanted very much.

'Hallo,' I said softly, and it sounded remarkably stupid.

He didn't move his head, only his eyes. The new focus stayed fixed, assessing me, too.

He was intelligently conscious, noting my strapped wrists, and the fact that I wasn't too comfortable. Again his tongue made an excursion out over cracked lips.

Our guard shifted his position and his rifle. Clem ignored the man. His voice, when it came, was almost normal.

'Your friends . . . didn't start firing until you were out of the plane.'

CHAPTER THREE

WHAT I WANTED to do then was curse Clem, loud and long. But I had to conserve energy, so I looked back at the fire. For the whole of this contact with the man I'd had the feeling that he was functioning as some kind of projection from a computer, a technician absolved from humanity in the mathematics of logic. And to look for a friend here was like expecting a reaction to 'how are you doing?' from a metal box with flashing electronic eyes.

Everything he knew about me had gone on strips of tape with punched hole symbols, these then fed into a machine which always came up with the infallible answer so long as a fuse hadn't blown somewhere. Certainly he had a lot of information for his computer, able to give it a really balanced meal which it could swallow without any burps of technological indigestion. I could fill in all the courses on that menu myself, starting with the *hors d'œuvre* of a somewhat unconventional youth in the Orient, through the entrée of what I had been up to in the last decade, a solitary trying to build his own little durable empire with ships and trade while the national empires in the area crumbled all around. There was very little indication of any specific allegiance on my part to loyalties beyond my own interest. I had shaken off any earlier slight attachments to Britain. As the European determined to survive in the new East I had openly traded with the Reds from time to time. I had been in Peking on a selling mission. My engines pushed Red junks over the

South China Seas. One of my businesses involved working with Chinese co-directors who almost certainly paid regular tributes to the big boss up north. Many of my friends could be labelled political unreliables and my trading fleet was now just about as suspect as anyone's trading fleet could be. Finally, I had agreed to assist American intelligence simply to find out the extent of their penetration into the areas of my interest.

That excretion from the box's intestines didn't require any detailed analysis at all. I played along with the Reds when it suited my bank accounts. And on this premise I had to be dealt with. The machine said so. The fact that in this case the machine was wrong was my little problem, one which inevitably faces the slight eccentric in an age when such eccentricity can only be interpreted in terms of mechanized psychological formulas.

I looked down at my knees. Those two knees covered by dirty trousers were a little oasis of the personal in the relentless desert of surrounding hostility. I stared at them.

The fire had turned to black smoke, its work done, a tall column tainting a purple night sky, the residue of a purge. Up near the wreckage a man went into a paroxysm of coughing, the sound, so violently beyond control, suggesting limits set on his mortality by lungs weakened from jungle damp. The leader's voice barked out again, producing a rustle of action through the grass. I looked up to see them carrying out their own casualty of battle. The scream I had heard must have come from this boy's throat. He was hit below the waist by a bullet which could have been a final shot from the plane or just a wild stray from an ill-sited cross ambush. The boy lay there unable to get up, but lifting the top half of his body, writhing to do this, propping himself on elbows as though to demonstrate that he had areas which were still functioning normally. He was talking, too, babbling with a desperate urgency to the leader who stood looking down, very much as he had looked down at me. But this boy wasn't going to be able to walk. He presented an even more acute problem than we did.

The solution to it was swift. The leader took his revolver from a holster and without even leaning down, shot the babbling youth in the head. One bullet, one sharp sound, that was all. They then carried away the body, adding it, a bit late, to the pyre, where only half charred remains would possibly complicate the task of investigators, adding a new inexplicable factor. A cloud of sparks went up, a little tribute.

I turned to Clem.

'I just hope you're going to be mobile,' I said.

His eyes were shut again, perhaps from the pain he had to endure.

The Malaysian Communist Party oath of allegiance apparently doesn't contain a clause binding recruits to total abstinence. I hadn't seen a looting of the plane before it was set on fire but this could have been carried out during one of my times of politic quiescence when I wasn't moving my head to watch anything because there was a boot too near it. But salvage there certainly was, all of it food and drink.

The food stocks went quickly, with a well-maintained discipline in the way these were portioned out. Someone who might have had sergeant's rank took pains in that dying red light to keep things approximately fair, one cooked chicken torn into as near equal portions as could be managed, with a ham for the rest, this chopped up into precise squares. Crackers and biscuits went out one each all around. There wasn't a hint of squabbling though it was clear everyone was hungry. Clem and I witnessed a fine demonstration of egalitarian sharing which might have been staged for our benefit but was probably normal practice. They shot a comrade who was no longer mobile, then neatly carved up a ham for the more fortunate survivors, and with no two-minute silence between one job and the other.

I didn't want anything to eat, but my throat was parched, and when they broached two cases of Coca Cola I called out for a drink. No one appeared to hear. I sat watching those bottles emptied and then the hard liquor being passed from hand to hand, some of the labels recognizable, Booth's London dry gin, Old Grandad bourbon, a vermouth, a Bell's 'afore ye go'. There seemed to be some wines, too, probably Californian.

Things began to have the feel of a party, the kind of party which would call for cabaret later, and I felt pretty sure that Clem and I would be it. I wished then, and perhaps he did, too, that Clem hadn't done himself quite so well in his mobile headquarters.

I had quite a clear picture of what might lie just ahead for us, fun and games inspired by mixed drinks. The prisoners would be given a sporting chance to run for it, Clem first, with me handicapped because more mobile. The performance couldn't be too long delayed either if, after it, we were to be added to a fire that still retained effective heat.

It was totally clear to me in those moments that my wild bid to save Clem was easily the most stupid thing I have ever done, impulsive lunacy which was going to produce the net result of two dead instead of one, and with no survivor to creep away to give an eye-witness account of the night's happenings. Further, my heroics hadn't even earned me minimal gratitude from the character they had been meant to rescue. Clem was going to take that computer verdict on me all the way, retaining to the last his deep faith in the reliability of machines as against the infinite potential perfidy of man. I was a no-good joe, just as he had intuitively felt from round one over there in Borneo, a by-product of collapsed empire who would sell out anything to keep intact a personal salvage from general wreckage. For me he had only burning red eyes. He was an impossible man to die with, let alone for.

I watched the last of the Old Grandad go into the leader, moving into a state that was vaguely euphoric, something suspended between a terror which has exhausted itself and a new one about to arrive. This lull was the eye in the hurricane and unfortunately you can't stay in its shelter for long, though it's restful while it lasts, almost permitting a return to personal norm. I even had time to wonder about how my Japanese assistant and new co-director, Ohashi, would run the business without me. Probably better than I had. And screened from the knowledge that most of our crews were undercover Reds he might go on using them for years, with a steady annual increase in Harris and Company's business the end result.

I think I was the first to hear the sound which came from somewhere over the jungle. Certainly none of the guerrillas reacted to it quickly, which was perhaps not surprising in the middle of a party even though the roaring soon became definite enough, suggesting a small tornado moving on a line that was going to include us. The air took on an unnerving localized turbulence with great trees lashing their top branches. I saw the leader swing around, his mouth opening for a shout that didn't come, or if it did was inaudible. The din was clearly mechanical now, a steady beat of engines, though the sky stayed an empty deep purple and no star constellations were shadowed.

I realized what it was just before I saw it. The huge helicopter blundered at us from only feet above the jungle wall, pushing down a whirlwind from rotors which flattened grass and the guerrillas, too. Men dropped into *lalang* for cover that suddenly wasn't available, fifty of them falling flat like worshippers before a sudden, terrifying revelation. The leader was down, as well, part of a ceremony of agonized respect.

A first run over was made at no more than fifty feet. It was a personnel carrier, with one of the big side doors wide back and men visible in the opening. They seemed to have guns. The machine gave an impression of being quite ready to convert itself into a low-flying bomber and probably grenades were ready for this role.

Forward movement ceased over the wreckage and a suspended cabin almost as big as Clem's shattered plane dropped down like a jerky lift. It hung shivering for seconds over still rising heat before the pilot gunned motors into a banked sweep around the field before an even slower return over us.

The guerrillas recovered from stunned shock. The leader was first on his knees, bellowing. He never even looked in our direction and the guard over us took off with the rest, towards jungle and cover.

Fifty guerrillas were running as the helicopter came lumbering back in an ungainly sideways manœuvre. The pilot gave chase, at twenty feet. Grass around the fleeing men turned into a flat carpet. Some of the Reds stumbled and fell, but got up again to run on. I saw white faces looking up at that thundering vengeance overhead but not one of our late captors raised a rifle to offer the resistance which would have brought down a hail of return fire. They just wanted away from that airstrip.

'The British navy,' I shouted. 'A long way from base. Rule Britannia.'

I looked at Clem. He had pushed himself up from his anthill and was shakily on his feet.

'We move,' he told me.

'Don't you want to be rescued?'

'Not by them. You got a car somewhere?'

He was trying to control a sway.

'It's about a mile away. And you ought to be in hospital. That thing will get you there in an hour.'

'No! Come on! Before they turn back.'

The helicopter was now going into a startling bank almost at the jungle wall and the last of the guerrillas seemed to be stumbling into safety.

'We could run into the Reds again.'

'Risk it,' Clem said, getting command of that sway.

I didn't have to stick with American intelligence. I could sit right where I was and be shortly surrounded by my own countrymen who offer such charming charity to the afflicted. On the other hand they would soon begin to ask questions, some of them not too easy to answer even if I did get my wits back.

I stood too.

'Free my hands,' I said.

'Not now. Where's the way out of this place?'

The overgrown track I had used in was beyond the burned-out plane. We started to circle the wreckage as the 'copter headed for us, and with a little spurt of speed.

'Don't look up,' Clem shouted, starting a shambling trot towards secondary growth which seemed a long way off. 'You lead.'

I got out in front. We must have made an interesting sight from above, one man with an arm in a sling, the other with his hands twisted behind his back, both taking an obstacle course around anthills while being pursued by one of man's most ingenious contraptions.

The shock of the blast wave from those rotors almost put me on my knees. What it did to Clem I couldn't see and I didn't risk a glance back. I was clinging now to a pious hope that the Navy, operating over land, would remain hesitant about using lethal weapons, for as targets we were quite perfect. I became horribly conscious of that hunk of metal suspended only feet above my head and sudden light down in a great white beam was almost demoralizing. I had the feeling that but for those mercifully towering anthills, arranged like anti-landing devices all about, the 'copter would have pulled on a little ahead to set itself down across our escape route. But the pilot remained conscious of the expensive piece of equipment he was handling. Further, he kept just a little behind us, which reduced the rotor thrust on his quarry. Probably the air was crackling with a radio request for instructions and I hoped that some duty brass back at H.Q. was sleepy and slow to react.

At any moment that machine could come low enough for some of its crew to risk a jump. And the damn manœuvrability of these things meant that an anthill could probably be used as a landing platform. When it came to getting away from armed men on the ground our chances would be greatly reduced. In my mind there was a bleat about the folly of thus running from your own side, even when your own side meant uniformed servicemen. It wasn't quite Clem's side, of course, which gave him a better reason for flight than me, but he was a long way from home and was going to have to use someone's charity to get himself back to base.

I reached cover first, not very effective cover, the new growth through the tarmac only going up to fifteen feet or so, but enough to force that 'copter into a rise. I looked back. Clem had fallen by another anthill, and the vast machine hung right over him, flooding down light into which he resolutely refused to look. He began to crawl. And as he did it a rope ladder dropped from the vibrating craft, a length of it which wobbled down into grass. Boots appeared on a swinging first rung.

Clem got up again. I saw his face if no one else did. It was the face of a man who isn't going to give up, even from staggering agony. His bad arm had fallen out of the sling and hung at his side. He ran towards me with a shoulder forward, an odd, crablike movement, with a drag on one leg. Trussed myself I could do nothing to help, and if I went out to offer a shoulder it meant the man behind the cockpit glass would have a very good look at me indeed. All this was Clem's exercise anyway. I was acting under a kind of moral duress and against my own instincts. I would have much preferred a plastic cup of lukewarm Thermos tea and young

British faces all around as against a continued blundering about in a tropic night which would only be memorable for sheer horror.

Clem reached me when the man on the ladder was still only half-way down. He was swaying on those ropes as though he hadn't received much basic training in this particular act, or perhaps he was used to having water under him when he did it. At any rate his caution was our asset, and it gave me time to see that we would be up against hunters equipped with walkie-talkies. This actually struck no terror to my heart at all, for these gadgets are totally useless in jungle tracking, even when that jungle is secondary. Certainly you can keep in touch with your mobile H.Q. up above but while you are doing that your quarry gets away.

Before I turned into deep cover I saw a second pair of boots on the ladder, but the 'copter appeared to be slightly upset by some fluke thermal, for it wobbled suddenly and the engines began to sound as though they were suffering from strangulation of the feed lines. Clem and I made fair speed, with me leading, but suddenly my head had taken all it could stand as a trail breaker. I stopped.

'Get my arms free. You ought to be able to do that with your good hand.'

'Don't yell!'

'Who the hell's going to hear with that row? Get me loose.'

It seemed to take a long time. I felt him picking away at the tape. We had lost light, both from moon and helicopter spot. In spite of that clanking din behind us I could hear Clem's breathing near my ear. The pace of this made me wonder how long he was going to keep on his feet. He sounded like an old man with asthma.

'I've got a hold,' he panted. 'Pull forward.'

Someone shouted from the edge of our cover. I moved as a kind of involuntary jump for safety and the tape peeled. Clem followed me up and completed the job. Free hands and a moderating pulse rate seemed to restore me back into normal sentimentality.

'Get your good arm round my shoulder.'

'Damn that,' he said. 'Just break trail fast. They're following.'

But I did have to help him a few times. The most spectacular was when we struck a swampy stream and stayed by it for moonlight even though I wasn't too happy about the direction indications. Clem fell in. He did it slowly and with considerable grace for an injured man, giving a little yelp of pain first, then slithering through reeds down into a slime which had been waiting there quite undisturbed for a few thousand years and had built up a considerable stench. It had also acquired a huge population of leeches and Clem lurched out from near waist deep, accepting my hand, with the little worms already feeding on his blood and with an ecstatic wriggling over its beef nourished quality.

'I've got matches. I'll strike one. Don't try to yank 'em off.'

'We can't wait.'

'Look, the 'copter is two hundred yards to the left of us. Which means the boys are right underneath. We're clear.'

He didn't believe me but was glad of the rest. I used a match to sizzle off the first of those unappealing parasites and then went on to nearly finish the box. The leeches only had a short breakfast.

'Any in your boots?' I asked.

'I don't know. Let them stay.'

But about two minutes later he eased himself down on a log and permitted me to take off his boots. We got a count of seven from behind leather. Clem's expression suggested that what was wrong with South East Asia was basically things like leeches. He also didn't like his own smell.

It took us an hour to reach the north-south highway. This was mainly due to my navigation which had to be intuitive and intuition has often let me down. But the hard metalling underfoot felt good, particularly in the stillness which had developed over the previous twenty minutes, the helicopter apparently having given up, taken on its wandering boys, and gone home. That was fine with me, the machine had served us well but any deepening of the contact was highly undesirable.

'How far is it to the car?' Clem asked.

'About half a mile.'

'Back towards the airfield?'

'Yes.'

We walked in shadow from verging trees just in case there might be anyone watching that road, though I was fairly certain that the guerrillas were in fast transit towards their safe mountains. We got to the trail leading in to the airstrip, and passed this, making for the wood where I had left my transport.

There is no rent-a-car service as yet available in the capital of Kelantan and the Fiat I was finally able to track down had first left the showrooms in 1937. It was an open tourer with a mouldering canvas hood as sun protection. It had a bulb horn fitted once as a classy accessory and now highly necessary because the brakes were erratic. There was a self starter, too, but in case this let you down the handle hung permanently under the radiator grille.

I approached this wreck with the feeling that we would probably find four flat tyres, but that wasn't the trouble, it was night damp depressing the plugs. I didn't put any strain on the shaky battery but went straight for the handle like one of those characters of 1903 when motoring was almost as exciting as a blood sport. Usually, when turning a handle you can feel the point of an engine's bid to come to life but the old car was flaccid and defeated.

'Is there a morning bus?' Clem asked from his seat beside the driver's where he had been holding out the choke with his good hand.

'I don't think so. Have you any money? The Reds left my matches, but took everything else. I saw them searching you.'

'I haven't my wallet either. What about those Reds? Where do you think they are?'

'A long way from here by now. They're not our problem any more.'

'Have you got a gun in the car?'

'No. You took my armament.'

I yanked again and something happened under the hood, a faint burp. I tickled the carburettor and then went forward for another turn over. There were two sharp cracks like cannon fire, followed by a roar.

'Keep that choke out!' I yelled.

The engine went on firing and even allowed itself to be revved back. I tried first gear and we jerked into movement, this almost vigorous, as though the Fiat had suddenly decided to approve of an early morning rise. We pulled up a gradient and out on to the road. I eased her up to eighteen m.p.h. and waited for vibration, but this didn't come. The needle started to climb towards the speed records of the car's youth, reaching twenty-three, then twenty-six, finally twenty-eight, still without the hint of a knock from her big end.

I took time off for a quick glance at Clem, risky with that loose steering. He had his eyes shut and was slumped down on sagging seat springs.

'You all right?'

'If you mean am I still alive, yes.'

The potential male nurse in me surfaced again, a character rich in sympathy of an easy sort for physical suffering.

'The pain must have been pretty hellish.'

'Oh, shut up,' Clem said.

So I just drove. There was now, beyond tiredness, a hint of exhilaration, elation at an escape from a situation with the odds at least a hundred to one against. I am always grateful when I'm allowed a miracle, particularly when one of these lets me have a little longer on this planet. My luck, on the whole, had been indifferent, but I've had more than any man's reasonable ration of miracles and they make luck superfluous, to say nothing of superficial. I have a secret conviction that if I ever start winning at cards or the races it will be a sign that the miracle issue is over. So I never gamble. I don't want to know for certain.

'There was absolutely no reason,' I said, 'for a Navy helicopter to be five hundred miles from base tonight and over the Kelantan jungle.'

'What?' Clem asked from the depths of a returned consciousness of three bullet holes.

'They don't patrol over Malaysia these days.'

'I could do without your speculations just now,' he said. 'Is this wobbling about the car or your driving?'

'The car.'

'Then give it all your attention.'

The Fiat's engine had never been quiet even when it was factory new and now, after a thirty-five year run-in, the thing bellowed, taking us through a pre-dawn tropic morning with all the discretion of a three trailer articulated truck. We heard nothing beyond ourselves and couldn't be expected to. The first indication that we were no longer alone was a sudden, violent flapping from the canvas hood, then the sharp noise of this ripping.

'What the hell is that?' Clem shouted.

I knew. The rotor down-thrust again. The Navy hadn't gone home.

We were on a gently winding road, a downstretch. The Kelantan river had joined us and was glinting through a thin row of trees. On the right was rubber, but set well back from the highway, which gave the 'copter adequate room for manœuvre just over our heads. I couldn't see how near over our heads, but from the sound added to our own it was pretty near.

The sudden artificial hurricane upset the Fiat which began to respond in a highly erratic manner to the wild sweeps I was giving the wheel.

The hood loosened from its windscreen fastenings and dropped on us, a stinking, ancient shroud. I had to take one hand from steering to clear my face. This might have been what the car was waiting for. We went straight at a bank. I fought that with a triple wheel revolution and we moved left towards the Kelantan river. The hood rose behind us like a sail and then detached itself completely as a piece of standard equipment, leaving Clem and me in a very open tourer indeed.

'Don't look up!' he yelled.

It was a message I'd had before. And anyway, I couldn't look up. No pilot ever fought a plane caught in turbulence harder than I was fighting that decrepit vehicle. From overhead we must have looked like a vintage movie comedy, one of those shots of an old car jerking back and forth over a road, filled with arm-waving passengers, and with a projector speed accelerated to stimulate laughter.

The helicopter stopped tailing to move right over its quarry, the snout of the thing about level with our boiling radiator and blocking out a good part of my moonlight ration. The full down-thrust of rotors let me share the experience of a new boy in a centrifuge seat being subjected to Mach One or whatever it is that starts to pull your face out of shape and loosen your teeth. The Fiat under my hands now had the feel of a large plastic duck being propelled through bath water at well below buoyancy level, liable at any moment to pop free and shoot out of the tub on to tiling. The cyclone encircling began to make us go a great deal faster than our engine revs or the gradient would have permitted and it was frightening to see the speedometer needle reaching forty-two miles an hour. It was like getting towards the end of a runway in an overloaded plane which isn't going to become airborne and is just at the point of going out of control. The seconds then became stretched in a horrible, suspended elasticity when a man's cerebration for once races ahead of time and it doesn't do him a damn' bit of good. The only possible hope lay half a mile ahead where jungle trees again bent lovingly over the road, coming very near to a natural arch which would certainly force the beast above to rise again.

There was no doubt whatever that we had been identified as amongst those present at the airfield. The others had got away, leaving only two candidates for interrogation and some very important people wanted us brought in for just that. I would have been moderately willing to oblige, but had got myself totally involved in keeping a piece of American security intact, this against all my sharp instincts of self-preservation and likely to be highly prejudicial to my personal interests. There was, of course, the fact that I was no longer technically a British subject, but I had a feeling that the battered old lion—still with a lair of sorts down there in the Singapore naval base—might be capable of reaching out a bandaged paw to give me a nasty cuff in the area of my vital business affairs. And if this happened I could scarcely expect much help from Washington. Or from Kuala Lumpur, either, for that matter. I could even find myself deprived of a new citizenship with no chance at all to recover the old, left one of those sad, stateless characters who try to keep a foothold on this planet with nothing to assist them beyond a U.N.O. ticket, which is a poor credit card.

The din had mounted above tolerance level. Any engine failure up aloft would see us a quickly squashed beetle. It was my feeling that if we had been able to hold anything like a steady course in the Fiat that pilot would have come lower than fifteen feet in an intimidation bid, but with our heaving about he couldn't risk it. Another possibility for him was to move his craft slightly to one side which would allow a grenade to be dropped into the car, an explosive finale, but one eliminating any possibility of bringing us back alive.

In fact the pilot's indecision lasted to the point where he had to allow our escape into the tunnel under trees, zooming up himself to get clear of them. The final kick back from his rotors was very nearly a last driving straw, and I couldn't quite believe it when we were running almost easily under shelter, our slalom progress ended. The racket ended, too. I said:

'The trouble with these little wars is that you never know really who the enemy is.'

Clem didn't say anything. I suspected he had his eyes shut again.

The Fiat's screeching brakes brought us back to some kind of motoring norm, though I now had to peer ahead into a gloom only vaguely penetrated by glow-worm headlights. I tried to remember what lay beyond this stretch of jungle, but couldn't. The 'copter's clanking was now inaudible beyond our own engine noise, but I could picture the thing hovering out there above the next open stretch of road like a horsefly waiting for a swimmer's head to surface. There was no doubt about it, they were taking their assignment to bring us in very seriously indeed.

I risked not being able to start again, switching off the ignition to coast down the gradient, though our lights didn't like no feed to the battery and almost packed in. The clatter from rotors penetrated again, but distantly. We moved towards that sound at a pace largely conrolled by a held handbrake and what I was half expecting happened, the roaring noise zoomed up, there was a coughing of exhaust, then a total deep silence.

'They've landed,' I said unnecessarily, yanking the car to a stop.

'What now then?' Clem asked, handing over all strategic planning to me. 'If you're counting on my being able to walk, don't.'

'They're laying a quick ambush for us down there. We don't run into it.'

'You mean to go back up this hill?'

'After a little. Give them time to get well clear of their machine so they can't just take off at speed.'

'Where do we get to . . . back up this hill?'

'Kuala Krai. Where there's a phone box.'

'How about cash for a call?'

'I'll reverse charges.'

'Who to?'

'A friend of mine at the Linguin mines. He's the manager.

He has a Piper to get him to the nearest bar quickly. He'll fly over the mountains and pick us up.'

'Just like that, eh? No questions asked. Why should he?'

'For the money I'll offer.'

'What do you do with the car when we get to this town?'

'Leave it.'

'The owner will make a noise about that. I'll bet this is a family heirloom.'

'I'll fix all that through the head boy at the Kota Bharu rest-house. He knows me.'

'You really own this country, don't you?'

He brooded about that, then said:

'What's going to be your personal alibi for this particular tropic night?'

'I was visiting a girl-friend.'

'I see. It's well known that you keep one in every state of the Federation? For occasional use?'

I had no comment.

'None of this is going to work,' Clem said. 'It's a feeling I've got. And there's something else. Pretty soon, if I don't want to have this arm chopped off, it's got to be seen to. And in a hospital. It wouldn't surprise me to be put in bed after surgery with a transfusion bottle hanging over my head.'

'Your arm will be seen to, but not in hospital.'

'Where?'

'In my house in Kuala Lumpur.'

'You've got another friend who's a horse doctor spare time?'

'I've got a friend who is the best surgeon in town.'

'Operates any place and no questions asked about the patient? Maybe you know he's sleeping with his pretty receptionist and his wife would shoot him if she found out?'

'You'll get the full works and no publicity,' I promised.

'It's against medical ethics.'

'Ethics can be stretched.'

'I hope so. It's quite important for me to get out of this country without ever having been in it, if you know what I mean?'

'I gathered that was the position.'

I switched out the car lights. We sat in a total, hot darkness. After a moment Clem said softly:

'It's quiet down there at the foot of the hill. But they're probably boiling up tea water on a primus. You people always stop your wars for the brew up that cheers.'

He was beginning to sound more like himself. After a moment he whispered.

'This masterly inactivity is getting on my nerves. Just what exactly are we waiting for?'

'Boots on the road.'

'And what's your plan when you hear them?'

'We leave. I don't think that helicopter will take off again without its full complement on board. It wouldn't want to have armed men wandering around without transport in a country that is now sovereign and sensitive about this. Even if they have walkie-talkies the boys will be called back to the mother ship. Which ought to give us at least half an hour of clear road.'

'In which to do what?'

'Get back to that rubber estate we passed and hide somewhere in the middle of it. While the 'copter patrols the road looking for us and uses up its juice. It'll have to go back to base long before dawn. Then we drive to Krai.'

'Terribly neat, Paul. But it all hangs on one thing. That this engine is going to start when you want it to. You're confident of that?'

'No.'

'So it doesn't start, what then?'

'I run for it. You get caught.'

Clem went silent. I was very conscious of the risk of trying to lure those men well up this road, but I had to buy time somehow. It also occurred to me that they mightn't just be airborne sailors, but active personnel from the late Sarawak-Borneo frontier fighting who knew all about night patrols on which boot clinking wasn't permitted. A really trained man could come right up to us and stick a cold gun muzzle against my cheek before I heard him. But fortunately someone boobed, a tactical accident of the kind which don't get in official despatches, a torch light came on a hundred yards down from us, a patch of brightness out into the roadway from just beyond a bend. A voice yapped and the light went out.

'Get working on that handle,' Clem said. 'And why the hell didn't you turn this thing?'

'Doing it would have made noise.'

I switched on, using the self starter floor button, and at once got a willing grumble. I put the Fiat in reverse and, rather as I had been expecting, she went better in this gear than in the two first forward speeds, probably because the ratios were less worn. The driving was slightly chancy, reversing with no rear spot, but my eyes had got a partial feel for the dark and we worked up a fair speed.

'This makes me feel really at home,' Clem said. 'Running from the enemy. But I prefer doing it in a jeep the right way round.'

CHAPTER FOUR

MICKEY DAVENPORT was a period character, an Englishman who
had lived abroad all his adult life and hadn't got word that the
right school background is now a positive social and economic
liability. No one had told him that these days, if you're wise,
you never hint at the terrible handicap of Eton or Harrow in
your past, claiming instead a heritage studded with horny handed
proletariats. Mickey, in a curious isolation from the realities of
his time, still brooded over the fact that his parents had sensibly
saved their money and sent him to Clapham Secondary. And to
surmount a totally imaginary disadvantage he assumed a strained
bid at the accent of long-dead empire builders, throwing an
'old boy' into nearly every sentence. His talk was weirdly
reminiscent of those cricket-playing English Hollywood actors
whose survivors are still hard at very highly paid work creating
an eighteen-ninety image of the British for mid-Western
Americans.

Dawn would have seemed a cruel time to get Mickey out of
bed if he hadn't once told me that he always made a point of
seeing the first shift down his mine. Here he had got his tin
mining traditions a bit mixed with those established for rubber
planters, but no one could say he wasn't keen, and it was the
keen chaps who rose to be managers, as he had proven.

The phone bell only rang three times and then there was
the operator's voice asking him if he would accept the charges.

'Eh? What's that? Where from?'

'Kuala Krai, the call,' sang the Malay girl, trying out her
English, a remarkable effort for that hour.

'Oh, well,' Mickey said. 'I suppose so.'

'I'm glad you agreed. Paul Harris here.'

'Paul, old boy!'

'Eating breakfast?'

'Oh, no, I don't have that until after muster. Just a spot of
tea now. And the old *papaya*. Up actually.'

'I thought you would be. I'm in a jam, Mickey.'

'Really? Good lord!'

'I've been sweating here in this box in case last night was
one of your K.L. evenings and you hadn't come home.'

'Oh, heavens now, I never go to the big city on a Wednesday.
Have to ration me gay life. Especially with the old girl off in
Majorca, what?'

He called it My-yor-ka, just like the natives.

'What I need,' I said, 'is your airplane. Now.'

'Oh? You mean up in Krai?'

'Could you, Mickey? Just come for us?'

'Us?'

'Me and a friend.'

'Some frightful Harris mystery, is this?'

'Well . . . sort of. Miss that first muster for my sake.'

There was silence at the other end. It was time to talk money.

'Of course I mean this as a hire. Commercial rates, I must insist on that.'

'Oh, my dear chap, don't be ridiculous.' His tone was warm. 'A hire, Mickey, nothing else.'

'Well . . . we'll talk about that later. And of course I'll come. Whereabouts in Krai?'

'We're not in the town. Betong rubber estate just north, about a mile and a half. There's a laterite road with plenty of clearance for the Piper. I could mark it if you like?'

'Don't bother, will find.'

'The road leads from the entrance to the estate, you can't really miss it.'

'Be with you in about an hour and a half, maybe.'

'I'm sorry to bring you over the mountains, but the mist ought to be clearing soon.'

'Absolutely. Not to worry, old boy. Cheerio.'

I blessed Mickey, then looked out of the box for a strolling policeman. There wasn't one. I dialled for the operator again and told her I wanted another collect number. She was quite cheerful about it.

This time the bell went for much longer. The voice which finally answered was sleepy and irritated. It was also rather mean about being asked to pay for the call.

'Betty?'

'Oh, it's you? Just a minute. I'll take this downstairs. Tom needs his beauty sleep.'

There was quite a long pause.

'Well, Paul?'

'I'm going to ask you to do something you ought to refuse.'

'Like going to bed with you, dear?'

'More so. Ethics.'

'I see. I'm not at home.'

'I need your help.'

'Of course you do. That doesn't mean you'll get it.'

'A friend of mine has been pretty badly knocked up.'

'That is not an adequate clinical description. Do you mean bullets?'

'Yes.'

'How did I guess? Ought you to be chatting about this?'

'No. But I've got to risk it. Betty, I know I shouldn't ask you to do this, but I have to.'

'And you do it with quiet confidence, knowing that I'll take any risks in the name of a beautiful relationship.'

'That's about it.'

'No, it's not! Bring your friend to the hospital. He'll have my personal attention.'

'I can't do that.'

'Then go to hell. I was called out last night. For surgery. I got to bed at three.'

'I'm sorry.'

'There's no need to go on saying that. You're not at all. You want something and you think the Harris charm is going to work over wire. Well, it doesn't. Not at this hour.'

'Tom . . . could be listening to this.'

'So he could. And so could your operator. I suppose you want me to turn a bedroom in your house into an aseptic theatre in twenty-five minutes?'

'You'd have three hours. And Ohashi would see to everything. You have his number.'

'No! I mean, I have his number but I'm not going to use it.'

There was a pause, then Betty said:

'Where are you?'

'Up north. Quite far.'

'You told me you were going to Singapore.'

'A change of plans.'

'A flat lie, you mean. How can you get down here in three hours?'

'By plane. That's arranged. The wounds are hæmorrhaging again. There is no question of a hospital.'

'Damn you! Do you know what you're asking for?'

'Private medical attention.'

'No! I'm to go out on a case of which there will be no record at all. I can't do it, Paul. I'm not even in general practice. You know perfectly well I have no private work. Bring your patient to the hospital and I'll keep things as discreet as I can. Use a false name if you want. That's not my worry.'

'It would worry the police. In a matter of bullet wounds.'

'So would a dead patient I'd treated privately and kept quiet about!'

'He's not going to die.'

'Then your worries are reduced.'

'He could still lose the use of an arm.'

'I'm not doing this!'

'Betty, it's not so long since I answered a call for help from you.'

'What? Why, damn you! You draw a parallel with that? You're a . . .'

There was a click as the line went dead.

I pushed open the door of the box. The street looked oddly dusty for Malaysia which gets frequent rain wash downs. The two-storey shops were all still shuttered, except for an eating place with a cart outside it on which were tubs of nightsoil for the paddies. The big harnessed ox was quietly chewing its cud while the owner breakfasted beyond strips of shelter curtain. You could smell the cart. The air was dead still and the morning mist hung low. I had cover walking away, total protection from helicopters.

Kuala Krai didn't have the feel of a place which had been put on a police alert for two escapees in a Fiat. The Navy hunt for us had been handicapped by a lack of liaison with the official forces for the maintenance of law and order in Malaysia and probably had been called off because of this. In these days of delicate new international balances quite a thing could be made of a buzzing on the public highway by a foreign aircraft. It was the kind of incident which could easily lead to an exchange of notes between Kuala Lumpur and London, and almost certainly someone down in that British base had thought of this and got cold feet, sending out the come home signal.

Beyond the town mist lay in fat tentacles across the road. I walked on the verge for silence, thinking about that cry for help from Betty which had reached me the night before I left on my excursion to Thailand. She was quite right. My response then hadn't earned me anything like the return service I was asking.

Clem had moved to the back seat of the vintage model, where the springs had stood up better to long service. He was curled up, with his eyes shut, his bad arm tucked in against his stomach. The bandages were still caked with jungle slime, which had dried off earlier, but was wet again from blood.

He didn't speak at once and when he did it was without looking at me.

'Well?'

'Everything's fixed up. A plane coming. No sign of an alarm out for us. We just have to wait. I've remembered I put some chocolate in that pouch. Like some for breakfast?'

'No. And don't ask me how I'm feeling.'

'I didn't tell our pilot to bring morphia. Thought it might put him off coming.'

'That's all right. A portion of pain is man's lot '

'There'll be a first-aid box in the plane. But if we try to use it that'll mean questions for which I haven't any answers.'

'Stop worrying. Just get me to that private doctor. You've laid that on, too?'

'Yes.'

'Once again let me congratulate you on your organization in this country. I wish mine were as good.'

I ignored that.

'Mickey shouldn't see your arm. I've got a windcheater we'll fit you into somehow.'

'I'm in your hands,' he said, without gratitude.

I sat down on the wide running board which was a feature of the Fiat, putting my chin in my fists. A few rows over from us a Tamil was making the day's first incisions in tree trunks and lowering the drip cups to catch the latex. If he was interested in an old car parked with two men waiting he had long ago learned to mind his own business. The Tamils have polished up the art of strict neutrality in a country where they are a racial minority not much liked by either the Chinese or the Malays. The tapper might be excited about the plane when it came in, but telephones weren't part of his world at all and he would never think of running to one.

I thought about Betty going back upstairs and into a cool box just large enough to hold twin beds. Tom and she lived in a sprawling wooden house of the type it isn't practical to air-condition, the best you can do is establish refrigerated areas. I wondered why they bothered even with that box. The temperature in their marriage was already cool enough not to require any artificial sixty-five degrees. She would be too angry at me to sleep again. Our relation, such as it was, continually provoked positive reactions of this kind, which was probably the main reason why she kept on seeing me. If what we had was love then there's not much cosiness in that state.

The sound which reached me was like a sewing machine motor under whining strain from a loose driving belt. I identified it and stood up.

As the 'copter came low over the screening roof of rubber trees Clem said:

'They haven't even taken time off for breakfast.'

The road out beyond us which was wide enough for Mickey's Piper was just perfect for a 'copter, and once they were down on it we had no cover at all. The area under these cultivated raw producers is kept neat and tidy, with visibility stretching for long distances down geometrically planted rows. And if we tried to drive out after their landing I suspected they might now be irritated enough to use bullets, at least at our tyres.

'What do we do, friend?' Clem asked.

'Hold our breaths.'

The green above was being flayed. I decided right then that I hated helicopters, you can do too much with them.

The Tamil saved us. Not a lot happened in his patterns and that clattering just above the crop he worked was too much, he had to see. He ran over thick leaves, stumbling once, then almost falling out into the road just at the moment a wheel of the under-carriage came dropping into our line of vision.

The man might have been killed. He was certainly caught by that down-thrust and put flat on his face against laterite. This enraged him. He got to his knees, a very black face lifted, one arm gesturing, indicating fury at this interference with quiet routine.

All books of service rules have passages in small print about how to treat the natives of a country you are patrolling, and those wheels suddenly went up again. The Tamil got on his feet. He seemed remarkably unafraid for someone of a race which is on the whole timid. And that presence beneath them of a man clearly interrupted on his lawful pursuits changed the pilot's mind about a ground check of this area. The choppers con-tinued their lift and the noise diminished.

'Search resumed at dawn,' Clem said. 'Mist and all. Who says the British Navy goes home at the first excuse these days? This calls for an overall reassessment.'

'Have you thought how interested they are going to be in a private plane landing here in a matter of minutes?'

'I told you hours ago this wasn't going to work.'

But I thought it still might. The helicopter couldn't have a forward speed of more than a hundred knots, which meant that if the Piper was able to land and take off again without inter-ference we could get away in it from air pursuit. At the same time it would be easy enough for the 'copter to pick up the light plane's markings and all kinds of messages to all kinds of people could result from that, which might mean that we were met at Kuala Lumpur airfield. If I had been on my own it would have been simple enough, I'd have asked Mickey to put me down somewhere over the mountains, from which point Ohashi could have come to fetch me in the Mercedes, but travel arrangements involving delay to establish alibis weren't the answer for Clem at the moment. I didn't like the way in which, between efforts to talk, he kept closing his eyes, as though without light pain was more endurable.

I climbed into the driver's seat and switched on the engine.

'We're going someplace?'

'Back into cover. There's scrub over at the edge of the rubber. I can nudge the car in and hide it.'

'What's the good of that when our Tamil friend has only to gossip over his lunch break?'

'I'll deal with the Tamil,' I said.

'He knows too much to be allowed to live?'

Clem's cracks were beginning to earn the silences they deserved. It was bumpy driving and almost beyond the Fiat's capabilities, but we made it, finding a clump of bamboo young enough to bow and let us in. Whether anyone would get that car out again under its own power was another matter.

'That was a horrible ride,' Clem said.

I left him, hidden with the car, and walked towards the Tamil who was back now at his rubber tapping but saw me coming. Long before I was really near I noticed the whites of his eyes. He was a senior man, entrusted with cutting the trees, a specialized job, and one he did on his own. Any excess of human activity in his area made him jumpy.

My Malay greeting didn't seem to be reassuring either. He was old enough to remember the troubles in the country and to associate the European with these. Already he was quite certain that a machine skimming his trees had something to do with two people sitting in a car. He wiped the palms of his hands on the lower part of a white shirt and faced me, a finely featured little man, almost coal black, with a feminine delicacy in slim wrists, thin arms, and enormous, sensuous eyes that would be a good feature for his daughters to inherit.

The southern Indians are a much nicer people than they are given credit for being either in their own country or abroad. They have been used for centuries to domination by tougher specimens than themselves against whom their main resistance has nearly always been a pliant gentleness as though, like well-rooted reeds, they had learned to bend and let the rough winds blow over. They are still, however, capable of sudden, explosive surges of anger which have proved the sharpest embarrassment at times to their bosses in New Delhi or in plantation bungalows. The ones in Malaya were brought in as indentured workers long enough ago to have allowed them two and even three of their shortish generations in the country, after which they are still in a sense aliens and highly suspicious of any attempts to intrude on their tightly coherent immunity. They remember that the Japanese chopped off a good many of their heads and suspect that the Chinese and Malays might also do the same if the right opportunity arose. The white man has left their heads alone but has a long record of exploiting their labour for big company dividends. He, also, is looked at without love.

'I'm in trouble,' I said, again in Malay.

That was *my* problem. A direct appeal brought no warmth into liquid eyes. His lips moved, but not for words.

'I need your help and I'm willing to pay for it.'

The very slight altering of his expression said that money is always useful.

'I can't give you cash. But I'll send it. Do you have an address I can use? I'll send a postal order for two hundred dollars. All you have to do is say that you saw no one in this rubber. A plane is going to land soon, and you can tell them about that. But not that you saw us getting on to it. Understand?'

He spoke then.

'They wouldn't believe me.'

'Then say you were in another part of the wood and saw nothing.'

'My work is here to-day, *Tuan*.'

'You went off to have a look at the work you had done yesterday. You just heard the plane. Two hundred dollars for that. And you can make it the truth by going away.'

'For this you pay me?'

'Yes. Have you a pencil? Write your name and address on a piece of paper.'

'The *Tuan* will not pay after,' he said with simple cynicism.

'I can only tell you that I will. I do not lie.'

He smiled. It was a comment on his experience of the West. But in the end he produced a notebook in which were jottings, probably notes on his trees, and with decided reluctance at the extravagance, tore a sheet from the back. He put down his name and address carefully, wetting the tip of the pencil with his tongue before writing. I put the paper in a trouser pocket and when he saw me doing this he was frightened of having committed himself, of allowing greed to triumph over prudence. He wanted then to run away. He turned back to his trees as to a norm for comfort, putting out a hand to bark he had himself scarred with a sharp knife. My need for his help was something alien, intrusive.

The Tamil was put to the test almost at once. I was just back at the bamboo screening when there was a noise from the main road, the grinding of gears as a car turned off on to that wide, laterite estate track. Clem was sitting up straight on the back seat.

'Planter's jeep?' he asked.

'No, police.'

'Sure?'

'Inspired guess.'

'Hope you've dealt with our friend the woodcarver?'

I hoped so, too. From behind bamboo we saw one of those long, low cars which are official status symbols in emergent nations. Out of it got three men in white uniforms. Almost at once they spotted the Tamil and there was a shout of the kind which means business. The Tamil went at a trot. He stood with a drainage ditch between him and the police while I just waited for an arm to lift and point straight at us. I thought about tyre tracks, there were plenty of them, a churning up of leaf mould which the slightest excursion under rubber would have revealed. But the morning was getting warmer, and the car certainly had an air-conditioner. The police got back into it, not thinking much of Tamils, reversing up the road with gearbox whining.

The tapper stood watching them go, then turned slowly and stared in our direction. I considered adding a bonus of fifty dollars, but decided against it. There was no need to start an inflation in the price of good deeds.

Mickey was late, for which I was thankful. The chopper was now completely inaudible, probably bumbling over some other estate looking for a dangerous Red called Harris known to be on the run with an American security man who, though wounded, was going to bring his man back to base in his own way and in his own time. Now that I had the minutes in which to assess things I realized that this was a pretty black Thursday morning for me, in fact just about a rock bottom morning in a career which had known a fair number of totally joyless days. I leaned back against that old car, longing for a cigarette I hadn't got. I don't know what Clem was longing for, probably sedation and a bed with white sheets.

'I'll take that chocolate now,' he said some time later.

I turned.

'Feeling better?'

'No. But my blood sugar is low.'

He ate slowly. Watching him didn't make me hungry. He had good teeth for his years and crunched without any nervousness about fillings, looking into the middle distance as he did this. I marvelled again how little time had battered Clem's face. It wasn't just the youthfulness which still shone through pain and mud splashes, but youth's total self absorption as well, which gives massive insulation against any outside penetration into a sealed core of private thought processes. He was a man who would, in the end, be too much for any woman, no matter what enthusiasm she brought to the task of training him to heel, and I remembered that his wife had left him. I wondered if tears had come into those Prussian blue eyes that day.

'I know you hate Europe,' I said. 'But what's your ancestry in it?'

He swallowed.

'I don't hate Europe, just limeys. My father was one. Everything good came out of England, according to him. And everything bad from the rest of the world. He was a college professor in Omaha. Which is a strange place for an Anglophile. It made for a curious home life. And turned me into a hundred per cent flag waving stars and stripes boy, which lasted until I went into journalism. Then I lost my wild patriotism probing American motivations.'

'Your mother was English, too?'

'Oh, God, no. She was a Pollack married in a moment of aberration by the professor. How do you like my neurotic background?'

'Not much.'

'I didn't either,' Clem said. 'But I'm right where I should be in this service. It takes a real nut case to get past the psychiatric screening we're subjected to.'

We heard a plane engine. Carefully I fitted Clem into the windcheater. In this he looked like a wrapped up but still not disguised casualty of the wars. Pain had again bleached his tan.

'How much did you pay that Indian to go away?' he asked.

I told him.

'Private enterprise certainly can hand it out.'

'Saving you is becoming more than a legitimate business expense,' I said.

He looked at me.

'Send the invoices to Washington. You'll get a printed letter of thanks back from the head of C.I.A. But no money.'

He was just slightly wobbly on his feet.

'Lean on my shoulder?'

'No.'

We plodded out into rubber and along under it, me watchful, Clem passive. The sound of the plane engine grew louder. The laterite road I had chosen wasn't in itself very wide, but it was a dead straight along the edge of a good half mile of rubber and with enough clearance beyond two ditches for the Piper's wing span. Any error of judgement on the pilot's part in landing would see him with a total wreck on his hands and I didn't know a great deal about Mickey's flying experience beyond the fact that he always seemed able to get home safely after a big night at the club, back up into his mountains in time for that first muster. And people who travel around in planes after a high alcohol intake either pick up some sharp subconscious skills or die early.

We stood just in the shade watching him come in. He flirted with the tops of rubber trees, throttled back, came down at about seventy to a few feet above the road, chose a new area on it, went up, then down again, skimming along packed red clay without even a bounce, the wings wobbling a shade but every thing splendidly under control. The final braking stopped the plane a hundred yards up from us and we were making slow progress towards it when Mickey jumped down to come running back with all the eagerness of a puppy just let out for its morning walk.

'Hallo, chaps. Sorry I'm a bit late.'

We weren't. He stopped then, gazing at us, and I got the impression that the way we looked gave him something of a shock.

'Engine was a bit gummy,' he said, with a few degrees less brightness.

He had an almost round face under remnants of what had once been sleek blond hair. His eyes were blue, but pale, washed with grey from the English skies of his youth. The tropics and years of gin had mottled a once delicate skin which had always gone pink on exposure, never brown.

'What do you mean . . . gummy?' I asked.

'Plug I should think. Have it seen to in K.L. I say, you two look as though you'd been having it rough.'

'We have.'

He stared in at the dark rubber aisles, suddenly uneasy about having taken on this hire.

'There's no one with a gun in there,' I said. 'Our troubles are over now you've arrived. Just get us home and accept our grateful thanks.'

He hadn't made the trip to earn thanks and this showed on his face.

'Together with the commercial price per flying hour,' I added.

The Piper had been bought second hand from a Singapore *towkay* who had thought it would be a good way to avoid the professional kidnappers lined up along the route to his summer palace, but he had got cold feet on this form of transport after being caught in a violent heat thermal over Johore Bahru, returning to armoured Cadillacs. The plane had been a bargain once, but had flown a great many air miles since, and you could see quite clearly a number of places on the bodywork which Mickey had touched up from a can of quick-drying enamel.

While Clem and I climbed thankfully up to the cabin our pilot fussed around outside like a used-car owner who has decided to make the old job do for another season. We heard him kicking the tyres.

Clem's breathing began to get noisy again, and just at the sill of the door he sagged. I caught him round the waist and swung him inside, past the front seats to the back where he would be less conspicuous. I got him down and saw that his eyes were shut. Fastening a seat belt took some doing and in the end Clem was more or less propped upright by it, not looking at all a happy traveller.

Mickey still hadn't joined us and I peered down to see him

worried, as though he had finally confirmed a hairline crack in wing metal.

'Let's get going,' I said loudly.

He swung himself up slowly, and as he was doing it I glanced down the road that was our take-off runway. Turning on to laterite from the highway was a car I had already seen that morning, the one containing men in uniform.

Any discussion of the situation, to say nothing of explanations, would have taken time we hadn't got. I dropped into the pilot's seat.

As the prop began to revolve I caught sight of Mickey's face in the doorway, astonishment, then outrage. I gunned the motor and what he said was lost.

'Shut that door!'

I got the brakes off and had us moving before he had quite done this. He seemed to be struggling with a lock in a kind of lunatic frenzy before turning on me. I counted on sheer stark terror as my ally to keep him inactive and got it.

'No!' he bellowed. 'No!'

The car, as I'd hoped it would, stopped. Then it began to reverse, rocking from side to side on the estate road in an escape bid. Jolting vibration eased as I got one Piper wheel off laterite, then stopped altogether. We were airborne. Mickey screamed. I saw that he was worried about what was happening to the wings. So was I.

We cleared the car roof by a foot or two and the jungle beyond the highway by some inches.

'For God's sake don't hold this angle!' Mickey howled. 'You'll stall her!'

So I levelled out a bit and the engine note altered. I was sweating. I got a glimpse of Mickey's face. It was awash, a kind of livid green underneath wet. The altimeter said two hundred feet. That seemed to me quite an achievement.

'You take her,' I said.

'Not now! Get some height!'

So I got some height, trying to remember everything I had been taught at the Singapore flying club before I became a drop-out. And that was some years ago.

At about a thousand, and with the engine only knocking slightly from strain put on a faulty plug, Mickey said in the voice of a broken man:

'Level off.'

So I levelled off, rather neatly. Mickey said:

'Never in all my life have I had a couple of minutes as horrible as those.'

'You've led a quiet life for the Far East, old boy.'

He produced a handkerchief. It was clear he hadn't yet got back enough strength to fly his own plane, much as he wanted to.

'Who were they? The car?'

'Police.'

'What?'

'I don't think they were able to take down our markings. You'll be all right. Did you tell anyone you were coming up here?'

'No.'

'Well, it's a long way off your beat. If you put us down somewhere and fly back to the mine you'll be all right. I think we'll give Kuala Lumpur airfield a miss, though.'

He didn't comment on that, just signalled me with one hand to vacate the seat of power, and reached over for the controls as he slithered heavily across my body. I could smell his fear. For a long time we seemed to be trundling straight at a mountain on a flight course of one thousand feet. Then he banked and we ascended spirally, the menacing rough country slowly spinning away beneath. The airspeed indicator said ninety knots. I glanced back to see Clem still with his eyes shut, apparently spared all excitements.

'Do you have a flying licence?' Mickey asked, his voice grim.

'Not now.'

This was stretching the truth slightly since my flying credits consist of one twenty-five minute solo up over a flat field. And when I landed that time my instructor, who had been wearing his crash helmet on the ground just in case I missed the marked places and swung over to take him in even where he stood sheltered by a shed door, came over and said very quietly: 'I think maybe you ought to stick to boats and fast cars, Mr. Harris.' I have always listened to authoritative advice, though my experiences at the controls still enable me to be critical of the way a captain of a Boeing 727 brings in his ship to the tarmac. There are good, indifferent and bad landings, and as an expert on the last I recognize these when I feel them.

It was nice to just sit in that plane with our troubles behind us and the pilot alongside being extra careful. We were high enough to avoid serious bumps and the flight was suddenly tranquil, if a shade on the slow side, still around ninety. Over the main spine of Malaysia to the starboard there was a bank of what looked like thunderclouds, these spiked by peaks and held apparently motionless. We were in bright sunlight and I glanced down at the jungle below, at once seeing a shadow travelling over it which was a little too far ahead to be ours.

The 'copter was doing more than our ninety knots and, while I watched, it decided to come up. The way they did that was unnerving, a straight ascent at speed.

'Mickey, what's your ceiling?'

'About twenty thousand. Why?'

'Get to it.'

'I will not.'

'We're being followed. Look down.'

He did.

'It's just the Army,' he said.

'Navy. And get up. As steep a climb as you can.'

'Paul, what the hell is this?'

'If he picks up your markings, you're in trouble. With us.'

'What kind of trouble?'

'Quite big.'

'I'm not risking any steep climbs with that plug.' Then he added bitterly. 'Thanks a lot for involving me in all this. Thanks a lot.'

We began to climb, the angle not impressive. That ascent below us, coupled with forward progress at the same time, was much more so.

'What's the Navy got against Harris and Company?' Mickey shouted.

'At the moment more than I like. Can't you risk a bit of speed?'

'I don't want to have to walk out of primary jungle. If we survived the crash.'

'Make for cloud cover over the main range.'

'That cloud's rough.'

He was thinking about hairline cracks, and all the holes he had filled up with plastic metal.

'If we head towards the high peaks they won't try to come up with us. And you could fly over that cloud.'

'Not this morning I couldn't. I'll take you to Kuala Lumpur. And I've never had a load I'd be happier to dump.'

He wasn't a man for the little emergencies. I looked at Clem. His eyes were open now. What he was thinking was not available for public issue. What I thought was that a little further delay in getting Clem medical attention was now unavoidable. At K.L. we might easily be arrested on touchdown. If you irritate the police in one place they send out quick messages to colleagues in the place they think you're making for. Our flight south had been observed.

'Change of plan,' I said. 'We'll go over the main range to Kampar. You can land on the edge of the club course. I've seen it done. Name your price, Mickey, I'll pay.'

'That's right, rub my nose in how you can buy anything. Well, you can't buy me another life.'

'Seven hundred and fifty dollars to Kampar?'

He said something I didn't hear. I guessed that he was thinking about that house in Majorca he and his wife were building against an early and permanent escape from the Far East. The place was costing much more than he had expected because he was being forced to put in an artesian well. With all the people from northern Europe squeezing on to those Mediterranean islands it won't be long before the limited water on them is more expensive than whisky in Scotland. You go to the sun to have a swimming pool and then can't afford to put anything in it. Escapism is becoming a highly complex proposition these days. California has got 'no vacancy' signs all over it like a rash and the French won't allow anyone but millionaires approved by De Gaulle into Tahiti. As for the West Indies, the only place where you can still buy land is on one of those small islands with a large volcano which the estate agents hope isn't going to erupt before the development is all sold out. Mickey needed money for his little slab of paradise where the brandy may still be cheap but nothing else is.

'One thousand dollars,' I said.

'Damn you!' he said.

I was losing another friend. It seemed less important than losing that helicopter.

Slowly we began to swing around towards the west and the altimeter went up to ten, then twelve, then fifteen thousand. Mickey was intensely worried about the noise his one little dependable engine was making and I couldn't really blame him. Our forward speed, even into the climb, reached a hundred and eighteen which was much better, and I peered down to see the helicopter looking discouraged. It had a full complement and a pilot who had already shown reflexes heavily conditioned by basic caution. I was fairly certain that they had not seen our markings and Mickey ought to be safe enough if he flew home at once with enough brush-on enamel to cover the whole Piper, converting it from cream and black to an all over more muted colour. I would probably have to pay for the paint, too.

'Mind if I use your phone?' I asked.

It was an extremely expensive piece of additional equipment and I wondered what had made him decide to install it. Possibly the handy instrument had been put in before the Majorca project had been decided on.

'Twenty dollars a call,' Mickey said, surly.

I took up the handset. Contemporary electronic devices never fail to astonish me. In less than half a minute I was through to the Lipis exchange and the girl down there asked for my number as if I had been in a box around the corner.

'And you are calling?'

'Kangar 2-274.'

'Hold on please, for your connection.'

All telephone girls seem to have taken the same charm course. Maybe they are only rude to other women. While waiting I noticed that the altimeter had touched sixteen thousand. We were about level with the top of the cloud bank over the main range and heading towards it. The 'copter I couldn't see any more.

There was a sound on the line.

'Hallo? Can I speak to Mr. Teng Ching Wok, please?'

'Speaking. As well as he can at this time in the morning.'

'It's nearly eight o'clock.'

'That's yesterday. Who are you.'

'Paul. I need your help.'

'Oh, bones of my ancestors. That man again. Don't you have any respect for civilized habits? I'm still in my bed. Where are you? Down in a bazaar disguised as a Tamil holy man?'

I told him where I was. He gave no sign of being impressed or curious, only sounded disturbed that we were headed in his direction. I asked him to lay on transport to have waiting at Kangar, hinting that in my present circumstances it would be unwise for me to attempt to arrange my own.

'You mean the cops are after you?' he asked with brutal frankness. 'Ready to pounce on a Mercedes driven by your Japanese gunman?'

'Perhaps. Only we won't go on about it. This call might just be monitored, though I think it is a bit early for them to have thought of that. What I need is some kind of well-sprung vehicle that is closed and can travel fast. Meeting us at your race course. With a lilo or stretcher in it.'

'You got a girl-friend with you?'

'Just an associate who needs his rest. I want a good driver. Not one of your truck men.'

'What's the risk to me?'

'Not much, if you watch it. I hate to mention this, but you are slightly in my debt, remember?'

'I remember, you blackmailing bastard.'

There was a moment's silence, then Teng added.

'I think I've got the very thing.'

That Piper was valiant, even with a sticky plug. She got over the cloud bank, keeping in sunlight all the way and only having to make the descent through a thin blanket of grey over on the other side of the range. Kangar gave us sun again and Mickey, concentrating on technique, put the plane down on to grass in a gentle three point I could never have achieved in ten years of practice.

'Thanks,' I said. 'You'll get your cheque.'

There wasn't a word from the pilot. I looked out of the window.

The transport was waiting. The Teng family money had been built up by a process of slowly acquiring all the businesses around the town which were still likely to flourish even in a recession year. One of them was undertaking. He had sent us a black mortuary van without windows.

CHAPTER FIVE

I SAT OUT on the lawn of my house in Kuala Lumpur waiting for the results of surgery. Betty had made no suggestion that I function as her assistant, having already organized my house-boy for that role. The cold calm of her reception of us had held a strong hint that I was to be dealt with after the patient. Clem had showed no signs at all of any prejudice against women doctors, just very glad to see someone in a white overall who looked qualified to get to work on him.

Home felt extremely restful. I stared at the view while chain-smoking cheroots, feeling human again after a clean up, if very short on sleep. Far below in Batu Road the traffic was thick, car windscreens flashing helios up to my hill. There were a lot of things to be done immediately and I didn't want to do any of them, for all that Ohashi, as one of the reception committee waiting on the verandah, had sent me a number of facial signals about an urgent need for top level action in the affairs of Harris and Company. I hadn't sent any messages back. Whatever the crisis my number two had been faced with in my absence I could top it with disaster so nearly total that it seemed to defy any kind of treatment. Dashing down to the office now for an emergency conference would only result in two, instead of one, being sharply unhappy about future prospects.

For the first time in my commercial life I had a certain sympathy with the man who has left his London city office on a Friday knowing that on Monday morning that horrible tradition of ringing a bell to announce a company liquidation will be brought into play for him. This afternoon, like the poor wretch's weekend, was my respite, a short space of ticking time in which a long-established norm appears to be continuing, tea on the lawn, neighbours in for drinks, the happy laughter of expensive children, the pedigree dog yapping. The imminent bankrupt can still mix a very dry martini in the solid silver shaker which won't be his next week. He can even go for a drive in the outsize Mercedes which will shortly be in the hands of the receiver. His garage will allow him credit for petrol and he can still cash a cheque at his grocer's, getting the usual smiles, soon to fade.

Clem's bombshell had hit me at a time when what the Singapore press has somewhat exaggeratedly referred to as my financial empire was stretched very tight indeed. Business in the Far East these days is much more of a gamble than it is anywhere else, and the shrewd executive spends a very large portion of his active hours sniffing the air for political change of the sort which can have acute effects on his trading interests. As a result of some concentrated sniffing I had decided, together with two Chinese gentlemen in Singapore and one rich Dane, all of whom had been notably good wind-of-change prophets in the past, that the end of the Malaysia-Indonesian 'confrontation' was about to happen, which meant the termination of what was really a state of war between the two countries. A new peace is a good time to get in on the ground floor with a fresh enterprise and to the bold in such a period can come rich rewards. Harris and Company, together with its affiliates, had decided to be extremely bold, and we had pooled our resources to build up a fleet of seven small cargo vessels of about three thousand gross tons which it was our plan to operate out of Singapore through all the vast network of Indonesian islands right to eastern Papua. We were out to capture the trade which had once made very prosperous indeed a subsidiary of the Nederland East Indies Line, an area of commercial activity sadly neglected for the past decade as a result of Soekarno's deep prejudice against doing business with what he calls so charmingly the 'neo-cols'.

The Lindquist, Harris and Hok Lin Shipping Company had been incorporated in Kuala Lumpur with the idea of trying to operate out of now independent Singapore, but, if this became too complex, using Penang as our home port. We had been lucky enough to get hold of three slightly too old ships of the right tonnage and draft in Europe and were building four more in Norwegian, Dutch, German and Japanese yards, priced out of Britain by rising labour costs. Already the new company was facing problems. Our three old ships were on the way to us and general conditions over in Java hadn't improved to the point where we could start trading, due largely to Soekarno's fantastic skill at holding on to office even when apparently stripped of power. 'Bottoms', as the trade calls them, not in active use, are a steady financial drain and it was beginning to look as though we might have to wait quite some time for any returns at all to balance a massive outlay.

My personal bill for a fourth share in all this had come to three-quarters of a million sterling, which is more money than I keep in post office savings. I had gone to my bankers for half a million, offering as security Harris and Company's junk trading together with my shares in the Dolphin engine consortium of

Jahore Bahru in which I have a forty-five per cent interest. Security was good and the banks had played with me, smiling. The remaining quarter of a millon totalled all my private funds for old age.

We had issued no public stock in the new company, keeping this as a reserve for the future, but if there had been a market quotation it would have remained sound enough despite delays to a trading start. Time was clearly on our side. What would certainly not be on our side was any disaster to Harris and Company which forced my major bread and butter activity into liquidation. And Clem, now my reluctant house guest, had the power to bring this about simply by issuing one public statement that I had been gun-running into North Vietnam.

I was still too de-hydrated from the jungle to be sweating as I sat under a sun umbrella, but in my normal physiological state I would have been. The facts were gruesomely simple. The news that I was dealing in arms to the Far Eastern Reds and, in consequence, sharply out of favour with Uncle Sam in the Orient, wouldn't now put me in any jail, but it could still mean the cancellation of contracts by nearly all the small traders who regularly shipped in my junks. There were other bottoms available, it is a competitive field, and no Chinese or Indian merchant wants the label of being a user of vessels blacked by the United States. It could be very bad for their business in the years ahead. And because of this I would soon have my entire fleet of motorized junks lying empty and silent in their home ports of Bintulu, Penang and Alor Star, with the crews clamouring for severance pay.

I tried to take a little comfort from the thought that the death of Kim Sung had eliminated Clem's solid evidence against me, but I knew perfectly well that an unofficial leak about one of my ships caught gun-running could still mean the end of Harris and Company.

If this were to happen what about my partners in the new L. H. & H. Shipping Line? I am old enough not to nurture too many illusions about business associates. I am fond of old Lindquist down in Singapore who is, in the private areas of his living, a sentimental man, doting on his grandchildren and prone to easy tears. But when it comes to his commercial interests those tears just dry up. I would have his deep sympathy freely given and he would almost certainly come up with a solution to my problems, sorting these out for me like a benign daddy.

It was the benign daddy I was afraid of, because I could foretell Lindquist's plan right down to the small print. He would point out that a respectable new business venture just set on its feet could naturally not afford to have the name of a gun-runner on its notepaper, therefore I had to be bought out. But buying me out wouldn't involve any actual payment at this stage. He would therefore, from the goodness of his old heart, take over my indebtedness to the now snarling bankers in lieu of that directorship and as a personal obligation in memory of his old friend, my father. As for the cash I had sunk in what would now be known as the Lindquist and Hok Shipping Company I could expect, in due course, to receive a handful of shares when there was a public issue of these, which could be any time in the next fifteen years providing trade was good.

As I now saw things extremely clearly indeed I was about to be stripped of my junks and left stark naked out in business areas where I had long been accustomed to moving about expensively clothed. It also seemed highly probable that I would somehow be squeezed out of my holdings in Dolphin Engines. When a business of my kind starts sliding this process almost invariably turns into an avalanche.

It was getting near to one of those situations in which a man sometimes decides not to stay in a world where he can no longer reach out for the silver shaker. But that wasn't my reaction. I was beginning to get good and angry.

Betty Hill was good and angry, too. She stood in front of me suddenly, with all traces of her recent professional activities peeled away, a woman just touching thirty wearing a simple green linen frock and about to give someone a piece of her mind.

'You look relaxed,' she said, still acid.

People in the medical business are not always as highly observant as they like to believe. I stood.

'Sit down.'

'No thank you, I must go home.'

'How's the patient?'

'He'll live.'

'I was afraid of that,' I said.

Betty has brown eyes. It's not a colour in which ice is usually noticeable, but it was now.

'So he's not a friend of yours?'

'I've had guests I loved more.'

'Doing your duty by him?'

'Put it like that.'

She took a deep breath.

'I'm not going to say anything, Paul, about you involving me in this. I came after all. The choice was mine.'

'Betty, I'm sorry.'

'You're not in the least. You've never at any time really stopped to consider other people. It's the secret of your success.'

She was being unfair. I had been considering her husband

for over a year. Betty and I were not lovers. Tom had always seemed to me the major reason for this.

'Your friend,' she said, 'is going to need a few things. A nurse for one. Night duty at least.'

'He's as bad as that?'

'Yes. He must have plasma soon. I can get it, but I can't get the drip apparatus. I mean, I can't just walk into my hospital and borrow the gadget for an unspecified use. A surgeon's black bag doesn't contain very much these days. As a matter of fact I don't carry one. I use sterilized instruments kept in the theatre and I don't have a personal bone saw with my initials on the handle. All this creates quite a problem when it comes to treating patients illegally.'

'I'm sure I can get hold of everything you need.'

'I'm certain you can. So here's the list. I want all these things waiting when I call this evening. And the nurse arranged for.'

'The nurse must be here by tonight?'

'I have no intention of sitting up with the patient myself.'

'This is going to be tricky, Betty.'

'I'm sure.'

'You have a lead for me?'

'None. There are three private nursing services in Kuala Lumpur. If you try to use any one of them I should think it will mean the police in your house by tomorrow noon at the latest.'

'Couldn't I get hold of someone who had retired from practice?'

'Not through me you couldn't. I'd say that this is a time to get in touch with one of your shady Chinese friends. How about that outsize playboy you once introduced me to? Who lives up north somewhere. I forget the name.'

'Teng,' I said. Betty hadn't liked my friend, which perhaps wasn't surprising.

She nodded.

'I'd have thought just the man to arrange something like this.'

She had a point, he was.

'Betty, you'll be coming back again yourself?'

'I've said I would.'

'Perhaps one more visit from you will be enough?'

'I've taken this on, Paul, and I'll come as often as I feel is necessary. You have a patient in your guest-room who should be in hospital. He'll be very weak for at least ten days. What I did on that arm was really major surgery. I took out two bullets. I thought you might want them.'

She opened a white plastic handbag and took out something wrapped in lint.

'Police evidence,' she said, handing it over, 'which could have me disbarred.'

I put the lint in my trouser pocket where it felt heavier than the small change.

'Will . . . the patient be able to use his arm again?'

'You avoid using his name out of consideration for me? Thanks. If he gets proper treatment that arm should be functioning normally in about six months. I'm good at my job. But I may say I don't like acting as my own anaesthetist. That, too, is a complete specialization these days. We all work in our specific compartments with very little overlapping. Only abortionists form complete units in themselves. I suppose I have that career in reserve if my name is scored off the medical register.'

'That won't happen.'

'Your guarantees don't amount to much in this area, Paul. There are some things your money can't settle. And I've just one more thing to say. When your house-guest doesn't need me any longer you and I are not meeting again.'

'In a place like Kuala Lumpur that will cause more talk than if we did.'

'I don't care!'

'I have an invitation to your cocktail party and I'm coming to it. Tom would think it odd if I didn't.'

'What Tom thinks is no concern of yours.'

There was something else on her mind. She had meant to hold it there, but suddenly couldn't.

'Paul, I bitterly resent what you said on the phone about my having wailed for help that night.'

'I didn't say you wailed for help. And I know I shouldn't have mentioned it.'

'You did, though. Piling up my debt to you. Laying claims against it.'

'Betty, I've said I was sorry.'

Her eyes were wide.

'You think I needed you that night as a frail female, don't you? That I had to have the right shoulder to cry on because of what had happened?'

'Not exactly.'

'Yes! I rang you after eleven that night because I had a deep human need of your company.'

'What's wrong with that?'

'Just the fact that it wasn't the reason why I suddenly asked you to take me down to Morib. I just couldn't go home to Tom, that's all. I needed to get down to the sea for a swim and I didn't want to go alone.'

'Betty . . .'

'Shut up and listen to me! Do you really think I was personally torn to shreds because that girl died on the operating table? Do you really believe that after all these years of practice that I go totally female about my job in that way?'

'Why shouldn't you?'

'Damn it, a surgeon can't! You don't tie yourself personally to a patient. I was sick all right, sick and angry. But not because the girl died under my knife. It was not my fault. What happened wasn't because I was inefficient.'

'I never thought so for a moment.'

'Really? Then let me tell you who did have that thought. My assistant at the table. And my anaesthetist. I saw their eyes above the masks. You know what their eyes were saying?'

She stood very erect on the grass, arms at her side, the white bag dangling from one hand, the other a fist. She might have been at attention for interrogation before a very senior officer, that hint of service experience in her bearing though I knew she hadn't had any.

'Their eyes were saying, Paul, that the girl just mightn't have died if one of my male colleagues had been in charge of the operation.'

'You imagined that.'

'Imagined it? God! I wonder if you can have the faintest idea of what a woman in my job is up against? And not only in this part of the world. All right, my assistant was Chinese and the anaesthetist a Tamil, and they don't really believe in women surgeons, or women anything. But I've had exactly the same looks in England when the responsibility was mine. An operation produces tension, but not emotional, nervous. This is true with every surgeon, male or female. But the woman has to contend with something more and that's a continuing male suspicion, however it may be disguised, about our basic capability in the role. When that girl died I looked up and saw exactly what I was expecting once again. The complicated operations of mine which have been successes didn't count at all. The thing right at the front of their minds then was that if Kemp had been operating that girl might have lived.'

She took a deep breath but held the rigid pose.

'Kemp! We're not supposed to say anything about our colleagues. But I'll break the rule. When Kemp is called out to an emergency at that time of night he has had a good dinner. And a good dinner with him consists of three whiskies first, a wine with food, and a fair whack at the brandy bottle after it. I've seen his hands shake, and not from nerves. Oh, no. He's a controlled alcoholic. But under those just slightly shaking hands the girl might have lived, because Kemp has got a slight extra something which is part of male mystique which is so bloody well propped up by other males. That's what those eyes by the table were saying to me. And that's why I went to a phone and wailed to you and got you to drive me to the sea. I was angry. I had to cool my anger.'

I remember her tears.

'Betty, what's wrong with caring about your patient?'

She stared. 'I've told you! In that way the patient doesn't exist to the surgeon.'

She swung around and walked off across my lawn. It is a wide lawn and it took her some time. She had the trim figure of the tennis player she was. The game strengthened her wrists, something she needed professionally. She wore her brown hair in one of those short, chopped all over haircuts which only require a comb run through them to look smoothly sophisticated, if you can find the right cutter. Betty had, probably a little woman she had trained herself, demonstrating what she wanted done with a pair of dissecting scissors.

I waited until I heard her car drive off and then sat down again. I remembered that the thing which had struck me at our first meeting was that Betty didn't care whether she was looked at as a woman or not. It was her big act for the world.

Ohashi shared with his age group, and behind certain Japanese mannerisms, that remarkable confidence in his own powers which is something that seems to be pretty universal these days, skipping lightly over national frontiers. It is fine that the young are sure of themselves and able to claim the rewards that this state deserves, but it might be finer if their assurance wasn't based on the apparent assumption that their generation has inherited from us a unique shambles, something that could never have come about under their control. Further, there is a considerable resentment that they have to spend so much of their valuable time rejecting our mess, either by protest or in more positive re-organization. Behind Ohashi's carefully groomed politeness I had detected this impatience often enough, and it was in his voice now on the phone from our office.

'Oh, I'm so glad you are now calling, Mr. Harris.'

I had made him a partner but he hadn't accepted the invitation to call me Paul. His deliberate avoidance of the casual might be due to a Japanese need to have someone on high towards whom a continuing obeisance of respect was almost obligatory, but I suspected that it was more likely to be his desire to keep the line of age demarcation drawn between us.

'Well, what's up?' I asked.

'Not good things. Mr. Lindquist in Singapore has rung me up many times in the last two days. Always he is asking where you are.'

'Did you say elephant hunting?'

'I say nothing.'

'Give me the crisis.'

'It is most serious. Government in Java is playing the field in connection with inter-island trading.'

'How?'

'Last week arrive in Djakarta German mission from Hamburg Bremen Lloyd company. For negotiations regarding small ships built especially in German yards to do job planned for our shipping company.'

'But they have no ships yet?'

'True. At the same time grave dangers of signing contract to build these with German efficiency. To operate under profit sharing arrangement with Indonesian government.'

'The devil,' I said.

'Most serious,' Ohashi agreed. 'Mr. Lindquist in much distress. Over the telephone he is shouting.'

'And what's his idea?'

'That you must go to Djakarta yourself. At once. On behalf of new company interest.'

'That would be fine. Only there is still officially a price on my head over in Indonesia.'

'I beg your pardon?'

'Something from before your time, Ohashi. But these people boast that they have long memories. I think if I showed up in Java I'd land in jail, at least. So for the time being this neo-col isn't risking it over there. One of the other partners will have to represent our interests. I suggest Mr. Hok.'

'I also made this suggestion. But Mr. Hok say political climate still unhappy for Chinese.'

'That's true enough. It'll have to be old Lindquist himself. It wouldn't hurt him to get off his behind.'

'You will phone Mr. Lindquist now?'

'No I won't.'

'What?'

'I'm not back yet, officially. You don't know where I am.'

'Mr. Harris, you cannot be understanding me correctly. This **is** *most* serious matter.'

'I'm capable of my own assessment, Ohashi. It just so happens that I have something on my hands which is considerably more serious.'

'Is this possible?'

'I'm sorry to say it is. Though I wouldn't have believed it forty-eight hours ago. Now listen, I don't want you ringing me up here, or directing any messages to this house. If I want to see you I'll come to the office. Meantime you are in complete charge. If you like you can tell them in Singapore that I rang you up from the north, where you can't get in touch with me again, and suggested that Lindquist deal with this problem himself. It'll make him angry to have to leave his air-conditioning, but he'll do it. And he'll do a good job when he gets there. They like grandfather figures over in the Java. And no one has anything against the Danes, lucky people.'

After a moment my co-director said:

'I am most unhappy.'

'That makes two of us. Good-bye.'

It took considerably longer to reach Kampar on a land line than it had from the Piper. Then I ran into the collection of secretaries which Teng Ching Wok keeps around him, all good-looking. Finally I got the town's big man himself.

'Teng, I'm stretching my credit just a little further.'

'You haven't any left,' he said.

'What's the matter. Didn't your van get home?'

'Sure, it got home. And that's a debt settled. Anything more I do for you needs a cash down payment.'

'I need a nurse,' I said.

'Your nerve cracked at last? I thought your voice sounded shaky.'

'A nice reliable nurse who is the soul of discretion and who doesn't know anyone in Kuala Lumpur. A trained nurse.'

'I didn't think you'd adopted orphans. Why should I have nurses available?'

'You have everything available. I want her by tonight. I'll send a hire up to you to collect. The nurse will probably be needed for two weeks. An older woman. Knits in her spare time. Live in and no shopping excursions into the big city.'

'I don't like this,' Teng said.

'I don't like it myself. Have the woman down on the *padang* so we won't involve your offices. Fanning herself under one of the palms. She'll be picked up in a couple of hours. I'll just have time to settle her in here before leaving for that new road-house up at the Gap where you will be my guest to dinner.'

'What?'

'We haven't had a good chat for a long time. And I'm told they've got a good cook up there. A Dutchman, but trained in near French cuisine over in Saigon.'

'Thank you, Paul, but the Gap is much too long a drive for me. And I have an appointment for this evening.'

'Tell the girl you'll be with her tomorrow. I'll meet you up there. And give my love to your wife.'

After a moment, and before hanging up, Teng said grumpily:

'Which one?'

I went along to look at the patient. The air-conditioning had apparently been turned up during surgery and the room had that clammy chill I don't like. I dialled sixty-five for the sake of Clem's health, then turned to the bed.

It was easy to see that blood plasma was called for. He seemed to have shrunk physically, with all the basic menace of his personality in temporary abeyance. What was left on that bed was a reminiscence of the boy who had once been, the high school cheerleader suddenly struck down by a first serious illness. He was propped up against pillows and a bandaged arm was laid across his chest. His eyes were tight shut and a breathing rate confirmed a withdrawal artificially induced. Betty had left a basin handy for post-operative sickness when he came out of a drugged sleep.

Clem would be immobile and incapable of any really positive action for about a week, if I was lucky. That was the time allotted me in which to get on good terms with the United States of America again. It wasn't a lot of time for the job involved, which meant finding out who was the Red's top undercover man in Kuala Lumpur. The computer said he was me. I had to be the first man in the world to successfully prove a computer wrong. I didn't, right then, fancy my chances.

I'm a sucker for advertising, even though as a business man I ought to know better. A really good toothpaste commercial has me switching my brands and the cigarettes I've cut down on have a special filter which takes the smoke through a new detarring compound not yet endorsed by any medical association. I gladly pay more for this brand than another that would let me furnish my house with free essentials like hi-fi equipment and collapsible electric underpants dryers.

I bought the Audi because I was challenged by the advertising which wondered if I dare drive one. I didn't need another car and it isn't faster than my Mercedes, but it is a kind of personal toy and to a near bankrupt offers the additional advantage of not using a lot of fuel.

The Gap is half-way to the east coast from Kuala Lumpur, at the peak of the pass through the mountains, and my time up to it even on that twisting road was very good indeed. You drive that little front wheel job into corners as hard as you like and she goes round them as steady as a ship fitted with stabilizers. The steering takes a little getting used to, so precise, and it's the ditch for the man who is casual with his hands on the wheel, but I am never casual about driving, it is an art in which I claim to be something of a perfectionist. So far I had met that advertising challenge, I had dared, and was still alive.

Teng Ching Wok believes that success in this world is something which ought to be underlined and he has a new Cadillac every year, trading in the old one with a lot of scrapes on its paintwork. I tucked my neat little box alongside the bonnet of a status symbol and went towards the door to the bar, pausing for a minute to sniff the mountain air which at four thousand feet held an almost north country coolness. A couple of thousand feet higher at Frazer's Hill they light log fires in the evening. Malaysia is that kind of country, you can drive into near temperate zones for a few hours to escape from the tropics. This is a stimulus to clear thinking, and one I needed.

Teng had bought himself a triple whisky and was looking gloomy over it. His outsize Chinese frame was covered by a white silk suiting over which some serf in one of his houses had laboured for an hour but which was already completely rumpled. He was a man for whom the drip dry creaseless had been invented but they weren't expensive enough. He looked up and his heavy, un-Oriental face had even more bloodhound sags in it than usual. The only thing really neat about the man was his black hair which looked as though it had been plastered to his skull with half a pound of scented axle grease.

'Hallo, old friend,' I said.

'Don't give me that. I've been waiting here for twenty-five minutes. This whisky is one of your Scotch rejects, only good enough for Oriental playboys.'

'I was settling in the nurse.'

He almost smiled.

'How did you like her?'

'Just what I ordered. And I'm not the one who needs her. What's her history?'

'Shady,' Teng said, and drank. Then he looked at me. 'My mortuary van driver thought your friend was an American. That right?'

'Yes.'

'Are you entertaining him by force?'

'Force hasn't been necessary.'

'But held in reserve?'

'I'm not making any statements.'

'Which means yes. Who is he?'

'A tourist.'

'Since when has Kelantan been tourist country?'

'Who said anything about Kelantan?'

'The newspapers,' Teng told me, unfolding one from the seat beside him. 'Been too busy to read?'

I had been. It was all there, right on the front page, much sooner than I would have expected. A British Navy helicopter, based on Singapore, but making a goodwill tour around Malaysia with a two day stop-over at Kuala Lipis, had been busy giving free flights to local schoolchildren in a bid to have them grow up pro-Western in outlook. Most nights it also took off on non-propaganda short training flights for new personnel and while on one of these over the main massif had spotted a fire. Investigation had revealed a newly crashed plane burning on the runway of a disused airfield. There were no identifiable markings on the smouldering wreckage and there was no mention of anything found in that pyre. The whole thing was billed as a mystery of jungle country and was markedly lacking in any reportorial guesswork. Even before a second read I got a strong feeling of an official handout which might or might not be followed up with more news later. There was not a word about a large number of men leaving the runway at speed or the pursuit of two others.

'Your guest a passenger on that plane?'

I thought a moment before answering.

'Yes.'

'Were you up there meeting it?'

'Yes.'

He smiled, an effort his cheeks resisted.

'You must really need me to be so friendly,' he said.

'I do.'

The bar was empty except for a British couple having their fortnightly evening out. I knew them slightly from the club in K.L., the husband in the rather dismal job of trying to sell agricultural phosphates to bored Malay farmers who operated on the principle that when a piece of land wore out you cut yourself a new slice out of jungle. The couple had exhausted all common small talk twenty years earlier and had since taken to the bottle. They weren't even interested enough in anything any more to listen to what we said. The wife kept lifting a cigarette to unfashionably red lips which dated her, but the husband had reached a dangerous age and wasn't smoking. In a couple of years they would be settled in Bournemouth and no happier. The days of the British Raj had terminated before they were able to get in on the final pickings and the husband gave the impression of brooding about this a good deal.

Behind the bar was a Malay boy who looked a stern Moslem and therefore a total abstainer, carefully mixing Western poisons with a certain relish at the thought of what they were doing to his customers' livers. A radio played, a continuous low whining which seemed to offer the performer no break for air at all.

'What makes you think the food's good here?' Teng asked.

'It doesn't have the feel of a place where the food is good. Do you know how many miles I had to drive to get here?'

A typical well-heeled Chinese, always thinking about his stomach when he isn't thinking about business. Women he never thinks about at all, just has them. I cut out all skirmishing.

'Who would you say was Mao's top man in these parts?'

'Eh?' He stared. 'What kind of a question is that to ask me?'

'I couldn't think of anyone better qualified to answer it. As the headman of your own big village, and the richest *towkay* for twenty miles in all directions you'll be down to have your throat cut if the Reds ever become ascendant again. And as a Chinese you'd make it your business to find out who was likely to authorize that throat cutting, in order to buy him off. Unless, of course, you're Mao's man yourself.'

'Very clever,' Teng said. 'But do you mind keeping your voice down?'

'Is Lum Ping active again?'

'How the hell would I know?'

'Teng, let's not play pat-a-cake. You'd know all right. Kampar isn't all that far from where the man who would like to be the leader of the Malaysian Soviet Socialist Republic still lives. Are any of your people being tapped for money again?'

'Not that I've heard.'

'Which probably means you make regular contributions to Lum Ping's pension fund.'

'If you think paying for my dinner also pays for that kind of talk, I don't.'

'Lum Ping's men attacked and burned that plane when it was on the ground. They killed everyone in it except the man in my house.'

Teng had gone very still. He seemed suddenly to reject both the whisky in front of him and his role as the man of two worlds. The bloodhound sags from good living were still there, but the sadness was synthetic.

'So you see,' I said after a minute, 'I know the old chief is active again. Just as you do.'

He put out the delicately boned, ridiculously small hand which most of their big men still retain, fingers prodding at the mat under his glass. 'What do you want from me?' he asked, in scarcely more than a whisper.

'Information about the Red feed line into this country.'

'I don't know what you mean?'

'Don't you? It's this. Supplies for the Reds are coming into Malaysia, in a big way. I know it because they are going out again.'

'In your ships?' he asked.

It could have been just a lucky shot, but I didn't like it. I didn't like, either, the way he turned his head to look at me.

'You haven't been caught?' he asked gently.

'I've been framed.'

Teng took time to fill his lungs, then he began to laugh. He made such a row doing this that the phosphate wife looked up, more than a little shocked, and suggested to her husband that they go in to eat. The Malay boy came out from behind the bar to clear away empty glasses and then, for the first time, moved over to ask if I wanted anything, and perhaps to get in on the joke. I ordered one of his bad whiskies.

Another boy from the dining-room arrived carrying those vast menu cards which are an almost certain guarantee that everything on them comes out of tins or the deep freeze, and in haste at that. We each got one and I glared at it, trying to remember who had told me about the new chef up here. Teng, at the suggestion of food, had become deadly serious again. Even his curiosity was in parenthesis for a time.

'Oysters?' he said. 'Oysters?'

'Australia,' the dining-room boy told us.

'Which means they'll be big and coarse. No. Rainbow trout? Ah! You know where I last had rainbow trout, Paul? Scotts, in London, a year ago.'

'How am I supposed to cap that?' I asked. 'With paw-paw in Moorea three months back?'

Teng became absorbed in ordering, but I knew that he was also using the recess to assess how things were with me, and how change might affect the slightly curious relation between us to his advantage. It's nonsense that rich men seek each other's company in plush surroundings in order to relax with their own kind. They do it to keep their eyes and ears open while pretending to be *bon viveurs*. The unguarded moment over the *flambé* has seen the start of many a commercial slide.

We went in to dinner. It seemed a long meal, with Teng watching me through most of it, and the food was undistinguished. The same radio voice had followed us through on wire, and that girl was setting an all time record for soprano warbling. The phosphates munched without much enthusiasm on the other side of the room. There were no other customers and the claret was hot, almost mulled.

'Next time,' Teng said, 'take me to eat in a night stall, will you?'

We skipped liqueurs and went out to sit in the back seat of the Cadillac where there was a cocktail cabinet with cut glass decanters, a little custom feature inserted at the customer's request. Teng did without travelling television because he drove himself, but he kept his cigars in a fitted, electric humidor and they were still indifferent Manila leaf. These gourmets always slip up somewhere.

'So the Americans are after you,' he said.

I knew he now had everything worked out. The chances were that at almost any time in the last five years he could have told, without reference to his files, what my assets were down to the small change I was carrying around in my pockets. And he certainly knew the extent to which my reserves were now stretched. He knew, also, that the slightest rip in the taut fabric of my affairs could see the whole thing tearing right across, with the impressive tent collapsing smack on top of the commercial Arab who sat under it smoking his water pipe and pretending to be at peace with the world. It would be absurd not to expect a rival Arab to get a certain private satisfaction out of a neighbour's disaster. It would also be foolish not to count on Teng nipping over to see if he could steal some of the cushions out from under the unhappy victim of sudden calamity.

'What have they got on you?' Teng asked, skipping any detailed interrogation, which wasn't necessary.

'Very little, thanks to Lum Ping and a few murders.'

'Was the plane some kind of confrontation?'

He was a great guesser.

'Yes.'

'I see. And you now have the only man who could really damage you tucked away in your house?'

'I do.'

'How long do you think you can hold things?'

'Long enough for my purposes.'

'Always the optimist,' Teng said.

'Sure. And I've survived some time in a fairly hostile climate. I intend to hang on. This is my country and no one is pushing me out, the Americans, Chinese, Malays or Reds.'

'Brave words.'

'I can afford them, with you by my side.'

He laughed again the noise loud even in that roomy car. I decided to chill his mirth just a little.

'Look, Teng, there is a noticeable change in the climate these days in our beloved country. Coming from on high in Kuala Lumpur. Too many foreign interests have too much power still to please the local politicians. And one of the effects of trouble with Indonesia coming to an end is going to be a great upsurge of pan-Moslem feeling. Moslem ascendency, in other words. Your people may control the economy of this country now but the break with Singapore has threatened that happy state for the lot of you. The Chinese in Java damn' nearly controlled that economy too, And look what's happened to them. The lucky ones are getting to Mao's China as refugees. That has struck me as very interesting. You wouldn't really expect so many of those free enterprise Chinese who made their money under capitalism, to be making a bee line to get back under the Red umbrella, but they are. Which suggests that their loyalties were pretty mixed while they operated in Java.'

'You're talking about the small shopkeepers,' Teng said.

'I wonder? As I see things what happened in Java could be happening here in a few years, your people on the run, even the ones who have been here for generations.'

He didn't deny this, it was one of his nightmares.

'The time may come when you'll need all your friends, Teng. At the moment I'm one of them. So stop rubbing your hands in glee over my present distresses. I want you to tell me whom you suspect to be the Red's big man in this country.'

After a moment he said:

'I couldn't even guess at that. I don't know who their man in Kampar is.'

'The man I'm looking for wouldn't even have to be a resident in Kuala Lumpur. It might be safer for him not to be. It's a small country. He could do his job from anywhere in it. Do you agree?'

'I suppose so.'

'But you won't help me with a hint?'

'I can't give you one.'

I looked at the side of his head and didn't believe him.

'He's likely to be one of your *towkays*,' I said, angry. 'There are sound profits to be made out of selling out to Mao. With insurance for the future thrown in as well.'

Teng said nothing. I reached for the door handle and pulled it down. Standing out on tarmac I looked back into the car.

'It's going to be a sad day for this country when the bulk of Chinese influence in it decides that the only hope for the future lies in backing the Reds against Moslem ascendancy. A very sad day, because it won't work. Just as it didn't work in Java. A lot of you will be butchered. Goodnight, Teng. And if you change your mind about letting me have information send a messenger. My phones won't be working.'

In the Audi I lit a tipped cigarette while doors banged as Teng changed seats. I let him away first, and followed down the mountain. The Cadillac lurched around bends designed by British engineers who were thinking of smaller cars. Teng drove with what he thought was style, but was really an invitation to an early death, the performance perhaps exaggerated by the knowledge I was tailing him and watching. With my window down because I hadn't air-conditioning I could hear the screaming of brakes ahead. I also heard rushing water sometimes and the lights of two cars kept swinging out over black drops tapestried with jungle. On the flat we both began to go fast, with the Audi hanging on at braking distance even when the needle climbed to eighty, eighty-five and then hovered near ninety. I began to let him have a little more room just in case an angry man lost control, but he flashed into the Kampar fork in a glitter of rear illumination which didn't respond to the goodbye flickers from my headlights.

Kuala Lumpur glowed in the sky ahead, my home, a new nation's touchy capital, the sleepy seeming tree-shaded city with its little hills a setting for old angers in new forms. I was alone on a long road as I had been so often before, not unhappy in the again hot tropic dark, but conscious of it as a vast area for concealment.

And I believed what I had said to Teng, that the peace of sorts we knew now could be but a respite between two horrors.

CHAPTER SIX

IN SPITE OF ALL that western man has done in the last hundred years which is shaming, I believe that he has none the less done a great deal more which is not, and that in the contemporary world our role shouldn't be based on any apology for the past or paralysing guilt from it. The guilt only earns us laughter, and is invariably interpreted as another symptom of decadence. It is probably a very good thing for the West to be burdened by conscience, but extremely bad policy to let this show when dealing with races who haven't yet evolved one.

I see the situation in South East Asia in terms of basics, and for me the basic in dealing with Red China, at least at the moment, is a line drawn and a firm statement: 'Not a step beyond this.' Such a statement may be morally indefensible in terms of enlightened liberalism, but against the plain, cold facts of continuing Chinese aggression it is effective. Further, it is something that the old man in Peking, and his generals and their successors, can't possibly misinterpret. I would be the first to admit that much of the South East Asia Mao hasn't yet taken over is in a mess, but I don't think the answer to that mess is to withdraw and let him have it. My stake is here, of course, which certainly prejudices me.

As someone very far indeed from being against general U.S. policy in this area it made me angry to be rejected by an American computer. I drove the Audi towards my suburban residence still very much in the mood of saying to hell with the C.I.A. and also to its man from Vietnam for whom I was providing free board and lodging, not to mention the best of medical care, while he—with returning consciousness—would be back at plotting my ruin.

Nothing sharpens to a finer point a man's appreciation of what he has managed to build up in this world than a sudden threat to it all. I put the little car up my driveway, and past those huge jungle trees I had preserved with such care, feeling that if I lost all this I lost my roots. And I liked my roots. They were well dug in to pretty fertile soil, watered regularly by heaven and sending out up above top quality leaves as an end product.

The steel meshed gate recently installed stopped me half-way on a sharp gradient and a flick of headlamps brought out my Sikh watchman, who was trying not to yawn. He took one look, then reached back into the concrete sentry hut to pull down a lever which released the gates and broke the electric current running all around my hilltop through steel fencing. Such precautions may seem a shade elaborate, but it is a country in which kidnapping the prosperous for ransom has become a top profession, and sometimes the mood hits me to sleep out on the lawn under stars, where I used to be rather exposed to this form of free enterprise. I also like to have my visitors properly announced, leaving me with all of five minutes in which to think up a good reason why I'm not receiving them.

I asked Gian Singh if there had been any callers that evening and was told that the lady doctor had been allowed through, no one else. Gian Singh's duty relief was at that moment doing a circular inspection of the fencing along the path inside it before the took over at the sentry box. My private world seemed expensively peaceful as usual.

One advantage of an adequate perimeter defence is that you can leave the house behind open to the night without worrying about bolts pushed home. Since my bungalow was of the sprawling type with arches on to verandahs, it had before the fencing, been a very bad burglary risk, but I now had my premium cut by sixty per cent. The inspector from the company had been particularly impressed by the electric current.

'Would kill?' he asked during our tour.

'Not unless you had a weak heart. Only meant to knock you out.'

'Children dangerous?'

'They couldn't possibly climb up. There isn't anything to climb on.'

The mesh was far too fine for finger holds and the well-spaced support columns were each wired to an alarm device which rang a bell in my bedroom and the guard box if anyone leaned a weight against them. The live wire ran ten feet above the ground and though a patient man with the proper cutters could have carved himself a hole into my grounds beneath this, he would have been sadly disappointed when, after patient effort, a hidden cable in long grass announced what he had been up to. I had put a good deal of thought into my defences and so had the security company who sent in the bill for them. In a troubled world if you want peace of mind you have to pay for it.

In my dimly lit hall there is a Japanese wax warrior, life size, picked up cheap at a Singapore auction, and now standing guard in full fighting armour with spear up at the ready. Looking at that defensive equipment for another age suggested that my own system might have also been designed to keep house guests from straying. When Clem was recuperating out in the garden, still pretending to be feeble, he would find a sudden dash for freedom and contact with his own local agent a somewhat frustrating procedure. Though he probably knew all about my fencing, along with everything else.

I went down to the sick-room. Teng's nurse was there, and I had to admit—looking at the woman—that I wouldn't have enjoyed coming back from a private dark to find her in attendance. Whatever had blasted her professional career, and I was sure from a first meeting that something had, she accepted the twists of fate with a gay spirit. Under black oiled hair pulled to a bun on her neck, and decorated with a pin ornament, her broad, just slightly greasy face at once suggested the comedienne. For death she had laughter, and for total disability giggles.

There was a plasma drip apparatus which would be charged to me—or my receivers—standing by the bed, but no longer in use. Beneath it Clem seemed unchanged, still with that rapid breathing, the pallor under tan, and closed eyes.

'How is he?' I asked.

The nurse got up from the cot which had been provided for her. It creaked and so did her bones under a covering of heavy flesh. She smiled happily and told me in Malay that Clem had been conscious for a time. This was apparently both unexpected and amusing. The fact that the patient had been able to drink a little beef tea provided by Chow, my houseboy, was also entertaining. There was clearly nothing for me to worry about.

To indicate that she had everything under control Mrs. Hasmah waddled over to the bed, tugging at a sheet and light blanket, thereby clearly demonstrating her training in a calling which demands that the patient, whatever his condition, must be strapped down into an invincible tidiness. A mussed-up bed and true professionalism can never live together and we are most of us doomed to die surrounded by grim, aseptic neatness. There was already a strong smell of disinfectant in the room, as though this had been sprayed about straight from the bottle on to Chow's highly polished teak floors. I felt an intruder and quite useless. Tomorrow would be time enough to see about the one bunch of flowers permitted to someone off the danger list.

I went to my own room where I was greeted by Taro, my Tosa hound. The dog opened both eyes and thumped his tail twice against the mat which is his bed, but didn't rise because he disapproves of late hours and anything out with a placid routine. I had noticed a certain slacking off in his sense of responsibility recently, as though he realized that the new fence relieved him of most of his job, and was quite pleased about this. He was also putting on a bit of weight, which meant that his walks were being adapted to Chow's convenience, something on which I would have to take action.

Taro watched me getting into pyjama trousers, certain that I meant to read in bed which he doesn't like at all. When all I did was put the Colt I had worn to dinner on the table near my pillow and then switched out the light, he sighed. Five minutes later there were snores.

I lay in the dark considering the possibility that I had been followed up to the Gap, but decided it was unlikely. My route out of the city had been devious and on the straight to the mountains the Audi had gone fast enough to shake off any pursuit. Teng didn't seem to have been tailed either, or at least there had been no one behind us on that descent of hairpin bends. I thought about Teng's ready laughter, deciding I didn't like it at all.

The dog's growl woke me. Taro is no alarmist, but he is also a great dreamer, and when there was no repeat I relaxed again, though listening. My house was built all of seventy years ago, and entirely of wood, which contracts in the cooler hours, this resulting in a small, steady orchestration of nocturnal noise. Wide board floors seem to creak under ghostly visitations from former owners and more than once I have been quite certain that the planter who originally built the place was back, pouring himself a triple gin and squeezing the fresh limes to put in it. I don't often use the air-conditioner in my room, preferring the night's own easing of heat and the subtle pleasure of stirring at about three in the morning to reach down for a blanket. Now a slight chill from the open window told me the time. There was almost no noise from the city.

I was just dropping off again when Taro bellowed action stations. His bark, when angry, seems to come from well down in his guts, a special tone. I heard him make for the window, then the thud of his paws on the verandah beyond it. I didn't follow that route, but took my Colt to the door. In the passage was a faint glow from the lamp near the Japanese warrior. I ran to another door and banged it open.

Mrs. Hasmah wasn't in Clem's room, but someone else was. A heavily shrouded light burned, enough to show Clem in the bed and a shape in front of a closed window. The shape had an arm extended out, pointed towards the bed. I fired at that arm, the Colt noisy. The plasma bottle crashed to the floor. Taro's baying seemed to be in the house again, as though he had come back to look for me. I hurled myself across the room but the shape didn't wait, the window behind had only been pulled to. I fell against the empty frame of it, one foot sending a revolver slithering across boards.

'Taro!'

The dog came from behind me, still baying. I cleared the window space for his jump through. He went out into the night again, shutting off the loud protests in his leap, switching to the hunter's growl. I didn't do a follow up. The intruder no longer had his gun which meant that Taro could deal with the situation on his own for the time being.

'Mrs. Hasmah!'

There was a shuffling from the corridor. I locked the window and swung away from it. Clem hadn't moved. He was still breathing at jerky speed. I went to the hall and switched on the lights. The nurse coming towards me wasn't finding this an amusing situation. Her plump face had sags in it.

'Tuan!' That was a wail, followed by near English. 'I go pee-pee. Tuan, I go pee-pee.'

'Just at the right moment! Why was the window in here open? The air conditioner is switched on.'

She had nothing to say, and brought plump hands up to her face, the gesture defensive.

'Look after your patient,' I ordered.

She started a bleating in Malay and this followed me to the front hall. Out on the drive there was no sound at all, nothing from Taro announcing a quarry cornered, stillness until the distant rumble of heavy night transport climbing a hill somewhere.

I called the dog again, then began to run down the drive towards the gates. Taro could be beyond the range of my voice, down in the heavy undergrowth on steep slopes.

Ranji Singh was emerging from his little guardhouse, an impressive white turbaned figure, black bearded, a retired policeman with the dignified air of a man who has long defended law and order by a sheer massive weight of personality. He cerebrated slowly, and if he had heard the shot hadn't yet permitted himself alarm. The sight of me in half a pyjama set didn't spark this off either. He merely stared, as though he found something unseemly in my activity.

'Someone's inside,' I panted.

He shook his head, denying this as a possibility, and was still at it when I reached him.

'A man with a gun tried to kill my guest.'

Shock opened his mouth. I went into the hut. There was a lever for the gates and above this a box like those for electric cookers, in which a light glowed red when the current was running through the fence. The switch was still down but the light dead, which meant that the current had been cut from the second control point in my bathroom. I remembered Taro's growl. It could have been someone passing through my room, a presence tolerated by the dog because my night visitor was accepted in the house.

Ranji Singh breathed heavily behind me, staring at the box with its dead eye. The light came on again, a glowing ruby. The Sikh gasped. I grabbed up a torch and pushed past him.

Taro's silence didn't make sense. I couldn't believe that a running man had dealt effectively with my dog. The Tosa was trained to make a noise before moving in to the attack. Further, when it came to bringing down a running man, the dog knew his business. He had come out with top marks from a six weeks' police training course, a quicker learner than the Alsatians or Dobermans.

I ran along the path inside the wire, shining the torch ahead, trying to check soft earth for any signs of a landing from a jump. Getting over that fence with the current off was relatively easy. I could have designed a gadget to do it quickly enough, a telescopic aluminium ladder fitted at one end with extending bars on to which could be hooked runged rope for the getaway. All that was needed was an accomplice inside the house working switches to a synchronized time-table. With the current off my defence system was useless.

I stopped to get my breath back half-way around my hill, just below the vegetable garden. It was very quiet.

'Taro!'

Almost at once the dog came into light, trotting down the path, wagging his tail. I stared at him. He had cost me a lot to buy, import and train, and I was fond of the brute as well. But right then I considered a replacement. It was his sheer happiness over inefficiency which shook me.

'And where the hell have you been?'

Taro didn't like my tone much and the tail slowed down. He paused, thoughtful, aware suddenly that the boss was a bit worked up. Things became still between us. Then there was a sudden crackling in the scrub growth not twenty yards away.

'Get him!' I said.

To redeem his reputation the dog at once leaped into action, but without a hint of a growl. I heard him thrashing up the slope and followed fast. There were loud sounds of canine joy and another noise suggesting that this wasn't being too well received. I found myself looking down on the back of a man who had suddenly given up crawling, who had, in fact, given up.

While Taro stood by with tail metronoming happiness a head came slowly round. The man on his hands and knees was my former personal assistant in Harris and Company, now co-director, Seki Ohashi.

Taro loved him, which perhaps wasn't surprising since they were both Japanese.

I had a long drink from my double whisky but Ohashi hadn't touched his. He kept looking at the Webley fitted with silencer, a bulky instrument found in a corner of Clem's room, solid evidence.

'All right,' I said. 'There was another man in the grounds and you chased him.'

'Dog chase me,' Ohashi complained. When he wasn't looking at the gun he stared at a Persian rug just beyond his feet.

'So you didn't see what happened to the other man?'

'No.'

'I still have to find out how you got in here. Don't tell me Ranji Singh took a bribe?'

'I . . . I come in doctor's car.'

'As her guest?'

'No. I am hiding. In boot.'

'How did you get into the boot?'

'She stops car by gates. Waiting to open. She talks to guard. I am waiting in bushes. Boot not locked.'

Ohashi's English is normally very good these days, but slips a bit under stress. It was slipping now. He isn't a man who ever seems to sweat much, either, but his forehead was bedewed even though his chair was directly under one of my antique, revolving fans.

'The doctor called about ten p.m. What have you been doing since then?'

'Sitting in Mercedes. In garage.'

'What sent you out on patrol at just the right moment?'

'From time to time I am going round the house.'

'A guard I hadn't asked for? An extra?'

'So.'

He bowed slightly from the sitting position.

'Come off it,' I said.

He looked at me.

'Pardon?'

'You don't expect me to believe that? The extra watchman, self appointed?'

'Also—I greatly wish talks with you.'

'I see.'

'It is most important that I speak with you, Mr. Harris. From what you say on telephone come many questions. It is my feeling you deliberately neglect vital business. I cannot understand. You do not do such things. So I must meet you.'

'Ohashi, I'm afraid you haven't really thought through your alibi. You should have put in the time in the Mercedes doing this. If you wanted a business conference with me in the small hours why didn't you appear when you heard the Audi drive in?'

'I not hear. I think I am sleeping.'

'Worn out from the responsibility of running things while I was away?'

He was beginning to look almost forlorn and might, in other circumstances, have made me feel a brute.

'I am needing sleep . . . yes.'

I could have made a crack about his three months' old marriage to a girl from Yokosuka, but didn't.

'Let me get this quite straight, Ohashi. You were wandering around my house at three in the morning hoping that my conscience was keeping me awake and that my light would suddenly go on. You'd then say a polite Japanese excuse me through my window?'

'Perhaps,' he said.

'Perhaps is about it. Perhaps maybe not.'

'The telephones in this house not working!' There was despair in his voice. 'I think surely some trouble is happening here.'

'So you decided to play faithful *samurai* with a personal check?'

His eyes remained fascinated by rug patterns.

'Thanks,' I said. 'Thanks a lot. And I'm grateful, too, for your having worked out that car boot trick. We'll watch this in future. Tell the Sikhs to check boots as well as whether something is huddled under a rug behind the driver's seat. We'll have real security up here provided I'm prepared to live entirely alone and shoot at sight anything that moves.'

He watched me drink some more whisky. A single drop of perspiration left his forehead and ran down one cheek, leaving a shiny mark like a snail's journey.

'Mr. Harris, you think I am lying?'

'Yes. And so badly it makes me regret having given you a seat on the board. I don't believe I've ever seen you frightened before. What's so terrifying about being a good *samurai*?'

'It is shameful . . . to be discovered like a sneak thief.'

'You're not ashamed, Ohashi. You're scared. And I know why.'

It was as if I had hit him. His body jerked upright. He looked at me from slits magnified by thick lenses, black framed glasses so much a part of his face that without them his personality seemed almost alarmingly diminished. I have watched the man standing polishing his specs wanting to beg him to hurry up and put the things back on his miniscule nose in order to give him a recognizable identity again. The lenses were in place now but I still wasn't looking at someone I knew well and a full realization of this made me feel a little sick.

I went over to a side table and refreshed my glass, deciding to do my talking looking at a Chinese painting on silk of the Kwangsi mountains. 'You didn't come through that fence to see me. You had to contact someone else.'

He made no sound.

'I said—there was someone else you had to see!'

'Mr. Harris, please . . .'

I turned my head. He was bent over as though to ease a stomach cramp. If something was paining him it was no worse than the pain I had, too. And it was no moment for mercy.

'Ohashi, you once told me about your family's *samurai* background. I took that to mean loyalty to anything to which you had committed yourself. I thought I was lucky to have some of that loyalty for my affairs. And for myself. I've gone on thinking I was lucky . . . until now. You little sod!'

His breath came in with a hiss.

'Please . . . please . . .'

The wail didn't impress me. I didn't raise my voice, there was no need in a room held by early morning stillness.

'In the last twenty-four hours it's been made plain to me that some remarkably detailed information has leaked about the workings of Harris and Company. I admit the leak was to people I was working for . . . just as you have been. For that's true, isn't it? You have been working separately for an American called Clement P. Winburgh? And the man you had to get in touch with inside this wire was him, not me. He's your real boss. And you've been feeding him facts about how we operate that should have been known only to you and me. Isn't that so?'

He made no attempt to defend himself. I stood looking at a bent back.

'Why in hell's name did you do this to me? Wasn't I paying you enough? Did you need money on the side to help cover the expenses of a new marriage?'

'No, no!'

'Then why?'

'I do not betray. I do not!'

'Most company executives would consider the feeding of confidential information to an outside source as pretty massive betrayal. What was your motive? I could perhaps understand it if we had been operating in any way outside the law. But we haven't been, as you know damn' well. Further I've never operated that way since you came into the firm.'

For a moment Ohashi kept the silence. Then he said:

'But not always so, Mr. Harris.'

'I see. The gun-runner accusation again. That's going to follow me for the rest of my life. But even you know damn' well why I was in those operations. I was against the then government of Indonesia. I tried to help considerable numbers of people in that country who were also against the government. And when I helped them over in Sumatra the place was already in armed revolt.'

'What a man does once . . . he may do again.'

I wanted to see Ohashi's face then. I came back to my chair opposite him and sat in it. And after a minute his eyes came up, as though to explore my face for the depth of my anger.

'So you were employed by the Americans to watch my current activities? From inside? From your unique position? They must have been delighted when I gave you that directorship.'

He swallowed. What I saw in his eyes reminded me suddenly of that curious aggression from Kim Sung.

'You say I am inside, Mr. Harris. But I am not so sure. Often I am feeling I do not really know how company operates.'

'What gave you that feeling?'

'You make me partner and I am no longer employee. But partner is not told everything. When Kim Sung comes to see you it is always a private meeting in your office.'

'Kim Sung was an old friend. I treated him as such. But we never discussed anything that was kept from you.'

'I see,' he said, almost with a reserved politeness, as though he had received the statement expected.

I was conscious then of a considerable weakening in my position as the man who has had his hand bitten by a favoured pet. The plain facts were that Ohashi, almost from the moment he had come into my business, had done as much for me as I had for him. There was no doubt that he had earned his right to be touchy about not being totally in the boss's confidence. In fact he *had* been in my confidence, but it was almost impossible to prove this. I swung off on a new tack.

'How did the Americans approach you?'

He was quite candid.

'In Kuala Lumpur restaurant. I think man is tourist with camera. He asks me about the city. But soon something else is plain. He makes me listen even though I do not wish. He tells me I am working for man who is dangerous. I am angry, but I have also doubts in my heart. You understand?'

'I suppose I can. Go on.'

'We meet again. It is difficult for me not to do so. I have many questions. He knows much of our business. He tells me that it is most dangerous for Japanese to become involved in such situation. He say to me that Japan must now play strict neutral role. And all her people also.'

'That man wasn't Mr. Winburgh?'

'No.'

'But you have met the man now in my house?'

'Yes.'

'Where?'

'Singapore. Last month when I go on business.'

'Fascinating. What did he tell you to do? Watch me?'

Ohashi nodded.

'Mr. Harris, by this time I am greatly troubled. There are things for which I can find no explanation. It seems to me possible that the Americans speak the truth. That Harris and Company front for other things.'

'What exactly made you feel this?'

'While you are working on plans for the new shipping company I am left in complete control of old business, all the matters of junk trade. I get the returns for this, routes of ship movements, all that. You hand it over. I am really running Kuala Lumpur office.'

'Not very sensible of me if I had something to hide.'

'This I also consider. But you are very confident man. Perhaps you think you are quite safe from Japanese assistant. Too clever for him.'

'I see. In what way?'

His hands were trembling slightly. He held them out in front of his body as though to watch that.

'Well—I discover serious discrepancies. In timing of junk voyages from captains' reports. I notice things like four days to load twenty tons of copra in small port. There are explanations for this, but they do not convince. Like delays in delivery. But these ports are collection points, where copra is stored to await shipment. So I add up and come to big totals in wasted time. One of Kim Sung's voyages spent nearly half of its trading days in port. The junks have fast engines. So it seems to me clearly that junks have other unreported activities, even long voyages. You understand?'

I understood all right. Ohashi had probed into an area in company affairs where I had been too casual by half. The profits had been sound and that had been quite enough for me. It was highly probable that when Kim Sung needed more time for his gun-running he simply pushed in false returns on ordinary trading and allowed a cut on his dirty racket to pass through the books of Harris and Company in order to keep me happy.

'You took what you had found to the Americans, Ohashi?'

He nodded.

'It never occurred to you to raise the matter with me? Or did you think it was dangerous to? That I might eliminate you for knowing too much?'

'I . . . I'm not sure. I am much confused. Also, the Americans are strong. In Japan they are still powerful influence. For me to challenge such authority is dangerous.'

'In what way?'

He shook his head.

'I'm not sure. Only troubled.'

'About your mother in Kamakura?'

'Maybe.'

He had been a boy during the occupation of his country. That time had left its marks. And it had also left a potent respect for power however well this might be camouflaged by good will. Ohashi's response to the authority of his youth wasn't surprising.

'You recognized Mr. Winburgh at once, of course, when I brought him here?'

'Yes.'

'Did you report back about his being in this house?'

Ohashi nodded.

'And you got orders to contact him as soon as possible?'

'That is so.'

'Well, you didn't manage to do that. Let them know about this, too. And suggest that any further attempts to get through to him are unlikely to come off.'

He stared.

'You mean . . . I must make contact with Americans as if . . . you know nothing?'

'Exactly. Just a little demand on your old loyalty. To Harris and Company, now somewhat bedraggled.'

Ohashi seemed to notice his drink for the first time. He lifted it in both hands, sipped, then put the glass back on a table.

'To be married makes man more timid,' he said.

'The responsibility?'

'So. My wife will have baby.'

'Congratulations.'

He looked at me. 'My heart very sick, Mr. Harris.'

'I know the feeling. If it's any comfort to you, and you can believe it, I had no knowledge of how our junks were being used. And that's the position from which I'm trying to fight back. It's not going to be easy. At the same time they've lost their key witness. Kim Sung is dead.'

His face showed no surprise. For a sub-agent on special assignment he was being kept well in the picture, much further into
it than I had been, which perhaps wasn't surprising since with
me they had merely been paying out rope.

'Go home now, Ohashi. Back to your wife. I'll give you a chit
to the gateman so he won't ask questions.'

'But . . . how can I help you?'

'That's a nice thought, in the circumstances. You can get in
touch with all our junks. Every single one, in all the fleets. I
want them collected at their base ports. They're not to leave
without orders.'

'What are you going to do, Mr. Harris?'

'Sack all the crews,' I said. 'From the captains right down to
the cook-boys. Harris and Company is starting from scratch again,
major assets a fleet of junks collecting barnacles. It's going to
play hell with our dividends. Only a miracle can save us from
total liquidation. Do you believe in miracles, Ohashi?'

He just stared at me.

'Most miracles,' I told him, 'call for a great deal of support
sweat from the beneficiaries. They're not just a free issue.'

CHAPTER SEVEN

The self-confidence Mrs. Hasmah had built up over the years
from her career as a successful sinner had been shockingly undermined by the events of one night. I saw Ohashi off home to the
Japanese wife who is always waiting—no matter what the hour
—with a smiling politeness for the return of her lord, and went
straight along to the sickbay. Teng's nursing discovery, if not in
a state of total collapse, looked very near to it. Something had
happened to her face, a rapid deterioration from wellbeing,
muscles gone slack leaving pouches of hanging flesh. She sat on
the cot bed, her feet just touching the floor, in an attitude of
dismal waiting, as though for some considerable time now she
had been going over her alibi only to find this as totally wanting
as I did. Certainly a nurse on duty has to answer the calls of
nature like anyone else, but she doesn't need to unlock a window
in an air-conditioned room before she goes off. It might have
restored the woman's morale just slightly to know that I had no
intention of notifying the police about an assassin in my grounds,
but I saw no reason to give her hope.

'*Tuan*,' she said in a near whisper, as though I had been the
executioner arriving with the dawn.

I looked at Clem in the bed. He was certainly having a long

rest, even for a man who has undergone surgery, still with eyes closed, and that look on his face of someone currently out of this world who may, or may not, be returning to it. His breathing continued unnaturally rapid. Mrs. Hasmah's one positive action appeared to have been a clear up of the mess made by a shattered plasma bottle, and the contraption for holding this was now pushed back against the wall as if to make a reminder of sudden violence as inconspicuous as possible.

I stared at the patient for some time and my total immobility allowed the nurse to rally slightly. She tried out a few cautious words in Malay:

'He's sleeping well.'

I looked at her.

'Where's your suitcase?'

'What, *Tuan*?'

'The one you brought with you. Brown leather.'

She went down on her knees to get it from under the cot, that position for a moment suggesting an alien piety.

'Just my things,' she said, half-heartedly stalling.

'Open it.'

She pulled the suitcase up after her and sat with it on her knees, her arms across the top, as though defending some basic totem of privacy. Then very slowly her fingers went out to the catches, releasing first one and, after more hesitation, the other.

One third of the contents were personal, but the rest suggested a first aid kit for an ambulance, remarkably complete. I inspected a number of items, lifting them out to do it. One of these was an unlabelled bottle containing enough morphia to poison a stable of horses. There were also at least a dozen interesting-looking ampoules without identification marks and a syringe. In a little box padded with cotton wool were some not too sterile-looking needles.

'You always carry all this?'

'I'm a nurse,' she explained.

'Nurses administer drugs only under a doctor's orders. Did Dr. Hill tell you to go on keeping the patient under sedation?'

'What, *Tuan*?'

'Were any of these drugs left by the doctor?'

'Well, no. But I'm a nurse. I must have them. For accidents.'

'The law doesn't say you must have them.'

But there really wasn't much use in threatening Mrs. Hasmah with a professional disbarment which had almost certainly already happened. The lady was now a free lance in areas untouched by ethics.

'Did you give the patient any sedation not instructed by Dr. Hill?'

She considered carefully the advisability of a lie, but decided against it.

'Only a little. He needed to sleep.'

The little accounted for that pumped breathing. It had also been designed to keep a target quite motionless against pillows. To this woman's credit had to be put the fact that she plumped for the truth when a situation rendered anything else useless. Mrs. Hasmah was a realist opportunist. And she was peeping at me now from this stance in life, rather hoping—from all she had heard—that it was my own position and as a result we could plot out some sort of working arrangement. It is slightly unnerving to be offered an alliance by a total sinner, as though the evil in you had suddenly surfaced and been identified.

I thought about putting her under interrogation. She was in an emotional state which might have made this productive, but there were two counts against, first that I had just ended such a session and felt slightly spent from it, and second, my questions would inevitably reveal to this woman the limits of my knowledge. Further, though she might confess a good deal, there was a point beyond which she wouldn't go. Even under stress Mrs. Hasmah was enough of a trained operator to reveal nothing about the people of whom she was much more frightened than she could ever be of me. It seemed policy for the time being to discipline her with only minor terrors. I picked up the morphia bottle again, feeling it fat in my hand.

'Are you in the retail business?'

Her eyes, which had been willing to meet mine, changed focus and moved around the room. She moved the suitcase slightly, as though finding it heavy on her knees. The lid back against her body made an exhibition bust of head and shoulders, and she was as soundless as bronze.

'There is a drive on to stamp out morphia addiction,' I said. 'I forget the exact sentence for local vendors, but it's stiff. As much as three years. You'd have been wiser to stick to raw opium instead of trying to move into the class trade. And you should have left your samples at home.'

She swallowed. Plump hands were suddenly added to the bust around the sides of the suitcase lid. The effect was odd.

'I am a nurse,' she insisted. 'I need these things.'

'So you always carry enough to deal with the injured in a major train wreck?'

There was no reaction to this cynicism about her role as a healer.

'Mrs. Hasmah, you're not going to get out of this house until your patient doesn't need you any more. And you're not going to get any messages out, either. I have a dog here who is very highly trained. He allowed you to pass through my bedroom to turn off the electric current in the fence because you had been accepted in this house. But I'm going to tell him now to watch you. Taro!'

I hoped my hound would take his cue and make an entrance. We both listened. There was a padding out in the passage and at this sound Mrs. Hasmah's hands disappeared behind the lid again. Her mouth opened. She had heard enough about the training of western dogs to believe that this involved a kind of witchcraft. And Taro, standing faintly bewildered in the doorway looking at us, was certainly impressive. He was still conscious of an earlier failure to match up to what was expected of him and his eyes retained a hurt from this.

'See this woman?' I asked in stern Malay. 'You're to let her go to the bathroom, but nowhere else. If she tries to get out of the house, stop her.'

A tail wagged to placate me, but also suggested message received. Mrs. Hasmah was now only visible from a plump chin upwards.

'Go back to bed,' I said, in English.

'*Tuan*, do not put the dog on me!' That was a wail. 'Please, not the dog!'

'He won't touch you if you do what you're told. But don't try to get out of the house. And no more attempts to shut off that current. He's a big dog, Mrs. Hasmah.'

'No!'

'It might be wise to call Chow as an escort if you have any reason to move about in the house. In here you'll be quite safe. Though when I'm not at home Taro becomes very keen about his duty.'

I felt fairly certain that I had the woman, for all her resource, nicely nobbled. Witchcraft still has its uses. Nurse obviously believed in it. She might even practise it herself as a spare time activity, but there wasn't going to be any counter spell to Taro.

I kept the morphia and helped myself to the ampoules.

'The doctor will give you what you need. And this stuff is going down my water closet. All you have to worry about now is getting your patient well again. When you've done that you'll be allowed to leave this house. But only then. Understand?'

She nodded. I went along to my bedroom where the dog offered me a couple of tail thumps from his mat, but continued to watch me with sad eyes.

I was out on the lawn having a late breakfast when Betty's Ford Consul groaned up the steep gradient in a lower gear than was necessary. Like so many doctors she treated a car with almost no respect, changing it every year before the thing started to fall apart from brutal use. The second-hand trade hates having to find customers for these medical discards, none of which have the life left in them the speedometer mileage would seem to indicate. I heard the driver's door slammed in a test of lock and hinges, then a silence. I had another cup of coffee and lit a cheroot, sitting there with the feeling of a man taking a deliberate use of leisure he hasn't got because a time bomb is ticking away under his life.

When Betty came down the front steps I was near them. She was wearing a white linen sheath on top of which would soon be a white coat for her round of surgical wards. She sent me a look which was very like the other ones I'd had from her since my return from the north.

'Pleased with your patient?'

'No, I'm not. That wretched woman must have given him some extra sedation, though she denies it. I made her open her bag but I couldn't find anything. He should have been conscious by this time.'

'He's lucky to be alive.'

Betty resented that professionally until I put her in the picture. Then she said:

'I'll go back in there and deal with that creature!'

'She's only an accomplice and I've dealt with her.'

Betty stared.

'Don't you feel that this has become a police matter?'

'Not exactly. The police mightn't be friendly to me.'

'So you're prepared to go on risking my patient?'

'Yes. He's getting more than he deserves as it is. And there's no medical danger, is there?'

'With that woman beside him anything could happen.'

'She was a nurse once.'

'Once is the operative word. I won't speculate as to what she does for a living now. All I'll say is that she isn't the type with whom I'm used to functioning. Paul, I feel very much like washing my hands of all this.'

'You've been saying that ever since I asked for your help.'

I held out an ampoule.

'Any idea what this is?'

Betty took it, broke off the plastic top with her finger nail, sniffed, then looked at me.

'Where did you get this?'

'Mrs. Hasmah. Confiscated. There were ten more and a bottle of morphia. Do you recognize the drug?'

'Helcramine, I'd say. Proprietary.'

'And you left those ampoules?'

'Certainly not. I left nothing. He'd had all necessary sedation. And further I wouldn't have given any nurse Helcramine. Are you sure that's all she's got?'

'I think so. Though I haven't shaken her to see if anything else falls out.'

'Paul, it's a shade disturbing to be treating unofficially a patient some people want to assassinate, including probably the nurse in attendance. It's my suggestion that you put your guest in a hospital ward at once. The fact that surgery has already been done can be explained somehow. I'm prepared to do that. And he'd be safe in hospital.'

'I don't feel that. Wards are fairly accessible. I think the risk to my friend would be greater.'

'I see. You refuse to consider me at all? I must warn you that I can't keep coming here twice a day.'

'Don't do it then. Clem's tough. The bullets are out, he'll survive.'

'That arm has to go into plaster soon!'

'All right, come back and do the job when you think it's about the right time. I agree that if you keep showing up morning and evening it's going to look more than social.'

She stared.

'So now I'm dismissed? I did what was essential and that's that.' She took a deep breath. 'You sit up here on your hill in the middle of the city and think because you're Paul Harris and have a wire fence around your place you can get away with anything!'

'Not anything. Just this. And privacy is what my guest wants, too. Very much. How long before he'll be sitting up with his eyes open?'

'I just don't know. It depends on how much Helcramine that lying bitch pumped into him. At the moment he looks about ready to be wheeled in for major surgery. Let me tell you something, I'll never do anything like this again, I don't care who it's for. I didn't sleep last night, sick with worry. And I'm not fit for hospital this morning.'

She did look stretched tight.

'Betty, I'm really sorry. I honestly didn't think about what all this involved. There was a lot else on my mind.'

'You knew a doctor and you got in touch with her?'

'Something like that. Look, I'd like to make this up to you in some way.'

'What way? I feel like a criminal at the moment. And nothing that I can tell myself alters the fact that I really am.'

'You've been giving help where it was needed.'

'Oh . . . hell! You're impossible.'

'Lunch with me at Yung Ching Wa's to-day.'

'What? Our little session just as usual? Heaven give me strength! You'll be lunching alone!'

Betty walked over to the car. The Consul door slammed again. She held the starter button down long after the engine was running, then managed to do something remarkable to the reverse gear and the car swept backwards in a lurching arc which slung its weight over on to the nearside wheels, sagging the tyres. She wound down a window while noisily groping for first and shouted:

'I've a damn' good mind to crash through your gate and wreck your defences!'

'You'd be fried in all that metal,' I called back. 'The heat's still on.'

The car went down my drive at some speed and I turned back into the house, making good time myself towards Clem's room, but taking care that my feet didn't announce this. In a trouser pocket the Colt I had decided to wear permanently for troubled times felt chilly through thin nylon.

Betty had arranged for another transfusion to thin down that extra Helcramine in Clem's blood, and the drip apparatus was forward by the bed again, with the feed line leading down into the normal arm. Mrs. Hasmah was in attendance, her broad back to me, and then she moved her stance slightly, bracing her body, leaning over. I saw the glint of a syringe.

'Push that plunger down,' I said, 'and I'll put a bullet in your hand.'

She went limp. The syringe fell to the floor. Before I could stop her she had put a foot on it, and there was a crunch of glass. She turned like an old witch from her brew, fury livid in her face, now no act of shocked humility, no excuse, not even a hint of fear.

'You go right on trying, don't you?'

She said nothing. Her eyes were chilly brown pebbles.

'It would be a public service to shoot you,' I told her in English.

The message reached her, showing that she understood English a lot better than had been admitted. But the defiance continued. She was an active combatant in a war which has a steady death roll. If you died doing your job you died. An earlier whimpering had been part of a false image of herself.

'Why bother with an assassin when they've got you on the job?'

She wasn't talking. She watched the gun, for a moment of slackening on my part.

'Chow! Come here.'

Taro arrived first, but his usefulness was over. I sent the dog away again.

'Get away from the bed, Mrs. Hasmah. Right away, over there.'

She moved slowly. Chow put his completely shaven head around the door as she was doing it, his pleasantly stupid face now marred by the resentment he felt at having his well-run house turned into a hospital featuring alien women.

'*Tuan?*' His voice was slightly sulky.

'We're going to lock Mrs. Hasmah in the small bathroom. The one with the grille over the window. She'll have everything she needs in there. You can feed her if you want to but I wouldn't bother. Let her coast on her fat. And if you do open that door see that you have Taro beside you. Because this woman is going to try very hard to get out and would think nothing of killing you to do it.'

Chow looked at the nurse for all of half a minute. Then he offered one of his rare opinions.

'I knew she was bad.'

It was spoken with the quiet confidence of a man who is guided by intuition and because of this has never needed brains.

I lifted the gun slightly.

'Walk, Mrs. Hasmah.'

The lady's movement down the passage wasn't too graceful, somewhat heavy swaying, as though her legs hurt from varicose veins. Even healers are afflicted by the common ailments.

Though I sell engines I'm not very mechanically minded and when I have to do something with a gadget I haven't dealt with before my fingers are slow. But it did seem logical that an empty plasma bottle should be disconnected from the patient. I set about removing that tube with what I thought was careful intelligence, but my technique jerked Clem out of his coma. It was startling to find his eyes watching me.

'Enjoying yourself?' he asked, through slightly blue lips.

I had my non-friend back again and was strictly conventional about the reunion.

'How are you?'

'Uncomfortable.'

He looked down at the feed point on his arm. I swabbed that hole with lint and alcohol, watched as I did it. It seemed highly probable from his expression that Clem was one of those people who have a deep-rooted dislike of the idea of someone else's blood in his veins, never quite able to shake off old wives' tales about how you acquired some of the donor's personality characteristics via plasma. Though in his case any change could only be for the better.

'Fancy something to eat?' I asked.

He thought about that.

'No. A cigarette.'

After a healthy rest from poison smoke his lungs protested and he coughed. This seemed to shake him back into life.

'What about my arm?' he asked.

'In time it's going to be all right, provided you get the proper treatment.'

'Sure?'

'The doctor's word.'

'Apart from being a girl-friend . . . how good is she?'

'Kuala Lumpur depends on her.'

He frowned.

'I've never rated European medicine all that high.'

'Sheer mid-western prejudice. I think you ought to have something in your stomach. Perhaps beef tea?'

'I had that boiled cow juice before, no thanks.'

'Something more solid?'

'Sure. A boiled egg'.

If I had loved him dearly I'd have been cheered.

'Not an underdone steak?'

'No.'

He had a small brandy, however, after I had brought in bottles highly unsuited to the sick room. The hand which lifted a glass shivered but steadied down once a contact with lips had been made. Clem was doing much better than he would have in one of Betty's aseptic wards, and though brandy may have been totally wrong for his post-sedated state it certainly put a touch of colour through waxy pallor.

'When I was awake before,' Clem said, 'I had a nurse. She looked like a walrus without tusks. Where is she?'

'Locked up.'

'You couldn't stand her face either?'

'She tried to kill you.'

He took that without any sign of sudden palpitations.

'How?'

'With a syringe. I don't know what was in it but it smelled bad. And there's a permanent stain on the expensive piece of Peking carpeting around your bed.'

'What made you think she wasn't just administering normal medication?'

'Because she was assistant to the assassin who tried to kill you earlier this morning. With a gun that time.'

'Oh,' Clem said.

He moved his bandaged arm slightly, testing whether the upper muscles still functioned and seemed faintly pleased about the results of the experiment.

'How did you stop her putting a needle into me?'

'By saying I'd blast her hand off.'

'As close as that?'

'Yes.'

'Thanks.'

'Don't mention it.'

'What about the gunman?'

'A bullet from my Colt knocked a silenced Webley out of his hand.'

He smiled for the first time.

'You been getting any sleep at all?'

'Not much. And take note that nurse is now locked in our third best bathroom. That's the one with the key on the hall side. If you should be up testing your legs I wouldn't advise you to peek in. Beyond those panels is a lady killer. If I read things right your enemies have issued an emergency order to all personnel that you are not to be allowed to leave Malaysia alive.'

The news didn't seem to do anything to check his convalescence.

'What happened to the gunman?'

'He got away.'

'Through your electric fence?'

As I had expected he was well informed. He probably even knew which picture my bedroom wall safe was behind. He asked for another small brandy which I gave him and then he wondered if there had been any contact with the police while he was resting.

'None at all. Our isolation from the world is complete. And I've hired two extra Sikhs to give us a double patrol around the wire night and day. I'm thinking of putting them on a bonus basis, so much for every hour that passes with no unauthorized characters getting inside.'

'How about essential services and the postman?'

'They're let through.'

'So I can write my Mum. What about a long-distance call?'

'The phones are dead.'

'You're a suspicious guy. Isn't it all terribly inconvenient for you?'

'I'm living in a dream world pretending that the last few days haven't happened. And Harris and Company is still just as solvent as it was last month.'

I lit a cheroot, a really brusque Java leaf likely to prolong any lingering nausea. Then I filled in more detail of a busy night, slowly, building up to the dog story, noting a certain tightening of his interest.

'Ohashi?' he repeated gently, as though he had heard the name somewhere but couldn't quite place it.

'That's right. My co-director and your man in Kuala Lumpur.'

Something flicked in blue irises, but that was all. After a moment he said:

'So it's checkmate?'

I leaned forward in my chair.

'You're damn' right it's checkmate. I've got you cooped up here like a chicken in transit to market. If you're good I may ship you on to Saigon later. But not until I'm quite certain you can't do me any harm over there.'

'Don't shout, Paul. I'm still frail. And actually I'm quite happy about all this security around my sickbed. I've been needing a real rest like this for a long time. You'll find me absolutely quiescent and docile.'

'Well, I'm not counting on it.'

Chow came in with the boiled egg, wafer thin toast, coffee, a starched napkin and the morning papers on a tray, just like room service at a Hilton. There is a strong maternal streak in Chow and his first real look at the patient set this twanging. He made clucking sounds as he set down the tray, hauled up a small table, tidied the bed and saw to all those other little details which are supposed to be a loving woman's role but can also be bought by a monthly salary to a carefully chosen domestic. I left them to it and went for a walk in the grounds, having a word out there with my head gardener who was one of the privileged allowed through the gate and whom I caught, happily, hard at work digging, to the surprise of us both.

Like nearly all Malaysian mornings it was a fine one, the hard sun making damp earth steam, with suddenly exposed worms wriggling like mad to get under cover again. A dragonfly hovered over my head in blessing and the taint of exhaust fumes from the city beneath was only very slight. The Tamil with the spade talked away about his plans for a new bank of bougainvillea as though nothing could ever threaten his totally stable world. My home was a kind of Valhalla for resting warriors and the only trouble was that very soon I had to drive down into the fray again while Clem lay in comfort with his too-active brain back to fast ticking.

I had now saved the man's life three times but there wasn't the slightest hint that he meant to put my name up for a citation. Quite the contrary, in fact. I was still public enemy number one on those computer returns, and the thought of this made me angrier. I went back into the house.

A lightly boiled egg and coffee can work wonders and Clem, propped up against fresh pillows, had the world under his hands again. Smoke trickled down from his nostrils on to the jacket of my best Hong Kong silk pyjamas.

'You certainly can pick servants, Paul.'

'If not crews,' I said.

He appeared to miss that.

'I had him turn up the air-conditioning. I hope you don't mind the extra current?'

'It'll be debited against my assets.'

'You're gloomy this morning?'

'Yes.'

I sat down again, sharply conscious that my guest-room was no longer that at all, it belonged to Clem. He hadn't moved from the bed and had no possessions scattered about, but everything was still his. The dog hadn't made this his base as yet, but that could start at anytime. Before long Taro might go out for his walk with a screwed-up message to the world under his right ear. Without any doubt at all Clem would have a way with dogs.

'What's eating you, friend?'

I looked at him.

'Just that I am still the accused and you are still the prosecution.'

He gave me the charm smile that had stayed with him ever since he was six months old.

'A kind of trussed-up prosecution, wouldn't you say? But still terribly interested in hearing the whole of the defence's case.'

'You know damn' well I haven't got a case.'

'But you're working on it? Well, I can wait. It must be my British blood gaining control at last. I'm prepared to do absolutely nothing while others run around. You're planning on doing some running around?'

'I need a sporting chance to make it effective.'

He grinned.

'I'm a great sportsman.'

'Okay. What do you know about Red supply lines into Malaysia? Just assume for a minute that I'm as innocent as I say I am.'

'Why, certainly.'

I glared at him.

'What I *guess* is this. There must be a central dump somewhere, fed from outside the country, with one supply line leading away from it up to Lum Ping's mob in southern Thailand and another to the west coast and from there in junks to Vietnam. I can see, too, why the Reds chose Malaysia as a central distribution point. It has direct access to the Indian Ocean for one thing, and your Navy isn't watching sea routes to Europe on that side of the country. Further, Malaysia is a heavy importer from the west just now, which provides cover for arms coming into the country hidden in normal-seeming shipments. Am I right in all this?'

'So far remarkably.'

'Clem, it's pretty obvious that your boys are fairly thick on the ground in this country. Which means you've had a watch on our ports and at least a fairly accurate check on what came through them. Have you discovered any arms at all hidden in shipments?'

He looked at the ceiling.

'Ah . . . no. Put like that.'

'You've checked Port Swettenham, Malacca, Penang, as well as Singapore?'

'To the best of our ability which, in spite of your suggestion that we're well dug in, is limited.'

'With negative results?'

'So far, yes.'

'Have you actually opened crates in bonded store and that kind of thing?'

'No statement.'

'All right, I'll pass that. Have you followed goods about which you were suspicous to orderers in this country?'

'On one or two occasions.'

'With no results?'

'Nothing conclusive.'

'Have you any idea at all of the location of the Reds' central supply dump in Malaysia?'

'We have some guesses.'

'But you can't point to a place on the map and say it's there?'

'I wouldn't do that.'

'How do you think the Reds are getting supplies to their central dump here?'

He reached out with his good hand for another cigarette, making a play of the invalid's helplessness, which forced me up to help him. He sucked in smoke, let it out slowly and then lifted his eyes.

'Actually, Paul, we had settled for your junk fleet based on Alor Star.'

I sat down again.

'So that's it? I'm in on the deal wholesale and retail? I shove the stuff in at one side of the country and take it out again on the other?'

He looked at the tip of his cigarette.

'You have a reputation for efficiency.'

'And just where are my junks on the east coast supposed to be picking up arms from Europe, or wherever they are coming from?'

'We thought Burma. Your Alor Star fleet operates up the peninsula in Thai waters.'

'But we don't go beyond them to Burma!'

'So you say. But you do go as far as the Andaman islands and
Burma would be on the way back, just a small detour.'

I could see what Clem was driving at. Freighters from Europe,
Russian or Polish, could unload their cargoes at Tavoy in
southern Burma, or perhaps even farther south at the little port
of Mergui, from which point my east coast junks could filter the
arms down into Malaysia. It was certainly a tortuous route, but
this was called for if the object of the whole exercise was total
secrecy. And, of course, it would be. A Red plan for a sudden and
major flare up in Southern Thailand meant that the guerrillas
in that area had to be supplied and with no leak as to how it
was being done. Any direct shipments from Mao's territory
would have to use the risky route through the American-patrolled
South China Sea. But the lanes between Burma and the west
weren't patrolled by anyone, just a vast area of empty sea. The
only east coast portion of that long peninsula stretching from
Bangkok to Singapore that would be watched at all was the
strip of Thailand coast on it. And all that my junks with hidden
arms would have to do as they were passing this was stay well
out to sea.

I sat there with the unpleasant thought that Clem just might
have stumbled on something which incriminated my east coast
fleet. I simply didn't know whether those junks had been running
guns or not. Kim Sung could have been in control over on that
side, too. And he might well have confessed to this during his
interrogation.

'All right,' I said. 'The guerrillas in Southern Thailand need
to get their arms through Malaysia. But Vietnam doesn't. Why
send junks from this country to Ho Chi Min when Iron Curtain
ships are carrying all he needs direct to his ports?'

Clem nodded.

'Sure, they are at the moment. But supposing the war escalated
some more and we blockaded Haiphong completely? Bombed
out the docks? It's right on the cards. And that would leave Ho
entirely dependent on the route from Red China to keep going,
which is the last thing he wants. Ho's idea is to play the field
with his allies, and to keep European Communism very much
in the direct help picture. That man looks ahead. He means to
keep going even if we do stop big ships from getting to his coast.
He then turns to the little ships. And before it is actually vital
to his interests he has an alternative system of supply by junks
worked out.'

'Meaning me?'

'And a lot of others now held in reserve. You were the pilot
scheme. Malaysia was the natural base for such a scheme, really
the only one with Indonesia now out of the picture as a potential

Red ally. This country is good cover, too, as you pointed out touchy about foreign snoopers on its soil. Don't imagine that we think Kim Sung's little cargoes were much of a contribution to Ho's war effort, they were nothing really. But they were establishing a route in. And it's mighty hard for us to control junk traffic, as the Reds know well. Which is why they are putting more and more emphasis on it.'

'And you saw me in total control of this operation through Malaysia?'

'Yes. It looked like we had everything worked out, except the matter of your central supply dump.'

I looked at him for at least half a minute.

'I'll pick some holes in all this, Clem.'

'By all means.'

'First point. I have only six junks operating out of Alor Star. None of my other ships go around to that coast at all. I'm sure you've found that out through Ohashi. That leaves six small junks with limited cargo capacity doing a ferry service between southern Burma and somewhere on the Malaysian coast. Each round trip couldn't be under a thousand miles. How the hell could six ships operating in this way bring down enough stuff to supply a small army in Southern Thailand and still have arms over to send out on Ho Chi Min's emergency junk route through the South China Sea?'

'Easy. You're using a lot of other junks besides your own. Your whole career has been starred with occasions on which you have happily collaborated with Chinese merchants and to mutual advantage.'

That was a gentle kick in the teeth, but I ignored it.

'By your information how many Chinese merchants have junk fleets trading regularly between Malaysia and Burma?'

'Three or four,' Clem said.

'With enough ships to do a big scale job?'

'It's possible. A number of unscheduled sailings even by small steamers could be thrown in for good measure.'

'Have you any record of such unscheduled sailings?'

'No comment.'

'Have you any evidence against Chinese merchants in the Burma trade?'

'Again no statement.'

'You're bluffing,' I said. 'You haven't a thing to back up desk theory. Now let me tell you something. If arms are coming into Malaysia in the quantities you suggest then they have to be coming direct to ports here from the west in big freighters. Since you haven't been able to discover how that's being worked, I will!'

He laughed. The shaking hurt his arm and he stopped.

'Delighted. Just you carry right on with that assignment.'

'Before I do I need all the help you can give.'

'That seems fair.'

'Clem, you must have a general idea of where this central dump is. Even if it's only guesswork.'

'Deduction, actually. We think you'd have your dump somewhere in the centre of the country, and in the northern half. It would have to be accessible to road transport and also provide a legitimate excuse for a great deal of traffic to it. There are a lot of projects in the country at the moment providing this kind of cover, but I will say that so far we haven't connected you with any of them.'

'That's a comfort.'

'You can't say I'm not putting my cards on the table. And in a way I'm really admitting partial failure.' He grinned. 'We feel that you looked for some place that gave you access to Thailand but not by any obvious route. Which sort of puts us near jungle country, possibly the main ridge. There could then be a secret covered trail all the way, ending up just beyond the area which you investigated for us. It's probably a long walk, but what's that to Chinese manpower specially imported for the job? They've had plenty of training at that kind of thing, down through Laos into Vietnam.'

'Are you suggesting a hidden road good enough for trucks?'

'No, not in that country. It'll be porterage all the way. Except where they use boats on that river. And porterage over the mountains down to the east coast as well. For that rendezvous with your junks. In both cases just a track, but well hidden from the air. And all this has been going for quite some time, too. There are indications that the big blow up in southern Thailand is scheduled for soon.'

This had been a local bogey for some time, America's main ally in south Asia suddenly squeezed from two sides, in the north by direct infiltration from Red-controlled territories, and in the south from the new guerrilla army it was known Lum Ping was building up. Clem had been up against a very acute intelligence problem. The Thais have allowed American troops into their country, but Malaysia remains highly touchy about independence and neutrality, a situation which makes the building up of a good undercover network difficult. It seemed probable that there were still a lot of big holes in Clem's spy net, even if it had caught me.

There was a sudden intrusion into the picture I was beginning to build up, and that was from the thought that Teng's enterprises would fit into it rather well. The town which he practically owned wasn't quite in the centre of Malaysia, but it was well north, and also directly at the foot of the main range which meant that jungle came down practically to its suburbs. It would be a long hike from Kampar to the east coast or to Thailand, but Chinese coolies could do it on rice bags hanging from their belts.

I was conscious of Clem trying to read my thoughts, but telepathy hasn't yet been put on any training schedules. When they get the technique of that perfected spying as a business is going to go into total eclipse, which will be a great relief of tension all around. And think of the money that will be saved.

'Time for a beer,' I said, getting up. 'Like one?'

'Sure. Talking has scraped my throat. Paul, I do admire your admirable control.'

'It's from a clear conscience.'

When I glasses of Carlsberg I stood looking down at him, sipping mine.

'Clem, why did you want to run from that helicopter?'

'It was British,' he answered simply.

'And this country is still a British intelligence sphere of influence? Americans keep out?'

'No. Mostly we have the happiest co-operation.'

'Mostly but not always. And you wouldn't be too keen to have certain British parties still functioning down in Singapore know that you had arrangements to clear small landing grounds around this country for quick private business trips in and out.'

'Well, you can put it like that.'

'You bet I can! The helicopter was out looking for you on information received. The papers say it was up north showing the flag of mutual defence to the cheering natives. But that was one big blind. A craft on a goodwill tour rests at night, it doesn't go out on patrol.'

'I'd have thought that,' he agreed.

'Singapore got the word about cute little village girls you hire to keep the grass down on certain remote selected strips. And they decided to pounce the next time the grass cutters went out. To catch you. And return you, via Singapore, to Saigon. Just a nice friendly little gesture to cut the C.I.A. down to size. You know something? I sense a certain conflict of interests going on over the body of prostrate Malaysia.'

Clem's one good hand crushed out a cigarette, grinding the butt down on to porcelain. He might have once again decided to give up the vice.

'Paul, don't start waving your new-found patriotism at me. It's one of your acts which I find yawn-making. Because if I ever met up with a good-going neo-colonialist, it's you. Though the rudeness may make you wince, you're in this country for the trading and damn all else. And friend, I've got a fat file to prove it.'

It pleased me to see him irritated.

'I have to go now,' I said gently. 'I'll be away for quite some time, possibly overnight. But Chow will look after you.'

'Sure he will. Depart with my blessing. I always like that Japanese ceremonial farewell, don't you?'

'What?'

'Kindly have deep regard for your health.'

The electrified gates clicked shut behind the Audi. There was always an odd little sizzling noise as the current went into circuit again. I drove slowly down the rest of my hill, the road curving through thick undergrowth topped by massive trees, each bend perfect for an ambush even thoug⸍ ⸍⸍⸍ ⸍⸍⸍⸍⸍ ⸍⸍⸍⸍ only five minutes away. I had thought of pu⸍⸍⸍⸍⸍ ⸍⸍⸍ ⸍⸍⸍⸍⸍ ⸍⸍ght down at the edge of my property, but it would have been too conspicuous and also cost twice as much. No one shot at me but as I approached two stone pillars marking the entrance to the public highway a man stepped out from amongst the traveller's palms where he had been sheltering.

I knew him well. He was a Singapore police inspector called Kang who, in these days of the island's total independence, should have no excuse at all for spending so much time in Malaysia. His answer to this was that the police forces had to maintain close liaison despite new and somewhat artificial national barriers. It was my belief that the man was paid more than his municipal salary for work done on behalf of interests who preferred to be nameless, but had their headquarters somewhere in London.

Kang wasn't dressed like any loiterer, impeccable as usual; his expensively tailored white suit with knife creases down the trousers. He wore a formal collar with hand-knitted scarlet tie, this in no way indicating his political convictions which had been tempered by years and seniority. Though you can never be absolutely certain I was reasonably sure that the inspector did not see his future in terms of Mao Tse Tung.

'Good morning, Paul.' His English was as smooth as the rest of him.

He opened the car door and got into the seat beside me.

'I'd like a lift into town, if you don't mind. I sent my taxi away. I was calling on you for morning coffee, but you're not being very hospitable these days. And I seemed to notice a slight excess of Sikhs. Surly ones, too.'

'I've been getting threatening letters.'

'I see. So now no one is allowed up there? Not even old friends?'

'That's right. I meet old friends by appointment at the club.'

'Difficult to make arrangements when your phone is disconnected.'

'There aren't many people I want to see. I'm living the life of a recluse while I give my liver a rest.'

'And you have no one staying with you?'

'I hate house-guests. They upset routine. What are you after me for this time?'

'Flying an airplane without a pilot's licence,' Kang said sweetly.

I nearly put the car in a drainage ditch, that steering is dangerously sensitive.

'Ridiculous.'

'You were seen through the cockpit windows by some very unhappy policemen up in Kelantan. Definitely at the controls and unmistakably identified.'

'Even if this were true, what has it got to do with Singapore?'

'I was called in for consultation.'

'Like hell you were! You got the word that I had gone to ground in Kedah and turned up two weeks later in Kelantan. A lot of suspicious minds decided that this might be dangerous to some security or other and sent you haring up here to look into things. On one of your overtime duties.'

'So you admit to being in the border jungles?'

'Yes.'

'What were you doing?'

'Prospecting for gold.'

'I didn't know the Americans were interested in Malaysian gold potential.'

'They're not. They've got all they need in Fort Knox. I wanted it for Harris and Company. I'm greedy.'

'You deny working for the Americans?'

'I work for myself.'

Kang sighed. It was audible above a very quiet engine. Then something extremely hard made contact with my left rib cage. I know a gun when I feel it.

'I hate to do things this way, Paul. And to an old friend. But you're driving us both to the airport. There are two seats reserved on the Singapore plane. It was considerate of you to come out from your fortress just in time to let us catch it.'

CHAPTER EIGHT

I DRIVE FAST enough to make fastening the seat belt a necessary precaution and had clipped the buckle at my waist on getting into the Audi. Unclipping it again for a sudden escape from that gun was an impractical proposition. Kang had kept himself completely mobile by not bothering about his belt. We moved into traffic in the direction of the airport with the silence between us chill enough to bring down the temperature even in the tropics and under a steel roof.

'Let's see your extradition order,' I said suddenly.

'It wasn't necessary to go to all that trouble.'

'I'm a citizen of Malaysia and you can't export me to Singapore in this manner. I have my rights.'

'Actually, in this case you don't. All the formalities have been arranged. It's relatively easy if you are a policeman. We'll be able to avoid customs, too.'

'Is this an arrest?'

'Nothing like that. You're coming south with me of your own free will to answer a few questions.'

'Thanks for defining the position,' I said.

He kept the gun against my ribs. 'Not at all.'

I took a deep breath.

'I have always suspected that under the smooth exterior you were at heart a twisted two-faced bastard.'

The inspector produced a modest little cough.

'All policeman become used to abuse early on in their careers. It has no effect on them at all.'

We came to a red light. If Kang noticed that I had brought the Audi to a halt behind a very large truck loaded with scrap iron he made no comment. I hated to do what was coming next to my nice little car, but there was no alternative. The truck began to move on amber, I waited for green, which put five yards between us. I slid into first, then jammed the accelerator hard to the floor.

In five yards lengthened to nearly six by the truck's movement we reached thirty miles an hour, smashing into the lumbering mass in front with force enough to sprawl me over the wheel and whack Kang's head hard against the windscreen. I don't know what happened to his revolver, but it ceased to threaten me. I got the belt buckle loose and jumped out into the road, blared at by a taxi and just touched by its offside fender. I made it to pavement and continued running. Behind was some considerable din, shouting, then the peep of a whistle which I didn't think came from Kang.

Batu Road offers a splendid selection of tributary lanes and I swung into one of them, then another, with such hue and cry as had been started soon left well behind. I walked, mopping my face. In the first shopping street I stopped a pedicab. I don't like manpowered transport and normally never use it, but one of those contraptions was the last thing a man on the run would be expected to jump into in order to get anywhere fast and it seemed policy to suggest that I was one of the world's leisured. So was the downtrodden Malay who did the pedalling. At one point he got up to seven miles an hour, but thought better of this and dropped back to five. He was also a bell addict and rang this continuously which almost guaranteed that no one would take the slightest notice of our passage.

Movement created a breeze and I sat in it wondering just what police procedure was likely to be in the case of a driver who hits and runs, but not in his vehicle. Their evidence was a crumpled Audi and identification of the owner would be a matter of about ten minutes even if Kang was in no state to assist them. They could then try to phone my home, which would draw a blank, or visit it, which would draw another, for I was quite certain that my retired policemen would never allow active members of their service through those gates without a search warrant. The offence in question simply didn't rate the issue of such a warrant. I had the feeling, also, that the inspector from Singapore wouldn't be spending any more time with his Malaysian colleagues than he could help, wanting to get clear to start up a personal hunt, and without official assistance. Kang wouldn't expect me to be thinking about food at a time like this, which made the restaurant I was making for seem the safest bet. It was certainly early for lunch but the place would be quite ready to give me discreet sanctuary at any time. I paid well for their discretion.

Yung Ching Wa's is a six-story Chinese house of pleasure, which means that it is mainly concerned with serving food. A lot of other things besides eating go on in the building during the twenty-four hours a day it is open, but all such minor activities are put in proper perspective by a continuous and splendid aroma of vast meals either being served or in the process of preparation. The building is nearly always noisy, with fat women waddling around in the passages amiably flashing gold teeth. It has a lift which is in constant movement, and around the open cage of this twist concrete stairs, also bearing a heavy traffic, these latter being regarded by contented clients as a suitable place in which to spit. Western standards of hygiene are unknown and would be thought ridiculous. Once or twice I have glanced through an open hatch into the kitchens, only to avert my head at once. The duck and mushrooms in chili sauce are a gastronomic triumph for which the place is celebrated as far north as Sungei Patani and Betty and I usually settled for that *plat de maison* on our weekly luncheon dates.

I paid my languid pedal man triple the correct fare, but to keep his mouth shut, not out of any extreme of humanity. The stairs were strangely deserted and I reached our fourth-floor private room without meeting anyone at all. Even the usually continuous clattering of a rope operated dumb waiter was silent and there were no high-pitched cries from the thousand or so girls who were connected with the establishment in one way or another.

By accident I had hit Yung Chin Wa's only siesta time and it was interesting that the cooks and others did take a period for rest, something I hadn't suspected. A little mental arithmetic suggested that this reduced the average working week in the place to a mere hundred and sixty hours. The Chinese restaurant business has sweated its labour for four thousand years and always will.

As a setting for romantic secret meetings the private room left a few things to be desired, the chief of these being a comfortable sofa. I wouldn't have thought that well-heeled Chinese business men had any masochistic streaks at all, but that expensive privacy was furnished with a hard wooden bench along one wall, two upright chairs and a table. There was also a mirror suffering from eroding damp, a Chinese pin-up girl calendar, a spittoon, one pot holding three dying canna lilies, and a telephone with a place of honour all its own on a little stand, for much business was conducted from these compartments for high living. The one window looked out on a ventilation shaft in the middle of the building and was the chief source of cooking smells. An electric fan on a bracket whirred day and night, stirring the tepid air but never managing to push out a reek of stale tobacco smoke.

Europeans almost never came here, using garden restaurants with tinkling fountains more suited to their fancy even if the food was greatly inferior. The phone which I lifted at once wasn't a pay instrument, local calls were on the house and, though you were supposed to leave the price of long distance, the average dinner check appeared to include six minutes to London. I got the airport at once and asked for a seat on the three o'clock flight to Penang.

'Name please?'

'Bonder,' I said. 'Eric Bonder.'

Eric is my banker, a full-blooded man, most of it in his face from whisky intake, who has a tendency to clap me on the back when we meet at the club bar, but I have always suspected that it would give him a kind of fiscal pleasure, if the day ever came, to let me know in the nicest possible way that Harris and Company were no longer considered a good bet for an extended overdraft. He would resent the liberty I had taken, but that didn't trouble me.

Service was always slow at Yung Ching Wa's, and during the siesta hour it took twenty minutes. The girl who arrived, yawning, was our usual attendant, little Miss Spring Anemone. It is a pretty name, but that was about all the waitress had got as her heritage, and coming from a hungry home she had settled in at Yung's to eat her way into the future. The result of a steady application towards this end was that, though only four feet eleven inches in height, she had to come through the door sideways.

'Oh, it's you,' she said in Cantonese, and with controlled surprise. She was chewing something. 'What do you want?'

'Tiger beer.'

'All right. You eating later?'

'Probably.'

'Your woman coming?'

'I don't think so.'

'Don't take the duck to-day. Pork.'

'What's happened to the ducks?'

She shook her head, keeping the chef's secret, edging her way back into the corridor, and pulling the door shut again which was an automatic reflex.

Without a meal to occupy me, and the company over it, sitting alone in that box was a little like making use of the waiting-room in a station on a railway line that is about to be closed down. Time didn't appear to move at all. Anemone brought me my beer, gossiped about the latest murder, and then decided that she wasn't paid to be a hostess. At ten minutes past twelve the phone rang, and the bell made me jump.

One of the things which is efficient at Yung's is the switchboard, it has to be to keep the clientele. Calls are put through at once, and to the right cubicle, just in case a guest, as a result of the news, has to make quick use of one of the seven separate exits provided. The building has so many annexes probing out in different directions that it is improbable that even a detachment of police could properly surround the place to plug all escape holes. An irate wife is simply no problem at all, and the staff are geared to deal with this routine. An acquaintance of mine had even been assisted to travel down from the fifth floor in the dumb waiter, with girls at each hatch level spinning the ropes through their hands.

'Ching Wa Tsu here,' I said in singing Cantonese.

'What?' It was Betty's voice.

'Well, correct that to Paul. It's nice you're coming after all. But you didn't need to ring up.'

'I am *not* coming. But a very odd thing has happened. I'm glad I've got you.'

Somehow that made me uneasy.

'Brief me quickly, dear.'

'Paul, what's been going on this morning?'

'Tell me about you first.'

'I was called down to casualty about half an hour ago. Normally I have nothing to do with it. If it's a surgery case I'm simply notified and . . .'

'Betty, I'm not interested in hospital procedure. Why were you called to casualty?'

'To meet a Singapore police inspector who had been brought in unconscious.'

'Did you say *meet* him?'

'Yes. You could say it was semi-social.'

'Oh.'

'You know about him?'

'Yes. Was he—ah—badly hurt?'

'Apart from an egg on his head, no. And no question of concussion.'

'That's a relief.'

'You mean you had something to do with the bump?'

'Indirectly.'

'Paul! You haven't hit a policeman?'

'No. Though I've done worse things. What did he want?'

'That's what I don't understand. Though I do understand enough to make me feel a little sick. Your friend was very smooth.'

'He always is.'

'They'd given him some tea. He was sitting there sipping it. He just looked up and said, terribly politely, "I'd be most grateful, Dr. Hill, if you could give me the name of the restaurant where you usually lunch with Mr. Harris. I find it has slipped my mind. Probably something to do with this bump." And then he laughed.'

'You told him?'

'But I *had* to! And why should I try to cover up from the police?'

'No reason. How long ago was this?'

'About half an hour. I couldn't get to a phone right away. Paul, he knew all about us! Have we been watched?'

'I have been. You're all right. Just forget it.'

'*Forget* it?'

'Look, Betty this has nothing to do with my meeting you for lunch here. It's just certain parties keeping tab. It's one of my career hazards.'

'And you don't think something like this happening is a career hazard to me?'

'Not in the least. But we'll go into that later. Just now I can't linger. And thanks very much for ringing.'

'Paul!'

Her cry seemed to linger in the little room, even after the click. I opened the door. The passage was still empty, though there were now some feet on the stairs, echoing from concrete. The lift was droning, too.

Inspector Kang had made the tactical error of incarcerating himself in a very slow-moving metal crate. He looked out at me between floors, and through two sets of decorated steel netting as I passed down. I nodded, then started taking three steps at a time.

Above me I could hear the self-operated lift go into an emergency stop. High up in the building the wheels of the mechanism clanged, then the counter weights changed direction. It was going to be a slow descent.

Mr. Eric Bonder, slightly less red in the face than usual, was passed through the barrier on to the tarmac without a hand coming down on my shoulder. The alien policeman from Singapore had held to his lone-wolf act and couldn't be everywhere at once.

I had a delightful flight north in a three-quarters empty plane in which the hostess, who could effectively swing her hips even coming down a narrow aisle, seemed much more concerned than these girls usually are about the comfort of her male passengers. And since I was for once a good deal younger than the other business men on board there was a truly personal touch in everything she did for me. She had tiny hands which fluttered like butterflies and then settled suddenly on a man's arm, or thigh. When I offered her a drink she said it was against the rules and accepted. We sat together for some time without bothering much about the view. It is a pleasantly informal airline in which the staff are permitted to be human in their approach, and Miss Lin told me all about her ambition for a career as a cabaret artiste. She had trained as a contortionist and did her act in two little strips of tiger skin, but was heavily handicapped by respectable parents who wanted her to marry and have a lot of Chinese babies. The air service had been a compromise, but a dream of true glamour still prodded her. She wished, she said, that she could show me the bit where she brought her head up under her buttocks and smiled at the audience. Miss Lin was certain this would be a show stopper, and so was I.

Disillusionment about my personal appeal only came as we moved into sight of Penang Island, when it turned out that the hostess had mistaken me for another European whose photograph she had recently seen in a newspaper and whose life work was booking floor shows for the big Singapore and Bangkok hotels. She gave me a smile as I got off, but this tinged with sadness, as though life was always letting her down.

I went over in the ferry from Port Wellesley thinking once again how much Penang reminded me of Hong Kong, the same island out in the water, the same high ground behind the city dotted with the homes of the prosperous, these getting bigger towards the peaks. The British have left curiously indelible marks and a tone of colonial life which refuses to be extinguished. The port has always just missed becoming a major one because Singapore is too near and sucks away the trade, but it has a certain charm from this, bustle moderated, the tempo of any day broken by long pauses for refreshing recreation which has tended to be based on alcohol. I had once, when uprooting from Singapore, contemplated moving my business headquarters to this island, but decided against it, chiefly because of that infectious tempo.

Not all empires have been built by hard unremitting toil. In portions of theirs the British quite often gained power, and from it riches, simply by being first on an unexploited spot and then socially ostracising anyone from other western lands who tried to muscle in until the wives of the interlopers forced their men to give up and go home. All of which makes the contemporary insolvency of the old motherland, now stripped of dividend-earning colonies, less surprising than it might seem. I know my secret weakness for the good life and in Penang could easily have gone to seed, taking Harris and Company with me.

From the bund I took a taxi to the offices of Lung Fing and Partners, Ltd. Lung was an old associate of mine. It would be too much to call him a trusted friend, but in the past our interests had coincided often enough for an understanding to have emerged to which Lung had come to attach some of the trappings of a blood relation. He always greeted me with a tear in each slightly rheumy eye and had on occasion said I was like a son to him. How long this intimacy would have stood up under no profits I don't know, but it had never been put to real test because all our deals made money.

When I had been engaged in close support of insurgent forces in Sumatra Lung had handled the supply end, and very deftly indeed, which was why I had come to see him now. This, plus the fact that he was the biggest contractual employer of lightermen in Penang, as well as owning half of the bonded go-downs. There was no lift to his third-floor offices, you went under cool and massive arches into cool and dim corridors and walked up.

The old man didn't seem to me a day older, but then he had always been too ancient to age. He rose shakily from behind a massive teak desk which ought to have emphasized the mortality of the frail creature who used it, but somehow didn't. The Ho Chi Min wisp beard he affected was blown back towards his ears from a central parting by a portable fan.

'Paul Harris!' he squeaked, holding out skeletal hands in a demonstrative gesture unusual with his race. 'My boy.'

'Hallo, Dad.'

He liked that.

'Always you call me Dad, eh?'

'You were always a father figure worth watching.'

'Sit down, sit down. There.'

I sat on his side of the desk where he could see all of me, old eyes taking comfort from still unwasted muscles. It took a long time to get around to business, in fact I never did get around to the real business at all, which would have been a sharp error in strategy. Instead I gave him information he already had documented about the new shipping company to which I was committed, indicating that I was out drumming up trade even before we had funnels re-painted in the new line colours which were to be red, white, and blue with a green strip zig-zagging through all three of these shades to indicate that we were cancelling out the bad old days. Penang was to be a major port of call and Dad, out of quasi-paternal sentiment, was going to see that a lot of crates in his sheds were stamped for shipment in our vessels.

He thought this very funny, one of the best jokes he had heard in months, good enough almost to bring on his asthma. When he had recovered sufficiently he wiped his face with a silk handkerchief and then practically whispered through it in Cantonese that, alas, his business had nothing to do with shipping as such, only unloading and storage. I ought to know this well enough, surely?

'My dear Lung Fing, the fact remains that you are the President of the Penang Chinese Chamber of Commerce, a director of the Ho Kwa bank, you own half the more ruinous property in the town, to say nothing of that new hotel. You're the big man, in fact. Everyone bows when you come into a room. It's why I feel so proud when you call me your son.'

The agitated rat noises came again. After them he said sweetly:

'You know I'll do what I can. And I wish you every success, Paul, every success. But a new company must establish itself. It must offer a unique service.'

'By which you mean cut rates outwith the local maritime agreement?'

He didn't confirm that exactly, only stroked his beard down into place on his shirt.

'Just what do you want?' That was cautious.

'At the moment I'm our company's promotion man. I'm contacting personally every potential customer of any size. And it occurred to me that the one person who could give me a clear lead as to what companies are using a good deal of shipping at the moment is you. After all, you unload for them. And you despatch out to Malaysian destinations. Nothing moves in or out of Penang that you don't know about.'

'True, yes. But to give this information . . . I'm thinking of business ethics.'

'Business ethics are something to insist on against your competitors. I'm not one of them. I'd never be such a fool as to set up in opposition to you.'

He liked that, too. After another half hour of palaver he agreed to give me a session with his head clerk, also aged, a man with whom I had dealt before and if not liked, respected.

It was an interesting hour out in that main office where they had to use electric light in the afternoon. When it was over I went back and took a ceremonial farewell of Dad. He didn't kiss me good-bye, but there was a moment when I thought he was going to.

I went down those stairs wondering how the old man ever managed to get up them. Perhaps he didn't, perhaps he lived in his office, the head clerk unrolling a bed-mat alongside the teak desk at eleven-thirty p.m. when it was time to bring a routine business day to its close. People who resent Chinese efficiency generally overlook the hours these orientals put in to amass their profits and spread their influence in the world. There are moments when I am unhappily certain that the swelling hordes of western clock watchers are due for some really nasty shocks in the next couple of decades.

The street outside still held the last light and was full of Chinese who hadn't managed the first rung in the success ladder and were without any expectations of charity from those who had, but remained undepressed about what life had done to them. Perhaps it is the climate, you may starve, but you won't starve cold.

I emerged from a long colonnade on to pavement flanked with huge palms, walking with a lot to think about and in the general direction of the old hotel where I was going to treat myself, after a series of gin Collins, to a good old-fashioned apoplexy inviting dinner starting with oxtail soup and ending with welsh rarebit, all nine courses served in the down draught from one of those vast bladed fans which look like propellers from obsolete aircraft. I had missed lunch and Lung Fing must have seen signs of this for he had asked me whether I was hungry. When I said yes the old skinflint ordered scented Amoy and a plate of half a dozen of the thinnest rice biscuits I had ever seen. He had then smoked my cheroots, inhaling them to stave off the craving for his daily pipe of opium.

I was fairly certain that I hadn't let Lung's head clerk see just how interesting I found an area of the facts we uncovered jointly, but they had certainly sent me off on a new line of speculation. I would never have made much of a scientist because I like to get my theory first by a kind of clutching intuition and then shape the facts to fit it. It's a much more entertaining course than a plodding progress to an inescapable conclusion. Anyway a considerable number of inescapable conclusions just aren't the truth, like Clem's on my activities. Perhaps I've been lucky, but at least six times out of ten my approach has worked out, and with some pretty wild theories as the original premise, too.

There was much to keep me preoccupied as I walked along, and I paid no attention to the traffic, not noticing a car that must have been slowing down to pull in parallel to my progress. Attention was smacked back to the outside world by a burst of sub-machine gun fire with me as the target. The fact that the first round of seven or eight high velocity bullets didn't hit target must have been due to the gunman not taking enough time to get his range, or perhaps someone in the car accidentally joggled his elbow. At any rate a great deal of irrelevant glass shattered beyond me. The second burst would have zeroed home all right if it hadn't been for the palm tree I was suddenly behind, a blessedly plump old specimen shaped rather like a sprouting pineapple. I could literally feel, so close had the two of us become, lead whacking deep into fibrous core, and after that second burst fronds crackled above my head from the poor plant's trembling.

Someone started to scream, though it wasn't me, my throat was parched dry as a prairie after a seven year drought and not a whisper could have worked its way up over arid roughness. The car was just moving, and I kept moving, too, around that splendid generosity of nature deeply rooted in amongst electricity cables.

I'm glad to say that I rallied to the point of putting one bullet from my Colt through a side window of the Austin saloon 1957 vintage. The hired killers had been told there would be no resistance and they didn't like this development. The Austin leaped away, leaving me and the palm and someone screaming, though the road seemed suddenly remarkably empty.

An avoidance of police interrogations is instinctive with me and a taxi travelling south was my next target. I didn't actually stop this with my Colt, but the driver braked noisily and let me in. If he had seen any of the action he didn't want to admit this, just accelerated fast, which was exactly what I wanted.

I leaned back on cushions and found a handkerchief. Dear, quiet, ex-Colonial Penang. Dinner was off. I was getting out of the place.

And then, rather late in the day, I remembered that Lung Fing's first cousin's son was Teng, that man who practically owned his town near the main mountain range.

I went south by train, even though this would mean getting up at an ungodly hour when no one would have any kind of breakfast ready for me. There is something infinitely soothing about a first-class, air-conditioned sleeping compartment. You are in transit, moving in life, but in a manner which puts no subconscious strain on the nerves, rolling on wheels towards a destination, with all the cosy certainty of arrival which kept the Victorians so happily immune to contemporary tensions. My door was locked and at Port Wellesley station I had bought a packet of British potato crisps, a cooked half chicken and a bottle of eight year old Glen Grant malt whisky which was miraculously sitting up on a buffet shelf behind the cash register. I had also bought a paperback *Gideon of the Yard* which promised to tell me more about police methods than I really wanted to know.

Another night I would have finished the *Gideon* before switching out the berth light, but I was suffering from a slight reaction to a day of some activity and I had also been generous to myself with the malt. It wasn't perhaps a deep sleep which took me, and I was woken from it by a heavier rumbling than had been the background noise, plus a loud, metallic clanking from just outside the carriage wall. I needed a moment to realize that this din meant we were on the bridge that crosses the South Perak river.

It was then I noticed a crack. The door I had locked was open an inch, admitting a dim light from blue corridor bulbs. I remembered that a pass key allowed the attendant in with morning tea. I watched, more frozen than alerted for action, as the crack widened. A hand came in for the switch on wall panelling. Something else came in, too, the snout of a heavy service revolver. There was going to be sudden light and then sudden death.

Probably a man with nerves in better shape would have waited until a door opened wide enough to reveal more of the assassin's body, but I had the sharp feeling of having used up my uncertain ration of luck for some time ahead. I fired at fingers on a switch, but from an awkward shooting position. The noise of the gun sounded loud enough to panic a train, but it probably didn't wake neighbouring sleepers if the bridge crossing hadn't already.

The door shut. I didn't hear the click. I got the berth light on and for a moment had the feeling of waking from a nightmare. Then I saw splintered panelling about the switch. The air-conditioning was dealing with a slight smell of toasted rubber. There was no one in the corridor and no one opened a compartment door to look out as we moved on to quieter track.

If the police decided to dig that bullet out of teak veneer and start up an investigation on the evidence it offered this was going to mean some embarrassing moments in the manager's office at the Kuala Lumpur branch of the Chartered Bank of South Asia and Australia. I was still travelling as Eric Bonder. The name was printed on a little card in a door holder.

I reached home decidedly red-eyed. You get that way sitting up through the small hours with a Colt on your sheeted lap, staring fixedly in one direction. Clem, however, against pillows looked as contented as a baby who has had a really good four a.m. feed and been properly burped for sleep after it. His blue eyes, clear and innocent, fixed on me. He concentrated for a moment, then said:

'Welcome home. How are things?'

'I've been looking after my health.'

'So I see. You might have had a shave before waking me. What time is it?'

'Six-fifteen. And all seems well up on the hill. No alarms, according to the guards.'

'None that reached me, at any rate. If I had a more placid home environment to offer I'd lure Chow away from you. I get the feeling you've never really made full use of the man's talents. Take a week off sometime with your feet up. I like it here.'

I looked at Clem in dead silence for some time. Then I said:

'Do you still believe I'm operating for the Reds?'

'Why do you ask?'

'I need a friend.'

He smiled.

'You've come to the wrong department. I'm not allowed to cultivate them. Though I'm prepared to be neutral even if I can't offer love.'

'Thanks.'

'Shave and have breakfast with me,' he suggested generously.

So I did that. It was early even for Chow's service, but he rallied to the occasion with a holiday offering of hot scones and bacon and eggs though I couldn't see a holiday ahead. We ate out on the verandah. Clem, in my absence and against doctor's orders, had become walking wounded. It was only with the second cup of coffee that I remembered my other guest in the bathroom.

'No trouble with your ex-nurse?'

Clem shook his head.

'Absolutely none. She made a bit of noise yesterday afternoon, perhaps for food. Probably Chow fed her because there was silence again. It looks rather as though she has opted for sleep in the bathtub.'

'I see your arm's in plaster?'

'That's right. The nice lady doctor. We got on fine. I've recovered from prejudice. I think she knows her job. But she was a bit irritated about having her car searched on the way in.'

'What did she say about no nurse?'

'Incurious. I told her the lady had gone. And from the state of my pulse and so on it was clear that Chow was doing a good job as substitute.'

'No sounds from the bathroom while Betty was here?'

'None that I heard. Anyway, your doctor wasn't in a very observant state. I think she had something on her mind. It could have been you.'

When I made no comment Clem nodded.

'How romantic are things?'

'Not very.'

'Because she has a husband?'

'There is that. And a lot besides.'

'Come on, come on, it does us all good to bare our hearts. And we've nothing in your file on this.'

'Betty isn't relevant to my file.'

'Everything is relevant, including your dog. Incidentally, that's a nice dog, but he's not properly integrated. You ought to get him a bitch and start breeding Tosas.'

'He does all right in the park without a home life.'

'Like you?'

'Shut up, Clem. I don't feel like talking about myself this morning.'

'We were talking about the lady doctor, remember?'

'What about her?'

'I'm interested in her background. She's good. Why is she out here?'

'A challenge to duty.'

'I didn't know people had those any more. This grows fascinating.'

I stared at a groomed lawn, part of the total tidiness about my domestic patterns.

'Betty came out here because ... well, it was a new opportunity.'

'Is she under contract?'

'She had one for three years. It's been renewed.'

'Let's get back to motivation. The British woman doctor coming out East. And not as a missionary, or anything.'

'You mayn't be so far off it with that missionary idea. She's the daughter of a fundamentalist parson up in the English Midlands. Brought up to strict Bible punching. There was an inflexible moral rule for everything. She lost faith, but still wants the moral rules. God is dead, but good works remain. No, that's not quite it.'

'What is?' Clem asked.

'I suppose the need for a purpose remains. She found her purpose in medicine. But the practise of it in Britain blunted the purpose somewhat. She came out here to get back to first principles. Also ...'

'Yes?' Clem said gently.

'I think the distinction of being a woman surgeon in an eastern country appealed to her. She's a bit of an actress.'

'And we're not actors?'

'Not as much. I don't think you see yourself as Clement P. Winburgh from the C.I.A. posed against a blood red Vietnam sunset.'

'You don't know me, boy. That's in my mind all the time.
What the hell do you think I do it for? The pay?'

'All right. You and Betty Hill.'

'Not a Harris girl at all, I'd say.'

'She's nobody's girl but her own. That's been the trouble. I
thought at first she didn't give a damn what other people
thought of her, women especially. But that's all the act. She
comes into a room deliberately not seeing anyone in it. She has
to be claimed, she never claims. You go out towards her and
maybe after a time she moves a bit towards you.'

'You've spent some nights gnawing the edge of your sheet
thinking about this?'

'Maybe I have.'

'The attraction is just raw sex?'

'I don't know. We haven't tried it out.'

'What? Oh, fellow, you need help. What's her husband?'

'A poet. He came along as Betty's guest. Then got a job
lecturing in English literature at the university here. Tom's a
simpler case, or at least seems so to me. A bottle a day man
because the world hasn't recognized his genius. Only the *New
Statesman*.'

'Any children?'

'One daughter aged seven. Totally spoiled by Mummy, Daddy
and the Chinese Amah. When Penny doesn't get her own way
she kicks everyone in sight. I've seen her do it. And no one has
ever tried to stop her with a good clout.'

'You resent the child as a challenge to your plans?'

'I have no plans,' I said.

'Why can't you choose a nice simple emotional set-up and
be comfortable?'

'It's not in my nature.'

Clem asked me to butter and Frank Cooper marmalade him
another piece of toast. While I was doing it he made a polite
inquiry about what I had been up to in the last twenty-four
hours. I told him most of the truth. From his expression it might
all have been any sub-agent's normal day.

'The situation is clear up to a point,' I said. 'Either the
Americans, the British or the Reds are trying to liquidate me.
I thought for a time of including on the list some of my business
rivals, but have left them out. Homicide is an admission of
commercial defeat. Still, the Americans, the British or the Reds
make up quite a large field for one man to play on his own.'

'Isn't it nice you've got a real fortress to come home to,' Clem
said with his particular brand of inhumanity. 'Aren't you worried
about helicopters at all?'

I looked at him.

'You don't mean you think that Kang might call in that goodwill flight again?'

'Why not, since he's tried all other ways to get you and failed? And there's plenty of nice smooth grass out there to land on.'

'But we're right in the middle of a capital city.'

'It wouldn't matter about them being seen. They just use temporary rotor failure as an excuse for a set down and apologize later. The whole operation wouldn't take long. By the time there was any real interest from the local police the machine could be twenty miles away. The weakness of perimeter fortifications in our time is that the chopper just pops over them.'

'I don't like this,' I said.

'Well, don't worry about it too much. If they land I'm going to tell them that I've been held prisoner here for the last six weeks and got shot by you when I was trying to escape.'

I got up and left. As a staff to lean on in time of trouble Clem was a piece of collapsible rubber. I went to my bedroom, reloaded the Colt, and took it along to a bathroom door. When I had unlocked this I kicked it open.

Mrs. Hasmah had opted for sleep all right, the long one. She was lying full length in the bathtub, clothed, and from each of her wrists was a trail of dried blood to the drain pipe. The razor blade was half hidden under one of her thighs, a Wilkinson stainless.

CHAPTER NINE

THE DEAD NEARLY ALWAYS seem almost unbelievably diminished, as though personality had been let out like air from a Lilo, what is left pitiable in its unimportance. Mrs. Hasmah would have killed me without compunction if it had been in her orders, but there wasn't even a reminiscence of menace in that slumped body. Coffined by the tub she looked composed in final immunity, ready for collection and disposal. In her case the collection had to be delayed for a time.

I checked that the passage was empty, turned the key, and locked the door. The nurse's case was on the floor. In it I found a dispenser packet of blades, as though the woman had travelled about equipped for all eventualities, even the need to slash her own wrists. It was impossible for me to assess time of death, though the body had passed beyond rigor mortis, already in that process of dissolution which made leaving it here for long out of the question. The little room didn't have air-conditioning, but there was an extractor fan which would have its use, and I switched this on. The sound of the motor might be heard by

Chow but would only suggest that the prisoner wanted air. It would also add a little to the time I had, though it was quite plain that the situation up on my hill had changed sharply. Clem might be nobbled for as long as I needed, and happily quiescent in this state, but a body in a bathroom left me with only hours before electrified gates had to be opened to allow in the police. I didn't in the least fancy the idea of a secret grave somewhere in my grounds, the law had to be brought in when I was ready, or at least when I hoped I was ready.

In the meantime it was important that no one else in the house found out about Mrs. Hasmah. Concealment ought to be relatively easy, demanding a small performance from me, then a key turned. Chow was fully occupied in his role as substitute nurse, my cook never came into the main bungalow and his wife, who cleaned, was far from bright. The two gardeners stayed in their domain.

Clem, of course, was another matter. He was well enough again to be acutely observant but I didn't feel that his shaky mobility would be up to any search of the premises. The bathroom he would use didn't adjoin this one.

As I was relocking a door from outside Chow came out of the sickroom carrying a load of breakfast dishes.

'We'll have to feed the woman,' I said, making my voice loud enough to carry through an open door and out on to a verandah. 'Fruit, milk and biscuits should be enough. Get these ready and I'll take them in. You haven't given her anything?'

He shook his head.

'I never went in. Why should I?'

It was clear from his expression that Chow's humanity was spasmodic and unpredictable. He had none to spare for Mrs. Hasmah at all. He mumbled something also as he went off but ten minutes later I had a tray on which were arranged modest little offerings for the dead and I took charge of it, feeling rather like an animist who believes that those who have left this life need solid sustenance for that first trying journey into another. I put the ceremonial food on a stool and left it, taking the key of the bathroom door along to the wall safe in my bedroom, locking it away. I then set my alarm for eleven a.m., swallowed a sleeping pill and lay down on my bed to build up the strength I was going to need.

But I didn't get the two hours I had rationed myself. Chow literally shook me awake.

'*Tuan, Tuan,* the guard! He wants to see you.'

Ranji Singh was already through the door, standing just inside it, turbanned and self-consciously dignified as always. He waited until Chow had left us and then launched into a policeman's account of his activities, this designed to show how strictly he had been adhering to duty. I knew it was useless to interrupt.

Ranji had been on wire patrol and had reached a point below the vegetable garden when something came out of the jungle wall beyond the fencing, flew over it and landed very near his feet. Before bending to pick up the object which he could see was a piece of paper wrapped around a stone he had inspected the heavy growth for any signs of movement from it, but had seen none. He had then called out in Malay the equivalent of 'Who goes there?' but, not surprisingly, had got no response. Since wire mesh made pursuit impossible my guard had listened most carefully and then, after making quite sure there was no sound of any kind, he bent down for the paper.

'The note, Ranji,' I said, butting into this placid, comprehensive report.

'It is for you, *Tuan*.'

'I guessed as much.'

The Sikh came stiffly over to the bed and stood as though it embarrassed him to see me relaxed, extending an arm with a sheet of paper at the end of it. This had been torn from a note-book, with the crumples now carefully smoothed out, probably all of five minutes taken over this proceeding. The letters were in square block printing designed to fool a handwriting expert and written with a biro.

'Paul Harris,

The eagle's nest appears to be under very complete observation by birdwatchers. Police? I can't get in. If you can get out meet me in the Botanic gardens today at one p.m. By the duck pond. Vitally important information. T.'

Teng had certainly not sweated up to my wire in person to deliver this chitty, which meant that he must have organized the whole operation of an approach to my house very carefully indeed, keeping his big Cadillac as a control centre a long way off, despatching first scouts to reconnoitre and then using a trained tracker who could get through jungle growth without being heard. He really wanted to see me.

I was inclined to agree with my friend's suggestion that it was the police down there, and not waiting to serve a summons for car wrecking in Batu Road either. Kang could so easily be in control of proceedings now, assigned local plain-clothes men as the result of a sudden order from a very high level indeed, which wasn't a pleasing development to contemplate.

'Ranji, isn't this the morning for the baker's van?'

'Yes, *Tuan*, it comes between twelve and one.'

'Be on duty yourself when it passes the gate. When you check it do you open those back doors?'

He claimed that he always did this, despite the fact that the whole van, behind the driver's seat, was fitted with racks right up to the roof in which were closely set sliding trays full of our local French bakery's goodies.

'This morning keep those doors open for long enough to let anyone hiding down the drive see the trays.'

'Who would be hiding, *Tuan*? Do you wish me to hunt in the woods for someone?'

'No, no, there may be no one there. But just do as I say. Open those doors wide.'

'Yes, *Tuan*.'

The order was understood, the reason for it was not. I could see that my guard, trained for long years to uphold the strict letter of the law, was beginning to have some doubts about his present employer, and only the need to supplement an inadequate pension still held him loyal. It was one thing to protect your boss from kidnappers, quite another to collaborate with him in out-witting former colleagues now lurking about the place. That word 'police' in the note had really upset him.

It was possible, of course, that the men in the woods weren't locals at all, but a detachment of U.S. Marines dropped in the night to rescue Clem and now hard at it digging a tunnel under my wire. But somehow I couldn't see this. Back in that plane cabin I had been given a strong impression that my now happy prisoner was under a big enough cloud with his own side to have him rated expendable, or if not quite that, at least no longer placed high enough on personnel charts to make him worth saving at the risk of an international incident.

Ranji left, taking with him doubts about my probity, and I got off the bed to get ready for a day in town which could so easily involve a need for my Colt. The baker's van eventually came grinding up the hill and I left the bungalow without saying good-bye to anyone.

There is a short stretch on the drive where neither the house nor the new gates can be seen, and I stood waiting there from twenty past twelve to quarter to one while the vanman gossiped with my cook. The bulky vehicle quite suddenly put in an appearance above me, free-wheeling in dead silence with engine off down a sharp slope. Brakes applied resulted in a terrible squealing and brought the van to rest almost sideways across tarmac.

The vanman was half Indian, half Portuguese which gave him the lilting Welsh accent that has taken over India, South East Asia, and now threatens the whole of England via the British Broadcasting Corporation.

'My goodness me, sir! But you have given me a terrible shock!'

'Sorry. I need your help.'

'But I am not understanding? I am supplying bread and cakes to your establishment. Is there some dissatisfactions?'

It is a mistake to envy the well-heeled. They have overheads undreamed of by the lower and middle income groups. I was waving money again, quite a sizeable sum, too. The vanman stared at the notes and only when what I wanted began to penetrate did his eyes shift to me.

'You cannot be meaning this, sir? I am to put my bread and my cakes in the bush-shes?'

'Just the two lower trays.'

'But what will happen to all the ba-king?'

My dog will get it. I'm paying you for loss. And something more besides. You can pick up the trays next week.'

Persuasion involved a transfer of notes to the man's hand. Even then he sat immobile and I went around to the back and began to pull out the trays myself. The scraping brought him, with an idea.

'Look, sir, we can put the ba-king in the other trays.'

'That'll take time.'

He had already started to work, frenziedly, forgetting that the buns were mine. Keeping them was sheer profiteering but a sudden crusade against waste had me at a moral disadvantage and in Asia one can't be casual about food, even from an expensive French bakery. I let the vanman hide his emptied trays to his own satisfaction and while he was doing it, squeezed myself down into the space these had left, roughly a foot and a half between floor-boards and a rack of teacakes. The man came back looking happy, as well he might. 'You are quite comfy, sir?'

'No. Get moving.'

The van was old, the back doors only just shut, and something had happened to the catch which meant this had to be carefully reinforced with a piece of looped cord. I had limited visibility through a gap, about a quarter of an inch, and lay there peering out, suddenly hit by gloom from the thought that my current prodigality in handing out money, a new development, was very likely a clear clinical symptom of impending financial disaster. No one has ever called me a mean Scotsman to my face, and I don't feel I've earned the classification, but I've never forgotten that my grandfather started up in Shanghai almost ninety years ago with total assets of seventy pounds sterling which, by diligence and a careful watch for sinful waste, he managed to increase some five thousand times before his demise, the good work carried on by my father at a much lower but still healthy rate of multiplication, this trust duly handed over to me in my turn. The race I belong to still secretly believes in that old saw about three generations from shirt sleeves to shirt sleeves and here was the third generation wildly handing out bribes to Tamil rubber tappers, private plane owners, and bakery vanmen, as though seized by a kind of compulsive madness. What my legal partner and fellow Scot in Singapore was going to say to all this I could well imagine. Russell Menzies can laugh off most things except extravagance with money.

We bumped down to the wire fence, were allowed through it without incident, and then coasted the rest of the way to the main road without benefit of engine because the vanman, even after his killing on the bakery market, couldn't shake off a habit of saving juice whenever possible as part of his fiddle on the running expenses of his vehicle. I lay there expecting the old crate to resist the starter when we reached the highway, which would probably mean that I had to lie under loaves of bread and the eyes of my besiegers for two hours while a breakdown truck come out from the city. But we were spared this, three and a quarter cylinders came to life with a jerk from second gear and our turn up the main road gave me a moderately clear view down it.

Parked not five yards from the stone pillars marking the beginning of my property was a rent-a-car Ford in which sat a man I knew well. Inspector Kang was smoking a cigar and looked fresh, as though he had only recently arrived to take over from an underling after a night in the city's most comfortable hotel and a very leisurely breakfast. As the distance between us slowly widened I waited for the inspector to reach out a hand to the starter button and pursuit. However, his usual sharpness seemed a little blunted this morning and he continued to sit motionless, apparently placidly waiting for a quarry who just might possibly walk away from his home, but if he rode, would certainly use the Mercedes.

I found it a shade disturbing that Kang wasn't in the least furtive about this watch at a mousehole. He looked like a man who has been given *carte blanche* authority, even to the point of a temporary command over a section of the local police. If this was the case it meant that the friends I thought I had in high places in Kuala Lumpur weren't so friendly any more. I was Harris the great unloved, and it was entirely possible that word had leaked already about a threat to my business interests, which meant that the smiles money puts on surrounding faces would now be gone.

Near the entrance to the Botanics I severed my connection with that purveyor of starch heaviness. He was cheerful, I wasn't. Like an over-tipped taxi driver the man came around to help me out.

'Oh, my goodness me, sir. You have flour on your suit-tings.'

I stopped that cloakroom attendant act.

'The money I gave you means no talking about any of this. Can you cover those missing trays?'

'Oh, yes indeed. There are many in store at the ba-kery. And my lips are sealed forever.'

He would squawk, of course, the moment half a degree of heat was applied.

The Botanics are always interesting, visited by exotic birds, but the featured attraction is a tribe of monkeys grown exhibitionists from being stared at. These put on a non-stop parody of intimate human behaviour which is more unnerving to the unprepared than the sickest late night revue. Sometimes, too, there are accidents of the kind which occur even in the best trained circuses. I was walking my dog once when a simian beatnik started to act a junky high up in his tree, swaying about on top branches, then slowly overbalancing to come plummeting down with ear-piercing shrieks. The trick, of course, was to catch the lowest limbs seconds before it was too late and then jerk upright to leer at a startled audience. But that little monkey didn't manage to catch the lowest limb. It was rather sad. The rest of the troupe gave him a full two minute silence before carrying on with the show.

Teng wasn't watching the monkeys, he was sitting in the Cadillac by the duck pond looking like a small town tycoon who always gets an inferiority complex when he comes up to the real bustle of the big city. Through the curved windscreen he observed my approach, but gave no sign, the scowl on his already marred face not lifting at all. Possibly it upset him that we weren't entirely alone in that part of the gardens, though I couldn't see any great threat to security from two Chinese *amahs* supervising three flaxen-haired children who had the high treble British voices which somehow suggests an inherited residue of racial arrogance.

These kids had certainly been born far too late for any easy confidence about their automatic position in the world, but when you are brought up with an *amah* always handy you can kick with impunity any time you feel like it, this tends towards an isolation—during formative years—from the real facts of our time. I've often wondered what happens to the little *amah* kickers when they get back to the second-class English suburbia which is on the cards for most of them, but I've never been in a position to find out.

The largest child, tall and rather bony, had lost interest in the monkeys and was throwing stones at a very Chinese-looking drake who continued a leisurely circuit of his domain, completely ignoring the little western barbarian. The girl turned towards me. She had a big featured face which seemed unlikely to fine down later into anything remotely approaching good looks and I had felt at our first meeting that her father's genes had been heavily dominant at conception, and that father couldn't by any stretch of the imagination be the poet she now called daddy. It was an uncharitable thought to have, but these do rise unbidden from time to time with most of us, unwelcome by-products of our natural powers of observation.

'Hallo, Penny.'

The child didn't smile and the tone of her response suggested a bored deb at a pre-wedding cocktail party.

'Hel-laow.'

Betty's daughter was growing up a long way from her mother's heritage of British non-Conformism. When I opened a door of the Cadillac the girl was still watching me, with a line between her eyebrows indicating concentrated attention, as though she had learned early that a precocious intelligence could offer a real threat in her contest with the adult world.

'Who's that?' Teng asked, his stare leaving no doubt as to what he meant.

I told him, and he at once started the car, driving away from the ducks, pulling up again under a vast durian tree where shade diminished the conspicuousness of the Cadillac. Then he heaved a very deep sigh.

'You can't have anything like my reasons for feeling sad,' I said.

'Paul, I've only just found out about that nurse I sent you.'

'Oh?'

'You must understand that I had to get someone in a hurry and did. There was no question of looking into credentials. Though I knew she was no longer a registered nurse and . . . the reason. What I didn't know is that she is active in the Communist Party. One somehow doesn't expect this with Malays. She comes from a village outside Kampar. And I can tell you I didn't get much sleep last night after I found out about her past. But there just wasn't any way of getting in touch with you.'

He looked at me.

'The American? He's all right?'

'Coming on nicely, thank you.'

'Oh. Look, go back to your house at once and throw that woman out. It's not safe to have her.'

'You came all the way down here to tell me this?'

'But, of course, I felt responsible. That so-called nurse could have been a deliberate plant. It's more than possible she has orders to see that the American doesn't leave your place alive.'

'What a good guesser you are, Teng.'

'You mean . . . she tried something?'

'Oh, yes. And failed. She's dead.'

I watched for a reaction. It came with elaborate slowness, like a Victorian actor registering stunned astonishment. Jaw muscles slackened, his mouth opened. The voice which emerged had a quaver in it. 'How?'

'A razor blade on her wrists. It seems she couldn't face up to reporting failure. The party she belonged to isn't understanding in these circumstances.'

'But . . . a dead woman? The police?'

'Only you and I know.'

'You've concealed the body?'

'Yes.'

He was staring.

'Why?'

'To buy time. I need it. There's a busy night ahead for me. Would you like to stay close during it?'

I got no response to this invitation. I was only given that over-fleshed profile again while he stared through the windscreen.

'Teng, you haven't by any chance been in communication with your father's cousin over in Penang?'

It positively hurt him to squeeze out the truth, but this came after a time.

'Yes.'

'Was my adoptive father greatly concerned about the attempt on my life? Or hadn't he heard?'

'He'd heard.'

'I thought he would have, somehow. Did he tell you about the train as well?'

'What train?'

'They made a second bid to get me on it. Death in a sleeping car. And do you know who I think "they" are, Teng? Lum Ping's boys. Someone has tipped off the Red leader that I'm still active. They want to stop this. Because they're highly jumpy just now. They don't want any premature leak of their plans in Southern Thailand. That would spoil the surprise element, which is such a great psychological factor.'

Teng's small hands were tight on the wheel.

'I wonder who tipped Lum Ping off?' I said.

His breathing suddenly became audible.

'Paul, you listen to me. Give this up now. All of it. Stop whatever you're trying to do.'

'Is this a recollection of old friendships just tearing you apart? Or am I getting warmer than any of you thought I would?'

'I'm not involved in any of this!'

'That sounds like a press handout. I never believe them.'

He had to look at me then. I don't think my expression was open and warm, it wasn't meant to be.

'I just don't know what you're driving at?'

'Very well, it's this. You didn't come tearing down here to warn me about Mrs. Hasmah. No one knew what was happening up at my house. You were sent to find out.'

'No! Mrs. Hasmah. . . .'

'Let's forget about the nurse. She failed. There was every expectation that she would succeed. And that absolute dead silence from my fortress was beginning to get on everyone's nerves.'

'You suggest I'm working for the Reds?'

'Teng, it could be that you're just sitting on the fence, with a foot scuffling the dirt on each side. I pointed out to you before that a lot of your big people are playing it that way and it isn't healthy. Maybe you're down here just as a message boy. Well, whatever the message, it's not accepted.'

It got so quiet in the car I almost wanted to switch on the radio. Teng was sweating.

'All right,' he said finally, and with a kind of bitterness. 'I'm a message boy. I don't expect you to understand. What do you know about the pressures Chinese like me are under?'

'Quite a lot. I just wish that more of them were resisting those pressures. I can take it you haven't?'

'You can . . . think any damn' thing you like! I got a message, yes. But not because I work for them.'

'What was it?'

'A phone call last night. A voice I didn't know. Chinese. I was told I was known to be associating with you. The man said he thought I had a better chance of seeing you than anyone else. And if I took you the message it would be remembered.'

'Blackmail.'

'All right, call it that. But I was thinking of you!'

'Sure. What were you told?'

'If you give up what you're doing now things will be made easy for you.'

He got that out in a rush and then stared at travel dust on the engine hood of his beautiful car.

'How will they be made easier?'

'Your business troubles will be ended.'

'I see. All my crews will be ordered to renounce their Communist Party allegiance and serve me faithfully as good little capitalists? What else?'

'There will be finance if you need it.'

I was really flattered.

'From mother China?'

'Paul, stop making a joke of this!'

'I know it's no joke. And if I don't play?'

'The man didn't say.'

'It's tremendous news they're unhappy enough to try and buy me off. Foreign currency doesn't come easy to them. I'm beginning to feel important.'

'You won't be . . . dead.'

I could have given Teng a little lecture on the ethical principles behind Harris and Company's operations, but it wouldn't have done any good, no one seems to understand them but me.

'What am I going to say?' he asked.

'You've got a number to ring? How about letting me have it?'

'There is no number! I'm to get a call.'

'When you do, tell them I made a rude noise.'

Teng's voice was harsh when he said:

'This could be the last time we meet.'

'And in some ways the thought is quite a relief to you. But it's a bit too soon to order the wreath.'

The car moved off the moment I was clear of it, and much faster than the park speed limit. But the drives are scenic, which means a devious twisting in and out amongst all those masses of labelled flora. The pedestrian paths are straighter and I strolled along one of them until I got to the cover of a vast, groomed clump of bamboo which looked like a setting for stuffed tigers. Then I ran fast, passing from the bamboo into a patch of artificially preserved jungle with a mock trail through it which had been sprayed with weedkiller. If there are any snakes in this nature reserve they all have their poison fangs removed before being granted visas into it. I can recommend the Botanics in Kuala Lumpur to the tourist who wants his tropics packaged and sterilized. You can see it all here as safely as you could from a movie house seat, and with smells added, together with more tree orchids visible in half an hour than you would come on in a week's ramble through the natural rough stuff.

I was in sight of the main gates when the nose of a Cadillac came poking down towards them. The car braked. A man came out of shrubbery, ran to the door flanking the driver's and got in. A moment later he got out again with a purpose, which was me. I knew this from the way the man was travelling through a park grown silent over the lunch hour. He was coming at the double towards the spot where I had last been seen.

Cover about me was flimsy. I went under the big hardwoods, hoping to merge with their shadow, but not too happy about the way secondary growth had been kept thinned. I could feel the faint stirring of a breeze which was wrong for jungle, the air should have been still and drained of oxygen.

There wasn't a long wait for Teng's assistant and probable postman. He came jogging down the path I had left at an easy lope which somehow seemed to put his feet weightless on packed earth. And then he stopped.

I had seen stops like this quite recently during my border expedition. It was the trained tracker's halt for frozen listening, something provoked by an extra instinct and apparently quite beyond the rational. It is as though anything abnormal to a particular place sends out some kind of psychic tremor which can be picked up on the invisible antennae of those who are equipped with these. Only one of my guides along the frontier had appeared to be in possession of this extra-sensory perception, the other man not a great deal more perceptive than I had been, and slightly in awe of his companion.

I had been slightly in awe myself, and felt this again as a head turned slowly in my direction. Teng's helper was no stranger. The man out there on the path had kept me company for two weeks in Thailand.

Shock did unpleasant things to my pulse rate, though I tried to keep this from my breathing. I remembered, not happily that dogs are supposed to be able to pick up the scent of fear at some considerable distance and anything a dog could do Ho Tai could do better.

I had never liked his eyes much, probably because you rarely saw them, he preferred even in shadow to shelter his intelligence behind slits that would have left a European blind. I couldn't see his eyes now, just the hollows in his skull which held them. He was massively strong, able to lift a rotting hardwood tree trunk and send it sloshing down into a sluggish jungle stream to make a bridge for our passing. I had seen him break branches for a fire with two bare hands, solid pieces of timber I would have needed to work on for some time with my little hatchet. It had been quite obvious early on in our journey that any matching of physical strengths was to be avoided at all costs. The matter hadn't arisen. It looked as though it might now.

He was at a slight disadvantage out there in leaf filtered sunlight, but I didn't see how this was likely to serve me. Ho Tai knew I was in the shade and almost exactly where. My identity meant something to him, there had been plenty of time for it to become established as part of his receptive patterns, and a radiation beyond my control, very much more potent than any smell of sweat, had stopped this man dead in an automatic recognition.

I have no explanation of this thing, it happens, and it is pretty horrible to witness it happening to you. I knew then what a fool I had been to let curiosity about Teng's assistant make me wait to see the man. The Botanic gardens are a big park, too far out from the city centre to be much used by lunchtime sandwich eaters, and probably Ho Tai and I had at least some well-wooded acres to be alone in. A body would be found in due course by the disinfectant squad or someone's imported Dalmatian, but that was no comfort. I could shout, but with small hope of help.

I remembered the man's hands. These had no hint of delicate

oriental boning, swollen from hard use. I was going to have to shoot Ho Tai before those hands got near enough to touch me, and the time to shoot him was while he was still exposed.

More of my life than I like to remember has seen a gun in my pocket available for use, but that use has almost always been as a threat of extra power in my possession. I didn't think this threat would serve with Ho Tai. He had an arrogance that would bring him on where another would be held. A bullet smacking near him would be likely to send the man lunging into shelter, and under these trees he could make a highly skilled use of cover I wouldn't be able to match. The stalker's total silence wouldn't be easy to match, either.

I had the feeling he would know when I reached for the Colt, that the lifting of my arm would flick him into action. My rigidity was acting as a kind of partial baffle to his complete perception of my presence, and he was now waiting for fear to betray me into movement.

The city intruded, a sudden, screeching violence, brakes jammed on, tyres skidding, then the explosive clang of metal being shattered by impact. It was as though a distant, practically unnoticed hum of town traffic had suddenly been turned up for catastrophe, and the hysterical shouting which followed a car crash reached us magnified, tearing away an illusion of jungle stillness under park trees. Ho Tai's weirdly held spell dissolved around him, and he stood there looking almost physically diminished, unnerved and spent, like a medium emerging from the trance state. His head turned towards that din from a boulevard and his hands lifted slowly. He wiped the sweat off the palms of his hands on his trousers.

Ho Tai didn't look back towards the shadow which held me. The cutting off of that reserve power had left him little better than a servant with specific instruction. He had been told that I was probably hurrying to get out of the park by the gate I had used to come in. Suddenly the man began to run. I let myself have the deep breath for which my lungs had been petitioning.

CHAPTER TEN

OHASHI'S MOTHER had continued to live on in her little house at Kamakura, declining politely over the years all invitations to come down to Malaysia for a long visit or to stay. It seemed rather as though she had given up the usual Japanese parental claims on an offspring until one day a letter arrived, quite a short one, in which the lady announced that she had found Seki a suitable wife in Yokosuka through the good offices of a well-known and highly reputable go-between. Son was expected to fly home the following week for the formal engagement party. Ohashi had translated the letter for me and been somewhat sheepish about the whole thing.

'It is necessary that I obey my mother's wish, Mr. Harris.'

'Even though you've never seen the girl?'

He bowed. 'Truly. My mother certainly most careful in choice.'

And Mrs. Ohashi senior had been. The bride arrived in Malaysia after only one meeting with my co-director, and that over ceremonial teacakes, wearing the polite, gently smiling expression of someone who has been taught to take life as it comes and never to indulge in extravagant hopes or romantic fantasies. Mitsuoko was representative of a new generation which seems to have taken to conservatism as a reaction against a post-war over-westernization of Japan, and if any contemporary influences had been brought to bear on her twenty years' experience of living, none of these showed. She came down the plane steps wearing kimono and thick flapping sandals, carrying an airline bag as though still slightly suspicious of this, and bowing with precisely the same degree of politeness, first to me as Ohashi's boss, then to her future husband.

The girl was pretty enough in an unemphatic way, but the thought that her entrance into a room could cause a stir of male interest would have shocked her to the core. That sort of effectiveness was left to geishas and whores, the respectable building their futures on totally unexhibitionist virtues. I had arranged a small party for the occasion which Mitsuoko's reserve rather kept from being a riotous success and though both Ohashi and I had sore heads the next morning, it was from alcohol resorted to in desperation and not the result of any really festive intemperance.

I must admit that I feel the Japanese approach to marriage has a lot to be said for it. In the first place, the parties contracted to each other for a lifetime under the same roof enter into the relationship with the massive advantage of having no personal responsibility at all for their situation, and if things don't work out can blame mum and dad and the go-between, not their own youthful folly. The psychological boost here from the start is obvious. And since true love is regarded by most orientals as slightly comic, if not downright indecent as an idea, its gradual erosion under wear and tear never becomes a depressive factor, because you can't lose what you never expected or even contemplated as a by-product of the married state. Also, the go-between takes his responsible job very seriously indeed, and does his best to balance temperaments, match social backgrounds, religious environments, and financial reserves, as well as doing a careful check of health records on both sides as far back as three generations. If there is anything at all to be said against this well-worked-out tradition it is perhaps that marriage by arrangement doesn't seem, on the whole, to produce a high degree of gaiety in the home. Everyone is just a shade too resigned to the inevitable from round one onwards and this naturally cuts down on the fun content.

It seemed to me that Ohashi was happy enough with his Mitsuoko, but that she hadn't done a great deal to increase his capacity for laughter which had always been fenced around anyway by a certain nervousness about what was permitted as risible matter. Then, too, in so far as I was concerned, I remained a shade uncomfortable about whether or not my colleague's wife liked me at all, which was of course just a hangover from the silly occidental desire to be loved for myself alone and not just smiled at because I was boss.

Mitsuoko always smiled and twenty-five minutes after I had left the Botanic gardens she opened a door to the apartment over the downtown offices of Harris and Company, the smile at once there, an instant ceremony of it. Mitsuoko's smile was just about as meaningful as the one that Japanese airline hostess is continually being shown offering to the world at large.

'Ah. Good day to you, Mr. Harris. You will please come into this house?'

That had been the idea which had brought me sneaking in from a back courtyard and up the service stairs, temporary sanctuary in these rooms which I had so expensively provided for my assistant.

Mitsuoko closed the door and continued smiling. If she had been washing up the lunch dishes or getting on with some cleaning, this didn't show. Not one of her oiled black hairs had drifted out of place. Her day kimono was bright without being frivolous. Her hands, folded together at navel level, suggested infinite leisure available in which to play gracious hostess.

'The weather is still very hot,' she essayed in her provincial school English. Since the weather in Malaysia always is, this didn't provide much of a talking point, but it had probably been one of the basic phrases in her text-book.

'Please enter sitting-room, Mr. Harris.'

What Ohashi's wife had done to that apartment had acutely depressed me the first time I saw it after they moved in. It was a gracious room, converted from the offices of moribund palm oil brokers, and at startling cost to me, long and low, with three windows on to a cool balcony which I had envisaged as a kind of terrace. Mitsuoko, an exile from the only reasonable civilization the world has produced, had decided to furnish the place as a continual reminder to her husband that he was in an alien land

and sojourning amongst glossy savages. She had packed in a vast amount of the kind of chain store furniture likely to produce a moan of pain from anyone with even moderate good taste, experimental chairs with chromium supports, sectional bookcases but with no books, a vast radiogram of shining, mixed veneers, a bright upright pianola, two cocktail cabinets which lit when opened, and fifteen or sixteen large and lurid oil paintings of the Malaysian scene done by a local artist for the station waiting-room trade. Under all this was a vast, hot jute carpet which fought for its share of attention with huge purple roses. Mitsuoko had been grimly determined that not even the faintest hint of traditional Japanese restraint should be allowed to mar her achievement and there was no *ikebana* flower arrangement, just pots of shiny leaved exotics scattered about, these climbing as high as seven feet and giving out a faintly repulsive smell which even whirring fans couldn't dissipate. On my first viewing the girl had used the air hostess smile, producing along with it a gentle impertinence:

'You like, Mr. Harris?'

That might have been the moment to state flatly that I saw through a plot to undermine her husband's easy content in South Asia and get him back to a paper-walled house in Kamakura as quickly as possible. Mrs. Ohashi senior had done a subtle job of wife picking which almost certainly meant that son would be resident in Nippon again by the time it came for proper rituals to be observed, with him as high priest, to mama's departed spirit. Mitsuoko would get the boy home even if this involved a steady but non-fatal dietary poisoning. And through it all she would wear that smile of sweet docility.

Once again I walked into a room offering a slow death of the spirit and with all my attention seized by its clutter. It was perhaps half a minute before I noticed that a chair in a corner by a terrace door was occupied. Inspector Kang was sitting in it.

'Hallo, Paul,' he said with the politeness which never deserted him.

I was near enough to the man to see now a patch of flesh coloured Elastoplast worn in the middle of his forehead. He was smoking and had been sipping beer. The Japanese hostess nips off at once when there are two men in a room likely to produce some rough male talk which it is better for her not to hear, but before she left Mitsuoko gave me a lager, a bow and that smile. I watched her bouncing sash to a door, with the thought coming to me that the girl could easily have given a gentle warning that alien forces were in occupation of her house. I didn't believe for one moment that she had been too frightened to do it. I turned to Kang.

'Very smart,' I said.

He shook his head.

'Not particularly. All I had to do was follow some baking, not too close. Though I made the mistake of deciding to follow you on foot in the park. Which meant that when your friend Teng decided he didn't like children I got left behind. It's a big park.'

'You know Teng?'

'I know nearly everyone in this country and in Singapore who has in one way or another made himself prominent.' Then he added, as though he paid the taxes on the place, 'Do sit down.'

I chose a contour model in his area and was glad of the support it gave my tired body.

'Your assistant had an early lunch,' Kang told me. 'He's gone back to work.'

'By arrangement?'

'Well, yes.'

'What hold have you got over him? I thought it was the Americans.'

'We used persuasion.'

'We?'

'I'm not alone. It seemed time to refer to higher authority. Sent for it, in fact. So I called in my chief from Singapore. He flew up. He's out on the verandah.'

This sent a twinge along my nerves. The inspector was not referring to his superior in the police force, but to the controller of his moonlighting. Down in the big city on an island I had sat in the cricket club over my drink and played a guessing game about which of the many prominent business men coming in for lunch was, in fact, also the branch manager for British Espionage South East Asia. It seemed obvious that he would be a business man, someone well rooted in commercial respectability and probably a pillar of the chamber of commerce. The game is an interesting one, and I'd felt I was getting warm once or twice but in actual fact had never really come up with a clear lead. My private sources of information had also let me down on this issue. The fact that this man with two lives was now hidden out there beyond masonry, but within earshot, was somehow acutely disturbing. His quick flight north seemed to give me a personal importance of the kind I didn't want at all.

'Is your boss going to stay faceless, Kang?'

'That's up to him.'

'I could dash out there and have a look.'

'I wouldn't,' the inspector said.

There was now a little revolver out on the arm of Kang's over-stuffed chair, mine was still in a trouser pocket. All I did was lean

forward, while Kang's finger closed over a butt, to peer through
the french doors. I saw the tip of one shoe, from the Bata cheap
range. The fragrance of the cigar smoke, however, said Havana
leaf which these days, certainly in the Far East, means the smoker
is in the real money.

Kang was watching me, his face suddenly rather stern, as though
a twinge from that bump on his head had reminded him once
again that I sometimes played by ungentlemanly rules. But his
voice stayed cool.

'All we want from you, Paul, is a straightforward account, as
honest as you can make it, of what you've been up to since you
signed on with the Americans. Don't skip anything. We have a
remarkable number of cross checks.'

My loyalty to Washington was pretty new and had been
subject to undermining stress. Besides, I had resigned, whether
this had been accepted or not. So I talked.

Kang didn't ask many questions and somehow, put into words,
my career as a spy seemed not only brief but starred with
ineptitude. I might have been convincing myself that this wasn't
a field for which I had been cut out at all, that the secrets I
uncovered best, and knew how to use when I had, were commercial ones.

There was a short postlude of total silence when I had finished
during which I drank lager.

'Want me to work for *you* now?' I asked.

'No,' Kang said, without hesitation.

'You aren't startled to learn that the Reds have a major supply
line through this country?'

'We knew they did.'

'Do you know more about it than Clem's lot?'

'It wouldn't be policy to answer that.'

'Then if I'm no use to you how about letting me go home?
I haven't had any lunch.'

'I think we might do that. And you can take a message from
us to Mr. Winburgh.'

'Delighted.'

'Just tell him that he can have a private escort out of Malaysia
and Singapore any time he asks for it. Or even a British Navy
helicopter flight if he would prefer that. Perhaps to some U.S.
hospital ship?'

'I think he'd prefer to travel by commercial airline if you'd
lend him the fare?'

'That could be arranged.'

'I can scarcely wait to get home with the good news. You get
tired of having your house turned into a hospital. And if you
send an ambulance for a body it will be allowed through my

gates. After a search, of course. You would like to have a look at that body?'

'Yes.'

'Make the collection in about an hour. With no more than one man besides the driver. And call off the local police watch on my place.'

'Paul, you're scarcely in a position to start laying down terms.' I smiled at him.

'I don't think my position is too bad. You can't touch me. The real problem now is getting my business back on its feet.'

'And that's going to be one helluva job,' said a voice from the verandah I have known well ever since I was a laddie in short trousers.

I don't think my jaw dropped, but it could have done. The figure blocking light was huge to the point of indecent obesity. He was a man who moved rarely, and then usually only to the source of his beer supply. He had lived in Malaysia for thirty years, been interned by the Japanese in Changi jail, survived to rebuild his interests to a point which at times threatened mine. He was my lawyer, and one of the three directors of Harris and Company, Russell Menzies.

I simply hadn't looked under my own nose for the man with two faces. But he had been sitting there in an office chair all the time, the perfect candidate, a practising lawyer and business man, with fingers in every conceivable pie from Mindanao to Christmas Island, unmarried, with no one in this world he cared enough about for his enemies to kidnap and use against him. Almost an untouchable, in fact, humanly speaking, who had plenty of Scotch sentiment but no heart. Anyone in Singapore, or indeed South East Asia, from blackmailed *towkays* to adulterous British wives caught in the act, could and did come to that office, sometimes dozens of them in one day. No visitors there, no matter how weird, would cause any comment amongst other tenants of the building. It looked as though London still knew how to pick its man on location.

'Doesn't this put an end to your security?' I asked after about a minute. 'Or do I have to swear another oath of secrecy?'

'A lot of use your oath would be, my boy.' He trundled to one of the many chairs available. 'As it happens I'm leaving the service. Handing over to my successor next month. And you won't find out who he is until he's also ready to retire.'

'I hope you're getting a knighthood out of all this?'

Russell put his feet on a small table. They had a tendency to swell up when they had to bear his weight for more than five minutes.

'Only the O.B.E. The thing they hand out to guitar players and designers of mini-skirts since we ran out of Empire. In my case for services to Anglo-Malaysian friendship. It's more than I expected from the present government and they've been remarkably considerate. On account of my phlebitis I don't have to travel to London to collect, which is just as well, since I wouldn't have gone any way. Too busy here.'

'Doing what, if you're retiring?'

'Saving Harris and Company from the ruin you've devised. It's the only active interest I'm retaining. And I'm doing it for the sake of your father and your brother. I was fond of them.'

I was suddenly conscious then of the year during which I had been under close observation from this man, most of what I was up to known to him, or at least guessed at, and never once in all that time had he contemplated using me as part of his network. It wasn't highly complimentary.

'How did you recruit Kang?' I asked.

'That's one of the few good things I owe to you. He was on your trail for something or other when we made contact. And a most satisfactory relationship it has turned out to be, eh, Inspector?'

'Better for you,' Kang said, which endeared him to me.

Russell ignored the comment.

'I'm moving up to this town, dear boy. To live with you, actually. It's vital that you have me available day and night during this delicate phase in your affairs. I don't like the climate here in Kuala Lumpur particularly, but I'll endure it. I'd even become a Malaysian if that would help, though it seems rather a surly thing to do just after receiving that high British honour. And I belong to a generation which doesn't switch nationality easily, just passports when this is called for.'

I stood up.

'Before you commit yourself too deeply to my affairs, Russell, there is one thing you ought to know. The company junk fleet is about to be mothballed.'

'Oh, I heard all about that from poor Ohashi. He is most distracted. And, of course, it's a bit of emotional extravagance on your part. Certainly find the ring leaders and sack a few. Disciplinary action, that sort of thing. But, my dear boy, you can't purge a whole fleet.'

'I can.'

'I'd be interested to hear how?'

'I'm hiring Dyaks.'

Russell's feet crashed to the floor.

'What? Those Borneo pirates!'

'Ex-pirates. There hasn't been a conviction against them for years. Further, they're totally untainted by Marxism. Out here

Marxism comes from China and they hate everything Chinese. And they know these seas like the lines on their hands.'

'You're being quixotic.'

'You've said that about some of my other plans. But they paid off in the end. Russell, I intend to have crews I can rely on as working for me alone.'

'You've tried Dyaks before.'

'I've tried mixing them with Chinese and that didn't work.'

'And you think you can train those fellows in your kind of trading?'

'Yes. It may take a year, even longer.'

'Who's going to finance you during that time? From all I hear you won't get credit from a bank or any of your Chinese associates.'

I smiled at him.

'You're coming up here to devote yourself entirely to my business in your retirement. Under these circumstances I should think you'd want to make that personal investment in Harris and Company which you've always avoided so far. Say a round hundred thousand pounds?'

Russell's eyes have always suggested an acute thyroid condition. Now they threatened to leave their sockets. It was rather pleasing to have rendered the head of British Intelligence South East Asia totally speechless. When he did make a sound it wasn't much more than a croak.

'Kang. Get me a beer.'

I waited until my co-director had a glass in his hand, then said:

'If Clem decides to accept your assistance out of the country how do I get in touch with you?'

'Through my office in Singapore, of course. I'm going back there on the three o'clock plane.'

'And the code word?' I asked politely.

He glared.

'There isn't one, damn you! Get out!'

The patient had suffered a slight relapse, probably brought on by over-exertion. He lay looking pale and back into that deceptive innocence again. He opened his eyes with reluctance.

'What was all that row in the passage?'

'Ambulance men carrying out Mrs. Hasmah.'

His eyebrows lifted.

'What's happened to her?'

'She became unconscious in the bathroom.'

Clem stared.

'Ambulance? You mean the police?'

'Yes.'

'And you let them in?'

'I had to.'

'They just took her away and no questions asked?'

'The questions may come later. But I hope not.'

He had no comment on that. I was quite certain that Clem knew his former nurse was dead. His surprise wasn't a very good act, probably because he really was feeling feeble. I believed he had been active. To a man with his training forcing back a simple mortice lock with a piece of plastic wouldn't be a very formidable task, even with one hand and shaky knees. He would have had the house to himself during Chow's lunch hour.

'Have you been exercising today?' I asked.

He looked at me, suspicious.

'I had a walk in the garden. Must have overdone it. Got back into bed with my heart thumping and thankful for the pillows.'

'I think you need better medical attention than you're getting here. And you can leave any time you want to now.'

'How come?'

I told him, in some detail. He didn't like any of it.

'So you were caught?'

'In a way.'

'One is either caught or one isn't.'

'All right, I was caught.'

'And by the British.'

'You make that sound as if the British were public enemy number one.'

'There have been a number of times in our history when they were.'

'Long ago.'

'Oh, sure.'

My news had soured him. I went out and took Taro for a circular walk around the grounds and then we both went back and lay on our beds. I stared at the ceiling and thought that though Russell had probably returned to Singapore on the three o'clock flight Kang certainly hadn't. They had both been a little too ready to let me walk out of the Ohashi sitting-room as though I was a totally free agent again, when both of them knew perfectly well I wasn't. The only relief to the pressures on me was the fact that the local police had been called off.

It is difficult for us to put our associates of long standing into a role totally outside anything we expect from them. I could see Russell as the perfect candidate for his undercover job, but still couldn't really picture him functioning in it. And I was almost grateful that he had retired so I didn't have to try. It wouldn't be easy getting that money out of a close-fisted Scotsman, but I was going to do it. As a replacement for my slowly vanishing Japanese assistant the lawyer would be less mobile, but with his contacts a positive magnet for any further financing we might need. And if I could get him on to the board of the shipping company as well, for something like a third of my interest in it, there was a fair chance that before long I would be able to take that long holiday in Scotland I had been promising myself for years.

The idea of sharing my house with the old beer tank wasn't exciting, but this, too, would offer positive advantages. Russell got on with dogs and I could safely leave Taro with him when I was in Europe. It would also mean someone for Chow to fuss over in my absence.

There was yet another point. Malaysia being what it is no one in the country was going to believe that Russell had been given the O.B.E. just for making money, and he hadn't apparently done much else. There was no record of his public beneficence to Singapore or, in so far as I know, even small contributions to charity. This all meant that the moment the honour was announced there would be much speculation about it, something that a grateful British government had apparently overlooked. In the end the truth, or an approximation of it, would leak, something which wouldn't do Harris and Company one little bit of harm. In fact, the news that such a man had now switched his complete attention to my company would scare the pants off some of my rivals. Spying at the top executive levels still retains a suggestion of slightly supernatural concealed talents. It might be sound policy for me to leak that news about my partner's past.

This sudden upsurge of kindliness towards an old party who, for all his years, still had a commercial potential, was sedative, and I slept almost content, waking to find Chow's tea-tray by my bedside with the pot on it stone cold. I ate a slice of cook's special marble cake, had a shower, and then began to dress for a party.

When I take time to do this carefully I can achieve a fair approximation to the conservative type who has always gone to the tailor his grandfather patronized and has never had to worry about the rent even under a left wing government. There was a special incentive to do this, for cocktails at Betty's meant fellow guests from pretty sharply contrasting worlds, her professional associates on the one hand, and her husband's on the other. It was as well to walk into that living-room uniformed for the group of your choice, and I much preferred the medicals to middle aged beatniks who had come to bring their light to an Asia which didn't want it.

Clem noted my suddenly acquired glossiness with an eye that held all the venom of a recently caged puma.

'Fun time now, is it?'

'That's right.'

'Choke on the caviar.'

'There is no need to be bitter. I warned you I was getting out of the spying business and I have. Just a civilian again. Tomorrow we'll make our plans for you.'

'Will we?'

He wanted to tell me that he made his own plans, but thought better of it. When I was at the door he called out:

'You won't be back for dinner?'

'I thought I'd have it at the club. You don't mind?'

'Why should I? Got your gun?'

That was slipped out to see if there would be an involuntary tightening of my upper arm against a chest holster, but all I did was grin at him.

'Just a social evening. To mark my retirement.'

'Settled your debts yet?'

'What do you mean?'

'All those bribes to get me to sanctuary. And especially that ham character with the plane. He gave the impression of being a man who likes prompt payment for services rendered.'

'As a matter of fact I have a cheque to him in my pocket, just in case we meet up at the club. Ohashi is taking care of the others. That relieve your mind?'

Clem was pale again. All the cerebration he was forcing on himself wasn't good for a convalescent who should lie still and let the world flow on without him. His act of being the happy prisoner had worn thin, as though a tension he was now under didn't leave him the reserves to play it.

I went thoughtfully out to the garage and stared at the huge car which at one time had come near to being the big love of my life. I didn't feel this any more, partially seduced from an earlier enthusiasm by that smashed Audi, but there was a strong residual affection and I walked around the brute thinking that the Germans do turn out a nice piece of machinery. There was, too, this evening the added satisfaction of the feeling that maybe, after all, the Mercedes mightn't have to end up in the hands of my receivers. And from that quiet inspection of a great hunk of property I switched to another check which had rather become one of my routines.

In our time it is so easy to attach a little gadget full of plastic explosive to the steering or ignition of a man's personal transport that I had cultivated the habit, when I felt that my car just might have been exposed to people who didn't really like me, of not jumping in casually and starting to drive off. A check doesn't take long and can be a life saver. I wasn't, therefore, totally astonished to find a small bakelite box attached to the fuel tank by suction clamps, but I was considerably shocked. For one thing that box meant that my perimeter fencing was just about the folly which

Clem rated it. The Mercedes had not, to my knowledge, been out since well before I went north to walk in jungle. The device had been stuck on it right here.

I read *Popular Mechanics* to keep up with the changing world and in a lay manner have a fair idea of what goes on in contemporary gadgetry. That box didn't look like a bomb. Further, in a car as big as a Mercedes a charge on the fuel tank is so far from the driver there's a fair chance he will escape the blast. This suggested strongly an electronic device which had rated an article to itself in my near-technical reading, a piece of current sophistication which sends out radio bleeps enabling a portable monitoring set to keep a reasonably accurate check on the car to which the sending device is attached. This cuts out an actual shadowing of the car you want to follow, with all the risk of being seen which that entails, but lets the pursuer keep out of sight, even quite a long way behind. Those bleeps are your guide, giving a sound picture of the quarry's direction and even speed. You follow as you like.

The gadget may not be as sharply useful on land as radar is at sea, but it was particularly suited to Malaysia where, once you clear the main cities, there aren't too many feeder side roads. And I could see that the moment I left town the monitor would give a pretty fair indication of where I was going.

In my mind there was suddenly a list of people who had access to this garage. It was quite a long list. I left the box where it was and drove down to the fencing, trying not to look with suspicion at the Sikh who let me out, and conscious all the time of a gadget sending out its steady flow of electronic messages. When I stopped at traffic lights somebody knew. The direction I was taking when I turned right beyond them somebody knew, too. It was no way to get into the party mood.

The Hill homestead was in the flattish southern suburbs of the city and a rather unfashionable area. It was a large, two-storey wooden house fringed with verandahs upstairs and down, which rented cheap because it had been the setting for two suicides and was reputed to be haunted by both these deceased. The one had been a public works contractor threatened with a bribery exposure, the other a discontented wife who was remembered at the club for her favourite remark that she would die if she had to stay in the country for another year. No one, including her husband, had really believed she meant it.

The place had large grounds, these well wooded and somewhat ill kept. Betty had no time for gardening and Tom no interest in it, and the Tamil they employed mowed some grass but mostly left it at that. It had always seemed to me highly depressive in general effect, the huge trees continuing to drip long after tropic showers had passed, with the ground underneath perpetually damp and highly productive of anaemic weeds. The drive twisted about in two acres as though trying to make the approach to the house as impressive as possible but only managing to increase a visitor's sudden sinking of spirits.

However, to-night there was a note of bustle, even a bid for gaiety, many lights, and at least a dozen parked cars, including Betty's Ford tucked slightly clear of the rest as if ready for a sudden getaway when the hospital called. There was no one around in the arrival area though the hum of people growing loud over drinks reached me. I didn't hurry towards the porch steps, suddenly uncertain of my welcome and rather caught by the feeling which hits the solitary from time to time that he is going to be the odd man out at a party entirely composed of couples, half envied and half distrusted because of his state. Further, whatever confidence Betty might have had in our security arrangements there was unlikely to be anyone in the room, including her husband, who didn't know all about those lunches at Yung Ching Wa's.

Penny met me in the hall, or rather she was posted there like a guard for family heirlooms, dressed in blue jeans and checked silk shirt as though the word about teenage dominance had reached her five years too soon and in that house the take-over had already started. I got no greeting, but it was quite probable that no one else had either, she continued to sit on a teak chair with her legs crossed, only removing her lips from the straw into a coke bottle for long enough to shout: 'Daddy!' then returning to her own interests.

Tom Hill was dressed for his side of the party, in white shorts suspended from the kind of waist which looks as though there had been a recent slide of flesh from an earlier chest development. His shirt was red and open necked, with long red stockings to match, and on his feet were Indian sandals. Twenty years earlier he had certainly had the sort of carved classic head which caught everyone's eye when he came into a room, but the carving had slipped here, too, and only his hair, now prematurely snow white, remained perfect, so shaped and tended it looked like a wig.

A decline from great beauty must be a hard thing to adjust to over the years and I have often felt sorry for those who have to do it. Very few of these unfortunates manage the job gracefully and Tom's whole living was now somehow a reminiscence of youth, with his talk an almost continual reminder of the period—just after World War Two—when he had been one of London's literary stars, with just enough talent to sustain that role. Within twenty-four hours of our first meeting he had given me the seventy-two page book of verse on which his then reputation had been based and the talent was evident enough in most of the pieces, though already flawed by a basic flimsiness of personality. His poems suggested the thin English tenor voice, charming in youth, but which is never going to be beefed up by solid feeding, soon to fade and be lost. Tom had not yet, to my knowledge, taken to drugs as a method of providing dubious fuel for the dying flicker of his gift, but a number of his colleagues out from home to similar eastern roles had gone in for the cheap opium and an output of gibberish, and the temptation could well be just in front of him.

He smiled at me. His teeth, along with his hair, were well preserved and as white.

'Well, if it isn't our tycoon. Are you relaxing to-night from a take-over bid?'

'No. Just from fighting one against me.'

'You chaps never achieve any security, do you? No matter how much money you make?'

'You have a point there, Tom.'

'I watch you, dear boy, with a kind of wonder. At your motivations.'

'Power,' I said, clenching my fists.

He laughed.

'Come and have a drink. I think you'll know everyone. At least in Betty's section. Mine may offer one or two interesting new faces.'

It depended on what you call interesting. I was given a gin and a woman from Hampstead Heath in iridescent beads who was on the way to Java to make a definitive study of *gamelin* music, financed by an American foundation in Poughkeepsie. She had spent the last two years, also under its auspices, writing a definitive work on the Japanese *shakohachi*, and was obviously highly trained at the art of getting dollars for worthy causes, in this case herself. She spoke of the United States with infinite toleration, as well she might, and once again I took a small vow to myself that if I ended up in a state in which it looked as though I would die rich I'd leave a will in which no trust, foundation, or any other organization for fostering the arts would have a chance to get their hands on one cent of my money.

The lady told me that the great charm of Americans was their utter naïvete, which was unquenchable, to which I said it would be a bad day for all of us if anything quenched it. Her face at once went blank with dislike and she swung around to get another drink. I drifted over towards the men in suits and ties, with their women, and was allowed in, if without any cries of joy. Down the middle of the room was a river of emptiness that might have been a frontier between two hostile states.

The other section was much the loudest. Strident cries came across to overpower our gossip. They were solving the problems of Asia and had all come to separate, definitive conclusions. One of the things I find disturbing about the large numbers of people these days who have skilfully avoided anything like real work is that they are invariably the most vocal. They are also, by sad default on the part of the workers, the creators of what passes for public opinion. We are in an age when noise counts for so much more than tiresome solid achievement. Anything which moves modestly towards its goal can't be with it, and gets kicked downstairs.

'You look hot, Paul,' said a gynaecologist.

And at that point our hostess came up with a jug of martini to which ice had been added and allowed to melt. She poured carefully before lifting her head. In her eyes was comment on my presence at the party. There was something else, too, a pain I had seen before, as though at times something drew Betty up to a sharp halt, forcing an introspection of the kind she usually avoided and which left her frightened.

'Can I see you alone?' I asked softly.

'No.'

'It's important.'

'Not to me.'

'What's happened to you?'

'Nothing I want to discuss.' She made her voice louder. 'So glad you could get *out* to-night.'

Betty went off with her jug, a dutiful hostess if not quite able to be a gay one on the fruit juice which was all she allowed herself. I had always had the feeling that her temperance was from heritage rather than a professional need to keep her fingers steady, and she seemed now to move amongst us not unlike one of the consciously godly surrounded by proclaimed sinners. She certainly gave an impression of having lost her own party, which was thundering on its ginned course. She served it as best she could, with her jug, with Malaysian small eats, and cigarettes, making deliberate intrusions on set pieces of screaming guests, but appearing defeated each time, glad of a little chore which permitted escape.

For the occasion Betty had her hair done in a new way, somehow lacquered straight up from her face. This seemed to me only to accentuate a boned firmness of jaw and put unnecessary emphasis on ears that weren't particularly shell-like. At times she came near to an individual beauty, but this wasn't one of them. Even her dress had fuss points on it which somehow mocked an athletic, but still very good figure.

There are only two things which give me a headache, a blow on the skull and a cocktail party. I wasn't drinking much, not from piety, but because these are not the conditions under which I like to do it. And after about an hour I went out for some air, totally unnoticed I thought, because for the previous five minutes I had been standing alone by open french doors without anyone trying to rid me of solitude.

There were broad steps down from the verandah into a section of garden now illumined from the house. This looked remarkably like a cemetery in which no one has been interred for a couple of centuries. Mosquitoes, wiped out in most of Kuala Lumpur by scientific oiling, had persisted here, though their whining was inaudible above that din from a vibrating building.

'Well, what is it?' Betty said from behind me.

Without the jug she looked oddly lost.

'Good news. The patient is leaving my house to-morrow. You don't have to come any more.'

'Oh. All I do now is send my bill?'

'Yes.'

'Did you make an expedition here tonight just to tell me this?'

I didn't answer. She watched me light a cigarette, then said: 'I've something to tell *you*. Tom knows.'

If I was supposed to reel with shock, I didn't.

'You mean he has told you he knows?'

'Yes. Last night.'

'Do we have to feel guilty over lunch once a week?'

'In a place like Yung Ching Wa's, yes. It's a call house for whores.'

'It's also the best restaurant in town.'

'Don't quibble, Paul. We went there so that our meetings wouldn't be known. And you suggested it that first time because you thought we were going to become lovers.'

'I did not! I would never try to seduce a woman on one of those benches. I took you there for the duck and mushrooms.'

'All right. We went there just to eat, once a week. But who is going to believe that?'

'I don't suppose Tom does?'

'No, he doesn't. And I didn't try to explain. It was his scene. High drama. When my husband starts to throw his soul around I have to watch him, there is nothing else you can do. And this was quite a remarkable performance. It started with humility. There's nothing really more embarrassing than humility.'

'Have a cigarette,' I said, opening my case. Betty rationed herself to six a day. She took one now.

'Thank you.' Her fingers trembled. 'Tom said he knew he hadn't been any use to me. But he wanted to know if we hadn't made something. He believed we had. It came down to Penny. It all hung on Penny, really, the thing we had made. And then I knew that . . . he was on to me there, too. And probably always had been. Right in the middle of his big scene I had the feeling he could name Penny's father any time he wanted to. But he didn't. That would have weakened his position. Penny was the trump card. He talked about the detail of life.'

'The what?'

'The little things, Paul. The good . . . small things. God in heaven!'

'Betty, don't cry.'

'I'm not going to. I know where I stand.'

'By Tom and against lunches?'

'Yes.'

'Betty, you told me that you had thought of leaving Tom after you'd been married for a couple of years.'

'That was when I met Penny's father.'

'But he wasn't a long term possibility?'

'Not with a wife and three children. Anyway, Tom needed me. He always has.'

But that wasn't why she had married him, and perhaps it wasn't even true. I couldn't see Tom, in his heyday, needing anyone. He had the whole of his own particular world. Betty had married a golden boy, stunned by beauty. It can be quite blinding when you have been brought up economically in a parsonage and more than slightly starved of it. They had met while the beauty still held and people still turned to look at that head, beauty with its attendant medical mouse.

'He tells me that I'm the chief source of his poetry,' Betty said. 'That he needs the pain I give him. How is that for an argument?'

'Lousy.'

'That's what I said, too. It made him cry.'

'All right, you can't stand seeing your husband's tears. What's for us? Occasional meetings in friends' houses?'

'Yes. You won't be troubled for long.'

'I wanted to marry you, Betty.'

'You had the idea at times,' she said.

In the house phone bells rang, from the hall and from a bedroom upstairs. Her head came up.

'I've never yet been able to play hostess without an emergency call from the hospital. The duty surgeon is operating already. What do you bet?'

I walked around towards the parked cars. In ten minutes Betty came out of the house by the front way, half running. She had changed. The party still roared behind her. She went to the Ford, got in, switched on the ignition. Nothing happened. I stopped her yanking at the starter button.

'Damn all cars,' she said. 'I hate the things.'

'Take mine. It's over there.'

She stared. Her face was pale, party make-up wiped off. There was only a faint smudge of mascara under one eye.

'What will you do?'

'Someone will give me a lift or I'll get a taxi.'

'Oh . . . all right. I'll get it back to you to-night somehow.'

'To-morrow will do.'

She got into the driver's seat of the Mercedes and smiled.

'You'll hate it if I nick this.'

'Yes. Don't. The car drives itself almost. Let it. You don't have gears to fight.'

She laughed.

'Good-bye, Paul.'

The move off was gentle. I waited until red lights were extinguished by a turn and then went over to where I had put the Ford's distributor cap under a stump. I lifted the bonnet, refitted the cap, and got in behind the wheel. It was only when I was in second gear that I had the impression of a face peering at me from bushes, white in the light from the house and against an almost jungle blackness. Penny's face. I braked, then accelerated hard again.

Before the main gates I switched out lights and stopped, getting out to check the main road. It was empty. If anyone was following a bleeping Mercedes they would have a short journey. I had a long one.

CHAPTER ELEVEN

The Linguin mine is seventy miles north of Kuala Lumpur, part of the way by the main route north to Perak, then on a branch off it which climbs three thousand feet to a pass over the main range. Just beyond the pass is a side track barred by a lift gate, and a Tamil is in attendance there day and night, controlling single line traffic over a private road. This pushes up for another two thousand feet, on a gradient starting at one in four and getting worse almost immediately. The track carved from canyon walls was designed originally for horse carts and, even though those horses climbed back up it without loads, they couldn't have had long working lives. A medium powered car on this now tarmacked route soon starts sliding back in ratios, settling for a groaning low before the top.

Linguin has been in operation for nearly sixty years, one of the few deep mines for tin in a country which mostly dredges this mineral from low lying surface workings. But particularly rich lode stone seams up in those peaks has kept the whole elaborate operation highly economic, justifying the expense of continually deepening shafts. The labour is entirely Tamil, which is unusual in mining, mostly third and fourth generation on the job, workers who live under the kind of open handed paternalism which reconciles them to an isolated life. Linguin was started with European capital and even after the Japanese occupation—when Chinese money moved into most things—it didn't move in here, and the concern is still entirely in the hands of a Franco-British commercial combine.

Those moonlit views, sharpened by swinging headlights, would have been tremendous if I had been able to look at them, but about all I got was a sense of increasing coolness and the occasional roar of a mountain stream spilling down over sheer drops. Up here even the flora changed, there were pine trees and heaths, and the gardens on top held English flowers not coaxed into sickly life, but growing happily, enjoying an occasional hint of frost.

Betty's abused car took the climb well enough, though its engine announced my arrival some time in advance and I reached the second gate to find the bar already lifted. The Tamil on duty here gave me a polite little salute of the kind which has rather gone out of fashion in recent years, suggesting that this particular Shangri-la still contrived to operate on rather antique patterns.

The mine wasn't in a high valley, but on a ledge beneath peaks, the shelf perhaps three miles long and about a third of a mile wide from steep final slopes to cliffs which spilled away for nearly a thousand feet. The area had long been cleared of any jungle and was set out with an almost Prussian neatness, the great spin wheels of the shaft lifts to the back, along with storage sheds and tin processing areas, while in front of these were the Tamil 'lines', tidy houses all whitewashed, and with their own gardens. Practically edging the chasm, only separated from it by groomed lawns, were the manager's bungalow and three others for technical assistants, these recently built in concrete and looking remarkably like transplants from European suburbia. Even those gardens seemed to deny the tropics, the shrubs in them under control and kept small, as though lush growth was against company policy.

I moved slowly along now level but twisting drives, not quite sure whether that passage through control points meant an automatic announcement of a visitor's arrival, but no one came out of Mickey Davenport's verandahless house to meet me, even when I slammed the car door. A dog barked somewhere, but that was all. I looked at the view.

It was screened by moon whitened night mist, but I remembered what it was like from visits here with my father, range upon range of jungle upholstered hills beneath. On a clear day the plain was visible in map detail, the Straits of Malacca beyond it steel blue, the far horizon as much as sixty or seventy miles distant. The windows of this villa offered quite a panorama, but they faced it with a kind of lace curtained smugness. I walked up steps to rap on something you don't often see in Malaysia, a solid front door. This even had a brass knocker from some Devon cottage industry, a moulded dolphin yawning at the world.

Nothing happened, though I began to hear a distant booming inside the house, punctuated by what sounded like rifle shots. It was Western hour on Malaysian television, the dialogue dubbed, but the action Hollywood. My second rap wasn't gentle and produced first a glow from a fanlight, then the door opening cautiously as if this was a desirable residential area which had recently been hit by a wave of armed burglaries. That door wasn't actually on a chain but Mickey gave the impression through a crack of being ready to slam it shut again quick and fast. It took quite some time for one eye to identify me, then he said:

'Good God!'

'Sorry to drag you away from *Stagecoach* and it's a horrible hour to call. But I had something on my conscience.'

He looked as though he had something on his. Though perhaps Mickey, for all his good cheer at a bar when someone else was paying the rounds, wasn't the sort of man to let bygones be bygones too easily.

'Where the hell have you come from?'

'Kuala Lumpur. I checked the club but it wasn't one of your nights to fly in. So I drove up to see you. I thought a personal delivery of this cheque would be more gracious. Especially since you feel I nearly killed you at one point.'

'You damn' well nearly did,' Mickey said, staring at the cheque.

I've had warmer welcomes but have learned to control touchiness and accept any. We went down a passage which bisected the building towards an opening from which came the television noises. The sitting-room had been placed at the back, away from the view, apparently with the idea that the manager could sit there and check that all his wheels were revolving properly. Though I had known Marjorie and Mickey even before I came to live in Kuala Lumpur it had been something of a club relationship, intimate after the third gin Collins, but somehow grown cold again the next morning. I had been asked to the rare parties they gave, but somehow had never managed to make it.

Now, looking around that contemporary sitting-room, I couldn't but remember the old bungalow which this pre-cast box had replaced. There had been a mongoose imported from India who lived under elevated teak flooring and frequently put on a snake killing act at sunset when it could be sure of a drinks' hour audience. I must have been about ten when I witnessed that, and it suddenly seemed long ago.

Mickey switched off the television with all the obvious reluctance of a host who has been interrupted just when he has settled in for a solid evening's viewing with his feet up and a bottle of whisky handy.

'I must say that was a long drive just to deliver a cheque.'

I smiled at him.

'But a fine night. I decided to break with routine.'

'I suppose you'd like a drink?'

'Thanks.'

While he poured he glanced down at the cheque I had placed on his chairside table, as though to see whether I had met promised liberality. I had, and this seemed to force him further into the role of a host.

'You've eaten, of course?'

'Actually not. Except some anchovies at a party. I rather thought you might be there. It was the Hills. Their big annual.'

'I don't know them well. She's almost never in the club, and Tom's so blasted arty. You've read those poems of his?'

'Everybody has out here.'

'They gave me the creeps.'

He glanced up at an electric wall clock which said eight fifty-three.

'Look here, my boy's gone, but I could make you a sandwich or something?'

And suddenly he welcomed the idea of getting away on his own for a time. I sat by myself in the living-room wondering if the phone here gave a little tinkle when an extension handset was lifted. After a few minutes I checked rather cautiously to see if the manager's line out of Linguin was in use. It wasn't.

Mickey was gone for nearly half an hour, returning with something more than a sandwich, hamburgers tucked into rolls which were so fresh they must have been plucked from deep freeze and popped into a quick oven. He was having one himself. With Marjorie in Majorca supervising the building of that house her husband had got into the bachelor habits of being handy about preparing odd snacks and this was just beginning to tell on his waistline. He needed wifely disciplines about him again, not being the type who could establish many of these for himself. I wondered then how much of his relatively successful career had been Marjorie pushing.

'That do you, old boy?'

Something near to clubhouse joviality had returned.

'Marvellous. Mickey, I want you to know that when I asked

for your help I thought it was a situation which just involved transport. Things got complex again while you were coming to us, and there was nothing I could do about it. I'm sorry you were put to risk.'

'Good lord, is this Paul Harris apologizing?' He grinned. 'I'm positively touched, old boy. I don't mind admitting I was livid at the time. And after. But, well . . .' He picked up the cheque, folded it and put it in a trouser pocket. '. . . this makes quite a difference. And you being decent about it. Sorry if I was stuffy and all that.'

'The police have made no inquiries about your plane?'

'None. I was in a bit of a flap that they would. But they can't have seen our markings.'

The plane had been identified all right, and no visit up here suggested the hand of Kang.

I was given another whisky. Mickey seemed to have forgotten about *Stagecoach*. He was now a man able to believe what he wanted to, that my longish journey had been taken on a casual impulse and as a bid to re-establish good relations. I had arrived at a time when the sharpness of his perception was more than slightly blurred by the drinks he had enjoyed before dinner and after. That stab of panic felt when he saw me on the doorstep had been sedated away by more doses from the dimpled bottle.

We talked about the house in Majorca. Marjorie was having some trouble with the local builders who claimed that the special jungle hardwood imported from Malaysia was blunting their chisels. Plumbers, too, were being difficult and had been caught trying to use Italian plastic drainage pipes not yet trial tested and likely to prove tasty to rats.

'It must all be costing you a packet,' I said.

'Don't mention it, old boy. But it's the one house we've built ourselves. We're determined to have it right.'

'When do you go to it for good?'

'In a couple of years.'

'A bit early for retirement, isn't it?'

'Well, I don't know. I'll be fifty.'

He waited for my surprise, which I gave him.

'Quite a number of companies out here are going along with this idea of early retirement at managerial level. The tropics use you up, old boy. Especially if you have to live with my kind of responsibility. Best to get out while you're still ticking over properly.'

'And if you've made your pile.'

He laughed.

'I won't say that. But the company's being quite generous. I get a big enough golden handshake to make me think they'll be glad to see the last of me. And a pension, of course. That's small, but . . . well . . . Majorca where the brandy's cheap and all that. And we'll have a little orchard, you know the sort of thing. Start a new life before the old arteries begin to harden. I might open a small shop, or something. I'm told a lot of our people do. Sell postcards to German tourists, what?'

He was suddenly too comfortable in a pink haze of contemplating future bliss, the simple life which, when reached, might last for seven or eight years before he got the bored man's nearly inevitable massive coronary. I let in some cold air.

'Your job's to oversee mine modernization before you go?'

That reached him through the whisky. Major developments up at Linguin were something he had never chattered about at the club. It seemed a shade strange that a great talker like Mickey had carefully refrained from any moan at a bar rail about a great deal of extra work put on him.

'It's a new pumping system and complete reventilation, isn't it?' I asked. 'That'll be tearing your mine apart.'

He stared at me.

'So you know one of our Singapore directors?'

'Not well enough to discuss Linguin. No, actually, I heard about it the other day over in Penang. As a kind of by-product of some investigation of my own. In the line of business.'

'Oh?'

His hand went out for the dimpled bottle but dropped before his fingers touched it.

'I was interested to hear about a major refit up here because it just could be an opportunity for Harris and Company.'

'How?'

'Well . . . when a company is going in for massive modernization you can sell them more equipment than they had originally planned for. I find this all the time. They get in the mood for spending money.'

Mickey had control again.

'This company doesn't. It's as mean as hell with capital expenditure. It's only doing now what should have been done twenty years ago. We're deep enough to have a real water problem and the equipment we had to deal with it was installed in the early thirties. I've been at them for years.'

'And finally got your way?'

'That's right. What are you trying to sell?'

'A new engine for your gallery bogies. Dolphin job. We haven't actually started to make it yet, but it's off the drawing boards and in prototype. An order from Linguin for thirty or so would be a nice little production start. I could demonstrate any time you like.'

He smiled.

'I see. So this wasn't just a social call?'

He lit a cigarette. His hand was steady.

'Look, Paul, I couldn't even initiate this without consulting the directors. They make the decisions. I'm just a kind of overseer of the modernization. Wimpole and Cleghorn are doing the new pumps and ventilation.'

I knew this and had been slightly puzzled. Wimpole and Cleghorn are a British firm who have suddenly, after a long period of rather solemn conservatism, got off their chairs and actually started selling. Some bright new boys in the concern have gone out into the world and in our part of it have managed to put enough contracts into the bag at one time to make their prices competitive. They have done this by deliberate rationalization, sending out British personnel to work on a number of projects consecutively, moving sharply from one to the other. It all makes the kind of hard economic sense which gives the feeling that the old country, with enough Wimpoles and Cleghorns, may still stay solvent.

'When do they move in here?' I asked.

'In a couple of months. The moment they've finished a Thailand contract.'

'Which they won against American competition?'

He nodded.

'They did, yes. Keen prices, old boy. Surprisingly.'

'I know. They've learned how to cut corners. And shipping in Polish freighters helps. That Gydansk company is undercutting our bottoms. And the Germans and the Danes. By as much as twenty per cent sometimes.'

'So what?'

'It's just smart of Wimpole and Cleghorn not to be patriotic about shipments, that's all. Just as it's smart of them to manufacture so much of their raw material under licence in Italy where production costs are a lot smaller.'

'You seem very interested in the firm?'

'All business men watch each other.'

'Well, you won't get much on them from me. I'm just the manager up here. I don't know the first thing about Wimpole and Cleghorn's affairs. My job is trying to keep the mine producing through all the mess they're going to make. When only half our old pumps and generators will be working and the new ones aren't in operation.'

'Trying time.'

'You can say that again. I'll be earning my money.'

In Penang the fact that the *Rialystock* had anchored a month before with two holds full of material for Linguin, and the *Poznam* with a similar cargo a month earlier hadn't really rung any bells in my mind. The almost sacred name of Wimpole and Cleghorn had kept them from ringing, together with the fact that Linguin itself was so immaculately free of any Chinese directorial influence. And questions had really only begun to bite as a result of that sleepless night sitting up with a gun in my lap in a railway carriage. Further, those queries hadn't coalesced into anything more than one of the Harris hunches which I prefer to keep to myself until I can shape the facts to fit, because so often the facts won't oblige. I was beginning to feel that this time they had, and that both Clem and the service Kang represented had been put off by the basic mistake of searching for a strong local Chinese scent when it might turn out that there wasn't even a whiff of China in phase one of the Red supply line through Malaysia.

All that was really needed was one man in the know at the reception centre and it made sense that this man wouldn't be Chinese either. Mickey was retiring early to a life in the temperate sun with a golden handshake from the Linguin directors . . . and who else? All the material the British company was going to need for the modernization was scheduled to have arrived and be in storage here at Linguin before even an advance party from Wimpole and Cleghorn arrived on the scene.

I looked at my host. For all the effective disguises undercover Reds can wear, and successfully for many years, I didn't believe for one moment that Mickey was a big man with them, or even a secret party liner. He fitted nicely into Category D, intelligent but with a potentially gelatinous backbone, sound to buy for one use and then allow to retire quietly. The East, and for all I know the West, too, is dotted with these characters, men who have provided for agreeable declining years by one big gamble and one big risk, and have got away with it, maintaining before and after a splendidly established and orthodox respectability. There is plenty of Red money available, even with balance of payment difficulties, for this kind of temporary hiring of souls. The chances were that Marjorie hadn't a clue as to what her husband was up to, and she might have been pushed off just at this time so there would be no chance of her tripping over one. Her function was to go ahead, to prepare that final nest, with only feelings of gratitude for Mickey's providence which would allow them a Spanish cook as well as the maid for housework, to say nothing of Pedro in the garden. Marjorie was a staunch Tory with political theories based on the old-fashioned adage of a fair wage for a fair day's work. She had avowed in my hearing that she would never set foot in Britain again because it had now become a land for gamblers and wide boys, with no room in it at all for the honest citizen. And Mickey, over that Majorca brandy, would approve her sentiments.

He was uneasy now, watching me as though a silence fallen between us had given him time to assess my reasons for showing up at Linguin at this hour, and these seemed flimsy. I wanted him uneasy. If he was the Red's local man, and this mine was their supply point for that line to Thailand and to the sea, then Mickey would be under very close supervision indeed from centre control. Almost certainly he would have orders that anything even slightly out of the ordinary happening at this sensitive point on their undercover route was to be reported back at once. It was highly unlikely that Mickey knew anything about two Red attempts to kill me, or even now why I had been in Kelantan. He was a temporary, down for dismissal after use, in no one's confidence, just a watchdog who would be well fed after a hungry spell of duty. But his half innocent report back to control would explode like a bomb at the other end of the line.

Or so I hoped and planned. It was a shaky plan, as so many of mine have been, a gamble in which I was putting myself in the most exposed position I have ever deliberately chosen.

'How about giving me a bed for the night, Mickey?'

He frowned.

'What's the idea? The drive back too lonely?'

'That, and the fact that I'd like to have a look in the morning at those ore cars of yours underground. I need to see what my engines would have to do. You have some pretty steep gradients?'

'Yes. But I can't just show you the mine like that. With the directors knowing nothing about it.'

'Why not? Say I came as a tourist, that you had no idea I was trying to sell anything. How about going down now? You've got a night shift working, haven't you?'

'No! I mean . . . yes, we have a night shift. But it's no time to take people round. Daylight would be better. And I suppose there's no harm in this. But for heaven's sake don't let the directors get even the hint of an impression I'm behind this. They're quite capable of thinking I was trying for a cut of the sale price.'

I smiled at him.

'I'll keep you covered, Mickey. But . . . ah . . . between ourselves let me say that I'd be most willing to remember afterwards any effort you put in towards fixing the deal. You know . . . a few timely complaints about the engines you've got. Liable to be a seize up in the production belt if you have to go on patching them up. That kind of thing.'

He stared. 'God! No wonder you make money. Palm oil all over the place.'

'Not all over. But you have to be flexible these days. Can you lend me a razor in the morning?'

'I haven't got a bed made up in the guest-room.'

'A blanket's all I need for your cool air. And I wouldn't complain about being asked to turn in now. Oh . . . how about some seconal? I'm off natural sleep.'

'The executive's complaint?'

'Well, I'm having some strain in one or two areas. A couple of tablets will do.'

He gave me three and a nightcap. The bedroom was completely square, and sealed for air-conditioning in a manner likely to keep me in a half claustrophobic wakefulness. Up here where night temperatures dropped steeply that gadget built into a window, and gently whining, was as unnecessary as it would have been in Tibet, but it went with the standardized building and king size deep freeze boxes.

Mickey closed me in and as he did it I noticed there was no key in the lock on my side. I was beginning to feel like a minor court official in the Egypt of the Pharoahs who had blotted his copybook and as punishment been prematurely sealed up in his economy model family vault. The seconal tempted for a moment but I flushed the tablets away into the drain of the wash basin and lay down in the dark with my thoughts.

These revolved around death, and the feeling that I wasn't ready for it yet, not having had enough living time to get my philosophies sorted out. Probably even the very old are continually asking for another postponement on these grounds and, if they get it, continue to waste the reprieve just living.

If my plan worked Red control would be coming up to Linguin in person. The job of dealing with me wasn't just something to be left to specialized killers, not now when I had reached home base. There were questions to be asked and I wanted a good look at my inquisitor, preferably before the session started.

The Colt was under my pillow. It's a potent weapon but having it close to me was less comforting than usual. I knew that Mickey would be phoning, it had been in his eyes when he left me, his uncertainty again, his doubt. There had been silence in the house for perhaps twenty minutes, then the doors opened, the bathroom cistern flushed, and finally the crack of light under my door went out. After about half an hour he came creeping down the dark corridor, standing beyond panels listening for a sleeper's breathing, which he got. A key mated with its lock, and turned.

My situation now had something in common with Mrs. Hasmah's terminal one, and I remembered her laugh for nearly everything. But as something to sustain you in a real crisis humour has its sharp edges. Men who have had particularly individual and dangerous roles in wars have told me how under stress there is no escape from overpowering loneliness, with comrades somewhere in support no comfort, and the thought of wife and waiting little ones at home not really assistance factors either. Ego is left facing itself and wanting to scream. If you are properly trained you don't scream. Right then my training felt very decidedly an X quantity, and untested.

We all tell lies about our insomnia, about nights spent tossing without a closed eyelid. Sleep was the last thing that should have come to me after hours of stretched out strain, but it did. And not just a doze. I went to sleep good and proper somewhere around one in the morning, fortunately waking, as I do quite often, in a motionless reserve which is a kind of testing of environment. A light on my face had certainly done the waking this time, and it was now probing my body, pencil thin, a tiny, selective ray. The ray steadied on my thrown out arm and into its beam came something else, a glittering needle descending.

I hit up with that arm, hard into something which felt soft. Breath sucked in above me, a moan just controlled. I groped for the Colt.

A ceiling bulb glowed. In the doorway stood Mickey, like a drunken ghost carrying a Smith and Wesson.

'He's awake!' Betty shouted. 'With a gun! Shoot him! Shoot him, you fool!'

Mickey's mouth opened. He lifted the revolver just slightly while I stared. He pulled the trigger. I saw a great deal of very white light.

Above me were stars, nothing artificial, but the big, low-hanging stars of the tropics which can sometimes seem menacing. There was one with a red tone. I felt no pain, just an intense heat.

'Mickey! Pick him up again! We're half way.'

'It's the blood . . .' Mickey said, in a childish whine.

'Oh! Come around here and take his feet then.'

'You can't carry . . . ?'

'Yes, I can.'

'Betty, wait! When they find him . . . how can you be sure they won't find a bullet wound?'

'After he's dropped three hundred feet, hit rocks, then dropped another few hundreds? Don't be an idiot! If you've never seen what's left after that kind of fall, I have.'

The stars came a little closer, like an eager audience. I was without feeling, but also without control. I knew that I couldn't move any part of my body. My voice might have worked, but I didn't experiment.

'It's all right for you! I've got to face the police. I've got to produce the explanations.'

'Keep your voice down! There will be no explanations. Because you don't have any. The last time you saw him was when he shut his bedroom door.'

'They might still find the bullet . . . ?'

'The bullet's not in his head. It's in the bedpost. We've got to get rid of that damn' bed some way. That's the problem. Not this.'

'You can say it. I've still got to face the police. I never thought . . .'

Her voice cut through his.

'Well, what do you suggest? We leave him here? With the gun artistically laid alongside. He'd recover. I don't think his skull is even splintered. He'd talk.'

'Oh, God!'

'God isn't around to give us a hand. We have to rely on our own planning. If you haven't learned that yet it's time you did. Now listen to me, I'll cover you every step of the way. You won't be alone. I'll do the thinking. But I can't drag him over the grass by himself. There'd be marks. Get him under the arms again and lift.'

In my head there was now sensation, not pain yet, but the feeling of something being slowly inflated above one ear, a great bladder that could suddenly explode. My fingers and toes held a tingling, like a recovery from cramp, and my lips felt bloated from a dozen bee stings. But I parted them, getting out audible words. 'She'll kill you.'

The lift didn't start. Mickey screamed. Betty came around and hit him hard on one cheek, emergency therapy for hysteria.

'You gutless pimp!'

Then she stood motionless, legs near my head, listening. The scream could have come from the jungle, not even probing through the surface consciousness of early morning sleepers. The night stayed still, no sound from those other bungalows near the manager's. Mickey wept.

'Where's the gun?' Betty asked. 'Didn't you bring it?'

'I don't know. I mean . . . yes, I left it. In the bedroom . . .'

'Stay by him. If he starts to crawl a kick will stop that.'

'Betty, what are you . . . ?'

The bladder by my ear exploded. I rolled over on dew wet grass. Mickey was saying something, but it was meaningless. I was making my own pain noises into the ground.

I don't know how long that went on for, perhaps a minute. Then I was obsessed, against pulsing sickness, with the idea of pushing myself up. There was no reason in this, just a need. I braced my arms and shoved. Mickey didn't try to stop me. I sat, slumped over, dizziness blinding, then it eased slightly.

My Mercedes was parked behind Betty's Ford, the long shape of it unmistakable in star sheen. A figure came round the bonnet, running towards us. Then it was circled by white, hard light. Betty stopped dead.

A voice shouted:

'Drop that gun!'

Betty lifted her arm and fired up the beam. She dropped flat. The beam lowered to cover her. From behind it came three heavy Luger coughs, bullets furrowing turf. Betty brought her arms over her head, as padding.

Light swung to us. Mickey yelled:

'Don't shoot! We surrender! Don't shoot!'

The bullet which came our way wasn't from the Luger. Light swung back, groping, finding a place on the grass now empty. It caught Betty running.

'Stop! I drop you!'

The voice was Ohashi's.

Betty didn't stop. She swerved out of light, which lost her for seconds. When it caught her again the Luger range was dubious, though the gun sounded twice more.

Betty ran on, no longer trying to escape light. At a three strand wire fence she jumped, clearing it, steadying on the few feet of solid ground beyond. Others were running across grass now, the light jerking. Mickey made blubbering noises beside me. I didn't close my eyes, I saw her go, over the drop. There was no cry at all, and the jungle slopes beyond didn't record that fall with any protest from startled birds. All we heard was a distant rattle of small stones, and this curiously delayed.

Mickey began to talk, as though Betty's disappearance released his tongue. He had a lot to say. This nightmare was no part of his real life at all, just an intrusion into it. His real life stretched for long years behind him, with an impeccable norm as its core. The intrusion couldn't really mean anything. He seemed to want confirmation of this from me, but didn't get it.

The light came towards us again, slowly. When it arrived it was beamed down on me. A voice rasped:

'Is there a doctor up here? You! A doctor?'

'What? Oh, no. He just visits. Clinics, that's all. Though we have a little emergency hospital. And there's a Tamil dresser. I think Paul could perhaps be taken there . . .'

'Where's the doctor?'

'Kampar.'

'Number?'

'Let me think.' Mickey now sounded rather like an old lady forced to deal with an emergency in the middle of her tea party. 'Oh, I know it quite well. Two something. Yes, two, two, four.'

'Put through the call, Ohashi. Ask for an ambulance.' To me Clem added: 'Lie down flat and don't move around.'

I was given a nice private room in Betty's hospital, with a view from the window over the tops of those jungle trees for which the city is celebrated. It was air-conditioned but when I asked to have a window open to allow in the sound of traffic and the smell of spiced cooking mixed with exhaust fumes, this was permitted. For twenty hours I had to lie flat as Clem had instructed, even though I no longer felt sick and the pain had been doped away. I wasn't allowed any visitors, but the house surgeon, a plump Bengali, came in frequently to bring cheer.

'We have been rather ingenious with you, Mr. Harris. Because we didn't think you were a gentleman who would like a permanent parting of one quarter inch wide. Also, it was somewhat too low on the side of the head.'

He laughed.

'I take it you mean scarring?'

'Quite. But this will not now occur. There has been a slight realignment of tissue to allow for renewed hair growth. Also, the top of your ear has been repaired.'

'Splendid. I fuss over my looks. What about headaches?'

'Unlikely. Your skull was merely chipped. Death only seared you in passing.'

The doctor had a positively literary turn of phrase. I suspected he had taken his B.A. first.

'When can I see the papers and get back into the world?'

'You are having no trouble with sight focus?'

'None.'

'Then perhaps this evening. Though there is to be no excitement, you understand? This is most important.'

When the papers arrived they were for two days, as requested, and I took them chronologically, stopped on page one of the first by a second banner headline.

TRAGIC DEATH OF KUALA LUMPUR SURGEON.

Dr. Elizabeth Hill, well known in the capital, and to a wide circle of colleagues in Malaysia, met her death by a drowning accident at Morib beach, apparently during the early hours of yesterday morning. Her body was found by a local fisherman and had been in the water for some time. It is learned that Dr. Hill visited the Central Hospital after seven the previous evening, and direct from a party in her house at which she was hostess. She was not, however, called upon to operate and left again within minutes, after which she was not seen until her body was recovered. Her car was found in the public parking at Morib. Her husband, Dr. Thomas Hill, the special Reader in English literature at the University in this city did not raise any alarm until the morning, since his wife was often detained at the hospital overnight.

It is thought that Dr. Hill had decided to drive down to the resort of which she was very fond for a moonlight bathe and, though she was a strong swimmer, the sea was heavy as the aftermath of a recent gale in the Straits of Malacca which increased the undertow at Morib. It is believed that she must have got into difficulties at a time when there was no one about to answer her cries for assistance.

Dr. Hill's tragic death will be felt keenly by her friends in medical circles both here and at Gemas where she was a consultant. During her years of service in Malaysia she has impressed all who worked with her as a brilliant surgeon whose presence was a great asset to our country, and the professional loss sustained by our medical services will not be easy to replace. Dr. Hill is survived by her husband and one daughter.

Our local paper has never been celebrated for the candour of its reporting, but that item read like some hand out from the office of medical P.R.O.'s, and as a piece of stilted whitewash was startling. I reached out for a bell and pressed it hard.

The nurse came in. She was Chinese and pretty, as I had been pleased to note when I first saw her.

'There's a plug down there for a telephone,' I said. 'And I want the instrument.'

She shook her head.

'Oh, no, Mr. Harris, that's strictly forbidden. You're to have quiet and rest.'

'If I don't get that phone I'll walk out of here in pyjamas.'

'I'll call the house surgeon,' she said, and fled.

Dr. Verisammy arrived with a syringe already topped up with sedation peeping from out the breast pocket of his white overall.

'Now, Mr. Harris, I am going to be quite candid with you.'

'Please do.'

'Conditions such as yours are very similar to concussion. Any excitement can have serious consequences.'

'If you don't want me excited let me use the phone. That's the only way to slow my present pulse rate.'

'But this is not allowable procedure!' That was almost a wail. Then he backed himself up. 'I am the doctor. You are the patient. I give the orders.'

After that there shouldn't have been any debate, but there was. It went on for some minutes, and at one stage Verisammy's hand fumbled up towards that syringe, but he decided against extreme measures when I started to get out of bed.

'Back, back! You must not try to stand! All right, two minutes only.' He waved both hands. 'And I accept no responsibility for the consequences.'

Though it was after seven Ohashi might have been sitting by the instrument in his office waiting for my call, the bell only rang once. We established personal contact again after the gap there had been in this, but with a certain crispness on both sides. His inquiries after the state of my health had the formal note of Japanese ceremonial, and from them I rather got the feeling that if I passed on from the sudden clot to my brain which Verisammy was expecting, my assistant would attend the funeral as a matter of professional duty. I probably owed my life to his off target shooting, but I saw no need to make a point of this. The young man was slipping away from the Harris orbit, in fact had already slipped.

'Is Mr. Winburgh back in my house?'

'No. It seems he has disappeared.'

I took a moment to digest that.

'And you have no knowledge of where he is?'

'That is correct,' Ohashi said.

He was lying.

'Is Inspector Kang still in town?'

'Yes. He has been wishing most urgently to see you but was not permitted.'

Things must have looked darker for me than the doctors would now admit if they had been able to keep that policeman from getting in to his victim.

'Kang has been in touch with you, Ohashi?'

'Indeed, yes. There has been much coming and going.'

It was a nice phrase which could cover a lot of activity, much of it not reputable.

'Can you get a message from me to the inspector?'

'Most easily. He is now in my office. He greatly rejoices that you are fit for visitors.'

Verisammy's authority must have been totally undermined for twenty minutes later Kang insinuated himself into my room with the gentle tread reserved for the mentally ill and perhaps dying. He took one look at me and relaxed. From the change in his expression the bandages I was wearing almost amused him.

'Do sit down,' I said politely. 'And you may smoke. The window is open.'

'Thank you.'

'Now what the hell is this?' I shouted, pointing at the paper spread out on my knees.

'I'll be ejected, Paul, if you are heard bellowing. I've been given five minutes.'

'We'll take as long as I need!'

'Very well. So that item surprises you? What did you expect to see, the truth?'

'Why not?'

'Naïve,' Kang said, delicately choosing the word. 'You, of course, haven't had time to think. I'm told that the bullet probably jarred your brain inside its protective pan.'

He remained bland under my eyes.

'All right, I'm punch drunk. But I'm still asking you why all this guff about Betty? And how did her body get from the bottom of a canyon in the mountains to a stretch of coast a hundred miles away?'

'It was transported. Together with her car.'

After nearly a minute, during which I tried to use my scrambled brain, I said:

'I don't remember the journey down here in the ambulance. I think I must have passed out there on the grass. Would you mind giving me the whole story from the moment I did?'

He obliged in simple words, rather like a man trying to make a bedtime story for kiddies out of something a shade more complex than these usually are. And the quick thinking ogre in the piece appeared to be Clement P. Winburgh, who also seemed to have taken a lot on himself for an alien in a country which hadn't granted him a visa. Round one had been to bring Mickey, still babbling, under control. This had been achieved by telling him that if he followed instructions he would be all right, which wasn't a policy line I would have adopted. Next had been the need to quieten down alarm aroused amongst immediate neighbours by the sound of shooting out on a lawn. This had been managed simply enough, by a whacking great lie involving me, to the effect that Mickey had been disturbed by the sounds of someone trying to break into his house. He had picked up his revolver and gone to investigate and when he opened the front door a figure had gone bolting away into the dark. He fired at it a few times.

I stared, speechless.

'Now don't get excited, Paul. You'll understand in a minute.'

This seemed improbable.

'Mr. Winburgh's service and mine may have seemed to be at cross purposes recently. But we're not basically. Far from it. We both wanted to find out how that Red supply line was operating and stop it. We also wanted no publicity about the whole business when it was uncovered. No leak at all, in fact. I suggest you use your imagination, if you can make it work. Just think of the real story in that paper—a major Red supply line through Malaysia, controlled by a Red supervisor neatly planted at the heart of life in this city. It would result in the biggest internal flare up since the country became independent. There would be a political crisis of the first order, just when a very real stability looks like being achieved. All hell let loose, in fact.'

'The truth is usually healthy in the end,' I said.

He looked at me, then fitted a new cigarette into his holder. The smoke from the last one was beginning to make me feel slightly sick.

'That's a nineteenth century concept, Paul, as you ought to know. This particular truth could have been turned to Red propaganda and most certainly would have been. Look at this carefully. Certainly we have uncovered the route they were using, but not until after it had been functioning for almost a year. They have sent enough small arms and ammo through this line to supply a small army up in Thailand, and that's what Lum Ping has got. The estimate is something in the region of fifteen thousand guerrillas waiting for their signal. The number may be a slight exaggeration, but may not. All this is bad enough, but not half as bad as the free publicity the Reds would get from the truth about their feed line. If the facts were made public, people on the fence all over South East Asia would say that if the Reds could get away with this in a country like Malaysia they could certainly do it anywhere else in southern Asia. And probably were. It could be a most unpleasant and dangerous chill to anti-Red morale. Can't you see this?'

I could, but wouldn't quite admit it.

'The tide's running against Red China at the moment with all their Red Guard atrocities. Their stock's low.'

'True. Let's keep it that way. The Linguin affair, made public, would send it up points.'

I changed tack.

'When did you catch up on Clem?'

'We followed him out of Kuala Lumpur. We were watching your Japanese. Mr. Ohashi collected his car and took evasive action around the city in it. Then he went to your fortress, was allowed in and came out again, presumably with a passenger. It was too dark to see who the passenger was, but we didn't need many guesses. My driver was a little awkward and they saw they were being followed. There was quite a chase up the Kampar road. It looked as though they had won when we became mixed with some heavy lorries on a succession of bends. And we made the mistake of going on towards Kampar for about five miles beyond the fork. Then we backtracked and made for the hills. The gateman at the Linguin road confirmed that we were on the right trail.'

It made a clear picture, Clem and Ohashi following the bleeps from a Mercedes driven by Betty, and Kang bringing up the rear of the procession.

'Your two services joined forces at Linguin over my inert body?'

Kang smiled.

'You could put it like that.'

'And how did you account for your combined activity to the people who live up there?'

'We said we were following up a rumour that the mine was to be sabotaged. This tied in rather nicely with the prowler their manager had shot. And no one was allowed close enough to identify you. The sabotage story also gave us an excuse for a thorough search.'

I controlled my reaction.

'You found what?'

'Nothing. The arms which had come in had gone out again. There is absolutely no evidence of the use Linguin was being put to. But Davenport has sung like a caged canary. The arms arrived concealed up in the middle of angled ten-inch pipes, held there by plastic sealing. The job of packing them in there was done at sea on board the Polish freighters, and they had the whole voyage in which to make things very neat indeed. The angled pipes were a good touch, too. You wouldn't expect to see through them in unloading and there were a great many of these. We have a feeling that the ship which is due next month at Penang will get orders to go somewhere else fast.'

'And are you now following up Red trails from Linguin north and east to the sea?'

Kang shook his head.

'No. The trails are of no importance now the source of supply is eliminated. Let the jungle take them again. A follow up would mean using large numbers of police and regular Army, which isn't possible if we are to maintain security on this matter.'

It wouldn't be possible even if they abandoned security. More than half of Malaya is made a no man's land by jungle, too vast to patrol even when you're fighting a war, and at the moment there was a technical peace in the country to which everyone was clinging as hard as they could, even the Reds for the time being. Lum Ping was being swept back into his cupboard under the stairs and the door shut tight.

I poured myself a glass of ice water, sipping it to bring down the temperature I'd developed.

'How about my friend Mickey?'

Kang didn't rush into his reply.

'I don't think you are going to like this, Paul. But in view of what I've said you must see that we can scarcely charge the man with assault on you.'

'Assault? Deliberate, attempted murder!'

'All right, any label you want. But the plain fact is we can't prosecute. The local police have co-operated with me up to a point but they haven't been brought into things officially at all. As far as they're concerned Dr. Hill's body . . .'

'Cut all that! What happens?'

'It's—ah—actually happened. Davenport was put on board an Air France plane in Singapore this afternoon. Bound for Europe. Now before you start making a noise, *think*!'

So I thought, about Marjorie and the villa in Majorca, and about hubby coming to it, the retiral a year or two earlier than had been anticipated, without quite so much money available to them as Mickey had hoped, which would probably mean they would have to do without that cook. Mickey would get his nerve back in time, to become the life and soul of expatriate parties of Britishers on the run from a Socialist Chancellor of the Exchequer.

'This is what you call a compromise peace, isn't it?' I said. 'Nobody wins.'

'Something like that, perhaps.'

'The trouble with our bloody age is expediency, do you know that? Everybody lives by it. It's the slogan done in red wool hanging on the walls of policy making rooms all over the world.'

'You're shouting again, Paul.'

'Sorry. I expect it's bad for your nerves.'

He smiled.

'You are actually taking it better than I had expected. Tell me one thing. When did you first get on to Dr. Hill? That was your exclusive line. No one else had it.'

I looked at him.

'I got on to her when it became obvious that she had murdered Mrs. Hasmah in cold blood in my bathroom.'

CHAPTER TWELVE

IT WAS KANG who needed the ice water then. He came around to help himself from the table by my bed, but before he drank he asked:

'You have proof?'

'Not a scrap.'

'Then why do you say it?'

'Because everything I was up to afterwards stemmed from a few minutes alone in that bathroom with a corpse in a tub. Mrs. Hasmah was a dope pedlar. Most of these are addicts themselves.

As long as she had access to her drug the woman was unshakeable. But in that cooler of mine she might have reached breaking point, the addict's hysteria.'

'You put the woman in there to bring her to that point?'

'Yes.'

'And Dr. Hill guessed what you were up to?'

'Yes. Mrs. Hasmah was her plant, through Teng. Carefully chosen at that. There was plenty of time to go into the question of choice between my phone call to Betty from the north and our arrival in K.L. She had already used Teng to have me tracked to the north, and she used him again. She treated Clem's arm and then told me I had to have a nurse, that I wouldn't get one in this town of the kind I needed. It was Betty who suggested that I contact my Chinese friend Teng, and believe me that came back into my mind later. The object of all that was to get the assassin over the wire to kill Clem. Finishing off a job that had been muffed up north. Clem was right on top on the Reds' seek and destroy list. He had been making too many private trips into this country. We'll never know who the assassin was, but I can have a good guess. My guide up in Thailand. Also supplied by Teng.'

'How did Dr. Hill know you were going to Thailand?'

'I had to tell her at one of our lunches that these would be interrupted for a time. I was off on a business trip. I wasn't on the Reds' seek and destroy list then, but I was down to be watched. And I was watched all right, practically led by the hand for two weeks by one of their murder squad.'

'Paul, how would Dr. Hill have access to that bathroom?'

'The key was on the outside of the door. A doctor washes hands after seeing a patient. Clem had said something about the nurse having gone and Betty hadn't seemed very interested. But she was interested all right. She knew that Mrs. Hasmah was in trouble simply because her patient was lying there getting better. So she turned that key and went into a bathroom with a hypodermic in her hands, to be received with relief by Mrs. Hasmah who right then wanted nothing more than a shot in the arm. She got it. An overdose. I don't know much about medicine but I know you can easily kill a junky that way. And Betty didn't need the woman dead, only right out. She then put Mrs. Hasmah in the tub and slashed her wrists. They were cut in the right places, neatly. It was all done in minutes.'

'This is all surmise,' Kang said.

'The packet of razor blades isn't. What would a woman like Mrs. Hasmah need a whole packet of Wilkinson stainless for in that leather trunk of hers? Betty slipped up bringing in those blades. It would have been better to use a pair of scissors I found in Mrs. Hasmah's sewing tidy. But the surgeon liked neatness, planned for it. Kang, I'm not pretending that all this hit me when I was in that bathroom with the door locked. Far from it. It was a kind of seepage for a long time, one thing after another coming through, until I had to admit a possibility. The last thing I wanted to do was admit it, but I simply couldn't get away from the feeling that the nurse was no candidate for suicide.'

'A drug addict?'

'All right, I know. But she still wasn't the kind who would kill herself, even in semi-hysteric depression. That stuck, I couldn't shake it off. I kept coming back to it.'

The inspector put another cigarette into that holder, not so neatly this time, it was a shade bent.

'I find it difficult, even with what we know, to understand Dr. Hill's motivations.'

'Because she was a western woman?'

'Perhaps that's it. I can understand a British communist doing undercover work out here, we've had that before. Even carefully planted like Dr. Hill was. But it seems to me that she was the wrong candidate for what she became. It's not idle to say that a doctor has a whole life, and a creative life, too.'

'She had two lives, Kang, and she saw both of them as creative. Betty had also lost one faith and found another.'

He shook his head.

'I'm not quite with you?'

'I don't know whether she got to know me well as part of her job, or as something separate from it. Probably a mixture of both. She may have talked to me to bring me out, to fill in the blanks in her file. At any rate I learned quite a lot about her past. She wouldn't see any risk in this, but the past does provide a key of sorts, sometimes. Betty's father was a preacher who took most of his texts from the Old Testament. It was a big family, he took that from the Old Testament, too. They lived by rules, under a stern God who was likely to punish you if you forgot your nightly prayers before you jumped into bed. Or sneaked off to the pictures instead of going to Sunday School. That was sin. So was dancing. It's hard for a Chinese to imagine the basic joylessness of a life like that. I mean a worldly Chinese like you, and living out of China.'

He didn't smile.

'There are still these sects in England?'

'There's even one where you can't sit down to a meal with people who aren't in your clump of the anointed. Betty's situation wasn't an extreme of that kind, but it was still that solemn paternalism over everything. She broke from it, she lost faith. But the point is it had once been complete, dominant. The rules were life, to break them was death. Her mind wouldn't let her believe any more. She was cut off from the family completely because of this, out on her own. She had to make a totally new life and she did this through medicine. Afterwards she filled up the personal with Tom and a child as well as lover or two when the marriage turned out badly. But there was still a vacuum from that earlier conditioning. Vacuums tend to get filled, in this case, by a new religion which she thought she could accept with her mind as well as feeling.'

'Feeling?'

'Yes, and near to the sentimental. I was kicked around up north just a few days ago by a guerrilla from your world. Better than your world, I suspect a lot of money. He was very far from being any kind of fool. But it wouldn't surprise me if certain selected passages from Mao could bring tears to his eyes. Betty and he had the same religion.'

'Chinese communism for Dr. Hill?'

'Why not? It was pure, it was absolute. Kang, I think Betty probably joined the British communist party some time when she was studying medicine. But like so many new candidates she was told to stay undercover. There are many more of these than the ones who appear on protest marches. But even in her under-cover roles she would still be subjected to party bickering over policy. This is a line as wavering as one on the drum of a seismograph. One week Jugoslavia is in, the next it's out. There is internal fragmentation over East Germany and Rumania, and all the time the Muscovites seem to be becoming more and more absorbed in bourgeois preoccupations. You mayn't need a dinner jacket yet for a night out in the Russian capital, but you wouldn't be mobbed these days if you wore one. All this lack of coherence would be almost unbearable for Betty. She had joined for a faith and she was in danger of losing a second one. That could have driven her to the Chinese line while she was still in Britain. They take on their recruits, too. No sign with them of the stern rules being relaxed.'

'A doctor, Paul, is no fool!'

'The man who kicked me around at the edge of the jungle wasn't a fool either. He was leading a hard and dangerous life for his belief. There couldn't have been any other motive. I don't believe he was on the run from anything.'

'But a doctor's position! The emphasis on the humanitarian.'

'Is it always these days? Betty was a specialist. She was a long way from the G.P. with the black bag. Much more a trained technician. She told me once that she sometimes saw a patient twice before operating, more often once and in emergencies not at all. There was a certain amount of after care in the surgical wards, but that was mostly left to an assistant. She could save a life or fail to save it, but was immunized from any real person involvement whichever happened. She had another immunization as well, a secret personal philosophy which lays down that the necessary goal to aim for is the greatest good for the greatest possible number. That's humanism sterilized by a statistical approach. It's happening in quite a number of areas.'

'So logic enabled her to kill? Personally kill, even though she was a woman?'

'It would have made her very angry to hear you say "even though she was a woman". Yes, Betty could kill personally. She was control in this area. When you have worked yourself to that eminence you have rationalized away the unpleasantness.'

'You're guessing, Paul!'

'I'm not guessing. I heard her shout to Mickey "shoot him". It was an order strong enough to make that poor fool obey, against every instinct he had. Betty was trained for command all right. She had earned it.'

Kang stared at the floor. I looked again at the newspaper on my knees, re-reading that amalgam of bogus news item and obituary.

'Betty must have gone home when she left the hospital,' I said. 'She was there to get a phone call from Mickey. Where was Tom?'

'He had gone on to another party from his own. Paul, do you think that man's a communist, too?'

'Probably. But not the kind you have to worry about. His variety is poster carrying and velvet jackets in Moscow. We've rather avoided talking about my friend Teng. How is he?'

'Quite well, I believe. In Macao.'

'I see. I wasn't sure for a long time, even after Penang, whether my fence-sitting friend had come down on the wrong side. Still, Macao's a nice place to sit in your hotel with access to your western bank accounts while you watch streams of refugees coming by from the thing you have been helping to build up.'

'We may get him yet. Even in Macao.'

'I think I'm sorry for Teng. He was just frightened.'

'And your feelings for Dr. Hill?'

'As you would say . . . no statement.'

He got up.

'It's a wonder they haven't thrown me out. It seems very quiet on this floor.'

'Mostly terminal cases,' I said. 'Put out that main light, will you?'

When Kang had gone I looked about for a switch to the remaining shaded bulb but couldn't find it. Perhaps there is always one they leave burning to keep the patient from any consciousness of being nearer to that total dark than most of the people walking around outside. Noises from the city had stilled down, like an agitated heart quietening.

Nurse came in to settle me for the night, tight with reserve from that terrible violation of the rules. She took my temperature but made no comment, just marked it up on the chart. I was asked if I would like some cocoa, but said no. When I was alone again I felt sick, but not to the point of ringing for a basin.

The figure standing by my bed was carrying an armful of American Beauty roses sent from Australia in cold storage and costing a fortune in Malaysia. In the dim light he looked like a man paying a first visit to a wife who has safely delivered twins. He wasn't quite sure whether to be madly gay, or weep.

'I hope I didn't wake you,' Clem said.

'No.'

'Can't sleep?'

'I've been lying here like a survivor from a war wondering why he fought in it.'

'Oh. Well, I brought you these.'

'Nurse will be delighted. They're my first flowers. What time is it?'

'Shortly after three a.m.'

'Scarcely visiting hours.'

'I came up in the service elevator.'

'An old C.I.A. dodge. Why?'

'Well, I didn't like the look of the gorgon at reception.'

'You'd better sit near the bed and keep your voice low. And put those flowers in the basin.'

'There's a bottle of whisky in the middle of them.'

I warmed to him, just slightly.

'What are all these tokens? To atone? To say you always knew I was pure in heart even though you had your suspicions?'

'Something like that.'

'Is Kang still looking for you?'

'Ohashi thinks so.'

'You've been hiding out with my Japanese boy?'

'No. Just in a place he recommended. Your favourite restaurant. Yung Ching Wa's. Those benches may be all right for love, but they're hell to sleep on. Still they got these flowers for me. Waitress's choice. And the whisky.'

'They can get anything.'

'I hear Kang's been hear. Did he mention me?'

'No.'

'He didn't even tell you I'd put the Mercedes back in your garage?'

'He didn't even tell me you'd pinched it. Was that at Linguin?'

'I ended our collaboration rather suddenly. I still want to get back to Vietnam my own way.'

'It's a long walk up the peninsula and around by Thailand and Cambodia. Who's financing you? Ohashi?'

'Uh-huh.'

'I've got a feeling that boy is slipping right out of my service.'

'You may be right.'

'Your firm offer better pensions?'

'Paul, you don't really mind.'

'No, no. You try to kidnap me for trial on trumped up charges, you wreck my business and pinch my newest director. I don't mind.'

'I practically saved your life up at Linguin. At least I held the torch.'

'Badly. The score is still three to one-half, my favour. And I hate you, man.'

'If you knew how hard it is to carry roses and a bottle of whisky with only one good arm you wouldn't say that.'

He sat down, looking tired and pathetic.

'Clem, who was your man inside my perimeter defence?'

'Ranji Singh,' he said at once.

'How long have you had him?'

'Ever since you hired a guard.'

'Through Ohashi?'

'That's right.'

'So your Japanese boy could walk in and out when he liked, too?'

'That's right.'

'What did you think when you found Mrs. Hasmah dead in that tub?'

'My first thought was that you'd done it.'

'And your second?'

'That another party had bought another of the guards. You really must scrap that fence. Or at least the current.'

'I'm going to. You never suspected Betty?'

'No. She was kind to me. Paul, would you mind if I borrowed one of those junks which have been assembled in Kuantan waiting for the boss to descend in Jovian anger?'

'Yes, I would.'

'Well, I'm going to do it anyway. Ohashi's downstairs waiting to drive me there. It's all fixed up.'

'You're going to travel home with a Red crew?'

'Ohashi says they aren't all Red. That you got carried away. He's picked the purest.'

'He's sacked.'

'He knows that. His wife is packing. How about letting me have a nip of your whisky, eh? One for the road. And they tell me the South China Sea is rough to travel on at this time of year. Steady north wind blowing.'

'From Vietnam,' I said.

He stopped pouring to look at me, puzzled.

'I never asked how you were feeling, Paul?'

'Weary.'

'Sure. Well, you can get plenty of rest in here. And there's Chow waiting for you up at the house.'

'Do me a favour, will you? You've had your drink. Drift. Quietly like a ghost.'

'If that's the way you want it?'

'That's the way.'

I didn't hear the door shut, but I heard it open again. Nurse stood by my bed, her mouth and even slant eyes round with outrage.

'I saw a man come out of your door. Just now!'

'Oh, well . . .'

'Mr. Harris! There are rules. We have to keep to them. You can't just do what you want in a hospital. You can't!'

'The last of my visitors. Your rules from now on.'

Ohashi had still to come, but formally, during the set hours, and probably bringing me a carefully chosen jig-saw to counteract boredom. We wouldn't have a lot to say to each other.

'Those roses are for you,' I said, seeing she was staring at them.

She stared at the whisky.

'You can take that for your boy-friend. I haven't got a taste for the good things back yet.'

'Mr. Harris, I'll have to report this . . .'

'It would save a lot of trouble if you didn't. And I'm feeling weak again.'

'No wonder!'

She went over and looked at the roses, then turned with a crackle of starch. She had been trained by a Scotch matron and had picked up that terrible professional third person.

'Well, then,' she said, tightening my one blanket. 'All we need now is to get comfortable, isn't it?'

'That's all we need, Nurse. Make us cosy.'

It sounded like a prayer, a kid's prayer by the bed before he dives into safety under a quilt.